KT-476-755

City of Light

City of Light

LAUREN BELFER

SCEPTRE

Copyright © 1999 Lauren Belfer

Text image copyright © Corbis
Maps by James Sinclair

First published by the Dial Press, Random House Inc., New York
First published in Great Britain in 1999 by Hodder and Stoughton
A division of Hodder Headline PLC
A Sceptre Book

The right of Lauren Belfer to be identified as the Author of the Work been asserted by her in accordance
with the Copyright, Designs and Patents Act 1988.

10 9 8 7 6 5 4 3 2 1

All rights reserved. No part of this publication may be reproduced, stored in a retrieval system, or
transmitted in any form or by any means without the prior written permission of the publisher, nor be
otherwise circulated in any form of binding or cover other than that in which it is published and without
similar condition being imposed on the subsequent purchaser.

This book is a work of fiction. Although certain historical figures, events and locales are portrayed, they
are used fictitiously to give the story a proper historical context. All other characters and events, however,
are the product of the author's imagination, and any resemblance to persons living or dead is purely
coincidental.

A CIP catalgue record for the title is available from the British Library

ISBN 0 340 74841 9

Printed and bound in Great Britain by Clays Ltd, St Ives Plc, Bungay, Suffolk

Hodder and Stoughton
A division of Hodder Headline PLC
338 Euston RoadLondon NW1 3BH

For my parents

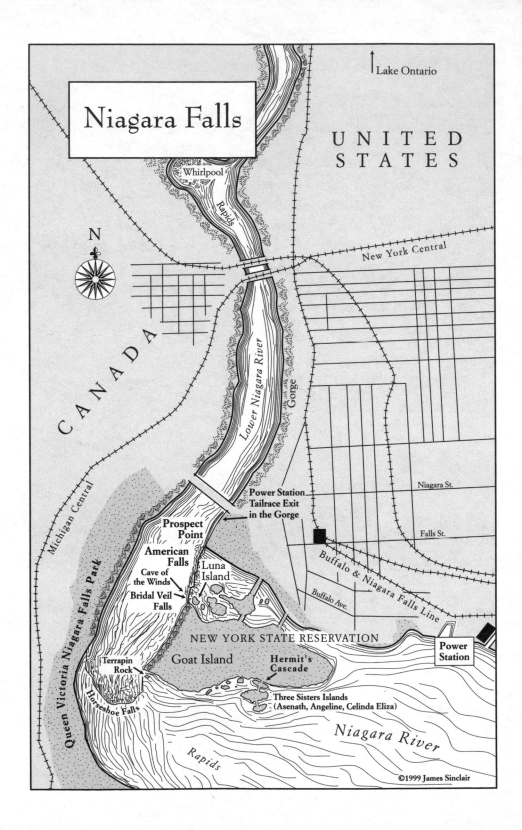

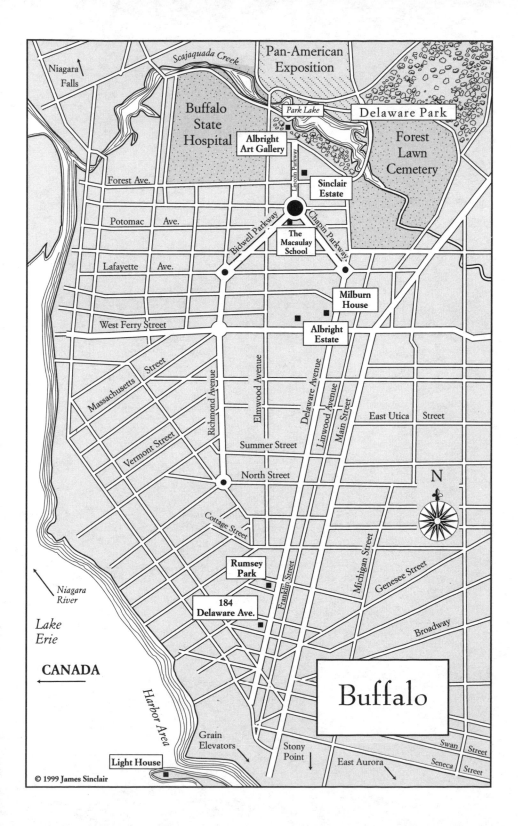

Niagara
Falls

Scajaquada Creek

Pan-American
Exposition

Buffalo
State
Hospital

Park Lake

Delaware Park

Albright Art Gallery

Forest
Lawn
Cemetery

Forest Ave.

Sinclair
Estate

Potomac   Ave.

Bidwell Parkway

Lincoln Parkway

Chapin Parkway

The
Macaulay
School

Lafayette   Ave.

Milburn
House

West Ferry Street

Albright
Estate

Massachusetts   Street

Richmond Avenue

Elmwood Avenue

Delaware Avenue

Linwood Avenue

Main Street

East Utica   Street

Vermont Street

Summer Street

North Street

N

Cottage Street

Niagara
River

Michigan Street

Lake
Erie

Rumsey
Park

Franklin Street

Genesee Street

184
Delaware Ave.

Broadway

CANADA

Harbor Area

Grain
Elevators

Stony
Point

East Aurora

Swan   Street

Light House

Seneca   Street

Buffalo

© 1999 James Sinclair

I am lucky: I know what people say about me.

To some I am a bluestocking, a woman too intellectual to find a husband. To others an old maid, although I do not consider myself old and I am no maiden. To still others, I've flirted with Boston marriages: I've lived with other women, they say, but I never have—not that way, at least; not the way they are implying. Nonetheless there is a certain benefit in being so considered: Wives do not fear their husbands spending time with me, and overenergetic husbands look elsewhere for their dalliances.

Yes, people misjudge me. They hear the title "headmistress" and assume a certain sort of woman. A woman without passion or experience. They never guess the truth of my life, and their assumptions lend me a freedom they would never credit. Thus has society given me room to maneuver. In secret, granted. But self-knowledge is, as the ancient Greeks might say, the only knowledge worth having.

And when I rise in the gray shadows of dawn, a cooling breeze coming through the open window, my hair flowing around me, my nightdress loose, my body warm beneath it, I gaze in the mirror and see myself for what I am: a woman of feeling, desire, even beauty. Then step by step I create the person I must be: The warm, free body becomes corseted and covered with a high-collared navy blue dress; the flowing hair is twisted into a tight bun; sturdy shoes take the place of bare feet. What do I hide? My joy, my memories, my dreams of those I've loved and what they might have been, my mind harkening back to the time when I knew them still.

Louisa Barrett,
1909

PART ONE

———◆———

Power

The city of Buffalo has, by the census of 1900, a population of 352,387, standing eighth among the cities of the United States. It leads the world in its commerce in flour, wheat, coal, fresh fish, and sheep, and stands second only to Chicago in lumber. In cattle and in hogs, only Chicago and Kansas City exceed it...Its railroad yard facilities are the greatest in the world, and are being increased rapidly...In marine commerce, although the season is limited to six months, Buffalo is exceeded only by London, Liverpool, Hamburg, New York, and Chicago.

Better still, it is a city of homes. Strangers view with delight its shaded streets and spacious lawns...

The Niagara Book,
by William Dean Howells,
Mark Twain, and others, 1901

The whole world will pay her tribute.

"The City of Buffalo,"
Harper's New Monthly Magazine, 1885

Chapter One

O n the first Monday in March 1901, in the early evening when the sound of sleigh bells filled the air, a student unexpectedly knocked at my door. I was accustomed to receiving visitors on Mondays before dinner, when my drawing room was transformed into a salon. Bankers and industrialists would stop by my comfortable stone house attached to the Macaulay School, knowing they would find professors and artists, editors and architects.

In those days, Buffalo was flush in an era of extraordinary economic prosperity and civic optimism. The city had become the most important inland port in America because of its pivotal location at the eastern end of the Great Lakes. Indeed, at the turn of our century, Buffalo had taken its place among the great cities of the United States. Many of the visitors to my salon were from New York City or Chicago, men who came to Buffalo at the behest of our public-spirited business leaders to offer their best work to the city. These included architects Louis Sullivan and Stanford White; sculptors Augustus Saint-Gaudens and Daniel Chester French. Years ago I met architect Daniel Burnham, and he invited himself for sherry with a man whose name I now forget and came again on his next visit to Buffalo. Soon they all came, presenting their cards with a note: "At the suggestion of our mutual friend . . ." Then the local people of distinction, with such family names as Rumsey, Albright, and Scatcherd, sensing an opportunity, came calling too.

They could do this only because I was considered unmarriageable. Because I was a kind of "wise virgin"—an Athena, if you will—these men granted me my freedom and I granted them theirs. Of course there were women at my salon—doctors, architects, artists. Those who had husbands came with them; those who did not came alone, or with the other women who were their life companions.

I liked to think that my Monday evening salon was the only place in the city where men and women could mingle as equals. The married and marriageable women of the upper reaches of the town were hidden away, given little room for interests beyond clothes, children, entertaining, and a bit of work among the poor. They led a limited life, which filled me with sadness and which I tried at Macaulay to change. I educated the young women placed in my care—the daughters of power and wealth—to expect more. I liked to think that I'd trained a generation of subversives who took up their expected positions in society and then, day by day, bit by bit, fostered a revolution.

In the past two years, the stream of visitors to my salon had become ever more fascinating and their concerns ever more urgent as they planned the design and construction of a world's fair called the Pan-American Exposition. Yes, Buffalo was to be an exposition city now, in the tradition of Philadelphia and Chicago. The Pan-American would celebrate the commercial links between North and South America as well as America's technological breakthroughs, particularly in the area of electricity, which was being developed at nearby Niagara Falls. Most important, the Pan-American's very existence symbolized and confirmed Buffalo's new, vital place in the nation. The exposition site was less than a mile from my home, and over eight million people from around the country and the world were expected to visit the fair during the coming summer. Debates about lighting, coloring, and schematic statuary took place before my fire, the gentlemen tapping their pipes against the mantel. Sometimes they called my gatherings a "saloon" instead of a salon, as if they were visiting the Wild West and I were Annie Oakley. I tried not to show them how much their teasing pleased me.

But on this particular Monday evening in March, I sent my visitors away by seven. There was a wet snow falling and a chill dampness in the air that made me want to be alone in front of the fire. My guests grumbled halfheartedly, though some of them were privately grateful, no doubt, to return home; here on the shores of Lake Erie we respected the icy storms of early spring. And although they might not admit it, more than a few of my out-of-town visitors probably yearned to leave business behind and move on to a relaxing game of whist in the mahogany-paneled confines of the all-male Buffalo Club. Even so, exposition president John Milburn was chagrined to be forced to cut off his conversation with chief architect John Carrère. "You're sending us out to talk in the snow?" he queried in the hallway.

"Absolutely," I replied. "You should walk the exposition grounds in the snow and evaluate your work right there—much better altogether." The men laughed as they gathered their coats and made their way out the door.

After they were gone, I sat in my rocking chair, resting my head, luxuriating in the evening. Then in the quiet, I heard my favorite sound: sleigh bells jingling on harnesses as the horses trotted down Bidwell Parkway, sleigh gliders swishing through the snow. At this hour, bejeweled couples cloaked in fur against the cold were on their way to dinner parties; snowstorms were never permitted to interfere with the social swirl. Closing my eyes, I conjured a scene in my mind: a dining room with French doors and a coffered ceiling, a long table laid for twelve, freshly polished silver, candlelight throwing rainbows through the crystal. I was forever apart from that life, observing it, never living it. Nonetheless I pictured myself reclining on a sleigh, the harness bells dancing, a bison skin pulled around me for warmth as snowflakes touched my face and I was carried to dinner at the estate of John J. Albright or Dexter P. Rumsey.

A knock at the front door intruded on my thoughts. Not wanting to be rude to latecomers, I rose and went into the hall. My Polish housekeeper, Katarzyna, had already opened the door, but she had not welcomed the visitor.

"People gone now. Visiting time finished," she said with a cut of her hand, as if to shoo the caller away.

The reason for her behavior was clear: One of my students was at the door, peering around Katarzyna to find me. Millicent Talbert, age thirteen, mature-looking for her years but possessed of an innocence and earnestness which at school made her the one who always missed the jokes.

"Miss Barrett?"

There was a hint of the Middle West in her speech. Millicent was an orphan who had come to Buffalo from Ohio to live with her aunt and uncle, who had adopted her. In the unlit doorway, Millicent was a shadow against the white of the evening.

"I'm sorry, Miss Barrett, I don't want to bother you, but—" She paused, glancing at Katarzyna. "May I speak with you? Just you, I mean. I watched from the corner and waited until everyone left, really I did, Miss Barrett, I didn't want to disturb you. I didn't want to cause trouble."

Millicent Talbert never stopped apologizing. For she appeared agonizingly aware at every moment that she was what the people of Buffalo called "colored." She seemed to fear that each time she stepped out of her own neighborhood her color was the only thing anyone noticed about her. And she was right. Among Macaulay's nearly two hundred fifty students, she was the first, and only, colored girl. Many parents assumed she was a gifted scholarship girl, but although she was gifted, she did not attend on scholarship. Her family paid full tuition and was also generous with donations. There had been some protest when I accepted her application, from parents worried about their daughters sitting next to a colored person in class, sharing a cloakroom with her, dining side by side at noontime. But Millicent was from a good family— meaning a *rich* family in society parlance—and the board of trustees had backed me more strongly than I expected. As it turned out, the girls themselves welcomed Millicent, I'm happy to say, regarding her as something of an exotic in their midst and befriending her with ease.

"I don't mind talking at the door, Miss Barrett, if that's better for you."

We might have been completely alone, the three of us lost in a wilderness of snow.

"Come in, Millicent." I reached out to her, bringing her inside. Her hands felt frozen, and I rubbed them between mine. "How long have you been waiting?" Instead of answering, she leaned into me for a hug of warmth. The snow on her hat touched my cheek.

"Katarzyna, please bring a pot of cocoa to my study for Miss Talbert. And hang this up, will you?" I said, as I helped Millicent take off her wet coat.

Katarzyna stepped back, her face revealing a combination of apprehension and disdain.

Giving Katarzyna a severe look, I hung up the coat myself and led Millicent to the study. I settled her opposite me before the fire.

"So, my dear, what prompts you to wait out in the snow instead of coming to my office in the morning?" I made my voice easygoing, knowing how Millicent's serious nature sometimes led her to fixate on things. I was prepared to be gentle with her: She was interested in the sciences, and I cherished a dream that she would become a scientific researcher. Her patient, exacting nature would be suited to such a profession.

"I didn't know what to think, Miss Barrett. It was"—she paused—"strange."

"What was strange?"

"We were walking home. I mean, I was walking *her* home."

Dealing with young persons can be frustrating. "I think you'd better start at the beginning."

"Oh." She glanced at me in surprise. Millicent was a pretty girl with pale brown skin, an oval face, soft features, and none of the awkwardness common to girls her age. "Well, today I went to the Crèche for my afternoon helping the kindergartners to read."

As part of the charity program I had instituted at Macaulay for girls nine and older, each student spent one afternoon a week at the Fitch Crèche working with preschoolers and kindergartners. The Crèche was one of the prides of the city, the first institution in the nation where poor mothers could bring their children to be cared for during working hours. The children were given meals, baths, education, and even medical examinations.

"On Mondays a lower-school girl named Grace Sinclair comes to the Crèche," Millicent said. I felt my body tense, and willed myself to relax. I mustn't show Millicent that I had any special concern for the nine-year-old named Grace Sinclair.

"She draws for the little ones," Millicent continued, oblivious to my reaction, "and she's good at it. Today she drew elephants that looked *so real*. Most of the children had never even seen a picture of an elephant! Then she imitated an elephant roaring—Grace is a fine mimic," Millicent assured me, "and everyone gathered round to hear her."

Of course I knew Grace could draw well. Of course I knew she was a fine mimic.

"Anyway, Miss Atkins always comes with the lower-school girls, and to keep an eye on us older ones too, I guess." For the first time Millicent smiled, shyly acknowledging my subterfuge for the supervision of older girls who wanted to believe that they needed no supervision.

"Today," Millicent said in a thrilled whisper, "Betsy Pratt got sick. She threw up in the cloakroom! It was disgusting! No one could go in there, the smell was so bad. Even after the custodian came to clean it. Miss Barrett—a man went into the girls' cloakroom! And—"

"Millicent," I interrupted. Girls this age switched from childhood to adulthood and back again as quick as lightning. "Everyone gets sick at one time or another. There's no need to make a fuss about it."

"Sorry, Miss Barrett." She pouted.

"All right, go on."

"Well, the matron was upset in case Betsy had a sickness that the little ones might catch, and so Miss Atkins decided to take Betsy home early, right away, even though her frock was still wet because of the"—she glanced at me guiltily—"because of what happened, and even though . . ."

As Millicent talked on, I felt myself slipping into the suspended animation that was my refuge whenever a young person began to tell me a long and complicated story.

". . . and this made a problem because Miss Atkins usually takes Grace Sinclair home herself, because Grace lives near school and Miss Atkins comes back to school after the Crèche. So Miss Atkins asked me if I would take Grace home when we finished at five and I did. We took the electric streetcar partway, and then we walked."

Now here was something important: entrusting a nine-year-old to a thirteen-year-old. Had Millicent been an Anglo-Saxon girl, Miss Atkins never would have done it. Instead she would have made a telephone call from the Crèche office and arranged for a housekeeper to pick Grace up, or called Grace's father downtown and asked him to send a sleigh for her. Or, if there'd been no other choice, she would have asked the favor of one of the many girls who lived closer to Grace than Millicent did. But because Millicent was colored, Miss Atkins felt free to treat her like a servant, trusting and exploiting her as she would a servant, by asking her to go blocks out of her way to take another child home.

The city—our neighborhood, that is—was quite safe, but in other parts of town—in the area where the Crèche was located, for example—there had been so many labor strikes, so many layoffs, so much hostility among the foreign groups, I suddenly feared that Millicent was trying to tell me that she and Grace had been assaulted on their way home. A young man roaming his neighborhood, on strike or laid off from his job, or unemployed since leaving school, had seen an opportunity to attack a daughter of the bosses who was out with only a dark-skinned servant girl to protect her. That's how it would have seemed to him. Or perhaps Millicent herself had been the target, because in our city the only work many colored men could get was as strikebreakers at the factories.

I asked, "Did something happen on your walk home, Millicent?"

"Yes."

I sat forward, gripping the armrests of my chair.

"Oh, nothing like that, Miss Barrett," she said, laughing nervously. "I mean, no one *bothered* us. But Grace said something . . . strange. So strange, I thought you'd want to know about it. It bothered me." Millicent's voice was breaking; all at once she was about to cry.

"It's all right, Millicent." I rubbed the back of her hand as she struggled against her tears. "Tell me when you're ready."

Finally she began. "Well, we were walking down Chapin Parkway and looking at the lamps coming on—it wasn't snowing yet—and I said, how beautiful it was, to see the lamplight on the snow. Even the old and dirty snow looks beautiful with the light on it. I said how lucky we were, to be out at sunset, the most beautiful part of the day, and"— there was a sudden shrillness in Millicent's voice, as she stumbled over her words—"and then Grace looked at me and said she wanted to kill herself."

Millicent stared at me, expecting a response. But as shocked as I was, I had learned long ago to withhold my reactions to what students told me until I was certain I'd heard everything. I didn't want to make snap judgments and perhaps miss the most important facts.

After a moment Millicent resumed, "She wasn't excited. She said it like it was the most natural thing she could think of."

She paused again, and I knew I must speak this time. But I mustn't frighten her, even as I was alert to every nuance of her words. "And what did you say, Millicent?"

"I said, 'You mustn't say that, it's a sin,' and she said, 'I can say it if I want, and I can do it too,' and she was mad at me, and I said—"

At this point Katarzyna carried in a silver tray holding the cocoa in a silver pot, a plate of shortbread cookies, and the flowered china she knew I liked to use for company. In spite of my upset, I was pleased that Katarzyna was trying to make up for her behavior in the hall. She placed the tray on a small round table, which she moved between Millicent and me. While I poured the cocoa, Millicent ate the cookies with intense concentration.

After she'd finished several, I asked, "You were about to tell me what you said to Grace?"

Millicent brushed the cookie crumbs from her skirt. "I—well, I didn't want to have a fight with her, so I tried to think of what you would say."

"Thank you, Millicent, that's very kind." My tone was more dismissive than I intended. I hated flattery. But I reminded myself that Millicent was unfailingly sincere. "And what was that?" I asked more gently.

"I said everything was so beautiful in the world—she should just look around at the snow and the lights, and listen to the sleigh bells, and she would realize. Was that the right thing to say, Miss Barrett?"

Her earnestness made tears smart in my eyes. "Yes, Millicent, you said exactly the right thing."

"Then Grace said everything *was* beautiful, she knew that, but she was a bad girl. 'A bad evil girl,' she said, and 'I want to be dead, so I won't be bad anymore.' I never heard anyone talk like that, Miss Barrett. I don't know Grace very well, but I remember helping to teach her to read, when I was younger. Remember how the girls in my class used to help the first graders with reading and math?"

Yes, I remembered.

"Remembering gave me an idea, and I said that if she killed herself, who would draw for the little children at the Crèche? Who would imitate elephants? The children would miss her. But Grace only said they would find someone else to draw for them. I didn't like it, when she said that. Oh, Miss Barrett, it was scary—she was so quiet about it. Like she'd really thought it through and knew exactly what to do."

I could see them clearly in my mind, making their way between a winter's-worth of snow mounds: Grace with her blond hair flowing in ringlets beneath her hat, the rabbit fur of her high-collared coat touching her jawline, her hands in a fur muff, her high-buttoned boots; Millicent beside her, wearing a coat expensive and well made, but plain-looking compared to Grace's, so as not to draw attention to the girl who wore it. So as not to elicit jealousy in someone who was capable of acting on that jealousy, because he was white and his daughter did not have as fine a coat as the daughter of a colored man.

"Then I remembered that Grace's mother died last year."

Less than a year ago, it was. At the end of September. On a pristine early autumn day, yellow just beginning to touch the green on the trees outside her window. Margaret Sinclair had been my best friend, and I missed her terribly.

"I know about things like that"—Millicent's reference to her own family was confident and matter-of-fact—"so I put my arm around her, and I said, 'Your mother would be sad if she heard you talk like this.' But Grace said, 'That's not true. Because when I'm dead, I'll be with my mother, and I'll be able to tell her that I'm sorry for everything bad I did, and she'll forgive me and she'll take care of me again, and that's why I'm going to kill myself, so I can be with her in heaven.' "

Millicent stopped.

"And then?"

"All of a sudden she made a snowball and threw it against a tree, and asked about—well, some gossip about one of the teachers, and she was giggling about it. That made me mad because I didn't know if she was just playing a game with me, about killing herself, or if she really meant it. When we got to her house she asked me to come in for cocoa and cake, but I was still mad so I said no, even though I wanted to, and then I came here."

For a long time I stared into the fire. One image filled my mind: Grace Sinclair as a baby. Her chubby cheeks, her silken hair, the delicate white bonnet her mother had knitted for her. How had Grace come to this dreadful point in her life? How and when had we adults allowed her to go astray?

For Millicent's sake, I roused myself. "You did well, my dear. Very well indeed. You've been splendid. Grace is lucky to have you as a friend."

Millicent's eyes lit up. "What will happen to Grace now, do you think?" Something occurred to her, eliciting a perverse, thrilling curiosity. She whispered, "Do you think they'll send her to the state hospital?"

The hospital, more formally called the Buffalo State Asylum for the Insane, was several blocks from school. With its two brooding towers that could be seen from almost every part of town, it was a specter that haunted the edges of children's minds.

"No, Millicent," I said evenly. "She won't be sent to the state hospital. She's only nine. As you thought, she's probably playing a game with those words about killing herself." I didn't believe it, but what else could I tell her? "She probably heard a grown-up talking, and she's imitating what she heard without understanding it. That's why a moment later she was throwing snowballs and giggling about her teachers. Well." I clapped my hands lightly, my signal to students that meetings were coming to an end. "I think it best that you not discuss this with your friends. We don't want anyone teasing Grace, do we? Of course you'll want to tell your family. But at school, it will be our secret." I squeezed her hand, knowing the hint of conspiracy would encourage her to keep quiet.

She looked toward the windows. "Miss Barrett," she said carefully, "does anyone really do that? Kill themselves, I mean. Is that something people do?"

Society's accepted answer would have been, "No, of course not." That was the answer her family and her minister would have expected me to give. Suicide was an unmentionable, shameful sin that reflected upon an entire family. But I couldn't lie to Millicent. Instead I said, "Grown-ups sometimes, but rarely. People have to be very misguided to do that; ill in their minds in some way."

"Never children?"

I said nothing. I was at a loss. I'd never known a student to commit suicide or even threaten it. Nonetheless, I'd had suspicions more than once among the upper-school girls . . . a senior whom I knew to be terrified of boats was said to have died alone in a sailing accident; a junior once died between evening and morning from what was labeled an "overwhelming fever." However, people did die in sailing accidents and did die of overwhelming fevers, so how could I know the truth?

"Never children. I'm proud of you, Millicent."

She smiled broadly, and perhaps feeling that a smile was inappropriate under the circumstances, she raised her cup and finished her cocoa. When she had also finished the cookies, I telephoned her aunt to send a sleigh to pick her up.

And then I was alone, with nothing but Grace Sinclair's face to fill my mind.

Chapter Two

There is a nightmare I have: I fall asleep at the end of a productive day and suddenly find myself trapped within the frothing, seething waters beneath the cataract of Niagara. The struggle is long. No one can help me. Black cliffs loom around me. Waves of mist blind me. Rainbows flash. Trout leap. My legs lock within the wet vise that is my skirt. Emerald-green covers my face, blocks my throat, until finally, I let the vortex take me. This dream comes to me two or three times a year, without warning. That is, with no attachment to any specific event that might inspire it. Nevertheless I do know why I have the nightmare.

My mother died of diphtheria when I was two years old, and my paternal grandmother came to live with my father and me at our home in Williamstown, Massachusetts. My father was a professor of geology at Williams College. He had married late in life, after years of complacent success, and he idolized my mother. Her early death left him forever with an expression of puzzled surprise, as if he were taken aback by a treachery he dare not define.

When I was seven, my father took me with him on a trip to Niagara. He had been to the Falls many times, but this was my first visit. With the acute focus of a child, I listened to my father explain the landscape: First there was the Niagara River, which divided America from Canada. About a mile above the Falls, the river was transformed into the rapids. At the Falls, the sixty-three-acre Goat Island divided the rapids, creating the American Falls on one side and the vast, curving Horseshoe Falls, which belonged to Canada, on the other. At the bottom of the Falls was the steep-walled gorge, which the water itself had carved through the soft rock. The gorge was seven miles long, and the river continued some seven miles farther, into Lake Ontario.

I insisted on these details because we weren't visiting Niagara as tourists. We had work to do. My father had come to study evidence of glaciation, and I was eager to help him. On Goat Island, we climbed down the long twisting stairway that led to the base of the American Falls. Following narrow wooden walkways, and soaked in spite of our rain gear, we made our way to the Cave of the Winds, behind the surging sheet of water. In the cave we took samples of limestone and shale. Then we climbed up the stairs again, nearly a hundred steps. My legs ached by the time we reached the top. After I rested, we crossed the stone bridges leading from Goat Island to the small Three Sisters Islands—Asenath, Angeline, and Celinda Eliza, far into the Canadian rapids. These islands were called the Three Sisters, my father explained, in honor of the daughters of General Parkhurst Whitney, a hero of the war of 1812. In their day, the bridges hadn't yet been built and early one spring, when the rapids were mostly ice-bound, the girls had bravely walked to these small islands and become the first females to visit them.

I could be brave too. I imagined myself, like Asenath, Angeline, and Celinda Eliza, tiptoeing through the shallows. The waters around the islands were calm and lovely, with gentle inlets and small cascades. My father and I visited in June, when the islands were a wilderness of rocks, flowers, bushes, and trees. Branches arched down to touch the water. Mallard ducks swam contentedly from cove to cove. Red-winged blackbirds flitted among the foliage, their yellow and red wing bars dense as velvet in the sunlight. A butterfly—a Painted Lady, my father said—lit upon my hair. Apart from the roar of wind and water, there was no sense—no hint, even—of the cataract nearby.

We picnicked along the tree-lined shore of the third Sister, Celinda Eliza. The stony ledge where we sat was magically smooth, for the rocks had once been underwater, my father explained: the unrelenting flow had polished them slippery as glass. Out beyond the sparkling shallows the rapids were like a green blanket, solid, thick, and strong. Yet here on Celinda Eliza, all was peaceful. The undersides of the leaves were lit with the rippling reflections of sunlight on water.

After lunch, my father became absorbed in searching for glacial erratics, boulders carried here by glaciers, sometimes from hundreds of miles away, while I became absorbed in the pebbles washed up along the shore, vibrating in the glimmer of the water's edge. One pebble in particular captured my attention. It was bright and shimmered like crystal or like a diamond. Yes, it *was* a diamond and I had to have it, for my father. I was a geologist, like him. A *diamond*—the finest gift I could ever give him.

A ripple of water carried the stone a bit further down the shoreline. Another took it a bit nearer the rapids, but I had to have it. I took a step toward it, the water touching the tips of my boots. I bent down, and reached . . .

"Louisa! Freeze!"

My father was grabbing my arm, pulling me back, making me stumble on the slick rocks, kneeling before me screaming, "Don't you ever do that again! That was a stupid, stupid thing to do! Don't you know how strong the current is? You could have been swept over the Falls in an instant!" And then, as I stood stunned within the circle of his arms, he began to cry, hiding his face against my shoulder, his rough gray beard scratching my cheek.

There had been no danger. I know that, now. Five or six steps would have been needed, at least, to reach the pull of the rapids. I have learned that many people—rational people—wade along the shores of the Three Sisters, cooling their feet in the bright shallows. I have come to understand that my father cried more because I was his only living link to my mother than because of any real danger. But when I was seven, his terror swept through me and became my own. Over and over I replayed the scene in my mind, but no longer was I standing in the reality of a half inch of water. I was wading—ankles, knees, waist, farther and farther into the rushing mass—until the soft blanket enveloped me.

After our visit to Niagara, my father came to believe that he could protect me only if he kept me near him, so when I completed the local elementary school, he decided against sending me to boarding school, which would have been customary for a girl in my position. Instead I was tutored for three hours each day by a succession of Williams College students. Under my grandmother's watchful eye, these young men taught me their areas of concentration—Roman history one day,

Chaucer the next, in a disorganized jumble nonetheless imbued with intellectual passion and rigor. In the summers, instead of spending peaceful days in Williamstown with my grandmother, I went with my father on expeditions to Colorado and Wyoming. When I was ten, we were stranded for two days by a frightening summer blizzard in the Togwatee Pass, in Wyoming, but because I was with him, my father thought me safe.

All this had an unforeseen effect: I learned to talk on terms of absolute equality with mountain men, Indian guides, and (most significantly) the eminently marriageable students of Williams College. I felt none of the awe that other girls—more properly raised girls—might have felt or feigned. I never learned to flirt or to simper. Perhaps the fact that I treated men as friends made it impossible for them to consider me as a wife.

My father was pleased to relent in his steadfast supervision when I was ready for college, a goal we'd both cherished, but he died while I was in my third year at Wellesley, so he never saw me graduate. My grandmother had died the year before. Now I was completely alone, with no family and an inheritance not even sufficient to cover my tuition. My father had had no income beyond his salary. What with paying for my tutors and financing his scientific expeditions (so that he might conduct them exactly as he wished), there was almost nothing left. I sold part of my father's rock collection in order to complete my degree at Wellesley. I had always hoped to follow my father's path: to work toward an advanced degree in geology, to teach at a women's college, and to continue our tradition of summer expeditions. The only graduate programs open to me, as a woman, were in Europe; therefore I would need to earn a good deal of money before I could continue my studies.

At Wellesley I had a close friend, Francesca Coatsworth, who was from Buffalo. After graduation, Francesca was returning home to begin an apprenticeship as an architect with the firm of Louise Blanchard Bethune. Francesca encouraged me to apply for a position at Macaulay, her old school. On her recommendation, I was offered an appointment teaching geography and history, a combination that seemed natural and pleasing. I took up my duties with excitement, knowing I had no choice, yet eager to make the most of the opportunity. In my heart, I believed Macaulay would be only a way station.

I surprised myself by choosing a city merely twenty miles from my nightmare of Niagara, but Buffalo was considered a place of promise and hope. Already it was called the Queen City of the Lakes, the greatest inland port in the history of America. And it was a city of glamour. Buffalo had sent two presidents to the White House, Millard Fillmore and Grover Cleveland. When I came to the city in 1886, Cleveland was in his first term in the White House. He had recently married young, beautiful Frances Folsom, who had grown up in Buffalo. She was wildly popular, with fan clubs dedicated to her around the country. There were sixty millionaires in Buffalo and scores who were almost millionaires. Their fortunes came from Great Lakes shipping, from railroads, flour milling, lumber, leather tanning, meat packing, soap, iron, wallpaper, banking—and, quite simply, land: from the fervent rush of commercial interests to establish a foothold in Buffalo. The city's daughters were being sent abroad to marry into the English aristocracy.

Outwardly, I prospered as the city prospered. In 1892, I became headmistress after only six years at the school. I brought Macaulay to prominence and doubled the enrollment, to close to two hundred fifty girls in grades 1 through 12. I instituted a college preparatory curriculum and, most important, made it fashionable. Girls from good families who had once completed their educations at finishing schools out of town now stayed home and graduated from Macaulay. Granted, not more than a handful were permitted to go to college, but all Macaulay girls attained a breadth of knowledge which made me proud. In addition to the standard subjects (including Latin), the girls studied chemistry, physics, and trigonometry. Many undertook the study of classical Greek. The curriculum was difficult, and new for women, but my girls rose to the challenge. I began a scholarship program, and although I had only limited funds (enough for one or two students per year), nevertheless Macaulay was recognized for educating the most talented among the working class. As an added benefit, my girls, probably for the first time in their lives, were forced to interact on an equal basis with the daughters of the men employed by their fathers' factories. I also formalized a program of volunteer work, to give my scions of power and wealth an awareness of the bleaker realities of their city. I wanted them to take this awareness into their marriages, each a gentle but persistent infiltrator.

Through all of this I never gave up my own goal, to undertake studies in Europe for an advanced degree in geology. My daily life in Buffalo felt transient, like a youthful, albeit fulfilling, lark. Yet as the years passed, almost in spite of myself I became settled. When the day came that I finally possessed the financial means to leave the city to pursue my own dreams, I no longer felt I could. I had invested too much, in emotion and labor, to leave the city behind. My moment of choice had passed.

Grace Sinclair lived in a Palladian house set back from the corner of Lincoln Parkway and Forest Avenue, less than a half-mile from Macaulay. A low brick wall surrounded the estate, with trees and shrubbery further shielding the house from the street.

The evening after Millicent Talbert's visit, I stood at the gate, my gloved hands upon the frigid grillwork, and I studied the house. A light, feathery snow was falling. Months had passed since I last stood here, and the house looked indefinably different. It glowed behind the barren trees with a brightness which wasn't entirely welcoming.

Grace Sinclair was my goddaughter. When her mother, Margaret, had died seven months ago, she'd left her husband, Tom, devastated. Margaret had been born into one of Buffalo's oldest and most prominent families, whereas Tom, although he was now the director of the hydroelectric power project at Niagara Falls, had endured poverty as a child in Ireland. Perhaps in part because of the difference in their backgrounds, Tom had adored Margaret, indeed worshipped her. After her death, he had retreated into himself. While still managing his business, he'd clearly wanted no visitors to his home during the time of mourning, and so I'd stayed away.

But Tom wasn't the only one devastated by Margaret's loss. Grace and her mother had been unusually close, and for weeks Grace had seemed dazed, going through the motions of daily life with little awareness of the details around her. I too had felt desolate. Struggling with my own loss, with the emptiness inside me which once had been filled by Margaret's warm, joyful laugh, I hadn't been as precisely attuned to Grace as I would have been otherwise. I'd seen her at school, I'd invited her out on the weekends; observing her slowly regain her equanimity, I'd gone no further.

That had been my mistake. Today I'd checked with Grace's teachers, who reported her to be "sensitive." I'd asked for specifics: abrupt shifts in mood, argumentativeness, a tendency to run away when challenged. Her teachers had responded to her actions with sympathy rather than strictness, as I myself would have reacted under the circumstances. Next I needed to consult with her father. This morning I'd sent Thomas Sinclair a note at his office, telling him to expect me at this hour. I opened the gate and made my way up the slippery flagstone path.

Grace herself answered my knock. She filled the doorway like an angel, the brightness of the hall making a halo around her. She wore a costume of scarves and shawls draped over one of her mother's tennis dresses.

In a life like mine, there are not many people to love. I loved Grace Sinclair.

"I raced from the third floor, Aunt Louisa." Breathing deeply, she gave me a quick hug and then curtsied with a teasing smile. "Good evening, Miss Barrett," she said in an Irish accent, acting out the role of an upper-class maid. "The master asks that you come upstairs to the library, if you please."

"Thank you," I replied, playing along with her. She grinned and beckoned me inside.

The hall was brilliant with a steady, glowing light. The sliding doors into the drawing room and dining room were open, and there, too, this odd light prevailed, revealing every detail: the classical pillars and coffered ceiling in the drawing room; the mahogany wainscoting and intricately carved mantelpiece in the dining room; and beyond, the willowy plantings and stone fountain of the glassed conservatory.

But Grace was oblivious to the peculiar brilliance of the light and was already making her way up the wide, curving staircase. I hurried to follow, smiling as I always did at the delicate statue of Hebe, Greek goddess of youth, which stood in the nook on the landing. The Tiffany stained-glass window above the statue was dark at this hour, but I remembered its woodland landscape of greens and yellows and the stream meandering into distant hills.

Suddenly, as I turned on the landing to begin the second flight of stairs, I realized how the house had changed. Instead of flickering gaslight, an electric glow as steady as day filled the rooms.

I stopped, leaning against the banister to look. To gawk. I had never been in a house lit by electricity. The change was—miraculous. I'd heard that in cities like New York and Chicago, the rich had been showing off their wealth by installing steam generators and electrifying their homes for the sake of novelty. But here in Buffalo, the old families had no need for novelty, and the nouveau riche emulated the old. Compared to this, the other homes I visited were shadowy and claustrophobic. Here the air itself seemed clear, vibrant, and somehow invigorating. All at once I knew why: Gaslight consumed the oxygen in a room; electricity did not.

Knowing that Thomas Sinclair was the director of the power stations at Niagara, I realized the light around me came not from a steam-powered generator at the back of the house, but from the lines of the Niagara Frontier Power Company. These lines already carried electricity from the Falls to light the city's streetlamps and to operate its streetcars. I felt the awe of witnessing magic: Thomas Sinclair had turned water into light.

"Grace, when did your father bring electricity into the house?"

Six or seven steps above me, she turned. All at once she looked like Margaret—the tilt of her head, the inquiring gaze, the way she leaned into the polished banister, with its scrollwork posts, as if posing for a portrait. The resemblance was like a knife in me, reminding me of the companionship and happiness Margaret had offered me each day from the moment we met.

"That was one of the first things Papa did, after Mother—" She stopped. Her wide-set eyes seemed to go blank.

"Grace?"

She stared past me, her face a deadened mask.

{23}

"Grace?"

Startled, she stepped back, then recovered. "And will you be wanting some tea, then, ma'am?"

I had been away from this house too long. I felt my absence with a cutting sense of regret. Margaret would have expected more from me. *I* would have expected more from me. But where Grace was concerned, my confidence faltered. That was the problem with love: It made me doubt myself.

She continued up the stairs. "Mrs. Sheehan and the others are out at a *wake*," she said, using the quasi-ghoulish emphasis typical of her age. Mrs. Sheehan was the housekeeper. "I'm looking after things for her until seven." She ushered me to the library. "Will you wait here, please, ma'am, while I see if the master is ready to receive you?"

She raced down the hall while I stood at the library door, watching. "Papa, Papa, Aunt Louisa is here!" she called. She knocked on a door at the end of the hall and went in without waiting for a reply.

Grace had always been boisterous, because no one had ever curbed her except to the limits necessary for her safety. She wasn't proper, or prim, or demure, or any of the other adjectives young ladies were supposed to be. She was both seen and heard, and openly cherished by her parents. The gossiping ladies of society said, disparagingly, that Tom and Margaret indulged her. They were indulgent, in the sense that they simply loved her, as odd as that would be in some of the other homes of the neighborhood, where the children were polished and groomed by nurses and nannies and presented to their parents for inspection once a day. Even more odd (according to the dictates of society), Tom and Margaret actually enjoyed spending time with Grace. Margaret organized her day around Grace's school schedule, using the housekeeper only for an occasional pickup or drop-off. Now and again I'd wondered whether Margaret and Grace spent too much time together, preventing Grace from learning how to be alone. However, in the context of the parental neglect which I typically saw, Margaret's excess was forgivable—especially in light of the secret of Grace's birth.

Apart from the doctor, I was the only person who knew that Tom and Margaret had adopted Grace. Often I wondered which other of my students were adopted, for surely some were. But all was kept hidden. After more than a few years of childless marriage, Margaret had feigned pregnancy when she learned that a child from a good family might be available for adoption. She'd worn padding and undertaken a confinement. Dr. Perlmutter had visited her regularly—*and* collected a fee for the nonexistent delivery, just to make everything appear normal.

I had been the intermediary, telling Margaret and Tom that because of my work, I was in a position to hear about such things. I had been the one who gave the assurances that Grace was from a good family, a family in which a properly raised daughter had been improperly supervised for one brief moment during which she'd made a devastating mistake. If this mistake became known, the girl would have no future—no possibility of marriage, no opportunity for college or work. No life, in short. Such was the punishment society exacted.

Margaret did a great deal of charity work and had enormous compassion. But in one of the—to me—incomprehensible hypocrisies of her class, she never considered taking an infant from the orphanage. Of course with a child from the orphanage, secrecy would have been impossible. There would have been forms to fill out. Legalities. There would have been hushed rumors and endless speculation about the infant's true parentage. As the child grew up, he or she would be forever judged by the community as a product of the poorhouse. But with Grace there were no legalities. No rumors. Only a good family, eager to forget. Grace could be presented to society as Tom and Margaret's true daughter. As she grew, becoming more and more like Margaret, copying her mannerisms, her tone of voice, her easy laugh, Grace did indeed become the true daughter that Tom and Margaret wanted.

Grace emerged from the bedroom and skipped back to me. "The master says will you forgive him, he returned late from the power station and he will join you as soon as he changes. Please make yourself at home in the library. I will leave you now, ma'am, having too much homework to dawdle!"

After a quick curtsey, she turned and ran up the stairs to her third-floor rooms. In most houses of this kind, the third floor was devoted to billiards and ballrooms, but not here. Grace had the entire floor to herself, divided into nursery, playroom, and art studio. If she hadn't learned how to be alone when her mother was alive, she must surely be learning now. I ached for her, even as I ached within myself, yet at this moment at least, she appeared as rambunctious as ever.

After her footsteps ceased and I could imagine her at her desk, I went into the library. This was the room where Margaret and I had always sat together, Grace playing at our feet. There was only one light on, the lamp on Tom's desk. The bulb was faint enough to give an impression of the gaslight I remembered. The room was exactly the same: the worn Persian carpets, the glass-doored bookcases, Grace's miniature rocker, the coffered ceiling with its quatrefoil design. Newspapers and magazines, folded back to mark the articles Tom was reading, were spread on the table. Papers covered his desk. He often worked at home. In the far corner atop a half-pillar was a plaster cast of the Nike of Samothrace. Scattered on the carpet between the two tall windows were Grace's pastel chalks and a pile of her drawing paper, untouched by the maid, a sign of Grace's unusually immediate presence in the daily life of the family.

I might have been waiting for Margaret instead of her husband. A chill passed through me. Frightened, I stepped away from the shadows, for Margaret *was* here, in the portrait that hung between the windows: Margaret at the time of her marriage, her dark hair pulled back, a few curls escaping at her temples as they always did, her eyes deep brown, at her neck the five-strand pearl choker she always wore in the evening. Her face held the bright, hopeful look of young womanhood.

When I came to Macaulay as a teacher, Margaret had graduated but was staying on to complete a college-entrance curriculum (not a standard offering before my time). I tutored her in Greek and Latin. Although I was several years older than she, we became friends. Like me, she had lost both her parents, and when we met she was living with her grandmother. Margaret was a Winspear, a member of the city's elite. Aided by a large private income, a lighthearted rebellion filled her, an irreverence which seemed to wake me up after the difficulties I'd faced upon my father's death. With her encouragement, I transformed myself into what I thought of as a "colorful character," in Oriental shawls and velvet hats. I cut a fine figure through society, I liked to think—tall and slender, blond and bold. The Macaulay girls emulated me; they thought me beautiful, then.

Margaret's grandmother permitted her to study as a way to fill the years before marriage, but when Margaret was actually accepted at Vassar, old Mrs. Winspear decided that she had to put a stop to such scholastic frivolity. She took Margaret on a world tour. This wasn't unusual: Many Macaulay girls enjoyed the Grand Tour before their marriages. However, Margaret and her grandmother eschewed Europe, where they had both traveled before, and went instead to the East—to Egypt, Ceylon, Singapore, Malaya. They spent five months in India, visiting maharajahs and walking in the foothills of the Himalayas accompanied by a troop of Sherpa guides and bearers.

When they returned, Mrs. Winspear had her victory: Margaret no longer felt a need for college. However she was now in control of her fortune, and she committed an act of rebellion more profound than going to college: She fell in love with Thomas Sinclair and chose him to be her husband. Sinclair was Irish, and he'd been raised a Catholic— two marks against him in her family's eyes. He'd also been born into poverty of a desperate kind. As a boy he'd worked in a glass bottle factory in Belfast. He'd been a "take-out boy," using tongs to take the half-finished bottles out of the molds and carrying them to the next step in the glassmaking process. He'd come to America alone as a teenager and risen by his wits, the gossips said—and the way they said it was not entirely complimentary.

While working at a railroad telegraph office in Scranton, Pennsylvania, Tom caught the attention of John J. Albright, a well-born Scranton native whose railroad associations would soon bring him to Buffalo. Albright paid Tom's tuition to his own alma mater, the Rensselaer Polytechnic Institute, where Tom studied engineering. Before his fascination with hydroelectric power, Tom made a fortune in the design and construction of railroad bridges. He was invited to Buffalo at Albright's urging by the private consortium of businessmen funding the construction of the power station.

Money triumphed, of course, and Tom and Margaret's union was finally accepted by the Winspears and thus all of Buffalo society. Tom shrugged off his Catholicism, and they were married at Trinity Church, the epicenter of the Episcopal establishment.

I liked Tom from the moment I met him, mostly because he made Margaret happy, but also because there was a focus and forthrightness about him that was missing in most young men (at least in my experience). Self-educated as a boy, he was well-read and displayed an enthusiasm for knowledge that was often lacking in those whose education came easily. He was purposeful while still being reflective; he was generous, funny, and welcoming. Never once did he object to the closeness Margaret and I enjoyed.

I often wondered if Tom and Margaret were aware of the disapproving whispers about them. If they were, they didn't care. They forged a marriage of rebellion. They gave up the endless round of dinner parties that marked formal society. Tom threw himself into the technological challenges of his position. Instead of being a hostess, Margaret made a commitment to settlement house work, teaching English to immigrant children and marketable skills like sewing to their impoverished mothers. To me she remained a loyal and supportive friend.

Gazing at her wedding portrait, I was stung by how far I'd come since I'd been Margaret's bridesmaid. I was no longer the young woman who'd pinned flowers in her hair, wore paisley shawls and garnet-colored skirts, and imagined herself in a pre-Raphaelite painting. Now my clothes were sturdy, my colors navy or gray. I could no longer risk being exotic.

Luckily the change for me came just when I was appointed headmistress. People began to remark on how I had "grown into" my position, becoming what they expected me to be. Margaret teased me about my newfound conservatism, but I didn't dare tell her the cause of it. More than once as the years passed, offering fewer and fewer possibilities, I found myself wondering, is this to be the limit of my fulfillment? I was now thirty-six, yet sometimes at school when I saw young eyes looking at me with respect, looking at me for guidance, I was surprised—who am I, but a girl like themselves, struggling to find my way?

No, I would not allow myself to indulge in the sin of self-pity. Firmly I turned away from Margaret's portrait and walked across the room. Hanging on the far wall, near Tom's desk, was a plainly framed architectural drawing of a railroad bridge. Tom considered this bridge, on a river somewhere in the West, his greatest achievement, although I could neither pronounce nor remember the name of the river it crossed. Beside the drawing were three fairly large watercolors I hadn't seen before and I set myself to study them.

The pictures showed the powerhouses on the shores of the Niagara River above the Falls. I'd read in the newspaper that two powerhouses had already been completed and put "on-line," as it was called. Two more were under construction on the American side of the river. On the Canadian shore, four powerhouses were also being built. Stanford White was the architect for the entire project (which as a whole was referred to as the "power station"), and the landscaping was designed by the Olmsted firm. In interviews Sinclair called the buildings "cathedrals of power," but I'd never understood what he meant. Now, looking at these watercolors, I did understand. The powerhouses rose beside the river like transcendent symbols of the holiness of man's endeavors.

"Lovely, aren't they?"

Thomas Sinclair stood behind me, looking over my shoulder at the pictures. Turning to greet him, I felt as if I were trapped between his body and the wall. He was tall, over six feet Margaret had told me, and strong. Tonight he wore a formal dinner jacket with white tie. His pale-brown hair was swept back, and he was clean-shaven. His cheekbones looked angular and precise; he was thinner than I remembered. Tom was in his midforties, but his face was smooth and unlined, his hair free of gray.

Whenever I saw him, which was primarily with Margaret, at home, his bearing disturbed me. There was a shyness and a hesitancy about him that was at odds with both his physique and his self-made wealth. He seemed to be slightly insecure about whether people were going to like him; yet at the same time, he obviously didn't care. He had the casual arrogance of a young street fighter.

"They were painted by someone you know," he said, leaning forward to focus on the pictures. Although he'd left Ireland thirty years ago, his brogue remained a gentle lilt at the end of his sentences. "Susannah Riley?" He looked at me with a touch of concern, saying her name as a question and implying that perhaps he should have asked my permission before purchasing the work of one of my employees. Susannah Riley was the art teacher at Macaulay. I was over-proud of her, for I had given Susannah her first job in Buffalo when she'd arrived here alone from the village of Fredonia, fifty miles to the southwest.

"Susannah is a wonderful artist," I agreed.

"Yes. I saw her work at the Fine Arts Academy exhibition last autumn. Those pictures of Niagara . . ." His words drifted off. "I liked the way she did the light on the Horseshoe Falls." He seemed embarrassed to be offering this bit of art criticism.

"Yes, I liked that too," I said, to encourage him.

"When I commissioned these paintings, I feared she'd be resentful—the scourge of industrialism, the wanton destruction of nature—the usual cant among these self-proclaimed preservationists." His hand cut through the air dismissively. "But she surprised me. She understood exactly what I was after." He turned to the watercolors. "These pictures are a comfort to me. An inspiration. Well." He stepped back and gave me a crooked grin that carried more than a little exasperation. "Making electricity is far easier than managing Grace, I can tell you. Please, sit down, Louisa."

And with the offer of a chair, he answered a question for me: by using my given name, he placed me within the family circle once more, where I'd been before Margaret's death. If he had called me "Miss Barrett," I would have been reduced to the woman he employed to educate his child. Instead, he would call me Louisa, and I would call him Tom.

He indicated one of the straight-backed chairs (considered more suitable for ladies) while he himself relaxed in a leather armchair, his long legs stretched before him, his elbows resting on the carved wooden armrests, his fingers forming a triangle beneath his chin.

"What can I do for you?" he asked, suddenly formal.

I took a breath, disconcerted by his abrupt shift from small talk. "I need to discuss a matter pertaining to Grace," I replied, as businesslike as he. I related to him the story Millicent had told me. As I spoke, his expression never changed. He's a wily one, I thought.

"Has she ever talked this way at home, Tom?" I asked when I finished the story.

He ignored my question. "Who was it who told you this?"

"Millicent Talbert. She's—"

"The niece of William and Mary Talbert."

I paused. "Yes." I knew only too well where this was leading.

"A story from such a girl, might it not be subject to . . . exaggeration?" He looked at me with raised brows. "Given the nature of her . . ."

He wished me to fill this in for him, to allow us to have a conversation of hints and nods and mutual understandings, nothing stated but everything comprehended. But I wouldn't give in to his urge for complicity, even though it would have been pleasant to smile at our mutual understanding, to let it bring us close. What Tom implied was what the overwhelming majority of Macaulay parents would imply. However, I had the responsibility to make a stand, to do as much as I could (little though it was) to grant Millicent Talbert a proper portion of respect.

I waged the battle gently. "We mustn't blame the messenger, Tom. Millicent was brave to come to me with this, instead of passing the story as gossip among her friends at school. The concerns she raised must be taken seriously. We must consider them, and be alert to any changes in Grace's behavior that might indicate—"

But his attention was gone from me. He'd turned his head and was listening to the faint singing upstairs, in Grace's rooms.

"I have been wondering . . ." he said slowly, "is this normal, do you think? This dressing up and imitating people, pretending she's acting out the plays and stories she reads at school? She gave me quite a fright the other day as Lady Macbeth."

I laughed, and he managed a smile. "I can imagine her as Lady Macbeth."

"Yes, it was quite a sight."

"That's perfectly normal, however. Girls at this age often play by taking on the identities of the people they study. I used to pretend I was Joan of Arc, conquering France on a white horse."

"Really?" He seemed taken aback.

"It was fun," I insisted. "Pretending to take care of the horse, especially."

"Well, here you see my problem, Louisa. Grace's life is so different from what mine was at her age. I'm happy for that, believe me—but it's not always easy for me to . . . judge her."

"And what was your life like at her age?"

"Ah. I'd already been in the factory for three years. But that's not a story for drawing rooms." He dismissed the subject with a flick of his fingers, and my heart went out to him for how lightly he wore his memories.

"Since Margaret died—" He stopped and took a deep breath before continuing. "Since Margaret died, Grace has been . . . well, we've both been . . ." Now his hints and implications were enough. "But she's never talked about . . . what Miss Talbert heard.She *has* been a bit more . . . dedicated to her costumes and her games. And to her drawing, of course. Miss Riley tells me she has a talent."

"Miss Riley?"

"Yes, Miss Riley comes to tutor her once a week. Should I have asked—?"

"No, no, that's quite all right," I said quickly. I knew Susannah tutored some of the ladies of the town, but I didn't know Grace was among her private students. The fact that neither Susannah nor Grace had mentioned it made me wary.

"Grace won't touch paints," Tom continued, "only pencil, charcoal and pastels. She's very obstinate about things that seem simple to me."

"Children sense their lack of power, so they gain what power they can by being obstinate about things that seem to us unimportant." Well, that statement came out a bit more schoolmarmish than I intended—undoubtedly a reflection of my jealousy over Susannah Riley's tutoring.

Tom sighed, glancing away. But when he looked at me again, his eyes were alight. "Why shouldn't she be obstinate? I'm glad she stands up for herself. Maybe this talk with Millicent Talbert was part of some play she was rehearsing."

I didn't respond.

"She's very ambitious—I do see that in her. She's always

dreaming up new plans for herself. I have high hopes for her."

Didn't he know that girls from nine to eleven were always ambitious, always dreaming up new plans for themselves? Didn't he know
that those plans almost invariably came to nothing? Mercifully, most
girls were not even aware of the nothing they were forced to embrace as
they grew older. They simply thought they had left their girlish fantasies
behind to take on the welcome obligations of womanhood: dinner parties, fancy clothes, and the interviewing of baby nurses. Sometimes I
despaired that I could do so little to help them.

I steadied myself. Who could tell? Perhaps Grace would find a new
kind of life, especially because her father would encourage her.

"Frankly, I've been grateful that she's had something to occupy
her time," Tom continued, "because I've been so involved with
business."

"Are you still enjoying your work?"

"It has its rewards," he said, suddenly brightening. "Recently I've
been devoting much of my time to persuading new industries to come
here to use the electricity we're producing. No sooner do they set up
shop than they're demanding so much power I've got to worry about
shortages! Then I'm racing to get more generators on-line. The aluminum industry is taking off like lightning. So is the production of
abrasives. I'm also planning the electrical exhibitions for the Pan-
American."

His eyes narrowed, as if I had unfairly accused him of something.
"We must each make our own consolation, Louisa. I didn't ask for
Margaret to die."

"And what consolation have you found in your business?"

He exhaled, regaining his equilibrium. "I have found light.
Literally. It's become a kind of religion to me, as *sac*rilegious as that
may sound: creating electricity from water, using alternating current to
send the electricity wherever it's needed. Most people don't realize
what it means. Of course everyone sees the new electrochemical industries at Niagara, and the street railway and streetlamps here in town,
and everyone talks about the steel plant we're building out at Stony
Point, but it's more than that—it *means* more than that, I mean.
Electrification is a fundamental change in the nature of life itself. I

know that sounds ridiculous, but it's true." He sat at the edge of his chair, leaning toward me. "Someday I'll send hydroelectric power to every farmhouse and every tenement in five states. Maybe the entire country. Certainly all of Canada. You see, Louisa, it's possible to change the world with electricity. When factories are electrified, machines will do the most dangerous jobs, not men. Factories won't need boys to work all night running cheap bottles from the benches to the ovens; a conveyer belt will do that. The boys can stay home and learn to read and write—with the steady light of electric lamps. Their mothers won't go half-blind, the way my mother did, sewing by kerosene. Farmwives won't be crippled from hauling water up from the wells all day long, every day of their lives; an electric pump will do that job."

The glow of commitment filled his eyes. And it *was* a glorious vision. I saw it with him: an end to child labor, an end to the beating-down that so many women endured simply to get by from day to day. I wanted to embrace that future with him—it was a miraculous place of hope and freedom, intoxicating to imagine.

"I tell you, Louisa, I'll change the world, and people won't be afraid anymore."

"Afraid?" I didn't understand him. "Afraid of what?"

"Afraid of the dark," he said easily. "Afraid of the night." He motioned toward the windows. "Aren't you ever afraid of the dark?"

"Well . . . when I was small, I suppose."

"That's the shield of gentility. I don't imagine that people who grow up in university towns are ever afraid of the dark—except as very young children, tucked up in their comfortable little beds, scaring themselves with thoughts of Indians in the wardrobe. People in the middle class, the upper class—no, they're never afraid of the night. Margaret was never afraid. But when you're poor, the darkness is like a blanket that suffocates you."

I didn't know what to say. I simply looked at him, knowing he was right, feeling pity for all he had suffered, and yet hurt that he seemed to be blaming me for things beyond my control.

"Forgive me, Louisa," he said, suddenly sheepish. "I've become a bit of a crusader, I'm afraid. Why don't we simply say that I'm involved with my work, and leave it at that?"

"It's quite all right, Tom, it's fascinating. I've never thought about electricity in terms of . . ." I heard myself speak the clichés that would return us to polite conversation, even though he'd shaken me. "Tom, why don't you take Grace out with you to the power station, show her how the machinery operates, discuss your plans."

"I don't think she'd find it very interesting, a nine-year-old . . ."

"You're wrong! She'd find it fascinating, because you do." An idea came to me, an opportunity for my girls. "I wonder if you might like to lecture to our seniors sometime. Whenever you have an hour. The young ladies at Macaulay would benefit from hearing your goals."

"Really? Well." He blushed, touching his pockets nervously as if searching for a cigarette before realizing it might be considered impolite to smoke in my presence. I had disconcerted him; the thought of it pleased me.

"You believe electricity is a proper topic for young ladies?" he asked.

"Virtually anything is a proper topic for young ladies when presented in the proper manner, by the proper person," I flattered him. One reason I hated flattery toward myself was that I used it so often to get my way with others; by others I mean the wealthy men of the community from whom I always needed money: to improve the science labs, to buy new books, to pay the custodian. "And most importantly, how will our young ladies assist their future husbands, if they're not given the opportunity to become familiar with the great challenges of our day?"

"Ah, yes. I see what you mean." He gave me a knowing look. "You're very . . . sneaky, Louisa."

"Oh, indeed. I'm rather ashamed of all the things I've been able to give my students through the subterfuge of training them to be better wives."

Why did I confess that to him? I chastised myself immediately. Granting him the leverage of such knowledge certainly wouldn't help me. That's what came of engaging in repartee: I lost sight of my own self-interest.

"You can't fool me, Louisa. I'm sure your 'sneakiness' makes you more proud than ashamed. Once Margaret said—well, never mind about that."

"No, please. What did she say?"

"Forgive me, Louisa, I promised myself I would never become the sort of person who spends his life quoting the dead." Sadness filled his voice. "But this reminds me of something I've been meaning to ask you. Margaret has the most beautiful clothes." I ached, that he referred to her in the present tense. "Three closets full. The latest fashions, needless to say."

Margaret had always loved beautiful clothes, and she'd always chosen them wisely: items that accentuated her own grace and beauty rather than making her into a mannequin.

"Grace uses the clothes for dress-up—with the results you've seen. But it's a pity they should go to waste and turn unstylish. I was thinking—you're about the same size as Margaret; maybe you'd like some of them."

I was so close to tears I couldn't answer; he must have realized, for he continued without waiting for my response.

"At home we always passed along the good clothes—and the not so good—when someone died. It was a bit of an honor, you know." His Irish brogue was stronger now. "Uncle Rob's Sunday suit going to little Tommy whether it fit him or not. Whether it needed patching or not." He stopped, and I saw that he too was close to tears. "Anyway, if you'd like to come over and look through some afternoon, just send a note to Mrs. Sheehan. Any day is fine for her, I'm sure."

I said nothing. I could never take Margaret's clothes. They would make me feel as if I'd shrouded myself with a ghost. Margaret, I thought, how could you have left us? Unmooring us both, and leaving us to drift alone.

"I don't feel ready, somehow," he continued, staring at the darkened windows, "to give those beautiful things away to strangers."

There was a heavy knocking upon the front door. Grace bounded down the stairs to answer. Tom checked his watch. "Odd, having a visitor at this time of the night." He turned his head to listen.

We heard the sound of a low voice identifying himself, and Grace's clear, high-pitched Irish accent: "Do you have a card, sir?" Apparently he did, and Grace brought it upstairs on a silver tray.

"Excuse me, sir, ma'am," she nodded at each of us. "A mister Karl Speyer to see the master."

"What?" Abruptly Tom stood. He took the card from the tray and studied it, as if doubting her words. "Excuse me, Louisa. This is"—he reached for the proper phrase—"an uncommon intrusion. Mr. Speyer is a business acquaintance. I'd planned to see him at a meeting at the club this evening. A problem may have come up that I must attend to immediately." He moved toward the hall. "Thank you, Grace." When he passed her, he touched her lightly on the shoulder.

As he went down the stairs, she walked slowly to the banister and stared after him, looking bereft. I joined her, putting my hand on her shoulder in the same place he had touched. I shivered when I realized what I'd done and pulled my hand away.

"Good evening, Speyer," we heard Tom say.

"Mr. Sinclair," was the curt response.

"No problems, I hope, to bring you here this evening?" Tom's tone held an ironic cast. "Come into the parlor." The parlor was a small room at the front of the house, next to the staircase and opposite the drawing room, which Margaret had designed for Tom to use when he conducted business meetings at home.

Grace turned to me with an odd expression on her face, like an appeal, for what I didn't know. "I wonder why he came here," she said, playacting no longer.

"He's just here on some business," I reassured her. "Something to do with the exposition, probably." We heard the parlor door close.

"But since Mother died, no one comes to see us, except our family, like you." Silently I blessed her for calling me family.

"Don't worry, sweetheart. Everything's all right."

"No, it's not! We're in mourning. No one is supposed to come here." She began to wring her hands together, her knuckles reddening with the pressure. Tenderly I separated her hands by taking them within my own. I couldn't understand why she was so upset.

"That's absurd."

Grace flinched at the sound of her father's voice raised in anger.

Now I remembered Karl Speyer's name. He was one of the engineer heroes of the power station. Working for the Westinghouse company, headquartered in Pittsburgh, he designed the turbines and generators used in the powerhouses. He was among the men extolled in the newspapers for genius and courage in the harnessing of Niagara.

"Don't threaten me, Speyer."

Tom was hesitant and shy no more. All at once, for the first time since I'd met him, I caught a glimmer of another side of him entirely; a side kept out of the drawing rooms and libraries of his private life, the side that must have filled his work life each day, to bring him from where he'd been to where he was now.

Speyer's voice in response was deep, his words muffled.

"Do you know what they're talking about?" Grace asked, calmer now.

"No, I don't."

"I do," she said carefully.

"Really? What?"

She gave me a sly smile that I didn't like. It made her look older than her years. "They're talking about electricity. About how much electricity—"

"God damn it, Speyer."

She paused, as if waiting for an echo, and then continued, dreamily, "Sometimes Mama and Papa would fight about electricity. I'd listen to them, just like I'm listening now. Except I'd be in my bedroom and they'd be in the library. Sometimes I'd put my ear to the floor, so I could hear them better. Sometimes Mama would cry."

I didn't know that Margaret and Tom fought about Tom's business. Although I realized I was being foolish, I felt hurt that Margaret had never shared this secret with me. Because of my jealousy, I spoke too hurriedly. "Grace, when people are married they often have disagreements about things. Then they talk about them, and sometimes even cry, and soon they understand each other better. They reach a compromise."

"You're wrong. My parents only ever had fights about electricity, and they never made a 'compromise.'" She dismissed the long word even as she showed pride in being able to use it.

"Electricity seems like an odd thing to fight about." I was torn, because I wasn't certain I believed her—especially because Margaret had never mentioned such disagreements to me. Did people really fight about electricity? After a moment's reflection, the notion seemed absurd. Nonetheless, I wanted to reassure Grace; to find a way to comfort her. "Didn't your mother want to electrify the house?" I asked gently.

"It wasn't that. Mama thought Papa was trying to take too much water from Niagara Falls. 'You won't be happy until we're picnicking on the precipice,' she used to say." Grace's imitation of Margaret's voice was uncanny, even though I'd never heard Margaret speak such a phrase. "I always think about that, because the words make something I learned at school: 'picnicking on the precipice'. That's called—" She glanced at me for help.

"Alliteration."

"Yes! Alliteration. 'Picnicking on the precipice.'" She seemed unduly pleased with herself, and I must confess to a touch of anger— the same kind of anger Millicent Talbert must have felt when Grace began to throw snowballs immediately after threatening to kill herself.

The anger led me to a blunder.

"Grace, when people have an argument, sometimes they say things simply for the sake of the argument. It's called a 'rhetorical device.' Your mother didn't actually mean that people would picnic on the riverbed at the Falls, she was just saying that to make a point. It's an absurd idea anyway. No one could take that much water, it's not possible to build a power station that big. You'd need a hundred power stations. Besides, the state has to grant your father's company options to use the water; the government would never grant options to use all the water."

She gave me that look young people have when they conclude that adults are beyond stupid. "You don't know what happened, do you, that made my mother die?"

"Grace, I do know," I said firmly.

Last year, Margaret had become pregnant. Grace and I had discussed this before. Of course Grace didn't know a crucial fact: that Margaret had not actually given birth to *her*, and this was a fact which I hoped Grace would never learn. Margaret was thirty-four, considered old to have a first child, and the pregnancy was difficult from the beginning. More than once Dr. Perlmutter had been called in when there was fear that she would lose the baby.

"I was here, remember?" I asked more sympathetically. "Your mother gave birth to her baby before the baby was ready, and the baby died, and your mother got sick from it." Even now, I choked at the memory. Margaret, dead in childbirth, like too many women I'd known through the years.

"No, before then. Sometimes I think I made her die, Aunt Louisa. She loved me so much, and I—"

Tears smarted in her eyes. I put my arms around her, and as if I'd finally given her the permission she'd been yearning for, she began to cry full out, leaning against me and reaching up to grip my shoulders.

"Sweetheart." Gently I stroked her hair. So this was the anguish that had caused her words to Millicent. "The sickness killed her. Her death had nothing to do with you. This happens so often. You know families at school where the mother has died, don't you?"

She nodded, even as her face was pressed against me.

"And then the children always think their mother's death is their fault—you can ask them at school. But it's not their fault, Grace. Try to believe me. It's not."

She pushed away a bit to look up at me. "But, Aunt Louisa, it wasn't . . . I mean . . ." She struggled to speak.

"Don't worry, Grace. Everything's going to be fine." I squeezed her shoulders.

"But I miss her so much."

"I do too. But I know she'd want us to be looking forward, to the future, not backward. She'd want us to try to be happy. Can you try to be happy for her?"

"Are *you* happy, Aunt Louisa?" I couldn't answer. "Are you?"

"I'm not happy, Grace," I admitted slowly, "but I'm doing my best. I'm trying to live the kind of life she'd want me to live."

Grace gazed off, thinking. "Well, I guess I'm trying to do what she wanted. I guess maybe she would be proud of me now." Eagerly she looked at me. "Shall I tell you the reason?"

Why did I have to speak at that moment? Why couldn't I just listen to what she might have told me? I berate myself, over and over. I thought I understood. I thought I was comforting her. I thought I knew everything, but my imagination had failed me.

"I already know. Because you're a good girl and you work hard at school."

Abruptly Grace pulled out of my arms and wiped the tears from her cheeks. "I hate electricity. Don't you, Aunt Louisa? Joan of Arc didn't have electricity."

"That's true, Grace. I was just telling your father that Joan of Arc was one of my heroines, when I was your age. I used to pretend that I was Joan of Arc."

"You did? How wonderful," she said with trembling glee. "I figured out today that all the people I ever loved to read about in history never had electricity. They always had candles. Queen Guinevere, Eleanor of Aquitaine, Lady Macbeth—but she's not real, maybe we shouldn't include her."

"Let's include her, why not?" Grace was herself again, and a conviction surged through me that her demons had been defeated. Relief made me feel light-headed. "History says there may have been a Lady Macbeth, and besides, Shakespeare tells her story so powerfully, she might as well be real."

"That's true," Grace said excitedly. "I never thought about it that way. Did you know that we can make candles right here in the kitchen? Cook showed me how to do it. I'll teach you. Come on." She grasped my hand and began to run down the stairs, but I managed to stop her about halfway down.

"Let's wait here for your father to finish his meeting, Grace. That's more polite. So he won't have to wonder where we are."

"He won't mind—"

"We'll stay here, Grace."

So we sat side by side on the stairs, and in the unwavering glow of electricity we enumerated our favorite characters from history and literature who had done quite well, thank you very much, without the lightbulb. This wasn't the time for me to talk to her about conveyor belts or electric water pumps. My only job now was to love her.

Suddenly she said, "I remember Mama and I used to sit right here on the stairs and wait for you to come visit us, Aunt Louisa. So we could open the door the second you got here. Did you know we waited?"

I hadn't known, but I did know that they were immediately at the door, always, to welcome me—drawing me in, showing me that I belonged. Even as a toddler, Grace on her chubby legs would open the big door for me, Margaret standing four steps behind her—Margaret in her exquisite dresses, with her porcelain skin and her openness to all the world, smiling with pride upon her little daughter.

"We had 'stair games' we used to play," Grace continued. "You know, finger games, with string. Like cat's cradle. I can do the cup and saucer. You know, that's the one where you . . ." Grace began to show me the moves in the air before dissolving into laughter at the intricate confusion of doing the moves without a string. "Mama always kept the string in her pocket, so we'd never have to look for it." Unexpectedly she knit her brows. "I wonder whatever happened to that string? I wonder if it's still in her pocket. In the dress those men put on her when they came to—" Grace gasped. I reached to embrace her, but she shook me aside, tossing up her head. "We can make another cat's cradle string! I'll show you how!"

At that moment, Karl Speyer came out of the parlor. We could see him through the posts of the banister. He was a big man with a thick dark beard, broad-shouldered, dressed in a fur hat and a bulky coat with a fur collar. He never looked up at us, so I didn't see his eyes. Maybe that's why I had the impression of the type of man whom a woman would be frightened to notice behind her on the street after dark. He let himself out of the house, closing the door gently.

Many minutes passed before Tom left the parlor. Grace was caught up explaining other finger games to me and didn't realize how long her father was alone. The telephone was in the parlor; most likely he was making a call. When finally he opened the parlor door and walked toward the stairs, he looked weary and preoccupied. But when he saw Grace giggling on the steps, her elbow resting on my knee, he stopped and smiled. He and I exchanged a happy glance, as adults so often do when they're caught in a moment's realization of how extraordinary children are. He began to walk up the stairs toward us.

"Everything all right?" I asked.

He shrugged. "Oh, I suppose so. My employee Mr. Speyer has a flair for the dramatic. And he seems to think he can get the better of me if he just keeps repeating his point." For an instant Tom paused, glancing aside at the scrollwork on the banister posts. "Well, I'm sorry you had to hear our little argument. Best if we all just put it out of our minds." He stopped before Grace. "Now then, my little girl, have you finished your homework?"

"It's too hard. The math is too hard."

"Come on." I rubbed her knee. "I'll review it with you for a minute." I stood and took her hands to pull her up. She looked pleased at the prospect of this unexpected treat. "But don't tell any of your friends. I can't have all the children asking the headmistress to help them with their homework!" We went upstairs, and soon after, the housekeeper returned and Tom left for his meeting at the club.

And I walked home alone, the streets alive with snowflakes that glimmered in the yellow haze of our electric streetlamps.

The next afternoon, I stood in the school's front office pondering the disturbing events of the night before. Speyer's unexpected visit, the ensuing argument . . . Tom's world and, although I could hardly credit it, Tom himself seemed somehow fraught with menace. By contrast, the school was like a haven of peace and predictability. Here I could offer my students, and myself and my colleagues, a respite from the perils outside. Here nothing mattered except learning and camaraderie.

Nonetheless, I had to give my girls the ability to deal with the challenges that would one day confront them. I'd just finished teaching the seniors a weekly class pompously titled "Philosophy of Everyday Life." There really was no other title for it, however, because we surveyed the history of philosophy with a practical goal: the discussion of moral standards and of the ethics by which the girls lived their lives. "All choices are ethical ones, opportunity and responsibility are inextricably linked"—those were the words written across the top of the blackboard. The class was my primary means of social subversion, and teaching it left me drained.

I was alone in the office for the moment, albeit in the company a marble bust, in the Italian Renaissance style, of a woman called "Modestia." She stared at me with a come-hither candor that wasn't strictly modest. A gift from a benefactor, she couldn't be put in a closet. I much preferred the Nike of Samothrace—the Winged Victory—who urged me to glory from her pedestal in the corner. The Winged Victory was quite fashionable; it seemed no home was complete until the Nike had been placed upon her pedestal, as she had been in the Sinclair library.

Modestia and the Winged Victory: two far different views of woman-hood, and how were we to steer between them? That was the dilemma I faced every day in the struggle to turn girls into women, to give them the confidence, knowledge, and inner strength to face up to the challenges outside. *Keep your rudder true. Make your lives count.* These were the precepts I tried to instill in the girls every morning when we gathered for chapel, the school organist guiding our procession with Bach or Handel. Undoubtedly I was overearnest in my morning messages, but how else to inspire the girls if not in terms of the ideal?

I glanced out the tall, wide windows toward the elm-tree forest of Bidwell Parkway. If I could walk through the mullioned glass, I would enter a winter woodland of dryads and nymphs—a chilly *Midsummer Night's Dream*, filled with intrigues as complicated as those among the girls right here.

I smiled at myself, for my fantasies, and realized once again that I loved this school. Like Grace, it was among the few things I *could* love. I loved the leaf-patterned shadows the sunlight threw across the walls; the hidden library nooks where girls went to read and dream; the stained glass window at the stairway landing of young women walking boldly into the future; the long hallways, their wainscotting carved into birds and beasts; the Elizabethan dining hall with its oaken tables and high, arched ceiling; the flagstoned central courtyard with its fountain, its urns of flowers, its marble benches, covered now with ice.

This was my home. I had a family here, a family I myself had created. The faculty was a band of scholars; the staff approving and supportive; the girls forever themselves. A sense of belonging filled me and held me close and grateful. Someone opened the front door and the scent of cinnamon rushed through the air. Mrs. Schreier, the school secretary, baked cinnamon sugar cookies at home and brought in a fresh batch every few days, placing them on a large platter on the reception desk just outside the office. Whenever anyone opened the front door, the incoming wind carried the scent through the halls, enveloping students, staff, faculty—and me. When I was away, the smell of cinnamon was always a wistful reminder of home.

After checking the afternoon mail, I was about to return to my own office upstairs, when a newspaper on Mrs. Schreier's desk caught my eye. WAS IT AN ACCIDENT? was the headline blazoned across the sensational *Buffalo Evening News*. I hated the yellow press, but I couldn't resist reading such papers when they came my way. Reaching for the newspaper, I was smug enough to believe the incident in question was indeed an accident. No doubt tomorrow's edition would declare this to be so. When I opened the paper to read the story, however, I was shocked. ENGINEER HERO DIES, read the inside banner. The accompanying article took up the entire page:

World-famous Karl Speyer, chief engineer of the Westinghouse Electric and Manufacturing Company as well as the Niagara Frontier Power Company, was visiting the Queen City from Pittsburgh to meet with leaders of the hydroelectric power project . . .

On and on went the article, describing what was known of Speyer's visit to the city, his professional credentials, his work for Westinghouse, his wife and two children in Pittsburgh, the shock and grief with which George Westinghouse received the news.

I paused to catch my breath and then read on: As best as the reporters could ascertain, Speyer had attended an evening meeting at the Buffalo Club with the leaders of the hydroelectric power project, including Mr. Francis Lynde Stetson of New York City, chief legal counsel to Mr. J. Pierpont Morgan, and Mr. Frederick Krakauer, Mr. Morgan's local representative. From what I understood about the financing of the power station's construction, J. Pierpont Morgan was by far the chief investor, although the consortium included such names as Astor, Vanderbilt, Biddle, and Rothschild, as well as several local men of great wealth. Tom (undoubtedly an investor as well) was the working director, answerable only to the consortium—which for practical purposes meant Mr. Morgan himself.

According to the article, after the meeting Speyer refused offers of a lift back to his hotel. He said that he was going to walk—not unreasonable, for the Iroquois Hotel, at Mainand Eagle, was less than a mile away. He needed some air, he said. But instead of returning to the hotel, he went to the Park. The time was after 11:00 p.m.

Where was I when this was happening? I thought back. At home. Asleep, after reading in bed. Yes, by then I was asleep, when several blocks away a man I had seen that evening was dying.

The men who'd been at the club reported that Speyer was abstemious in his personal habits. I understood this to mean he wasn't drunk when he set off on his midnight walk. The newspaper considered the possibility that he hadn't walked at all but had hailed a cab when he was out of sight of his colleagues to take him on the two and a half mile journey to the Delaware Park lake. The driver was asked to step forward, if such were the case.

A diagram showed the trail of his footprints across the iced-over surface of the lake, the weak spot where he fell through, and the place some five or six feet beyond the hole where his body had been discovered, contorted beneath the ice. The reason his body was discovered so soon, the *News* explained, was that a Mr. Jacob Hoffman, the manager of the boathouse restaurant, had been standing at a second story window of his domain enjoying a morning cup of cocoa when he saw the footprints, the hole in the ice, and the suspicious bulky darkness just beyond. He telephoned the police immediately.

The *News* speculated about whether Speyer had drowned or died of exposure; doctors offered varied opinions, awaiting the autopsy. The paper also raised several obvious questions: Why was Speyer walking across the ice in the middle of the night? Was anyone with him or following him? Did he see the posted danger signs and choose to ignore them? Thus far, the *News* reported, the police had discovered no indication of foul play.

The report concluded with this comment:

> *"His death is a tragedy for the development of hydroelectric power throughout the United States," Thomas Sinclair, director of the Niagara Frontier Power Co., told the* News *this morning.*

"I was privileged to work closely with him for many years. We enjoyed a pleasurable reunion at the Buffalo Club last night. I hadn't seen him in several months. He was like a brother to me, and I shall miss him," said the shocked Mr. Sinclair.

Quickly I folded the newspaper and put it away. For what possible reason had Tom neglected to mention Speyer's visit to his home? Why had he lied? What possible reason could there be to lie, except some personal involvement? Had Tom used the telephone in the parlor after Speyer's visit, as I'd assumed last night, and if so, whom had he called? To make what arrangements?

Even as these questions riveted my thoughts, another came too, one more personally pressing: Surely Tom knew that I would read his lie in the newspapers. Now I, as well as he, carried the burden of this secret.

Chapter Three

I f Frederick Law Olmsted had been a painter, Buffalo would have been his canvas. Beginning in 1868, he created in the city a vast system of parks linked by forested roadways wider than the boulevards of Paris. Olmsted had come to Buffalo at the invitation of a group of civic-minded business leaders, many of whom had served on the Macaulay board of trustees. Each time I stepped out of the school, I entered Olmsted's vision as if I were walking into his mind, surrendering to the eloquent unity of every avenue.

Delaware Park, where Karl Speyer drowned, was about a half mile from school, within easy walking distance. After reading the *News*, I completed a few items of work and by four-thirty I put on my cloak and set off. I followed Olmsted's regiments of trees, rows of six across, up Bidwell Parkway, around Soldier's Place, and onto Lincoln Parkway. The clouds were gray, the air damp and cold. I crossed streets slushed with a winter's worth of snow. Water seeped into my boots. At Forest Avenue, in front of the Sinclair estate, the west wind—the ice wind, from Lake Erie and the Niagara River—whipped around me, burning my cheeks. Olmsted's vision embraced me nonetheless. I felt exhilarated by the majesty of the trees.

At the end of Lincoln Parkway, atop a slight hill, Delaware Park opened into a startling vista of three hundred fifty acres. From where I stood, I could see a wide expanse of open meadows, gentle valleys, and tree-covered hillsides, all shaped around an ornamental lake, its shoreline gently curving. Just north of the park (primarily outside the park boundaries, on land which had been a cow pasture), the Pan-American Exposition was nearing completion, its gaudy Spanish Renaissance turrets and domes rising above the park trees. Of the dozens of structures in the exposition only two were designed to be permanent, destined to remain standing within the park itself: the New York State Building, a white marble Parthenon which I could just glimpse to the northwest; and beside me, on a knoll to my left, the half-finished Albright Art Gallery, inspired by the Erechtheum. The Albright Art Gallery and the New York State Building were surprising additions to the park. The other park buildings, such as the boathouse and the bandstand, had been designed by Olmsted's partner Calvert Vaux, and they retreated into the trees, leaving nature preeminent. But these two edifices dominated their hillsides as if trying to prove that man, not nature, was the most noble creation on earth.

The gallery looked far less than noble this afternoon, however. Idle, horse-drawn delivery wagons surrounded it. A disordered collection of union men on strike marched back and forth in the mud. Some of their placards advertised the various socialist workers' parties.

Here and there on the construction site, Negro men labored, self-consciously ignoring the shouts of the unionists. The Negroes were strikebreakers, of course; unions did not accept Negroes as members.

As I continued down the park roadway in the direction of the ornamental lake, I heard the protesters shouting at one another in languages incomprehensible to me. I spoke German, French, and Italian, but I couldn't even identify the languages these men were speaking. Hungarian, perhaps, or Slovak.

Reading the placards, I did understand that today's strikers were stonemasons and plumbers. The gallery's construction had been plagued by strikes, and people now accepted that the Albright would not be completed in time for the exposition. Whispered jokes claimed that Mr. Albright himself arranged the strikes, to deflect attention from the fact that he couldn't afford to pay for the marble needed to complete the project. I had personal reasons for hoping these whispers weren't true: Mr. Albright, the man who'd sponsored Tom at college and encouraged him to come to Buffalo (and who was also Grace's godfather), was on the Macaulay board of trustees. I didn't want to lose his yearly donations.

I was about to cross the roadway when one of the strikers, a thin, small man with a neat beard, broke ranks and, still holding his union sign, ran across a field of metal pipes. Without warning he began to beat a colored worker. The colored man attempted to shield his head with crossed arms. Again and again, the striker lifted his placard as a weapon. Blood began to pour down the face of the colored man. Other Negroes ran from far-flung parts of the construction site to help, but they were so few compared to the strikers who now joined their comrade, shoving the Negroes aside, that nothing could be done. Two foremen, recognizable because they wore neckties with their work clothes, observed from a safe distance.

The colored man was now on the ground. All I could see of him were his trousers, dirty and gray.

What could I do?

What could I *do*?

I glanced around for assistance but saw no one.

In a sick agony of helplessness, I turned away. I had read about incidents like this—many incidents like this—in the past few years, but I had never seen one. I felt as if there were a private civil war going on in the nation, one that people like me were sheltered from. Should I have thrown myself between the colored man and the striker? Would that have been courageous, or foolhardy? How could I judge? How do any of us make the judgment of how far to place ourselves at risk to help others? Finally I spotted a lanky police officer lounging nearby. He gave me a lopsided grin and shook his head, as if to say, what will these savages think of next?

Shaken, trying to close my mind to the shouts reverberating behind me, I crossed the road and walked toward the broad flight of stairs leading down to the water, struggling to keep my steps straight and steady. I tried once more to surrender to Olmsted's vision as it spread before me: the lake, curved and meandering; the bare trees, thick upon the hillsides; and on the distant shore, about a half-mile away, Forest Lawn Cemetery steeply rising, stone angels reaching their arms to heaven.

Down on the lakeshore promenade, barricades blocked access to the ice as policemen, detectives, reporters, and photographers vied for space, unaware of—or ignoring—the strife I had just witnessed. To them I suppose it was simply one more addition to the genre labeled "labor unrest," whereas the drowning of a world-famous engineer hero in an ornamental lake—well, that didn't happen every day. Near the lakeshore bandstand, a crowd of twenty or so of the curious had gathered on the promenade. The crowd included more than a few nannies; their small charges, looking fat from layers of blankets, were strapped tightly into wooden sleds. Ponies pulled several of the sleds, the nannies pulled the others. The entire area was covered with dirty snow warmed by the steam of horse manure.

I made my way down the wide row of steps, the wind at my back, and took my place among the crowd. All these people, come to see where a man had died. They moved along quickly. A nod, a homage—a sense of, well, it wasn't *me*, not this time, at least—and the person walked away, replaced by another. The ponies tossed their heads, their harness bells jingling. The clouds were low and dense. All at once I was at the front of the shifting crowd, pressed against the barricade at the edge of the frozen lake. Part of the lake was devoted to skating, the ice smooth and well-tended. The area beyond was roped off, its rough surface marred by hard, irregular snowdrifts. Speyer could not have strayed beyond the ropes accidentally.

I climbed up a nearby snow mound to see better and tried to imagine the scene as it must have looked to Karl Speyer. Last night, a light intermittent snow had fallen. Speyer must have thought he'd stepped into a dream: the Spanish turrets, the Greek temples, the far hillsides covered with stone angels spreading their wings. Awe must have filled him. He must have felt taken outside himself to a blessed place where ice never broke—indeed he had walked halfway across the lake. The detectives, stepping gingerly on strategically placed wooden planks, carefully examined the footsteps leading to the break where he had fallen. Speyer was a big man, wearing a bulky coat. In March, the snow-covered ice could be unpredictably treacherous. A stream moved beneath the surface, the Scajaquada Creek, flowing from the cemetery to the Niagara River.

What did it feel like, to fall through the ice? To sense a heavy winter coat become heavier with a weight of water? How long did he struggle—searching for a bit of air, frantically scraping his soon-bloody fingernails against the ice to dig himself out, disoriented finally, unable to find the hole where he'd fallen? Could Thomas Sinclair, the husband of my best friend, the father of my goddaughter, have had something to do with such a death?

The wind shifted. Gradually the sky cleared. Often this happened in Buffalo—the weather changing half a dozen times a day, at the mercy of the winds of Lake Erie. Did I have a responsibility to go to the police to report Speyer's meeting with Tom, to disclose Tom's lie? Not yet, my intuition told me . . . I would watch and wait, and learn what I could, before betraying Margaret's husband, Grace's father. All at once sunlight glared off the ice, blinding me.

"See anything?" asked a man's voice directly behind me on the snow mound.

Startled, I lost my balance, slipped, and instinctively reached for the man's arm to keep myself from falling.

"Forgive me for surprising you." His voice was refined, with the unmistakable inflection of the elite. I released his arm and smoothed my skirt. "See anything out of the ordinary?" he asked again.

Instead of answering immediately, I gazed out at the lake. We hadn't after all, been introduced. "No, I don't see anything."

"Ah. Too bad."

The man bounded down the snow mound and I appraised him quickly. He appeared to be a gentleman, but a man of the arts rather than of business, judging from his tweed trousers and the longish cut of his coat. Carefully he moved a brightly polished wooden camera box and tripod away from a group of gawkers.

"Let me help you down," he said, offering me his hand.

"Thank you, that's quite all right, I can manage."

In four light steps I was beside him. He was a rumpled figure, about my age, taller than me, his face smooth-shaven. His dark hair curled haphazardly, yet there was an elegance in his bearing. All this I noticed in the instant before I remembered that I mustn't allow him to engage me in conversation. I looked away, concentrating on the lights coming on in the boathouse restaurant.

"Did you know him?" the man said.

"I beg your pardon?" I asked, without looking at him.

"The deceased." He spoke the word with a grand irony. "Did you know him?"

Did I? Did watching someone go out a door after an argument constitute "knowing" him? I didn't know what to say, which was just as well since I didn't want to say anything at all.

"Forgive me for presuming to question you." So, he was a gentleman. I turned ever so slightly toward him. He took off his hat and pressed it against his chest. "I should have introduced myself. Franklin Fiske." He bowed. "I arrived last week from New York City. My distant cousin is married to Mr. Dexter Rumsey of this city. Maybe you know her: Susan Fiske Rumsey."

"Yes, of course!" My relief must have shown on my face—my feeling of, how delightful, to meet a man I can speak to!

Fiske laughed. "I'm amazed—although after a full week of it I suppose I shouldn't be—by how quickly any reference to my distant cousin brings me friendship in this city."

"Well, we are basically very friendly here—among those we know, of course," I added with a smile. In Buffalo it was axiomatic that "to know a Rumsey is to know enough," so I accepted Franklin Fiske without question. Dexter P. Rumsey was the president of the Macaulay board of trustees. Reliable rumor said that the Rumsey family owned half the land on which the city was built.

"Did you know him?" Franklin Fiske asked again.

"Mr. Rumsey?"

"No, the deceased," Fiske said, exasperated.

"Not exactly," I said without thinking. A mistake, and Fiske caught it.

"That's an unusual response," he said smoothly.

"Why are you asking the question?" I couldn't control the irritation in my voice.

"Ah." He paused, as if we were playing chess and I'd checked him. "Point well taken. I only ask because there's been quite a bit of speculation amongst the journalistic boys"—he motioned toward a group of gentlemen, as rumpled as himself, who were warming their hands over a fire they had built in a barrel with detritus from the construction site—"about the circumstances of Speyer's death."

"You checked with them?"

"Well . . . I happened their way. I used to be one of them. A foreign correspondent for the New York *World*—at your service, ma'am." He clicked his heels and gave a mock salute. "Sent out to pasture at my own volition after acquiring a near-fatal illness in the Philippines during our nation's glorious and on-going suppression of that island's democratic insurrection. Although I've given up on journalism, Cousin Susan nonetheless hides the children whenever I come to call, fearing my corruptive influences. I, however, have always considered myself morally upright despite my profession. I see by your dress that you, ma'am, like dear Cousin Susan, are a lady. I hope I have not damned myself forever in your eyes by admitting to my former profession."

I laughed.

"A laugh? That is your response?"

"I have great admiration for your profession—your former profession, Mr. Fiske. It is one of the few open to women. I have great admiration for the women who practice it." Ida Tarbell, Nellie Bly—they were heroines of mine.

"Yes, I know several of those women. Maybe one day—under the proper circumstances"—he raised his eyebrows invitingly—"I'll tell you about them." He gave me a crooked smile. "Now that I've engaged your sympathies, I'll treat you to a bit of my sad tale. Having left the realm of pencil pushers, and being utterly free from entanglements, emotional or otherwise, I am now fulfilling a longtime dream and pursuing art photography." "I'm forging my own, profoundly innovative area of photo-pictorialism, to wit: artistic pictures of industrial sites. Factories, machinery, that sort of thing."

I recalled Susannah Riley's watercolors of the power station. "That's fascinating, Mr. Fiske. Art should try to capture the beauty of the industries that are transforming our lives."

"Indeed," Fiske agreed noncommittally. "At any rate, I had an appointment with the deceased this morning. We were going to go to the power station together, and I was going to take photographs of a special generator of which he was unduly proud. Alas, he never appeared. Stood me up. By afternoon, I learned the reason why: He'd been previously engaged—under the waters of this delightful lake. I came here hoping to find someone who could tell me why."

"You're rather lighthearted, under the circumstances."

"Well, yes, that's my professional demeanor. Or rather, the professional demeanor of my former profession. Others have their own demeanors. For example, some of the boys told me that Thomas Sinclair—you know who he is, don't you? The director of the power project?"

Tensing, I glanced away. "Yes."

"Well, Thomas Sinclair was holding forth in his office this morning about how poor 'Karl' was like a brother to him, and one of the few men with whom he'd never exchanged a harsh word, and—"

"Really?" Too late I realized that I'd let myself sound surprised.

"'Really?' 'Really' what?" He was clever, was Franklin Fiske. With his posturing he'd lulled me into complacency, and now he pounced. "Why are you surprised by that?"

"Well, simply because—well, I should think one's brother is the person that one constantly *does* exchange harsh words with. At least in childhood. Of course, I've never had a brother," I added lamely.

Franklin Fiske simply gazed at me, leaning forward to study my face. "Forgive me," he said softly, "but what is your name?"

He disconcerted me. I stepped back, my heel digging into the snow mound. Snow slipped into the top of my boot, making me shiver. Nonetheless I said firmly, "Louisa Barrett." Still he stared. "I am the headmistress of the Macaulay School." There it was, my title—my ultimate, automatic, but somehow hollow defense.

"I thought you must be Louisa Barrett."

"You thought no such thing."

"I certainly did. I'd been told to look you up, to stop in at your Monday evening salon. You're the talk of New York, with that—"

"You're lying."

He burst out laughing. "Forgive me for teasing, Miss Barrett. You're an easy mark. But indeed I was told to look you up. By an editor I know. Richard Watson Gilder."

I stiffened. Richard Watson Gilder was a supposedly talented poet and the editor of the *Century* magazine. He was also a close friend of former President and Mrs. Grover Cleveland.

"I met him once," I said, hearing the belligerence in my voice. "Many years ago."

"Did he do something that upset you?" Fiske asked.

"Not at all," I said quickly, regretting that I was so transparent. "His snobbery was not to my liking."

"No surprise there," Fiske admitted. "Nonetheless Gilder told me that more recently a few of his friends had enjoyed stopping in at your 'saloon' for a bit of conversation on Monday evenings. He described you in great detail and quite truthfully, for a poet: tall, slender, blond, sensitive and basically shy—although sometimes appearing on the surface bossy and know-it-all. In short, a schoolmarm with a heart of gold."

I felt myself beginning to blush.

"And you see, Miss Barrett, I guessed that you were you, because what other lady of society would be here, walking alone—without a female relative, paid companion, or carriage—at what may soon be declared a murder site? I've been warned that you do exactly as you please—within the bounds of propriety necessary to retain your job of course. Yes, I've been told that you behave exactly as if you were one of us."

"One of you? One of whom?"

He appeared extremely pleased with himself. "Don't worry, Miss Barrett: not a journalist. Not even an editor or a poet. No, something much less evil—I hope: a gentleman. A gentleman free to saunter over to a murder site any time he chooses."

He made this oddly insightful comment so flirtatiously that I felt quite flustered. I took refuge in my schoolmarm disguise. "Now Mr. Fiske, I don't believe—"

"The clouds are reflected in your eyes, Miss Barrett," he interrupted, cutting my attempt to patronize him. "White against blue, like the sky." I wasn't used to men treating me as if I were attractive, and I was stirred as he stepped closer. I met his gaze. The clouds were reflected in his eyes, too: White and gray merging with green, a flick of yellow near the center. "Gilder left something out—which is how very beautiful you are, for a woman who's been able to embrace the advantages of a man. How very alluring, the line of your jaw." He almost touched me. I inhaled sharply. "Are you sure you didn't know him?"

"Who?"

"Karl Speyer."

So much for flattery. "Why are you convinced that I did?"

"Because in my experience, people seldom spend more than a few minutes at the site of a shocking public death without some reason. Most come to gape with family and friends and then move on to dinner. But others—those who come alone, who wait patiently . . . well, they're interested in something else." His voice dropped almost to a whisper, and he leaned toward me. "Perhaps they're here for professional reasons, like my friends over there." He motioned toward the journalists, who were now joking with a policeman who'd come to warm his hands—the same lanky officer who'd shrugged off the beating of the Negro strikebreaker. "Or like the detectives and various other public servants hanging about conducting what they like to call investigations." He flicked his hand at the men making their way across the ice, taking measurements. "Or even our local representative of Mr. J. Pierpont Morgan: the esteemed Mr. Frederick Krakauer, dozing in the bandstand over there as he steadfastly protects his employer's monumental investment in the power station."

Quickly I turned to look and indeed, there he was, the man I'd seen recently at lectures and concerts and heard rumors about, bundled up in a thick coat, long scarf, and fur hat, exhibiting his usual look of unfocused but somehow watchful sleepiness. Although Krakauer was not at all on Tom's level, he might easily be thought of as Tom's local supervisor.

"Or perhaps they're even here for artistic reasons—to photograph the beautiful lake, for example. Olmsted's masterpiece." Fiske's face was close to mine, his breath warm on my forehead. "But otherwise, Miss Barrett, there is a personal reason for the visit. An intimate reason, even. Relating to their own lives or the life of the deceased. You stood five minutes on that snow mound, staring at the ice. The detective had his eye on you."

I glanced around, but no one was watching.

"Don't worry, he's moved on to other quarry. But I decided to stick with you, determined to discover the reason for your—concern, shall we call it?"

Don't threaten me, Speyer.

There was a wall in front of me, constructed of all I needed to protect. Grace. Tom. Myself. I resolved to be silent for the moment about my suspicions regarding Tom and Speyer and instead to discover whatever I could on my own. I took a deep breath. "Mr. Fiske, you may know 'people' but you do not know me. I am pursuing a study of the efficiency of the police department. I visit the scenes of possible murders totally out of civic concern."

With that I pushed my foot against the snow mound and strode up the steps. Without looking back, I waited at the roadway for a delivery wagon to pass, and then I resolutely followed Olmsted's tree-lined parkways back to my home.

Chapter Four

Y|ou are to be congratulated, Miss Barrett," said Dexter Rumsey from his place at the head of the table. In his early seventies, Mr. Rumsey held himself straight, like a vicar. He was thin and bald, with a tightly trimmed white beard. Despite his unassuming manner, he was acknowledged to be the most powerful man in the city. "Let us be the first to say it."

"Hear, hear." There was a pleasurable pounding on the ornate dining table in the second floor meeting room of the Buffalo Club, reserved the third Friday of every month for the eight-man Macaulay School board of trustees. The board felt that midday was the proper time to discuss issues relating to a girls' school, and the Buffalo Club served the best midday meals. The fact that women were not permitted in the Buffalo Club was tacitly ignored by the porter at the door each time I appeared, thus proving Franklin Fiske right: I did enjoy the privileges and comforts (such as they were) of a man.

The Buffalo Club was certainly comfortable. The meeting room boasted a white coffered ceiling, ivy-patterned wallpaper, and a thick Persian carpet designed to absorb the many and varied secrets—business and otherwise—that were exchanged here. Tall windows with burgundy-colored velvet curtains overlooked graceful Delaware Avenue, although my trustees were not the type of men who spent time gazing out of windows.

"To you, Miss Barrett," said John J. Albright, raising his glass of brandy. In his early fifties, Albright had a squarish face accentuated by round glasses; the rest of his body was elongated and overly thin, as if he had the arms and legs of a marionette. His grayish-brown mustache was carefully trimmed. Mr. Albright had started his career as an agent for the Philadelphia and Reading Coal and Iron Company, collecting twenty-five cents on each ton of coal shipped through Buffalo. Enough tons were shipped to make him a millionaire. Now he was developing a vast steel mill project at Stony Point, south of the city. "Our sincere compliments."

"To Miss Barrett," the others joined in.

I wasn't happy. The men gathered around the table were obviously withholding something important from me and using it to have a bit of fun at my expense. They looked altogether too smug, and I resented their teasing.

We had just enjoyed a hearty luncheon, although not nearly as hearty as we would have had years ago when I first became head-mistress—portliness, per se, no longer being the ultimate measure of a man's success. Nonetheless, we'd managed to partake of oysters, shrimp bisque, lobster Newburg, filet mignon bordelaise, and a variety of individually sized cakes. These men of my board of trustees did nothing in moderation. The fat ones were very fat, and the thin ones, like Albright and Rumsey, were so thin as to be ascetic.

Of course the best of the hearty eating dated back to the days of Grover Cleveland—lawyer, sheriff, mayor, governor, president—whose portrait, triple chins and all, gazed at us from the wall. Lacking any school business to deal with today (I suspected these meetings were held so frequently because the men around me appreciated the opportunity to see Mr. Rumsey), our conversation had begun an hour and a half earlier with a discussion of the new portrait of Grover Cleveland that the club was planning to commission from Lars Sellstedt. It would be a more noble portrait than the one before us now. A portrait more worthy of a two-term president, albeit a Democrat. Full-length, with the White House in the background.

Plans for the portrait had elicited a host of ribald comments from these barons of industry and capitalism.

"We should pose him with Mrs. Halpin and the boy," one said, referring to Cleveland's notorious affair with a widowed shop girl in the 1870s and the resulting illegitimate child. While acknowledging the boy, Cleveland had refused to consider marriage to Mrs. Halpin, who was known to have bestowed her favors on other well-to-do men of the community. To console herself, she'd begun drinking, and Cleveland arranged to have his son taken from her by force and adopted by an established local family. When Mrs. Halpin refused to accept this separation, Cleveland had her committed to an insane asylum, where she remained until she saw "reason." The story was hushed up at the time, but it became public when Cleveland ran for president in 1884. The press ran wild with the revelations, printing material so lurid that newspapers had to be kept hidden from children. The incident became a national trauma, which I'd followed in disbelief from Wellesley. Suffragists even called Cleveland a "male prostitute."

Although my board members could joke, fifteen years later, in '84 they'd felt intense mortification. To his credit, however, Cleveland never denied the story and told his aides and friends to tell the truth. *Ma, Ma, where's my Pa?*—that became the Republican rallying cry in the election. *Goin' to the White House, ha, ha, ha*, the Democrats had added sardonically after Cleveland's victory.

"Instead of the White House, maybe a German beer garden would make a better background, don't you think?" someone offered.

I removed from my mind any recognition of the identity of these speakers, to save the embarrassment I would feel on their behalf. I was certain these men had voted for Cleveland; they were the type of reform-minded Republicans who'd taken pride in becoming Mugwumps and supporting the Democratic ticket in '84. But they had little personal respect for the roisterer they'd considered "unclubbable" even after he'd finally become a member of this club when he was mayor of the city.

Certainly President Cleveland was coarse. And certainly he preferred German beer gardens to the more refined pleasures of the Buffalo Club—but that had endeared him to me then. Apparently he liked nothing better than to rise up at a crowded beer garden and sing from his favorite song, *There's a hole at the bottom of the sea, there's a wart on the face of the moon*. Even after he'd become governor, there were tales of visits to Buffalo that included late-night drinking binges and good-natured fisticuffs on downtown streets.

"We could include the beautiful *Mrs*. Cleveland in the picture," someone piped up.

"Should we put in any bruises?"

This was greeted with guffaws. During Cleveland's unsuccessful reelection campaign in 1888 (that was the election in which he won the popular vote but was defeated in the electoral college), there'd been whispers that he beat his popular young wife—so many whispers that she'd felt compelled, or had been compelled by her husband, to deny the rumors publicly. Of course rumors denied are rendered only more convincing.

"If we included Frances, most men would wonder whether we were showing husband and wife or father and daughter!"

Now this comment was below the belt, so to speak. Frances Folsom Cleveland was indeed twenty-seven years younger than her husband (Cleveland had paid his respects to her upon her birth, for she was daughter of his closest friend). However, there were men in this room—including Mr. Rumsey—who were married to women far younger than they: With death in childbirth so common, what was a man to do but find ever-younger women to partner him in the challenges of life's journey? Someone was needed to supervise the staff that looked after the house and children. Mr. Albright had found the easiest solution to this problem: After his wife died, he advertised at Smith College for a governess-companion for his daughter and within two years married his new employee.

Ah, Louisa, you're becoming cynical. But the idea of being married to one of these men sent a shiver of horror through me. With the fat ones, their stomachs alone would dominate the bed. How would one find the necessary parts? As to the thin ones, touching them would be like consorting with a skeleton.

The group having exhausted the question of President Cleveland's portrait, someone turned the conversation to the continuing preoccupation in the yellow press with the possibility that Karl Speyer had been murdered. This caused me to glance around nervously, but as the lobster Newburg was being consumed, no one noticed.

"The accusation is absurd!" declared George Urban, Jr., talking with his mouth full. As president of the company which controlled local distribution of Niagara's power, Urban had attended the meeting on the night of Speyer's death. Urban was clean-shaven, with small eyes and heavy features. Perhaps because of his striking physical similarity to our former national leader, Urban had been one of Cleveland's earliest political backers. His family had made a fortune in flour milling, and I liked to imagine him covered in a pall of white flour dust, the dust of his family's millions. Oddly, and to wide acclaim, Mr. Urban cultivated green roses. The only green roses in the United States, and ugly things they were. Last year I was forced to wear a green-rose corsage at graduation. Urban proudly told the gathered school community that he had made the corsage himself. "Whipping up such nonsense is not only dangerous—it casts aspersions on the entire power project! We should put a stop to it!" Urban proclaimed.

"Hear, hear," came the boisterous agreement. Despite their desire to scuttle the controversy, however, Speyer had died just ten days before, so in fact the continued coverage was understandable. Nevertheless, I understood Urban's concern: Every time Speyer was mentioned in the papers, the power station was also mentioned, and usually when the power station was mentioned, Tom was mentioned. Although no accusations had been directed against Tom or any of the leaders of the power project, the constant publicity was both undesirable and awkward: It might begin to interfere with profits.

"Let the coroner do his work, and then we'll all know what happened," Urban went on. "Although why we can't just order the coroner to say it was an accident and be done with the whole thing, I don't know."

There was a long pause while everyone looked at Mr. Rumsey, who concentrated on his lobster Newburg, clearly unwilling to respond. The other men began to debate the idea in blunt terms, obviously for Mr. Rumsey's benefit. Was I shocked that these men had control over the coroner—even though attempting to influence such an official was undoubtedly, if only theoretically, illegal? No, I wasn't shocked, since they had control over everything else. If challenged, they would explain that they used their power for the overall good of the city. And certainly the city had become extremely prosperous under their protection. My only surprise was that they would discuss this matter in front of me. Either I was so powerless as to be invisible to them, or they considered me an integral part of their group. Either way, I was wary.

The men continued their debate. Still not looking up, Mr. Rumsey patiently finished his food. Finally he put down his fork. He cleared his throat, reducing the room to abrupt silence. "I spoke to Butler over at the *News* about his inflammatory reporting concerning Karl Speyer's death," he said quietly. In addition to the phrase "To know a Rumsey is to know enough," we might have said, "To hear a Rumsey is to hear enough." Dexter Rumsey spoke quietly, and he was always heard. "Butler told me, somewhat surprisingly, I must say, that as publisher he has no interest in the truth or falsity of the accusations of murder. Apparently there hasn't been much else to report on, and his only interest is in selling newspapers. Well, I could hardly interfere with his pursuit of business, now could I?" Mr. Rumsey asked with a wry smile.

And that put an end to any discussion about dictating the coroner's report.

Unobtrusive waiters changed the plates and disappeared, and talk moved on to the labor unrest and strikes which were disrupting construction at the exposition. I glanced at Mr. Albright, but he nonchalantly concentrated on his filet.

"With all these strikes and riots, the only ones they're defeating are themselves," someone offered derisively. "They know they can't win anything. They should just buckle down and get on with things."

"Or 'things' will get on without them."

The men laughed. Oh yes, they made brave jokes. But I knew they were worried, and not just about the exposition. Their own businesses were vulnerable. Dynamite was all too easily accessible. Haymarket, Homestead, the Pullman strike—these words were like a litany of disaster in their minds. Less than a decade before, an anarchist had attempted to assassinate Henry Clay Frick in Pittsburgh. Of course we'd had nothing that severe, not here. Not yet. But we could. At any time. In the last twenty years, the population of Buffalo had more than doubled. Three-quarters of the populace was now foreign-born: German, Italian, Irish, Polish, Croatian, Russian, and every nationality in between. Unemployment was at 19 percent. Socialists were stirring up trouble. There was no end to the permutations of anger and hatred, and so our embrace of civic glory became all the grander in counterpoint to the undercurrent of fear.

Someone said, "If these strikes continue—well, unlike some places, we don't have an endless supply of coloreds to bring in to work the line."

"And we won't have any if the unionists keep lynching them," someone else jested. The man I'd seen beaten at the gallery over two weeks ago hadn't died of his injuries, according to the *News* (which devoted three sentences to the incident), but he would never fully recover and most likely never work again. Because of Speyer's death, the park had been filled with police that day, but none would come to help a Negro. Nor, sadly, did I.

"Well, the Italians are breeding like rabbits—we can draw from them."

How did my graduates manage to live with such men? My chastity was much the better fate. At this moment I wouldn't begrudge a socialist mob storming the club.

What would I do if I weren't *here*, I asked myself, allowing my mind to drift: become Annie Oakley, shootin' 'em up through the Wild West? Or the keeper of a real saloon, in Wyoming or Montana? Become a relief worker at a New York City settlement house? Or a settlement house doctor? Alas the necessary training to become a doctor was so onerous that only very wealthy spinsters could achieve this ambition; I would need a sponsor. Maybe Mr. Urban would be my patron, if I promised to wear a green rose each day in his honor. Or I could become Nellie Bly, circling the world in seventy-two days to beat Jules Verne's fictional record and then writing a book about it.

The muted rattle of silverware and the rustle of linen interrupted my thoughts; the waiters had arrived to clear the table and serve the brandy. The men passed around cigars. The room began to fill with the floating blue pall of cigar smoke, which my luncheon companions seemed to find so comforting. Perhaps I should take out a cigarette and begin smoking myself—an act that would horrify these men if it came from a wife or daughter (although I knew that their wives and daughters smoked in secret—secretly from them, that is).

But I would never take out a cigarette. I enjoyed some of the advantages of a man, but I knew only too well the proprieties I needed to observe to maintain my position. The cigarette I would save for the long sojourn I enjoyed at the Twentieth Century Club on the third Friday of every month after my long sojourn here. I was already luxuriating in the expectation of it. The Twentieth Century Club had been founded by Macaulay graduates and was now ensconced in a lovely Italian Renaissance-style building just a few blocks from this bastion of manhood. Each time I approached, simply gazing at the second floor covered veranda soothed my spirits. When I entered the columned, skylit main court after facing the stresses of masculinity, one of my former young ladies could be counted on to exclaim something along the lines of, "Oh my God, Miss Barrett has come to us *reeking* of cigar smoke! Quick, bring her a drink!"

Yes, my graduates—at least within the confines of their bright and airy clubhouse—were a joy to behold. Widely traveled, they never stopped educating themselves, and yet they wore their learning lightly. They organized reading groups, lectures, philosophical debates; they hired professors from the university to give courses in history and geography. They performed scenes from Shakespeare. When I met my girls at the club, I knew my work had not been in vain.

Just when my thoughts had reached this point of yearning for my own kind, Mr. Rumsey refocused my attention by offering his congratulations, and the others followed suit.

"Yes, yes, Miss Barrett, we are very pleased," offered John N. Scatcherd, a round-faced, boyish-looking man who controlled a conglomerate centered on lumber, railroads, and banking. "We hope you will be very pleased too."

Well, this must be some surprise indeed, for them to put on such a show about it. Round and round they went, congratulating me about my good fortune. I did not appreciate it.

"How seldom in this life do any of us have the privilege of bringing a colleague truly extraordinary news." That fawning remark, delivered with a Georgia-born lilt, came from Dexter Rumsey's son-in-law, Mr. Ansley Wilcox. At forty-five, Wilcox had the distinction of having married not one but two of Dexter Rumsey's daughters. Not at the same time, of course. Among other useful endeavors, Wilcox directed the citywide Charity Organization Society, and I hated him, for he had instituted in Buffalo the cruel distinction between the "deserving" and "undeserving" poor, denying innocent children charity because their parents were inebriate or "immoral."

If Wilcox was holding forth, the time had come for intervention.

"Forgive me, gentlemen, but—"

"You see, I've won, haven't I!" John D. Larkin broke in, his glee propelling him up from his chair. Mr. Larkin was our mail-order soap millionaire: "Factory to family" was his motto. No one would have dreamed that his lovely soaps had their genesis as the by-products of the city's horrific stockyards and packing plants. With his thick but smoothly cut graying hair and beautifully trimmed gray beard, Mr. Larkin shone with cleanliness and ever gave off a pleasant scent. "I knew if we teased her long enough she would begin with 'Forgive me, gentlemen'! You each owe me five dollars and I expect it promptly," he declared, slapping his hand on the table before resuming his seat.

The necessity of repressing my anger made me blush. I could only hope that they wouldn't notice. But naturally Mr. Rumsey did notice.

"Forgive *us*, Miss Barrett," he said, breaking into the merriment, which he had never joined, and silencing it. "We did not intend to discomfit you. But you see, our news *is* extraordinary."

"Go ahead and tell her, Rumsey," said Mr. Albright.

"Hear, hear."

"Yes. Well." Mr. Rumsey fingered the red legal folder on the table beside his place setting. A gray satin ribbon held the folder shut. "This week we have received word of a substantial—a more than substantial—donation to the Macaulay School. An endowment which will transform the building and the opportunities within it. This endowment is given entirely in cash, and I have begun investigation into proper investments."

He paused.

All these men had funded the school generously over the years. More than generously. For them to speak of substance, for them to be impressed, for them to feel such astonishment at a figure that they made a game out of revealing it—well, it made me nervous. I felt the bite of suspicion and doubt.

Mr. Rumsey untied the satin ribbon, then glanced through the papers within the folder. John G. Milburn, the school's attorney, rose from his place and went to stand behind Mr. Rumsey, helping him to find the appropriate documents.

"These here, Mr. Rumsey," Milburn said in his cultivated British accent. Born in the north of England, Milburn, at fifty, was a commanding figure—handsome, debonair, and charming. In addition to serving as legal counsel to most of the men in this room, as well as to their various companies, Milburn at the moment was amassing glory as the president of the Pan-American Exposition. Local rumor was that President McKinley had him under consideration for the position of Attorney General, although I would be surprised if he actually received the nomination: McKinley was a Republican, Milburn a Democrat. "You might begin with this one," he advised.

"Thank you, Milburn."

Mr. Rumsey read through papers he must surely have read before, but that was typical of him: to proceed slowly. I was lucky to have him as president of the board. He had a scientific and philosophical bent; his support for new and serious courses of study was steadfast. At last, in stentorian tones, he read aloud:

"The Macaulay School is hereby awarded an endowment of one million dollars, the yearly income from which is to be used solely at the discretion of Miss Louisa Barrett, headmistress, with an immediate release of fifty thousand dollars in principal, for work to begin."

I was stunned.

"This endowment is made in honor of the late Margaret Winspear Sinclair, class of 1886, by her husband, Thomas Sinclair."

Mr. Rumsey stopped and looked at me, waiting for my response. In the silence I heard only one thing: *Don't threaten me, Speyer.*

I said nothing. Mr. Rumsey looked slightly surprised, then went on. "In view of this gift, we think it only proper to offer Sinclair a place on the board. An unusual step, I know, given that Sinclair is somewhat—new to the city."

That word *new* was freighted with implication. Mr. Rumsey turned to Mr. Albright, who, as Tom's sponsor, might be expected to speak up for him. But Mr. Albright merely gazed at his coffee. He himself was somewhat new to the city, having arrived only in 1883. But his newness was different from Tom's.

"Nonetheless we deem it appropriate to offer Sinclair a place," Mr. Rumsey continued. "With your permission, of course, Miss Barrett." Again he paused. "Miss Barrett?" He leaned forward, eyeing me carefully. "Do you approve?"

Why would Thomas Sinclair give such a gift? Why would he part with so much, when half as much, a quarter as much, would make a profound impact on the school?

"Miss Barrett?" Mr. Rumsey sounded concerned.

I glanced at Albright. How much did he know about this? His face remained impassive.

"Miss Barrett?"

"Yes, yes, of course I approve," I said angrily.

The men nodded knowingly at one another. They would expect anger. Anger would be considered part of my obstinate character. Well, I *was* angry, because I had no choice in the matter. This was a gift I couldn't refuse or even question.

And yet, no matter why the money was given—possibly it was simply a memorial to Margaret—it would bring the school improvements I had dreamed about for years. These dreams filled me, smothering questions of why and wherefore, and my dreams became words: "The things we will do . . . a chemistry laboratory, a theater, a new art studio, scholarships—"

"Not too many scholarships, Miss Barrett," someone said at the other end of the table. I ignored his identity and the affable laughter which greeted his remark.

"A swimming pool, a running track, a new gymnasium designed for basketball—my girls love basketball."

I realized I was blushing badly now. The gentlemen around me were smiling—with kindness. They weren't smug, they weren't complacent; they were my friends, my supporters. They'd always shown me sympathy. Anything I'd wanted, they'd given me. Ten years ago, I'd asked them for a sabbatical leave—to visit Europe, I told them—and they'd agreed without demur and given me a grant to cover expenses. When I returned, the position of headmistress awaited me. I was the orphaned, nearly penniless daughter of a college professor, but they accepted me as an equal among them. They gave me a place at their table. They championed the cause of women's education. They even allowed Millicent Talbert to attend the school. And I had repaid their trust.

Yes, they were generous, sensitive, and kind. They embraced the future. They were among the beneficent lords of the nation, the most wonderful men I had ever met. Each was a father to me. The father I had lost.

I covered my face, unable to hold back my tears.

"Well, gentlemen, here's something we shall have to keep among ourselves," Mr. Rumsey said gently. "Old Tom Sinclair has made our Miss Barrett cry."

Chapter Five

The generators gleamed black in the sunlight that poured through the long, arched windows of Thomas Sinclair's cathedral of power. One week after I'd learned about the endowment, I stood with my eighteen senior girls and our guide on the wrought-iron observation bridge that spanned Powerhouse 1. The ten generators—alternators, to be precise, our guide explained—were aligned in a row beneath us. They were mammoth, their outer edges spinning so fast as to be invisible. With their unceasing whir, they might have been alive. When I first saw them, I caught my breath—we all did, gasping as we edged single file onto the bridge. Men walked among these leviathans. Men stood at the switchboards, checked the gauges, adjusted the levers, calmly controlling and directing the machines that rose around them. Bands of color from the stained-glass transoms colored the men's faces blue and red.

The powerhouse was pristine and glowing, its white enameled brick walls polished clean. There was no hint of factory grit. The hum of the generators filled the room like a drape of velvet, soft and pliant. The windows were so wide and tall as to create the illusion of no walls at all. High at the far end of the room, like a rose window in a church, was a stained-glass rendering of the symbol of the power project: the American and Horseshoe falls surrounded by forest, as in the days of the Indians, and shot through with a lightning bolt.

Tom was right, there was a sacredness here, a deep urging toward awe that the builders of Chartres and Bourges must have felt. A person could worship here, turning himself over to a greater power; finding comfort and fortitude in its strength. Architect Stanford White had fulfilled Tom's conception, sparing no expense to create a masterpiece.

Outside, the Niagara River passed, dense and purposeful, its ice floes a shock of white against the water's brilliant green. Because of its roiling, the river contained so much oxygen that its color seemed uncanny. The Falls were only a mile away. The power station had been built right at the edge of the reservation, the land reclaimed from commerce in 1885 to create the first state park in the nation. Outside the river was fierce and turbulent; but here, amid the generators, the power of nature had been subdued by the power of man.

"Yes, young ladies, feast your eyes on the largest hydroelectric alternators on earth! Five thousand horsepower each," announced Billy O'Flarity, our guide. Upon our arrival this morning, O'Flarity had received us with extravagant deference. We hadn't yet seen Tom. Indeed, I hadn't seen Tom since the night Karl Speyer died. Of course I'd written him to express my thanks for his endowment. He had responded with this invitation to visit the power station.

Despite my better instincts, I had continued to read the often extravagant speculations in the yellow press about Speyer's death. If the coroner's report turned out to contain only what Mr. Rumsey thought it should, I rationalized, I needed to have my own information. Unionists, nature lovers, professional rivals, thieves: the newspapers considered these the most likely culprits in Speyer's death. Mercifully, no reports, thus far at least, had implicated the leaders of the power project. Therefore I still felt secure withholding from the police my knowledge of Tom's argument at home with Speyer and his lie about it later. I could still cling to the hope that my suppositions were wrong; I prayed so. Yet the matter gnawed at me, my fears made worse by a creeping suspicion that Tom was in fact using the endowment to bribe me into silence . . . otherwise, why would he have presented it that way, suddenly and without warning?

"Yes, you're lookin' at ten percent of the electric power generated in the United States of America—and it can go anywhere we decide to send it," O'Flarity was saying in his Irish brogue. He smiled benignly upon us. His wavy hair was white around his face but progressed through various shades into a pure carrot color that curled over his collar. His white eyebrows were thick and brushed upward, waxed into position, I wagered, because I'd never seen such gravity-defying eyebrows. The blue of his eyes faded into white. Although his clothes were not flamboyant, he wore them flamboyantly—two vests of contrasting plaids, both frayed, a silken ascot, and a white shirt with billowing sleeves. He was like an impoverished showman, a carnival barker like so many in the town of Niagara Falls, with its fire eaters, stuntmen, and museums of horror. The only difference was that Billy O'Flarity wasn't showing off America's Fattest Lady or the World's Tallest Man, but a symbol of the future come to life.

"Right here, right before your very eyes, you are witnessing the transformation of the world, from the age of steam to the age of electricity!" Extravagant phrases, but true nonetheless.

"Over there's the switchboard platform—made from nothing less than the finest Italian marble. See how smooth it's been polished? Notice too the polished faces of our handsome switchboard operators!" A few of the girls giggled, but more blushed, and O'Flarity beamed with pleasure. "Yes, indeed, you've got every single thing you need to operate the generators right on that platform: your bus bars, your rheostats, your handsome young men. Any questions?" He raised his eyebrows in appeal. "No? Well, young ladies, I'm not surprised. Overwhelming, it is, to see for the first time these miracles of human ingenuity. Let us leave this temple of power to the edification of the next group of visitors, and I'll show you how it all works."

With a well-rehearsed dramatic flourish—throwing an imaginary scarf around his neck—he turned on his heel and led us back the way we'd come, down a narrow flight of stairs and through a vaulted passageway. He walked with a swaggering limp that might have been fabricated solely to add to his style. I herded the girls before me, taking my place at the end of the line to make sure no one wandered off. Thus I saw the girls as a group, dressed virtually alike in long dark silk skirts and high-necked Holland shirtwaists, hair twisted up at the back of their heads. Alas, a timeworn image came into my mind, making me sentimental just when I wanted to be stern: the memory of these girls only a few years ago, their skirts at their calves instead of the floor, their hair bouncing freely behind them, big bows propped on the tops of their heads. Now they were grown, almost ready for college or coming-out parties or both. In most ways, they were out of my control. Either I had made them into what I wanted them to be, or the cause was lost.

As we entered the high-ceilinged presentation room, O'Flarity took a pointer from the bin near the door. Diagrams and maps covered the walls, and there were working models of machinery, some with water gushing through them. Groups of tourists, including a party of Japanese gentlemen, vied for space. The power station had become as much a tourist destination as the Falls. Considering the expense that must have gone into this presentation room, Tom and his partners were obviously eager to show off what they had created.

"Now, ladies, gather round, gather round," O'Flarity said, his words echoing with other words in other languages against the marble floor and tiled walls. He drew us together around a scale model of the Niagara River region from Lake Erie to Lake Ontario.

"Now for a bit of background. The men who built this power station—the greatest men in our great nation—paid for it out of their own pockets. Without any public offerings. Without any help from the federal government—that's right, zero was the amount of money that came from Washington. Their names are Morgan, Vanderbilt, Belmont, Biddle, Rothschild, and Astor—not to mention many from right here on the Niagara Frontier. They put up millions of dollars with no guarantee of return. And why did they do it, I ask you?"

"To turn a profit?" Maddie Fronczyk asked.

I stifled a laugh. Maddie was softly round, her blond hair braided around her head. Her family was Catholic, from Silesia, a region on the Polish, German, and Czech borders. I feared some of the girls teased her about looking as if she were in Silesia still, but Maddie took everything in stride. She attended Macaulay on a scholarship that Margaret had established years ago for the daughters of industrial laborers. Her father had worked here at the power station before his death. Perhaps because of her background, she seemed older than her years, certainly older than the other seniors around her.

"It's an excellent example of the function of the profit motive in a capitalist society," she continued.

What had she been reading in her free time? The element of ironic humor in her words was lost on her peers, but I enjoyed it immensely.

O'Flarity, however, was indignant. "You are wrong, young lady! The men who paid for this power station did it for the good of mankind—to run our industries, to light the darkness. They saw a need and they filled it. They are heroes! *They* took the risk, they had the courage—they transformed the world!" He tapped his pointer against the floor.

Maddie smiled as if forgiving a child for misbehaving, but the other girls looked impressed. I didn't interfere. I made it a policy to stay in the background when I took the girls on field trips. People didn't expect enough from these girls, and it was my job to expect more. To make them expect more from themselves. My primary duty here was to protect their virtue.

O'Flarity glared at each of us, as if awaiting further challenges, before continuing. "Now I'm sure you're all wondering why Niagara is the most perfect site in the world for a hydroelectric power station," he said, like an accusation. "I'll tell you. First, the Niagara River is not a river. It's a strait, linking two bodies of fresh water, Lake Erie and Lake Ontario. Because it's a strait, we have a continuous, steady, even flow. This is extremely unusual, and I hope you'll never forget it. The Great Lakes are a huge reservoir behind us"—he thrust out his arm expansively—"where water exists for nothing but to go over the Falls. And we've got a second advantage here at Niagara, which is that we aren't off somewhere in the woods. We're at the absolute center of the best commercial routes in the country, adjacent to the major metropolis of Buffalo."

Now he cleared his throat and spoke with a certain reverence, gaining from the girls an even closer degree of attention. "The farsighted heroes who built this project"—he glowered at Maddie—"realized they would need to send the electricity away from the Falls to make it truly beneficial. Therefore they opted to utilize alternating current. Over the objections even of the great Thomas Edison, they chose alternating current: That's how brave they were. These details are important, dearies, so you must bear with me, you must stretch your minds."

Only Maddie flinched at his deprecation; the others may not have recognized it. "Nowadays we accept alternating current as the most natural thing in the world, but even a decade ago it was radical! Thomas Edison—now, he's done a lot of good in the world, don't get me wrong—but he devoted himself to direct current, clung to it, no matter what evidence anybody gave him to the contrary. That was *his* profit motive talking. Direct current was his baby. But the problem was, direct current has to be used within a couple of miles of where it's generated; it's got a low voltage, it can't just be sent anywhere. Luckily the farsighted George Westinghouse believed in *alternating* current, which can go places. This is what brought on the so-called Battle of the Currents, which some of you may have heard of."

I, at least, recalled the bitter Battle of the Currents: Thomas Edison electrocuting stray dogs in front of reporters to try to prove that high-voltage alternating current was dangerous to bring into homes. But Edison did not mention that high-voltage alternating current was never brought into homes; the voltage was always stepped down by transformers before it was used. In addition, scientists like Edison always talked in terms of home use when virtually no homes used electricity; factories, industries, streetcars, yes. But homes weren't wired (except for those of men like Thomas Sinclair), and I'd never heard anybody even discuss the mass wiring of homes.

"So what exactly is alternating current?" O'Flarity pondered aloud. "I'll tell you. It was invented by the greatest genius of all time, Mr. Nikola Tesla. I myself have seen Mr. Tesla, right here at the power station, during one of his visits. I'll never forget it. He's a gigantic man—in mind and body; I'll wager he's over six and a half feet tall, and thin as can be; he's all brain! Now, as to this alternating current: Mr. Tesla saw it one day in a flash of genius while he was walking in a park in Budapest—that's the general part of the world he's from, in case you're wondering what he was doing in such a place. Alternating current is what we call a polyphase system. It keeps reversing its direction. Forward and back, forward and back. It's created with a rotating magnetic field. The way it works is . . ." As he spoke on, in increasing complexity—and I was impressed by his knowledge—the girls' eyes glazed over. After a few moments O'Flarity realized he'd lost his audience and tapped his pointer hard on the floor, startling them.

"Ladies! Rouse yourselves for this bit of insight: Our electricity can go anywhere in the state, anywhere in the nation! It can be put onto what we call a grid: flick a lever right here at Niagara, and someday you'll be lighting up Albany or Cleveland or Chicago or Ma and Pa's farm out in the boonies somewhere. And it's cheap. Cheap and plenti-ful!" He eyed the girls with mock lasciviousness. "Which no one would ever say about *you*, my dear young ladies!"

Well, that remark certainly caught their attention. More than a few of them covered their mouths to hide their giggles.

Sternly I cautioned, "Mr. O'Flarity."

"Yes, ma'am," he acknowledged, bowing his head with a grin. "You have a harsh mistress, girls—as you should, as you should. All right, follow along, every one of you," he said as if addressing a troop of obedient house pets.

He moved to the next model, a side view of the powerhouse itself. "Now, here is how a powerhouse operates." He used the pointer to show us the relevant spots. "The water from the Niagara River enters the canal outside the building here, flows into the sluices of the forebay, then down the penstocks to the turbines." His voice rose in excitement with each item. "The water makes the turbines spin, the spinning moves the alternators, and *voilà*, electricity!"

The girls applauded him.

"After it does its work, the water flows through the tailrace—that's a fancy word for a tunnel—and discharges into the gorge down below the Falls. Okay?" He glanced around to gauge the girls' comprehension. In spite of their enthusiasm, they looked a bit confused. "Here it is again: We take the water from the river above the Falls, use it to gener-ate electricity, then discharge it into the gorge below the Falls. The water we use never goes over the Falls at all. Don't worry if you can't understand, it's a lot to take in all at once. Questions?"

"What happens after you've taken all the water from the river?"

Well, that was an insightful question. Abigail Rushman had asked it, peering at O'Flarity over the glasses perched at the end of her nose. Abigail was the daughter of a dry goods store owner, a man who had become very rich very recently. Never thin, Abigail had gained a bit of weight this year and taken on a plodding studiousness. From little things she'd said to me during the past months, I sensed that her mother was pressuring her about coming-out parties and young men. Also, I sensed that her mother chose her clothes: bright colors (though still within school regulations for seniors) that didn't suit her. Several times I'd spotted telltale threads from bows or ribbons that had been ripped off. I was pleased to see Abigail paying attention and participating.

"Take all the water?" O'Flarity protested, almost jumping on her. "Impossible, my dear. We'll never have a shortage. Our supply is as limitless as the Great Lakes themselves."

"What I meant was, after you take all the water to make electricity, there won't be any left to go over the Falls."

"Ach," he said dismissively. "You've been listening to the madmen outside."

Driving through the power station gates, our carriages had passed a group of demonstrators protesting any diversion of Niagara's waters. These were the so-called nature lovers who were constantly writing letters to newspapers and magazines to condemn industrial development at the Falls.

"Fact is—and this is what the madmen outside never tell you— we're saving Niagara Falls. Saving it from itself. The tiny amount of water we're taking out for electricity—less than three inches on the depth, and the depth is maybe twenty feet at the Horseshoe—that tiny amount helps to preserve what the madmen say we're destroying. The Falls are weak, *weak*. Let me show you."

He limped over to a wall diagram of a cross section of the rock strata of the Falls. "Here at the top, you've got your hard limestone, but underneath you've got soft shale. Every day, the water erodes that shale down, beats that shale back, until the limestone layer is just sticking out alone. Eventually the limestone cracks, breaks off, falls down. Then the shale gets beaten back again, and the limestone on top crashes down again, over and over, every day, until someday the Falls will be nothing but rapids. By taking some of the water, the power station is actually lightening the burden—rescuing the Falls!"

I nodded in recognition. My father had talked about this. The Falls receded on average several feet per year. Over the millennia, the Niagara River had cut a gorge seven miles long.

"Understood?" O'Flarity knitted his brow, the tufts of his eyebrows meeting in the center as he stared at Abigail.

"Yes, but—"

"Good." He smiled graciously. "Well, my dears, the time has come for the *pièce de résistance*, as the Frenchies say. Gather round then, and I'll share my own little secret." He urged them closer.

"I wasn't always crippled as you see me now. Oh no, once I was strong and handsome as—well, as Mr. Sinclair himself. Allow me to show you." He was whispering, as he must whisper to every group. He began to fold up the cloth of his pants leg. "I got a wooden leg here, you see." He pulled down his sock.

"Mr. O'Flarity," I warned.

"Ah, quite right, ma'am." He folded his pants back down. "Impressionable young ladies. Quite right. Well, well. Visit me some-time without your headmistress, girls, and I'll give you the full effect, if you know what I mean." He winked, but the girls, I'm proud to say, just caught each other's eyes and shook their heads: They weren't falling for this. "Begging your pardon, ma'am." Chastened for the moment, he gave me a nod of deference.

"All right then, let me tell you how I came to get this wooden leg." He turned back to the cross-section model of the power system. "You see this tunnel? The tailrace? Yours truly is one of only three men in history to fall from the wheel pit into the tunnel and live to tell the tale. Yes, ladies"—he tapped his pointer on the model—"that's one and one-quarter miles through the tailrace, and that's where I went. Twenty-six and a half feet per second, twenty miles an hour—that's the velocity of the water. The trip takes three and a half minutes. I popped out at the water's edge—just below our beautiful steel arch bridge. It was winter, and I fell, *wham*, onto the ice, frozen solid, and went skid-ding a hundred yards with my leg twisted up. Had to be taken off above the knee, it did." He lifted the stump (covered by his pants) to show it off. "Mr. Sinclair paid the medical expenses himself, seeing how noteworthy it was to have me alive at all. I'm always grateful to him."

The girls stared at him in shock.

Evelyn Byers finally asked, in her typically coy but rebellious tone, "Why didn't you drown in the water tunnel, Mr. O'Flarity?" She had the come-hither look of the bust of Modestia in the school office. Her father controlled a Great Lakes shipping empire.

"My dear miss," he said seductively, "I didn't drown because I held my breath!"

"You did not!" Evelyn blushed.

O'Flarity appeared pleased with himself. "You're right. The day this happened, we were still testing things out. Only two generators online, so the tunnel wasn't full up the way it is now. It was only about a quarter of the way full. Pitch-black in there. You can't understand how black it was, like a black wall you're smashing into." He slapped a fist against his palm. "But I says to myself, 'Relax, Billy, you know where you're headed—right to heaven's door. Just enjoy the ride.' And so I did, like a baby floatin' down its mother's"—he caught himself and glanced at me—"well, floatin' down."

That was a close call. I'd never hear the end of it from these girls if he made an actual reference to the birth canal. As it was, judging from their faces they hadn't realized where his thoughts were headed (except for Maddie, who caught my eye, but she would never tell).

"'Course it was cold as hell"—he glanced at me again—"I mean, cold as all get out, and I had the echoes of my buddies' prayers following me all the way: 'You're a good fellow, Billy-boy. We won't forget ya'—that kind of thing. It wasn't exactly a comfort. And I didn't much enjoy getting discharged through the air and onto that icy reward. Still, it made me famous.

"Afterward I said to Mr. Sinclair, I'm not putting myself at risk again. I'm better off showing visitors the wonders of this power station and telling the tale. Being a boss wise beyond his years, he saw the truth of this and put me in a place where my talents could excel, impressing young ladies like you." The girls (with the exception of Maddie) continued to stare at him with wide-eyed wonder.

"Excuse me, Mr. O'Flarity," I said, in my best schoolmarm style. "Perhaps we should move on?"

"Yes, of course. Yes." He cleared his throat and a change came over him, from a seducer to a teller of ghost stories. As he leaned toward the girls, his tone was now filled with *faux* terror. "From here, we take the elevator down—down—down into the darkness of the wheel pit." He shivered. "I warn you—and only once do you get the warning: the depths, the blackness, the spin of the turbines, the never-ending churning of water through the penstocks—they could terrify persons much stronger than you, my darling girls!"

He was right. The elevator cab, with its ornate, wrought-iron filigree, clanged against brick-lined rock as it swayed down ten flights, through a trench lit only by bare, hanging electric bulbs. The penstocks—huge metal tubes filled with rushing water—loomed before us. The noise was deafening. The air smelled dank. Abigail Rushman reached for my hand, and I squeezed hers in reassurance. O'Flarity and Addison Barker, the Negro elevator operator, exchanged a knowing smile. As we neared the bottom of the wheel pit, the flywheels and the turbines came into view, delicate, shadowed, eerily beautiful with a mist of water glistening around them.

At the lowest level, we stopped. "One hundred and thirty-two feet down, we are!" O'Flarity announced. He got out, positioning himself on a steel platform. He opened a trapdoor in the floor and pointed downward with satisfaction. "There it is, my dearies," he shouted above the roar. "The tailrace, surging beneath us. You feel the power of the earth down here, don't you? Pressing against us. But we're holding it back, eh, ladies? For now, we're holding it back."

In spite of his showmanship I shuddered, and I felt grateful to return to the surface. In the presentation room, a young workman awaited us.

"Peter!" Maddie ran to embrace him. He was tall and blue-eyed, with dark blond hair turning to brown; a thick curl fell across his forehead. He was neatly dressed, wearing a tie, and looked to be in his early twenties. The girls gathered around him, a bit aghast. They would probably remember this young man more clearly than the wheel pit.

"Miss Barrett," Maddie said, her arm around his waist, "I would like you to meet my brother, Peter Fronczyk." As he stepped forward to shake my hand, he seemed embarrassed by the attention.

"Ach, ach," O'Flarity interjected. "So, Petey-boy, this is the famous sister who went to the city to get herself schooled, eh? I'd keep a better eye on her if I was you, my lad. Strange ideas and manners she be getting there—socialist tendencies, if you ask me."

"It's nothing but what I've picked up from Peter," Maddie said, teasing them both, "if you can get that into your thick head, Billy O'Flarity."

As she said this, I saw the glimmer of another culture, one she kept hidden from us at school. Although Maddie boarded at a house across from Macaulay, her family lived at Echota (meaning "city of refuge" in Cherokee), the model village designed by Stanford White for the power station workers. I felt as if the community of Echota were now revealed to us, with its own rules, standards, and jokes. I understood why Maddie never seemed bothered by the teasing of other girls: She wasn't at Macaulay to find a group of friends, but solely to get an education.

"Well, my dears," O'Flarity said, "this young man is a specimen of our switchboard trainees." He said the words with a touch of irony, giving Peter a shrewd glance. "Yes, ladies, we've got over four thousand workers here and every one of them a prince. But our management plucks these especially intelligent and charming boys out of the line and teaches them to monitor the thing itself—invisible, all-powerful electricity!" He paused, relishing his own verbal flourishes. "Management does this in particular with boys who show signs of being good union organizers. Girls, you couldn't find a better organizer than Pete here—up until about, what, six months ago now?" O'Flarity laughed heartily.

Peter looked sheepish, but still managed a smile.

"Now then, Petey, and not meaning to be rude, what takes you away from your classes to come slouching with us?"

"Mr. Sinclair's assistant found me and told me to join you." The earnestness of his manner reminded me of my father's students, those young men, grown-up boys, really, who were constantly eager to discover the right thing to do and then do it rightly. "Miss Barrett, I'm instructed to tell you that Mr. Sinclair is occupied with telephone calls to New York City this morning. He will join you if he can."

"Excuse me, please, Miss Barrett." Abigail Rushman pulled on my sleeve. "Can we see the outside part now? The intake canal?" I was pleased that she'd broken away from the generalized swoon over Peter Fronczyk. "I heard it's famous."

"You don't have to tell *us* how famous it is!" O'Flarity exclaimed.

"But I'm trapped, Pete—I got some Swiss engineers coming in. Thinking about building a power station in the Alps, they said in their letter. You want to take these young ladies out, since you're freeloading with your sister for the morning?"

"Yes, I'll take them," Peter said shyly.

I thanked Mr. O'Flarity and tipped him, and then we retrieved our coats from the reception area and followed Peter outside.

When I'd visited Chartres Cathedral years before, my first glimpse of it had been from far away. The cathedral had seemed to rise from misty wheat fields, alone, pure, and noble. Of course, as I got closer I discovered that the cathedral was surrounded by a bustling town, its buildings blocking the view. Therefore the image I always cherished was the first one, the towers and buttresses emerging on the horizon from a field of wheat.

When we walked out of Powerhouse 1, Peter taking us through a door on the river side rather than the formal entryway we'd used when we'd arrived, I felt as if I'd come to a Chartres that had no village to conceal it. The four cathedrals of electricity existed in proud isolation along the windy riverbank. The damp, weighty snow of early spring encased the expansive landscape. Like white fire, morning sunlight glinted off the windows of the two powerhouses now complete on the Canadian side of the river. Just beyond the powerhouses, the transmission lines began their journey upriver to Buffalo, cutting the sky like taut ribbons of black.

Peter led us down the carefully shoveled path to the intake canal—"three hundred feet wide and two thousand feet long, and we can expand it whenever we need to," he explained—and I imagined what the scene would be like if the powerhouses did take all the water. Most likely the machinery could never take every drop; a little would always escape, and we could ice-skate on what remained. What a joy that would be, to glide on skates to Canada and back. And although I shivered now in the unremitting wind, I could visualize the summer, when we would picnic on the precipice amid gentle rivulets and streams.

Suddenly a huge blast rocked the pathway beneath our feet. Gulls shrieked. The girls stopped and turned to me, immobilized, waiting for my reaction. Quickly I made myself impassive—that was always my trick to gain a moment to figure out what was going on, before giving them guidance. For my own guidance I turned to Peter. He was smiling, so I smiled too, and the girls relaxed. "Look," he said, leaning against the canal railing and pointing to the river. "They're using dynamite to break up the ice."

Indeed, there were men walking on the ice at the mouth of the canal. They wielded poles and pickaxes, prodding and pushing at the ice to break it up before it entered the canal. As they worked, they jumped from ice floe to ice floe, hats pulled low over their faces.

"With Powerhouses One and Two, there was a mistake in the design," Peter explained. "The sluices aren't low enough to pull in water from below the ice, so the men have to keep the ice out of the canal, to stop the sluices from getting clogged. When Three and Four are on-line, you won't see men doing a job like this. The new sluices are lower, with better gratings too."

"What happens if someone out there slips and falls into the water?" Evelyn Byers asked with a thrilled shiver at the horror of it. "He could get caught in the current and be carried over the Falls. Or if the ice he was working on was already in the canal, he could get pulled into those sluices and sucked into the turbines!"

Peter simply looked at her without replying.

"Yes, and it happens all the time," Maddie said angrily, stepping in front of her brother. "If you read the local paper you'd find out it happens at least once a week."

"Now, now, Maddie," Peter said, patting her shoulder. "Where would your friend see the local paper? Besides"—Peter turned to Evelyn, who looked more emboldened than hurt by Maddie's outburst—"the men know the risks. They know exactly what could happen, at every moment. They try to be careful." Peter stared at the men on the river. "Well, come on," he said, rousing himself and chucking Maddie under the chin. "Let me show you one of the wonders of the world: The new tailrace for Powerhouses Three and Four."

The sound of the wind filled the tunnel, its roar carrying away the echoes of our footsteps. Water seeped from the walls, puddling on the floor. Peter carried a lantern, which threw our shadows high against the curving brick walls. The tunnel was shaped like a horseshoe, the floor curving downward, the walls curving out and up, meeting in an arch high above our heads. Although Peter held up the lantern, we still could not see the ceiling.

"Isn't it beautiful?" he whispered, exultant. "It's made from masonry and concrete, lined with four layers of bricks. It's made to be filled with water." His voice was edged with wonder. "Once it's filled, no one will ever see it again. Unless it has to be closed because of a problem. But I'm sure there'll never be a problem. The design is too perfect. Every time I come down here I feel like I've got to get the memory of it inside me, to last forever." Slowly he turned in a circle, holding the lantern high, transfixed, a look of longing and wistfulness on his face—in stark contrast to my girls, whose primary concern was their wet feet.

"Ugh," said Evelyn, walking on tiptoe, trying to find a dry spot. "Why didn't we get rain boots before coming down here?"

Peter laughed, the spell that had taken hold of him broken. "There are underground springs all through the surrounding rock. That's why we get this seepage, until the tunnel is completely sealed."

"That wasn't my question," Evelyn said morosely.

"Now, now, enough of that." He shook her shoulder as if she were one of his sisters and she positively flushed, forgetting her wet feet altogether.

"This is the tailrace for Powerhouse Three," Peter said. "Up ahead, it merges with the tailrace from Powerhouse Four to make a single tunnel. Come on, I want you to see the interlink."

Evelyn hurried to his side. I smiled to myself as I gathered the others.

We had been alone in the tunnel, but as we approached the interlink we heard voices, growing louder, and saw the crossed shadows thrown by dozens of lanterns. Men were moving through the interlink and down the main tunnel. There was an animal stench in the air, explained when we saw a mule pulling a cart of bricks.

And then the interlink opened before us, vaults and archways wide and soaring, architecture and engineering melding into an extraordinary creation. I was filled with amazement. So this was what artists meant when they spoke of the sublime. Meanwhile men put on rain gear, gathered tools, ate lunch, rested. The interlink seemed nearly as wide as a town square. There were more than a few Negroes among the laborers; Tom was known for paying high wages and hiring without regard to race, but as we walked further into the interlink, I saw that, among other jobs, the Negroes alone were responsible for the dozen or so mules that were stabled to one side, baled hay piled high.

The workmen gazed at my girls frankly and made certain gestures which caused their eyes to widen. Joking in languages I couldn't understand, the men began blowing kisses at the girls. We shouldn't be here, I realized, but Peter was oblivious to the situation.

"The men are going a mile down," he said excitedly, pointing toward the main tunnel. "To the outlet, where we're doing the final work. We're hoping everything will be done by the time President McKinley visits in September, when he comes for the exposition, and then he can personally throw the lever that will put Powerhouse Three on-line, and—"

"Ladies, good morning, forgive me for not joining you sooner."

We turned, and there was Thomas Sinclair striding into the interlink with no regard for wet feet. He held a lantern, and in the crisscrossing shadows he seemed taller than everyone else. His suit was impeccably cut, his hair perfectly combed. All conversation stopped, replaced by a murmured "'Morning, Mr. Sinclair, 'morning, sir."

"Good morning, everyone, thank you," he said, turning to the group at large like an actor basking in applause. He looked sincerely happy, and although the men now moved more briskly toward their work, several couldn't conceal an indulgent smile when they passed him, as if he were a roguish child and they were proud of him. In a way he was their representative: the one among them who had made good. Even so, I could see how, in this environment power surrounded Tom like an almost-visible aura. He could afford to be charming and boyish; he could afford to elicit genuine affection from his employees, because there remained something ineffable in his manner that would prevent anyone from ever challenging his authority. Watching the faces of his workmen, I saw that they'd do anything he asked of them; the only question was, how much would he ask of them? Would he ask any one of them to commit murder? Had he?

"Well, then, Peter," he said, "let us escort these fine ladies upstairs, shall we?"

"Yes, sir, I'm—" Peter looked abashed, only now realizing that he'd been imprudent.

"Come along." With a pleasant smile Tom spread his arms as if to gather us up like ducklings. He ushered us back the way we'd come, not in any hurry, with Peter looking increasingly concerned and Tom looking absolutely relaxed but gazing away from us, into the middle distance, as though to render us invisible to the stares of passing workmen.

When we were in the isolation of the tunnel, Tom joined me at the end of the line, slowing his pace until we were separated from the others. "Good morning, Miss Barrett," he said evenly. Of course he would address me formally when I was with my students. "I hope you'll forgive Peter's enthusiasm in bringing you to a place that even your ladies most likely found inappropriate."

"Not at all. They were perfectly comfortable, particularly in the admiration of your employees."

"Yes, I thought they would enjoy that best."

"Peter wanted us to see the tunnel," I said in his defense. "He thought it was important. He called it one of the wonders of the world." In the lantern shadows, I couldn't read Tom's expression. "And it is. One of the wonders of the world."

Tom turned to me, his face entering the light. Slowly, a puzzled surprise came into his eyes, as if he were seeing me for the first time. Seeing me, not Margaret's friend, not Grace's godmother. His look disquieted me. He raised his hand and almost touched my cheek but instead took my arm as if to protect me, from what I did not know.

I have relived what happened next again and again. Not so much during the day, when there is enough around me to fill my attention, but when I lie in bed at night and close my eyes—that's when the scene comes back, the moment-by-moment unraveling of it. Again and again I feel the urge to run to help, although my arms would have been useless. Sometimes, if I drift into sleep with the scene still in my mind, I see something that never happened: myself, there beneath the steel casing. Trapped. Screaming. Myself, watching myself in a detached, naive agony that asks, how has this come to pass?

Back on the main level of Powerhouse 3, Tom led us to the closest exit, but the doorway was blocked by a huge piece of machinery being wheeled in on temporary railroad tracks.

"The other side then, ladies." Tom led the way down the length of the powerhouse, which seemed as long as a big-city railroad platform and was filled with construction debris: ladders, piles of tiles, discarded equipment, the remnants of wooden scaffolding. The unfinished generators rose beside us, each seeming about two stories high and as broad as a small house. Laborers clambered over and around them. The men wore overalls, or baggy trousers with two shirts and a vest for warmth, and cloth caps. Many smoked long-stemmed pipes while they worked. As we passed, each man paused for a moment to touch his cap and murmur the now familiar greeting, "Morning, Mr. Sinclair." Tom called out to many by name, exchanging quick jokes.

When we neared the end of the powerhouse, we realized that something extraordinary was taking place, and we stopped to watch. I stood next to Tom, Maddie and Peter beside us, the girls arrayed behind. A crane, attached to tracks along the wall, high up near the ceiling, was poised over the tenth generator. The crane chain held a huge, hollow generator casing, its top covered with a tarpaulin. The casing was being lowered on top of the generator, although the process had just begun. If the generators were about two stories tall, then the casing was being held about four stories above our heads. Looking up, watching the casing slightly sway, I felt vulnerable and afraid. Tom and Peter took the situation in stride, however, so I tried to emulate them. The crane operator leaned out of the pulpit (as Tom called it) and watched what was taking place beneath him, making changes to the crane position. About ten men stood below, around the generator base, waiting to guide the casing into place.

What was truly extraordinary was the work of another man, who stood atop the casing itself, as high and confident as a flying trapeze artist at the circus—except he wore no safety harness, and there was no net beneath him. Holding the chain, he called directions to the crane operator while simultaneously using the weight of his own body to ease the casing into position, taking a few steps one way, a few steps another way, making subtle adjustments. Astride that massive casing, he looked like an ancient hero, Hercules perhaps, taming a monster.

"This is the new generator my chief engineer, Karl Speyer, was working on before he died," Tom explained. There was a catch in his voice—from regret or guilt, I couldn't tell. "It produces four times more electricity than the others, with the same amount of water. I wish he was here to see this." He sighed. "Well, it will have to serve as his memorial, along with the others we're building from his plans."

Suddenly, the casing swayed as the crane shifted too far to the right. Everyone gasped. But the man gripping the chain simply shouted a few choice words to the operator, who gave a good-natured shrug. Relaxing, the other workmen laughed, glancing first at Tom to gauge his reaction. He was smiling too.

"Isn't that Rolf up there?" Squinting to see better, Maddie took a step forward.

"Yes, I think it is," Peter said. He placed a hand lightly on her shoulder to stop her from going closer.

Maddie turned to me, her eyes alight. "Rolf was a friend of my father's," she explained. "They used to play chess together. He lives near us."

The first hint of what was to come was an aching sound like a deep, slow groan. With that groan, the chain ever so gradually began to slip from its ties; gently, as if its moves were choreographed—a dance of metal and men—until abruptly the casing angled steeply to one side. Rolf gripped the chain above him with the strength and confidence of the god he was. For a long moment he swayed. Then the chain began to slip through its bounds. He struggled to climb it, to reach the steadiness of the crane itself, but as the chain cascaded through its ties, Rolf cascaded with it, desperately trying to pull himself up until all at once the chain ended.

And then, like a scientific experiment on gravity, the chain and the casing and the man began to fall, coming toward us, closer and closer, until all appeared to reach the floor at the same moment. The man expelled his breath in a long "ahhhh" as he landed on his right shoulder, his head hitting the dirty floor like an afterthought. The long, slithering chain rattled around him. The casing hit on its edge, making a hollow, reverberating *ping*. Then it began to fall over. Toward the chain. Toward the man. In that millisecond, the man might have rolled over and escaped. In that millisecond, someone might have reached for him and pulled him to safety. But he was dazed. We were all dazed. And perhaps the millisecond only seemed that long, as it burst into eternity.

The casing fell on the man's arm. He didn't call out. He simply looked at the chunk of metal that pinned him down, looked at it with surprise and confusion, as if not exactly understanding what it was, or how it got there. Someone screamed, and screamed again, and I realized that the screaming came from beside me, from Maddie—"Rolf! Rolf!" she cried—and I clutched her as Tom and Peter and the workmen ran forward. I gathered my girls and pushed them into a corner, out of the way. I turned them, so they wouldn't face what was happening, and they obliged like marionettes I could arrange for my pleasure.

All except Maddie, who wouldn't turn, who wouldn't stop screaming. An alarm sounded. The workmen tried to rig another chain to pull the casing off the man's arm. A bottle of whiskey appeared, and Tom held it to Rolf's lips. Tom held the man's hand and spoke to him softly. Finally a medical crew arrived. Tom shifted to make room. His suit, from knees to ankles, was seeped through with blood. Then the chief of the medical men opened his case and took out a saw.

"Peter," Tom called with a preternatural calm, never taking his attention from the man stretched on the floor beside him, "escort the ladies to their carriage, will you?"

"Yes, sir."

Peter came to us and wrapped Maddie in his arms, pressing a handkerchief over her mouth to quiet her crying. He took us outside, into the frosted, ice-bearing air, the sky deep blue, the high clouds white and sailing, as if we'd entered heaven itself. But I didn't sense the presence of any god in this heaven.

On the walk to our carriages, I steeled myself to absolute calm. There would be time enough later to cry. Time enough to talk, to try to find explanations. At this moment, we had only our dignity to protect us, only propriety to guide us.

As we approached the power station gates, I saw the demonstrators who had been standing in the cold for hours to protest the theft of Niagara's waters to make electricity. "What the Lord has given, let no man taketh away," their leader exhorted his followers. He was a thin man, with a white beard and long, wispy white hair. He was small but stood on a crate to make himself tall. "The waters of God's river belong to God. The falling waters lead to God! God sees, God knows, God has sent me here!"

Quietly I asked Peter, "Who is that?"

"His name is Daniel Henry Bates."

"Would Thomas Sinclair put himself in the place of God?" Bates shouted. "Would he? Yes, he would. Do not doubt it: for I know the secrets of Thomas Sinclair, I know the desecration he plans. Nothing, *nothing*, can he hide from me!"

Peter said, "He's the founder of the Niagara Preservation Society. His followers call themselves preservationists. He's from Harrisburg, Pennsylvania." Peter too had taken refuge in propriety. "I hear he col-lects roses; he has hundreds of kinds of roses in his garden. Well, he won't find many roses around here." Peter sighed. "Each day when I come to work, I hear him invoking the name of God in his protest against us. But isn't God light? Am I right on this, Miss Barrett? Isn't it God's work we're doing here, by making light? Or is it a sacrilege? Are we just imitating the power of God? Trying to take God's power onto ourselves? Does God approve or disapprove?"

His earnestness brought me close to tears. "I don't know, Peter. I don't know. Perhaps your priest . . ."

"Oh, yes. Father Mroz. He has dinner with Mr. Sinclair every other month. He's got a beautiful church at Echota and the most beautiful vestments any of us has ever seen. I've never heard Father Mroz criticize the power station or speak up for better safety. You must forgive my sister," Peter said abruptly. Maddie walked alone, ahead of and apart from the rest of us. "Our father died that way— close to it, at least, when Powerhouse Two was built. She wasn't there, of course. She could only imagine the accident. Until now."

"I'm sorry, Peter. I didn't—"

"After that, when Henry Perky started building his factory for Shredded Wheat, well . . . the rest of the men in the family went to do construction work over there. Except for me."

Like a carnival barker selling nutrition, Henry Perky had come here two years before. He'd advertised that his factory would be utterly modern, absolutely clean, and astoundingly well-lit. With missionary zeal and apparent sincerity, he claimed that Shredded Wheat, which he had invented, could not only transform individual lives but would save the world. He called his factory, which was scheduled to open in May, a "temple," so I suppose Shredded Wheat was the deity worshipped therein.

"My mother and my sisters—excepting Maddie, of course—have already got jobs lined up over there to make the Shredded Wheat after the factory opens," Peter continued. "Now I'm sure Maddie will start in on me to make the move too. I could probably get some kind of supervisory job there. But Shredded Wheat's not exactly on the same level as electricity. Not to me, I mean."

"Hey, Fronczyk! You robbing the nunnery?" a man shouted from the other side of the road. Judging from the placard, he was with a group from the National Brotherhood of Firemen and Oilers who walked a picket line.

"Not the nunnery!" another man called. "Mrs. Monroe's more likely!" This was greeted with guffaws. A few of the girls bit their lower lips, struggling to control the giggles that couldn't be suppressed despite what they'd just seen. Poor Abigail, though, looked around at me in confusion, as if to say, "Mrs. Monroe, who's that?" Evelyn took her elbow and whispered an education in her ear.

"Greetings, gentlemen," Peter called to them with a wave.

"How kind it is of management to say hello. Glad to see you haven't forgotten your old pals."

"Oh, think nothing of it," Peter said, putting on a British accent.

"He'll come running back to us someday, just wait and see."

After we passed them, Peter said, "I was an organizer once; O'Flarity was right about that. I suppose I did get enticed away by the bosses; sending union organizers to management training is one of Mr. Sinclair's favorite tricks. But I've got to think of my own future, and my family, not just the movement."

I was surprised that work could continue with one of the unions on strike. "Don't the unions all strike together, in sympathy with each other?"

"Oh, this is more of a slowdown than a strike. Got to keep everybody in practice. There's always somebody out here, marching around."

Three open carriages waited to take us back to the train. Peter gave Maddie a hug before helping her into her seat. She had stopped crying, but her face was a blotchy red. Strands of hair had fallen from her bun. The other girls shied away from her as they took their places.

When the girls were settled, I took Peter aside a few steps. "Thank you for looking after us. I'm so sorry."

"Yes. Thank you."

"The man's family, perhaps the school could—"

"That's not for me to say. But don't worry yourself, Miss Barrett. This sort of thing happens all the time. Falls, drownings, electrocutions. Two or three a week. More, sometimes. During the unlucky weeks." He stared toward the river. "It's all reported in the *Gazette*, except nobody reads the *Gazette* but us! Tourists don't read the *Gazette*; they're too busy searching the Falls for some kind of 'holy experience.'" Suddenly he turned to me, words rushing from him. "Please—don't think I'm ungrateful for the work. The work is good. The pay is good. Mr. Sinclair makes improvements when he can. He even pays for medical care—personally pays—when men are injured on the job. Guess he couldn't get the other directors to agree to having the company pay; I never heard of Morgan, Astor, and that crew paying for amputations." Peter gave a short, bitter laugh. "We've got safety classes we're required to go to, teaching what to do when someone's in electric shock—which isn't much, but still . . ." He paused. "The accidents we have inside the powerhouses are nothing compared to what the men outside suffer. The linemen, the cable splicers: they're climbing thirty-five-foot poles and falling off every day. They have to deal with kids who think it's fun to throw stray wires onto the lines and short them out. I wonder why the nature lovers haven't figured out how to do that yet; maybe they haven't taught themselves enough about electricity to know how it works." He shrugged at the irony. "Anyway the men outside, they're dealing with the thing itself: eleven thousand volts flowing through the lines. 'Hot stick men,' we call them."

I remembered a newspaper article that had stayed in my mind because it had seemed so strange: Last year in Baltimore, the "hot stick men" had gone on strike, not for higher wages but for a reduction in the voltage.

"Hot stick men," Peter repeated meditatively. "One false move . . . well, that's true for all of us in this world, isn't it, Miss Barrett? No matter what we do." His face seemed ready to crumple. "One false move and it's over."

The girls were subdued as we waited for the train. The Buffalo and Niagara Falls Electric Railway, the line was called, fifty cents each way, a half-hour trip. We boarded and spread out through the car, most of the girls wanting a window seat. Maddie sat opposite me, staring out, Peter's handkerchief crumpled in her hand. I sat quietly waiting for her to show a readiness to talk.

The girls said nothing during the trip. I too said nothing, because soon I would be called upon to say something—clear, cogent, and comforting. When we arrived back at school, we would gather for class, and I would need to give the girls an explanation. I was responsible for them; responsible for the kind of adults they turned into. I had tried to teach them to feel the anguish of others, to think for themselves, to search, evaluate, and take action in order to make some contribution to the world. What could I say to them, in the face of what we'd just seen, to reinforce all that?

If I were a minister, I'd tell them that what we'd seen was God's will and Rolf would have his reward in heaven. But I found that argument offensive. When I first came to Macaulay a twelve-year-old student was killed, her body mangled, at a railroad crossing. "Emily looks down at us now from heaven. Happiness glows around her. She tells us to be happy for her, not sad, for she is in a better place. She is at peace with the Lord," intoned the Reverend Holmes at her funeral service at Westminster Presbyterian Church. At that moment I lost faith with organized religion.

I looked out the window and saw that we were passing the power station: a group of lovely buildings arrayed along both sides of the river. The long windows reflected blue sky and billowy cumulus clouds. If I were a unionist, I'd tell the girls that we must fight harder now for safety standards so such an accident would never happen again. If I were an industrialist, I'd say that Rolf had made his sacrifice for the greater good of mankind. If I were a preservationist, I'd say that God himself had allowed the chain to break, to prove the sacredness of nature and the hubris of man.

The train curved away from the river, following the double row of power lines. Like an artist's exercise in perspective, the rhythmic alternation of poles and cables created a stark beauty across the landscape. Up ahead a horse-drawn cart was parked in the snow between the double row of poles. As we passed, I saw on the side of the cart a sign for "The Niagara Frontier Power Company." Directly beneath it was the company symbol of the Falls shot through with a lightning bolt. The horses' breath steamed. Two men climbed the poles, the "hot stick men," making repairs and checking the lines.

At that moment past and future seemed to merge: the silver-black lines cutting the sky with their burden of electricity; the wooden cart with its horses stamping their hooves impatiently; and the men, frail as ever, climbing the thirty-five-foot poles without safety harnesses, working with wires that carried eleven thousand deadly volts. As Peter Fronczyk had said, one false move and their lives were over.

Chapter Six

I'd give up everything for you. You know that, don't you? Home, position . . . everything I have could be yours." Amiable teasing filled Francesca Coatsworth's voice; she always concealed what was most important to her in a veil of irony. "I'll take you around the world, if you like."

Sitting side by side at her drawing table, we were about to review the architectural plans she'd prepared for the addition to Macaulay that Tom's endowment had made possible. On this Friday afternoon in early April, the warming light was soft through the mullioned bay windows as the time neared six o'clock. The wind-roar amid the giant maples around the house muted all other sounds.

"We can start by spending a few weeks sleeping the day away on the deck of a ship."

Every year at this time Francesca pressured me to go off with her, and every year I refused, no matter how tempting the proposed journeys might be. I had to refuse, because for Francesca, more was involved than simply the trip itself. She expected something in return . . . a degree of intimacy that made me uncomfortable, and her continued expectation brought a line of tension to our friendship. Margaret Sinclair and I had never made demands on one another. We were simply best friends, our relationship a given. With Francesca, however, I felt her shrewd looks upon me, her evaluations and calculations, her apparent confidence that somehow, some way, she could convince me to change my ways. Nonetheless, I clung to her friendship: she had brought me to Buffalo; we shared a wealth of memories and a similar way of life; and I relied on Francesca to be my cover if ever a wife began to question her husband's presence at my salon.

"We can dine at the captain's table every night; a mixed blessing, granted, but some people think it's fun."

We were ensconced on the top floor of her family house on Cottage Street. It was an eclectic mansion of huge pocket doors, long windows, mansard roof, and spiky turrets: a stereotypically brooding combination of Beaux Arts and Gothic. After the deaths of her parents, Francesca had turned this third-floor ballroom into an art studio, a retreat of hanging silks, Persian rugs, and wide sofas, her work area spread beneath the arched windows. From her drawing table, we gazed across the tops of the trees, at Lake Erie and the Niagara River; both shimmered with sailing ships. Beyond the water was Canada—so close, like a touch away in a painting. Canada made Francesca's dreams of flight seem real, for there it was, a foreign country at her doorstep.

"You need only say the word, and *poof*!" Like a sorcerer, she opened her fist in the air, flinging magic. "We'll be gone."

"It's easy to threaten to give things up when you'll never be asked to do so," I said.

"Even so. I'll hold the school plans hostage until you say yes." She spread her arms over the drawings and rested her head upon them, her dark-red hair flowing down her back, overwhelming the silver filigree clip at the crown of her head. Curls touched her forehead and her cheeks. Francesca was lithe and slender. Although on business assignments she wore the shirtwaist and corduroy skirt proper to a professional woman, her hair tidily pinned under a hat, at home she favored the loose, pseudo-medieval garb made popular by the pre-Raphaelites. She had met with much success in the years since she'd returned to Buffalo from Wellesley. In addition to many private homes, she'd designed two classroom buildings for the university, and she was assisting now with the design for a downtown hotel.

"I think Asia would be a good choice for us this summer," she continued with a touch of wistfulness. "Angkor Wat. We'll mount an expedition into the jungle. How many bearers will we need, do you think?"

Francesca tended to be romantic because she could afford to be. Her family was one of the oldest and wealthiest in the city. To care for the house and garden, which she had inherited from her parents,

Francesca employed seven people. She had been named Frances at birth, but changed her name to Francesca after visiting Italy during her Macaulay years. Her parents had traveled the world with their children—as a toddler she'd been carried through the Himalayas strapped to a Sherpa's back.

"We'll have separate staterooms on the boat, if that would fulfill your sense of propriety. We needn't actually share rooms, after all, to be together."

If I accepted her offer, the day after the Macaulay graduation I would be whisked off to New York City, outfitted splendidly with custom-made clothes that fulfilled her idea of the proper attire for female explorers, and soon we would board a ship headed wherever our fancy took us.

"No one need ever know if there were intimacy between us. A kiss, an embrace, an unbuttoning of all those buttons that go down your dress."

That teasing tone took her a long way. She raised her head to look at me more directly. In the fading light, her brown eyes turned black.

"Sometimes I think I should just throw you across the table and have my way with you. What harm would there be?"

How easily I could have taken her hand, or caressed her thick hair in all its shades of auburn. Even kissed her cheek, so smooth in the fading light, like a child's.

"Francesca," I said gently, "I don't think—"

Abruptly she sat up, twisting her hair into a coil. "Yes, yes, I know. But I must say in my opinion chastity is overrated."

I felt sick inside from my loneliness. "Chastity *per se* has never been a goal of mine."

"Well, you've certainly fooled me all these years. Really, Louisa, I'm tired of being your cover—lurking in the background so the ladies don't get jealous of your dealings with their ever-so-handsome husbands."

Her anger surprised me. She'd always said that being my cover was a good joke. I felt our friendship shift, leaving me bereft. "Thank you, Francesca." My eyes filled with tears. "Thank you for being my cover and allowing me to conduct business freely with the ever-so-handsome men of the town."

"I'm not interested in your thanks. Just look at you: all your beauty wasted. Hidden away and covered up. What are you saving yourself for? To grow old alone? I should think you'd be grateful for some companionship. For some passion, even."

"Yes, I would be grateful. Of course I would." My voice was trembling.

Finally she realized I was trying not to cry. She rubbed the back of my hand. How lovely she was.

"All right, I'll never mention it again. Especially because . . . well, I've been planning a comeuppance for you." Her irony was mixed with sadness, as if she too were hiding tears. "This was your final chance."

"Whatever do you mean?"

"Simply that I have another interest developing. A requited interest. I may no longer need to bother you with my bribes of trips around the world." She gave me a brave smile. "I wanted to offer you one last opportunity to see the error of your ways. But as you persist in your misguided notions, you'll have a surprise. Soon. This evening." All at once she appeared exceedingly pleased with herself.

"Francesca—"

"Jealous, are you? Thinking of changing your mind while there's still time?"

"It's unfair to invite me to dinner when you have something unpleasant in mind."

"Not in the least unpleasant, I assure you. Other guests are coming—fascinating, each and every one. Besides, we have the Macaulay plans to review. I'd like to show them off tonight."

She assumed her brusque professional manner, putting on her glasses, turning on the gaslight on the wall beside the window.

"So," she said firmly, "let's see if these meet with your approval."

And they did. Indeed they did. The plans were magnificent, inspiring enough to force merely personal worries out of my mind. The new wing would be constructed behind the school, on land we already owned. The exterior would be Gothic Revival, with turrets, eaves, and towers to match the present building. On the lowest level (actually the basement), there would be a swimming pool with intricate tile work and windows near the ceiling, cleverly concealed on the exterior to allow for light but prevent spying by the Nichols School boys (Nichols was the male equivalent of Macaulay, and its denizens were known for their mischief). On the ground level, there was a new gymnasium with a balcony all around that could be used as a running track. Above that, new chemistry and biology laboratories. On the top floor, an art studio with slanting skylights.

"I've made the tower stairs begin in the art studio, so the girls can go off alone with an easel to draw the sunset or do whatever girls like to do these days when they go off alone. *I* did nothing but dream—except once or twice when I stole a kiss in the music room."

"You did no such thing!"

"If you insist, Miss Barrett." She smiled coyly. "But you can't expect the standards in my day to match your standards!"

She paused, studying me with a curiosity that changed to concern. "Louisa, do you have any idea why Thomas Sinclair gave you all this money?" I stiffened. "Not that I'm complaining. But it's the talk of the drawing rooms."

I could well imagine. Happily such talk hadn't yet come to my salon, which might be considered too close to home for open speculation. From the phrasing of her question, I deduced that no one had made a link between the endowment and Speyer's death. But of course no one knew about Speyer's visit but Tom, Grace, and me. Even so, I couldn't share my worries with Francesca. Our interests weren't the same here. Francesca loved gossip and relished scandal. She had the freedom to enjoy them both, for even if they touched her personally, her position was secure. Unlike mine. I could never totally trust her, not the way I'd trusted Margaret. Some things were just too exciting for Francesca to keep to herself. Not foreseeing any harm, she might pass along something I'd confided in her, telling it as a secret, of course, and someday those told secrets could return to vex me.

I offered her what I had developed into my set response. "Mr. Sinclair probably wants to give his daughter more opportunities as she gets older." I tried to sound impatient with the entire issue. "And there's Margaret's memory too: I'm sure he wants to create something lasting in her name."

"But it's too much money for that. There must be something else."

"Frannie, it may seem like a lot of money to me, and even to you—forgive me for saying so," I bantered, "but it may not seem like a lot to him."

"Well, the money really isn't the point, is it?" she said, irritated. "People think he's trying to buy something." A streak of fear passed through me, but immediately I tried to shake it off. People couldn't have made the link between us—it was impossible. Impossible. "There's talk of what it might be. Position, perhaps. Forgetfulness."

"Forgetfulness?" I queried.

"Like an apology. For Margaret."

"What about Margaret?" I asked, hearing myself sound defensive.

"Oh really, Louisa, you're so dense." But I knew what she meant: because people disapproved of Tom—because he was Catholic, and Irish, and born into poverty—they liked to pretend that Margaret had been mistreated by him, to vindicate their disapproval. I'd never seen any evidence of that, however, and I'd seen Margaret almost every day. Or perhaps the apology Francesca referred to was simpler: Tom had taken—stolen—one of the princesses of the city and essentially killed her with pregnancy; his gift to the school helped to make up for his theft.

Apparently bored with the subject, Francesca stared out the window at the growing dusk. The Canadian shore had turned a deep, shadowed green, the western sky above it shot through with pink and purple. From our eyrie at the high bay windows, we ourselves might have been part of the sunset.

Abruptly she said, "How are the girls coping with the accident they saw at the power station?"

I was taken aback. "How do you know about that?"

"Oh, I hear everything, you know. Eventually. A girl tells her mother, her mother tells one of my all-too-many cousins, that cousin tells another cousin who tells me. What does it matter how I heard?"

"Only that we agreed, the girls and I, that it was something we wanted to keep private. Just for immediate families."

"Afraid there'd be more concern for the girls than for the man himself?"

I paused. "Frankly, yes."

"And you were absolutely right. I haven't heard much mention of the man—but the girls, the poor girls! How people worry for the girls! Have no fear, though: No one's criticizing you for taking them there." Francesca cocked her head at me: "Everyone knows that your motives are eternally above reproach. What happened is viewed more as another mark against Sinclair. So how are the poor girls?"

"They were shocked at first. But now—this is a horrible way to put it—they are inspired to do better. They're inflamed with the passion to improve things. Evelyn Byers has even spoken to her father about the safety of the crewmen on his fleet, if you can believe it."

"Did he tell her to tend to her knitting?"

"No. He said he would investigate. Possibly having heard that before, Evelyn herself investigated, and now she reports that something may actually be done. She's even offered to borrow against the funds she'll be coming into when she turns twenty-one to pay for the improvements. Maybe there really will be more to her future than flower arranging."

Suddenly a feeling of futility swept over me. "So you see I am doing some good in my life, Francesca. I haven't wasted all my time since Wellesley."

She hugged me tightly, in friendship, not passion. "No one ever said you had, Louisa. You've transformed the lives of all the girls who've been at Macaulay under your care. You should feel proud."

"I see that man—Rolf was his name—falling over and over when I close my eyes at night. That we were even there to see it feels like a sacrilege; like a violation of his dignity. I wonder how he'd feel, if he knew he'd 'inspired' my girls."

"He probably wouldn't care a hoot about 'your girls.' Why should he? And what you should care about is that maybe you've rescued Evelyn Byers from a life of nothing but diamonds and lace. Seeing the accident didn't miraculously change her. She was changed before—by you. The accident simply gave her an impetus to act."

She squeezed my shoulders and shook me a bit. "Come on now,

snap out of it. Shall I tell you the rest of the drawing room gossip? That'll get your mind off things. People are wondering," she said with conspiratorial glee, "whether there's more than coincidence in the two recent events relating to the power station."

"Which two events?" I asked, confused.

"Come now, Louisa. Don't be naive. First the chief engineer drowns, under a sheet of ice, no less, and even after almost a month of work the police still can't seem to figure out anything to say about it."

She was right: There'd been no official report yet on Speyer's death, and I'd wondered what Mr. Rumsey was waiting for. But I would never share that question with Francesca. At my salon, I'd listened carefully for any loose bits of information that might be circulating, but everyone seemed to agree that Speyer's death was accidental.

"Then a generator casing—that's what it was, wasn't it?" I nodded. "You wouldn't believe some of the descriptions I've heard. Anyway, a generator casing falls on an experienced workman—"

"What are you implying?"

"Obviously there's more than chance at play. Hasn't that occurred to you?"

Until this moment, a link between Speyer and Rolf had not entered my mind.

"What everyone's debating is, who is to blame? Is it the handsome parvenu Mr. Sinclair, with his million-dollar endowments to little girls? Is it the God-fearing preservationists? The union militants staging a *coup d'état*? Or maybe, just maybe, could it be J.P. Morgan's own representative Frederick Krakauer, stirring up trouble for reasons best known to himself?"

"Accidents take place every day at the power station," I said, forcing myself to sound dismissive about her speculations. "We just never hear about them."

"If we never hear about them, how do you know they happen?"

This was absurd. "They're reported in the local Niagara Falls newspaper."

"You read the local Niagara Falls newspaper?"

"I've been told by someone who does."

"Who?"

Why was she pushing me on this? "I've been told by—" Suddenly I didn't want her to know about Peter Fronczyk, didn't want him and Maddie pulled into the round of gossip. "By someone in a position to know. Someone far from the intrigue you are so absurdly implying."

"Absurd? *Moi?*" She laughed with joy.

There was a light knock. "Sorry—am I early?" A woman stood in the shadows at the open door. Suddenly I realized that the room had become dark; the sunset had passed into night. "The young lady downstairs said to come up."

How deftly her words—"the young lady downstairs"—pegged the background of our visitor. A woman like Francesca or Margaret would have said "your girl" or, if she had visited before, simply the servant's name. Only someone who'd grown up without servants would refer to the maid as "the young lady," as if she were the equal of herself.

"Come in, come in." Turning on another gas lamp, Francesca went to greet the visitor, taking her hands and bringing her into the light. Only then did I recognize her: Susannah Riley, the Macaulay art teacher. The painter who'd done the watercolors in Tom's library and who tutored Grace in drawing. So this was the person on whom Francesca had set her sights as my comeuppance: the young woman from Fredonia who'd come to the city only a year and a half ago and to whom I'd given her first professional opportunity by hiring her at Macaulay. How quickly she had insinuated herself into our lives.

"Look who's here, Louisa," Francesca was saying. I rose to give my greetings, filled with proper *politesse* even though I wasn't accustomed to socializing outside school with junior faculty. Furthermore, Susannah's developing friendship with Francesca made me wish I could disappear.

"Good evening, Miss Riley. Miss Coatsworth and I were reviewing the plans for the addition to the school. You are going to have a wonderful new art studio."

"Yes, I know," Susannah said eagerly. "The entire addition is going to be beautiful." So: Francesca had shown the plans to Susannah before showing them to me. I glanced at my friend, but she was studying Susannah with frank admiration.

Susannah was an odd one to elicit such attention. I knew from observing her classes that when she taught, confidence filled her, and she was precise and blunt with both her criticism and her praise. But outside the art room, she sometimes appeared unsure of herself and vulnerable, like a child finding her way. She was thin and small, probably just five feet tall, and her clothes always seemed too big for her. Tonight, with her regulation shirtwaist she wore a lavender necktie that almost shouted "artistic." Her boots needed polishing. Her dark hair was pulled into a thick, disarrayed bun at the nape of her neck. Yet seeing her here tonight I had to admit, as much as I hated to, that there was something alluring about her. Her lips were thick, her features sculpted, her eyes big and dark. Her expression was simultaneously childlike and womanly, innocent and knowing. With a shock I realized that the vulnerability I saw in the faculty room at school could easily be an act. The thought of her as Francesca's physical intimate made me cringe.

"I was sorry, Miss Barrett, to hear about what happened when the girls visited the power station."

Obviously she was already well within the loop of gossip.

"Yes, it was unfortunate," I said, too brusquely. Quickly I changed to an alternative topic. "I saw your watercolors at the Sinclair home when I was visiting recently. They were remarkable—and quite realistic, I was surprised to see when I went to the station."

"Thank you, Miss Barrett." She gave me a wide-eyed, almost flirtatious look. I'd seen that kind of look before: on the faces of young women attempting to please and flatter wealthy older men. That Susannah was using this type of pseudo-innocent enticement with me was noteworthy: I wondered what she wanted. "I tried to show the beauty of the natural world around the power station, so the buildings wouldn't overwhelm the nature."

"You found the perfect balance," I assured her, maintaining the rigors of courtesy.

"Hi-ho, where are you, Frannie?" a man's voice called from the hall. "Awfully dark up here." All at once there was a bustling of arrival as the other guests came up the stairs: Dr. Charles Cary and his wife, Evelyn Rumsey Cary; Louise Blanchard Bethune and her husband,

Robert; and bringing up the rear, focusing on everything around him with a curiosity that wasn't strictly polite, the man whom I had met at the lakeside: Franklin Fiske.

For several minutes there was much high-spirited banter. Dr. Cary took upon himself the chore of lighting the rest of the lamps, while teasing Francesca about her Bohemian ways. All at once the room was bright, the darkness nothing more than a kind of curtain filling the tall windows. Francesca had grown up with the Carys, both of whom were supremely self-confident and supremely fun-loving. Fresh-faced and thick-haired, growing into portliness, Charles Cary was a medical doctor. His wife (Dexter Rumsey's niece) was an artist of some repute and dressed the part, in flowing gowns. Tonight she wore magenta velvet.

And then there was Louise Blanchard Bethune. Francesca had done her apprenticeship at Mrs. Bethune's firm, Bethune, Bethune, and Fuchs (Louise Bethune was in partnership with her husband). Mrs. Bethune had accomplished what women like me were always told was impossible: She enjoyed an apparently happy marriage, she was successfully raising a son, who had a bent toward medicine, and she was a well-known architect. She didn't pursue small domestic commissions, those which would be considered more appropriate for a wife and mother. No, she had designed factories, and a women's prison. Through all of this she'd managed to remain a slight, feminine figure, friendly and helpful to other women. She'd suffered none of the dire consequences that traditionalists promised women who broke with their "proper" roles (such as insanity), so naturally I was more than a little jealous of her. Standing alone beside the unlit fireplace, I watched Mrs. Bethune befriend Susannah Riley—or more accurately, Miss Riley befriend Mrs. Bethune, standing close to her and praising—as I could clearly overhear, even at a distance—certain small details of one of her designs.

Soon, however, my attention was captured by Franklin Fiske, who was undertaking an intent peregrination around the room as if he were a thief looking for something to steal. He examined the Macaulay plans, Francesca's drawing materials, the bookshelves, the furniture. No one objected or even noticed. Of course he was an appealing figure, with an open, eager face: the type who's always forgiven his indiscretions. He was dressed more formally than when I'd last seen him beside a snow mound, and I realized how attractive he was: tall and well-built, with sharply angled cheekbones, the late-day shadow of a beard upon his smoothly shaven face, his dark hair curling in disarray. "Byronic" was the word that slipped into my mind; he looked like a tousled, world-weary Lord Byron. I laughed out loud at the exaggeration just as Fiske was turning his attention to me.

"Miss Barrett, how lovely to see you. What makes you so happy this evening?"

"Weren't you ever taught that it's impolite to ask personal questions of virtual strangers?" I asked jokingly.

"No," he assured me seriously. "I was never taught that." He gave me a sudden grin. "Well, I must say, you were quite right last month when you said that people here in Buffalo are very friendly among those they know. Thanks to Cousin Susan, all doors open to me." He motioned broadly to embrace the room—and to welcome Evelyn Rumsey Cary as she approached us. Evelyn had a full face, and she always wore an exquisite pearl choker to conceal her somewhat thickening neck.

"Louisa, I'm so pleased you already know Mr. Fiske. Apparently he's exceedingly creative," she noted, "although he hasn't actually shown us any of the photographs he claims to be taking."

Quickly Franklin said, "So, Miss Barrett, how are you proceeding with your study of the efficiency of the police department?"

At that I blushed. Such were the rewards of blatant lying.

Evelyn was surprised and fascinated. "Louisa, I didn't know you were—"

"Oh, it's only a minor study," I said, cloaking myself with modesty. "When I get the time—"

Luckily we were interrupted by Francesca's butler passing around the sherry. The group came together in an informal circle.

"How awful for you, Louisa, to go to the power station and see an accident," said Dr. Cary. I glowered at Francesca, who was standing opposite me. She shrugged.

"Thank you for your concern," I replied.

Franklin offered, "I was out at Niagara last week." Silently I blessed him for changing the subject, if only slightly. "Instead of spending numbing hours gazing at the mighty cataract, I visited all the electrified factories that are springing up near the power station. I took photographs too, for your information, Mrs. Cary." He actually chucked her under the chin. He certainly fit into this world with ease, as if he were born to it—which he was, I reminded myself. "Well, what I saw was amazing. Companies are coming from all over the country to use the power of Niagara, and their profits are astronomical."

I felt certain that these companies were searching out local investors to aid with start-up costs: my board members were getting richer and richer, and Mr. Milburn was gaining more and more clients.

"The factories are working twenty-four hours a day, using totally new processes: electro*chemical*, electro*lytic*, electro*thermal*. They're making aluminum, graphite, silicon carbide—I don't even understand what these things are, but there's a huge demand for them. They couldn't even be produced without electricity, and lots of it. Just look at silicon carbide."

Evelyn groaned.

"No, bear with me, Ev." Ev: most likely fewer than a handful of people felt entitled to call her that. "Silicon carbide is produced by a new company called Carborundum. As best as I can understand, it's an abrasive that's used for grinding wheels. And grinding wheels, I'm happy to inform you, are the *sine qua non* of modern industry. Silicon carbide is created in the most incredible way: The people out there make up a mixture of sand and sawdust and this and that—their own secret recipe—and then with electricity they heat up their furnace to seven thousand degrees Fahrenheit—" He paused, looking puzzled. "Or maybe it was four thousand degrees Fahrenheit—either way they make it hot, and with this tremendous heat their secret mixture is miraculously transformed into a little pile of crystals. These crystals constitute the fabulously profitable silicon carbide."

Dr. Cary nodded eagerly as he followed Franklin's explanation.

"There's also a company called National Electrolytic, involved in the production of something called 'chlorate of potash.' I spent fifteen minutes with the director of that company—while setting up my camera, of course"—he acknowledged Evelyn with a raised brow—"and I still have no idea what 'chlorate of potash' is or does."

I warmed to Fiske for his enthusiasm, for his openness to experience. That he combined them with irony and self-deprecating humor made him even more appealing.

"But whatever chlorate of potash is or does, it's beyond doubt miraculous. The entire industrial strip at Niagara—miraculous. I stepped into the future, and it was wonderful. A new world for a new century. Do I sound trite, do I sound clichéd?"

"Not at all, Fiske," Charles Cary answered. "I'm hoping there'll be medical breakthroughs to come of it."

Ever soft-spoken, Louise Bethune said, "I just received a commission out there for a new factory, an extension of the Pittsburgh Reduction Company. For aluminum."

"Congratulations," Francesca said, reaching to squeeze her friend's hand.

"The new, artistic factory," Fiske mused. "Incredible potential—for my photographs, I mean."

"Wait." Suzannah Riley's faltering voice broke in to the conversation. "Think. That's the problem—everyone goes full ahead and no one ever stops to think. Those factories need electricity twenty-four hours a day, just as you said, Mr. Fiske." Her voice grew stronger. "They steal the waters of Niagara Falls to make—what? Grinding wheels? 'Chlorate of potash'? Is that really the future we want, a future that turns the sublimity of Niagara into grinding wheels?"

"I don't see why not," I said. An urge to strike her down filled me. "It's just a small bit of water that they're taking to make electricity. There's still plenty left for people to look at. And why shouldn't the water do something useful? The Falls has too much water for its own good, anyway. You must know that, Susannah, spending so much time out there painting. The constant rock slides. The erosion. And anyway"—I was enraged now, and I couldn't say why—"who are we to say that aluminum and silicon carbide and whatever else Mr. Fiske mentioned don't help humanity more than water falling over a cliff?"

"But Miss Barrett." All at once Susannah was close to tears, yet still she stood up for herself. "They'll never stop. You know that. They'll keep going until Niagara is bare rock, from the rapids to the gorge."

She covered her face, weeping. Francesca wrapped her arms around Susannah and took her off to a corner, whispering, "There, there . . . you shouldn't take these things so personally, we're just talking, just making conversation."

The others gathered around me in an awkward silence. I felt thoroughly embarrassed.

"You're right, Louisa, you know," Dr. Cary finally said. "Too bad she became upset, but you *are* right. Take some comfort in that."

"Thank you," I said, deeply ashamed that I had attacked someone younger and more inexperienced than I.

"She's highly artistic, that's the trouble," Cary continued. "Too emotional for her own good. Too wrapped up in her own concerns—that's the artistic temperament."

"Aren't I 'artistic'?" Evelyn asked, taking mock offense.

"Yes, but you're older, my darling. You handle it better. And you have me to keep you steady."

Evelyn laughed joyfully, and her laughter restored our equilibrium.

Two more servants came upstairs. From the dumbwaiter they took china and silver, then platters laden with sliced meats and finely prepared vegetables; I caught the scents of mint, orange, and Indian chutneys: Francesca's repasts were more exotic than those of the Buffalo Club. The servants arranged the dinner on a buffet table at the end of the room. This, I thought, is my moment to depart. I couldn't tolerate the notion of sitting down to dine with Susannah after the scene I'd created. I told the company that I'd stopped by simply to see the plans, and now I needed to move on to a previous engagement. There was little notice; Francesca had stationed Susannah on the couch, and the others were admiring the buffet. Charles Cary made a point of saying that he and Evelyn would see me on Monday evening at my "saloon," as he so kindly put it.

The stairwell was infused with the enveloping, misty gold of flickering gaslight. Halfway down, I suddenly heard a step behind me. I stopped and turned, unreasonably frightened.

"Miss Barrett—I hope your departure has nothing to do with me," Fiske said, hurrying to my side.

"With you? Why should it?"

"Well, historically I've noticed that people tend to flee the room once I've arrived."

I smiled. "How unfortunate for you."

"Indeed, it is a sorry fate. But seriously, I feared I might have embarrassed you with that question about the police."

"That was the least of my embarrassments tonight."

"I didn't intend to embarrass you. I only wondered how your study—"

"Think nothing of it, Mr. Fiske."

"But I can think of nothing *but* it," he insisted.

"My study of the police interests you so?"

"No, no—that I might have embarrassed you so much that you felt the need to leave."

"You certainly seem to have an elevated view of your own importance."

"I knew it! You're leaving because of me, just the way you left the park because of me. When I would like nothing better than for you to stay and permit me to bask in your lovely presence." There was just enough humor in his voice to allow him to get away with this rigmarole. Even so, I sensed that to some extent, at least, he was serious; he reminded me of Francesca, veiling with irony everything of importance.

Of course he *was* attractive, he *was* suitable. We stared at one another. Could I risk even one step toward him? Immediately I felt wounded, cut by the insecurity that overwhelmed me whenever a man approached me as if I were a desirable woman.

Although I made myself sound amused, sadness filled me as I forced him away. "Go upstairs, Mr. Fiske, before you miss your dinner." Hastily I turned and continued down the stairs, feeling his gaze upon my back.

The next day, Saturday, I took a walk at noontime among the budding trees. Bidwell Parkway to Soldier's Place to Lincoln Parkway. I exchanged greetings with students and parents, friends and acquaintances. A clear, icy scent tinged with last autumn's fallen leaves filled the air. Sparrows flitted to collect whatever they could find in the softening soil. And there they were, in the distance, coming toward me: Two figures on horseback, one big, one small. I stopped where I was, to watch them. They made their way slowly along the bridle path.

The little one . . . for nine years I had walked this path, hoping to see her. Watching her grow: from infant carriage to sled; from wobbling steps to running; from pony to horse. I never let her realize that she was the reason I walked here. Nor did she suspect. Many people walked along the parkway, and all of them knew one another.

"Aunt Louisa!" she called, catching sight of me. She galloped toward me, cheeks ruddy, hair flying. Bells jangled on the horse's harness. She reined him in beside me, her movements precise, well-taught. "This is Rowan." She was proud of herself. Excited. Catching her breath. Straightening his mane. "Papa got him for me. For my very own." For several years Grace had taken riding lessons at the country club, north of Delaware Park. "This is the first day I've ridden him outside the training ring. I named him Rowan because he's a roan—isn't that funny?"

Yes. Funny. What a frail vessel Grace was for the weight of my affection.

"Isn't he cute? Oh look, there's Winnie—I need to show her Rowan!"

And with that, she was off.

Her father approached me. For a moment I couldn't look at him, beset as I was by worries about Speyer, Tom's lie, and the endowment.

"Good morning, Louisa."

All at once I realized that I mustn't let him suspect my uneasiness; I must behave with absolute normality. "Good morning, Tom," I replied evenly.

He stopped where she had been, touching his hat in greeting. His eyes looked very blue against the sky. He wore a camel-colored riding jacket, well-cut.

He seemed shy, his demeanor completely different from the last time I'd seen him, when he'd been a commanding, powerful figure. Now he appeared awkward. Or perhaps I was the one feeling shy and awkward as I contemplated my conflicting emotions toward him— curiosity, attraction, fear. What was he capable of? How could I know?

I pressed down on the horse's nose, on its white blaze. The horse pushed up against my hand in its version of a greeting, then nuzzled my neck, its hair tickling my cheek. I wanted to hug it tight, to hide my face against its withers.

"Grace seems content today," he said. I followed his gaze. Up the street, too far away for us to hear their conversation, Grace had dismounted and was showing her classmate Winifred Coatsworth (one of Francesca's many relations) the wonders of Rowan. I might have entered a child's picture book, one designed to show how small things seemed when they were far away and how big they became when they were close.

"She isn't . . . edgy today, the way she sometimes gets." He dismounted and stood beside me.

"What do you mean, 'edgy'?"

"Oh . . . I don't know exactly. Sensitive. Noticing every little thing."

Up ahead, Grace wrapped her arms around Rowan's neck and kissed him.

"The horse is good. Keeps her busy. Maybe that's the whole trouble: She needs something to keep her busy. She takes care of him. Worries about him instead of thinking about . . . well, instead of missing Margaret."

I was silent; I didn't want to say, you and I have more than enough to keep us busy, but we still miss Margaret.

"How are you, Louisa?"

"Well, thank you." I looked past him and upward, at the branches dotted with green like a gossamer net. "How is Rolf?"

"Recuperating. Thank you." In my mind once more I saw Tom's tenderness as he knelt on the dirty floor beside the injured man. "It's kind of you to ask."

We began to walk side by side toward Grace, Tom holding the horse's reins loosely in his hand.

"Lovely day. You can sense the life beginning to stir within the earth," he said, sounding very Irish.

"Yes."

Everything had slowed; again I had that image of us caught like illustrations in a book. Now we were in a tale of King Arthur, I with my flowing cloak, the wind blowing loose my hair, the pictures sumptuous.

"She has Margaret's smile."

"Yes."

"You and Grace have the same hair color."

This pleased me. "Hardly," I replied, brushing back the tendrils around my face. Pushing a few under my hat. Was it a betrayal of Margaret, for her husband to pay me a compliment and for me to feel pleasure in it? Had he actually paid me a compliment, or simply made an observation? My love for Grace made it feel like a compliment. "My hair has darkened since I was her age."

"It's just that she spends more time in the sun."

"Even so."

"By the way, I've turned down a position on the Macaulay board."

"Why?" I asked, surprised. At the very least, a position on the board guaranteed entrée to the city's decision makers. Was Tom really so determinedly independent, so cavalier, that he didn't desire this advantage?

"Unlike many of my colleagues, I feel no need to lunch with Mr. Rumsey once a month." Quickly, with a dash of humor, he added, "Will you feel comfortable managing all that money without me?"

"Yes, of course."

"Good." He was entirely matter-of-fact. If he were trying to bribe me, wouldn't this be the moment to say something? To confirm my continued . . . cooperation, as it were? We walked in silence. A palpable silence which I breathed in deeply, willing it to fill me like a reassurance that my suspicions were groundless. I looked around. Everything glowed; everything was itself, only more so—the trees taller, the houses bigger, the sky brighter, the parkways longer and wider.

"Louisa." Tom stopped and turned to me. He looked troubled. "I've been meaning to ask a favor of you." He paused.

"Yes, Tom. Of course." The favor was something to do with Grace, I felt certain. Or him and Grace. Or the three of us together—Grace, Tom, Louisa—the permutations spinning through me. I felt more trusting of Tom than I did of a stranger like Franklin Fiske; I could allow myself to relax around him, if only a bit. After all, because of Margaret and Grace, Tom was like part of my family.

"I've heard from Maria Love that she plans to disband the breakfast carts. You remember, the ones Margaret organized outside schools in the immigrant neighborhoods."

I felt irrationally disappointed that he'd shifted away from personal matters. Were there tears in my eyes? Did I reach for my handkerchief to cover them? Although the trees were no less beautiful, the parkways no less wide, they were rendered abruptly normal, whereas a moment before they'd been extraordinary.

"Well—it's a bit difficult for me to talk to Miss Love." He flashed a shrugging smile. The redoubtable Miss Love had placed herself in charge of much of the community's philanthropy.

"Yes, I understand."

"I'd like to keep the carts going. There's no question of money: We paid for the whole thing from the start. Do you think you could talk to Miss Love about it? When you're not busy, I mean. Try to bring her around? If it's no trouble to you. For Margaret's sake."

I felt as if there were a transparent screen between us.

"Yes, Tom. Of course." What else could I say?

"Thank you. I appreciate it."

"Yes."

He touched my shoulder in gratitude, and we continued our walk toward his daughter.

Chapter Seven

This was what happened when you accepted a million dollars from someone: You felt compelled to do favors for him. Or so I brooded the following week, having been forced to leave school on a Wednesday morning to meet Maria Love at the place and time most convenient for her. With festering annoyance I walked eastward on Swan Street toward Michigan Street. Once this part of the city had been refined and elegant. Beaux-Arts town houses with mansard roofs bespoke a glorious past. But over the years rail lines and factories had divided the neighborhood, and now the town houses too were divided—and redivided and divided again, to pack in more and more immigrants.

I wasn't late, but already Miss Love waited for me on the steps of the Fitch Crèche, her headquarters. She stood impatiently glaring from left to right, examining the neighborhood for unfortunates who might need her assistance. If I were an unfortunate, I would flee at the sight of her. She was a tall woman, almost six feet, and ramrod straight. Her tight corset made her top half seem as if it were about to burst out of its lustrous silk and lace. She was sixty-one years old, and each passing year made her stronger and more confident. She gave new meaning to the word regal, and even attended costume balls dressed as Elizabeth I (no acting required).

Spotting me, Miss Love offered a clipped wave, turning her hand from the wrist. On her jacket lapel was a corsage of green roses, undoubtedly a gift from Macaulay trustee George Urban, Jr., who obviously knew how to curry favor. The three long feathers in her hat swayed precariously in the breeze. She carried an oversized leather handbag, filled with God only knew what implements of assistance. I braced myself: Louisa, you must try to remember all the good she's done.

And she had. Miss Love had devoted her life to doing good. She'd been inspired as a girl, when she'd heard the story of a toddler who'd burned to death because the child's mother, in a misguided attempt at protection, had left the youngster tied to the kitchen table when she went out to work. To stop such tragedies, Miss Love established the Crèche to care for the children of poor working women, day and night if necessary. And she'd accomplished much more: She'd helped to establish settlement houses and employment bureaus and schools where immigrant women could learn English and train to be cooks or seamstresses. Worried about consumption, cholera, and diphtheria, Miss Love arranged for the children at the Crèche to receive free medical care, and their mothers got the same. Every ethnic group was included in her efforts, even Negroes, who were so often left out. On a visit to the South when she was young, Maria had seen a slave auction, and the experience had marked her forever. If she'd been born a man, she could have been anything she chose—governor, U.S. senator, even president. But as a woman, political life was closed to her, so her immense ambitions, energies, and wealth were focused on good deeds.

"Louisa Barrett, at last!" she announced, stepping forward, gripping my arm, and abruptly leading me at a quick pace down Michigan Street. "I'm conducting a visitation."

The exaggerated precision of her elocution was such that children who weren't terrified of her were reduced to (private) gales of laughter. She was well known for performing in amateur theatricals and had even gone on tour to such far-flung cities as Cleveland and Toledo with a group organized by Dr. Cornell, our local impresario. Rumor had it that she was devastating as Cordelia.

"A deserving family has been brought to my attention." She might have been Christ himself, and alas the unfortunates being visited had best regard her as such if they knew what was good for them. Miss Love towered over me, partly because of the feathers in her hat but also because of her thick high heels, not the type of practical shoes one would have imagined her in and which I myself had worn hoping to please her. Well did I know the necessity of ingratiating myself with Miss Maria Love. A few whispers from her to Dexter Rumsey could destroy my position. And I wanted my girls to be able to do volunteer work at the

Crèche. It was an eminently suitable place for them: The impoverished children's families were thoroughly examined to make certain they were neither profligate nor inebriate, so my students' parents need not worry that their daughters might be exposed to immorality as well as poverty.

Miss Love treated people well or badly in proportion to how closely they followed her advice and how grateful they were for the privilege of doing so. She had always treated Margaret badly, because Margaret had never followed her advice and never shown her the least bit of gratitude. Alas, being on Maria Love's bad side had repercussions, because she was the power behind the Charity Organization Society, a group which had organized the churches of the city to dispense charity in their specific neighborhoods, without regard to denomination. Ansley Wilcox (my board member and Dexter Rumsey's twice-over son-in-law) was her figurehead and collaborator, the two of them building an empire governed by their own unchristian views of what constituted Christian charity.

The breakfast carts exemplified this. Studies done by philanthropic groups showed that children did better in school if they had a good breakfast. These studies also showed that children from poor families often had no breakfast awaiting them at home in the morning, except maybe some weak coffee or tea. Margaret had the idea of the carts, which would bring fresh bread, milk, and fruit to public elementary schools in "affected neighborhoods." Any child, whether he or she had had breakfast or not, whether his or her parents were married or not, inebriate or not—*any* child could grab something to eat and continue on his way to school.

Maria Love and Ansley Wilcox abhorred this plan. There was no control in this plan. Anyone—anyone at all—could take free charity under this plan. This plan would be responsible for the sinking into degradation of hundreds of formerly self-respecting poor children—because they would be getting something for nothing! *All* of them, the good and the bad together! Better that these children come to Maria Love, be properly evaluated as to whether their parents were profligate and/or inebriate, and then, if they passed muster and did some work that Miss Love found for them—delivering messages or sewing on buttons or making paper flowers, depending on their age and sex—then their parents might be given a penny a day with which to buy the children a proper breakfast.

As luck would have it, Margaret was very rich, and of course the rich can do exactly as they please. So Margaret set up her breakfast carts, Miss Maria Love be damned. But with Margaret gone, the carts were now under the Love/Wilcox jurisdiction.

"Hold tight to your possessions," she cautioned as we turned onto Seneca and walked toward South Cedar. The streets teemed with raucous life: saloons, whores, peddlers, horse carts, dirty children running amok or blocking the street with baseball games. Poles, Jews, Italians, Irish, Russians—pressed together in a jumble of languages. We pushed our way around fruit vendors and dry-goods peddlers. Women wearing shawls and kerchiefs shopped beside others in shirtwaists and hats, the Old World mixing with the New. Clothes hung from windows to dry. Garbage cluttered the curbs, rotting vegetable peelings mixed with dog-chewed bones. Flies swarmed around the carcasses hung outside a butcher shop. The nearby factories filled the air with acrid soot, and there was another smell too, one which I couldn't exactly identify, something like burning yeast.

"This neighborhood takes on more and more the look of the Godless Orient," Miss Love said, not bothering to lower her voice. Probably she assumed that no one around us spoke English. "How well I remember the slums of Constantinople." Miss Love never let you forget that she had "gypsied" (as she called it) around the world more than once. "Well, we do what we can."

"You have done more than anyone, Miss Love, to help the lives of the deserving." Margaret or Francesca would have heard the irony, but Maria Love was immune to irony.

She stopped, turning to me, staring down at me as people jostled around us. "Thank you, Louisa, thank you. I take that to heart, coming from you. I have the deepest respect for you."

"Thank you, Miss Love." She always called me Louisa, I always called her Miss Love. We resumed walking. "I am grateful for your respect." And oddly, I was. This was her power: She had a charm that could sweep people into her net, trapping them before they understood they had been snared.

"You have earned my respect, Louisa—never forget it."

This seemed like my moment.

"Miss Love, I've come to see you—"

"That question, Louisa, we will address later," she declared, squeezing my arm to get me across the street as if I were in danger of being trampled by a horse cart. Mercifully she let go of me on the opposite side. I caught the look of a teenage boy, who studied her with incredulity. I couldn't help but smile, and I covered my mouth with my handkerchief to hide it.

"Louisa," she whispered, leaning down, suddenly sensitive to those around us. "I know this is a filthy neighborhood and the people smell worse than the streets, but we must try to pretend we are accustomed to it. Whatever we do, we must not cover our faces with our handkerchiefs!"

"Yes, Miss Love," I whispered in return, quickly putting my handkerchief away and biting my lip to stop the urge to laugh.

We arrived at our destination, a derelict-looking town house. She stopped abruptly, and I bumped into her.

"Sorry, Miss Love."

"Not all at, my dear." The bumping necessitated an adjustment of her hat. She was like an awkward giantess who thought herself a swan. By now several street urchins had gathered to follow us and stare at her. She ignored them, although I would have thought them her natural constituency.

Standing at the bottom of the town house steps and staring up at the blackened door, she took a deep breath, girding herself for the battle ahead. "Well, Louisa, onward with courage!"

The front hall smelled of kerosene, onions, and the garbage piled just inside the door. She led us to the rear of the house, to the back stairs, faintly lit by the soot-encrusted skylight above. At the second floor, the smell from the communal water closet pierced the air, choking me. On the third floor, Miss Love rapped once at what looked like a recently installed door and opened it without waiting for a response. "Never wait for them to answer the door, Louisa," she whispered. "Gives them too much time to hide things."

The room we entered was lit by a small kerosene lamp on a table in the corner. A woman sat in a chair beside the table, darning a child's shirt while an infant slept on her lap. Three other children of about eighteen months to four years ran to the woman when we entered. They appeared basically clean—hair combed, faces wiped—but the eighteen-month-old toddler seemed bowlegged, a sign of rickets. Their eyes were red and rheumy. The children pushed against their mother's chair.

The room had no windows, so it must have been carved out of a larger room when the building was divided—thus explaining the new door. There was an unmade bed on one side, a sink and stove on the other side near the table, and laundry hanging from a line tacked along the wall. The floor no longer looked like wood; had we been on the plains of Missouri, I would have identified it as hard-packed mud. Miss Love stared at the children for a long moment before addressing their mother.

"Signora Gambuto." Miss Love spoke Italian, which I understood, although Maria Love's Italian wasn't the sensuous, musical language one usually thinks of; it was more like stiffly formal English translated literally into Italian. "I am pleased to make your acquaintance."

The woman nodded wearily, as if she were well-accustomed to tall Protestant women wearing large feathered hats visiting her at odd hours of the day and night.

"I have been told by a reliable source that your lawful husband brought you to this great nation of ours only to desert you and your legitimately conceived children. Is this true?"

Again the woman nodded.

"I am further told that never does the scourge of alcohol pass your lips."

The woman looked as if she didn't understand.

"You never take money that should be spent on food for your children to indulge yourself in spirits."

The woman shook her head firmly no.

"*Brava!*" Miss Love was extremely pleased. "I can help you."

She opened her huge handbag, the repository of all assistance for people in distress, willing or not.

"I have noticed more than once that respectable women of Italian origin are greatly skilled at laundering. Therefore I have secured a job for you as a laundress at this address." She gave the woman a piece of paper. "Bathe before you go and dress as if for church. While you are at work you shall bring your children to the Fitch Crèche, at the second address on this paper, where they shall be cleaned, fed, and examined by reputable physicians. They shall be cured of any illnesses, and they shall participate in organized play. In addition, at the Fitch Crèche you shall take English lessons after work as well as lessons in sewing—for I have further noticed that with proper training, women of Italian origin make excellent seamstresses. Thus I shall give you the opportunity to improve your lot in life. I see you are sewing now—excellent! Upon the completion of your daily lessons, the children will be discharged into your care. Agreed?"

The woman opened her mouth to speak, but Miss Love gave her no opportunity.

"Fine. Toward the end of the summer, I shall arrange for you and your children to enjoy a brief sojourn at one of the delightful farms to the south of our city. There you shall help with the fruit harvest. Your children especially will enjoy this honest labor in the Lord's own sunshine, among the company of many of their upstanding compatriots, I assure you. This sojourn will also help you and your children to avoid the scourge of tuberculosis. Excellent." Pausing, Miss Love beamed. "I am certain you will find yourself profoundly satisfied with this turn of events and give thanks to God at your church. Should your priest give you any difficulty about accepting Protestant charity, ask yourself what he has done for you lately."

The woman's eyes rounded in horror.

Miss Love laughed. "No, no, I was only joking. I am well-acquainted with all the religious practitioners of this city. We work together now—united for the common good. And when your priest opens a Crèche you may certainly go there with my blessing."

Miss Love glanced at the laundry hung along the wall. "I'm glad to see you keep up with the washing." Then to me in English: "No matter what people say about them, Louisa, I have always found that Italian women keep up with the laundry." Then to Signora Gambuto in Italian: "Now then, we shall provide you immediate assistance by washing the dishes and sweeping the floor, so you may take a moment's rest from your labors." Back to English: "Come, Louisa, to work! And stay sharp," she added, *sotto voce*, "in case there are any bottles hidden away."

We washed the dishes, made the bed, and swept the floor without finding a single bottle, I feigning the great enthusiasm that Miss Love seemed actually to feel, while the woman and her children watched us as if we were out of our minds. I had to admit that Miss Love was nothing if not practical. I'd heard many a tale of well-meaning charity women who would visit a family like this, give theoretical instruction on how to bathe the children, for example, and then neglect to leave behind the bar of soap with which to do it: such women simply didn't realize that some people can't afford to buy soap. Miss Love, I knew, would never make such a mistake.

"It is example, Louisa, example," Miss Love explained as we worked, "that these people crave more than anything. Simply by showing them the proper way to make a bed"—which for Miss Love meant very tightly despite the lack of a top sheet and the loose weave of the single blanket—"we have uplifted them."

She did a final inspection and decided we were finished.

"Well, then, signora, I am very busy and must leave you now. However, you are obviously a woman of refinement who wishes to improve herself. Therefore I will give you my card. If you need help, you may show the card and ask for me personally at the Crèche."

She handed over the card, which the woman accepted cautiously, holding it by the corner with two fingers and slowly reading aloud, groping with the sounds of English: "Miss—Maria—Love."

Oh, the joy of it. The sheer thrill to be alive to see such a thing. For Signora Gambuto had said—not "Mar*i*ah" Love, which was the proper Delaware Avenue way to pronounce Miss Love's Christian name—but "Mar*eea*" Love, as if Miss Love were herself Italian—perhaps even an Italian immigrant! An Italian immigrant about to begin work as a washerwoman!

Miss Love looked utterly abashed. Profoundly surprised and discomfited.

"Signora Gambuto, forgive me, but I must tell you, for your own good, that in this country, names such as mine are more properly pronounced 'Mar*i*ah.' I'm sure you grasp the difference. Good day to you."

She turned her back on the unfortunate woman, and moments later we were on the street.

There was much harrumphing before she was able to speak again. "Well, well, all right—I'm willing to forgive her. Apart from that regrettable interlude at the end it was, in fact, a most gratifying visit. How inspiring, to work with a woman who sees so clearly where her best interests lay. They aren't all like that, I can assure you. Some must be cajoled none too gently on the road to righteousness." We began walking back the way we'd come. The smell of burning yeast was stronger now. "I told President Cleveland, when I was at the White House in '94, that some must be cajoled none too gently on the road to righteousness."

Because Miss Love never let any one forget, we all knew that during the Cleveland administrations she'd made annual visits to the White House to attend "private" receptions. These private receptions included dozens if not hundreds of similarly well-connected citizens, although Miss Love never mentioned them.

"Now, Louisa, I assume you've come to me to discuss the so-called breakfast carts." Over the years I'd given up trying to figure out how she gathered her information. Perhaps she was simply good at making educated guesses. "There is nothing to discuss. The carts are anathema to all the Charity Organization Society is attempting to accomplish. There is no self-respect or self-discipline in running past a cart, grabbing breakfast, and running into school. If children need breakfast, their families can go to their churches, be properly evaluated, and receive what they need, no more, no less. I find it unfortunate that you find yourself in the position of doing the bidding of Thomas Sinclair. This is what comes of accepting money from unsavory sources."

We turned a corner. At the end of the street, beyond the tenements and the acres of railroad yards, there was a wall of fire. A grain elevator was burning, which explained the yeasty smell in the air. With the next burst of wind, grain dust floated around us. Dozens of grain elevators lined the sheltered waterways off the main harbor. Because of its location at the eastern end of the Great Lakes, Buffalo received grain shipments from the entire Midwest and led the world in its production of flour. Despite extensive scientific investigation, however, spontaneous combustion remained a constant problem in the wooden grain elevators, and this neighborhood suffered from the consequences.

"Why do you say 'unsavory'?" I risked. "The endowment is in Margaret's honor; most likely some or most of the money was hers."

After staring for a moment at the fire, Miss Love placed a hand on my shoulder and leaned close to my face, her hat feathers flapping in the wind. Behind her, the sky was a smoky gray.

"I know everything that goes on in this city, Louisa. Remember that. If I'd been Margaret Winspear's grandmother, the girl never would have married him. I gave them both fair warning. Margaret and old Mrs. Winspear, I mean." She shook her head at the sorry spectacle of two misguided souls ignoring her advice. "And Margaret wasn't happy, you know. She lived to regret her choice. She should have listened to me when she had the chance."

"I never noticed that Margaret was unhappy," I said in the confused, innocent tone I feigned when contradicting Miss Love. "She always seemed happy enough to me. And I saw her . . . well, almost every day."

"Harrumph," Miss Love replied. "Well then. The question you must ask yourself now, Louisa, is what to do with this so-called gift he's given you. Can you return it, you're probably wondering."

That I was certainly not wondering. I had no intention of returning the money. She, however, considered the option for a good long while as she studied the flaming horizon.

"No," she finally concluded, turning to me, "money is money, whatever the source. What you want to avoid is undue influence. Happily Sinclair had the wisdom to decline a position on the board. I suppose one must respect him for that, at least: He knows his place. Especially while there's still this public controversy about the death of poor Karl Speyer—a charming man, I must say; I met him once. I can't understand why Dexter hasn't ordered the coroner to release a report. The death was obviously an accident. Obviously." She regarded me shrewdly, as if expecting me to confirm her opinion or at least offer some new information. After all, I attended the Macaulay board of trustees meetings and she did not. Miss Love might claim to know everything, but some things remained beyond her ken.

Of course I would reveal nothing. I made my expression deferential and expectant: I was young, simple Louisa Barrett, waiting to be enlightened by Miss Love. I didn't need to say a word to appease her.

"Well, well . . ." she concluded complacently after studying my face. "Dexter has his reasons, I'm sure. At any rate, Louisa, I shall make myself available to advise you step by step in the coming months."

"Thank you."

"My pleasure entirely."

She adjusted her hat, as if to say, that's that, another problem solved. "Now then, if you go down Seneca to Main, you can get the streetcar. I trust you know the way from there. I must say however that I sincerely hope you will walk back to Macaulay—much better for the constitution. I must continue on my rounds. Good day to you, Louisa."

With that she was off, striding down the street into the wall of fire. As I stared after her, I felt a yearning to tell the tale of her "visitation." To share every detail . . . her huge handbag; the tightness with which she made the bed, almost ripping apart the blanket; Mar*ee*a instead of Mar*i*ah. But with whom could I share these details? Not Francesca, enjoying her rounds of gossip. Only Margaret; only she would appreciate every nuance. In my imagination I began forming the words to tell her—before being brought up short by the realization, which still shocked me sometimes, that she was gone forever. As the feathers bobbing on Miss Love's hat became smaller and smaller in the distance, my aloneness pressed hard against me.

Chapter Eight

I 've got a terrible chill." Just past 8:00 p.m., on the Tuesday after my meeting with Miss Love, Franklin Fiske wheezed and coughed at my doorway, his handsome features contorted with discomfort. "I haven't been myself since I went to the Philippines two years ago. My health has been terrible." Behind him, a heavy, windblown rain filled the night, dampening my face. "I need your help." He wore a striped scarf around his neck and a soft cap, both soaked and reeking of wet wool. Incongruously he held a large black umbrella propped closed beside him like an elegant walking stick.

"I'm not your mother."

"No, but you're the only mother surrogate I have in this city, apart from my landlady, who's invariably tipsy by eleven a.m. Surely you wouldn't want me going to her."

I sighed, none too happily, at the thought of what curious neighbors might say if they saw me inviting a man into my house after dark, but I couldn't very well turn him away. "All right, come in then." Katarzyna had left a short while before, and I found myself wondering whether Fiske had watched from across the street, hidden among the trees of the parkway, waiting for her departure before knocking on my door.

After settling him in the rocking chair beside the fire in my study, I went to the kitchen to make him tea with lemon and honey. By the time I returned with the glass in its filigree holder, his chill seemed so improved as to be completely gone. He had stretched his legs toward the warmth of the fire, his hands were folded behind his head, and he appeared to be absolutely comfortable.

"Feeling better?" I asked.

"Oh, quite. Quite completely better as I bask in the pleasure of your company."

"What do you want from me, then?"

He sat up quickly. "What makes you think I want something?"

"Compliments like that always imply a desire for . . . something."

"You're simply unused to compliments."

"That's true." I sat down opposite him.

"But now that you mention it, I did have a few questions to ask you," he admitted guiltily. "And something rather important to tell you. Privately. Away from the so very . . . heady atmosphere of your 'saloon.'" Fiske had attended my salon the night before, as indeed he had each week since I'd seen him at Francesca's, but he'd never attempted to speak to me alone. "My ploy was amateurish, I grant you, but it's one that's never failed me."

"How encouraging. Do you use it often?"

"Yes. Often," he assured me with clearly feigned innocence.

"So what is it that you wanted to ask me and to tell me?"

Instead of answering, he picked up his glass of tea. Its pale shade caught the reflection of the fire. He turned the glass slowly, rubbing the filigree holder, studying the permutations of color.

"A million dollars," he said meditatively. "A tidy sum. Simple to pronounce. Congratulations."

Rain lashed against the windowpanes. Trying not to sound impatient, I said, "Would you get on with it, please?"

"Yes. Of course. My first question, Miss Barrett, is this: Before your presence in the Sinclair home on the evening of Karl Speyer's death, did you have any inkling that this endowment was . . . in the works, as it were?"

I forced my expression into impassivity, although I was staggered. How had he learned I was there? My insides knotted in fear of what he would do with his knowledge, and of what he might want from me. "What makes you say I was visiting the Sinclairs that night?"

He sighed. "Well, if you insist on my going through this step by step . . . I learned through badgering my professional colleagues—my former professional colleagues," he corrected himself, "that part of Sinclair's unofficial alibi for the night of Karl Speyer's *adieu* was that he was at home with his daughter and his daughter's godmother before the meeting at the Buffalo Club. The scribblers didn't think the fact newsworthy enough to print, and never pursued it. They were also influenced, I'm proud to report, by their unwillingness as gentlemen to inflict upon an innocent lady the ignominy of seeing her name in the newspaper on anything but the society page. And evidently—remarkably—they seemed not to know the identity of this 'godmother.' Just out of curiosity, I asked Cousin Susan, 'Who is Grace Sinclair's godmother?' Well, wasn't I surprised to learn that she was you! You—the very person I met at the park lake the day after Speyer's death, studying the crime scene out of concern for the efficacy of the police department."

So . . . he knew I'd been at the Sinclairs, but he didn't know that Speyer had visited too. Therefore he knew nothing.

"To return to my original question: Before your presence on the evening of the . . . death, I think, is properly objective, of Karl Speyer, had Mr. Sinclair given you any expectation of monetary reward?"

I was under no obligation to Franklin Fiske. I was not required to answer his questions. Who was he, after all, but an art photographer ingratiating himself throughout the city for reasons unknown? This conviction made me bold enough to be silent.

He eyed me speculatively. "Well, how about this: did anything unusual happen at the house while you were there?"

I wanted to throw him out, but I wouldn't let myself be that dismissive: I couldn't afford to make an enemy of Susan Rumsey's cousin, and besides, he would most likely view any intemperate reaction as a sign that I was hiding something. Noncommittally I said, "You're certainly forthright, Mr. Fiske."

"I won't do you the insult of trying to sweet-talk it out of you," he said with sudden—startling—anger. From the intemperance of his reaction, I concluded that he *was* hiding something. "Nor do I have the time. I've been here over a month now, with little to show for it."

Little to show for it . . . that slip confused me, but also gave me an edge. "Why, Mr. Fiske, haven't you been working hard with your picture-taking?"

"Whatever you know may have significance far beyond what you can imagine, so why don't you simply tell me," he demanded.

He stared at me, waiting. I stared back at him.

He glanced away. Finally he said, "You may be interested to learn that news of the million-dollar endowment was all the rage last weekend when I attended a kind of court-of-Marie-Antoinette 'informal' luncheon at the estate of Bronson Rumsey on Tracy Street."

Bronson Rumsey was Dexter's older brother. He was well into his seventies and in failing health; he was retired from business.

In an abrupt shift, Fiske continued lightheartedly, "I must admit I'm having trouble keeping those two old Rumseys straight. Bronson and Dexter. I've had to invent a mnemonic for them: *Dexter lives on Delaware, Bronson in Beaux-Arts on Tracy.*' It's not perfect, not as rhythmic as I would like, but it'll do. Dexter, of course, is the one I'm most interested in, because of his close link to you."

Again I did not respond. After a few moments of silence, Fiske resumed, "Well, as I was saying, Sinclair's gift provoked much speculation, beginning with: Who would ever have imagined he had so much money to spare, and for such a worthy cause? This was the view of the ladies, most of them Macaulay graduates, and there was endless discussion about what dear Miss Barrett might do with this donation. The gentleman were glumly silent on the endowment issue—undoubtedly to deflect any notions that they too might be in a position to give away so much to so worthy a cause.

"Then there was the matter of the reason he gave the money. Did he have a guilty conscience perhaps? For presuming to marry where he shouldn't have? However, I must say I sensed that Margaret Sinclair wasn't exactly liked by her peers. Apparently she couldn't go 'calling,' because all her time was taken up teaching English to immigrant brats. Not only that, but she and her husband turned down dinner invitations in order to stay home and dine with their child! Who has ever heard of such a thing? And absolutely terrible for the child too, my lady friends assured me."

Now that he was using Grace for his verbal flourishes, I had to intervene. "This is not a joke, Mr. Fiske. And furthermore it's none of your concern."

Patiently he sipped his tea. He stared into the fire. His face was soft in the firelight, his eyes shadowed. At last he said, "In this case, the ladies may be right: Your goddaughter certainly is a handful, isn't she?"

"Whatever do you mean?" I demanded brusquely, and he looked at me with surprise.

"I'm just making conversation. Whatever do *you* mean?"

"Oh, people can be so judgmental about children." I tried to sound nonchalant. "Especially people who spend little time with them. Seeing the worrisome in the normal and then totally missing something that's actually wrong. Tell me what happened, that made you say what you did."

Despite my effort at detachment, he appeared worried. "Well, as I told you, I was over at the Bronson Rumsey estate for a luncheon. It was some sort of birthday party, although I'm not sure whose. An infant's, I think. Don't be upset that you weren't invited, it was all family—which I am, of course," he added wryly, "although I must say the family seems overextended: Miss Maria Love was in attendance. Did you know that she's related to that lovely couple Dr. Charles and Evelyn Cary?"

"Yes."

"How exactly are they related again?" For a moment, brow knit, he attempted to figure out the complex genealogy of the Carys and the Rumseys, who were forever intermarrying.

"I won't illuminate you on that now. About Grace Sinclair?"

"Oh, yes. Did you know that the Pan-American Exposition was once a three-hundred-fifty-acre cow field for the grazing of the prized Rumsey herd? Special Holsteins, I think. Or maybe it was Herefords. Short-horned, I believe I was told. Or was it long-horned? Whatever it was, it was supposed to be the first herd of its kind in the United States. Did you know that?"

"Yes, Mr. Fiske. I dare say everyone around here knows about the Rumsey herd."

"And the money they must be making from the rental of the land to the exposition committee!"

Good grief, he nosed his way into everything. "I dare say, Mr. Fiske."

"Did you know that the Rumsey money originally came from the tanning business? That's means they made leather."

"I know what tanning means," I said impatiently.

"You must forgive me my constant curiosity and enthusiasm, Miss Barrett. I find the ins and outs of this so-called Queen City of the Lakes to be quite mesmerizing. The city is a true microcosm of the world, and I love a microcosm."

"You were saying about Grace Sinclair?"

"Ah. Yes. Grace Sinclair was there, at this indoor family 'picnic,' as a guest of Cousin Susan's daughter, Ruth. Soon there arrived a veritable gaggle of other little Rumseys, from all the Rumsey houses around the estate. Apparently Mr. Bronson owns a preternaturally large plot of land and has kindly built a separate house on it for every one of his many progeny. There were enough grandchildren to—well, to stage a dramatic tableau from *Macbeth* in the conservatory, which is exactly what they did."

"Ruth and Grace are reading the play in school this year," I explained. "It seems to be seeping into many areas of their lives."

"An odd choice, for little girls."

"You'd prefer to keep them occupied with *King Lear*? Or perhaps *Coriolanus*?"

"I'd prefer to keep them occupied wherever I'm *not*. At least the preparations kept them busy for a while—a full hour, during which I could enjoy the crowd. There was one nonfamily entry: our friend Mr. Krakauer, J. Pierpont Morgan's man, snoozing in a chair in the corner. I've noticed that Krakauer never elicits conversation with anyone, although he is charming when approached—as he frequently is, bearing as he must the burden of the reflected glory of the magnificent Pierpont. Miss Love went to speak to him, unleashing her own inimitable charm."

"And the performance?"

"Oh, yes. Exactly what one would expect. The witches' brew, with more witches than scripted. Masses of giggles. I followed Mr. Krakauer's example—a Morgan-endorsed example, one must assume—and snoozed the time away. What was interesting came afterward. Cousin Susan, being an affectionate type, went to hug her daughter by

way of complimenting her on the blissful pleasure brought by her performance. Then she turned to hug Grace too. But Grace turned stiff as
a board, as they say, and shouted, 'You're not my mother, get away
from me, my mother's dead and I wish I was too.' Or words to that
effect. All the time she was saying this, she was pounding her leg with
her fist, which I must admit was disturbing. Then she ran outside—
without her cloak, as one worthy matron noted in shock—and hid out
there among the fountains and gazebos and half-naked statues. After a
minute little Ruth ran out to find her—with her cloak on, I'm glad to
say, and Grace's slung over her shoulder. The other children followed
shortly, like a mass migration of cloak-clad little antelopes. Meanwhile
the other adults continued their luncheon festivities as if none of this
had happened. Sometime later a nurse or a nanny or a housekeeper—
whatever these women are called—came to get Grace, but by then she
was inordinately happy about some apparently excellent tree-climbing
she and Ruth had undertaken and all was well."

My heart was beating fast. Hide everything; steady my voice: "Did
Susan Rumsey or anyone else speak to the housekeeper about what had
happened?"

"Not that I noticed. But by then we were on our third serving of
dessert and I was distracted. So, what do you make of it?"

I willed myself to appear indifferent. "Nothing, Mr. Fiske. Nothing
at all."

"Oh." He looked put out.

Shift the subject, I told myself. "What's your stake in all of this, Mr.
Fiske? What's your concern with endowments, and a widower and his
daughter? Or even with me?"

"Perhaps I wish to be your protector."

I laughed bitterly.

"No, I mean it. From the moment I saw you perched on that snow
mound by the lake, I've been quite swept up by you. I can't get that
image of you out of my mind." I gazed at him in bewilderment; could
he be sincere? Had he been sincere at Francesca's? I could no longer
trust myself to judge correctly.

More seriously, he continued, "I must say you are naive to think
you can maintain your equanimity among the forces at work here."

That, at least, I could judge. "Forces at work? You've missed your calling, Mr. Fiske. You should be writing Gothic melodramas instead of doing—what is it again that you say you do? 'Artistic photographs of industrial sites'?"

"Ah." He leaned toward me, elbows on knees. "You've hit on the very thing I meant to tell you tonight." He took a deep breath, exhaling slowly. "I'll be blunt, which I sense you prefer. The fact is, I have not given up newspapering, as I led you to believe when we first met. No, indeed. I'm sorry I had to mislead you. I'm here in secret—as a reporter for the New York *World*."

"Please don't tease me, Mr Fiske."

"No, I'm not. I assure you."

I thought back: his presence at the lakeshore, his well-cultivated intimacy with the upper echelons of the city, his pressing interests in matters that theoretically weren't his business. Everything he'd done, he'd done for a hidden cause. I felt as if the pieces of a puzzle had clicked into place.

"The *World* has a great tradition of covert work," he was explaining. "Nellie Bly, among those women journalists whom you once told me you admired—and a personal friend of mine, I will say in my favor—has often undertaken such assignments, and although I regret deeply that I may have caused you—"

"What are you here to investigate?" I interrupted.

"Ah. Thank you," he said, obviously grateful that I had accepted him. "Irregularities in the development and operation of the hydroelectric power station at Niagara Falls."

"You're joking with me now, Mr. Fiske."

"No, I assure you."

"It's impossible."

"No.

"Mr. Fiske," I interrupted wearily, "there is nothing 'irregular' about the development of hydroelectric power at Niagara Falls." Even as I said it, I doubted my words; I heard Grace: *All they ever fought about was electricity.*

"I wouldn't be so quick in your assumptions," Fiske insisted. "As you know, I had an appointment to meet Karl Speyer at the Iroquois

Hotel on that same fateful day that you and I met. As I may have explained, he and I were planning to visit Niagara together, so that he could show me a piece of machinery of which he was tremendously proud. He'd even named it after himself: the Westinghouse-Speyer, he called it. I believe it was a new type of generator that made more electricity with less water."

Yes, I knew it only too well; I saw it at night when I closed my eyes.

"Karl Speyer was concerned about the profligate use of water. For you see, although he was justifiably proud of all he'd accomplished at Niagara, he'd already shared with me, when I just happened to visit him at home in Pittsburgh the month before, a healthy skepticism about the goals of the people who happen to have control over his creation." Fiske stared at me fixedly. "Poor Speyer met with an 'accident' before he could meet me, as we know. Speyer was a romantic, or so the theory goes—one theory, that is. He went to view the park in the moonlight, although the night was snowy."

"We have a lovely park here, Mr. Fiske. People come from around the country to see it. Olmsted and Vaux—"

"I know all about the park, Miss Barrett. I also know something about the character of Karl Speyer, which is that he was unlikely to visit a park after dark in a snowstorm for the purpose of admiring the work of Olmsted and Vaux. No, this man was murdered. I would like to know exactly why, and by whom. Evidently we can't rely on the police or the coroner to tell us; as I'm sure you've noticed, there's been a distinct lack of official conclusions." I forced myself to meet his eyes. "Something you said that day, by the frozen lake—by the murder site— led me to believe that you would like to know as well."

"What was it that I said?" Of course I knew.

"When I told you that Sinclair had claimed that Speyer was one of the few men with whom he'd never exchanged a harsh word, you said, 'Really?' as if you were surprised. That 'Really?' seemed significant to me, Miss Barrett. What did it mean?"

"It meant nothing. I was 'just making conversation,' as you were only a moment ago."

Abruptly he stood and walked over to the shelves that held my father's rock specimens.

"You're interested in stones?" Fiske asked over his shoulder.

"My father was a geologist. That's what I've saved of his collection."

"How did you decide what to save?"

"I saved what I liked best."

"That's an intriguing way to do it, without thought for value."

"What I didn't like was worth enough to pay for my last years at Wellesley."

"Ah. They're beautiful." He began to pick them up, one at a time; to caress and cradle them. Possessively, I hurried to join him; I felt an irrational fear that he might mistreat them, these few objects I owned that my father had touched.

"This one is curious. It has snowflakes in it."

"It's obsidian. Snowflake obsidian." I almost snatched the rock away, but managed to hold back my hand. Standing close beside him, all at once I remembered that we were alone in the house. He smelled of pipe tobacco and a citrusy shaving lotion. I could see his chest move as he breathed. "Sometimes I think it's magical." I rubbed the snowflake obsidian where it rested in his palm. I looked at his face, and our eyes met for an instant before we both glanced away. "Look at this one. Polished sodalite. You can see yourself in it, like a mirror."

Gently he put down the obsidian and took the sodalite, holding it up to the gaslight.

"When I was young," I said softly, letting down my guard, "my father took me with him on his expeditions. I had a miniature hammer and chisel. I knelt beside him in the hills of Colorado and Wyoming, knocking away at the rocks."

"I wish I'd known you then."

"I met Indians, and mountain men. When my father died, that entire way of life closed to me." Remembering my father's death brought me back sharply to the present.

Perhaps to show his sympathy Fiske offered, "My father died when I was eight."

Automatically, still feeling my own sadness, I said, "I'm sorry."

"He was a Unitarian minister."

"Really?" Now I smiled. "There it is again, 'Really?' infused with meaning."

"And its meaning in this case?"

"I was raised as a Unitarian. Although I now attend the Episcopal church for the sake of the school."

"Yet another of the small compromises involved in being a head-mistress." He too showed a touch of a smile. "But it's something we have in common, at least: We're both presumably free-thinking and undogmatic. That's good to know."

I could feel myself easing into a sense of comfort with him. A sense of friendship. "Did you consider becoming a minister?"

"Never. I studied history at Columbia College, and afterward, being too much of a misfit for anything but minding other people's business, I joined the *World*. I was attracted by its crusading zeal. By old man Pulitzer's passion to better the lives of the oppressed and powerless."

He gazed at me as if I were a quarry in the forest, then turned and walked to my desk, examining what he found there.

"Why are you always looking at everything?"

"Because I have no life of my own and nothing whatever to offer anyone except what I discover about them. For example: Here I see a small photo of our esteemed former president Grover Cleveland. What is that doing on your desk? Did you know him when he lived here?"

In spite of myself I blushed; busily I rearranged the stones, hoping Fiske wouldn't realize. The photo had been on my desk so long that I'd stopped seeing it. "Cleveland had left Buffalo before I moved here."

"How can you keep a photo of a man whose strongest belief was that a president has no authority to interfere with anything that happens to occur in the nation he happens to be president of?"

"Here in Buffalo his political reputation is somewhat different. Here we remember him when he was mayor and put a stop to patronage and bribery." Regaining my composure, I turned to him. "And I admired him at the end of his first term as president, when he spoke to Congress about how industry should be serving the people instead of vice versa. About mansions next to tenements. I remember his exact words. That the people were being 'trampled to death beneath an iron heel.'" I sighed. "I was idealistic in those days. I thought industry would take his words to heart. At any rate, I got the photo around then," I added wearily.

"He'd certainly forgotten that speech by the time he sent troops to put down the Pullman strike. And when he did nothing to help the starving after depression hit in '93. Oh, no: six hundred banks may fail but that's not the proper realm for presidential action; oh, no: coal strikes, textile strikes, rail strikes—can't let a president get involved with any of those."

"Yes, you're right, he did betray my ideals—as well as his own," I said angrily. "Maybe he finds it even more difficult to live with himself than I do. I hope so. And let us not forget that many would say the *World* was single-handedly responsible for electing him president in the first place."

"Touche." As the reform candidate, Cleveland had been extravagantly championed by the *World* in '84.

I forced myself to relax. "Nowadays I keep the photo on my desk for a different reason: as a constant reminder of the value of following the rules."

He looked bewildered, and I was glad. "Meaning?" he asked.

When I didn't respond, he waved aside the perplexities of Grover Cleveland. "Well, be that as it may. I do need your help, Miss Barrett, but not because I have a chill. I want you to help me to discover who killed Karl Speyer—or who ordered him killed—and why. I also want your help exploring bribery and various other types of corruption and greed involving the power station, quite separate from his death."

I could not accept this. "Now you will think me naive and idealistic, Mr. Fiske, but I believe these are good men, these men who are united to build the power station. I know some of them. I've seen the power station—"

"You know nothing. Just because you don't see little girls getting their fingers caught in machinery doesn't mean the management has turned altruistic and decided to devote itself to the good of humanity."

"The power station is different. The men who are building it, they do it with their own money, without guarantee of profits, and they give away what profits they have—witness Thomas Sinclair, with his million dollars to Macaulay."

"My dear Miss Barrett," Fiske said in a tone of exasperated patience. "What they give away is nothing compared to what they have. They're causing themselves no sacrifice by giving money away. And don't be fooled by the 'sacrifice' of millions spent to build the power-houses, because millions more will be realized as more electricity begins to flow, as more industries take it on. I've dealt too often with men like these. I've come to see that the truth exists in inverse propor-tion to the sincerity with which they discuss their noble deeds."

"What makes you so cynical?"

"I served time in the Philippines, remember? I saw our fine and honorable American soldiers using the too-aptly named 'water cure' to exact confessions from prisoners; of course the prisoners weren't white so it didn't matter. But you can see that I come by my cynicism honestly. This is not a parlor game to me."

"I thought your newspaper was in favor of American intervention in the Philippines. Indeed, I thought your newspaper virtually insti-gated American intervention in the Philippines."

"Quite right. So you'll be glad to discover I'm not a sycophant. Now when I hear our beloved President McKinley urging upon us our God-given duty to 'uplift and Christianize' the 'heathen' of the Philippines, most of whom happen to be Catholic, when what he really cares about is selling them things they don't need—well, my cynicism quite overwhelms me."

He touched my arm. "Miss Barrett, I came here to follow a trail. A trail of money, power, and avarice. I would like you to join me on this quest."

"I know nothing of these matters."

"But you do. And you know you do. That's the reason I chose you to help me; I haven't told anyone else what I'm doing here, only you. That's because you're apart from them but simultaneously part of them. You're accepted by them. You're 'one of the boys.' You lunch with them at the Buffalo Club. They let their guard down with you, make jokes in your presence that they would never make in the presence of their wives."

He was right, of course. How quickly he had pegged me.

"I ask you only to listen, Miss Barrett, and wait until the facade slips. Then report back to me."

"You mean, betray my friends and spread malicious gossip."

"Well, that's one delightful way of looking at it. You could also look at it as helping your country."

"Indeed. How so?" I asked skeptically.

"The *World* believes—and by happy coincidence I agree—that the utilities should belong to the people."

"The *World* believes?"

"Yes, I realize this is coming from the very same editors who brought us the glorious war with Spain. Nonetheless, they're correct on this point. Electricity should be a public service, not a commodity sold to the highest bidder. The electricity created at Niagara belongs to the people. Not to the industrialists, not to the nature preservationists—a gaggle of geese there, if I've ever seen one, and self-righteous to boot— but the *people*. Even the poorest of the immigrant masses—even they— should have a stake in the profits of Niagara. You may be interested to know that in Europe, governments own and operate power stations; common citizens get priority in the use of electricity, not industry. People get their homes lighted first, and what's left goes to make chlorate of potash."

"But at Niagara the *people* aren't paying to build the power station."

"No, but the power station is using the water of the people's river and the people's Great Lakes. Karl Speyer understood this and was trying to preserve the river and the Falls."

"The *people* never did much with the water before, except gawk at it; excuse me—admire its supreme beauty. Besides, the state of New York, presumably the protector of these people you claim to represent, has given the power company the options to use the water—"

"In what darkness were these options given, I ask you? And given away for 'free.' Whose palms were greased to bring about that bit of chicanery? I told you: Bribery is one of the hypotheses I am here to prove."

"You've reached your conclusions before completing your investigations?"

"Well, of course. How would I know what to investigate if I hadn't already reached my conclusions?"

"I see your point."

"But seriously"—he was almost pleading with me to agree with him—"the water of the Great Lakes belongs to all the people, not just the people wealthy enough to exploit it. That means you, and me. You do see that, don't you?"

"I see that you are a crusader. Or perhaps a preacher, like your father."

"Miss Barrett. Please, let us at least acknowledge the fact that the public should own the profits from Niagara."

"By what means should they do so? Through the state government which you yourself have just accused of corruption?"

He sighed. "I believe—and I'm not alone, I assure you—that electricity is a basic human need. Here in your home you have running water and steam heat—these are considered necessities. Why not electricity? Don't you want electricity?"

Of course electricity was a wondrous gift, but I hadn't grown up with it, and so having it at home didn't seem essential. "Not particularly, no."

"Oh, you're impossible. I'll ask you to look at it purely from the perspective of money, then. Imagine all that could be done with the profits to help the poor. The state could establish—"

"Why, Mr. Fiske, I do believe you're a socialist," I jested, attempting to put an end to what was beginning to feel like a harangue. "I myself have always stayed out of politics."

"No one can stay out of politics forever, Miss Barrett."

"Loyalty to my friends is more important."

"Is it?" He looked at me disparagingly. "And if your so-called friends have committed murder in pursuit of their goals?"

"If Karl Speyer was murdered, who exactly do you think murdered him?" I demanded, even though I wasn't sure I wanted to hear his answer.

"Not Thomas Sinclair personally, that much is obvious. I visualize more of a Henry the Second/Beckett scenario: 'Who will rid me of this troublesome priest?' I believe Speyer was about to blow the whistle on him."

"Pardon?" I asked incredulously.

"I mean, reveal what he's really trying to do: take all the water of Niagara and turn it over to industry."

I paused to think. What was my goal here? Grace. The protection of Grace. I focused on her, to keep myself from making any confessions to Franklin Fiske that I might regret. "I will not betray my friends for the glory of your newspaper."

"Your name would never appear publicly. Besides, you're in this now whether you like it or not. Why not put your access to good use? These men have nothing to hide from a woman like you—someone they can't see, even when she's with them."

"You have an odd method of persuasion."

"You say you don't like flattery. Besides, I think it's wonderful to be invisible. I wish I could be invisible."

"That you could never be."

He stepped closer to me. He put his hands on my shoulders. "The *World* believes in heroes and villains. Why not be one of the heroes?" He increased the pressure of his hands on my shoulders. All at once I was tempted. Tempted in every way—intellectually, emotionally, physically. "Why not step outside yourself? Future generations will thank you for it. Why not—"

Future generations . . . Grace. I stepped away from him. "I'm sorry, Mr. Fiske, but I can't help you."

He stared at me for a long moment. "Well, nothing ventured, nothing gained," he said magnanimously. I led the way into the hall and retrieved his coat. "Don't hesitate to contact me, should you change your mind," he added hopefully.

And with that he was gone.

Chapter Nine

G race . . . she was more important to me than the waters of Niagara, more important than Franklin Fiske's hypotheses, or Karl Speyer's death. How could I know that they were all linked? At that moment I only knew that Margaret was no longer here to take care of Grace; now I held that responsibility and held it willingly.

Thus, several days after Fiske's visit, I walked up Elmwood Avenue on a brisk afternoon heading toward the state hospital. I tried to put Fiske's Henry II/Beckett scenario out of my mind and focus only on my goddaughter, but nonetheless my thoughts drifted . . . Could I have misjudged Tom all these years? Would he stop at nothing to achieve his goals? Even now I couldn't permit myself to believe him capable of . . . but was I deluding myself? My mind went in circles—and inevitably circled once more to Fiske's image of Grace at the Rumsey luncheon, pounding her fist into her leg and saying she wanted to die. I felt incompetent with her, useless; I had helped so many girls at school, but Grace, somehow, I couldn't reach.

Which was why I'd made an appointment with Dr. Austin Hoyt, the superintendent of the hospital. Already I saw my destination ahead: the red medina sandstone towers with their mansard roofs; the high fence; the tall trees, offering refuge to the patients huddled beneath the canopy of branches.

As a group: that's how I forced myself to see the patients as I made my way up the drive. About thirty men and women, separated by sex, spread out along the paths. They gardened with intense concentration. Here and there nursing sisters stood like sentinels, watching them. Guarding them. From each other? From themselves? The patients were all slightly off-balance, their hair too thick or thin to match their eyebrows, their shoulders oddly angled to their heads. They were a people of extremes: the very thin working next to the very fat; the very short next to the very tall; their faces were terribly long and wrinkled, or perfectly round and full. None of the men's regulation muslin trousers fit properly: Either bony legs emerged between cuff and sock, the skin pasty-white; or the trousers were rolled up at the ankle over and over into a thick bulge. Each person was off-kilter by just a notch, and thus separated from those who walked free on the other side of the fence.

Grace didn't look anything like these people. I grasped at a hope that therefore she would never be among them.

The Buffalo State Asylum for the Insane. Designed by H.H. Richardson, in the Romanesque style. The complex faced due south; sunlight was one of the treatments. Frederick Law Olmsted and Calvert Vaux had designed the landscape, covering over two hundred acres with billowing trees and rolling meadows. There was space for one thousand patients in linked pavilions that curved along the crest of a hill. Nonetheless, rumor held that the hospital was perpetually over-crowded, two or three patients bunking in the rooms designed for one. Still, before the hospital, the insane had been relegated to poorhouses or ignored on the streets. Now they enjoyed (if that was the word) farm labor. They grew their own vegetables, milked their own cows, raised their own pigs. They possessed a bubbling brook to stroll along. A baseball diamond. A music conservatory. A greenhouse. The hospital was like a paradise at the edge of the city. How I longed for a paradise. I was tired, worn down by vigilance.

I met Dr. Hoyt at his office. He suggested that we talk outside, and so we walked together along the curving paths. All the paths curved; curving paths were considered therapeutic. Crocuses and daffodils spread wild across the lawns. Hoyt looked like a youthful Santa Claus (although not so much like Santa Claus as to be mistaken for one of his patients). Over the years, I'd seen him at lectures, concerts, and art exhibitions, where his bluff heartiness could spread good cheer around a room. But this was the first time I'd consulted him. I couldn't trust the opinion of Grace's family doctor, a kindly old man who treated all the children of Delaware Avenue and who undoubtedly knew as little about why a girl would talk of killing herself as I did. I also wanted the opinion of someone who didn't know Grace personally and could be objective while still understanding her background. Dr. Hoyt was the only choice. However, I didn't know if I could trust him; I intended to approach him cautiously until I could parse out his loyalties.

Through the greening tree limbs, I glimpsed the two square towers at the top of the hill, visible for miles around.

"You know, Dr. Hoyt, my girls have the distinct impression that you stare at them from those tower windows. That you sit up there in your study day and night, watching everything that goes on in the city below you. The idea gives them hours of pleasurable terror—as well as a few serious nightmares."

His blue eyes truly twinkled as he looked at me, and he rubbed his white beard (much better trimmed than Santa's). Taking my elbow, he guided me around a turn in the path. We were the same height, but his girth was such that there was little room on the path for me. My skirt brushed against the bare rosebushes, getting caught here and there on the thorns.

"I'll let you in on a little secret, Miss Barrett," he whispered dramatically. "There is nothing up in those towers except pigeons—and the evidence of pigeons. The towers are empty. Hollow. Purely for show."

"Really?" I glanced back at them. "I'm . . . shocked!" And I was, although I made it sound like a joke; the towers had haunted me too. "Please don't tell anyone else, Dr. Hoyt. Their hold upon the imagination must never be diminished."

"I agree totally, Miss Barrett." He gave my elbow a squeeze and leaned closer to my shoulder than was strictly necessary for conversation.

With this intimacy inflicted upon me, the moment seemed propitious for confiding the reason for my visit. So I told him the story of Grace Sinclair, never giving her name, never revealing that she was adopted, but providing sufficient details, I hoped, for him to reach a conclusion.

When I finished, we walked some moments in silence across the crest of the hill, studying, in the far distance, the marble outlines of the Albright Art Gallery and beyond that, the Spanish cupolas of the Pan-

American Exposition. At the bottom of the hill, the meandering Scajaquada Creek reflected a ribbon of sunlight through the valley.

Finally Hoyt asked, "What do you think is the cause for concern here, Miss Barrett?"

"Well—that the girl will do exactly as she threatens and take her life." Why was he asking, when the answer was self-evident?

"What makes you think her words are more than just talk, the kind of talk children that age habitually engage in?"

"I've never heard a child threaten to take her own life."

"Your experience perhaps is limited." His voice was heavy with condescension. "Children will say almost anything to gain attention."

"Almost anything, Dr. Hoyt," I replied, mustering my defenses. "There usually remain some areas about which they have scant knowledge."

"You speak as an indulgent schoolmarm, not as a physician."

I waited until I could control myself. "The girl and her mother were very close. One might have to say unusually close, compared to other families in the neighborhood."

"Mothers and daughters should be close."

"After the mother died . . . well, the girl seems to have become overly emotional. Her reactions are too extreme. One minute she's . . . nervous, and the next she's as happy as . . . well, as a child."

"She *is* a child, Miss Barrett. Children are known for such extremes."

"Sometimes, but not always, she blames herself for her mother's death."

"That is a natural part of mourning, for any child."

"Yes, but—"

"Now, now," he said, to reassure me.

"Well, there's another area of concern. From things the girl has said, I fear there may once have been a certain . . . tension in the home. She has spoken of arguments between her parents . . ." I let my words drift into implication. But I myself didn't understand the meaning of the implication: I couldn't very well say to him, her parents argued about electricity.

"Miss Barrett, you have never been married. Had you been, you would realize, I assure you, that such arguments are the commonplace of daily life. It must be difficult, I realize, for you to find a way to evaluate that which you yourself have not experienced."

Hold back your anger, Louisa. Laugh it off. "But Dr. Hoyt, we're not consulting about me." I tried to sound flirtatious.

"Of course not, my dear," he brusquely replied. "Surely I did not imply such a thing. You are emotional and disjointed today."

He was trying to humble me. Because I wasn't married. Because he assumed me to be inexperienced in ways of the heart and the body—a nun in relation to men. He presumed certain facts about me, and defined me to himself in a way that bore no relation to my actual life.

I realized that I should confide nothing more to Dr. Hoyt. That anything I said could be used against me. The instinct for self-preservation that I had assiduously developed over the years came to the fore, protecting me from this fragrant garden. Flatter him, my instinct told me. Twist him to my own benefit. Then walk out the front gate and forget everything he's said.

"Please understand," he continued, "the tears of marital discord are commonplace. How else is the fair sex to get its way? The domestic argument, or series of arguments, overheard by your young student probably had to do with an overexpensive piece of silk. Or a brocade for new curtains when the old curtains still looked fine."

"Yes, Dr. Hoyt." I pretended to mull this over. "I begin to understand. You are right. Undoubtedly."

"You describe the girl as having artistic tendencies. These must be properly channeled, to direct any concomitant emotional waywardness. I trust you to see to that at school. As you say, the girl's mother recently died. It's only natural that she should speak in ways that are to us unaccustomed; that she would seem different from her old self. I am certain that when her time of mourning is complete, she will return to her usual cheery disposition."

"I'm sure you're right."

"What I find more interesting, Miss Barrett, is your concern. Your particular concern. You, a woman with so many students to care for . . ."

We stood beneath the spreading bower of a purple beech, the

leaves fresh and new—pure, brilliant color. We gazed across the lawns to the hospital farms.

"Please sit down, Miss Barrett." He indicated a wooden bench that circled the tree trunk. He sat beside me, a bit too close. He placed his arm along the back of the bench, as if he were stretching.

"Have you considered why you should have this particular concern?" He raised his brows in an inviting manner. "Perhaps you don't understand your own mind. Obviously I don't know the identity of the family in question . . ." He paused over this phrase, so I knew that he suspected. In spite of Fiske's journalistic machinations to discover it, the fact that I was Grace's godmother was no secret. "But if there is a young daughter involved, is not the widowed father a man of your own age, of solid position, a man for whom you may feel some sense of attraction?" He placed his hand upon my shoulder. He patted me. From a distance, an observer would think he was simply comforting me. "I have no desire to invade your privacy or gain intimacies to which I am not entitled, Miss Barrett." He rubbed my shoulder carefully, bit by bit, as if he were examining the bone for a fracture. "I simply caution you to keep in mind your own motivations, in everything you do. As I would caution anyone." He shifted so that he faced me. It seemed entirely possible that in another moment he would kiss me.

"You are so insightful, Dr. Hoyt." I clapped my hands lightly, as I did when a student interview was at an end. I stood. His hand drifted down my skirt to the back of my knee—his idea of a sheltering embrace, I was certain. "I'm so grateful for the time you've spared me in your busy schedule. I shall certainly take your words to heart. In the meantime, Miss Francesca Coatsworth awaits me!"

He leapt away. It never failed: Francesca's name, when properly invoked, had the power of a witch's spell. He covered his protruding belly with a flat hand as if to protect himself from an assault.

"No need to walk me out, Dr. Hoyt." I couldn't resist one more turn of the knife: "Before I see Miss Coatsworth I must stop at school to review my monthly report for Mr. Rumsey—Mr. Dexter Rumsey, that is; the head of my board of trustees, as you may know. Mr. Rumsey holds you in the greatest esteem. He has mentioned you to me. During one of our frequent meetings."

"Anything I can do . . . any time . . . a pleasure . . ." He appeared positively frightened of me. Although none of my questions had been answered, I felt a thrill of accomplishment.

He gave me a quick handshake and I strode down the sylvan paths, indulging myself with the certainty that I would never need to visit Dr. Hoyt again.

Chapter Ten

T hat night, as I lay in bed, Dr. Hoyt's accusations came back to me. Did I really know too little about life to make realistic judgments? Alone in the darkness, I found myself agreeing with him. I recognized all that was lacking in my experience. Over the years I'd had to close myself off from so many of the wonders of life, simply to survive. And yet . . . the scent of spring was flashing through the night breeze. I got up and opened the window wide, letting the sweet air envelop me, feeling it caress my skin. Returning to bed, drifting into sleep, faces went through my mind: Grace, Tom, Franklin Fiske, Karl Speyer bundled against the cold . . . in the softness of this particular night, none of them could trouble me.

When I woke in the morning, a perfect snowdrift the size of two plump stacked pillows had formed along the wall beneath the window. Shivering in the cold as I got out of bed, I knelt beside it. My knees turned chill through the gauzy spring nightdress, and I felt a surge of happiness when I looked outside from my second-floor perch. During the night a windless blizzard had blanketed the daffodils and the hyacinth, and the great elms on the stately parkways. Snow covered each tree limb, outlining it white against the blue of the morning sky. Spring blizzards . . . my city was known for them, a gift from the Great Lakes.

I ran my hands through the light, dry snow. I rubbed it against my face. I tasted it, crisp knots of cold melting in my mouth like ice cream. Suddenly reckless, I threw the snow into the air, handfuls and handfuls, higher and higher, sparks of it lit by the sun like private fireworks falling upon my face, sharp and cold.

But as joyful as this was, I had work to do—and I was thankful for it. Always there was work, filling my life and warding off my fears.

As usual on the weekends, I was dressed and had breakfasted by nine. I intended to use this quiet Saturday morning to review a stack of scholarship applications, and went next door to my school office. Because of Tom's gift, I could accept six scholarship girls in the coming year. So much good would come from the endowment . . . today I felt as if I could almost put aside my apprehensions about the reason it was given.

I had dozens of applicants. Most of the girls were recommended by my colleagues in the public school community. These educators knew that without a compelling reason to stay in school, such as the improvement in expectations made possible by Macaulay, even the most gifted would be forced by their families to take full-time factory jobs or care for younger siblings. Few parents saw an intrinsic value in the education of daughters.

With a sense of urgency, I read through the forms: the daughter of a stevedore, mother deceased. A girl with nine siblings, whose father had been a grain hauler killed in the labor disputes of '99. The daughter of a hotel clerk, of a railway telegraph operator, of a printer. A girl who lived at the Remington Settlement, on the worst part of the waterfront. The child of a police sergeant. And on and on. That the girls received excellent grades and participated in a wide array of activities was a given; that they were more gifted than many of the girls who paid fees at Macaulay was also a given. What I had to determine was who would fit in and benefit most from what the school had to offer. I needed to find a flexibility of temperament and a touch of innocence. I couldn't accept those who had been embittered, for they might close themselves off to what the school could give them and became resentful of the easygoing wealth of their new peers. I hated myself for making such judgments, but I knew no other way to separate one girl from another; I could only follow my instincts.

Hours passed. I barely noticed the morning turning to midday as I read the personal essays each girl had been required to prepare. My book-lined office, with its mullioned windows and Persian carpet, glowed with reflections of sun on snow. I felt as if I were in a high tower, all alone, while my mind was filled with images of construction sites, grain elevators, steamships—places I rarely saw, flowing across the applications in my hands.

"Excuse me, may I come in?"

Startled, I looked up to find Millicent's aunt, Mary Talbert, at the door.

"Yes, of course, Mrs. Talbert." Unreasonably frightened, I rose hastily, upsetting the paperwork spread across my desk. "There's nothing wrong, I hope?"

"No, no, nothing wrong. Forgive me for approaching you unexpectedly. Your housekeeper told me I might find you in your office and guided me, not without misgivings, through the perhaps-secret corridor leading from your parlor." Mary Talbert was a solidly shaped but elegant woman, somberly dressed in the same style she encouraged for Millicent: clothes that were well made and expensive but never drew attention to the person who wore them. Her skin was a smooth, dark honey color, her brown eyes intense.

"I did not wish to cause you . . . embarrassment," she said, with an ironic glimmer in her eyes, "by visiting during school hours." Her voice was deep and sonorous, like that of an opera singer or a minister, each word precisely enunciated as if she were reciting the Psalms.

"You could never—" I began the expected protest.

"I believe you understand what I mean, Miss Barrett."

Alas, I did. When she had brought Millicent for a tour of the school, all eyes, teacher and student, had followed them wherever they'd gone, from library to chapel to classes. As I could not shoo the watchers away without calling more attention to them, I'd simply ignored them, as had Mrs. Talbert and Millicent.

"Won't you sit down, Mrs. Talbert. Shall I make tea?" Immediately I regretted the phrasing, which turned the making of tea into an imposition. *Would you like tea?* Would that have been better? Or, *I was about to make tea, would you like a cup?* A fruitless line of debate, for the question was asked and couldn't be taken back. Conceivably Mrs. Talbert had heard nothing odd in it, and my uneasiness reflected only my own self-doubt.

The truth was that Mary Talbert both intimidated me and filled me with guilt. She was more qualified for my job than I was, but because of her race she would never be offered a position like mine. She was the daughter of a barber. She'd attended Oberlin College, become a teacher in Little Rock, Arkansas, and the principal of a high school there. She'd come to Buffalo when she married William Talbert, a wealthy real estate man from one of Buffalo's oldest colored families.

Although only about fifteen hundred Negroes lived in Buffalo, many were well-established. The city boasted a strong Negro professional class, with doctors, lawyers, and educators. William Talbert was president of the Buffalo Colored Republican Club, and because of his real estate interests he was on good terms with Mr. Rumsey—which undoubtedly accounted for the board's quick acquiescence to Millicent's Macaulay application. Talbert worked as a city accountant, although he was called a "clerk" because colored people weren't officially permitted to work for the city in such professional positions. Because the Buffalo public schools had a policy against hiring married women, Mrs. Talbert couldn't pursue her teaching career after her marriage (happily, race wasn't the determining factor here: there were quite a few Negro women teaching white pupils in the public system). Instead of teaching, Mrs. Talbert served her community.

"Thank you, Miss Barrett, for the offer of tea, but I have only a moment." She still stood.

We were caught in a play, the two of us, saying our prepared lines. We had so much in common. We could have been friends, we would have been friends, had our skin colors been the same.

"And I don't wish to interrupt your work." She motioned to my desk.

"I'm reviewing scholarship applications." I tried to sound light-hearted, making small talk. "Always a wearisome task."

"Is that so? In my years as an educator I never had the privilege of reviewing scholarship applications."

I must remember never to make small talk for Mary Talbert. "Do sit down, Mrs. Talbert. What can I do for you?" I asked briskly, resuming my own seat.

My harsh tone seemed to suit her more than my attempts at *politesse*. She settled herself opposite me. "First, I have come to discuss Millicent. She has been upset these many weeks now over her encounter with Grace Sinclair. I didn't come to you initially because I believed Millicent's distress would pass. However I fear the incident has captured her imagination. You see, Grace Sinclair's threat comes from a point of view somewhat alien to our community. I suppose we, or at least the friends and associates Millicent meets at our home, are so involved in fighting for the future of our race that we seldom have time for thoughts of—suicide." A gentle smile played at the edges of her lips.

"Millicent handled herself very well with Grace," I said. "She stayed calm, she commented sympathetically and reassuringly, and she tried to show Grace her value to the community—a profound insight on Millicent's part. I reassured Millicent on this at the time."

"Yes, and Millicent took comfort from your words and your concern for her. My concerns, however, are somewhat different. How was it, I wonder, that Millicent was accompanying Grace Sinclair home to begin with? Millicent is not a servant, to be assigned whatever job needs doing."

"I have spoken to Principal Atkins of the lower school quite frankly about this point, and it shall not happen again."

"I am grateful to hear it. I hope it shall prove to be the case."

Why was she doing battle with me? "I do not excuse Miss Atkins. Nonetheless, I believe Millicent took a certain pride in the responsibility entrusted in her, to escort the younger child home."

"Yes, indeed, she was quite irrationally proud of that, and I did not attempt to open her eyes to the true facts."

We looked at each other for a moment. "Mrs. Talbert, let us posit a hypothetical situation: How would you feel if Millicent's Sunday school teacher were forced to ask her to escort home a child of your own community?"

"That would be different."

"It would be both different and the same. As I say, I am not excusing Miss Atkins's breach of protocol, but rather asking that you put the situation into perspective. Now then," I continued, before she could interrupt, "moving on to Millicent's fears for Grace, I think we can explain to Millicent what I myself have come to believe: that Grace was indulging in a bit of hyperbole, not uncommon at her age, saying phrases guaranteed to shock, with little knowledge of what her words actually meant."

I didn't believe a word of that, but it sounded plausible.

Mary Talbert simply stared at me, as if looking right through me—seeing my pretenses, my lies, the balancing act I performed to maintain my position.

"Yes. Indeed. You are right, Miss Barrett," she finally offered. "In your position I would say exactly the same. I shall reassure Millicent in this way and reiterate her own fine behavior."

Again she stared at me, and I forced myself to meet her gaze.

"I must say, Miss Barrett, that I wish it were not necessary for Millicent to attend the Macaulay School."

I flushed with anger. "That the Macaulay School exists at all is a blessing to the young women of this city."

She looked taken aback. "Please don't misunderstand me—I meant no personal offense." She paused. "I did not explain myself properly. I do not wish Millicent to be . . . fooled is possibly the best word: Attending classes with white girls, dining with white girls, sharing a cloakroom with them—when she will always be the stranger in their midst."

"After everyone adjusted, there has never been a problem at school."

"That is part of my point: that someday someone might act on behalf of your innocent white girls, to 'protect' them from the stranger in their midst."

"As we are speaking frankly, I must say you are exaggerating."

"Perhaps. I hope so. It is also my hope that one day there will be a school in our own community that will provide Millicent, or at least the girls who come after her, with the standards and expectations that Macaulay provides. In the meantime, yes, I am grateful for what Macaulay offers her. I only hope that the school will never do her any harm."

"I trust not, Mrs. Talbert." My anger ebbed. I glanced out the window, then searched for a means of conciliation. "Do you miss your own teaching?" I asked.

"I do not feel that I have stopped teaching. I have simply broadened the perspective of my teaching: organizing my people, working toward suffrage, fighting lynching, helping newcomers to find steady work by providing vocational training to give them the skills they need. Everything I do is teaching."

How meager my own endeavors seemed in comparison. "I once considered going to the South to teach colored children," I confessed. "When I was at college."

"Why didn't you?"

"The salary was low, of course. And I—well, frankly, I had no family, no outside income, I needed to support myself. I needed— wanted"—I stumbled over my hypocrisies—"a certain standard. Then as time passed, other . . . considerations kept me here."

"Materialism triumphant once again," she joked. But the joke stung.

"I admire you tremendously, Mrs. Talbert."

"Don't idealize me, Miss Barrett," she said forthrightly. "I've only put my hand to what I've found in front of me. And of course William Talbert has given me a certain . . . standard, as you put it, that I would be loathe to give up in order to return to the public schools of Arkansas." She nodded, acknowledging our common ground.

"This brings me to the second reason for my visit today. In about a week's time I shall be appearing before a meeting of the executive committee of the Pan-American Exposition, to make a plea. I would be honored if you would accompany me to that meeting—at the Buffalo Club, needless to say." Sarcasm filled her voice.

"What is the nature of your plea?"

"As you may know, I lost what I call the first battle of the exposition: the attempt to force the committee to invite a Negro to join their ranks."

This battle had been conducted primarily in the newspapers, and I remembered it well. The Pan-American was the only recent national exposition not to have a Negro commissioner.

"Now what I feared has come to pass: the exposition will include on the Midway a display of plantation life with 'happy darkies' shuffling through their days, performing songs and selling miniature bales of cotton. The 'original' Uncle Tom's Cabin will be displayed. But nowhere will there be a comprehensive exhibition of the achievements of my people. Oh, there may be a passing reference here and there, hidden away in the machinery building or the agriculture building," she said dismissively, "but nowhere will there be a coherent presentation. This must change, Miss Barrett." She tapped her fingers on my desk, a crusading spirit sharpening her face. "If *they* would have us ignore their 'darkies' on the Midway, then *we* must have a pavilion devoted to our accomplishments."

She lowered her tone a notch, taking me into her confidence. "This matter is also a personal embarrassment to me, because I successfully lobbied the National Association of Colored Women to hold its biennial conference in Buffalo in July. Miss Love was kind enough to volunteer the use of Lyric Hall—whether she checked with the management, I don't know!" This was a bitter joke, because Lyric Hall was run by the Women's Educational and Industrial Union, a broad-based settlement house, and its managers were, more than most, at Miss Love's mercy.

"As things stand now, my compatriots will visit the exposition and see only that which we have fought to leave behind." Her public persona slipped away, and she looked deflated. "And there is another reason, one that may be closer to your heart: Millicent. Our situation as a race is fraught with challenge. Five years ago, as you know, the Supreme Court approved systematic segregation throughout the South under the Jim Crow legislation; lynching has become commonplace in southern states, where there are perhaps as many as three lynchings per week, according to reliable reports. What kind of future are we to create for Millicent?"

Here I had no doubts. "Millicent is very bright. She can aim for whatever future she chooses."

"So it would seem to you, from your lovely office high above the fray."

"I admit to a degree of isolation," I said smoothly.

"Will you endorse this endeavor by joining me at the meeting? You will be proving to the commissioners that our view has support within the educated white community. I intend to stress the economic benefits that the NACW conference will bring to the city. We expect several hundred attendees, and many women will be bringing their families." There was an almost imperceptible weakening in her voice, as though she knew her effort to be doomed and was preparing herself for an unwinnable fight.

"Mrs. Talbert, I sympathize with you, truly I do. But I do not become involved in public disputes."

"Your presence would endow my plea with profound validity for these men."

"I will speak to Mr. Rumsey about it privately."

"You would need only sit in the back of the room—your support would be symbolic, rather than active."

"Isn't Maria Love the person you should be asking? Especially if she's already arranged for the use of the hall for your convention. I've never known her to hesitate in the face of a battle, and she knew most of the commissioners when they were boys. Probably even spanked them when necessary. She's the one who'll get you what you want."

"Yes, Miss Love has always been a friend to my community." For a moment, Mrs. Talbert remained silent. Then she continued thoughtfully, "Miss Barrett, have you ever noticed that there is a certain type of reformer who likes to help only the helpless? Who takes it as a personal affront when the people he or she wishes to view as subjugated become independent?" Unexpectedly Mrs. Talbert's eyes now danced with playfulness. "Have you ever noticed that type of reformer?"

"Why, yes, indeed, I have—right here in Buffalo." Gently I acknowledged her game. "I've also noticed how very annoyed such reformers become when they see other people filling the place that they believe should be theirs."

"Yes, I've noticed that too."

"Well, Mrs. Talbert, perhaps I shall join you. I will consider it."

"I have one more reason for asking you, if truth be told."

"Yes?"

"The idea of standing in front of a row of rich white men scares me." She smiled broadly, her face transformed into beauty.

What could I do then, but accept her invitation?

After I said good-bye to Mrs. Talbert, I focused again on the scholarship applications. I began to separate out the candidates with real potential, pausing regretfully over each borderline applicant. How long, I wonder, was Grace watching from the doorway before I looked up to find her secretive smile bestowed upon me? I glanced over and there she was: her cheeks red from the cold, her eyes bright blue against the white of her rabbit fur hat, her entire being suffused with the brilliance of a snow princess. How I loved her.

"Hello, Aunt Louisa. I was watching the school with my spyglass. Was that Millicent's aunt who came to see you? After she left, I told Papa we must go and get you and take you sleigh riding."

"Sleigh riding?" I hadn't gone sleigh riding for fun in years; just the mention of it filled me with a delight I hadn't felt since childhood.

"Papa's waiting downstairs."

I went to the casement window. Parked in front of the school was the Sinclair sleigh, long and sleek, black with red trim, the metal work curving into fanciful arabesques. Two mahogany-brown horses with bells dangling from their harnesses stamped at the snow. Tom reclined on the velvet seat, a bearskin blanket spread loosely across his legs, his head resting against the seat back. He smoked a cigarette, blowing the smoke into the sky. I hadn't seen him in two weeks, not since I'd met him and Grace horseback riding on the parkway. I'd written him a note after my visit to Maria Love, explaining my lack of success, and he'd replied with a gracious letter of appreciation for my attempt. Seeing him there in the sleigh, my worries about Speyer seemed absurd; Tom could not have made Margaret so happy if he'd been capable of such a deed against his colleague, or so I told myself. Of course if we don't want to believe something, denial is so very easy . . . and on some days it's easier than others.

Of more immediate concern was that there might be gossip if I went sleigh riding. However, I was Grace's godmother; and in addition, despite the inroads of Susannah Riley with Francesca, I was still commonly considered beyond romantic involvements—with men at least. I glanced at Grace, then back at the sleigh. The scene glowed as if it were a painting waiting only for Grace and me to enter the places intended for us.

As we drove away, I saw diamonds in the treetops. Diamonds of ice, blowing in the breeze. We rode down Chapin Parkway to the circle and so to Forest Lawn Cemetery. Passing through the cemetery's whimsical gate, we joined our neighbors amid the tree-covered hills and curving paths.

Angels and obelisks covered the hillsides, but there was nothing morbid here. As in so many cities, the cemetery was a favorite place for picnics in summer and snowball fights in winter. No one came here from the narrow streets along the waterfront, or from the neighborhoods where people spoke languages different from ours. Or had skin of a different shade. We who idled here were like an extended family, at ease and at home.

Today children built snowmen and played hide-and-seek among the sandstone mausoleums and the marble peristyles. Their parents strolled the grounds, unconcerned about separation from their little ones: the guard at the gate was conscientious, keeping out everyone he didn't know, and since everyone inside knew virtually everyone else (whether living or dead), any lost child was invariably found.

So many were here among my students and their families, among the sixty millionaires and many near-millionaires of Buffalo, and among the doctors, attorneys, ministers, artists, and architects who served them. Yet despite these many visitors, the cemetery felt blissfully uncrowded; there was more than enough room for all of us to spread out among the lofty tulip trees and the broad beeches, to find sheltered glens lined with white-barked birches where we could linger beside still ponds.

Coming toward us now was Maria Love, with a sleigh full of her grandnieces and grandnephews: mischievous little Carys and Rumseys, one or another continually tumbling off the sleigh and into the snowdrifts. Without slowing the horses, Miss Love circled the sleigh around and reached out a hand to retrieve them. A trio of men named John approached us, all members of my board of trustees: John Milburn, bestowing his charming smile on one and all; John Albright, birdwatching with his youthful second wife; John Larkin, the mail-order soap king, gleaming as he always did with the cleanliness bestowed by constant use of his own products. Even his hands gleamed, and undoubtedly because of this, he rarely wore gloves. Mr. Rumsey drove past, tipping his hat like a minister offering his blessing upon us all. His daughter Ruth, he told Grace, was home with a cold; bad luck, we agreed, for her to miss such a glorious day.

Grace sat between Tom and me. She held my hand and sometimes touched her father's arm or rested her head against his shoulder. She asked to tour the cemetery and so we did: around the spring-fed Mirror

Lake surrounded by flowering, snow-covered crabapple trees, white on pink; along the cascading Scajaquada Creek, where a great blue heron fished slowly along the shore; across stone bridges and into hidden vales of oak trees. Scattered among the obelisks and angels were stone portraits of dead children, captured in their playfulness and hurry, snow like shawls around their shoulders.

Grace appeared serene and at ease. After my useless consultation with Dr. Hoyt, I could only feel relief that at this moment, at least, she was fine. When she spotted a field of violets poking through the snow beside a small Gothic steeple, she pulled at Tom's sleeve.

"I want to pick some for Mama."

Tom brought the sleigh to a stop, and she slipped out. A flock of white-throated sparrows fluttered up as she approached. She spent some time among the violets, carefully gathering only the most perfect.

As we watched her, Tom said quietly, "I never dreamed I'd see Grace picking violets for Margaret's grave. Before we were married, Margaret asked me to bring her here to pick violets for *her* mother's grave. This is the same spot. I remember the steeple." Then he fell silent. How different this day would be if Margaret were with us. We'd probably be throwing snowballs at each other now, or having a contest to see who could throw one the farthest; Tom and Grace would be the finalists, and Tom, of course, would let Grace win.

Finally Grace returned with the flowers sheltered in the crook of her arm, and we drove to the area near Margaret's grave. Tom tied the horses, and we climbed up the hillside, Grace leading us. When I slipped on the snow, Tom caught my elbow. This was the highest hill of the cemetery; President Fillmore was buried at the top. Margaret's grave was three-quarters of the way up. A rabbit hopped away from the marker as we approached, its white tail bobbing in the snow. Laughing at the sight of it, Grace turned to us, her smile making me yearn to hug her. When we reached the grave, Grace stood still as if saying a prayer, then placed the violets beside the stone. The flowers were velvety purple against the melting white. Only a stone marked Margaret's grave now, but on the anniversary of her death a carved angel would take its place above her. Grace wiped the snow from the stone so we could see the lettering. *Margaret Winspear Sinclair, 1866 to 1900.* I bit my lip, trying not to cry; I didn't want Grace to see me cry.

I had stood here with Tom last September when Margaret was buried. Grace wasn't with us. Because she was distraught, Tom had allowed her to stay home with the housekeeper during the funeral and burial. The Winspears had clucked their disapproval at Tom's decision. The funeral and burial were exactly what she needed to see, they argued, to help her with her mourning. They appealed to me. Generally children did attend burials, but at that moment I was too distraught myself to judge or advise. The Sinclair house was so confused the morning of the funeral: people turning up from everywhere, food being served in every room, muffled greetings exchanged, hugs bestowed upon me by friends whose names I couldn't remember. I hadn't slept in days. Grace threw a tantrum, kicking the maid who tried to help her dress, throwing a dish of applesauce against the wall of her playroom, screaming for "Mama" over and over. In retrospect, I realized that Tom had been right to keep her home. Finally that evening, as Tom had tucked her into bed and I had given her a good night kiss, a numbness—an utter blankness—descended upon her. She slept for fifteen hours, and when she woke, for weeks that blankness became her refuge.

"I wonder if Mama sees us now." Grace didn't sound sad today, only matter-of-fact: a child who had been raised to believe in heaven and still had no reason to doubt its existence. "Remember how much Mama loved the snow? Remember that time she helped me build the biggest snowman anyone had ever seen, on our front lawn? Remember how we dressed him up in your silk top hat and scarf?" she asked Tom.

"Of course," Tom said. "As I recall I donated some old boots to him too."

"I remember, Papa." She hugged him with pleasure. "I remember."

"And then *I* came over to admire him," I said.

"Yes, Aunt Louisa, I remember! I wrote you a special note of invitation."

"I still have it."

"I remember everything about that snowman," she said proudly.

Remember, remember, remember. So much of our lives had turned into remembrance.

"I'm sure Mama sees us now. She watches everything I do," Grace assured us. "So I always have to do the right thing. That's why lately I never do anything wrong." She gave Tom and me an impish grin. "Sometimes I like to pretend she visits me. Sometimes when I spin around really fast like this"—she twirled and twirled in the snow—"I get dizzy and I can see her out of the corner of my eye, just like she's sitting over there!" At the end of a twirl she stopped suddenly and pointed at a gravestone farther up the hill. She looked stricken, as if she'd truly expected to see Margaret; or as if she had seen Margaret, at just the edge of her vision, and now Margaret was gone. "Did you two see her?" she asked.

"No, darling," Tom said gently. "We didn't see her."

"Neither did I," she said, bereft. Grace took Tom's hand and mine, making a chain of us, and we stood for a long moment looking through the trees toward the park lake and the half-built art gallery beyond it. In the sharp, clear air, the towers of the asylum seemed close upon us. I studied Grace's now-placid face. I wasn't surprised that she would attempt to conjure up Margaret's being. Children were always telling ghost stories, and at church the ministers made angels and the afterlife sound like a certainty. Therefore why wouldn't her beloved mother always watch over her, and even visit her now and again? I grasped at something Dr. Hoyt had said, that Grace simply needed to pass through the time of mourning and then all would be well. I tried to believe this was true. Yes, I said to myself over and over, at heart my goddaughter was fine, and she always would be.

I glanced at Tom, to find him looking at me. He seemed to be searching my face, for what I didn't know. Then, almost as an afterthought and only for an instant, his searching look turned into a shy smile.

When we returned to our sleigh at the bottom of the hill, we came upon Seward Cary, one of Maria Love's adult nephews. He was a thin, long-faced man with a passion for polo, who never seemed to have enough to do to fill his time. "How about a race, Sinclair?" he called, standing in his cutter. His breath steamed in the cold. "Up on the flats." He motioned towards the northern part of the cemetery.

"You're on, Cary," Tom responded. The gentlemen of our city had a love of sleigh racing. On Richmond Avenue, on Delaware, even here in the cemetery, they liked nothing better than to race in the brisk air.

Hesitantly Grace said, "I don't want to race."

"Now, now, little girl, a bit of a race will do you good," Tom said, with more than his usual touch of Irish brogue.

Up on the flats, Tom pulled alongside Cary's sleigh. Earlier races had drawn a small crowd. The route was discussed, positions were adjusted. Both men stood. Someone offered to give the signal: A whip snapped against a tree trunk—and with it Seward was off, whipping his horse and whooping, Tom right beside him. The bystanders shouted. The wind lashed against us, burning like ice crystals into our skin. Our sleigh heeled as we curved around a bend, and I gripped the railing.

"We've got him," I thought I heard Tom say into the wind.

Grace clutched my hands and pressed her face into my skirt, making a mewling sound and trembling—altogether more scared than she should have been. At her age, she should have been enjoying it. Nonetheless she was terrified, and I couldn't see her this way and do nothing to help her.

"Stop, Tom!" I shouted. My eyes watered in the wind. He did nothing to stop. He couldn't hear me. I shouted again. Still he couldn't hear me. I pulled at his arm. "She's frightened!"

He glanced at me, bewildered, and looked down at Grace, her arms wrapped around my legs, her face hidden. Then he did slow the horses, from a gallop to a trot to a walk until he stopped them completely—or they stopped on their own accord, feeling the strength leave his hands. He sat down. Up ahead Seward Cary gave a cheer in the joy of his victory.

"She was frightened, Tom," I said quietly. "Even if she had no reason to be."

He stared at Grace and then at me. Not in anger or regret, or even with concern for his daughter. He simply looked confused, as if he were in a foreign land and the language I spoke—although he was supposed to know it, had even studied it—was so different from what he expected that he couldn't begin to comprehend it.

By the time we left the cemetery, however, all was forgotten. Grace seemed happy again, rubbing her father's arm, pressing against him once more. He too seemed to have put the incident from his mind. But as I gazed at her, watching her glance flit from one spot to the next, I realized that she defied my understanding, defied every small reassurance at which I grasped. She was like water slipping through my hands.

We turned onto Delaware Avenue, heading downtown. The late afternoon sun left bands of color across the snow. The horses went at a steady trot, the mansions and churches flashing by, the lawns broad and snow-covered, the branches of the double row of elms meeting overhead. Suddenly downtown opened before us in its glory: City Hall, its Gothic tower surmounted by statues representing Justice and Commerce, Agriculture and the Mechanical Arts. The post office, with its tall, slender campanile. And the new skyscrapers, taller than church spires. Yes, we had skyscrapers in Buffalo.

We passed the Prudential Building, designed by Louis Sullivan: thirteen stories high, built of steel, covered with terra-cotta carvings of vines and trees that soared upward like an impenetrable forest to surround the oriel windows at the top. The decorations made the building seem even taller than it was, and the terra-cotta glowed deep ocher in the sunset.

"Look well at that, Grace," Tom said. "Thirteen floors and no electricity. Steam-powered elevator and gaslights. I don't know how the workers stand it, being in the gaslight all day. Well, we'll improve on that soon, eh?"

"Yes, Papa," she said, though I sensed she wasn't listening. "Look, there's where *you* work!" Excited, she stood and pointed to the Ellicott Square Building, a few blocks ahead.

"Right you are, my girl."

Designed by Daniel Burnham, the Ellicott Square Building was ten stories tall and covered an entire city block. It boasted six hundred offices, forty stores, sixteen counting rooms. It was the largest office building in the world, but it, too, had no electricity.

There were other magnificent buildings everywhere around us. Downtown Buffalo was designed in the early 1800s by Joseph Ellicott, whose brother had worked with Pierre L'Enfant on the design of Washington, D.C. The downtown streets radiated from wide public circles that created an aura of nobility and civic triumph. At the end of every southward-running street, the grain elevators rose stark on the horizon. Beside the elevators were the coal trestles, the biggest in the world, and the railroad yards; and in the harbor were the masts of the lake schooners and the funnels of the freighters, symbols one and all of where the money came from to make this magnificence possible.

When I was a child, and later at Wellesley, Boston was the city I visited for a treat, but Boston was staid and self-protective compared to Buffalo: Here we had the freedom of the frontier, the freedom of never-ending expansion. We were a city "full of beans," as I'd once heard it described. A city of wonder. We'd sent two presidents to the White House. We were an exposition city, like Chicago and Philadelphia. Suddenly a sense of gratitude swept through me—to be here, now, in this sleigh, gliding through the most exuberant city in the nation. The city's exuberance was mine; the city itself was mine.

I felt overwhelmed; shaken by my sense of belonging.

This winter, hotelier and restaurateur Ellsworth Statler had opened a Viennese café, the first café we'd ever had, in the central light court of the Ellicott Square Building. No matter how many times I visited the Ellicott Square Building, when I entered the light court I was astonished. It was covered with glass supported by curved metal braces. Huge chandeliers hung from central arches. At each end of the court, curving staircases with intricate banisters led to the shops on the balcony. The building was designed around this central court for a very practical reason: to bring natural light into the inner offices.

Now that dusk was upon us, gaslight suffused the court. Everyone of importance was here. Mr. Statler himself, a net of smile lines around his eyes, a thick mustache dominating his thin face, showed us to a table. Francesca waved from a corner, where she sat with Susannah Riley, who had her back to the crowd. Maria Love was at a center table (naturally), surrounded by her rambunctious little Carys and Rumseys, their faces now covered with evidence of hot chocolate and cake. Nearby, Susan Fiske Rumsey sat with her cousin Franklin, his photography equipment piled on the floor beside them. Mrs. Rumsey smiled her greeting, while Fiske simply nodded at me by way of recognition, and I appreciated his discretion. For the first time, I focused on the fact that I was the only person to whom he'd revealed his secret. Knowledge, of course, is power; why had he given me such power over him? Why had he trusted me? I caught myself staring at him for a beat longer than modesty dictated; hastily I shifted my gaze away. Tom and I continued our peregrination across the room. We said hello to everyone we passed and everyone said hello to us, each strand of the city knit tightly together.

The only person we didn't say hello to was Frederick Krakauer, "Morgan's man" as Fiske called him, who slouched, hands folded across his broad abdomen, in a straight-backed chair near Maria Love's table—near her table, but pointedly not at her table. Looking as if he were lightly dozing, eyes half-shut, he regarded us all with a forbearing smile while Miss Love studied him speculatively.

Once we were settled, Grace ran off to join a group of children who were playing a complicated game of hopscotch across the marble mosaic floor. She received an effortless welcome from them. All the girls were Macaulay girls, all the boys went to the Franklin School and then to Nichols. How wonderful it was, to gaze upon children who had nothing more to do with their time than devote themselves to the self-imposed rules governing jumps across a patterned floor.

Tom too gazed at the children, but with a preoccupied look. Perhaps he was remembering his own youth, or perhaps he wondered only about the propriety of lighting a cigar in mixed company. Grace's hair flew as she jumped. And then Tom startled me.

"You know," he said, almost to himself and still watching Grace, so that I had to lean close to hear him, "sometimes I look at her and realize that I've completely forgotten, for weeks or for months, that she's not really my daughter. That's surprising, isn't it?"

He turned to me, and because I had already leaned close to hear him, we were now very near to one another, his eyes dark in the gaslight. Suddenly I felt shy and flustered.

"Well, no, it's not surprising. You've had her since she was a new-born."

"At the beginning I used to wonder, what did the father look like, and the mother. I used to conjure them up in my head. Then after a while it didn't seem to matter anymore. But now, when she makes some gesture I don't recognize, I wonder if it's something she's gotten from . . . those other people."

"Or from herself."

"Yes, but what is a self?" he asked with a hint of a smile. "She's so much like Margaret. I remember catching her when she was very young, just two, maybe three years old, following Margaret around the house and imitating her walk, arranging her shoulders and her head to be like Margaret. It almost broke my heart. You can't even imagine what it feels like to remember now. It haunts me, how much like Margaret she is."

His voice caught. Shifting his body, he looked away. I started to reach out to him, to comfort him, then pulled back my hand, frozen by the impropriety of touching him in a public place. After a few moments, his knee brushing mine beneath the narrow table, he turned to me again, his face composed.

"You're still the only person who knows, Louisa. Apart from the doctor, of course." He glanced around. "Sometimes I wonder which of my neighbors' children aren't really theirs, and they have to keep the truth hidden the way Margaret and I do." There it was, the present tense, cutting into us. If Margaret were here now—well, she and I would be chatting together while Tom most likely would have gone off to join the gentlemen who were smoking and discussing business by the balcony stairs. "Do you ever wonder what happened to the poor girl who gave birth to Grace? Do you think she ever thinks of her?"

I felt myself blushing. But before I was forced to answer, the bulky form of George Urban, Jr., arrived at our table, on his way, he told us, to bring the good news to Frederick Krakauer that despite the unex-pected storm—and extremely icy it was, out at Niagara—the lines had held, the electric power had not gone down. The generators were still transmitting current, the factories were still churning out aluminum, the streetlights of Buffalo were still illuminated.

The truth of this we later discovered ourselves when we left the Ellicott Square Building and found the streetlamps ablaze. Grace gave the lamps not a thought; we'd had them nearly five years now, virtually a lifetime to her. She took them for granted. But to me, they remained a small evening miracle, like a nightly blessing.

As we rode home, bearskin blankets covering our legs, Grace fell asleep. She leaned against her father, her face like an angel's. I wished there were a way to keep her close to me forever. I ached, that soon she would go to her home, and me to mine.

On Chapin Parkway, Tom said, "Would you mind if I took Grace home first, to get her out of the cold?"

"No, of course not. That's best."

He headed down Lincoln Parkway to Forest Avenue. We drove through the gate of the estate, up the shoveled drive, and stopped under the *porte cochère*, which was lit by an electric bulb in a fixture designed to resemble a gas lamp.

And then we saw that the beveled-glass window of the entry door had been smashed. Tom stared at the door in silence.

The groom, pulling on his coat, ran out from the coach house. "Good evening, sir." Irish. Black-haired. Young, but self-possessed. All the Sinclair servants were Irish. Did Tom find some kind of comfort in that? Were they more deferential to him, or more to be trusted?

Without preliminaries, the groom jumped into the explanation. "Mrs. Sheehan heard the noise just after dark. It was a torch. Thrown from pretty close, probably, and pretty hard. Burned the hallway carpet. Could've been worse, if Mrs. Sheehan hadn't been dusting the pieces on the mantel in the drawing room." He paused for Tom to respond, and when Tom said nothing, he continued, "We searched, but we couldn't find anybody or any traces. Not even footprints in the snow. They must have used the drive. Damned cheeky."

"Yes." Tom sounded oddly untroubled.

"Mr. Sheehan didn't want to telephone the police without your approval."

"Good. No need to telephone the police. Take hold of the horses, will you? I'll get Grace settled before seeing Miss Barrett home."

Tom went to the door, giving it a cursory examination before propping it open. How aloof he was. For him, aloofness was a kind of power. He did not invite me in, but took Grace in his arms with the utmost gentleness, keeping her wrapped in the blanket. Turning in his arms, she sighed. He spoke tenderly to her, words I couldn't hear except for their reassuring tone. I had never been given the chance to speak to her with such words, to use such a tone.

"I won't be but a minute, Louisa."

In the hall, he was joined by the housekeeper and butler. The Sheehans were both gray-haired and thin, with an almost military bearing; they were one of those married couples who come to look like one another after long years together. They began talking about the window, pointing out the burned patch of carpet, but Tom silenced them, nodding toward Grace in his arms. He carried her up the stairs, Mrs. Sheehan following while her husband carefully pushed the door almost shut: closed enough to keep out the cold, open enough to show me no offense.

Soon Tom returned. Mrs. Sheehan would help Grace to change her clothes, then tuck her into bed; despite her forbidding appearance, the housekeeper was kind-hearted. As we rode away, Grace's third-floor light was on. The horses' bells jingled sharply in the cold night air; if Grace had awakened she would hear the cheerful sound.

"Albright was telling me the other day that I must get a governess-companion for Grace," Tom was saying. "Told me she needs more than a housekeeper looking after her. Advised me to put an advertisement at Smith College, or even Vassar. But not Wellesley, he told me—Wellesley girls are too headstrong! I'm sure he was thinking of you, Louisa." He batted my shoulder good-naturedly as he turned the sleigh onto the street. "Anyway, I told him, seeing as what happened when *he* brought a governess-companion into the house, I thought as I wouldn't! At least not yet." He laughed. "But Albright assured me that a pretty governess was probably just what I needed. 'Fix you up in no time,' he said."

I liked Susan Fuller Albright, the Smith College governess John Albright had married. She was from New England Shaker stock, which made her unusual and interesting. But I couldn't allow the thought of her (and the implications about a possible stepmother for Grace) to deflect me.

"Who do you think threw the torch?" I heard my voice echo beneath the snow-covered trees.

He waited a long moment before answering, and then said with studied indifference, "Oh, a thief, don't you think?"

"A thief? A *torch?*"

"You're probably right, Louisa." Suddenly he was treating the matter as a joke. "Couldn't have been a thief. Much more likely that the house was set upon by nature lovers. Someone from the Niagara Preservation Society. Daniel Henry Bates himself. Singed his beard in the process. Or maybe the perpetrator was a disgruntled investor in the Buffalo Gas Light Company. Or a member of the lineman's union—a 'hot stick man'. Or maybe—now here's a thought—maybe it was Frederick Krakauer. Although he doesn't seem like a torch thrower himself. But surely Mr. Morgan provides him with discretionary funds to cover the hiring of torch throwers. I wonder how you'd put that down on an expense report. Honestly, I imagine; I'm sure Mr. Morgan insists on honesty: 'five dollars, torch thrower with good aim.'"

"Why are you talking this way?"

His smile faded. "Ah, Louisa, everyone's impatient with me these days."

"Why should people be impatient with you?"

"I'm sure they have their reasons."

"What reasons, what people?" I knew I sounded proprietary, but I couldn't help myself.

"People in hot pursuit of their own agendas. I wish them luck, one and all."

"But don't you care if—"

"Of course I care, Louisa. I particularly care about Grace. About her safety. But what's the point of upsetting the household? Or upsetting you? It was obviously an act meant to frighten us, not to burn the house down."

"How can you know that?"

"Because it was done when the servants were awake. And because someone who wanted to burn the house down would have thrown the torch through the front windows, onto the curtains."

"Maybe whoever did it was just incompetent."

"That's possible," he admitted grudgingly.

"Why won't you telephone the police?"

"The less notice, the better. I don't want to give whoever did it the satisfaction of a public investigation."

"But ignoring it might prompt whoever did it to do something that would be impossible to ignore."

"A risk I'm willing to take." Suddenly he became angry: "If you want my hunch, it's Bates's gang. They make everything personal. Sometimes I wonder if they've got a spy on me: Their propaganda shouts things about me that I'm only vaguely aware of myself." He smiled as he said this, his anger quickly waning. "I'll just have to get a spy on them—tit for tat! Well, let's not think about that now. Let's think about what a wonderful day we've had. Let's think about a snowball fight."

He stood and reached to grab a handful of snow from a low-hanging branch. Before I knew what was happening, he'd put the snow down my back. It tickled and made me shiver even as I laughed. He put his arm around me, pressing me close to him and gripping my wrist to prevent me from trying to pull out the snow.

"Be careful or I'll toss you into a drift," he whispered.

And with that whisper, an image of the park lake came into my mind. An image of Karl Speyer writhing beneath the ice. I pulled away from him.

"What's wrong? Have I taken liberties?" There was a touch of irony in his voice.

After managing to remove the snow, I wrapped my arms around myself. I stared ahead, reluctant to respond.

"You'd better tell me. I can't let you go home unless you tell me. Shall we spend the night sitting in the sleigh outside school?"

In spite of myself I relaxed a bit. "Well, it's just . . . I was surprised, when Karl Speyer died, that you didn't, I mean—"

"That I didn't mention to the journalists his impromptu visit to us earlier that evening?"

"Well, yes. Exactly." I was taken aback by his frankness.

"And you've been harboring this question for weeks now, have you? Torturing yourself about my sins of omission? With no one to talk to and nowhere to go with your worries?" He was trying to make me laugh and had finally succeeded.

"Yes, to all those questions, yes."

"You should have come to me right then, Louisa, and asked me about it," he said gently.

"I felt—shy."

"Shy? You?"

"Yes, I'm very shy. Once you get to know me."

"Mmm, I see what you mean," he said, not believing me. "Let me explain, then. I didn't tell the reporters or the police about Speyer's visit because it was irrelevant. I'm trying to run a business. How can I do that, with police and reporters swarming over me? Speyer and I had a discussion we'd probably had five times before. We disagreed on a certain policy that I won't bore you with, and whenever it came up, I won the argument. I am the boss, after all. But he kept pressing his point, and that's good: I don't like yes-men around me."

"Some people think you arranged his death."

"No one I know, I hope."

I didn't think he'd ever met Fiske. "No one you know."

"Good."

"But you see, when you gave all that money to the school . . . well, naturally I wondered—"

But I couldn't say it. I couldn't say, I wondered if you were trying to bribe me into silence.

By now we were on Bidwell Parkway. Silent himself, Tom rode down to Elmwood and turned to come up Bidwell beside the school. In front of my home, he drew the horses to a stop.

Then I realized that he hadn't denied the accusation; he'd asked a question, he'd made a joke—and he'd let my implication about the endowment and Speyer's death stand unchallenged. Distressed, I reached for my reticule and pushed the blanket from my legs. Although I was upset, I had to maintain dignity and politeness: I turned to thank him for the day—and found him calmly studying me.

"Don't go yet. I have a confession to make." I didn't move. "The truth is, I made a mistake with Karl Speyer. I let myself show how angry I was, because he came to the house instead of talking to me at the office or even at the club. I raised my voice. If I hadn't raised my voice, you wouldn't have found anything amiss, now, would you? You'd have simply been grateful that I'd kept your name out of the newspapers. I violated my own rule, which is to make my voice softer, not louder, when trying to make a point. A trick I picked up from old Dexter Rumsey."

Even now he didn't deny my implication. "But then why—" I began, prepared to challenge him.

"No, don't say anything." He put his fingers to my lips for a half-second. His hand smelled leathery from the reins.

"There's something else I must tell you, seeing as you've virtually accused me of murder," he said amiably.

"Tom—"

"Quiet, now." He brought his hand to my lips once more. "Since our discussion, what, six or seven weeks ago now, I've been keeping track of Grace a bit more than I used to. I've been bringing more work home instead of staying late at the office. I've been reviewing papers in the library, that kind of thing. Grace has been joining me, doing her drawings and her homework. So we've been working together, you might say. And I've been watching her. I'm discovering—to my surprise—that she begins to remind me of someone. Of you, in fact. Or rather, you begin to remind me of Grace."

There was a subtle strain of threat in his voice. Dread crept into me, tingling in my fingertips.

"Not her manner—that's like Margaret. But her features. Her—your hair, your eyes, your jawline." No, I wouldn't challenge him now, and he knew it. Twisting the reins around one hand, he touched my face, one finger moving across the line of my jaw. I didn't move. He pushed back my hat, rubbing his fingers into my hair. He whispered, "Yes, I see you in her, and her in you. What does that mean, do you think?"

Abruptly I turned away from him and fumbled for my key. "It's our Anglo-Saxon Protestant blood." I tried to sound lighthearted even as I trembled. "It makes us all look alike. Sometimes in class, I can't tell one girl from the next. Thank goodness for the scholarships you're funding, to bring some fresh features among us. I'd best be going." I was careful not to look at him. "Thank you for the lovely day." I slipped out of the sleigh, not waiting for him to accompany me, and hurried up the path.

I was panting by the time I shut the door behind me. I pressed myself against the wall, gasping for breath.

And then the tingling sound of sleigh bells reached me. Thomas Sinclair was driving home.

PART TWO

———◆———

Possession

"I have tried so hard to do right."

Former president Grover Cleveland,
before his death on June 24, 1908

Chapter Eleven

W|hat is the measure of a man?

Is it physical? He was of medium height with dark-blue eyes and rich brown hair. His mustache was thick and long. He weighed over two hundred and fifty pounds, but during his time heftiness was a sign of prestige, of the enviable comfort needed to consume so much food. His weight was also a reflection of the German beer gardens he frequented, where he enjoyed sausage, sauerkraut, and innumerable steins of beer.

What is the measure of a man?

Is it professional? He was the impoverished son of an impoverished clergyman. Struggling to find his way, he settled with an uncle in Buffalo. He became a clerk in a law office, taught himself the law. Gradually he progressed in his chosen field, impressing one and all with his probity, his honesty, his hard work. He was elected sheriff and never shirked his duty, even when duty included the role of hangman. In 1881, he was elected mayor. He promised to end corruption, and he did. Over and over he vetoed city contracts that had been awarded by graft. The "veto mayor," they called him. In 1882, he was elected governor. "Public Office Is a Public Trust"— that was his slogan, and it was revolutionary. With unwavering courage, he confronted the forces of corruption, fighting patronage and the vested interests. And in 1884, he was elected President of the United States.

Stephen Grover Cleveland. Yes, there was much to admire in him. People said his rise was meteoric. In three years, he went from mayor to governor to president. Some said it was Buffalo that catapulted him to glory, Buffalo that spoke for him—the city like an explosion of power and might withstanding every economic downturn. Buffalo, the city every American wanted to feel touched by, an emblem of hope for the nation.

What is the measure of a man?

Is it moral? In public, he projected steadfast integrity. He took pride in being a reformer, battling bribery and kickbacks. He struggled to put an end to the spoils system which had ruled political life for years. But in private, his standards were different. Perhaps this is true for most men, however—their private transgressions are harmless enough, as long as they remain undiscovered. Perhaps we should simply be grateful when, in at least some arenas, these men put duty and honor first. And yet . . . Cleveland aspired to the highest office in the land: Should he have been held to a higher standard than other men, in order to inspire the nation by his example?

During the Civil War, Cleveland avoided service by paying a Polish immigrant to replace him in the fighting. Of course there was nothing illegal about this; many estimable men did it, and Cleveland at the time was the sole provider for his mother and sisters. Nonetheless his decision to avoid the draft was considered somehow . . . unpresidential.

A bachelor until age forty-nine (when he married twenty-two-year-old Frances Folsom in the White House), Cleveland spent his Buffalo evenings drinking and carousing. There were pranks; practical jokes; fisticuffs on the street outside his favorite saloons; blunt language and blunt pleasures with women who expected nothing more. Even after he became governor, no visit home was complete without a good-natured brawl.

And then there was the shop-girl widow Maria Halpin, the child she bore him, and the whole sad, sordid tale I knew so well, of how she expected marriage and began drinking to console her shame; how Cleveland arranged to have their son taken from her by force and adopted by a well-regarded family; and how she was committed to an asylum until she accepted the separation.

What is the measure of a man?

Was he an incorruptible reformer, or profligate philanderer? An apostle of rectitude, or an inveterate roisterer? Was he moral or immoral? Honorable or dishonorable? Or was he simply a man, a prism of good and bad?

In 1888, President Cleveland was defeated in his bid for reelection by Benjamin Harrison; Cleveland won the popular vote but lost in the electoral college. He had refused to campaign, considering it beneath the dignity of the presidency to beg for support. In his final message to Congress, he gave the speech that I'd quoted to Franklin Fiske; that I quoted so often to myself as if I could gain strength from the fact that he had once harbored such notions: that he had noticed that trusts and corporations were becoming "the people's masters," that fortunes were being built "upon undue exactions from the masses."

But no changes resulted from his words, and soon he himself seemed to have forgotten them.

Out of office, Cleveland refused to move back to Buffalo. He was bitter. When he had won the presidency, the most aggressive office seekers had been from Buffalo, self-serving acquaintances and even friends pressuring him for bounty, for a share in the spoils. He refused to give that bounty; after all, he had run on a platform of reform. As a result, these supposed friends neglected to invite him to their homes during his first summer vacation as president. This wounded and offended him. Of course he had other reasons for refusing to move back to his hometown. He hated the city now, hated it with an unforgiving passion because in Buffalo his enemies had unearthed the stories of Mrs. Halpin and her child, of his draft avoidance and his easy living. He blamed the city when his own deeds came back to haunt him.

So the former president and First Lady settled in New York City, where Cleveland became "of counsel" to the firm of Bangs, Stetson, Tracy, and MacVeagh. The "Stetson" was Francis Lynde Stetson, J. P. Morgan's legal counsel, and Cleveland and Stetson were close friends. Each morning Cleveland rode the omnibus to work while quietly, far in the background, his supporters laid the plans for another run for the presidency.

In May of 1891, after much effort, Cleveland's true Buffalo friends, among them the men of my board, especially Milburn, Urban, and Wilcot—those who had no need to share in any spoils—finally persuaded him to visit his hometown. They would ensure that the city redeemed itself for its overly aggressive seekers of personal gain. Now the city would make amends for the rumors that his political opponents hadn't allowed to be forgotten. The city would show him its true, self-less adoration—and prepare a golden place for itself in the second Cleveland administration that people assumed was at hand.

The former president traveled to Buffalo by train with a few assistants and friends but without his wife, who reportedly awaited the birth of their first child. A boisterous contingent of well-wishers met him at the station and brought him in pomp to the new, elegant Iroquois Hotel. While in the city, Cleveland visited old cronies, gave speeches, made time for a fishing expedition to one of the forested islands in the Niagara River. And he attended an evening reception and buffet dinner at the Cary residence at 184 Delaware Avenue. At this reception I made his acquaintance.

The Cary residence: a rambling, ivy-encrusted Gothic pile presided over by the widowed Julia Love Cary and her younger sister, Miss Maria Love. Although the house truly belonged to Mrs. Cary (having been built by her now-deceased husband), somehow it had come to be known as "Miss Love's house." Throughout the wide hallways, Cary and Love ancestors smiled wistfully at one another from oil portraits and from marble busts placed atop heavy pedestals; so weary were their expressions that I often thought the ancestors would have been happier locked in the attic. The appurtenances of wealth filled the house: carved fireplaces, mahogany wainscotting, high ceilings with intricate plasterwork, a colonnaded music room.

But there was nothing staid about "184." Indeed any approach to the front door was greeted by squealing children and barking dogs. Julia Cary had seven children, who by 1891 were beginning to marry (they married Rumseys, mostly) and have children of their own. All these children knew other children, and one and all they came to "184," creating an atmosphere of barely contained chaos. They adored their aunt Maria. Miss Love permitted excesses among her own young that she would never tolerate among the needy souls at the Fitch Crèche.

The reception. I see the scene once more. I see Julia Love Cary, a haglike woman who too often wears a tiara. I see Maria Love, behaving as if *she* were the president. And I see you, Stephen Grover Cleveland, standing on the receiving line. You are more handsome than I expected. You are charming. Jovial. Polished and glowing, with a joke or a quip for everyone. Yes, you are justly renowned for your fine sense of humor, for your good-natured teasing. Your voice is deep and strong. You reach out to shake my hand. You place your left hand atop our linked hands, rubbing my knuckles. Your skin is soft. Your eyes—cliche that it is—twinkle with friendliness. Power surrounds you like an aura, and you take pleasure in treating the aura lightly. Your associates stand ready to fulfill any wish. They call you "Mr. President." Everyone stares at you, even as they pretend to gaze at their companions. Everyone pauses to overhear your jokes. Everyone says how well you look. You're in your fifties now, but you look better than ever, or so they say. Married life must agree with you, they say—and there's a secret pride in this because you married Frances Folsom, one of our local princesses, and now her vibrant glamour is mixed with your power.

After shaking your hand, I circulate among the guests. As a relative newcomer to the city, surrounded by people who've known one another for years, I feel a twinge of nervousness at such receptions. I'm still simply a teacher; Miss Love was kind to invite me. I wear what I think of as modified exotic garb, a nearly off-the-shoulder dress of claret-colored silk and a fringed embroidered shawl. I'm grateful when Dexter Rumsey (even then on the Macaulay board) comes to my side and offers me his companionship, publicly displaying his approval. Maria Love's grandnieces and nephews, known for their mischief, live up to their reputation and let the birds out of the cages in the conservatory. Canaries circle overhead, diving down to steal crumbs off our plates, adding to the general mirth.

After completing your duty on the receiving line, you wander from group to group. All in the room are alert to where you are at every moment. Suddenly Dexter Rumsey, beside me, says in his fatherly way, "You should have your chance to chat with the President, Louisa. Young people do enjoy such things, I've observed." He sighs with mock weariness. "I myself am feeling a bit beyond presidents. But come along, then."

How kind he is to me. He leads me to a group that includes attorney John Milburn and his wife, Patty—and you. He explains to you that I am a teacher, come to Buffalo from Wellesley College. You focus on this for a moment, and then the conversation moves on.

Standing there listening, at first I notice only Patty, with her dark eyes, fine clothes, and an unexpected look of apprehension that now and again flickers across her face. Patty once taught school in Batavia, a village about forty miles east of Buffalo; now she gives money to the Free Kindergarten Association, which provides schooling for poor children. I met Patty when I first moved to Buffalo, and I thought she would be a natural ally for me, a friend even. But instead she seems always to focus her eyes just slightly away from mine. She befriends only the upper echelon, the wives of her husband's clients. Her home is celebrated for its gracious hospitality; for fine food, warm fires, and scintillating conversation. The poet Matthew Arnold once stayed with the Milburns, at the suggestion of the city fathers.

Perhaps Patty will not meet my gaze because I remind her of her alternate fate, of what she could too easily have become: a spinster schoolteacher like me, one step away from poverty. Patty has no trouble, however, focusing on your eyes, Stephen Grover Cleveland. You relate for her benefit the story of how in years past her husband always carried law books beneath his arm when walking on the street. "I used to wonder if he was trying to absorb law through his armpits!" you jest, your voice booming. We laugh heartily; your laugh is the most hearty of all. No doubt you are remembering that John Milburn was your most staunch local defender during the Mrs. Halpin crisis. Others join our group. You step away to greet a new arrival. Many guests move into the dining room to partake of the buffet. Groups form and re-form until the moment comes—Dexter Rumsey turning aside to consult his brother—when all at once you and I are alone.

Possibly you noticed when you clasped my hand on the receiving line, or when we stood with the Milburns, that I wore no wedding band. Francesca Coatsworth is one of the few other young women here without a wedding band, and already most people assume that she and I maintain a *ménage*. You, however, know nothing of these local assumptions. You speak of education for women. Of civil service reform and tenement house reform, of settlement houses, education for the poor, milk carts outside public schools, a gradual end to child labor. Bit by bit you use my own passions to lure me until, in the most gracious phrases imaginable, you invite me to your suite at the

Iroquois Hotel. To continue our discussion without the pressure of your public responsibilities. You are formulating policies on these issues; you are looking ahead; you need knowledgeable assistance, private advice.

I have often wondered: If I'd had other passions, would you have discovered them just as quickly and used them against me? If I'd been a woman of society, would you have professed a passion for fox hunting? Had I been an artist, would an analysis of the latest Saint-Gaudens monument been your means of seduction? If Francesca had been your quarry, would you have shared your excitement for the Home Insurance Building in Chicago, or the new Wainwright Building in St. Louis? Was every step that you took with me a false one? Or can I cling to the idea that you admired me just a bit? That in some way I was special?

At that moment I certainly felt special. More special than I had ever felt in my life. You thought that I could help you. Around us, everyone glanced your way, as if you were the sun.

What is the measure of a woman?

I was in my midtwenties then, without family, without private means, dependent on my own work for my support; college educated, which in itself pegged me as unmarriageable (despite the fact that your beautiful Frances Folsom had been a college girl). Already I was called a bluestocking.

And I was an innocent. As a girl I'd always been told that men would attempt to take advantage of me—but you had been the *president*, you were married, you were much older than I; I trusted you as if you were my father. I didn't hear the code words you used, I heard only that you wanted to fulfill the promise of your own best instincts. You wanted to do good for the country—and I would help you. Even Patty Milburn, she of the fine clothes and warm hospitality, even *she* you did not ask for help.

You glanced around the room with a touch of suspicion. "Don't tell anyone," you said lightly. "I don't want any jealousies. Or anyone trying to tag along."

This last was said jokingly, but I knew what you meant: You still harbored bitterness over the press of office seekers among your Buffalo acquaintances; of people thinking only of themselves and of the spoils you could dispense.

"I should be allowed *some* privacy." Warmly, you laughed.

Of course you should be allowed privacy; how else could you formulate new policy?

"Don't worry, I'll manage this." How pleasant you were. "Go off now and talk to your friends. I'll send someone for you later."

You spoke as if I were a child.

The former president traveled in the company of his close friend Richard Watson Gilder, the editor of the *Century* magazine. Gilder was a far different type from Cleveland: slight, cultivated, effete. In addition to his editorial skills, Gilder was the prolific author of endlessly praised, pretentious poetry. He nurtured a concern for the body politic. He and Cleveland had crusaded together for civil service reform. Gilder hungered after Cleveland's every word.

Toward the end of the reception, just after the president had said his farewells (of course no one would leave until he left), Mr. Gilder came to me. With a slight bow and a gaze that went over my left shoulder, he told me that he would be delighted to escort me to my next appointment. He would meet me outside. His carriage driver wore a white carnation—I should look for that.

I had no trouble finding the proper carriage. We took a roundabout route to the Iroquois, I assumed to give the president time to return to the hotel. During the drive, I attempted to converse with Gilder. Enthusiastically I said, "Mr. Cleveland is concerned about tenement house reform."

"Oh, I dare say," Gilder replied indifferently. With deep absorption he stared out the carriage window, discouraging further conversation. Part of me realized even then that his indifference was toward me, not toward the issue that he himself vehemently endorsed in his writings. I understood even then that he would extend himself only to someone who mattered. But I easily dismissed Richard Watson Gilder; after all, he was not the one invited to consult privately with the president. Most likely he feigned indifference to conceal his jealousy.

At a certain moment best comprehended by himself, Gilder gave a

signal to the driver. Several minutes later the carriage pulled up to the
back entrance of the Iroquois Hotel, far from the Beaux-Arts flourishes
and lurking journalists at the front.

"If I were you, I'd place your shawl over your head," he said before
getting out of the carriage. And that was the last he said. I assumed he
had an overdeveloped sense of propriety. Nonetheless I draped the
shawl stylishly around my head and shoulders as if I were protecting
myself from a rainstorm. I followed Gilder into the hotel and along a
circuitous route that took us past ironing rooms and pantries. We
walked three flights up the back stairs and entered a long hall punctu-
ated by imposing doorways. Gilder hurried along the hall, checking the
numbers. Finally he knocked at a certain door, opened it without waiting for a response, and motioned me inside. Quietly he shut the door
behind him.

I was in an unlit entryway.

"Come along then," I heard the president say from a room at the
end of the entry gallery, and I walked toward his voice.

The suite's opulent sitting room was decorated with heavy curtains
and hand-painted wallpaper, feathery forest scenes in the style of
Fragonard. The former president looked up from a newspaper. He had
changed, taking off his shoes and his jacket and tie. He wore a silk paisley dressing gown over his trousers and open shirt. This surprised me.
But then I realized he would want to relax after his day's full schedule.
There was a glass of brandy on the well-polished table beside him. He
smoked a cigar. The night was warm and humid. The air in the room
was oppressive. I felt pressure in my chest from breathing the cigar
smoke. Not knowing what else to do, I stayed near the door.

"Well," he said, looking me up and down, evaluating me. From the
look that came into his face, he seemed to relish what he saw. "Good
evening." He stretched out the words meaningfully—although for what
meaning I had no idea. Stubbing out the cigar in the crystal ashtray, he
got up, lumbering, and padded toward me across the thick carpet, the
silk of his dressing gown rustling.

I stepped back, to the wall beside the door.

"You're certainly a beauty," he said.

"Oh. Thank you." I flushed in embarrassment. I felt pleased by the compliment but startled that he would notice my appearance. I still didn't understand. My bewilderment seemed to please him.

"First-timer, are we?" he asked, smiling. I didn't know what he meant. I was unprepared when he took my shoulders and pulled me close and kissed me, filling my mouth with the acrid taste of cigars. There was a line of perspiration along the top of his mustache, and it dampened my cheeks.

I tried to push him away. "What are you doing?" I choked.

But my pushing only made him tighten his grip on my shoulders. "Playful, are we?" he asked, not displeased.

"I'd better go," I blurted out. "This isn't—I didn't—I'd better go." He pressed me hard against the wall. He was big, so big—Big Steve, his friends had called him when he was young—and I struggled but couldn't escape. His body surrounded me like a supple barrier, present wherever I turned.

"What lovely eyes you have." Holding my chin, he moved my head slightly back and forth. "Dark blue, eh?"

I couldn't respond.

He gazed at me indulgently. "Now, now, my dear. Don't be like that." He touched his forehead against mine, rubbing for a moment. "And besides, wouldn't you like to know what it's like? What the poets sing about?" He nuzzled my neck, whispering in limpid tones. "Haven't you ever wondered?" He kissed along the line where my cheek met my hair. "Any girl as pretty as you deserves to know everything life can offer, eh?"

"Please. Let me go," I begged.

He patted my hair. "Go where?" His touch was gentle. "Mmmm? Where exactly is it that you want to go?" His voice was tender. "Do you want to go running down the hall and into the lobby where everyone will see you? It's very late, for a young lady like yourself to be out alone. And in a hotel, of all places." He rubbed his private self against my leg. "What would the reporters think? And I'm sure the reporters are still there—they always keep a close eye on me when I travel. The local reporters, I mean. The ones who'd have no trouble determining your identity." I felt myself about to cry. Tears caught in my throat. "And even if you escape the lobby unscathed, how will you get home?" He rubbed his private self harder, adjusting his body so that his bulky middle didn't interfere. "How would you find a hansom driver who wouldn't talk? Or will you walk home, do you think, miles and miles through the streets?" Again I struggled against him, and he grabbed my wrists, hard. "No, no. You stay now, and I'll make sure you get home safely. And secretly." Letting go of my wrists, he put his arms around me and pulled me tighter against him. His breath was warm upon my ear. "And really, my dear"—now his forearms pressed against my back to hold me while his fingers pulled down my hair—"I think it'll do you good. No one will ever know. I promise you. You'll never be put to shame. It's too late to change your mind, anyway." He rubbed harder, his legs entrapping me. "Too late."

And he was right. How could I get home without his help? Without his help, I would be compromised beyond repair. I would lose my job and I would never find another—not teaching, that is. Any dream I'd ever had would be over. I hated myself for my ignorance. All of this was my fault: I hadn't known the code, I hadn't understood the subtext of his words. It was too late now, to go back. His promise of secrecy was all I could rely on to protect me.

I stopped fighting him. I became impassive, like a small, trapped animal.

"So." In his pleasure he lengthened the word. He kissed away a tear upon my eyelid. "Good girl." Nonetheless, when he pressed his lips to mine, pushing his tongue against my teeth, instinctively I turned away, his saliva leaving a band across my cheek. Laughing he caught my face in the palm of his hand. "Still shy?" He tapped my nose with one tender fingertip. "No need to be shy with me."

He guided me to the bedroom. When my footsteps became reluctant, he gripped my wrist and twisted my arm behind me—laughing still, as if it were a game, my resistance a show that pleased him more and more. The bedside lamp was lit. The bed had a brocaded canopy.

It wasn't necessary for me to undress completely, that would take too much time, he said. With hurried fingers, he fumbled with the buttons of my dress, letting the silk fall to the floor as he pulled at my underclothes. The petticoats and the corset stayed on. He took off his trousers and undergarments, taking the time to fold them over a chair. He left on his shirt and dressing gown. Then he folded down the bedspread, keeping it even and neat. He lay upon his back and smiled at me encouragingly. But when I didn't join him, he sat up suddenly and grabbed me. "None of that now," he said, his smile gone—but gone only for an instant. In a tone that could only be described as loving, he added, "It's natural to feel nervous the first time. But it won't be so bad."

He moved me into position atop his legs. He put my hands around his private self, his hands over mine. He made my hands rub him, up and down.

"There you go, there you go," he said, his voice gentle, his grip crippling. Up and down, up and down, his hands over mine. Abruptly he placed his hands behind my head and pushed my head down—I didn't know what he wanted, didn't even know what he was thinking. In confusion I glanced at his half-closed eyes. He grunted in response. He shifted, pulling my body into position over him and pressing me down upon him. There was resistance, beyond my control, my body not opening to him. I had no notion what to do. He was displeased. His smile turned to a grimace. He used his spit to ease his way, gripping my hips and moving me to his exact pleasure.

I wondered then, as he pressed inside me, more than hurting me, *this* is the great and hidden knowledge of life? *This?* This is what men and women have whispered about and created elaborate rituals to sanctify? Is this how it is with your wife, Frances, she who came to you as innocent as I, she who claims publicly to adore you? Is this what she adores? Your stomach like a rubbery cushion, propping her up? Or are you different with her? Is it possible to be different?

I stared at the brocaded canopy. I didn't know how long it would take. But suddenly he gave a self-satisfied sigh, and it was over. He rested, smirking. Sweat glistened on his forehead. I didn't move.

After a few minutes, the president instructed me to leave. He was finished. Besides, he didn't want to keep his assistant secretary, who would take me home, up late when they had another busy day tomorrow. "And we can't rely on poor Gilder to get you home," he added. "*He's* undoubtedly off somewhere resting his *nerves*." The president chuckled as if this were a very good joke.

Delicately, he pushed me off him. When I stood, the offal of his body flowed down my thighs. I dared not make a show of wiping it away. The smell of it made me gag. I pressed the back of my hand against my face to block the smell. I dressed as quickly as I could, my fingers shaking. This time he didn't help me.

An overly thin young man with ruddy cheeks and glasses waited outside the suite. The assistant secretary. Without looking at me, he led me to a carriage that had pulled in close to the hotel's back door. For the sake of anonymity, the carriage dropped me at the deserted park, leaving me not far from the lake where one day Karl Speyer would drown. From there I walked home through deserted streets, trying to steel myself against tears. Tears would do me no good now. Besides, I had saved myself: I should be proud, I told myself over and over, defending myself against despair, fighting off self-pity. I had saved myself. I gripped my shawl across my chest as if it could protect me.

In those days, I lived on the top floor of a house on the far side of Elmwood Avenue. My landlady was an elderly woman of genteel poverty; my rent allowed her to maintain her home. Her hearing was such that she never noticed my late-night footsteps.

After that evening in 1891, I never tried to write to the President. He must have understood me well. Too well.

Yes, you must have seen my type before, Stephen Grover Cleveland, and known that I would never betray you. That I would never blackmail you or attempt to contact your wife, because I had too much to lose. I had a position to maintain, and any scandal would hurt me more than you. Most likely from the moment of our introduction, you knew that I was safe. Yes, I protected you well, Stephen Grover Cleveland—mayor, governor, president.

As the days and weeks and years went by, gradually I found a way to live with my anguish. Often I was barely aware of it; it resurfaced only when a man looked at me with affection, approached me to offer love, the way Franklin Fiske had on the stairs at Francesca's. Over the years there'd been several such men: a history professor at the university; a physician-researcher at the General Hospital; the headmaster of a New England boys' school, whom I'd met at a conference in Boston; even a young architect at Louise Bethune's firm. From the first hint of their interest, the pain, the shock, and the fear swept over me once more. Panicked, I took refuge in my professional position as I pushed the man away. During my times of composure, I forced myself to think of that night as a scientific experiment: I had learned, as you had said I would; that what I learned was disappointing—well, what more can be expected from an experiment? Not joy. Not comfort or reassurance. I had learned something else too: that I must never be trapped by ignorance in anything I did. I became ever-alert, ever-watchful, ever-searching for the code words by which society functioned, for the subtle nods and lifting eyebrows that signified everything—but only for those who understood. I made it my overriding goal always to understand.

And then there was Grace. Unforeseen. Unforeseeable. How far-fetched, the idea that those few minutes amid the cigar smoke shadows could produce the miracle of Grace. Within three months I realized that I must make a plan.

My plan included the protection of you. In those days, in spite of everything, I still had high hopes for you; I blamed myself and my own ignorance for what had happened between us. I still saw the future with your name emblazoned upon it. Yet I realized that even as I protected you, I must protect myself from you. The fate of Mrs. Halpin was clear in my mind, and it terrified me. There must be no opportunity for you to steal my child, to put me into an asylum. I would look after myself better than that unfortunate woman had. Furthermore I knew that your 'friends' would never allow you to face another moral scandal; they would resolve any such scandals themselves, silently and lethally, before there was even a whisper of public exposure.

This was the terror I faced. An appearance of normality must be maintained at all costs. There was no question of my starting the autumn term. I requested a leave of absence for the coming year from the Macaulay board. This would also give me the following summer away; other faculty members had taken such sabbaticals. I explained to the board that I wanted to spend time in New York City investigating new trends in education for women. I also wanted to travel to the Continent, where I'd never been. I wanted to renew myself among the cathedrals of France and the ruins of Greece.

How touched the men of the board were, how excited, to contemplate the increased knowledge I would bring to their daughters. Not only did they approve my request with more alacrity than I had expected, they awarded me, unasked, a generous study grant. A more than generous study grant. And with their money I went to New York and found a sanctuary.

When I was at Wellesley, a well-known woman, a Wellesley graduate—never mind her name—had come to lecture. She was working to establish a settlement house on the Lower East Side of Manhattan to help the immigrant poor. Her lecture had been inspiring. She'd invited us to join her if we shared her passion. After the lecture I spoke to her at length, but my path after graduation led me to Buffalo, not New York. Nevertheless I kept up with her work and her success through Wellesley publications. She now lived at the settlement house with like-minded women and devoted herself to teaching and charity.

She was the person I approached for shelter. I wanted to take refuge with someone who was a stranger—not someone who might care about me or ask me questions. Just someone who would give me a room and a job, and direct me to a physician when my time came. And so there, in New York, I became simply one more sad lady in a long gray coat, making my way through streets crowded with people who had no interest in me whatsoever.

Day after day I despaired over what would happen to the baby that was growing within me. Certainly I would lose my position if the board learned the truth. Without a job, without family, without money of my own, I had no means to raise a child. But I could never give the baby to an orphanage and surrender my claim on him, or her, forever. Unreasonable plans jostled in my mind. I could pretend to be a widow, change my name, move to San Francisco or Vancouver or Guadalajara, for surely teachers were needed in such places. And yet . . . the child and I might be safe in such a place, but life would be hard; harder than I wanted it to be for my baby.

One day when I was walking along the Battery, staring at the ships in the harbor, an idea came to me:

Some months before I met Grover Cleveland, my best friend, Margaret, had confided to me her despair that after several years of marriage she'd not yet had a child. Suddenly the solution I'd been yearning for spread before me like a flash of inspiration: Margaret and Tom would become the parents of my child. I would return to my position in Buffalo, where I would watch, and help, my child grow. Margaret and I shared the same values, the same ethics. She was generous, tender, and loving. Of course I knew Margaret better than I knew Tom, but Tom had always seemed to me upright and moral. I admired his courage and all he had achieved. Margaret and Tom loved each other; their marriage was stable and happy. And of course they were both rich. Their child's every material need would be fulfilled. Margaret and Tom would create a mirror image of how I would have raised the child myself, if only circumstances had been different.

I wrote to Margaret from New York and said that the leader of the settlement house where I was staying (while conducting my board-sanctioned research into trends in education for women) knew of an innocent girl who had found herself in an unfortunate position. This girl was from a good family (not from among the immigrant hordes one might associate with my settlement-house acquaintance), and she hoped to find an equally good family to raise the child she would bear but could not keep.

After a few weeks, Margaret wrote back to say that she and Tom, after much discussion, were interested in adopting this child. Margaret had some questions, however, which had to be addressed before plans could move forward. Was I certain that the parents of this child were not Italian? Not Spanish, Greek, Russian—was I certain that the parents had no link (except one of philanthropy) to the immigrant communities of the city? Would this child grow to have Mediterranean-type skin? Did the child have Jewish blood? (She did not mention Negro blood, which to her must have been beyond imagining.)

I was saddened by this letter even as I responded to it with reassurances. Despite her independent nature and her work among the poor, Margaret harbored, like an unerasable part of her soul, all the prejudices of her class. But who among us does not? Who among us, if we strip away the veils of self-righteousness, would take the chance she and Tom were taking without at least a modicum of reassurance?

To answer Margaret, I spun a tale. I created a play in which I was a character, although not the lead character. I created the innocent girl who had found herself in this unfortunate situation. I described my visit to the girl's home. She turned out to be a child, really, no more than fifteen. Since the deaths of her parents, she had lived with her grandparents in a substantial home in the East 70s, off Fifth Avenue (how much more authentic, I told myself, than a house actually on Fifth). The grandparents were kindhearted. They blamed themselves for what had happened to the girl. They were telling their friends that the girl suffered from consumption. When the girl's time neared, they would take her out of town and tell everyone that they were traveling in search of a cure.

I related to Margaret every detail of my visit: being ushered in by the butler; walking up the curving staircase; meeting the grandmother, whose family name I recognized; entering the girl's bedroom, where she lay upon a canopy bed, surrounded by dolls, blond hair curling around her face.

Perhaps I overdid it. But so clear was my vision that I couldn't help but add details, more and more. The pastel drawings of children on the walls. The pile of books on the bedside table. The girl's modesty, her obvious intelligence and wish to do the best she could for her child.

The father of her child . . . well, this was more problematic, I realized as I prepared my letter. A bounder, yes. A man who took advantage of a young girl . . . who could it have been?

All at once I knew. Of course! The girl's older sister was married to a member of the English aristocracy. "It is my understanding," I wrote to Margaret, "that during a recent holiday, this so-called gentleman took advantage of his young sister-in-law, then returned in due course to his English estates with his wife, who, I am assured, is ignorant to this day of what transpired."

Perfect. A sweet American girl taken advantage of by a cad who is nonetheless an English nobleman. With misgivings I remembered after I posted the letter that Tom had been born an Irish Catholic, not likely to respect the English aristocracy; but he never protested, and maybe he appreciated the irony.

At any rate, this was the provenance I created for the child I bore to President Grover Cleveland.

My story had the desired effect. Margaret wrote back to say she and Tom would be very pleased indeed to adopt this infant. She would begin telling her friends and family that she was with child at last. She would wear a pillow around her stomach and increase the stuffing bit by bit. Embracing her latest adventure, she made a continuing joke in her letters about the need to reshape this ever-enlarging pillow with scientific care.

Only Dr. Perlmutter knew the truth. She had persuaded him to play along because society would think something amiss if the esteemed doctor were not seen entering and leaving her house with a certain frequency during her confinement. She and Tom had already decided on names, she wrote: If the child were a boy, they would name him Thomas, after his new father. If it were a girl, they would name her Grace, for by the grace of God they had found her.

When my time came, my acquaintance from the settlement house took pity on me. She found a local doctor. She secured a place of privacy for the birth itself, which went as well as could be expected. She traveled with my infant daughter and a wet nurse to meet Dr. Perlmutter in Albany. He took the infant with him to Buffalo, accompanied by a new wet nurse whom he had hired in Albany. The Albany nurse looked after Grace in a second-class compartment while the doctor relaxed in first class, telling one or two friends he met along the way that he had been visiting a cousin in the state capital. The nurse returned to Albany on the same train. Dr. Perlmutter knew the infant was intended for Margaret and Tom, but he did not know that I was its mother.

When I had recovered from the birth, I went to Europe. I visited the places I had dreamed of and felt as if I didn't see them at all. My attention was focused on imagining the baby now ensconced in the mansion at the corner of Lincoln Parkway and Forest Avenue.

When finally I returned to Buffalo, shortly before the start of school in September of 1892, a letter awaited me from the board. In formal language the letter informed me that upon the retirement at the end of the year of the now-elderly clergyman who had established Macaulay nearly forty years before, I would become headmistress; I would move into the house next to the school.

I barely glanced at the letter, so eager was I to see Grace. At the Sinclair home, the maid ushered me up to the library. Margaret sat in a rocking chair, the baby in her arms. My baby. Grace. I was startled. She was so much bigger than the newborn I had last seen. Now eight months old, she was round and tumbly as a bubble. Her eyes were still blue, her hair still blond. Her baby clothes were soft and fine, decorated with lace. She smiled and giggled at her mother. At Margaret.

Happiness glowed on Margaret's face. "Don't tell me anything more about her parents, Louisa. I want to pretend she has no parents at all, that she was brought by angels. In fact, she *was* brought by angels."

Margaret snuggled Grace close against her neck. "You'll be her godmother, won't you, Louisa?"

I felt dizzy. I had lost forever the right to hold Grace that close, as much as I yearned to—and how I yearned to press that round baby body against my heart; to feel that smooth skin against my cheek. I was consumed by the urge to grab her—to run down the stairs with her and out the door, my future and hers be damned. Even if we were in the poorhouse, at least we would be together. We *must* be together.

No. Focusing all my strength, I steadied myself. Grace's future was the only one that mattered, and her future had to be here, where she could have everything she needed. Not simply money, but family too: a mother *and* a father.

Dreamily Margaret repeated, "Yes? You'll be her godmother?" I nodded my assent. I knew then that I would never tell Margaret the truth. I would never step into the bond of her love for Grace, because if I did, I might hurt Grace . . . Grace, whom I must now protect whatever the cost. I watched Margaret cuddle her. I loved Grace, and also I loved my friend. My best friend. I would never bring her guilt or anguish by revealing the true parentage of the child she cradled. Now, for the first time, and forever, there would be a secret between us.

I knew that Grace would be sent to Macaulay. I knew that throughout her childhood and youth, I would be in charge of her education: seeing her every day, watching her grow, training her mind, with luck becoming her friend. Closer to her perhaps, as she got older, than a "mother" ever could be. I would be the one she would confide in. Perhaps. Perhaps.

And so our lives would pass. Grace would grow up to be smart, beautiful, confident, and happy. If she wished, she would go to college. With luck, she would return to Buffalo to marry. She would have children of her own. As I grew old, I would be always with her, she always with me. Her children would be my grandchildren. I saw no other future, nor could I imagine one.

And so our lives passed. Margaret adored Grace. Tom was a wonderful father. Grace did well in her studies. She learned to ride. To play the piano. To draw. As I had hoped, I was part of her daily life. The bond between Margaret and Grace grew ever stronger. Although I was outside that special bond, nonetheless Margaret, Tom, and Grace made me feel like a member of their family, which was enough; which had to be enough.

Then one day Margaret died. And now Grace talked of dying too.

Chapter Twelve

N ext item: Presentation by Mrs. William Talbert." In his role as chief officer of the Pan-American Exposition, John G. Milburn tapped his gavel. The sound echoed through the Buffalo Club's unadorned public meeting room, where Milburn and his fellow commissioners sat behind simple tables on the dais. The day was unusually warm for April; although the windows were thrown open, the curtains hung limp in the quiet air.

The room was sparsely filled and most of the petitioners looked fidgety, coming as they were to discuss problems. We'd waited over an hour through discussions of faulty plastering, misaligned statuary, and leaky flower urns for Mrs. Talbert's name to be called. Everyone looked a bit sallow, which wasn't surprising: This was called the Yellow Room for the all-important reason that its walls and curtains were yellow. Large enough for communal meetings, the Yellow Room was hidden away at the back of the building on the ground floor. Women were permitted in this room if business warranted; women were presumed to find the color yellow soothing, although I certainly didn't. Perhaps I was more manly than I gave myself credit for, I'd thought as I took my seat with Mrs. Talbert when the meeting was first called to order; I much preferred the bracing opulence of the intimate luncheon room upstairs where the Macaulay board gathered.

While we'd waited in the muggy heat, listening to the plasterer enumerate his excuses, my mind had begun to wander . . . to Tom. I recoiled at the memory of our encounter in the sleigh outside school. Knowledge, of course, is power. By letting me know that he had guessed my secret, Tom had assured my silence about Speyer's visit more securely than any amount of money could have done. Nonetheless I surmised that I still had room to maneuver, for although

Tom had guaranteed that I would not go to the police, I continued to harbor facts that he wanted to suppress. There were still no official conclusions on Speyer's death; until there were, Tom's position was precarious, whether he was actually involved with the death or not.

I pondered, not for the first time, whether I'd lost all sense of proportion. Perhaps Tom's explanation of his motives regarding Speyer was truthful. Perhaps I should simply be grateful that he'd kept my name out of the newspapers, and listen to the intuitive voice inside me that said he was no murderer. Maybe he'd shared his supposition about Grace and me simply to bring us together—to bring him and me together, that is, and my suspicions were merely another proof of my panicked determination to push away any man who approached me with affection. Maybe he'd believed my lame explanation about the resemblance between Grace and me, and I was the one, knowing the truth, who couldn't let the matter go . . .

"Mrs. Talbert, welcome," Mr. Milburn said, capturing my attention. The porter ushered Mrs. Talbert to the table and chair strategically placed before the dais. "Please, make yourself comfortable," Milburn continued, his demeanor warm, his tone unctuous. With his bold, handsome features, Milburn looked like a statue of a Roman emperor; from his elevated position as president of the Pan-Am, he gazed upon his subjects with benevolent pride.

Mrs. Talbert took her position with her head high and her shoulders straight, her face grave and reflective, as if she were a minister coming to the lectern in church. Her dress was somber yet rich. She placed her notes upon the table but she did not sit, nor did she glance at her papers. The dozen or so businessmen arrayed on the dais wouldn't have known that she was nervous. Only I knew, because she had told me so during the ride over in her carriage. She had offered (graciously, for it was out of her way) to pick me up. I could only pray that she was right to come here instead of approaching Miss Love or Mr. Rumsey privately. Either way, time was running out for her: The exposition would open officially on May 20, and although some of the exhibitions would not be complete by the twentieth, plans needed to be well along by now, certainly.

"Thank you, Mr. Milburn and gentlemen of the committee." Her

deep, sonorous voice carried throughout the room. She paused, looking at the men one by one, garnering their attention. "I bring to you
today a question of business. Yes, business." She nodded and looked
around, as if to confirm with everyone that business was the most
important question that could ever be contemplated.

"In this mighty city we are now engaged, one and all, from every
race, from every background, in an exalted endeavor: the creation of
the greatest exposition in the history of our nation. There is hard work
involved, there is sacrifice. But we shall achieve our goal." She glanced
at the commissioners mischievously, as if sharing their secrets. "How
much more glorious our efforts will be if the deity sees fit to reward our
sacrifices." Suddenly she smiled. She knew that for the honor of serving
as commissioners, all these men had invested heavily in the exposition;
the honor of serving of course would be rendered even more wonderful
if their investments returned solid profits.

"To this end, with the needs of the city as a whole foremost in my
mind, I have arranged for the National Association of Colored Women
to hold its biennial convention in Buffalo in July and conduct its work
amid the splendors of our exposition city. The most eminent among the
Negro race will participate in this convention. We expect several hundred attendees and their families. Large revenues will flow into the city
from the generous leaders of my race." She paused, possibly waiting for
a hint of gratitude; instead the men were impassive.

"But"—her voice rose—"what will these leaders see when they
tour our great exposition? Will they see monuments to the achievements of our race? Will they see recognition of our goals for the
future? Will they be compelled to visit the exposition again and
again—paying their fees each day—to absorb all that can be learned
from such an educational presentation?" She glanced around in
reproach. "No," she said with dramatic force. "They will see the 'original' Uncle Tom's Cabin. They will see 'old plantation life'; 'happy darkies' singing and dancing; they will be offered miniature cotton bales as
'souvenirs.'" She gazed at the commissioners with a look of profound
indignation.

"At the Paris Exposition of 1900, there was a comprehensive exhibition of our achievements as a race, and that exhibition received

highest honors. It was prepared by my esteemed friend and colleague Mr. W. E. B. DuBois. I am certain Mr. DuBois could be persuaded not simply to recreate but to improve upon that presentation here—if he were given a place for it. Are we to be outdone by Paris? Are we to let a European city take precedence over an American city?" Disdain filled her voice. "Never! *Our* city must be at the forefront! Furthermore, what is the example we wish to give the world as we face the twentieth century? How do we want Buffalo to be seen in the eyes of the world? As bigoted and backward, or tolerant and forward-looking? Gentlemen, on behalf of my race I say to you, let us embrace the future together. Let us give a bold signal to the world that Buffalo has arrived!"

After a moment's pause, she sat down. I felt the urge to applaud but stifled it as the gentlemen on the dais maintained their impassivity. No one said a word. Milburn examined his notes. The silence continued. Finally Milburn looked up from his papers. "Thank you, Mrs. Talbert, for your strong presentation. We shall take your request under consideration."

She studied him, her head tilted, a querying smile on her lips.

"Thank you, Mrs. Talbert," he repeated with a touch of impatience.

She tapped her fingers on the table.

Milburn gave a small bow, his dismissal clear. "Thank you. Now then, the next item on our agenda." He shuffled the papers. "The plumbing difficulty at the Alt Nurnberg restaurant on the Midway."

A trembly high-pitched voice responded. "Yes, Mr. Milburn." The plumbing contractor, his plaid suit hanging on his thin frame, rose awkwardly and hurried from the back of the room.

Mary Talbert had no choice but to relinquish her seat at the table.

She strode far ahead of me down the front path, beneath the spreading elms, as if we hadn't come here together. Her carriage waited outside the gate. When he saw her, the driver, an elderly, fastidious Negro, got down and opened the door. Motioning him back to his position, she turned to me at last, standing beside the carriage and waiting for me to catch up. She breathed deeply, her chest rising.

"Mrs. Talbert," I said, before she could speak, "each time I complete a parley here with our esteemed male friends, I treat myself to a drink at the Twentieth Century Club among the comforts of our female compatriots. Would you like to join me? It's just up the street— it might have been constructed for this special purpose!" I made myself sound cheerful. I knew she had been humiliated, but what choice did we have now except to make the best of it? Although there'd never been a Negro guest at the Twentieth Century Club, my position was such that no one would challenge me if I brought her. Her visit would be at least a small effort in the right direction.

She stared at me, her expression intense and focused. Under her pressing gaze, I suddenly felt that I'd been transformed into her enemy.

"Why didn't you second my opinion?" she asked quietly. Too quietly, as if she were holding herself steady with a vise.

"There was no point to it. Nothing would have been gained. I would have been speaking out of turn."

"Out of turn. How many battles have been lost by people reluctant to speak 'out of turn.' To me, 'out of turn' is a self-serving and self-fulfilling prophecy. A fear of coming out on the losing side."

I chose to ignore her accusation. "Sometimes a public argument is not the best way to accomplish goals. Surely you know that. Sometimes—"

"This is a game to you, isn't it, Miss Barrett? A game of wheedling and dealing and going off to your club when you've met with a setback. If you had stood up for me the newspapers would have noticed. A point would have been made—and gained—even if the result were the same. You have the most extraordinary pulpit in the city, and you throw it away."

"My position is not a pulpit, Mrs. Talbert. And I hold my position at the sufferance of those men in there. If I lose my position, I have nothing."

"You underestimate yourself—purposefully, to abnegate your responsibilities. To rationalize your lack of action."

I waited until I could control my voice. "I will forgive you the ferocity of your words, Mrs. Talbert, because I know the justice of your goals. And I know that you could hardly express your anger toward the gentlemen in there, so perhaps it's easier to express it toward me."

Staring at me fixedly she did not reply.

"Before you condemn me, however, I would remind you that *you* have no position to lose. You live to fight another day from the resources of your husband's home. You travel from battle to battle in your private carriage, your driver at your command. As you would urge me to battle, so I would urge you to mercy."

"Yes, mercy," she said with irony. "Justice tempered by mercy—one of the laudable goals of our nation." She laughed bitterly. Then she said, "Well, I must get a report of this meeting into the newspapers. I must organize a letter-writing campaign. I must consider alternatives. I have no doubt that I shall be defeated, but even in losing battles there is victory if more allies are brought to the cause."

"I wish you luck."

For some reason she softened. "Why *don't* you challenge those men? Dare them to dismiss you. You may be surprised to find them reluctant to turn you away. You may finally discover your value to the community."

"I would like to help you, Mrs. Talbert. Truly I would."

"Then you must."

"I cannot."

"Your job is so precious you will not risk it? What is the worst that could happen to you? If you were dismissed here, you would find other cities eager to snap you up for the very independence you had shown. Our nation is wide with opportunity—for whites like you, I mean. There are many cities that would be pleased to welcome a woman of your experience. We in Buffalo may think ourselves the center of the world, but we are not."

"It's not arrogant provincialism that keeps me here. I'm committed to my girls; they too would lose if I lost. I'm sure you understand that education remains a tenuous privilege for them, whatever their class or race."

"There are schools for girls in many cities, and at Macaulay someone would be found to replace you."

"Nonetheless, I cannot go to another city. This is the city where I must remain."

She continued to gaze at me intently, and I fought the urge to look away. "So. Something personal holds you back," she said dismissively. "Woe to us all when we let the personal hold sway over the fight for justice."

With that bit of self-righteousness, she departed. I stood at the gates of the Buffalo Club and watched her carriage drive along Delaware Avenue toward downtown until it merged with all the others and I could find it no more.

Something personal. Yes.

Later that afternoon I stood at the balustrade on the second floor of the Macaulay School and watched the girls coming and going from their classes. They were a gently chattering stream of bows and ribbons, high-buttoned shoes, leather-bound notebooks, and sharpened pencils. Soon I would see her, the one I waited for, my heart skipping a beat at the flash of her smile. But at school I would make no special signal; I would show no one that I nurtured special feelings for her. Here she was one of many, and it was enough. Enough that I should come upon her by chance in the library, working with a partner, their notes for a research project (on the lives of polar bears, perhaps) scattered across a table. Enough, that on the way to the dining hall I might see her in a corridor sharing a joke with her friends. That when I observed a basketball game, she might be among the players, pleated uniform skirts flying with every jump. Or that when I looked out at the flagstoned central courtyard, I might see her reading on the marble bench beside the fountain, purple rhododendron flowering behind her. She was everywhere, filling the school I had made for her.

My school. My refuge. Away from Mary Talbert and crusades I could not join. Away from Thomas Sinclair and his steady, observant eyes. Away from Franklin Fiske and his theories and accusations.

Here I was safe, and here I could make her safe. My daughter.

Chapter Thirteen

"Miss Barrett, we have a problem," declared the mother of Abigail Rushman. Well, I appreciated people coming to the point, particularly in view of how rare that was in the circles I frequented. Still, it was nonetheless surprising.

Mr. and Mrs. Rushman were unlike their daughter. Ostentatious and flamboyant, they had entered my office with a flourish. Mrs. Rushman prolonged the flourish with an extended unwrapping of fur boas, worn even though the weather was now past the point of such trappings. But fur boas impressed no one if they were in the closet. It was the day after my visit to the Buffalo Club with Mary Talbert, and I wasn't in the mood for fools.

The Rushmans were new to Buffalo. They owned a group of five- and ten-cent dry goods stores, called F. E. Rushman, which had proliferated throughout Ohio and western New York. There were rumors, which I'd heard via Francesca, that Rushman was the Anglicization of a long and unpronounceable German name. But Mr. and Mrs. Rushman didn't appear to be immigrants themselves. They were stalwart supporters of the socially prominent Westminster Presbyterian Church— although again, rumor purported that once upon a time, in an unidentified portion of the Midwest, they'd attended (let us gasp together!) a *Lutheran* church.

Mrs. Rushman sat down opposite my desk, and her husband stood beside her.

"Our daughter—" Mr. Rushman began.

"—has gotten herself into a difficult position," Mrs. Rushman interrupted. "Pregnant. Let's just say the word so no one gets confused."

Of course. How could I have missed it? I'd blinded myself to it altogether, expecting such a situation from a free-spirited girl like Evelyn Byers, but never from the sober Abigail. In the months since I'd first noticed, during our visit to the power station, Abigail had continued to put on weight. When I'd spoken to her about it, she'd quickly turned the topic to her studies, sharing her pleasure in a new area of interest, natural science, especially the study of butterflies. Never gifted, she was now eager to pursue this small area of endeavor, so I'd ignored her weight problem and focused on getting her advanced assignments from Miss Price, the science teacher, and practice in scientific drawing from Miss Riley.

"Don't worry, Miss Barrett"—Mrs. Rushman lifted her hand as if to ward off my objections—"we don't blame you and we don't blame Macaulay. Far from it. We know how it happened, don't we, Fritz?"

"Yes, I suppose we—"

"Exactly. We blame ourselves, but no good comes of blame. We are Christians and we know God forgives us."

"Then why have you come to me?" Unlike Christ, I was under no obligation to forgive.

"Well," she announced meaningfully, "you know Fritz has become one of the commissioners of the exposition?"

"No, I don't think I did." Vaguely I recalled his presence on the dais in the Yellow Room of the Buffalo Club. "Congratulations, Mr. Rushman," I said, although I wasn't impressed. No doubt he had purchased a large number of exposition bonds in return for this honor.

His wife accepted my felicitations on his behalf. "Yes, yes, thank you, we're thrilled. But just so, we must maintain certain standards now. Which is what brings us to you. You understand?"

"No, I'm afraid I don't." Of course I did, but I wasn't going to make this easy for them.

She sighed impatiently. "It means that we can't leave town with her because everyone will know the reason—leaving town just as the Pan-Am is about to open, and Mr. Milburn already promising the commissioners invitations to his Bastille Day ball for the French ambassador. And Abigail can't leave town alone, because everyone will realize then too. So we're counting on you to find something to do with her, to get her out of the way with no one knowing." Suddenly Mrs. Rushman's belligerent surface cracked and she seemed about to cry. Her husband put his hand on her shoulder.

"We thought, well, we assumed—" Mr. Rushman hesitated. "Seems like something that must have come up before." He looked at me hopefully. "So you would know what to do."

"Yes," his wife broke in. "That's exactly what we thought. It's the sort of thing that's come up before and you would know what to do."

I paused. I wasn't about to reveal to them whether "this sort of thing" had come up before, although of course it had. "How far along is she?"

"As best as we can figure out—and of course we haven't taken her to a doctor—about six months."

"Six months! And you never noticed?"

"Did you notice?"

"No. However I did notice that she was putting on weight."

"Was she?" said Mr. Rushman, concerned. "Hasn't she been getting enough exercise? Has she been overeating? I thought she liked sports. Did you notice she was gaining weight, Cassie?"

"Of course not," insisted Mrs. Rushman.

Please God, protect me. I took a deep breath. "Have you any idea who the father is? Perhaps it's not too late for a wedding."

"If only—" Mr. Rushman began.

"Impossible!" his wife interjected. "The man is married. He's a very prominent man in the community," she reported with emphasis and pride. "You would recognize his name if I mentioned it—which I certainly shall not!"

She had the temerity to proclaim this as if I were a common gossip.

"Of course we never should have let him be unchaperoned with Abigail, but how could we say no?" Mr. Rushman turned up his hands to show his helplessness. "They had interests in common. That's how they met, pursuing these"—he whipped his hands in front of his face as he searched for the proper words—"these common interests!" The breath went out of him, leaving him deflated. "He put us in a very awkward position," he offered flatly.

"He promised Fritz a position among the commissioners, and he followed through—we can't fault him on that," Mrs. Rushman said. "He also arranged for us to be invited to dinner at the Rumseys—and I'm not talking about the Dexter Rumseys, Miss Barrett, I'm talking about the Bronson Rumseys! At their beautiful home on Tracy Street." Obviously Mrs. Rushman hadn't recognized a vital truth: In our community, the retired Bronson Rumsey might be the epicenter of glamour, but his younger brother, Dexter, was the center of power. "Miss Love was there! She even approached me on the subject of assisting her with a charity project."

"So you offered up your daughter's virginity in exchange for dinner at the Bronson Rumseys?" Oh, Louisa, that was needlessly harsh, I chided myself. But sometimes the constant effort of self-restraint became too much for me.

"Certainly not, Miss Barrett. You exaggerate. We allowed him to spend time with her, pursuing their—common interests, as Fritz says, and we were quite innocent of what followed."

"I see."

Alas, I did see. Everything. The Palladian mansion on North Street. The house's emptiness in the late afternoon, when Mr. Rushman was at his office, Mrs. Rushman was out paying calls, and the servants were preparing dinner. It probably happened in the Gothic revival library, there on the deep sofa, or on the velvety Persian carpet, while Abigail's homework lay untouched on the desk. The only odd part was that Abigail didn't seem the type to attract the attention of the kind of man they had described.

"Does he still spend time with her?"

"Certainly not! What do you take us for? And we haven't told him a thing, in case you're wondering!" She looked as if I'd insulted her. "We've told him only that she's too busy studying for her final examinations to spend time visiting. But we have reason to believe that he suspects. That he is concerned. He is a gentleman, so he would be concerned. But he doesn't pry."

"We still approve of him," Mr. Rushman assured me.

"Obviously," his wife added. "Now here is the point, Miss Barrett: We must find something to do with Abigail and the infant. Will you help us?"

"What about your minister?" I asked. "The Reverend Holmes may have experience with such matters."

Mrs. Rushman flushed. "This is not the sort of thing the Reverend Holmes would want or expect among his parishioners."

"Ah. Quite so."

"You *must* help us, Miss Barrett," pleaded Mr. Rushman. "There's no one else we can ask."

I stared out the window at the trees, the leaves a delicate pale green. It would be difficult. Obviously Dr. Perlmutter, who had been Margaret's doctor, was the man to call. But at six months—would that be enough time for a childless wife to prepare for an adoption by pretending to be pregnant? And Abigail would need to leave the city. But as her mother said, leaving just before the opening of the exposition would be tantamount to admitting that something woeful had occurred. Abigail would be "gone to the bow-wows," as my students so succinctly phrased it.

I must have paused for some time, because Mrs. Rushman began to pull at her husband's sleeve. "Tell her, Fritz, tell her," she said in a loud whisper.

"Oh, yes. Yes," he fumbled, touching his pockets. "Miss Barrett." He cleared his throat. "We are in a position to offer you a good amount of money." He stepped back in response to the derisive look I gave him. "As a donation to the school—not to you personally."

"I will not mix money with a girl's misfortune."

"Don't be so upright," Mrs. Rushman snapped. "The school can always use the money."

Before Tom's gift, I probably would have agreed with her. I would have accepted the offer, visions of new gymnasiums and science laboratories floating before my eyes. But Tom had given me the ability to take the high road.

"No. I will not accept your donation. But I will try to help Abigail. Is there anyone in your family without obligations, who might be able to leave the city with her?"

"I suppose Fritz's mother could go out of town with her," Mrs. Rushman admitted grudgingly. "But she's seventy-eight and frankly her English isn't the best."

"What language does she speak?"

"German, if you must know, although I don't see why it's relevant."

"Would the senior Mrs. Rushman be willing to do this?"

Mr. Rushman slowly brightened as he realized this plan might work. "Yes, I think she would. And she's completely reliable. Totally on the money in spite of her age." As he relaxed, he seemed to melt into a kindly man, justly proud of his accomplishments and of his family. "From the time I brought her over from our farm outside Frankfurt, she's been my best advisor. She didn't want to come here at first, refused for years, but after—"

"That was a long time ago, Fritz," his wife broke in, putting an abrupt stop to his reminiscences.

I said, "Before I decide anything, I need to speak with Abigail."

"Whatever for? You won't get anywhere with her—she says no to everything these days. She won't wear the beautiful clothes I buy her, or if she does wear them she pulls off all the bows. She won't even think about her coming-out party—I've got to make all those arrangements myself! I don't know what to do with her."

I said nothing, waiting for the echo of her dismal words to die away. Then: "I must ascertain what Abigail would like to do with the child who is, of course, hers."

"That's an unusual way of looking at it," Mrs. Rushman opined.

"Yes, I suppose it is."

Two hours later, during the senior study hall period, Abigail Rushman sat before me, round-faced and childlike, her books piled on her lap. Farsighted, she wore reading glasses suspended from a woven cord around her neck. She looked so forlorn that I pulled a chair next to her instead of facing her from behind my desk.

"Your parents have been to see me, Abigail."

"Yes," she whispered.

After that, I didn't know what to say. Although this situation had come up before, it had never been brought to me personally for a solution. Indeed, my knowledge of previous situations was based on supposition, for I attuned myself to every shift in normal customs. Seven, eight times over the years I'd known something like this was occurring, even though those involved said nothing directly to me about it and I said nothing to them. Two of the situations had been obvious: Girls pulled out of school in their senior years and married to men not strictly suitable, their babies born several months "premature." But the more typical situation involved girls abruptly taken on grand tours, or sent to help needy relations in the West, or enrolled in exceedingly obscure boarding schools far away. I always wished I could talk to these girls and console them, but part of understanding the code was the tacit agreement not to break it. Parents would never want me discussing intimate matters with their daughters; to do so would be considered outside my proper role. Furthermore I would never tell a girl to keep one of our discussions secret from her family; I would never put a girl into that position, or indicate to her in any way that her parents might not always deserve her full confidence. So despite my better instincts, and knowing only too well the heartbreak these girls were suffering, I did my part to maintain the status quo.

Yet now, with Abigail, perhaps I could finally do more. "Is there anything you'd like to ask me, Abigail?"

"Do you hate me?"

Poor child. "Of course not, my dear. Why would you think that?"

"Because what happened . . . it's so different from the . . . standard you set for us."

"Standards are goals, aren't they? Goals that we all struggle to live up to, as we try to be good people. To be the kind of people we ourselves can respect. Do you think you've let yourself down, with what's happened?"

"I don't know. Everything is so confusing. The gentleman, he was so kind and sweet to me. I didn't realize. I mean . . ."

A chill swept through me.

"I didn't expect what . . . what he was going to do. I didn't realize about . . . I mean, no one ever told me." She stopped, biting her lip and staring down at her books.

"Yes, I understand." And of course I did. The habits of society hadn't evolved much since my own youth. To this day, with their fathers' encouragement, boys of Abigail's age were "educated" by certain women in other parts of town. Every now and again I heard whispers among the matrons at the club about girls receiving strictly unidentified diseases along with their wedding rings. But daughters were kept in complete ignorance of sexual matters, with nothing to fall back on for knowledge but disjointed rumors passed by older brothers, or easy-to-discount tales related by the few girls who spent time on farms. Most girls had no way to defend themselves against seduction, or even to recognize it; no way to say, this far but no farther. Oh, yes, they were told over and over that men would attempt to assault their virtue and they must never give in. But they were told in such a way that they expected the assaults to be aggressive. Faced with sweetness, with tenderness and vulnerability—or even with deeply veiled innuendo, as I had been— they were helpless. Unfortunately parents did not consider it part of my job to teach them otherwise.

"And he really was nice to me," Abigail assured me. "I mean, he never meant to hurt me. We met because of the butterflies. We were both looking for butterflies in the upper meadow of the cemetery. It seems like a long time ago now." She shook her head sadly. "It was at the end of last summer, when we met. We had so much to talk about. He knows everything there is to know about trees and birds and butterflies. I bet there aren't many grown-ups who like butterflies!" she averred. Then she sighed, crestfallen. "My parents won't let me see him anymore or even talk to him. He must be wondering what's going on. His feelings must be hurt."

There were tears in her eyes. She looked no older than Grace.

"Will I be able to graduate?"

Graduation was in a month, when she would be that much bigger of course, but everyone was accustomed to seeing her overweight. I made a quick decision. "Yes, Abigail, you shall graduate."

That brought a grin which she tried to repress.

"Have you thought about what you would like to do with . . . the baby?" There it was. The word finally out.

Her eyes widened with bewildered surprise. "It's hard to think about. I mean, about it really being there." She glanced at her stomach. "Do you really think it's there?"

"Your mother seems to think so."

"But how does she know? She asked me a lot of questions and said she'd hit me if I didn't tell her the truth, and I *did* tell her the truth, and then she got my grandma and they pressed their hands all over my stomach and decided a baby was there."

"I'm sure they were right, Abigail. Now we must decide what to do."

I gave her time to think this through. "Well, my mother and my grandma say I can't keep the baby, so I guess I'd like the baby to go to a family that doesn't have a baby and needs one. It doesn't have to be an important family. Just a family that could love a baby."

Then her composure broke. She leaned against my leg to cry. I placed my hand on her back to comfort her. After a few minutes I said, "Up, now. Up."

Rising, she gazed at me with open, absolute trust.

"You must focus on the good you can take from this experience, Abigail." I hoped I didn't sound pedantic. The line between sanctimony and encouragement was blurred. Yet how could I greet innocence except on its own terms? "I admire your courage."

I squeezed her hands, and she gave me an unsteady smile. "Thank you, Miss Barrett. I'll always do my best from now on."

Chapter Fourteen

I wouldn't put it past any man to feign an interest in butterflies to get what he wanted from an innocent girl. Nonetheless, I didn't allow myself to engage in idle speculation about the father of Abigail's child. It wouldn't help me or Macaulay if I greeted a prominent man of the community with a too-knowing look, let alone an impulsive glare of condemnation.

A few days after the Rushman visit, while I was still trying to map out the proper course of action for Abigail, I received this note:

> My dear Miss BarretÏt,
>
> I wish to discuss with you, privately and confidentially, a matter relating to the Macaulay School. Kindly visit me at my office, in the administration building at Stony Point—where we may be assured of privacy—at your convenience. Shall we say this Friday at eleven a.m.?
>
> With thanks,
> J. J. Albright.

Such a request, from a member of the Macaulay Board, could not be ignored, even during school hours. So on Friday, I undertook the train ride from downtown Buffalo to the massive steel mill complex rising along Lake Erie at Stony Point, less than ten miles to the south.

Only a few years earlier, Walter Scranton had negotiated with Buffalo business leaders about moving his Lackawanna, Pennsylvania, steel mills to a new, better location on the shores of Lake Erie, close to the cheap electricity of Niagara and easily accessible to ore shipments from the Mesabi Range in Minnesota. Scranton had quickly found the local investors he needed: my board of trustees in action once again. One city we were, cut like a diamond, every facet a glittering reflection of the whole.

As one of the leaders of this new steel-mill consortium, John J. Albright had been responsible for organizing the purchase of the land, nearly fifteen hundred acres. He'd been able to buy it cheaply by misleading the owner into believing that he was looking for a flat piece of property on which to grow the millions of flowers needed for the Pan-American Exposition. Apparently Albright hadn't actually lied about his intentions, he'd simply played on the seller's assumptions. When the deal was complete (the legal documents prepared by John Milburn), it was hailed as brilliant. With the addition of something called a "timber crib breakwater" (carefully diagramed in the newspapers), Stony Point would have the best harbor on the Great Lakes. The steel complex would one day compete with the Carnegie works in Pittsburgh. Or so the newspapers proclaimed.

From the train window I saw miles of ill-made shacks forming a town of squatters. Here lived the thousands of workers who had come to construct the technological miracle which would one day—or so it was advertised—produce a million and a quarter tons of steel a year. The workmen were like an ancient army camped across the plain, accompanied by food and water wagons, as well as the requisite camp followers.

The train stopped at the gates of the construction site and I got off. Before entering the complex, however, I paused. The air was acrid, stinging my eyes. Dust gritted against my teeth. At the end of a road lined with infant trees and carefully paved with asphalt (in addition to his other endeavors, Mr. Albright was our local asphalt baron), the administration building rose in almost shocking Beaux-Arts magnificence atop a gentle knoll. Beyond it, Lake Erie shimmered, light reflecting off the water to lend an unearthly halo to the monsters before me . . . yes, fifteen hundred acres of monsters: gruesomely shaped derricks, dredges, gantries, cranes and engines belching black smoke. With a touch of anxiety, I began my walk toward Albright's office. Around me were rail lines by the dozen, going nowhere; narrow bridges crossing the sky; electrical lines in a dense weave. And there was sound: dull thuds, high-pitched screeches, small explosions, whistles, bells—whether of warning or alarm or happiness at the shift's end, who could tell? Before I was halfway down the road, all the sounds blended into one sound, a vibration that never ceased and became more a feeling than a hearing, passing through my body.

A few years before, Stony Point had been a forested lakeside wilderness. Now it was—this. Yet I had to admit that some of the monsters were beautiful. I had to stop to admire them, as they bathed and baked in the sunlight: slender smokestacks in towering rows; graceful lighthouses (or so they seemed) with bells on top; the machine shop like a crystal palace. In their way, these monsters were as beautiful as the forest they had replaced. STEEL WORKS WILL RISE LIKE MAGIC—that was one of the headlines I remembered. There *was* magic here: I was surrounded by a magical forest of the future.

When the secretary ushered me into his office, John J. Albright did not stand to greet me. He simply looked up from the work at his desk, his glasses catching a glare of light.

"Good morning, Miss Barrett," he said graciously. He was terribly thin, but he always looked like this, year after year unchanged. "Thank you for coming. Please, make yourself comfortable. I'm at a tricky spot here."

He returned to work. Tools were arranged neatly across his broad, polished desk. In addition there was a stack of white boards, and a container of pins. As I approached, I realized that he was mounting butterflies, flashes of color dense beneath his long, delicate fingers. Don't leap to conclusions, I cautioned myself.

His office was what I would have predicted: the intricate scrollwork of the ceiling; the wide leather chairs; the flowing brocade curtains at the tall windows; the thick Persian carpet; gaslight rather than electricity. Nevertheless there was one important difference from the standard-issue industrial mogul's office: The paintings were by Corot, misty-green scenes of sheep, lakes, and shepherdesses, feathery-leafed trees rising around them. Mr. Albright enjoyed landscape paintings, particularly from the Barbizon School, although he couldn't be called a connoisseur. He simply collected things, from the canvases that would one day go his art museum in Delaware Park to the mounted butterflies that adorned one wall of the office.

His "tricky spot" continued, and so with Corot's vision in my mind I went to the windows. As so often happened in Buffalo, the wind from Lake Erie had changed the day. Clouds now covered the sky, painting the scene in shades of gray. If the office had been on the opposite side of the building, I would have seen the lake, huge as an inland sea; I would have seen the grain elevators and the skyscrapers of Buffalo, comforting as home. Instead I felt as if Albright and I were in a boat run aground in a landscape created by Jules Verne or H. G. Wells, no longer magical but desolate, the derricks and gantries looking like giant insects. For a split second the Pan-American Exposition flower garden that might have been exploded before me: millions upon millions of flowers in rows of rampaging color, roses, daffodils, lilies, tulips—butterflies flitting among them.

"Did you have a pleasant journey?"

I turned to find him staring at me. In his gray suit, with his graying hair and mustache, he was as stark as the landscape outside, the dead butterflies offering the only colors of life within the narrow orbit of his being.

"Yes, thank you. It was brief."

He chuckled. "Indeed. We are close to the city but far away."

"Quite so," I replied.

He returned to his work. His every gesture was meticulous. Suddenly there was a long screech outside. A bell began clanging. A fire bell, maybe, or an ambulance. Albright tilted his head, frowning, listening. When the bell ceased, he resumed work. Albright had the overwhelming ease of a man born to great comfort. He had no need to rush, no need to think of my responsibilities. His own convenience was the motivating force with which he passed through the world. Soon, perhaps, he would sojourn at his retreat on Jekyll Island in Georgia; soon he would visit his so-called cabin in the Adirondacks. What need had he to hurry?

I approached the desk and stood beside him, to feel the presence of his body. Had he fathered Abigail's child? It seemed unlikely, he with his asceticism, she with her solemnity. And yet—so far—he had fathered six children in two marriages. There must have been pleasure in such fecundity. Pleasure to spare.

"What kind of butterfly is that?" I leaned close to him to examine the specimen. He glanced up at me, surprised, perhaps, by my nearness and meeting my eyes for an instant. Immediately he looked back at the butterfly.

"This is a Colorado Hairstreak, sent by my man in the West." He tilted up the mounting board for me to see. The butterfly had large patches of purple and orange, shaped by bands of black. I never understood the satisfaction derived from killing such exquisite creatures in order to mount them on the wall. "I'm preparing a gift for my little daughter Elizabeth." He paused, giving me a quizzical look. "Do you like butterflies?"

Who would admit to not liking butterflies? "Yes. Of course."

"This is one of my favorites." He opened the wooden box on his desk and delicately used tweezers to remove one of the specimens. "Cloudless Sulphur."

A beautiful name. Cloudless Sulphur. The butterfly was completely yellow, even the body and antennae. Not the sallow, dingy yellow of the meeting room at the club. This yellow was pure and brilliant, like a bit of morning sunshine captured upon the earth.

"It's surprising, to see something so pure," I offered.

"Yes." He studied me, his brow knit. "It is surprising. I'll mount it for you as a gift. Yes"—he seemed to drift off into his own thoughts—"a gift."

"Mr. Albright, I don't think—"

"No, please, you are in need of a gift. You deserve a gift. Indeed you do." He nodded his head hard, as if sealing the deal. "I won't have it mounted today, however," he insisted petulantly. "You won't be able to take it home with you today. Please don't assume—"

"Oh, no, indeed. I would never expect to take it home today," I reassured him, wondering what convoluted path had made him defensive. "Whenever you're ready will be fine with me."

"Well then, that's settled," he said with happy relief. "Do sit down, Miss Barrett." He motioned to the chair on the opposite side of his desk. "I'm most grateful to you for coming all this way. Did you tell Sinclair that you were coming?"

"No. Why should I?"

"A question, nothing more." He waved it away. "I'll get right to the point, then. I find myself in the position of asking a favor of you. Two favors, actually."

Here it comes, I thought: his admission of guilt. Evenly I said, "Whatever I can do. I'd be honored to assist you."

"You know, Miss Barrett"—he leaned back in his chair, crossing his arms across his chest—"I have often observed that things happen in this life which are difficult to explain. For which no one is to blame." He sat up a bit. "Now there's a bit of a rhyme, eh? 'Difficult to explain, no one is to blame.'" He beamed at his cleverness.

"Yes."

He watched me for a moment before beginning again. "Indeed I have often observed that life is filled with trials and rewards. With challenges that give us the opportunity to do our best. To become all we can become. To do what is right. So the Good Lord would have it—I believe, at least. Well"—he sat up straight, moving his chair toward the desk, rubbing his hands together—"enough said on *that* matter. And spring is here at last. Makes us all feel better."

I beg your pardon, Mr. Albright, I felt like saying. What are you trying to tell me? If this was a code, its meaning completely eluded me. I could understand how the owner of the land we were sitting on had been persuaded to sell for a song because he thought a flower garden was going to be built here instead of a steel mill. I leaned forward. I smiled brightly. Why not bring on a confrontation? "Mr. Albright," I said charmingly, "Are you acquainted with a Macaulay student named Abigail Rushman?"

He looked terribly confused, his eyes narrowing. "I didn't say that. Why do you ask?"

"She has a great love of butterflies."

"Ah," he exclaimed happily. "Good for her. A fine interest for the young. You might show her your Cloudless Sulphur—when it's prepared."

"Yes, I shall. What a good idea. I may even give it to her. As a gift. In the summer." In the summer, Abigail would give birth to her child.

"That's as you wish." He appeared indifferent to the prospect of me making a plan to give away his gift before I had even received it. "How well I know the pleasure we butterfly lovers find in the acquisition of new specimens. Now, Miss Barrett, the second favor."

He stared at the Corot on the wall beside his desk. He seemed to be collecting his thoughts, pondering how to begin. Finally he said, "You must tell Tom Sinclair that I have my finger in the dike, but I can't hold the waters back much longer." He smiled at me thinly. "That turn of phrase is a good joke, don't you think? In this context, I mean. 'Finger in the dike . . . holding back the waters.'"

"I don't precisely understand it." Was Albright trying to warn Tom that the authorities were closing in on him regarding Speyer's death?

"I'd assumed he'd taken you into his confidence."

"About what?"

"Well . . . about what he's doing. Out at the power station. You're certainly a person worthy of confidence. I've always had the utmost confidence in you. I would trust you with anything."

"Thank you."

"You're welcome."

How should I play this? I decided on continued confusion. "But why would Mr. Sinclair take me into his confidence about his work? I rarely even see him."

Mr. Albright glared at me as though convinced he'd caught me in a lie. "You see him often enough. After all, you *are* godmother to young Grace." Suddenly his mood shifted. "Of course, you and I have that in common. Being Grace's godparents, I mean. I'd almost forgotten. It's as if we're related to each other, being godparents to the same child. Well, well. I hadn't thought of that before; hadn't put two and two together. Good, good. At any rate, Sinclair will understand my message," he concluded in a non sequitur.

"Why don't you tell him yourself?" I inquired firmly.

"Oh, I have, I have. We're very close, as you know. At least we once were. Before these . . . matters came up, and I found it necessary to distance myself. I still feel responsible for him. You don't help someone for years and whatnot and then just turn your back."

"No, of course not."

"I'm hoping that hearing my message from you, with your

mutual . . . connections, will be more persuasive for Sinclair than hearing it once more from me. If you follow."

I hesitated. "Not exactly."

He sighed. "I'll try to be more clear." He thought for a moment. "You see, Miss Barrett, in America we have always had equality of opportunity. This is what I tell these unionists when they come to me." He waved his hand in irritated dismissal. "I'm giving men an opportunity here at Stony Point—an opportunity to work. What they do with that opportunity is their business. But unions—they don't give equality of opportunity, do they? They make everyone exactly alike, make everyone part of a faceless mass. A cog in the industrial machine." The distaste in his voice was palpable. "But equality of opportunity—*that* is America. Sinclair knows this better than any of us, coming from where he's come. He didn't stay where he began and spend his life organizing a glassmakers' union, now did he?"

Albright stared at me, expecting an answer to this rhetorical question. "No," I admitted to appease him.

"And just as we must have equality of opportunity, so too nothing can be given away for free. Destroys the motivation. The incentive, if you will." He stopped. "I don't see how I can be more clear than that."

"You're referring to unionization at the powerhouses? Or here at Stony Point?" I asked in bewilderment.

"Neither! Whatever do you mean?" Now he looked bewildered too. "Why would you think that?"

I didn't respond.

Exasperated, he demanded, "Why this subterfuge? Sinclair knows very well I won't betray him—you can tell him once more that I won't be party to what he's planning, but neither will I betray him."

"What is he planning?"

"Miss Barrett. Disingenuousness doesn't become you."

"No, honestly. I don't know. But I feel I *should* know, don't you? Especially since you clearly assume I *do* know."

For a long moment he studied me. "Well, we've worked ourselves into quite a conundrum, haven't we," he observed. "Well, well." He glanced around the room, his fingers drumming the desk. When he looked at me again, there was something sinister in his eyes. "Miss

Barrett, have you ever seen a butterfly called the Blue Morpho?"

"No, I haven't." My voice caught from nervousness.

"It's a South American butterfly. A tropical butterfly. I've coveted it all my life. It would be easy enough to acquire," he assured me. "I've men collecting for me around the world—I just need to give the word. On the other hand, I've been hesitant to let the Blue Morpho join my collection, for fear that acquiring my heart's desire will serve only to harken my demise." He smiled in appreciation of his own jest. "A Blue Morpho is a large, brilliant azure butterfly. The few specimens I've seen are remarkable. But what's truly remarkable is that the undersides of the wings are drab brown, with small orange-black eyespots. When the Blue Morpho alights, on a treelimb, for example, it seems to disappear." Intently he stared at me. "Rather like you, don't you think?"

Was he threatening me? I clutched at my independence and attempted to affirm that I too was a person to be reckoned with: "Mr. Albright, forgive me for changing the subject, but I was surprised, on the train ride out here, to see the squalid encampment where your employees live. Such a situation hardly compliments the work you do here. Something should be done about it," I added more confidently, my fear dissipating as I saw a wary expression appear on his face. "You should build a model village for your workers, like Echota, out at the power station."

"All in good time, my dear," he replied carefully.

"Why don't you at least clean things up a bit. Otherwise by summer you'll have typhoid. Or cholera. Who'll build your steel mill then?"

"Women like you are always trying to improve the world," he said bluntly. "How glad I am that I rescued Susan from such a fate."

Susan Fuller Albright, the governess-companion from Smith College. Obviously his words were intended as an insult, which I ignored.

"Aren't you worried that your men might revolt, living as you force them to?"

"Not very likely. I do believe they need the work."

"At the least, you provide fertile territory for union recruiters."

After a long moment, and carefully staring at one of his Corots on the wall, he said, "What would you know about that?"

So, I had scared him. He could visualize me as a spy, or a socialist. "I know absolutely nothing about it. But I will say that you'd best do something to help those men, Mr. Albright, or I'll see to it that Miss Love is informed."

"You blackmailer!" he suddenly cried, delighted. "Yes, yes—I certainly shall do something before Miss Love can be called in to help." He began to laugh boisterously. "Miss Love: our own local battle-axe. What would we do without her? You've certainly given me the most effective threat I've heard in years. I'll remember that one. Well, well." He wiped his brow with his finely pressed handkerchief. "In the end I suppose we'll recognize that it's you women who've single-handedly made the world free for capitalism. What would have become of us without your petticoat brigades lending a hand to the downtrodden? It's my favorite irony: wives, daughters, and sisters righting the wrongs of fathers, husbands, and brothers. Men victimize and women rescue. A neat little trick. Who needs socialism, or communism, when Miss Love can be called in at a moment's notice to redress all wrongs!"

Done with his laughter, Albright pushed up his glasses to rub his eyes. Then he folded his thin hands over one another on the desk.

"My dear Louisa." His use of my first name was a subtle recognition of my subordinate position. "One good turn deserves another, don't you think?" He cocked his head and gave me a look I can only describe as lascivious. I wouldn't have been surprised if he'd now made an ungracious request. A request that required the locking of the door.

"You've come all the way out here for me, so I'll give you some advice: Go back to the city, deliver my message, and then ask Sinclair his plans. Once you know, never tell anyone and stay as far away from all of this as you can. I wouldn't want you, of all people, to get caught up in any . . . complications."

"Might these complications relate in any way to the death of Karl Speyer?" I asked, risking frankness.

He looked sincerely taken aback. "No, not at all. Why do you ask?"

"Just wondering."

"Ah, well . . . I'm afraid I really must return to my work now."

I didn't move. I remained silent until I had his full attention. "Mr. Albright, did you have anything to discuss relating to Macaulay?"

Gently he chortled. "Everything we've discussed is related to Macaulay, my dear. I should have thought that obvious."

Angrily I walked down the asphalt-paved road, cursing its Albright-sponsored smoothness. What was I to do with this warning he'd given me for Tom? Obviously I would have to pass it along, but how foolish I would feel, repeating Albright's nonsense about his finger in the dike—especially because I had no idea what it meant.

Workmen were streaming in and out of the gates: a change in shift, I assumed. As I crossed to the train station, I saw a man handing out flyers—calling to his friends, reaching to shake hands, trying out greetings in several languages and enjoying his inability to master any of them. I took a flyer from him and looked at it as I waited on the railway platform, the wind from the lake whipping my skirt against me. As I read, I felt surprised that the flyer was handed out so openly.

Debs's appeal to you!

There was a blurry picture of the fiery socialist labor leader Eugene V. Debs, thin, bald, and bespectacled.

We stand for you! Can you and will you understand? We are of your class and we have resolved to free ourselves from wage-slavery.

Are you with us? You must be unless your eyes are blind, your heart dead, and your hand lifted against your own wife and child.

Socialism is the hope of humanity, the light of the world.

Here is our hand, brother, give us yours.

"Miss Barrett? Is it Miss Louisa Barrett?" a man's voice inquired. Startled, I looked up. I recognized him immediately—the man who was the talk of the town. I crumpled the flyer and slipped it into my jacket pocket. "I thought so. Well met, well met." As he reached for my hand, he took off his hat and bowed slightly from the waist. His thinning brown hair, combed over the crown of his head, was so thickly pomaded that the wind didn't lift it. He wore a plaid-patterned beige suit of a thick tweed. His entire manner was warm and affectionate, as if we'd been friends for years, when in fact we'd never been introduced. But of course he knew me. That was his job: to know people. "What a happy coincidence."

I had an uneasy suspicion that our meeting wasn't a coincidence at all. For here was Frederick Krakauer, Mr. Morgan's man. "You've picked a lovely day for a tour of the steel mill. Lovely." He gazed at the gray sky suspiciously, as if wondering why it didn't cooperate with his convictions.

Meanwhile, the train arrived on the other side, discharged its passengers, and circled around for the trip back to the city. When it pulled up, Krakauer took my elbow lightly to guide me down the platform. "Allow me the honor of escorting you back to the city."

Instinctively I pulled my arm away from him. "I'm hardly in need of an escort, Mr. Krakauer." Then I realized my mistake; I must not offend him: Who could tell what ears he whispered into? As graciously as I could, I added, "Should you wish to accompany me, however, your presence will make the trip much more . . . mutually entertaining."

He paused. "Yes, I think so," he finally agreed, as though my words had taken him a moment to unravel.

We boarded, I took a window seat facing the direction we were going, and he sat opposite, facing me. His bulky presence seemed to fill the double seat. He gave off a sweet tobacco scent, but not of cigars or cigarettes; a pipe, most likely. The train whistle blew, and then we were moving.

At first we sat in silence, but as we passed through the squatters' camp Mr. Krakauer began to offer his views on humanity. "How curious it is, Miss Barrett, that this little community is not what it appears. No, no, it's not one large shantytown for the workers of Stony Point: It is many small shantytowns—one for the Poles, one for the Italians, one for the Slovaks, for the Croats, for the Czechs, and on and on. Even the coloreds have their pitiful circle. Each group has its own territory and God help them if they step over the invisible boundaries because they won't live to see the morrow!"

I didn't honor his prejudice with a response.

"Barely pays to build them real housing, at the rate they're killing each other. Not to mention losing arms and legs on the job. I don't know how poor Mr. Albright keeps things going! Do you know, there are over four thousand injuries a year and on-site fatalities average one a day? Extraordinary. And yet men keep lining up for the work." Krakauer patted his belly, looking pleased with himself for being able to pass on this inside information. With his smooth skin, his age could have been anywhere between forty and sixty.

"Mr. Albright worries about strikes, but *I* say, when you've got the men working twelve-hour shifts, who has time or energy to organize a strike!" This time he waited for my response.

"I see what you mean," I said noncommittally.

"Now, Mr. Sinclair over at the power station, he's got different ideas. He's all for taking care of his workers—giving them proper houses and even education. And not just them, but their families too! Can you beat that?" Krakauer shook his head at the naiveté of such notions. "I suppose we'll just have to wait and see which is more profitable in the long run." I had no doubt that Krakauer had already made up his mind on that score.

"Well, I'm certainly happy to have this chance to speak with you. Unfortunately I wasn't present for your tour of the powerhouses—although I heard about your visit, yes indeed I did. Well, I can't be everywhere at once," he admitted sadly. "Even Mr. Morgan doesn't expect me to be everywhere at once. I can only do my best, and try to be where I need to be, at any moment."

I couldn't resist the temptation to tease him. "It must be difficult, to judge where to go. Where you'll be needed most."

He sighed, thinking me sincere. "Yes, that's the toughest part of my job."

"Mr. Krakauer," I said gently, "What exactly is it that you're doing here?"

"Here? On this train?" He looked astonished. "Why, going back to Buffalo."

"No, here in general. At the steel mill. At the power station. In the city and all around it. At one social event after another. Week after week, month after month—my girls are beginning to regard your presence as highly suspect."

He chuckled good-naturedly. "Yes, yes, I have daughters myself. I know what fun they have with anything out of the ordinary."

"Yes, they do."

"My dear Miss Barrett." He leaned toward me appealingly. Almost apologetically. "I'm here for the reason everyone knows I'm here: I'm Mr. Morgan's man and proud of it, and I'm looking out for his interests wherever they lead me."

"What are his interests?"

"Oh, he has many interests, Miss Barrett." He leaned back, smirking, puffed up with vicarious glory. "More than any of us can ever imagine. But he manages to keep track of everything, I can tell you. That's why I'm here. Just think: If you'd invested a fortune to build a hydroelectric power station five hundred miles from your home, and you'd encouraged your friends to do the same, wouldn't you want someone on hand to look after your interests?"

"Yes, of course."

"Good." Suddenly there was an edge to his voice. He regarded me with narrowed eyes.

"So . . . you met with Mr. Albright himself today."

He let the statement float between us, and I wondered at what point he had begun to watch me.

"Mr. Albright's on your school board, isn't he?" Krakauer asked rhetorically. "You must have a great deal to discuss," he added, inviting me to confession.

"Yes, indeed," I said, creating a story and feigning enthusiasm for it. "Mr. Albright and I share an interest in butterflies. He had some specimens to show me. It is my fervent hope that one day Mr. Albright will donate his butterfly collection to Macaulay."

Mr. Krakauer gazed at me quizzically, apparently unsure whether to believe me. "Did you enjoy seeing the steel mill?" he inquired accusingly.

"Enjoy is not precisely the word I would use."

"Ha ha," he guffawed, slapping his knee. "I understand what you mean. Good for you." His reaction, so at odds with my expectations, made me even more cautious.

Carefully I said, "What is Mr. Morgan's interest in the steel mill?"

He looked taken aback. "Forgive me, Miss Barrett, but I'm

surprised at you. A person like yourself, asking a question like that. Why anyone who reads the newspapers . . ."

No doubt it was for the best, that he think me stupid. Finally he added, "It's a delicate dance we do here, Miss Barrett. A delicate dance." He raised his eyebrows, as if challenging me to ask him to go on.

"Yes?"

Unexpectedly he shrugged, then shifted on the seat, leaning forward elbows-on-knees to speak confidentially. "We've had so much success with the hydroelectric power project, you know. Sinclair's got a gift for bringing in business. Graphite, abrasives, aluminum, you name it. That old Irish charm, eh? Nobody can resist him. The investors are already seeing a return! Isn't that extraordinary? Especially considering that work is still in progress. Well Mr. Morgan certainly is perspicacious, and I'm certainly proud to be his man."

"Quite so, Mr. Krakauer. Hearing you talk makes me wish *I* could be Mr. Morgan's man!"

"Oh, my dear lady, that would be impossible." He looked aghast.

"I know, Mr. Krakauer." I patted his sleeve. "I'm only joking."

"Oh," he said, discomfited but not displeased. "Anyway, it's been an education to me, learning about these new businesses, finding out how the power station works. Learning about turbines and penstocks and generators. A real education. You know who taught me the most? Poor old Karl Speyer." Krakauer regarded me frankly. "Poor fellow. Some people say he was murdered. Yes, murdered," he assured me disingenuously. "Forced at gunpoint to walk across the ice to a weak spot where he fell in and was left to die." Seeing the scene through Krakauer's eyes, suddenly I visualized him being the one to force Speyer on this death walk. Yet what would J. P. Morgan gain from Speyer's death? I couldn't imagine. And besides, surely there were easier ways to kill a man than forcing him to walk across a frozen lake— especially a man who journeyed regularly to Niagara Falls, where sudden death—accidental or otherwise—was a common occurrence. "Falling through the ice," Krakauer mused. "It's the sort of accident that could happen to any of us, isn't it?"

"I hope not, Mr. Krakauer. What a horrible way to die."

"I don't suppose any way is easy," he replied with the matter-of-fact confidence of someone in a position to know.

We stared at each other. Krakauer had a slight smile on his face. Trying to change the subject, I asked, "Mr. Krakauer, do you think it will be necessary—I mean, some people say that the power station will have to take all the water from Niagara to meet the demand." I fought an urge to avert my eyes. "Do you think that's true?"

He waited a long time before answering. "Well now, 'all' is a relative term, Miss Barrett," he said thoughtfully.

"It is?" I asked, wide-eyed.

"Yes, indeed. 'All' is a relative term. That's what Mr. Morgan believes. He told me so himself." Krakauer gazed out the window with intense concentration, remembering, I felt certain, the day that J.P. Morgan, in the shadows of his library, had passed along this precious bit of information.

"Then it must be true—I mean, that 'all' is a relative term," I said, and I wasn't teasing, for if Morgan had said it, then for all practical purposes it was true. "Mr. Krakauer, I may be wrong on this—and you know best"—how was that for wheedling?—"but I thought there were some kind of state controls on the water. From the state of New York, I mean. That companies had to rent the water or option it, they couldn't just take as much as they wanted."

He bestirred himself. "Yes, yes; true, true. There are state controls, it's all very strictly supervised. Mr. Morgan insists on very strict attention to details like that."

Then his manner shifted once again. He seemed to be trying to appear blasé, slouching back in his seat, but in fact his eyes were intent upon mine. "Miss Barrett, how well do you know Thomas Sinclair?"

I was uncomfortable in Krakauer's stare and felt myself blushing. I looked away. "His wife was my best friend. She died last year."

"I know. I'm sorry for you. Tell me about her."

I didn't dare conceal information from Frederick Krakauer. I must choose carefully, what to tell and how to tell it. I must tell him only what he surely knew already. "Well . . . she attended Macaulay. That's how I met her. Mr. Sinclair has supported the school generously in her name."

"So I've heard. He's an extraordinary character. A man of force and integrity."

"Yes."

"Understands the power station like . . . well, like nobody else. Some of the boys know a little of this, a little of that; but Sinclair, he knows the whole shebang. He's got the whole thing in his head." Krakauer tapped his temple. "Anything happened to him, the rest of us'd be in big trouble." Krakauer made this sound like a joke.

"Yes."

"He's self-made, as you probably know. Worked in a factory as a boy. Extraordinary, how far he's come. Mr. Morgan finds it—well, extraordinary. But that's America for you, isn't it? That's America all over."

"Yes."

"The only place in the world like it. I mean, here I am, never even finished school, and I'm Mr. Morgan's man."

"Yes. It's an honor."

"So it is." He paused, for too long a time. He cleared his throat. "I wonder if Thomas Sinclair ever . . . remembers"—Krakauer gave the word intense meaning—"those days. In the factory, I mean. The people he knew . . . his fellow workers, you'd have to call them. His peers, compatriots, comrades, may we say? Of course he was just a boy. But I do wonder if he ever thinks of them. If he's ever in contact with them. No telling where they are now. What their . . ." He searched for the word. "What their . . . inclinations might be."

I sensed the crumpled Debs flyer in my pocket. I couldn't meet Krakauer's gaze. "I wouldn't know."

He sat up, spreading a hand on each tweed-covered knee. "No, of course not. How could you possibly know." He was silent for a moment. Then, abruptly, "It's hard to believe, but Thomas Sinclair actually gives every single one of his workers a ham for Easter! Pays out of his own pocket. A ham! Now, I ask you, Miss Barrett, what does your average Serb or Croat want with a ham for Easter?"

"Well, I guess that's America for you, Mr. Krakauer."

"Mmm." He nodded thoughtfully. "Right you are there, Miss Barrett."

Tentatively I said, "If you're wondering about Mr. Sinclair's old friends, maybe you should ask him."

"Thank you for the suggestion, but it's not the sort of question a man in Sinclair's position would take well to, now, is it?" There was a harsh undertone in his voice. "That's why I was asking you."

All at once I was truly frightened of him. Irrationally, wildly frightened. My heart was racing. I fought the urge to fist my hands together. "Truly, Mr. Krakauer," I said quietly, in a tone I knew sounded like pleading but that I couldn't control. "I don't know."

He didn't respond. I wasn't certain he'd even heard, for he had turned to the window and his gaze was unwavering. The squatters' shacks had given way to South Park and its glass conservatory, which in turn gave way to the grain elevators. Now our rail line joined dozens of others in a band of tracks half a mile wide, leading to the vast coal trestles of the Lehigh Valley Railroad. Leading to the Buffalo Harbor—the greatest inland port in the history of America, people called it; the sixth busiest port in the world. There—so close—were our skyscrapers, dwarfing the church steeples, outlined against the fat white cumulus clouds that now swept the horizon. How beautiful was our city, how exquisite; it filled me with awe. And all the while, Frederick Krakauer stared out the window with that look of his, watchful but unfocused. Concealing and protecting the interests of Mr. J. Pierpont Morgan.

Chapter Fifteen

G reetings, all!"

On the first Monday evening in May Elbert Hubbard arrived at my salon with a flourish of high spirits. Elbert was the founder of the Roycrofters, an artists' community in the nearby village of East Aurora. He was decked out in his uniform of Stetson hat (long brown hair curling around its brim), farmer's brogues, loose corduroys, flannel shirt, and flowing cravat.

With Elbert's arrival, mail-order soap king John Larkin abruptly quit his conversation with board member John Scatcherd and left my house without a word to anyone, not even to me. Elbert's sister was married to Larkin, and as a result Larkin was privy to certain private moral irregularities that Elbert himself shrugged off with a sheepish grin.

Once upon a time, Elbert had been the marketing genius behind the Larkin Soap Company, but in early 1893, with a hefty financial settlement, Elbert left the company to take on the mantle of "writer." Now Elbert was famous throughout the country—throughout the world, he would say—as Fra Elbertus, the Inspector General of the Universe. His magazine, *The Philistine*, (which was basically an advertisement for himself, filled with his homilies and fooleries) had one of the highest circulations in the country.

After everyone heard the front door slam behind the retreating Larkin, Elbert called to me across the crowded drawing room: "Miss Louie! A pleasure to see you, as always. And a pleasure to see how popular you've become!" Elbert beamed as staid businessmen excused themselves from conversations with several artists who'd come to Buffalo to work on the exposition and gathered round him instead, patting him on the back and asking after his health. The artists responded with stiff, chilled smiles. They knew Elbert was not of their ken. He was a master salesman who'd decided to put his talents to the cause of "art" as he defined it. They doubted the quality of the work produced by the Roycroft shops; more important, they could never forgive Elbert the work's mass appeal. But businessmen adored Elbert, and he basked in their adulation. To date, Elbert's greatest commercial achievement had been the publication of a little story called *A Message to Garcia*, a paean to the loyal and unquestioning worker (he who was becoming so rare in these days of labor unrest and unionism). This little story had sold millions of copies, especially in bulk orders from railroads and other industries, which passed it out among workers and clients alike as a kind of management-approved "inspiration." It had even made its way into the military, where generals ordered it distributed to their troops.

"I am here to discuss the role of the Roycrofters at the Pan-American!" Elbert proclaimed to one and all. "We have much to offer the Pan-American, but—does the Pan American have anything to offer us? Who will be the first to tell me?" He didn't have to wait long for a response: John Milburn was already at his side.

Elbert's community in East Aurora included a printing press and bookbindery, a furniture-making shop, and leather and metalworks. The colony was based on William Morris's Arts and Crafts movement in England, which fostered individual craftsmanship as an antidote to industrial mass production. To the Arts and Crafts ideal, Hubbard added what he might have called a good dose of American ingenuity— i.e., commercialism. The Roycrofters sold their work far and wide, aided by a variety of bonus offers.

After his conversation with Milburn about possible Roycroft exhibition space at the Pan-Am, Elbert sought me out.

"Your 'saloon' is the best place in town to do business, Miss Louie, and I'm indebted to you," he said loudly, giving me a welcome public endorsement. "Gentlemen, I'm off to a lecture at Lyric Hall on the evils of hydroelectric power development at the Falls. Anyone wish to join me?"

If Elbert was going, then of course everyone (except the artists) did wish to join him, myself included. Only a half hour before, my guests had been deriding this lecture, but Elbert was sure to make it fun and probably create some fireworks along the way.

There was a pleasant, misty drizzle outside. Several of the men had carriages, offering enough room for all of us. After everyone was settled, Elbert and I found ourselves in his carriage alone. As we set off—two misfits, unbound by the conventions that trapped our peers—a plan occurred to me.

About ten years earlier, Elbert had carried on a love affair with a schoolteacher in East Aurora named Alice Moore. This was a close-kept secret. Alice had moved to Boston and given birth to a daughter. Although there was talk of divorce, Elbert and his wife, Bertha, who had four children, patched things up. Bertha was a gifted miniaturist and took an active role in the artistic production at Roycroft, decorating books and porcelain; I wouldn't have been surprised to learn that Elbert had avoided divorce because he didn't want to lose Bertha's talents.

At any rate, this was the matter that had caused the rift between Elbert and his brother-in-law John Larkin. I knew the details because Elbert's sister had confessed the story to me one day in a torrent of tears when she was in my office discussing the spring fund-raising fête. She and her husband sided with Bertha, she told me; her brother was selfish and self-indulgent. She and Mr. Larkin no longer wanted anything to do with him.

I liked Elbert and he liked me, and I saw no reason to change my opinion. I'd met Alice Moore once at a teachers' conference before I knew of her relationship with Elbert, and I remembered her as being straitlaced and puritanical, even within the context of schoolmarms. She seemed an odd choice for Elbert, but who was I to say? I believed Elbert maintained some degree of contact with her; Alice had recently gone out West to teach after settling her daughter with her relatives in Buffalo (how different my life might have been, if only I'd had some family, somewhere, to help me). In his writings Elbert spoke in favor of free love and equal rights for women, and he touted the virtue of following one's heart—topics undoubtedly designed to please Alice, wherever she was reading them.

"Elbert," I said, sidestepping into my plan, "you know how you're always lauding the virtues of 'free love'?"

"Why, Miss Barrett, is this a proposition? I always thought you went quite the other way. Won't Miss Coatsworth be shocked? However, now that you mention it, I must say you have a radiance about you that I've always admired. Quite artistic. I do admire women of intensity. Of thoughtful intensity. Of probing intelligence. In short, I've always admired *you*, Louisa. Therefore your wish, my dear, is my command." He placed a hand upon my knee.

Laughing, I returned his hand to his own knee, squeezing it to keep it there. "Thank you, Elbert, for your admiration. I must assure you that I do not 'go the other way,' as you so elegantly describe it, but Miss Coatsworth is an excellent foil, don't you think? Her mere existence seems to answer so many questions about me, without answering them at all."

"You're a sly one, Louisa." He regarded me with renewed respect. "Almost as sly as me."

"Oh, that I could never be," I assured him.

"Is there no chance for me, then?" he asked with mock regret.

Patting his leg, I said, "Not today, Elbert, dear," although it was difficult for me to understand why, since he was most attractive, with his pouting brown eyes and smooth skin. He smelled pleasantly of woods and grass—undoubtedly a special scent he was developing to compete with his brother-in-law's perfumed soaps. He was gentle, easygoing, and comforting. In short, he was everything against which my girls had no defense. Around him I felt none of the fear that beset me with other men. Loving him would be much too easy, and for that reason, probably, I felt no inclination to do so.

"May I inquire as to the origin of your unexpected though not unwelcome question?"

"One of my students has found herself . . ." I searched for the words, "in an *awkward* position, as they say." I raised my eyebrows meaningfully. "One of the results of free love that its proponents seldom address."

"Yes, indeed," he admitted wearily.

"At any rate, she's a shy girl who stumbled into her difficulty more out of innocence than wickedness."

"Or so she would have you believe."

"Perhaps you're right," I acknowledged. "But no matter. The

family has asked me to try to find some . . . solution for her. It occurs to me that Macaulay could sponsor a summer apprenticeship with the Roycrofters, and this girl could be the recipient of the first scholarship."

"An interesting idea. Where would the money come from to support this apprenticeship?"

"At the moment I have some discretionary funds at my disposal." I planned to ask the Rushmans to donate the money anonymously.

"Is the girl artistic?"

"Not that I've seen."

"A fine opportunity, then, Louie, to instill some artistry in her. What makes you think her secret will be safe with us?"

"Because it will please your sense of righteous rebellion to keep it safe."

"True enough."

"She must live in your own house. Bertha will not object?"

"Bertha will understand the—a—social significance of our action. The girl would be expected to work, however. Bertha could assign her various tasks in her room. Watercoloring borders, that kind of thing."

"She is the type of girl who is only too happy to help."

"Mmm," he pondered, "I've met that type before. Quite irresistible."

"In this case you'll steel yourself against temptation."

"Yes, yes, all right." He gave me one of his bad-boy looks.

"Now then, this girl has a special love of butterflies; one might even say that butterflies have contributed to her current condition." I regarded him wryly. "Perhaps Bertha could set her to painting butterflies. She understands them in all their permutations."

He looked at me with bemusement. "Are you implying something?"

"Oh, yes, indeed," I said, enjoying his confusion. "At any rate, she travels with her grandmother."

"An immigrant grandmother?"

"Yes, in fact. German. From a farm, I believe."

"Can she cook? Strudel? Sausage? How I love immigrant grandmothers."

"I thought you would."

"With the addition of the grandmother, I shall be more than happy to help you—I shall be grateful to help you!" With relish he rubbed his hands together. "Well, then, I leave the details to you. Just keep me informed."

And with that he took the liberty of kissing me hard on the forehead, to seal our agreement.

When we arrived, Lyric Hall was already crowded, for lectures were fashionable. Buffalo was a city that attracted lecturers: Mary Wollstonecraft Shelley, Lucy Stone, Matthew Arnold, all had graced Lyric Hall. Tonight we would hear Daniel Henry Bates, the man who'd led the protest at the power station on the day I visited with my seniors.

I knew Tom wouldn't be there; he and Margaret had never attended public lectures. Over the weekend I'd seen him briefly at home when I'd dropped off Grace after having lunch with her at the club. He'd tacitly ignored the import of our conversation in the sleigh outside school—he'd made his point, of course, and didn't need to repeat it. With some embarrassment I'd taken him aside and told him Albright's message about the finger in the dike. I was completely disconcerted when he burst out laughing. "My friend certainly has his own inimitable sense of humor, doesn't he?" Tom observed.

"But what does he mean?"

"Oh, he doesn't mean anything."

"But then why—"

"Albright likes to make little jokes. Please don't give the matter another thought. Now then," he said abruptly, "what am I to do with Grace this afternoon? There's a problem that needs solving."

Even as we resolved that they would play tennis, I couldn't quite convince myself that Albright's words were meaningless. Albright might be eccentric and his remark about the dike odd, but he wasn't a fool—far from it: he was one of the city's commercial geniuses, and he, like the other members of my board, undoubtedly had a strong monetary interest in the power station.

Tonight, as our group looked for seats at Lyric Hall, this remained a conundrum in my mind; but I had delivered the message and now it was Tom's issue to resolve. Finally we sat three quarters of the way back, taking up a row opposite an oversized portrait of the Marquis de Lafayette, who had visited Buffalo in 1825. The marquis stood awkwardly on a grassy knoll holding a top hat and walking stick and wearing what looked like extremely high-heeled boots. Such were our heroes.

Because of the rain, the gaslit hall smelled dank. Looking around, I spotted Francesca near the front. My student Maddie Fronczyk and her brother, Peter, sat halfway back. Franklin Fiske was near them, and he gave me a surreptitious salute. On the side aisle sat Frederick Krakauer, looking unusually awake (for him). When he saw me, he stood and waved, causing me intense embarrassment. I wanted him as an ally—or at least not an enemy—but I didn't want him waving to me in public as if we were friends. Mercifully, no one seemed to notice or if they did, assumed Krakauer was waving at my companion: For here as everywhere, Elbert was the center of attention, people turning to stare at him, friends calling out their greetings, strangers coming to shake his hand, to all of which he responded with a never-flagging grin.

Finally everyone was seated. Glancing through the program, Elbert whispered, "I'm suspicious of anyone who uses three names, aren't you? Horrible affectation."

"You are never guilty of affectations," I responded.

He beamed. "At least not *that* affectation."

Bates entered the hall from backstage, accompanied by a small group of supporters. They seemed a dull, conservative lot, but among them was Susannah Riley, who stood out because she was much younger than the others. Bates held her arm, at one point gripping it hard for support as he grimaced in pain. Mostly likely he suffered from arthritis and was too proud to use a cane. He was thinner than I remembered, almost gaunt. His white beard and long hair were uncombed and wild; his eyes flashed.

"Ah," said Elbert appreciatively, "I see he's cultivating the Old Testament prophet look. A smart move, in this context."

Susannah's presence surprised me only in that it was so public, such a forthright statement of allegiance. She'd do well to be more cautious, I thought, or the men in my row would think twice before allowing their wives and daughters to indulge in art lessons taught by a woman they would consider a radical. Looking graceful tonight in a simple dark-blue silk dress, Susannah helped Bates to his chair beside the podium. He whispered to her for several seconds, and she nodded in agreement. The others in the group had already proceeded to their seats in the reserved front row, so she was alone with him, evidently a close confidante. Finally she took her seat.

Courtesy of the newspapers, I now knew more about Bates than I had when I saw him at the power station. He had become involved in the nature preservation movement after an outbreak of typhoid in Harrisburg, his hometown, was traced to the Susquehanna River's polluted waters. He traveled the country crusading for nature-related causes. When he wasn't crusading, he tended his rose garden and wrote books on roses.

Miss Elizabeth Stetson, the director of the museum of the Society of Natural Sciences, gave the introduction. With her prim shirtwaist, severely pulled-back hair, and glasses perched at the end of her nose, she aggressively proclaimed herself to be one of us: one of our happy band of unmarried professional ladies who were considered past their prime before they reached their midtwenties, taking on a perpetual middle age that stretched from roughly twenty-five to fifty-five.

When Bates took the stage, grasping the lectern, he studied the crowd for a long moment before beginning in a strong yet measured tone. "What are we talking about, when we talk about Niagara?" He paused, looking from face to face. "It is this: transcendence. Sublimity. The divine. Yes, when we talk about Niagara, we talk about the Lord God. We talk about how the Lord God, millenniums ago, fashioned a great monument to himself. And that monument is the miracle of Niagara. As Ralph Waldo Emerson has rightly told us, nature is a manifestation of the divine. The contemplation of nature leads us to the divine. And so when we stare into the green waters of Niagara . . ."— once more he paused—"we are staring into the face of God."

"Hogwash," Elbert whispered.

"Now, what is it that the power company wishes to do with this manifestation of God?" Bates gazed around, waiting for an answer. Abruptly his intonation turned harsh: "The leaders of the power company intend to take God's miracle and turn it into bits of steel and aluminum and electric light." He spat out the words. "They tell us they'll only take a teeny, weeny, insy, binsy bit of water," he said like a child, pressing his fingers together to show the small amount, squinting to see it.

He pounded his fist on the podium, jolting me. "But we know them, don't we? We know that their 'tiny bit' is anyone else's ocean. We know they won't be happy until not one drop of water flows across Niagara's precipice. Has not their own prophet declared this policy? Their own 'President of the International Niagara Commission,' their prophet of darkness—Lord Kelvin."

William Thomson, Lord Kelvin, was a renowned British physicist with an expertise in electricity.

"Listen to what 'Lord' Kelvin says: 'I look forward to the time,' he tells us, "when the whole body of water from Lake Erie will find its way to the lower level of Lake Ontario through machinery. I do not hope that our children's children will ever see the Niagara cataract'! So speaks 'Lord' Kelvin," Bates said derisively.

On and on he went. My mind began to wander. An image came to me, of how pleased my father would have been to see Niagara without water. To climb the Falls like any other rock face, simply to study what was there.

"People think me an impractical man," Bates said, shifting tone and regaining my attention. "An unscientific man. An uncompromising man. And I admit it: I will not compromise my faith. But to you who would find it easy to dismiss me as a fool, know that I too have a practical side. I know what will happen—I see it happening already: the American Fall is shrinking, becoming narrower and narrower in its channel. Soon the American Fall will be nonexistent. Dry rock from the shore to Goat Island. Then the broad Horseshoe Fall will begin to shrink, narrower and narrower and so to nothing.

"Hear it now!" he cried. "As the power company in its greed takes more and more of our God-given heritage, Lake Erie itself will become unnavigable—this is fact, not faith. The water level will sink—even in the great harbor of Buffalo ships will run aground. This is fact, not faith. More than ten million gallons a minute, they're taking now: Isn't it enough? Over a foot off the depth, they're taking now: Isn't it enough?

"I have even heard it said"—here his voice dropped, letting us in on a secret—"that at night, when no one is watching, they take thirty-four thousand cubic feet per second to feed their foul industries! When will it be enough?"

"Do you think someone is paying Bates to do this?" Elbert whispered. "Do you think he really believes this nonsense?"

"I think he believes in himself."

"Well said, Louisa. I should make that one of my homilies: He who believes in himself believes in whatever he says."

"Quiet, Elbert."

"Yes, ma'am."

Bates too turned quiet. "Ask yourself this, my friends: Who owns the Falls of Niagara? Is it the lovers of nature and God, or is it J. Pierpont Morgan?"

At the mention of his employer, Frederick Krakauer sat up suddenly, startled out of a quasi-nap, and looked around confusedly, wondering what he'd missed.

"Is it J. Pierpont Morgan and John Jacob Astor and Nicholas Biddle and your own Thomas Sinclair and John Albright"—Bates was raving now—"and George Urban, Jr.—"

His words were drowned out by the cheers of his supporters in the front row. Susannah stood to applaud. Everyone else was silent. Bates nodded at his followers in gratitude, then motioned for Susannah to sit.

"Oh yes, they will try to trick us," he continued. "They will tell us that electricity is good for us." He laughed disparagingly. "That it brings us wonderful things. But let's be honest here. No one but the rich will ever have electric lights. Gaslight makes for glorious streetlamps, and horsepower has willingly pulled our trolleys for generations."

"I wonder if he asked the horses about that," Elbert said. I bit my lip to stop myself from smiling.

"For the common man, electricity has created nothing of value and never will! And so my friends, let us unite. Let us rise up together and take control of our God-given heritage."

"You don't think he's a socialist, do you?" Elbert pondered.

"We—yes, we—have the ability to create the future. Will we create it in the image of God or the image of the devil?" He glanced around. "I know I am only a David, fighting a Goliath. But in this fight I shall never tire. I will fight to victory or to death. My troops are here before you." He motioned to his followers in the front row. "I must warn you that soon the day may come when we will be forced to take matters into our own hands. When we will be forced to fight in every way necessary to fulfill God's will. But we fear no jail. We know that for each of us who is silenced by prison bars, another will come to take his place to fight for the glory of Niagara. God is with us: This we know. Did not God himself pull the devil's engineer Karl Speyer beneath the ice to drown? A big, tall, proud man—sucked helplessly into the holy water of God. Was not his death a sign of what God has in store for all who anger him?"

"Well, here's an interesting new theory of Speyer's death," Elbert mused. "I wonder if Bates has shared his idea with the police. How exactly would you investigate such a theory? Would you begin in a church, do you think? But what denomination? Trinity Episcopal or Westminster Presbyterian? Or would you go right to the source and visit St. Anthony of Padua?" he asked, referring to the Roman Catholic church downtown. "Or even Temple Beth Zion!" Beth Zion was our primary Jewish congregation.

I didn't respond. I had no humor regarding Karl Speyer. Again I envisioned his bulky form, bundled up in a fur hat and a heavy coat with a warm fur collar, heading out the door toward death.

Now Bates's voice was a stage whisper, hissing. "I am a fair man, for God teaches both justice and mercy. So I will tell you: I have here a list"—he took a folded sheet of paper from his jacket pocket and held it up in his fist—"a list of New York State inspectors being bribed to look the other way while the power station steals God's water. I will not humiliate the men on this list by reading it aloud. Not yet."

Around me, the crowd murmured and mumbled—except for the board members in my row, who wore looks of studied boredom and indifference, revealing nothing. Franklin Fiske had referred to bribery when he visited me; I glanced sharply at him, but he too appeared determinedly indifferent. Where would Bates get such a list, I wondered, before remembering Tom's concern about a spy.

"I am satisfied for now, that those involved should know that I possess this list. And that I will use it. When the time is propitious."

"He's got nothing," Elbert said dismissively. "If he did, he would at least unfold the paper. Show us that there's something written on it. It could be completely blank. Nonetheless," he admitted, "it's a convincing tactic. I could learn from this fellow." Elbert made a note in his pocket diary.

"And so I invite all of you to join me in this holy fight—this crusade for Niagara. To you who are leaders of the project, I invite you too— even you—to repent your ways, to enter God's forgiveness, to join us in our holy war to recapture the great cataract of Niagara in the name of the Lord!"

Appearing exhausted and vulnerable, and amidst the cheers of his followers, he collapsed into his chair beside the podium. He covered his face with one hand as if he were praying. His supporters rose in a standing ovation, but he kept his face covered. Clapping with a kind of fury, Susannah Riley turned to search the crowd. Tears glinted on her cheeks, and she did not wipe them away. She seemed in a religious ecstasy, swept up in the moment, her face shocking in the purity of its beauty. Francesca half-stood to acknowledge her, and Susannah's sudden smile was like a brilliant jolt of love that made me avert my eyes, ashamed to have invaded their intimacy.

Elbert was saying appreciatively, "Yes, yes, he certainly has dramatic flare. He'd make a top-notch salesmen. Just need to get him a better product. Maybe he could do a book for us. On roses. *Roycroft Roses.* He could barnstorm the country. Make a fortune." Elbert made another note in his diary.

Miss Stetson took the podium. Meanwhile Susannah hurried onto the stage to give Bates a quick hug of reassurance. As she turned to leave, she squeezed his hand between both of hers and then slipped away. "In the interest of free and open discussion," Miss Stetson said with flat objectivity, "we have asked Mr. James Fitzhugh, acting chief engineer of the Niagara Frontier Power Project, to give the rebuttal." Surprisingly, Bates's supporters in the front quickly calmed, returning to their seats.

Mr. Fitzhugh was in his early thirties, clean-shaven and pale. He had been Karl Speyer's on-site assistant.

"Thank you, Mr. Bates, for sharing your opinions," Fitzhugh said with a touch of nervousness. He arranged his papers on the podium and cleared his throat. "First, I wish to say—and here I speak for the entire staff and directors of the Niagara Frontier Power Project—that we share your concerns. The preservation of an adequate scenic effect at Niagara has always been foremost in our minds. The Falls at Niagara are a source of daily amazement and spiritual comfort to us all."

This was greeted by hostile mumbling from the front row: The preservationists would consider Fitzhugh's remarks hypocritical and disingenuous.

"Let me say too, that the notion of taking all the water from Niagara is irrational on its face. No one could possibly take all the water. The technology to do so does not exist."

So Fitzhugh, like Krakauer, regarded "all" as a relative term.

"Furthermore, our charters from the state of New York would never permit us to take all the water. Water use is strictly controlled and we are subject to frequent inspections."

"And who's paying the inspectors' salaries?" someone in the front shouted.

Fitzhugh ignored the question. As he began to read from his prepared statement, I knew he would not address or even acknowledge Bates's threats and innuendoes; Fitzhugh would say only what he'd been told to say.

"The most important point to realize is that our work is in fact saving Niagara. As many of you know, the Falls suffers a natural recession of as much as four feet per annum or more, on average. In other words, the cataract is destroying itself. In the thousands of years since its creation, the cataract has cut a gorge some seven miles long, from the Queenston Bluff to its present location. By lessening the water's incessant grinding at the limestone and shale of the escarpment—even by such small amounts, mere inches on the overall depth—we significantly slow this natural process of destruction."

I saw my father diagraming the process for me, showing me how the soft rock broke down. A relentless retreat, he called it: five hundred feet per century. Someday Niagara would be gone. How I missed him. How I yearned to be held again within the aura of his affection. To be his child again. Forever. To feel his beard scratch against my face as he kissed my cheek.

"As we take water from the river, we remain alert always to our charters from the state of New York." Like an echo, Fitzhugh's voice invaded my mind. "Solemnly we vow to preserve Niagara for the enjoyment and contemplation of future generations."

I sighed. Fitzhugh was appealing enough, and he spoke with a measured calm that I appreciated after Bates's dramatics. But he was an innocent compared to Daniel Henry Bates; a lamb in the lion's den.

"Mr. Bates visits us from the esteemed city of Harrisburg, Pennsylvania," Fitzhugh continued. "Therefore it is easy for him to speak of Niagara as if it existed only as a tourist attraction. But for those of us like myself and Mr. Thomas Sinclair and, I would guess, most of the audience here tonight—those of us who make our homes on the Niagara Frontier—benefits beyond tourism derive from the production of hydroelectric power at Niagara.

"First, this power reduces our dependence on coal. No longer are we at the mercy of the labor unrest which so often disrupts the coal industry. I'm sure no one here has forgotten last year's devastating six-week strike, which pushed coal prices to extortionist levels. In the first months of 1901, however, our electrical output was equal to more than one thousand tons of coal a day. Furthermore, as electricity replaces coal, there is a concomitant natural purification of the atmosphere. In other words, the air becomes cleaner. Easier to breathe. Here too, as with saving the Falls, our interests commingle with those of the nature preservationists.

"In addition, the power station has created jobs for this area— thousands of jobs at the power station itself and at developing industries throughout the area, including the steel mills now under construction at Stony Point."

Clearing his throat, he ruffled through his papers. "Now to the specifics of power generation. Mr. Bates grossly exaggerates in his reports of water usage. But in order to understand the true figures and their meaning, the numbers must be put in context. When you understand the volume of the Falls, you will understand how little impact the power station has."

He took a deep breath and, so to speak, plunged in. "The natural flow of water over the Falls is two hundred and two thousand cubic feet per second, or five and a half billion gallons per hour. This is the equal of five million horsepower. The depth at the center of the Horseshoe Falls is estimated at approximately twenty feet. Mr. Bates's diversion figure of thirty-six thousand cubic feet per second is absurd. The maximum capacity of each station is no more than nine thousand cubic feet per second, or seventy-two thousand horsepower."

"Ah," Elbert whispered, "he's trying to slip something past us, telling us the usage for one station, when they have, what, two on-line, another coming? Sneaky little bastard." From Elbert, that was a compliment.

"In actuality, the power station diverts approximately seven million gallons a minute, which equals no more than three to six inches off the depth at any given time. Such usage is minuscule within the overall context, and completely unnoticeable. The accusation that water usage increases at night is patently false, as well as illogical. Apart from those few industries which operate twenty-four hours a day, demand lessens at night."

Could this be a trick too? I had thought that the whole point of electrolytic and electrochemical industries was that they *did* operate twenty-four hours a day.

"An aggregate of daily water use—"

Sotto voce, Elbert said, "I've had enough of this." He rose beside me. "Excuse me, Miss Stetson. Forgive me, Mr. Fitzhugh." With his voice carrying through the hall and capturing all attention, Elbert bowed to them both. "An inspired and passionate presentation for the engineers and mathematicians among us, but I can keep silent no longer."

Fitzhugh looked stunned, moving backward to find his chair and sitting down with a bump beside Bates, who kept his face shielded with one hand.

Elbert stood proudly tall. He was renowned for his lecture tours (and for the high fees he received for them), and many in the audience probably felt themselves lucky to be hearing him speak for free. "The real issue here, if I may be so bold, is not cubic feet per second or gallons per minute or horsepower per hour or year or century." He waved off these details. "The real issue here—and a great truth it is—has been ignored. Must *I* speak to it? Will no one else rise up to share the great truth that has been ignored?"

Pausing to build dramatic impact, he looked around with a benign, forgiving smile. "Will no one offer unto this debate the truth that Sinclair, Albright, Astor, Vanderbilt, Biddle, and all the rest are as much heroes as Daniel Henry Bates so obviously thinks he himself is? Will no one speak for the industrialist heroes among us?

"Let me paint their picture." He waved his arm expansively, as if to create the illustration on the wall. "There they are, straddling the continent: investing their money, putting their families' futures at risk, changing the nation with the discoveries they have helped bring into being. They are the new explorers: the new Columbus, the new Ponce de León, the new Henry Hudson. They are the ones willing to open themselves to new ideas. They are the ones who find the engineers and inventors and support them through the long hard hours of dark struggle until the coming of the light. They are the ones who offered a haven to Nikola Tesla with his alternating current, Charles Martin Hall with his aluminum, Edward Goodrich Acheson with his carborundum. Ladies and gentlemen, I propose a round of applause: to the industrialists!"

And he got his applause, all right. Indeed he had electrified the crowd.

"Now, I must also say"—and here he took on that self-deprecating, I-know-how-naughty-I-am look that let him be all things to all people—"being just an old-time socialist, as many of you know . . ." Grinning, he glanced around the room, eliciting a few laughs. "Mr. Bates raises one interesting question, and that is, who does own the Falls of Niagara?" Honest bewilderment seemed to suffuse his demeanor. "Mr. Bates would have us believe that 'lovers of nature and God' own the Falls of Niagara. One presumes that Mr. Fitzhugh would vouch for ownership by the titans of industry. At the moment, the only people who appear to own the Falls are those who are in a position to exploit it. And I find Daniel Henry Bates to be as exploitative as Thomas Sinclair!" The audience began to shift in their seats uncomfortably.

"Let us debate this question: Who owns the Falls? Not the land itself, now so graciously preserved as the reservation—" He bowed toward the men (most of them in our row) who had spearheaded the movement for the state park years before. They noticeably did not meet his gaze. "But the water that flows over it. Who owns that water? Surely not our friends from the nature preservation movement. Nor the eminently trustworthy and incorruptible bureaucrats of the state of New York." This garnered a few laughs. "Nor their fellows of the royal province of Ontario. Nor even the noble industrialists wealthy enough to build power stations.

"Once we know who owns the waters, then we will know who owns the power so graciously produced by the power company. We will also know who owns the profits from the power being so graciously produced by the power company. And then we may even be surprised to discover"—he paused for effect—"that the common citizenry own the profits. Who should administer those profits on behalf of the citizenry is a question that I, your humble servant, am unable to answer."

Abruptly Elbert sat down, to absolute silence. "Well, that certainly shook them up a bit," he whispered to me, looking pleased.

John Milburn rose—as I could have predicted. Needless to say, he was the attorney for the Niagara Frontier Power Company. "May I interject a word here, Miss Stetson? With due respect for the speakers thus far, I wish to enter this debate from a somewhat different angle. An approach closer to the truth, I believe, than what we have heard. Far removed from the threats of violence and defamation presented here tonight. Such threats have no place at civilized gatherings in a nation founded on democratic principles." He paused, allowing this rebuff to Bates's tactics to register with the audience.

"I am a God-fearing man," Milburn continued. Elbert gave a loud sigh. "I worship my God each week at Trinity Church, as many of us do."

"Mmm. An appeal to crass elitism, not always bad," Elbert now reflected.

"It seems to me—and I'm more than willing to consult the Reverend Davis on this issue—that God made the earth for the glorification of man. God has given the great Falls at Niagara to man, for man's benefit. In the sight of God, men are more important than waterfalls. In Genesis 1:26, the words are clear. Forgive me if I compress: 'And God said, Let us make man in our image, after our likeness; and let them have dominion . . . over all the earth.'

"Therefore we see that the question of ownership is irrelevant: God owns the waters, and gives them to man to do with what he will, for the benefit of others. Is there any greater benefit than the easing of backbreaking labor through the electrification of factories? Is there any greater benefit than the lighting of the darkness? Are these not amongst God's greatest blessings? Is not the power that we produce at Niagara a holy thing—as blessed surely as the sight of water pouring over a cliff? Let us not forget that we are making light at Niagara. Is not light the symbol of God incarnate?" He paused, looking over the crowd with the persuasive sincerity of the attorney he was, playing us as if we were a jury. "And if light is the symbol of God incarnate, then electricity is a manifestation of the divine."

Oh yes, I thought; let us make something more of Niagara than water falling over a cliff. Let us allow Niagara to transform the nation. God grant that one day we may walk across the riverbed in peace, without the surging water to entrap and haunt us.

"Yes, I know I wax philosophical. But most people truly do know me"—nodding towards Bates, Milburn treated us to his most charming smile—"as a practical man. So I shall continue in a practical vein: Like Mr. Bates, I believe that we have the power to create the future. Will we permit the vast, God-given natural resource that is Niagara to go to waste? Never. Never! Let us remember that Buffalo's future and the future of Niagara are one and the same. When the work at Niagara is complete, we will become the greatest city in America.

Let us embrace our future—and let us permit our future to embrace us."

The audience's uproarious approval effectively brought the meeting to a close. When I looked around, I saw Susannah Riley staring at John Milburn with a fixed expression of hatred in her eyes.

Chapter Sixteen

I warned Francesca to tell Susannah to stop. Or at least to be less public. I could not be put in the position of defending her. "If the board comes to me with complaints," I said, "I'll have no choice but to let her go."

We were walking along the second-floor balcony of the Market Arcade in the late afternoon, the Saturday after the lecture. We passed tiny shops filled with specialities, from the rarest cigars to the finest lace. Sunlight filtered through the skylight. The arcade led from elegant, refined Main Street to the rather different Washington Street, with its outdoor Chippewa Market. The Chippewa Market was a pastureland of carts and stalls frequented by women wearing babushkas and shawls who haggled over the price of live chickens. Shawls spanned cultures, however, and shawls had brought us to the Market Arcade today. Francesca was looking for a cashmere shawl, and she was in a self-indulgent, cashmere-shawl frame of mind.

"I have no control over Susannah," she said with sardonic pride. "As the poets say, I can only love her."

I caught myself on the verge of harrumphing but quickly stopped myself so as not to slip into the demeanor of Miss Maria Love. Reasonably I said, "If you love her, then you must try to protect her."

"I can't protect her. She makes her own decisions. I've offered her everything, I assure you, to get her into my grasp. I've even offered her a trip to Angkor Wat."

"Angkor Wat! I thought that was *my* special reward. You're certainly feckless in your affections."

"No, just determined to get there. To Angkor Wat, I mean. But Susannah won't even consider it. She can't leave the city while the 'battle for Niagara' is going on; while she's saving her little bit of the world." Francesca shrugged mischievously. "I'll just have to wait for her to lose all her teaching positions and all her painting commissions because of her 'radical' ideas, and then in poverty she'll come begging to me to rescue her. You know how I love to rescue people. I even rescued you, don't forget, bringing you here from Wellesley when you had not a place in the world or a penny to call your own."

"Yes, indeed you did," I acknowledged.

"So I shall certainly not urge Susannah to caution; I shall urge her to greater excess, to hasten the day of my victory!"

A group of ladies, wives of professional men we knew, approached us on the narrow balcony. Their skirts brushed together in a rustle of silk. Among them was Dr. Perlmutter's youthful wife, beautifully attired in red plaid. Francesca took my arm and giggled intimately against my ear. The ladies passed us single-file with knowing glances.

When they were out of earshot, Francesca whispered, "How was that? More flirtatious than was even necessary, eh?"

"Oh, I'm most grateful." And I was, even though part of me felt wretched that for so many years I'd required this subterfuge.

"Now, on to other matters," she said. "Miss Love and Mr. Wilcox have bestowed a favor upon me."

"Whatever do you mean?"

"Good! I've surprised you. I feared you might have heard a rumor of it."

"Of what?"

"I've been appointed president of the Infant Asylum."

"The Infant Asylum?" There was an Orphan Asylum on Virginia Street, but I'd never heard of an Infant Asylum.

"It's a newly-created subdivision of the Orphan Asylum. I suppose they had so many undeserving newborns left on the doorstep that they had to set up an organization solely for them. Miss Love wants the babies to have a building of their own, but that's in the future. Right now they're housed on a single floor of the Orphan Asylum, within squalling distance of the 'diseased and infectious' older children, as Miss Love describes them. Doesn't she have a lovely gift for language? Anyway, the job will primarily involve begging my friends for donations. But there'll be oversight too, and some administrative work.

Would you like to know the charming way she informed me of my appointment?" Francesca squeezed my arm, obviously relishing the tale. "She didn't politely ask if I might be interested. Oh no, not her. She invited me to tea at 184 and she said, 'Frances,' she always calls me Frances, 'we both know you'll never have children of your own, so you might as well look after these God-forsaken creatures.'" Francesca did an inspired imitation of Miss Love's regal tones. "'I wouldn't dare send a young wife over there, with all that corruption and degradation, but *you* can handle it.' Of course! Corruption and degradation—just my *métier*."

"Couldn't you refuse her?"

"My dear Louisa." She put her arm around me. "Refuse Miss Love? I'd never work as an architect again."

I had known that the obedience rule applied to me; that it applied also to a woman of Francesca's position was consoling.

"I went over there yesterday. To see it. The Infant Asylum." She turned, leaning against the balustrade, looking all at once unsure of herself. "Louisa, it was like—it was like some kind of hell. The filth. The smell. The crying. And it seemed—well, I was too afraid to ask anyone, any of the matrons, I mean, but it seemed like all the babies were dying. That they were put there specifically so that they'd have a place to die. The matrons use the sheets for shrouds. That's one of their biggest expenses, I found out when I looked at the account books: the sheets they use for shrouds." Her eyes glinted as they teared. "Well, I was wondering . . . I mean"—she struggled to keep her composure— "seeing as *you'll* never have children of your own, and *you'll* never be a young wife, so we needn't worry about corrupting and degrading *you*— I was wondering if you'd go there with me sometime and take a look at everything and give me advice. I can't do it alone, it's too much for me to do alone." For once her irony had deserted her.

"Yes, of course, Francesca. Of course." I leaned to hug her, touching my cheek to hers.

Later that afternoon, as I made my way up the Rushmans' curving drive, I felt especially saddened by Francesca's description of the Infant Asylum. I had a five o'clock appointment to meet Abigail's parents to tell them my plan. The Rushmans lived in one of our newer mansions, the trees around it thin-limbed. The house was on North Street, our second most fashionable street after Delaware Avenue. However, the Rushmans' abode was near the intersection with Richmond, perilously close to less elite thoroughfares. Perhaps for the Rushmans, being able to say "North Street" made up for any middle-class views from the windows.

The man of the house was visiting one of his stores, Mrs. Rushman explained as she received me alone in the library. I didn't know where Abigail was. In this room, where I had placed the beginning of Abigail's difficulties, the Persian rugs were thick and silent, the sofas deep-burgundy velvet, inviting and pliant. The leather-bound books in the floor-to-ceiling cases looked never-touched; undoubtedly they had been purchased in bulk and placed upon the shelves by height.

Motioning me to a straight-backed chair while she herself sank into one of the sofas, Mrs. Rushman asked bluntly, "What is it that you propose to do?" Her voice carried a hint of dismissal, as if she were addressing a social inferior. I steadied myself with the thought of her daughter; I was doing this for Abigail, not for the woman before me.

Equally blunt, I said, "I've determined that Abigail and her grandmother shall go to East Aurora after Abigail's graduation and stay with the Roycrofters for the duration of her confinement. We shall announce that she has won a prestigious artistic fellowship, which you and your husband shall fund—anonymously, of course. She will spend the summer learning how to watercolor and practicing the art of illuminating manuscripts. She will be under the special protection of Mr. Elbert Hubbard and his most reputable wife, Bertha. Mr. Hubbard understands the circumstances and is willing to be of assistance. Despite his reputation for flamboyance, I assure you that he is trustworthy in this regard. I will take on the responsibility to speak with Dr. Perlmutter to make arrangements for the birth and adoption of the baby."

There was a long pause. I heard a clock ticking. With each tick Mrs. Rushman's broad features became more pointed and tight. "The money is not an issue, but East Aurora is totally unsuitable," she said, her lips a thin line. "You've chosen badly, if I may say so, Miss Barrett." There it was again, the not-so-subtle condemnation of my role. Did she assume this attitude to hide her shame and responsibility for what she had allowed to happen to Abigail? I could only hope so.

"Why is East Aurora unsuitable?"

"Abigail is not an artist."

"She will learn to be. I imagine she'll enjoy it. And East Aurora is lovely in the summer. Restful, I assure you," I said, with what I hoped sounded like a warning.

"There has never been an artist in our family. It is completely unacceptable. You must find something else."

My eyes narrowed. "Well, that is disappointing, Mrs. Rushman," I said slowly. "I'm sorry you feel that way, because art is so fashionable for women these days." I paused to let the notion sink in. "Witness Alice Glenny—Mrs. John Clark Glenny—called upon to paint the murals for the New York State Building at the exposition. And Evelyn Rumsey Cary—Mrs. Dr. Charles Cary—designing the official poster for the exposition. And what a beautiful poster it is! It would be impossible to find two women more . . . ladylike than Mrs. Glenny and Mrs. Cary. Two women more . . . welcomed at the Rumsey estate—and I'm speaking here of the Bronson Rumsey estate. Of course for Mrs. Cary, née Rumsey, the estate is her family home." I sighed. "Both ladies have mentioned to me that they may one day offer Macaulay girls the opportunity to assist in their studios. What a chance for Abigail, gone to waste."

This was a lie, but the two gracious ladies in question, both of whom frequented the Twentieth Century Club, would intuitively cover for me if faced by an assault from the likes of Mrs. Rushman.

"Really." She bit her lower lip, mulling over the matter in this new and appealing light. "It's true that Abigail has always leaned toward the artistic. Maybe I've been wrong to discourage her. She's *very* talented, you know," Mrs. Rushman assured me. "Mrs. Cary would be the first to recognize her talent, I'm sure. Yes." She clapped her hands with childlike glee. "I'll announce the award of Abigail's prestigious artistic fellowship at dinner this evening. You can let me know how much money to send you whenever it's convenient. Tonight we're dining at the Freddy Coatsworths—Francesca Coatsworth's second cousin," she added with proud confidentiality. "Possibly you know the Freddy

Coatsworths." Her tone indicated that she was quite certain I did not. "Your paths most likely never cross, however, as they have only sons, not daughters."

"Oh, Mrs. Rushman," I said modestly, "in my position, I'm lucky enough to be on familiar terms with all the important families in town, daughters or no."

When I returned home, a large pile of mail awaited me. I flipped through it at my desk, pulling out two items for immediate attention: a large envelope from Tom and a note from Franklin Fiske.

When I opened Tom's envelope, however, I discovered that his message was nothing more than a note too, attached to a larger sheet of paper. After a moment's confusion I realized that the large sheet was a mock-up for an inside page of tomorrow's *Express*. The note, in Tom's precise handwriting, read simply, *Dexter Rumsey sent this to me. I hope it sets your mind at ease.*

The article, marked as page 3, filled less than a third of the space across the top of the page. DETERMINATION IN PARK TRAGEDY, the headline read. The article reported that the coroner, in an official report to be released on Monday, had unequivocally concluded that Karl Speyer's death was accidental. The article went on to review the circumstances surrounding his death on March 5 and the stringent investigation conducted by the police. There was some discussion of the medical difference between death by drowning and death by exposure, which I skipped after a few words because the details made me queasy. The article concluded with a quote from Tom, in his capacity as director of the power project, to the effect that we might all rest more peacefully now, knowing this tragic matter was finally resolved.

I reread Tom's note: Mr. Rumsey had sent this to him. He hoped it would set my mind at ease.

I leaned back in the chair and closed my eyes to think. The coroner's conclusion had a certain logic, but was it true? Moreover, did Tom believe it to be true, or did he know it to be false? Step by step I parsed the matter out: First, Mr. Rumsey had offered the *Express* the opportunity to print the story before the official findings were released. The

Express was our most prestigious newspaper (Mark Twain had once been its editor), and it had notably abstained from the sensational speculations about Speyer that had filled most of the other papers. The *Express* could in fact be called Mr. Rumsey's favorite newspaper. Undoubtedly Mr. Rumsey had dictated the placement of the story on page 3, where it would be noticed but not create a fuss.

I wasn't surprised that Mr. Rumsey had given the *Express* the opportunity to print the story first. What did surprise me, however, was that Mr. Rumsey had given Tom the opportunity to read the story first. The coroner's report said Speyer's death was accidental, the least controversial of all possibilities. What had Mr. Rumsey hoped to gain by withholding it for so long? All at once I felt chilled, as a comprehension of his purpose crept upon me. He must have withheld the report as a kind of warning to Tom. As a way to say in effect, if you attempt to cross us, we have the power to destroy you—by truth or falsity, what does it matter? At this moment you are safe; we have issued a report that frees you, but next time we might make a different decision. *I have my finger in the dike, but I can't hold the waters back much longer.* I was slowly beginning to grasp the meaning of Albright's seeming nonsense.

And yet . . . if Mr. Rumsey felt the need to make this oblique warning, he must have believed that Tom was a threat to him—to all of them. Suddenly I perceived Tom as an independent center of power, able to withstand and even manipulate the others. This explained why he so easily turned down a position on the board: he truly did not feel the need to lunch with Mr. Rumsey each month. Mr. Rumsey had nothing to offer him. Now I saw why people like Maria Love distrusted him. He had no need or desire to be part of their group, and that was frightening to them. Even Krakauer and Albright were frightened: Why else would they attempt to approach him through me? They were all frightened—why, I still couldn't say. In a full-scale dispute between the two sides, who would win? What would be the leverage that would determine the final outcome?

I would have to watch, and wait, to understand. And then I realized that the report, even if it were true, bore no relation to truth whatsoever. It represented only what Mr. Rumsey, in his wisdom, had decided the city should believe.

Bitterly shrugging at these intrigues, I pushed the newspaper page aside and turned to Fiske's note:

My dear Miss Barrett,

I have a confession to make: I have never visited the Falls of Niagara. I'm thinking I'd better see them before certain friends of ours turn them into a barren cliff.

Will you honor me with your insights—uncompromising and unfrivolous—on an excursion to the Mighty Cataract?

Fiske

Well, that was certainly a change of pace. A man was asking me to join him on a pleasure excursion? Unheard of! I reread the note searching for ulterior motives but found none. Nor did I find even a hint of coded seduction. I found only friendship . . . and the friendship was welcome to me. After my dispiriting analysis of the Express article, Fiske had provided what felt like a jolt of freedom—an opening for me to step out, if only for a day, from the strictures which bound me.

I hadn't been to see the Falls (as distinct from the power station) since my visit with my father years ago. This was actually quite an accomplishment, if not an oddity: to live so long in Buffalo and never visit the Falls. Margaret had taken Grace to the Falls often for picnics, traveling home with Tom when he finished work. She had frequently urged me to join them, but if truth be told, I was afraid to go—afraid to face again my father's admonitions and my father's tears. His irrational fears had become mine, and I even felt flashes of reluctance that Grace should visit the Falls so often. Alas, I couldn't stop her, for the decision had been Margaret's to make.

Today, impulsively, almost as a harmless protest against Mr. Rumsey's control, I decided to put my fear aside. As I wrote my acceptance, suggesting to Fiske that we visit the Falls on the upcoming Friday (school met for only a half-day on Fridays), I congratulated myself for having no impediments of propriety in my way. A supposedly middle-aged intimate of Francesca Coatsworth need not worry about society's view of an excursion to Niagara with a cousin of Mrs. Dexter Rumsey. Yes, I had the independence of a man, as Fiske himself had once pointed out, and I resolved to make the most of it. Furthermore, Fiske had trusted me with the secret reason for his presence here, and that alone meant I could trust him in return.

After ten years of keeping secrets, I valued—perhaps too deeply—the sharing of them.

Chapter Seventeen

I stood near the base of the American Falls, on the wooden walkway, slippery as ice, perched across the jagged rocks. I gripped the guardrail as best I could, my fingers stiff from cold. I was shivering; by force of will I stopped my teeth from chattering. Billows of mist, radiant white, swept past me in waves, concealing and revealing the cliff that rose one hundred eighty feet before me. My eyes ached from the blinding glare, my neck throbbed from staring upward, my hearing was numbed by the dual roar of raging wind and falling water. That roar enveloped me, and each wind gust soaked my face.

"Miss Barrett, do you—" Franklin Fiske's words dissolved in the reverberations around us. He put his arm around my shoulders to steady us, to warm us. The overwhelming power of the Falls—the fear inspired by the Falls—made this closeness possible; made mutual protection our only concern.

We were dressed alike, in yellow oilskin coveralls and hooded coats. On our feet we wore white felt slippers tied with whipcord. Despite these precautions, we were soaked through. Even though the day was warm—it was a bright spring day in mid-May, I reminded myself—Fiske's wet hand was frigid as he placed it over mine on the railing. We had changed into these useless and absurd outfits up above, at the top of the cliff, in the Goat Island dressing house. They were required attire for the Cave of the Winds tour, which Fiske was set on taking. I had seen the cave with my father and would gladly have let my memories remain unchanged, but Fiske said he wanted to see it with me, and so I acquiesced. After changing, we had made the dizzying climb down the narrow, twisting stairway that led to the bottom of the Falls. Along the way our guide, stocky in his own oilskins, had commenced the standard recitation of foolhardy stunts, gruesome accidents, and never-ending suicides in the history of Niagara: men going over in barrels, children tumbling in by mistake, upright citizens being hypnotized by the rapids and leaping to their death—until Fiske had cut him short.

"We're here for God, not the devil," Fiske said, and only I caught the irony in his voice.

Our guide, undoubtedly dependent on tips to survive, commenced a new recitation, this one on the holiness of Father Hennepin, the Franciscan friar who had "discovered" the Falls two centuries before. Then he went further back, to the "savages" who were here even before Father Hennepin. "The savages worshipped the Falls, that they did," he assured us. "Sent their prettiest maidens over in canoes, without their shirtwaists on—or so the story goes. Made their gods very happy, I'm sure." He turned to wink at Fiske. "Not a fate you'd want for your own little lady, eh, sir?" Beneath the shadow of his hood, the guide's face appeared a mask of black whiskers.

Fiske didn't respond, but the guide wasn't waiting for an answer anyway. We'd come to the bottom of the stairway, and he led us gingerly down a rocky ledge and onto this precarious walkway leading to the Cave of the Winds. Nearby, three fishermen formed our only company, casting for sturgeon and bass in a sheltered pool formed by a semicircle of fallen rocks. From their enthusiastic expressions, I knew they'd had excellent fishing today.

"Is it different?" That's what Fiske seemed to be asking me now. We were alone; the guide had walked on ahead, giving us privacy.

"Is it different?" Fiske repeated, bits of his words carried off on streams of wind.

"Is what different?"

"The Falls."

I looked at him uncomprehending.

"Because of the water they're taking out to make electricity."

Oh. I studied the surging mass, trying to recreate my visit with my father. We'd stood directly here, at the base of the falling water, he with his hand on my shoulder to protect me. A spray like glistening icicles hit my face. No, there was no change; the Falls were exactly the same. The water was alive. Like a primeval beast. What more could Daniel Henry Bates want than what was falling before us? How much more frightening, how much more overpowering did the waters need to be for the transcendence Bates sought? For God to touch us as we walked the earth?

I turned to Fiske and shook my head. "No, nothing's changed."

Our guide, himself gripping the guardrail, motioned us toward the final walkway that led behind the cascade itself. All at once he was in a hurry; he probably had a daily quota to meet. We followed his direction. The Cave of the Winds wasn't really a cave, but rather a deeply curved space beneath a wide outcropping ledge. The water surged over the ledge, making a kind of veil in front of the "cave." As a result, this part of the Falls was known as the Bridal Veil. One day—a day that no one could predict, a day which could be today, this instant—the ledge would break off, the unrelenting force of the water pounding it down, the Falls destroying themselves once more.

As we walked on, the wind became even stronger than before, beating us back, refusing us passage. Inching along, I felt as if I were pulling myself through a blizzard, the guardrail my only safety rope. Finally we were beside the sparkling sheet of water. I yearned for the shelter of the cave. A few more steps and we were behind the water.

At first the cave seemed black. Airless and suffocating. My chest ached from the struggle to breathe. Wind-borne sleet slashed my face. Eels which somehow lived in the cave twisted at my feet, around my felt slippers, slimy as they touched my ankles; my father hadn't known how the eels had gotten here, yet here they always were. Then slowly the fish and the sleet both seemed to disappear. The sunlight became a green-white iridescence through the sheet of water, and the water became a sheet of light, a transparent wall moving with such unflinching speed that it seemed not to move at all. Peace descended upon me—eery, luminous, calm.

And then I saw the rainbows . . . in perfect circles on Fiske's face, and at his feet. Spinning. Turning, end on end. Suddenly he was within them—his entire being, suffused with rainbows . . .

He was staring at me, his expression perplexed. I lifted my hands and realized I was covered with rainbows too.

We saw all the sights that day. We traveled on a small electric train down the gorge that the Falls themselves had excavated. We stood on the cliffs above the whirlpool, where the river turns at a right angle and the water, four hundred feet deep, curves upon itself with tranquil-seeming determination. Later, walking on the slender suspension bridge that led across the lower river to Canada, we paused to watch red-tailed hawks chase each other down the gorge, soaring and lunging before returning to their nests high in the rock face.

Crossing into Canada, we tried to avoid the hucksters, barkers, and petty thieves who made the Canadian side of Niagara a third-rate carnival. This rapacious atmosphere lessened my appreciation of the Horseshoe Falls, but not Fiske's. He yearned to admire the twenty-five-hundred foot-wide Horseshoe from every angle. Finally he exhausted me. So while he took the *Maid of the Mist* boat trip (to the very base of the Falls), I enjoyed high tea on the still-gracious terrace of Clifton House.

Fiske and I were perfectly at ease with one another. Almost without noticing, we had begun to address each other informally, using first names. Not for the first time, I envied his confidence, his self-effacing trust in himself. I wished I could be as open to experience as he was. He seemed to take pleasure in observing everything around him, whether he judged it good or ill. A decade ago, I had lost my ability to accept the world with such unmitigated pleasure; I had become a prisoner of myself. Wistfully I wondered, would I ever be able to change, to become more the way *he* was? The idea felt like a bit of magic glimpsed in a dream, far away and never reachable no matter how fast we run to capture it.

When Franklin returned to the terrace of Clifton House, searching me out among the crowded tables—several women turning to stare at his handsome profile after he passed them—I couldn't help but smile at how lucky I'd suddenly become. In my imagination an entire future opened before me, with him at its center—marriage, children, a home to share. How enjoyable this vision was, even though it would only ever be a fantasy.

Franklin must have seen the joy on my face. "Are you laughing at me?" he asked.

"I suppose I am," I replied. He pulled the brim of my hat over my eyes.

Late in the afternoon we returned to the American side of the Falls, where Franklin retrieved his photography equipment from the Great Gorge Route train station. We intended to spend what remained of our day exploring Prospect Point, Goat Island, and the Three Sisters.

Unlike the Falls themselves, Prospect Point and Goat Island did look different to me: more lush, more wild than I remembered, the vistas more open. The last time I'd been here, the riverbank had been chockablock with advertising signboards, pulp and paper mills, brick mills, sheds and shops. In addition, every viewing section had been blocked off by competing owners who demanded separate payments to see the Falls. In 1883, however, then-governor Cleveland had signed the legislation to create at Niagara what became the first state park in the nation; this was the first time state funds—public funds— had been used to purchase land to preserve scenery. Designed by Frederick Law Olmsted to reflect his vision of what Niagara must have been like centuries before, the Niagara Reservation opened in 1885 and admittance was free. The reservation encompassed the riverbank for one mile upstream as well as all the islands in the rapids.

Even before the reservation, however, the Three Sisters Islands had been beautiful. At the stone bridge leading from Goat Island to Asenath, the first of the Three Sisters, Franklin leaned across the balustrade to study the glistening waterfall—only several feet high and about thirty feet wide—known as the Hermit's Cascade. It was named after Francis Abbott, an English eccentric who was drawn to Niagara around 1830. Abbott lived alone and bathed daily in the tranquil, tree-framed pool beneath the cascade . . . until June of 1831, when he walked into the river beneath the Falls and drowned, whether by accident or suicide no one knew.

"The water is so calm," Franklin said.

"So it seems."

"I feel like I could wade in it. I'd like to, in fact." The day had become exceedingly warm. "Perhaps I will!" He began to walk around the balustrade to the riverbank.

"Don't," I said harshly, gripping his arm. Suddenly I saw my father, pulling me back. The scene was before me in perfect clarity, turned crystalline by fear: A little girl leans into the water to capture diamonds, and her father pulls her back.

Franklin looked at me with surprise. "The current is tricky," I said diffidently, glancing away. As tears smeared my eyes, I remembered my father's love. Struggling to make my tone sound cheerful, I added, "I wouldn't want to lose you."

For a long moment he said nothing, simply staring at me in puzzlement. Then, "At least I'll take a picture of the cascade."

Lightly, shaking off my tears, I asked, "Oh, Franklin, what are you going to do with all your pictures?"

"Well, I do need to be faithful to my own disguise. When I get a big pile of them, I'm going to ask John J. Albright to give me an exhibition at his new art museum. You can introduce me to him."

"You're incorrigible."

"Thank you—my specialty."

While Franklin set up his equipment, measuring the light and adjusting the tripod quite as if he really were a professional photographer, I crossed onto Asenath. I roamed among the quiet streams and overgrown eddies, and I watched mallards frolicking among the reeds and indolent swans gliding as if asleep. I climbed over black boulders as smooth as polished obsidian and slippery damp from the never-ceasing vapor of the cataract. Gradually I wandered across the bridges from Asenath to Angeline and so to the last sister, Celinda Eliza, down paths lightly shadowed by the pale green of spring, amid red-winged blackbirds, blue jays and waxwings; through glades of columbine and buttercups and ferns. Brightly colored butterflies flitted around me.

I had made my way through a stand of blossoming dogwoods when suddenly I saw before me a living painting, framed by tree limbs: Susannah Riley, painting at her easel, tendrils of her hair tossing in a gentle riot around her face; and beside her, focused on a smaller easel, biting her lip in concentration, her straw hat tied tightly under her chin so it wouldn't blow away, Grace Sinclair.

It was a moment of perfection, but all I felt—banishing any other consideration—was jealousy, anger, and loss. Grace had come here with Margaret, had set up her drawing pad, just so, with Margaret. They had told me about their afternoons here, regaled me about every turn of the water, every flight of the red-winged blackbirds, every change of blossom and leaf as spring turned to summer and summer turned to autumn. Filled with pain at the memory, with anguish at the idea that Susannah would dare step into Margaret's place, I strode forward.

"Grace, why aren't you in school?"

The two of them looked up, startled. But when Grace realized it was me, she shrieked with delight and ran to me, taking my hand.

"Aunt Loui—I mean, Miss Barrett, what are you doing here?"

So . . . she regarded her trip as an extension of school; she would call me "Miss Barrett," our rule for school. My anger diminished.

"Come and look," she insisted. "I'm doing an oil painting! Look!" She pulled me to her canvas. It was a rendering of the scene before us: the quiet, flower-filled glen, the rocky inlet with its tracery of sunlight. Although the underlying sketch was confident, the colors were muddy, obviously the work of a beginner. "Miss Riley keeps telling me to keep the colors pure, but it's hard."

Breathing deeply, I forced myself into equanimity; I'd been foolish to become upset, but Margaret's presence was so immediate to me still. "You've made a fine start, Grace."

Susannah Riley's picture of the same scene was fluid and alive. She had focused on the light, on the distinctive shading of every object in its path and on the spectrum of shadows in its absence. She had recreated the scene by transforming it.

"This is extraordinary, Miss Riley," I said.

"Thank you," she replied simply, stepping back to stare at the painting. "The hardest thing to capture, for me at least, is the way the light bounces off the water onto the lower leaves of the trees. To me, that's the most beautiful part about being by the water."

"I feel that way too," I said, surprised that here, of all places, we might find common ground with one another.

"But it's so hard to get that reflection just right. Each bit of light is like a different facet—"

Now it was Grace's turn to be jealous. "This is the first time I've painted *plein-air*, Miss Barrett," she interrupted. "That's French for 'outside.' And it's the first time I've used oils!"

"Grace Sinclair!" Susannah said in the strict schoolmarm tone which I managed to use with every student except Grace. "You should know better than to interrupt when adults are speaking—or when anyone is speaking, for that matter."

Grace looked properly cowed, staring at her feet. "Yes, Miss Riley." Probably I had hurt Grace at school over the years by my inability to be strict with her; I'd let her become headstrong and willful, because I couldn't bring myself to discipline her strongly. Even now, I couldn't bare to see her unhappy.

"You've picked a fine subject for your first oil painting, Grace," I reassured her. "The best possible." Then I remembered. "Why aren't you in school?" I didn't let myself say what I felt, which was, Miss Riley, how dare you take Grace out of school and bring her here alone?

"Miss Barrett, it's Friday! Remember? We get out early on Friday."

Ah, yes. She was right. She was here on Friday afternoon for the very reason I was here on Friday afternoon. My upset had made me forget.

"After I got home Miss Riley came to fetch me and we came here on the train. We were here before we knew it!"

So theoretically everything was fine. And yet . . . there was something about their presence here that I didn't like, something beyond my yearning for Margaret. I sensed something inappropriate which I couldn't precisely identify.

"Miss Barrett, did you know the train is run with electricity from Papa's power station?"

"Yes, I did know that."

"Maybe we can all go home together. On the train."

Well, that pleased me. I glanced at Susannah to learn whether she had other plans, but she was staring at the rapids and either hadn't heard or didn't object.

"Yes, Grace, that would be lovely," I said. "Why don't you finish your work. I'll continue my walk, and we can meet again later."

Susannah bestirred herself. "I'll come with you a few paces, Miss Barrett." She put down her brush and palette. "Grace, you work hard and surprise us with all you've done when we get back," she instructed.

As we began to meander along the shore, Susannah said, "It surely is a beautiful day for a trip to the Falls, Miss Barrett. I understand why you came. I always come out here on days like this." When we were safely out of Grace's hearing, she continued, "I'm glad to have a few minutes to talk to you alone. Francesca—I mean, Miss Coatsworth, mentioned that you were worried about my beliefs . . ." After only a few years among us, Susannah had already learned to speak in ellipses.

"Your beliefs don't worry me." Consciously I took on the manner of Mr. Rumsey.

"Well, she said you thought I shouldn't be fighting for what I believe in."

"That's entirely up to you."

"But Francesca thought it might be better—I mean, she thought you might prefer, that I shouldn't be so public."

"The issue is entirely what you prefer. The school continues forward, with or without any particular individuals. You are the only one who can decide your own . . . priorities, is the best way to describe them."

"Oh." She thought for a moment. "Yes, I understand."

We walked on, rounding the shoreline. A blooming forsythia blocked our view of Grace. Susannah turned and gazed out over the rapids; the waters of the Niagara River looked lazy, like a thick blanket. The Canadian shore on the far side of the river was a hazy, evanescent green.

Suddenly I realized that this must be close to the spot where I had tried to capture diamonds for my father. The topography looked familiar, imbedded in my memory from that day long ago, but something was different. Gradually I realized that the island was bigger than I remembered; the shallows were wider. Now I saw what I hadn't been able to see before: how much water the makers of electricity had indeed taken from the river; how much land had been uncovered. Yet there was still enough water—more than enough—for anyone so inclined to find God among the rapids.

I stood at the shallows, staring out. There was a sprinkling of little islands in the rapids, nothing but rocks really, covered with quivering shrubs and bent trees that somehow clung on through the torrent of wind and water. Susannah stood close beside me. As she looked out at the water, there was a strangeness about her, and she bore a probing expression I couldn't comprehend.

"It's mighty, isn't it?" she said quietly. "People are foolish when they think they can control it. It could sweep them away in an instant." She took a step forward, the water lapping at the toes of her boots. The current flowed at over thirty miles an hour, and yet the water appeared almost completely still.

"How wide it is," she said. "Do you see how each tilt of a wave takes on a different reflection? That's never really been captured in the paintings of Niagara—all those separate tilts. A sky or a cloud or a tree reflected in each one. Sometimes I stand here and think how easy it would be to wade in and touch those tilts. To be part of them. To let the water buoy me and carry me gently on its back. That color. That green. The river water's filled with air—that's what gives it the color. Did you know?" She glanced sharply at me, but she didn't wait for an answer. "Sometimes I want to float there. To be part of the color. The air in the water would hold me up. It would be comforting, to be part of that color."

The moving water was hypnotic. She took another step, water surrounding the soles of her boots. She spoke as if from a trance. "Do you ever want to float there? Do you ever imagine what it would be like? The water lifting your body and carrying you away? No sense anymore of right or wrong? No need to fight for anything. Just resting. Floating and never sinking. The water is like God, isn't it?"

She gripped my hand, like a child crossing the street, hesitant but eager. She took a half-step forward. And another half-step. I myself took a step into the rapids. Her words had lulled me. Water seeped into my boots, cooling but not cold. She was right: The water *was* like God. It would bear me away with dignity and cover me with oblivion. I wanted to give myself over. To embrace the oblivion and merge with it and rejoice when the water and I were one.

"What a terrific spot for a picture!" Franklin came up behind us. "You two are getting your boots wet, you'll regret that later."

Franklin cautioned us too loudly. He began to set up his equipment close beside me. Too close. Stepping into the shallows himself. Protecting me with his proximity. I shook myself out of the trance and realized that the water was near my ankles. I was farther into the rapids than Susannah, who in fact hadn't stepped in farther than the arch of her foot. What could I have been thinking of, to forget myself, and my past, so completely?

"Miss Riley, we meet again," Franklin said, reaching out his hand to her in such a way that he placed his body between us. Then I realized that he'd been frightened. There was perspiration along his hairline, and he breathed deeply from running. Could he really have believed I would walk into the water? Did he somehow think that Susannah was a threat to me, that she intended to . . . I studied her, but she was simply herself—a frail young woman seven inches shorter than I was. No . . . Fiske was overreacting, as my father had; there'd been no danger then, there'd been no danger now. Susannah came here frequently; she knew what was safe and what wasn't.

"Mr. Fiske," she replied, holding her hand back for a moment and then, as if feeling she had no choice, reaching out to shake his with a quick, cutting motion.

"I read in the guidebook," he said, "that there's at least one suicide a week here in the summer months. Although the guidebook calls it one 'accident' a week. That's gruesome to think about. Did you know that?" He addressed both of us, but Susannah answered.

"Yes," she said, turning away. "So I've heard."

"Where have you two been!" Grace called, skipping up the path, looking not the least bit worried but rather peeved that she'd been

ignored for so long. She stopped about ten feet from us. "You two got
your boots wet. How could you, Miss Riley, after you made me promise
not to get near the water? That's not fair. I want cool feet, too. I'm
going to—"

"Stay back, Grace," Susannah warned sharply. "Miss Barrett and I
were scouting scenes to paint when a wave caught us. If you get your
feet wet on purpose I'll never bring you here again."

I was surprised by the depth of anger and fear in Susannah's voice.
Grace sulked for a moment, but when Franklin invited her to help him
with a photograph, she perked up. The scene was so incongruous: the
trees waving in the breeze; the dappling misty sunlight; the delicate
wild flowers and flitting birds; the mirror-smooth rocks; the peace of a
springtime glade late in the afternoon—a few steps from the oblivion of
the Falls.

Franklin let Grace take the exposure. Afterward, she glanced at me
with a contented pride that made my entire life seem worthwhile.

The next day, this appeared in the afternoon newspapers, under the
front-page headline, TRAGEDY AT NIAGARA:

*James Fitzhugh, age 31, acting chief engineer of the Niagara
Frontier Power Company, devoted his life to Niagara Falls.
During his lunch break he made a habit of walking along the
river. When the weather was fine—as it was yesterday—he
often went as far as Goat Island and on to the Three Sisters.
Yesterday he apparently made a misstep and was swept to his
death. His battered body was discovered upon the boulders at
the base of the cataract, just before sunset. The police have dis-
counted foul play.*

*"We can only assume that some tragic accident overtook
him, on paths that were well-known to him," said Mr. Thomas
Sinclair, director of the power station. "His work was first-rate
and vital to the nation. I doubt the truth will ever be discovered.
The entire staff of the power station grieves with his family."*

*Readers will remember the accidental drowning in
Delaware Park Lake earlier this year of Mr. Karl Speyer, chief*

engineer of the power station. The two events appear to be unrelated.

When informed of Mr. Fitzhugh's death, Mr. Daniel Henry Bates, leader of the Niagara Preservation Society, commented, "The cataract has claimed him as her own."

PART THREE

Prosperity

I was...at Buffalo in October 1861. I went down to the granaries, and climbed up into the elevators. I saw the wheat running in rivers from one vessel into another, and from the railroad vans up into the huge bins of the warehouses—for these rivers of food run up hill as easily as down.

The work went on day and night incessantly; rivers of wheat and rivers of maize ever running. I saw the men bathed in corn as they distributed it in its flow. I saw bins by the score laden with wheat. I breathed in the flour, and drank the flour, and felt myself to be enveloped in a world of breadstuff...

I began to know what it was for a country to overflow with milk and honey, to burst with its own fruits, and be smothered by its own riches.

North America
by Anthony Trollope, 1862

Chapter Eighteen

onday, May 20. The Dedication Day of the Pan-American Exposition. It was a city holiday, and the schools were closed. Tom had asked me to look after Grace for the day. Theodore Roosevelt, vice president of the United States, led the ceremonies. Nothing else was worthy of attention. The death of James Fitzhugh four days before—who could even remember it? No one.

Except for me. Fitzhugh's death haunted me. First Speyer, now Fitzhugh: the power station's chief engineer and his replacement. An announcement was promptly made that Tom would take over the duties of chief engineer, adding to his already full schedule. I knew the police had labeled both deaths accidental, and yet . . . although I had no proof, I believed more than coincidence was at work. What could these deaths possibly accomplish, however? And for whom? One conclusion was that someone wanted to cripple the power station. But to what end? Besides, the deaths of two people could never disrupt the inevitable progress of electricity. Another possibility (one that Fiske had mentioned) was that Speyer particularly had wanted to force policy in a direction that Tom—or other directors of the station—had disapproved of. But Tom himself was the one in charge, so why would it be necessary to resort to murder just for the sake of policy?

These questions were like a puzzle that defied solution, and they gave me no rest. Meanwhile the newspapers were looking for answers as well, but the journalists took a different approach, indulging in extravagant speculation about whether the dark forces of the supernatural were involved. The papers also printed graphic descriptions of how the thrashing waters had torn away Fitzhugh's clothing and battered his body. But even these lurid details were soon swept away by more pressing matters, such as: Would the vice president's hoydenish daughter Alice travel with him and his wife to Buffalo to see the exposition, and, if so, what would she wear? Every publication in the country focused on us—on Buffalo and its Rainbow City, as the Pan-American was dubbed because of its brightly colored pavilions. We had become the center of the nation.

The idea of glory was like an infection that struck us down, rich and poor, immigrant and native-born alike. We who lived in Buffalo looked only to the future. We became passionate optimists. We could feel to our fingertips all we would achieve through our work and dedication. We understood our future as if it were alive. No vision was too far-fetched. If alternating current could send electricity long distances—and the Pan-American Exposition was a celebration of electricity—anything could be accomplished. Electricity: it seemed like magic, but it was science. Magic had become science, science had become magic, anything was possible and the future was ours.

At 11:00 a.m., Grace and I followed at the back of the crowd while Tom gave the vice president a tour of the Pan-Am's Electricity Building.

"Can you see Papa?" Grace asked, standing on tiptoe in her patent-leather shoes. She wore a pleated sailor dress, sky-blue with white piping, the collar wide across her shoulders. With little success, she tried to peer around the all-male bodies pressing toward Tom and Roosevelt, among them my board members, other businessmen not quite worthy of the board, the commissioners of the Pan-Am, and assorted city officials including our titular mayor, Conrad Diehl. Mrs. Roosevelt and Miss Roosevelt (*Alice is here!* the newspapers gushed) were off being entertained by the Women's Committee (i.e., the wives) at the Women's Building. But Grace wanted to see her father's presentation, and so we moved along behind the tobacco-scented crowd, examining X-ray machines and washing machines, electric motor cars, irons, toasters, and gramophones, each one a marvel.

At the end of the building was the sleek electric transformer which stepped down the voltage of the alternating current sent from the power station at Niagara so it could be used here at the exposition. This item elicited much gentlemanly admiration, particularly from

Roosevelt, whose detailed questions revealed the depth of his interest. The vice president, attired in a formal morning coat, relished everything, no matter how small, alternately clucking with approval and booming with enthusiasm. Tom appeared taken aback by Roosevelt's unalloyed excitement. As the stocky vice president grew ever more ebullient, Tom, tall and polished, turned ever more diffident, creating a pleasing study in contrast.

Soon, Grace's attention began to flag. "Would you like to go outside?" I whispered. She nodded, but glanced guiltily at her father. "He'll understand," I reassured her. "He'd probably prefer to be outside himself." She turned to hide a smile, and quietly we slipped out.

Stepping into the noontime brightness, I squinted, and the scene came into focus like a mirage shimmering in waves. On the far side of a half-acre of apricot-colored tulips, about twenty Negro women dressed in formal white marched in a circle. They wore the purple sash of the National Association of Colored Women. The fringes on their white parasols swayed with every step. They might have been a group of well-to-do society ladies enjoying a spring fête, except for the color of their skin, the repetition of their walk—and Mary Talbert, who climbed onto a crate in the middle of the circle. In her deep, sonorous voice, she called, "What are you afraid of, Mr. Milburn? Are you afraid of civil engineer Benjamin Banneker? Are you afraid of heart surgeon Daniel Hale Williams? Are you afraid . . ." On she went, through a litany of Negro achievement.

Although I hadn't spoken to Mrs. Talbert since the day we'd parted in anger at the Buffalo Club, I knew that her fear had come true: the Midway boasted the exposition's only coherent reference to Negro life and history, and it was "The Old Plantation." The promoters proudly advertised that it was manned (womaned and childrened) by "genuine southern Negroes" portraying "happy slaves." Nevertheless Mary Talbert hadn't given up the battle for recognition. "Mr. Milburn, give us our black Edison—Granville T. Woods—and you may keep your 'Old Plantation.' Give us Jan Ernst Matzeliger and his lasting machine, and you may keep your display of 'happy' slaves."

"Isn't that Millicent's aunt?" Grace asked. "What is she talking about?"

"She's upset because Negroes are only being remembered for slavery, not for all the good they've achieved."

Grace thought about this. "She's right, it's not fair," Grace said with the forthright conviction of the innocent.

"I know."

About a dozen police officers lounged nearby. They glanced at the protesting women and occasionally shrugged, shaking their heads as if to say, what foolishness. A few repressed smirks.

"Mr. Milburn, where is your courage?" came the challenging call.

Obviously Mrs. Talbert was attempting to provoke an incident, to gain attention and publicity. Probably she wanted to be dragged away to a police wagon, but the police must have been instructed to do nothing, to ignore the women. Even the reporters and sketch artists who waited for the vice president paid no attention, as if Mrs. Talbert and her protest had been made to evaporate, as evanescent as a true mirage in the beating sunlight.

Several groups of exposition visitors did pause to listen, however: two youngish ladies arm-in-arm; a family with three children dressed in their Sunday best; an older couple, the wife holding her parasol close over her head. They heard Mary Talbert's words and then they moved along, apparently uninspired, as she soldiered on. "Mr. Milburn, are you afraid of scientist George Washington Carver? Are you afraid"—then suddenly, urgently—"Mr. Roosevelt—hear us, join us!"

I turned. The vice president was striding out of the Electricity Building with Tom beside him.

"Mr. Roosevelt!"

Talking with animation, undoubtedly plotting the future of electricity in America, the vice president didn't glance up or take his attention away from Tom. For him, Mrs. Talbert's impassioned pleas must have been nothing more than background noise. The retinue of men in formal morning coats followed behind the vice president, all heading to a luncheon reception on the roof garden of the nearby Electric Tower. After lunch, they would go up to the very top, over three hundred eighty feet high; from there, they hoped to observe the mist column of Niagara in the distance. Even on their short walk up the esplanade, they strove to establish a hierarchy in relation to Roosevelt, positioning and repositioning themselves in a kind of minuet. Not one paused to gaze at the glimmering geysers in the Court of Fountains, or at the seventy-foot cascade in front of the tower. They certainly had no time to listen to Mary Talbert.

Except for John Milburn. When he stepped out of the doorway he did pause, he did listen. While others made their way around him, he stopped about ten feet from Grace and me. He saw.

"Mr. Milburn, we appeal to you!"

Steadily he observed the scene. The brightly painted pavilions. The profusion of tulips. And the disturbance—created by a collection of colored women—to his day of glory; to his moment of precisely balanced perfection, the apex of years of labor. He seemed to look slightly to the right of Mary Talbert, the way his wife looked at me. Two young couples, prosperously middle class, the women bright and lively, paused close to us. As they listened to Mrs. Talbert's continuing oratory, their faces fell into looks of disgust. "We paid good money to see *this*?" one of the men asked. Mr. Milburn turned sharply to stare at him. The speaker was beefy yet slick. I pegged him as a salesman—just the kind of upstanding citizen with a bit of disposable income that Milburn wanted to attract to the Pan-Am. The exposition needed many, many such ticket-buying visitors to repay the huge private investment that had gone into its construction. "We should get a refund!" the salesman said, only half-joking. He and his friends shook their heads in distaste as they wandered away. Milburn's eyes narrowed. He stared at Mary Talbert and her friends with contempt, his famous charm far from evident. Gradually he steeled himself into an expression of profound indifference and walked away.

"Mr. Milburn, where is your courage?" she called behind him. But he never looked back. When he was too far away to hear, she studied the few passersby stopped before her. "We invite all like-minded citizens to join us!" A small group of gray-haired matrons came near. "Ladies, join us! Ladies, show your strength! Show your power! Join the fight for justice!" They continued walking. Then her glance arrived at me, focused on me. "Ladies, join us?" There was a catch in her voice, an abrupt shift from demand to question; a begging for support; an admittance of despair—her inner self suddenly revealed and open to any knife.

Flushed and embarrassed, angry and guilty, I hurried Grace away.

While we picnicked on the shore of a small island in the exposition's Mirror Lake, the necessity of staying away from Mary Talbert's battles gnawed at me. Of course I wanted to join her, if only to give John Milburn a much-deserved comeuppance. But as I gazed at Grace feeding crumbs to the ducks, I recognized my choice—which was no choice, for only one path opened before me: Grace.

After we ate, I tried to keep her away from the dubious attractions of the Midway, such as Chiquita the Cuban Midget (she entertained in a miniature house and conversed in seven languages) and Bonner the Educated Horse (he solved addition problems, but only in the presence of his trainer). The Midway, in the northwest corner, was the commercial center of the exposition, and it provided a sharp contrast to the public-spirited displays on the esplanade, which were dedicated to such elevated topics as agriculture, transportation, and of course electricity. Grace was determined to see the so-called ethnological exhibitions on the Midway, apparently at the urging of Miss Atkins, the lower-school principal. She'd encouraged the girls to seek out the mighty educational experience of watching human beings displayed as if they were animals in a zoo. Luckily I was able to steer Grace away from the Old Plantation and the "happy darkies" who were its advertised inhabitants; even so, we spent a gruesome hour going from Africa to Hawaii, from the Philippines to Japan, observing "joyous natives," most of them barely clothed, pursuing their "usual" lives. There were rumors that the "natives" might actually be actors. However, Grace was taken with the presentations, so I hoped there was some educational value concealed in them. She especially liked the Eskimo Village, with its igloos and kayaks.

After the Midway, Grace and I decided to take a gondola ride. A maze of canals wove through the exposition to create an illusion of Venice—a sweet-scented, idealized Venice, and after the Midway a haven of peace. We glided beneath carved bridges decorated with classical sculpture; we passed hanging gardens and miniature waterfalls. The exposition's extravagant Spanish Renaissance architecture surrounded us in a riot of colors, from deep red to warm ivory. We were shaded by the orange and bay trees which had been brought in from California by the hundreds to decorate the exposition grounds.

Was it beautiful, this city of the imagination brought to life? From here on the gondola it was. From here it seemed eternal; there was no sense that it was merely a plaster stage set that in six months would be bulldozed back to farmland.

I lay my head on the cushions, closing my eyes and luxuriating in the gentle breeze that touched my skin. That was when Grace said, with the delighted slyness of a child relishing special knowledge, "I have a secret that you don't know."

I didn't even open my eyes. "That's what makes it a secret."

"See if you can guess."

"You'll have to give me a hint."

"All right. It's something Papa said to me last night. Well, a talk we had."

"That's something I could never guess."

"Then I'll have to tell you. Open your eyes." She shook my shoulder lightly, and I opened my eyes halfway. Playfully she confided, "We talked about whether it would be all right if he began courting a lady." She said it in Tom's Irish lilt; I could hear his voice. "He said he wouldn't do anything like that without asking my permission, because if he and the lady decided to get married, then I would have a stepmother."

I could only stare at her, a sick feeling knotting at my insides.

"You see, I have surprised you!" She clapped her hands in triumph.

"Do you know who the lady is?"

"Well it's *you*, of course. Who else would it be?"

"Did he say it was me?"

"No, he didn't say it. He didn't have to say it, I knew it; I told him right away."

"Grace, you're just using your imagination." I chucked her chin. "It could be anyone. It could be . . . Miss Riley, for all we know."

"It can't be Miss Riley. She's too young to marry Papa! Besides, it has to be you because there's no other lady I've ever even seen him talking to. I mean for more than a few minutes."

"I'm sure he talks to ladies when he's away from home and you don't see him."

"No. He doesn't," she assured me. "And it has to be you because you're our best friend."

"Well, thank you, Grace," I said, momentarily warmed by that same sense of belonging I'd felt when Margaret was alive.

"Besides, you're my godmother and Mama's friend, so it's only right that he should marry you. That's what people do."

"That's what people sometimes do," I explained. "I don't think he was talking about me, Grace. You must put that out of your mind. Your father has never regarded me in that way." And any time I had sensed in myself a glimmer of regarding him in that way, I'd pushed the thought aside, both because of my own anxieties and because it felt like a betrayal of Margaret.

"But there *isn't* anyone else," she insisted.

Realizing she must be nervous at the idea of a woman she didn't know becoming her stepmother, I rubbed her hand. "I'm already your godmother. That will never change, no matter what."

"And now you'll be my mother! Just like my real mother!" She lunged to hug me, throwing the gondola off-balance. Water splashed into the boat. I felt staggered by the realization (one which I'd steadfastly forbidden my conscious thoughts) that simply by marrying Tom I could become her mother; legally I would *be* her mother. This reality superseded any passing fantasies surrounding Franklin Fiske which I'd indulged at Niagara; perhaps it could supersede even my fears. I could become Grace's mother: the idea fixated me.

"Be still, stay in middle," the gondola driver hissed in an accent that sounded like genuine Italian, not actor's Italian.

Chastened, Grace repositioned herself. Suddenly she pulled at my sleeve. "You won't say I told you, will you?" she asked, eyes wide. "We promised not to tell anyone. You'll act surprised when he asks you, won't you? Please?" She was begging now. She grabbed at my hands. "He'll be angry if he finds out I broke a promise. Please don't tell him I broke a promise!"

I didn't answer, mystified by how desperate she seemed.

Again she demanded, "You won't tell, will you? Will you?"

"No, Grace." I caressed her cheek with the back of my hand. "I won't tell."

At four thirty, I took Grace home to rest. There would be fireworks at nine, and despite her protests a nap was in order. While she slept, I went out on the second-floor terrace to rest on a cushioned chaise in the shade of a tall elm tree. The maid brought iced tea and strawberries with cream. The yellow light of late afternoon filtered through the leaves. The house was built on a slight elevation, and from the terrace the entire exposition spread before me: domes, turrets, and spires in a panoply of exoticism. Sunlight sparked off the sixteen-foot gilded statue of the Goddess of Light atop the Electric Tower, creating a daylight star.

All around me was the Sinclair estate. Lying on the chaise, I drifted into its luxury: tennis court, conservatory, bathing pool; the formal garden with its two-tiered French fountain filling the air with a faint murmur of falling water; beyond it, the English garden, lush and wild, a carefully overgrown maze in the middle; the raspberry patch; the butterfly garden, a gift to Grace on her first birthday from her godfather, John J. Albright.

My imagination opened. Yes, *I* was the chatelaine here. The house and garden were *mine*, by right of marriage. I was Grace's mother in the eyes of the community, I was Thomas Sinclair's wife; we were a family. Margaret would feel pleased, not betrayed. I would fulfill the promise of her lost life. I would be with Grace every day, as she had been.

There would be other rewards. My mind leapt: I held court here, my Monday night "saloon" transformed into a true salon that filled the house. Musicians played Schubert in the garden, acting troupes performed Shakespeare beside the fountain. No longer bound to dress the role of a staid schoolmarm, I wore the fine clothes I loved and could now afford. Not only did I continue my work at Macaulay (Tom was not the type of man to object), but I funded as many scholarships as I pleased, the board be damned. Every problem dissipated in the ease of wealth. Patty Milburn tried to meet my eyes, but now I could afford to look past hers. Anyone who'd ever called me a bluestocking or an old maid or a spinster learned to be jealous of *me* finally.

Somehow in the gondola, Grace had given my mind permission to travel in this direction, and now I embraced the safe harbor Tom could offer. Tentatively I began to ponder our possible intimacy . . . but what could I imagine? What experience did I have, with which to formulate my yearnings? Only my evening with former president Cleveland, only this: the rubbery mass of his stomach buoying me; the anguish as his body prodded into me; the too-warm liquid that he left, slipping down my thighs.

Stop! I told myself. I rose from the chaise, banishing self-pity as well as the fantasies to which Grace had led me. I straightened my high-collared gray dress. Looking like the proper headmistress I was, I went inside and down the hall to the library to find something to read.

At first I was sun-blind, startled by black forms rising before me. Waiting for my eyes to adjust, I breathed deep a combination of dusty books and lilac-laden air. The silence was as dense as the shadows. The windows were thrown wide, the gauze curtains lifted by the breeze. One by one the pieces of the room came clear, in tones of sepia: Susannah Riley's watercolors of the power station; the plaster Nike of Samothrace glowing soft white on its pedestal in the corner; the small framed photograph of Margaret on Tom's well-ordered desk.

I went to look at the photograph, picking it up from the stand. Margaret with her dark hair and eyes, gazing at me. Would she want me to take her place? In all the years I'd known her, I'd never told her about my evening with Grover Cleveland, and she'd never asked me about Francesca, although she must have heard the rumors. I suppose she was too well brought up to inquire directly, and I never confessed: the thought of discussing a Boston marriage (real or feigned) with beautiful, confident Margaret embarrassed me deeply. And after Grace was born, I wanted Margaret to believe in my supposed liaison with Francesca, so that she would never suspect that I was the woman who had given birth to the child she cradled in her arms.

A shiver passed through me, at the closeness of death. The room was no longer a haven of warmth and peace, but a place haunted—by

Margaret. The barrier between us—the line between life and death—became permeable and frail. I could feel her everywhere around me.

I put the photograph back, fighting an urge to flee.

And then on the desk I saw it: a dark red folder, labeled "Water." A small granite paperweight—an eagle in flight—held the folder closed. My sense of Margaret flowed away.

"Water." Such a strange title. Not water power or water leases, not water charters or rentals or options. Simply "Water."

Who would not have opened it?

We all take refuge in our moral certainties, our smug sense of "*I would never do that!*" Blithely we condemn anyone who would. Yet faced with the choice, we do open the folder. Just this once, we think. Just this once won't overturn a lifetime of rectitude. God will understand. And so the deed is done, the smug certainties still safely in place.

The files were extensive. I recognized Tom's overly precise handwriting, the writing of someone for whom the mere act of putting words together was an unexpected gift. Now these sacred symbols of the alphabet covered page after page, letters and numbers arranged in a code I couldn't break. The column titles, however, I could understand: "Westinghouse-Speyer," "Usage," "Kilowatt hours," and the initials "cfs." Cubic feet per second, I realized after a moment's confusion. "Full capacity," with a future date, repeated again and again at the bottom of the pages. There was a copy of a bill from the state legislature defining the limits on the amount of water that could be taken from the Niagara River above the Falls. There were guarded communications from Francis Lynde Stetson, J. P. Morgan's attorney.

I heard muted coughs from upstairs as Grace woke.

An urgency crept into me: I mustn't let Grace discover me reading her father's papers. There were only a few pages left. The key to Albright's warning, to Rumsey's warning, was here—if only I could break the code. My hands were shaking. Initials—that's what the last pages revealed. Initials with ever-increasing amounts of money beside them. Initials with dates—dates of inspection.

Grace called dreamily from upstairs, "Aunt Louisa?"

I flipped through the file again. Where was the link I had missed? It was here; it had to be. But I was lost.

"Aunt Louisa, where are you?" Grace was awake now.

Fingers trembling, I stacked the pages as neatly as I could and closed the folder. I returned it to its spot on the desk, slightly to the right of the photo of Margaret. I put the eagle paperweight on top and hurried outside to the terrace. Once more I was sun-blind, this time from light instead of darkness. Before my eyes I saw lines of black numbers and letters, repeated over and over with precision. I heard Grace's voice coming from the third-floor window; she asked if I was all right. I said that I was. Gradually my vision cleared, yet still I was blind. I saw, but I could not understand.

Mrs. Sheehan brought us an early dinner in the playroom; she would be leaving soon to attend the exposition with the rest of the staff. As we were served that meal, I recalled Signora Gambuto's family a few miles from here, living in less space than Grace's staircase landing. Nonetheless I enjoyed our dinner, nursery food that it was (ending with the compulsory graham crackers and cinnamon-sweetened apple-sauce).

By the time we finished dinner, we were completely alone in the house. The sense of emptiness was eery. Anyone could come in, and we would never know, never hear—the doors were too far away. I had a childlike unease about glancing at the windows or at the staircase for fear someone would be there, watching. With this tinge of apprehension, I changed into a silkier version of my usual schoolmarm garb, making me look just like myself only more so. Grace put on a whimsical, dropped-waist white dress that made her look quite elegant.

In the hour remaining before the fireworks, Grace and I sat side by side in her art studio, and she took me through her stacks of sketches. They were neatly divided into still lifes, landscapes, and "figures from life," as she called them. Gradually, after ten, then fifteen, then twenty of them, I felt tedium sweep over me. I was a teacher, accustomed to seeing children for a few hours at most. As much as I loved Grace, this extended visit was more time than I'd ever spent alone with a child, particularly one who viewed me as on call. I suppose if I'd been more experienced as a mother, I would have made her play by herself for an hour or practice the piano. But I had no such experience, no knowledge of how to put her off without hurting her feelings; and she, thrilled to have a willing audience, had no reason to stop the incessant chatter. I went into a daze, responding to her with the surface of my mind, while my real thoughts strayed in a jumble of questions and desires. So dazed was I that I didn't focus on the group of life drawings that Grace began to display. I managed to register the housekeeper. The cook. "Look, here's Papa sitting in the chair you're sitting in, with his shoes off." "Here's one on a hot day when he unbuttoned his vest." "Look, here he is wearing his paisley dressing gown."

The everyday life of a family—although I actually knew very little about the everyday life of a family. The pictures portrayed what I imagined the everyday life of a family to be. I offered Grace an appropriate "lovely," or "how careful you are with the flow of the fabric," and she smiled and went on to the next drawing.

And then suddenly the next drawing turned out to be something different. At first I couldn't comprehend what it was. Grace was already hurrying to hide it when I roused myself to take it from her. It was a document. A document like the ones I'd seen in the folder on Tom's desk.

"Where did you get this?"

Grace blushed. She pushed a lock of hair behind her ear. "Oh, I was working with Papa at his desk," she explained. "That's when I made this picture, see, of him at his desk." Nervously she flipped through the pictures, finally holding one out to me: Tom at his desk, wearing a suit, pen in hand. "This piece of paper must have gotten mixed in by mistake. I'll return it later. He'll be angry if he finds out it's missing."

"Yes, I'm sure he will. You'll return it before we leave for the fireworks."

"Yes, Aunt Louisa." Taking the document from me, she put it aside on a shelf and gave me a sudden, beguiling grin. "Now, this is a special picture because it's of Papa holding Fluffer!" She took it from the bottom of the stack and unveiled it like a magician producing a treat from a hat. Fluffer was a long-haired, broad-tailed cat. "Papa didn't want to hold her, because she sheds all over, and that's why I named her Fluffer. Mrs. Sheehan doesn't even like her to come in the house. But I always bring her in. I told Papa he had to hold her—for my education. He always does whatever I want him to do, if I tell him it's for my education." She winked at me. "A cat and a person in the same picture. Miss Riley will be happy."

And so we drifted on.

How many lives we lead, each of us. How many lies we perpetrate as we balance one facet of ourselves against the next. At that moment in May, my daughter, Grace, young and lovely, already nurtured a nest of secrets while I, oblivious, was consumed with her protection. I never realized that everything I needed to know about her had been laid before me, if only I'd been paying attention.

Chapter Nineteen

M ay I present Miss Louisa Barrett," Tom said.

Jovially Mr. Roosevelt bounced my hand in his. Was I thrilled to meet the vice president? Certainly I did not object. But my memories made me cynical toward politicians who were generally praised for their probity.

We'd gathered beside Delaware Park Lake, a crowd of chosen ones bearing such family names as Rumsey, Cary, Love, Urban, Scatcherd, Coatsworth, and even Winspear, vying for position around the beacons of Roosevelt, his wife and daughter. We waited to board the lavishly embellished rowboats that would take us to watch the fireworks from the water. Alice Roosevelt charmed the gentlemen while the ladies surreptitiously studied her, hoping to learn her secret; I'd seen girls like her before, however, and "spoiled" was the only adjective that came to my mind. Above us the star clouds of the Milky Way shot across the heavens, bright and clear.

"And this is my daughter, Grace."

Roosevelt leaned down to her. "I saw you in the Electrical Building today, hiding there behind the morning coats. Nothing escapes me! A fine thing in a girl, to show an interest in the future. Keep it up!" Boisterously he batted her shoulder in playful camaraderie, but Grace stepped back, looking more abashed than amused. Roosevelt straightened when we were joined by a gentleman whom I immediately recognized—slight, effete, with a curling gray mustache and the look of an evil spirit. My insides constricted and I forced myself to stand straighter to make up for the cringing feeling within me. "Eh, Gilder? A fine thing, for a girl to care about the future."

"Indeed, sir." Richard Watson Gilder, editor of the *Century* magazine. Well, he certainly was a friend to power: first Cleveland, the

Democrat; now Roosevelt, the Republican. Of course both men were reform-minded, and Gilder was nothing if not reform-minded.

"Know these people, Gilder?" Roosevelt asked.

"I've met Miss Barrett," he said smoothly. Apart from Cleveland's private secretary, who'd taken me home that night, Gilder was the only person who knew about my visit to a certain hotel suite a decade ago. At any moment he could use the knowledge he sheltered to destroy me. "We became acquainted during an earlier administration."

Roosevelt heard no sinister undertones. "Good. The big fella here is Tom Sinclair, head of the power station and a damn fine job he's doing with it too. And this is his daughter, who's training to be an electrical engineer." Roosevelt pushed the brim of her hat over her eyes. He gazed around to see if he needed to make any more introductions, but for once the sycophants had provided a wide berth. So he asked Tom a complex question about the stepping-down process for alternating current (Grace listening with her hands around her father's arm), and Gilder turned to me.

"How very good to see you again," he said quietly. He stood too close, but I wasn't going to give him the satisfaction of stepping away. What a horrible little man he was! He must have arrived this afternoon, for I hadn't noticed him among the group at the Electrical Building. Or maybe he'd been elsewhere garnering praise: He was being hailed far and wide for some banal inscriptions he'd written for various exposition pylons and entryways.

"I've certainly enjoyed reading your inscriptions, Mr. Gilder."

He averted his eyes. "Ah, yes. Well, thank you. Very kind of you." He adjusted his tie in false modesty. "My, my, it's almost, what, ten years since we met, Miss Barrett?" Was he purposely trying to torture me, or was this simply his natural demeanor? "How well I recall it. When our esteemed former president Mr. Cleveland was between terms. A time of upheaval."

"Yes."

"Well, you are as lovely as I remember. More lovely, in fact. And you've come so far and accomplished so much. Many of my friends have enjoyed visits to your home—and they report back to me on your every activity! They sing your praises, but I reveal nothing!" He gave me a long, meaningful grin.

Could it be that he was attempting to seduce me? Did he think that because I'd once been at the mercy of Grover Cleveland, I'd now be at the mercy of him? He leaned closer while I ran a string of cutting responses through my mind to have one at the ready before I remembered: I couldn't possibly reject him. I could only add one mistake to another, one lie to another, caught in a circle of helplessness.

"It's a wonderful thing, when a beautiful woman brings intelligent men together." Close to my ear, he spoke softly, yet in the tone of public exposition. "Indeed it is vital in this era of our nation's expansion that we maintain the salons of intellectual rigor." His breath was warm on my cheek. "I understand that at your salon for example, plans were made—"

The vice president glanced our way. "To the boats!" he declared abruptly. He strutted off and inwardly I blessed him for his need to be always at the center of attention.

Gilder rushed to take his position on Roosevelt's left; after all, a vice president only has two sides, and in this case his wife had claimed the other.

From our boat on the water, the exposition beside us was like an imaginary kingdom come to life, a city without shadows or substance, its reflections rippling on the surface of the lake. Rather than illuminate the buildings with arc lights that would reveal—well, solid buildings—the lighting designers had chosen to outline the structures with small incandescent bulbs, hundreds of thousands of them, creating the illusion of structures without walls. Compared to this, the fireworks were a magnificent anticlimax, bursting over us in forty-one glorious varieties (according to the program) and promptly forgotten. Afterward, the dignitaries piled into the carriages waiting to take them to a reception at the Buffalo Club, open to women on this night of nights. Being still in mourning, Tom would not attend the reception, and I opted not to as well, to avoid the lurking Gilder.

On our walk home, in the press of the common crowd, we came upon my student Maddie Fronczyk and her brother, Peter. Maddie's thick blond braids were wrapped around her head and covered with a scarf. Peter was as handsome as ever, unassuming and appealing, with a wayward lock of blond hair falling across his forehead despite his continual efforts to push it back. He was escorting Maddie home, to the house opposite school where she boarded on the top floor, close to the watchful eyes of the two Macaulay teachers who lived on the lower floors.

To my surprise, Tom invited all of us to his home for refreshments on the terrace. Peter hesitated, most likely uncertain whether it was appropriate for him to visit his employer socially, but Maddie, ever forthright, accepted for them both.

With the staff out, Grace was in heaven, fancying herself in charge of the house. She found a lemon cake in the pantry and carefully instructed Maddie and me on where to find lemonade and the various glasses, plates, and silver that Mrs. Sheehan considered appropriate for use outside on the second-floor terrace.

Maddie didn't attempt to conceal her awe at the house. "How wonderful, to visit a robber baron *en famille!*" she whispered with delight as we climbed the stairs behind Grace. "I could manage to be happy here."

"Yes," I agreed as we passed beneath the Tiffany window. "It would do."

"What are you two whispering about?" Grace demanded.

"About you, of course!" Maddie said, pretending to chase her up the stairs.

When we joined the men on the terrace, Tom had already poured whiskey for himself and Peter. He'd lit candles on the glass-and-wrought-iron tables beside each chair. He seemed comfortable in his role as host. Meanwhile in the broad, shifting shadows, Peter looked ill at ease and younger than his years, out of his element, like an eager boy given his first glass of spirits and furtively trying to learn the proper way to drink it.

We sat down, and Grace served the cake while we talked and laughed about nothing of importance. How I liked Maddie. She was bright, confident and without conceit. Unlike most of my students, she neither feared nor worshipped me. Yet soon I would lose her: Next month she would graduate, and in the autumn she would enter Cornell University on scholarship. I projected a sea of possibilities onto her: Perhaps she would become a doctor, a scientist, an attorney . . . no matter what, a leader among women. I hoped she would feel that I had prepared her well.

Peter slowly relaxed while Tom told amusing stories about some of the power station's more eccentric employees. There on the terrace, an observer might have concluded that we were equals, one and all. But the sense of equality was nothing but a trick of the candlelight.

Gradually we fell into a comfortable silence. Tom stared toward the exposition, at the Electric Tower that looked like a transparent net of light. Grace stretched out on the chaise where I had lain in the afternoon. In the quiet, the warm calm of the evening swept around me— the soft breeze shifting, the sweet scents percolating as if from a thousand roses, the crickets calling, the high vault of trees protecting. Yet as the minutes passed, we seemed to wait with an increasingly unnatural patience—for Tom, as if he were the center around which we moved, the person for whose benefit we spoke even when we were speaking to one another. Oblivious to our waiting, absorbed by the view, he slowly sipped his whiskey. The murmurings of the French fountain in the garden seemed louder in the stillness.

Finally Tom turned to us. "Before electricity, we would've had to close the exposition at sundown. Gives us a bit of a chance to serve the public, eh, Peter?" he asked wryly.

"I hope we always serve the public, sir," Peter replied.

"Yes, let us flatter ourselves with the conviction that we do." Tom stretched his legs before him. "Well then, Peter, what are the men saying about poor Fitzhugh?"

Peter looked a bit shaken by the question. "What do you mean, sir?"

"No talk about supernatural forces pulling him into the water? The same supernatural forces that might have had a hand in the death of Mr. Speyer?"

"I read about those supernatural forces in some of the newspapers," Peter admitted. "Along with curses, hexes, all kinds of nonsense—right there in the newspaper," he added indignantly.

"Yes, I read all that nonsense too," Tom said. "The point is, did anyone believe it? Any of the men, I mean. Anybody thinking God is no longer on our side, as it were? That we're holding court with the devil?"

"No, sir. I can assure you on that."

"And no one's thinking Fitzhugh might have walked into the water on purpose? Because of some . . . upset about his work?"

"No, sir. Not at all." The idea of suicide seemed to shock Peter. "We all knew Mr. Fitzhugh. He was always coming around to check on everything. Always asking questions. Not to criticize—just for the love of it. He never would have . . ." Peter couldn't say the words *he never would have walked into the rapids on purpose*.

"Good," Tom said with finality. Abruptly he changed the subject. "Well, if I'm not mistaken you've nearly completed your apprenticeship. Soon we'll be congratulating you on becoming a full-fledged operator."

"Yes. Thank you." Even in the candlelight, I could see that Peter blushed.

"Any regrets on leaving your friends behind?"

"Friends?"

Tom sat up. "If we may call them friends. How about 'colleagues'? That sounds better, doesn't it? From the International Brotherhood of Electrical Workers."

The stillness grew deeper around us. Nothing seemed to move. I could hear Peter's breathing as he tried to determine the best way to answer. He might have been on trial for the crime of association—was that a crime? As the silence lengthened, I remembered Frederick Krakauer, in the train returning from Stony Point, attempting to convict Tom of a similar crime.

Finally Peter stammered, "I . . . well . . ."

Benignly Tom said, "Let us assume that you have left them behind. They're a reckless group, if I've ever seen one. You don't seem reckless. When I heard they were debating whether to secret away a stash of dynamite, stick by stick—"

"How did you—" Peter began, then abruptly stopped.

Tom let the silence drag on, as if silence itself were a technique of interrogation. Then quietly he said, "How can I conduct a business if I don't know what's going on? If I don't know what my workers are thinking and plotting and planning?"

Maddie, beside me, gripped the armrests of her chair. I sensed that somehow her brother's future was at stake. I realized I was now seeing the subtle mastery Tom possessed, the power as pure and unalloyed as Mr. Rumsey's.

How could I ever have allowed myself to be lulled into thinking he was a man with a clear conscience, or incapable of doing harm to further his own interests?

Tom leaned forward. "I need to protect them from foolishness and stupidity. From doing things they'd regret later. Can't be a good father without knowing what the kids are up to—that's what my dad used to say. Got to make sure they don't get into trouble with the law. Can't allow them to blow up their own jobs, if you see what I mean."

Although Peter said nothing, I did see what Tom meant: he alone was keeping back the union-smashing forces Frederick Krakauer's employers would be only too glad to release.

At last, with surprising boldness, Peter spoke up: "The union men are still my friends, but I don't regret training to become an operator. I think I know what's best for myself and my family."

Tom leaned back, looking pleased. He took a sip of whiskey. "We may have something in common, you and I." There was a gentleness in his voice, like a father speaking to a beloved son. They were like father and son: They shared the same height, the same coloring, the same occasional shyness. But with this difference: Peter, terribly handsome, was still a boy, lanky, not fully grown into his body, his features smooth and innocent. Tom was strong and at ease with his strength, his features handsome but worn at the edges: a man poised at full maturity, old age still beyond imagining.

"When I was young," Tom continued, "I was lucky enough to be helped along my way by a man who took satisfaction in helping others." Tom could only have been referring to Albright. "In response to my gratitude, he said only that he was one who'd gained the most."

Now I warmed to Tom, sentimentalism be damned. How could I know that he was drawing Peter in—like a fisherman playing the line.

"I try to give opportunities to those who've worked hard and made sacrifices for what we're all trying to achieve."

Peter said nothing, risked nothing.

"I remember your dad. A fine man, he was. When a family's given so much . . ." His words drifted off. But what exactly was Tom offering Peter—and in return for what? Just when I thought he might come to the point, Tom put his glass on the table beside his chair and got up. "Well, look at that girl, will you? Asleep in her party clothes."

And indeed she was, her arm spread across the pillow of the chaise.

"Louisa, would you help me get Grace into bed?"

Looking eager to escape, Maddie rose. "Peter and I had better be going. Thank you, Mr. Sinclair, for—"

"No, thank *you*. Grace and I have been too isolated these last months. It's good to have company."

He walked to the chaise and stood beside it, his suit jacket pushed back by his hands on his hips, while he considered the best way to lift Grace and carry her upstairs without waking her.

"Peter," he said, still looking at Grace, "would you and Miss Fronczyk mind staying a few minutes to walk Miss Barrett home, since you're going in that direction? The staff may still be out, and of course I can't leave Grace alone."

"That's quite all right," I said. "I can walk myself home." I hoped I sounded cheery. I didn't want to go home, at least not yet. I wanted to stay here, I *needed* to stay here. To learn if Grace's supposition about her father's intentions could possibly be correct. Suddenly, unexpectedly, I felt desperate to belong; desperate to find a safe haven where I could finally rest after my years of concealment and maneuvering. God help me, but in my own weariness I was thinking of attaching myself to a man who perhaps condoned murder or may have committed murder himself. "I've walked these streets many times, day and night."

Deferentially he said, "I'm sure you have, Louisa. But please, allow me my sense of responsibility. I can't let you walk home alone with so many dangers lurking about."

I wasn't accustomed to people looking after me, and now I discovered I didn't entirely like it, in spite of my yearning for shelter. I wondered: Who was I, in his eyes? A forthright schoolmarm the equal of any man, or as much a lady as Margaret, respected for her virtue and in need of masculine protection? "Come now. What dangers?"

Gently he said, "I simply prefer not to take the risk."

Chapter Twenty

I checked the statistics: we're lucky if three percent survive to their first birthday," Francesca whispered so that the skulking nurses wouldn't overhear. "So ninety-seven die, for every hundred who come in."

Francesca and I walked slowly through the Infants' Ward of the Orphan Asylum. A Gothic edifice, the orphanage was at least forty years old, with long windows and open wards. The quatrefoil ceilings were shadowy and cavernous above us. Our footsteps echoed. A heavy rain beat against the windowpanes, and the air around us was clammy and dense, as if all the oxygen had been used up. Rusting in neglect, metal cribs stretched down the ward; infants lay swaddled within them, sometimes three or four to a crib. The babies were pinch-faced, their skin drawn tight across their skulls from dehydration. Their cheeks were pimply and peeling. Here and there between the cribs, stolid women dressed in black sat on stools and held an infant to suck at each breast. Was this really where the judgment of the Lord was passed upon us? Was this really the Lord's design, to punish the innocent for the sin of their making? How was it, that people managed to twist God's teachings to justify whatever they pleased?

"I corresponded with the director of the Infants Hospital in New York City," Francesca said. Her words sounded hollow against the tiles. "He wrote back that Italian women make the best wet nurses. So I managed to dismiss the old wet nurses, who were all Russian—why, I don't know—and utterly worn out anyway, and I brought in these women, but even they—well, how do you keep up with the demand?" She glanced at a woman who was struggling to burp one baby while the other still cried for food. The smell of unchanged diapers made me gag. Two orderlies tried to manage the diapers, and they appeared to treat the babies gently, but obviously it was an endless, unwinnable process.

The dates the babies had been brought in and their presumed dates of birth were posted from signs hung on the cribs. We stopped beside a crib that held four infants. The youngest babies were the fattest, the oldest were the thinnest. Here was a three-month-old, wizened and gazing at the ceiling unblinkingly. At three months Grace had smiled and brought her little hands together—or so Margaret had told me in a letter while I was in Europe. Here was a six-month-old, hollow-eyed and still, with sores around its eyes, skin so white as to be transparent, the red and blue of arteries and veins throbbing across its skull— approaching death at the age when Grace was rolling and sitting and squealing on her blanket in the garden.

How easily Grace could have been condemned to this, to this holding pen of human beings awaiting death. The fact that she had avoided this was nothing but chance—a lucky chance that Margaret and Tom had wanted a baby; if they hadn't, who knew whether I would have been able to support her on my own, despite my best attempts? I felt a stabbing pain in my stomach and tried not to bend over, not to let Francesca notice my anguish, not to let her wonder why I couldn't view all this clinically, like a problem to be solved.

I closed my eyes partway, to see only in fragments. Enough to walk at Francesca's side. Fragments: Francesca's high-buttoned boot. A fringe of cashmere shawl. A skirt of rustling silk. My friend had statistics to keep her steady. She had a purpose, a goal. Despite her initial hesitancy and misgivings, she had now turned into an avenging angel.

"I put together some reports the doctor in New York sent me and figured out that from 1896 to 1897, three hundred sixty-six infants were brought to his hospital and twelve survived the year. Twelve. So their survival rate is about the same as ours. I don't know whether to feel proud or angry that we can meet the New York City record." She swished her skirt around a cart. "It's called Wasting Disease, but it's nothing but neglect. I went to see Miss Love at 184 and asked her if she really knew the conditions here. She sat there offering a plate of cake crumbs to a canary and told me that most of these children are bastards anyway and we mustn't let ourselves get sentimental over them. God will do his work, she said. And she felt compelled to add that she never would have entrusted me with this mission if she'd known I'd turn sentimental. Do you think she really wants them to die?"

I managed to whisper, "I don't know."

"I thought better adoption procedures might help, but when I asked Miss Love about that idea she was very negative. For the entire asylum, all ages. Seems there once was a time—a pre-*Lovian* time—when 'ladies of the night' came here looking for recruits. When farmers came looking for laborers they could raise up like workhorses. They especially wanted these younger ones, who wouldn't already know how to talk back the way the older ones did. Miss Love informed me proudly that she put a stop to both the adoption and the talking back." Francesca strode ahead, as if hard work alone could constitute a slap at Miss Love. She stopped at a crib in the corner.

"Now, here we've actually got one who's made it to fourteen months." She turned to look for me. "Come on, Louisa," she said impatiently, tapping the crib railing. I forced myself forward. "Maybe this proves Mr. Darwin's point, for only the truly fit can survive this charity home. This boy's ready to be transferred to a regular orphans' ward. Of course the statistics are better there, because most of the children are brought in when they're older—when their parents die of consumption or the father deserts them and the mother can't manage to feed them on her own. But a lot of them have rickets or get it here, so they're not that much better off."

The child who proved Mr. Darwin's theories sat alone in a metal cage; his crib had caging across the top, so he couldn't climb out. His name, George, was written on a tag attached to the crib. He didn't move or call for attention. He simply stared at us. At fourteen months Grace had been a terror, talking gibberish with conviction, racing through the house on ever-stronger, pudgy legs, crawling under tables to play hide-and-seek with Margaret and me. But not George. His legs were spindly. His expression was blank. I felt suddenly as if I were looking at an animal in a zoo. There was a huge, horrible abyss between us. We might have been from different species, incapable of communicating, even with our eyes.

A faintness grew within me. I couldn't breathe. My vision was going black, while Francesca talked on and on. Like an echo I heard her words, then suddenly felt her hands grip me as I began to fall. "Louisa, are you all right?"

"Yes, I'm—" Pulling her along even as I used her for support, I hurried to the end of the ward, where the stairwell had wide windows that I pushed open. The wind blew rain around me, the cool, clean rain of early summer. Outside, the landscape was enveloped by the month of June, but inside, seasons were irrelevant, defined only by heat or the lack of it. Rain splattered on my face and neck, and slowly my breathing eased.

"Louisa. I know it's horrible, but why in the world . . ." Francesca was chastising me. By my own choice, she could never understand me. How I yearned for a hand upon my shoulder; for words of comfort. But I could only get them by confessing the truth, and although part of me yearned to share the truth, such words gagged in my throat. "I—I must have eaten something that didn't agree with me."

"Yes. You must have." She seemed to believe me. Such a good liar I had become. "When you're better we'll go down to the office. I have some ideas I want to discuss with you. I want to hire someone who knows about infant development. I want to—"

"I'm sorry, Francesca, but I can't help you here." I stared out the window at the tree limbs tossed by rain, too humiliated to meet her eyes.

"Why ever not? Don't tell me you're too 'sentimental' for it? Maria Love be damned, I'm going to set up adoption procedures, I'm going to hire doctors, I'm going to design a separate building for the babies and see that it gets built—there's a real chance to make a difference here."

"Yes, Francesca, but not for me. I can't make a difference here."

"Why ever not?" she said again, her anger mixing with petulance. "It doesn't make sense. You're just being squeamish. You'll get used to it. I did. You're the perfect one to work with me. We'll never have children of our own. We owe this to society. To the city."

"No, Francesca," I insisted. "No."

"I think you're being selfish."

I didn't answer. Better she think me selfish than know the truth.

How could I tell her that here, but for fortune, was Grace? How could I tell her that I saw Grace in every crib?

On Sunday morning, the day after I'd toured the Infant's Ward, I sat in Trinity Church near the Tiffany stained-glass window of the archangel Gabriel. Gabriel's robes were stark white against a swirling opalescent background of blues and purples, like the end of the world as imagined by the poet William Blake. But Gabriel himself was serene, suffused with light. He seemed neither male nor female. His face was beckoning and forgiving, all-knowing yet reverential. His eyes gazed not upon the surface of things, but to the spirit. Gabriel . . . the angel of the Annunciation. In Islam, the angel of truth. Whenever I came to Trinity, I sat near him. He was a solace in my loneliness; he offered me a path to transcendence. Today he eased the anguish that I'd felt among the dying children, even though he had no answer as to why God allowed such a place as the Infants' Ward to exist.

"Louisa? Is anything wrong?" Startled, I looked around to find Tom standing beside me. He touched my shoulder. Embarrassed, I stood too quickly, fumbling with the hymnal on my lap. Tom took my elbow to steady me. The service was over, and the church smelled of incense and lilies. The transoms were open, and the winds of Lake Erie purified us. The sepia-toned air glowed with a mist of dust motes. The custodian, a graying Negro employed for the sake of charity, muttered as he rearranged the prayer books for Evensong. Otherwise Tom and I were alone. Grace must have gone off with the other children to play on the parish house lawn.

"Louisa?" He sounded worried.

Not looking at him, I rearranged my shawl. "I'm fine. Thank you for asking."

"What were you staring at?"

"The window." I glanced at it. The shadow of a bird fluttered across the colored glass. Tears welled in my eyes, from the beauty of it. "It's a comfort to me." I stopped, feeling I'd revealed too much. "I don't know why," I added hurriedly.

"A comfort for what?"

I studied him then, carefully, the way he sometimes studied me: the blue eyes, the clean-shaven cheeks, the pale brown hair swept back from his forehead, his features muted by the sanctuary's hazy light. He looked diffident, without the edge of domination he'd shown that evening on the terrace. I felt the loneliness of us both. And at that moment I loved him—regardless of what he had or hadn't done—perhaps simply as a friend, perhaps only selfishly, because he had come to me, thinking me distressed; of all the congregation, he was the only one who noticed.

"My mother used to go to Mass every day—really believing it all, not just dragging us over on Sundays because it was her duty. I come here mostly for Grace's sake, not my own, I'm sorry to say." He held the corner of the pew, massaging the polished wood. "Louisa, I—" He stopped. "I thought—" He looked aside, seeming at a loss. Then his mood shifted, or at least appeared to, as he resolutely took on a tone which allowed him to feel more at ease: "Grace seems to have gotten a notion in her head that we should get married. Just about assaulted me with it not too long ago. Did you know?"

So, her confessions in the gondola had originated even more in her imagination than I'd assumed. "She passed on something to that effect."

"Well, it's an idea with certain attractions, don't you think?" The Irish lilt in his voice allowed him to get away with such indiscretions. "You were Margaret's closest friend; I feel I know you well. You're everything I could ever want in a mother for Grace." He spoke without a trace of irony, as if he'd forgotten our conversation in the sleigh—although my own apprehensions made me feel certain that he had not forgotten.

"That's hardly a recommendation for wifehood," I replied, matching his tone.

"Now, now, wait a minute . . . I'm sure people have married for lesser reasons. And of course you're very beautiful. I noticed that even when Margaret was alive, if you'll forgive me for saying so." His beguiling look forced me to smile. "I wouldn't mind having a woman around the house, I must admit. You know how Albright keeps telling me to advertise for one—it seems so much easier just to ask someone I already know."

"Tom, if you don't stop teasing I won't know what you mean."

"Ah. Sorry," he said, not looking sorry at all. "The fact is I mean every word I say." I couldn't respond to this; I felt flustered and unsettled by how quickly he was moving us along. "But the teasing is part of my nature. You'll have to learn to live with it. Margaret learned to live with it." Then his smile faded. "None of this is as easy as Grace would like, is it? Sometimes Margaret is so alive in my mind."

"In mine too."

"It's only been ten months."

"I know."

"Of course you know." He touched my shoulder, consoling me. "This morning Mrs. Sheehan came upstairs to bring me a cup of coffee in the library and for an instant I swore I was hearing Margaret's step on the stairs. I felt everything else just . . . disappear, and she was the only thing left." He studied the archangel Gabriel for a long moment, then turned to me abruptly. "But I do care for you, you know." He slid one finger across my cheek, and I felt like cringing away from him even as I yearned to embrace him. Instead I couldn't move. "Maybe we should agree that in a year or so we may possibly have an understanding with one another."

"Yes," I said, the tension easing out of me. Because of Margaret, everything would proceed slowly; because of Margaret, bit by bit I could overcome my fear, step by step imagination could evolve into reality, and I could become Grace's true mother at last. In that time, too, I would surely learn the truth about Speyer and Fitzhugh—if in fact there was any other truth to be learned. I felt as if my best friend had returned to offer me a gift. "Yes, I would agree to that."

"Do you think possibly having an understanding in a year or so will appease our little girl?" he asked.

"No, I don't think so."

"Neither do I," he agreed. "Well, that's part of growing up, isn't it? Learning to wait for what you want. A new experience for Grace. And, perhaps, for me."

Chapter Twenty-One

U sually after the Macaulay graduation in mid-June, my Monday evening salon went on hiatus. I hated entertaining in the hot weather and in any event the good families left Buffalo for their summer homes along the shores of Lake Erie, in the Genesee River Valley, or in Newport, Rhode Island. But not this summer. My salon ceased as usual, but because of events surrounding the Pan-American Exposition the good families stayed in town and the world came to them.

To all of us. Parties and receptions filled my days. I saw Franklin Fiske at many of these parties, and he was unfailingly kind. I never saw Tom, however. He'd sent me a note the week after our meeting at Trinity Church to tell me that he was consumed with business. I had to admit that this was a relief. In retrospect, I'd startled myself by how quickly I'd agreed to the notion of an understanding with him. As the days passed without the pressure of his presence, however, I gradually developed more confidence in the idea of marriage sometime in the future.

Meanwhile the newspapers were filled with stories of what had been dubbed the "the race to the finish": the number of days left until September 6, when President McKinley was scheduled to visit the power station and push the lever that would put Powerhouse 3 on-line—if it was ready. Work was being conducted in twelve-hour shifts, twenty-four hours a day. The papers were documenting every aspect of construction, every test, every difficulty no matter how minor (in the articles Tom referred to these as "challenges," not difficulties); profiling everyone from engineer to janitor, searching for heroes. And in the eyes of the newspapers (albeit not the establishment-bound *Express*) Tom had become the greatest hero of all. While he was working, Grace spent the long summer days visiting friends and taking tennis, swimming, and riding lessons at the country club. I had breakfast with her every other morning. Most days, Tom had already left for the power station by the time I came to call or had simply spent the night out there, leaving Grace in the capable care of Mrs. Sheehan.

Each week brought new dignitaries to the Pan-Am, lured by special events in their honor: University Day bringing academic officials; Opera Day renowned musicians; national days bringing troops of ambassadors and princelings, the local families vying to provide their entertainment and accommodation—such privileges generously bestowed by John Milburn, never a man to overlook a detail that might someday result in a reward to himself.

We became a city transfixed by expectation.

On July 9, the National Association of Colored Women convened its three-day biennial convention at Lyric Hall. Miss Love invited me to attend the first day. Ordered me, would be a better description of the note she sent. But no matter, entering Lyric Hall I felt an assuaging of my guilt about not joining Mary Talbert in her protest at the exposition. The hall was decked out in banners of purple and white, the NACW's colors, symbolizing royalty and purity. "Lifting As We Climb" proclaimed the central banner across the stage. Miss Love had staked out a row toward the back, not far from the portrait of the Marquis de Lafayette. Every Caucasian woman who came in the door was peremptorily called to join her. We made for a small group: myself and several reform-minded ladies, seated primly in our row while around us several hundred Negro women beautifully attired in white or purple greeted one another with excitement. They ignored us.

In a white lace dress, Mrs. Talbert stood at the front of the hall answering questions, making notes, passing out leaflets, directing people to their seats. Her protest at the Pan-Am had garnered no attention whatsoever—at least not in *our* newspapers, although undoubtedly the Negro papers had covered it. Nonetheless she was still organizing, her demeanor forthright and proud; she buried any despair she might feel under a veneer of steadfast commitment.

I sat between Miss Love and Miss Mary Remington, a short, stout, and formidable lady originally from Massachusetts. She'd established her own settlement house in Buffalo—the Remington Mission—in the worst part of town. Unlike Miss Love, she actually lived at her mission among the destitute, with her loyal friend Miss Alice Hyde. Miss Remington was rumored to be both gracious and affectionate toward the many who came to her for assistance. Miss Love viewed Miss Remington as her chief female competitor in the charity circuit.

After everyone who could be expected to join us was in attendance, Miss Love announced to no one in particular, "When I was a girl my mother hid runaway slaves in our stable. Our stable was a station on the Underground Railroad!"

I'd heard this before. More than once. No doubt Mary Remington had too.

"How well I remember the day I saw a slave auction in the South," Miss Love continued, nostalgically reminiscing. "I've always been lucky enough to travel. Nearly fifty years ago, that auction was, but I recall it as if it were yesterday. An entire family separated—each to a different owner. I can hardly bear the memory. It's an inspiration."

"What did you say, Miss Love?" asked Miss Remington pointedly, and not because she was hard of hearing. She leaned across me, and because of her bulk, I had to press myself against the back of my chair.

"An inspiration."

She caught Miss Remington's astounded expression.

"To reform, of course!" Miss Love snapped. "An inspiration to commitment!"

I sighed. It would be a long day, sandwiched between these two. Programs were dispensed. Over the three-day convention there would be lectures and discussions on such topics as the convict lease system, and nurse training for colored women. Several presentations would be devoted to the ever-increasing prevalence of lynching. The women would discuss whether Federal legislation would be formulated to help curb lynching. Indeed every lecture would end with a call to action— with practical steps women could take to confront the challenge.

Mrs. Booker T. Washington gave the keynote speech. She spoke about the achievements of the Tuskegee Institute, where Negroes received high-level vocational training as a path toward economic prosperity and equality. Applause was tinged with an undercurrent of critical comment. Even I knew about the debate between Booker T. Washington and W.E.B. DuBois. Washington focused his work on economic advancement for Negroes, and he had made concessions on the issue of enforced segregation in return for racial harmony and for support from the likes of Andrew Carnegie. DuBois, on the other hand, rejected segregation and believed that political action was the only route to equality for Negroes.

After the keynote speech, a thin, earnest woman from Chicago gave the first lecture, on the subject of the establishment of free kinder-gartens for Negro children in the Midwest. With discussion time, this lasted about an hour. The next topic was a consideration of the state of Negro teacher training, an issue of much concern and debate. As the time passed, the hall grew stuffy. Negro and Caucasian alike, we fanned ourselves with our programs.

Finally, at 3:00 p.m., Mrs. Talbert took the lectern to give the day's concluding remarks. She stood silently for several moments, garnering the room's attention. After thanking the lecturers, she said, "Now we will disperse for the day, and many of us, I know, are eager to tour the Pan-American Exposition, for both pleasure and education—for plea-surable education!" There was a smattering of laughter. "Before you go, I must confess to you my great disappointment that despite my best efforts, the exposition pays no formal recognition to our achievements as a race. Accept my apologies, for having failed you." For a moment she bowed her head in humility. "And yet . . . I cannot accept that all is lost. No, I will never accept defeat. I believe we can still make a differ-ence." Several women cheered. "Therefore I am calling today for a leaflet campaign. If each one of you takes only five leaflets each day to distribute among the visitors to the Pan-Am, our request will turn into a groundswell of support, and I pray—I know—that the public will rise up with us to demand our rightful place at this, the greatest exposition in the history of our nation!"

"Amen!" the women called. There was conversation all around and questions were called out as the women pondered more action than simply a leaflet campaign. As righteous passion surged around me in the stifling heat, I felt a need to escape. Immediately. Their cause was hopeless. Bidding good-bye to a surprised Miss Love, forcing my way around Mary Remington's wide legs, I left. I didn't have the strength to be part of hopeless causes.

———————•◆•———————

Wanting a bit of a walk, I took the streetcar only partway home, listening to the other passengers chat in German, Italian, and Polish. I disembarked at the corner of Main and Allen streets, the atmosphere around me raucous and commercial. From there I strolled across Allen to Delaware Avenue—several short blocks, bringing me to peace and tranquility. All at once I was in a different city altogether. On Delaware, the elm trees along the sidewalks met overhead in a green arch, while across the wide lawns sprinklers swirled in a flash of diamonds. Lawn mowers whirred, and the breeze carried the scent of fresh-cut grass.

At this hour of the afternoon, in the warm, quiet shade, there were few people around and fewer vehicles, just the ice wagons, making their slow journey from house to house, the horse's hooves muffled by the heat-softened asphalt. Regardless of its architectural style, each house had French doors and ivy vestments; tall upper windows filled with gauze curtains that swept in and out upon every breeze; and stone flowerpots brimming with blue and orange blossoms. My girls, when they were Grace's age, viewed the entire avenue as their private domain. On summer days, when the mood struck them, they would go from house to house on their horses and beg treats from the cooks at each kitchen door.

At the corner of North and Delaware, at the top of the hill, I turned and looked back over the city. Beyond the skyscrapers, church steeples, and grain elevators, Lake Erie shimmered in the distance. High clouds drifted across the sky. The air was so clear I could see even the smokestacks at Stony Point. Along the lakeshore, freighters, steamships, and commercial schooners glinted in the sunlight, while beyond them sailboats caught the wind for pleasure, colorful spinnakers unfurled. To the west were the beckoning green hills of Canada. Less than fifty years ago, escaped slaves had made the journey across the Niagara River at night to freedom. Buffalo, the final stop on the Underground Railroad: We had so much to be proud of.

I continued walking up Delaware, past two mansions designed by Stanford White in the style of Italianate palaces. Then I passed Westminster Church, with its soaring Gothic spire.

"Miss Barrett?"

I turned to find Franklin Fiske wheeling toward me on his bicycle. Hailing me on the street, he'd used my family name, and once again I appreciated his discretion. He came to a stop at the curb and dismounted. Suddenly I realized that I hadn't seen him in a few weeks.

"Where have you been, Franklin?" I asked as he brought his bike onto the sidewalk beside me.

"In and out of town," he explained. "Serving time in the state capital, basking in the summer beauties of Albany while interviewing state water inspectors."

"Was that interesting?" I asked, skeptical.

"Oh, being a water inspector is a most unusual job," he assured me. "You go to a power station, let's say right here at Niagara for the purposes of argument. Pad and pencil in hand, you stare at the water flowing into the powerhouse sluices for a good long time. You stand alone and uninterrupted. Then you pronounce the amount of water being taken as absolutely within legal limits. Thank you for noticing my absence." Looking around at the deserted street, he asked, "Might I walk beside you? If it wouldn't scandalize the town, that is. And if your errand isn't secret."

"I'm walking home. And yes, you may walk beside me."

While he pushed his bicycle by the handlebars, I felt the sense of his body there beside me: tall and slender, the dark hair, the smell of him—a touch of sweat on this hot day mixed with his citrusy shaving lotion, the lemony scent of it cutting through the heat.

"This is a nice sidewalk," he observed.

I laughed at his excuse for conversation. "Yes, it *is* very nice. Red medina sandstone. One of the prides of the city. Brought here by barge on the Erie Canal."

"You're certainly a font of knowledge."

"Part of my job description: experienced schoolmarm, font of knowledge."

"You shortchange yourself."

"That, I assure you, I would never do. You're very fashionable these days, wheeling around town."

"Yes, it's true: I am fashionable."

"I've never been on a bicycle."

"Try mine," he offered.

"No, thank you," I said firmly. "A woman in my position must be properly attired for wheeling." The Buffalo Women's Wheel and Athletic Club recommended sturdy knee-length bloomers and thick stockings.

"Quite right," he agreed with mock-seriousness. "A woman in your position must always be properly attired. Whatever she's doing," he added in a voice that hinted at unseemly implications. When he saw that I ignored them he continued, "This is a wonderful city for wheeling."

"You can thank Mr. Albright for that. He arranged for the asphalt. You may not know that Buffalo has more paved streets than any other city in the nation."

"Really! Good to know. A conversation opener: 'Mr. Albright, I certainly have been enjoying the asphalt. And what was your profit in it, may I ask?'" Before I could object to his profit-motive explanation for all local endeavors, he said, "Speaking of Mr. Albright, I've also been taking my camera to Stony Point. The perfect time, when everyone in charge is busy with the exposition, to mosey around in pursuit of 'artistic' industrial photography."

"And what have you found at Stony Point?"

"The construction of a very large steel mill. A veritable 'city of steel.'"

"Nothing new there. You could have found that out by reading the newspapers."

"And for once the newspapers are right! I can confirm with my own eyes that they are not exaggerating. A most unusual discovery for a newspaperman to make, believe me. A first, in my experience. I have an urge to cable Mr. Pulitzer to report 'newspapers correct on city of steel.'"

"And did you receive a warm welcome out there?"

"Not at all," he said happily. "I had to spend days ingratiating myself with the middle-level bureaucrats while the bigwigs were in town showing themselves off to the various dignitaries come to see the Pan-Am. Of course I planned my visits around the absence of these self-same bigwigs. The bureaucrats became very talkative, I'm pleased to say, once they discovered my innocent, useless—dare we say unmanly—dedication to photography. They quite let themselves go. Verbally, that is, the way another class of men does with you, my dear Louisa." He tipped his hat.

With a nod, I acknowledged the double-edged compliment. "Did they tell you anything useful?"

"No . . ." He dragged out the word. "Not directly useful to me. But useful for another story. My esteemed leader Mr. Pulitzer considers himself the champion of the immigrant classes, as you know, and that steel mill is a hazard to immigrants if there ever was one."

"You mean the shantytowns?"

"Yes, partly. But you've got shantytowns outside every new industrial complex. The bigger problem is that the whole place is electrified and the men don't understand one whit about electricity: they trip over wires, they step into puddles that have wires in them, they touch connections. They're getting electrocuted like there's no tomorrow and since most of them don't speak English, you can't even explain what's happening and why. You'd need translators for fifteen languages if you even wanted to try. Your friend Albright doesn't care, because for every man who's down, there's ten waiting to take his place. I'm writing it up. Hoping the boss will send someone to look into it. My esteemed employer loves a crusade, you know. Feather in my cap to give him one." Apparently he'd exhausted the issue of the steel mill, for next he said, "Now, here's a question I've often pondered: When does one say 'macadam' and when does one say 'asphalt'? I must inquire of the copy editor at the paper. Where are you coming from?" he asked, the sudden shifts in the conversation startling me.

"The biennial convention of the National Association of Colored Women. At Lyric Hall."

"Oh, yes." He looked annoyed with himself. "I forgot about that. Well, I can't be everywhere."

"Frederick Krakauer once said the same thing to me."

"Then it must be true. When were you talking to him?"

"We met—" All at once I didn't want him to know about my visit to Albright at Stony Point. Franklin was always seeking implications and permutations, as if we were all caught in a giant web and awaiting his dissection. "We met by chance. He was rather charming, in his highly distinctive way."

"I'm sure of it: distinctive charm is undoubtedly part of his job description. But this convention of colored women . . ." Franklin mused. "It seems to me I've been hearing about that. There's a woman named Mary Talbert involved, I think?"

"Yes," I said, puzzled about what he might have heard.

"And she's been raising trouble at the exposition?"

"Has she? I saw her protesting when Roosevelt came, but I didn't think—"

"It's coming back to me now. None of this has been reported, of course, so in that respect her protests don't officially exist"—he raised his eyebrows and nodded in recognition of our joint understanding of the realities of the city—"but apparently she's been making a pest out of herself. Printing leaflets and lecturing from soapboxes—all very harmless in the scheme of things, but no doubt there'll be more of the same during this convention. I sense that our esteemed Pan-American investors wouldn't want to lose a single paying customer because of a bunch of colored women forgetting their place—at least that's how our more distinguished citizenry seems to see it. Ah well, just another facet of the ever-fascinating microcosm that is your city."

He glanced at me sidelong. "I've missed you," he said quietly.

"I've missed you too." And I had: I'd missed his conversation, and even his admiration.

"In addition to everything else," he said nonchalantly, as if it were of no importance whatsoever, "I've been looking into possible links between the late and lamented Karl Speyer and the youthful James Fitzhugh. Beyond the obvious link of profession, I mean."

"And have you found any links?"

"Not yet," he admitted cheerfully, "but I'm sure there's something out there, just waiting to be stumbled upon. I don't suppose you've discovered anything you want to tell me about?"

This question angered me, but I forced myself to sound light-hearted: "Franklin, I told you I wouldn't betray my friends. Why are you pressing me about this again?" I demanded, my anger slipping out.

"What do you mean?" he asked, looking genuinely bewildered.

I trusted him enough to answer honestly. "I feel as if you're using me, by asking a question like that."

"Using you? I'm sorry. I never meant for you to feel that way. I simply thought, well, I imagined we could be together on this . . . you know"—he glanced away for an instant—"together. I've always thought, theoretically, I mean, that there'd be something wonderful about being united on a crusade with someone, fighting the good fight, two together, swept up in the romance of it all . . ."

He looked at me for affirmation. Was I tempted? Tempted to blend politics with romance, betrayal with love, two like-minded people united to create a revolution? Theoretically, like him, I could see the appeal in such a life, but for myself . . . well, perhaps I'd spent too many years carefully watching the world and calibrating my every reaction to suddenly dedicate my entire being to the changing of it. He waited for some response from me. Then: "*Have* you discovered anything?"

An image came into my mind: the documents on Tom's desk. The lines of writing; the figures, the initials, repeated over and over, amounts of money beside them. Could this be evidence of bribery, the very bribery Daniel Henry Bates had been talking about in his lecture at Lyric Hall? All at once I perceived that it might be. But did this realization mean that I should join Franklin's crusade? Was his battle now my battle, too? A sudden impulse toward confession captured me.

"Franklin." I stopped walking and turned to him. I placed my hand over his, where he held the handlebars of his bicycle. We were at the corner of Delaware and West Ferry, near the Milburn house and the Albright estate. The wind from the lake swept around us.

"Yes?" he said urgently, placing his other hand over mine, believing this was the moment that would unite us.

"I . . ."

"It's all right," he said, his voice both reassuring and eager. "You can tell me."

"Several weeks ago—" But I couldn't go on. The image of Grace came before me. Grace and Tom, both. I couldn't betray them. I wouldn't. I exhaled in frustration at the conflicts inherent in my position. "I'm sorry . . ."

Our friendship would be over now, I knew. He would walk me home, of course, because he was a gentleman, but we would never speak again, beyond the demands of politeness. How deeply I regretted this—but he was the one who'd made me choose.

Then Franklin surprised me. "All right," he said simply. His eyes reflected the color green—leaves and mown lawns. "I won't mention it again. No hard feelings, I hope?"

"No, I suppose not," I said, caught off-guard by this turn in my expectations. "Of course not."

"Well, that's all right then." He brushed a windblown lock of hair back from my face, making us friends again.

And so we continued our walk. I felt worn down by the crisscrossing subterfuges that ruled my life, and I took refuge in the beauty around us. At the circle we turned onto Chapin Parkway. Elm trees in five widely spaced rows basked in the yellow mist of late afternoon. Chapin truly was a "parkway." With only a few houses on each side, it was like a radiant, ceremonial path into a forest. I felt (not for the first time) as if I were living within the mind of Frederick Law Olmsted; I'd become a figment of his imagination, Franklin and I stepping into his painting of the perfect city.

We entered the yellow mist. At Soldier's Place we turned onto Bidwell Parkway: There was my house, outlined in the raking light; there was the school rising in its Gothic splendor, construction scaffolding across the back and part of the roof.

It was close to six o'clock. All was quiet. Was this early for the construction workers to have stopped for the day? I couldn't precisely remember their hours; sometimes certain elements needed to dry before the men could move on to the next step and so the foreman let them off early; on others days, they worked straight through to sunset.

Nonetheless the sight of the deserted scaffolding broke into my reverie. Even here, at this small project, going on less than a month, there'd been labor disputes and walk-outs. One morning there'd been a picket line from the carpenters union in front of the school; this left me in the uncomfortable position of being simultaneously irate at the delay and philosophically sympathetic to the cause. Last week the contractor had had to hire two nonunion bricklayers who happened to be Negro to get a certain bit of work done while the fine weather held. Francesca had warned me that this might lead to repercussions, but she and the contractor had felt the need to press ahead.

"May I invite myself in for tea?" Franklin said.

"Yes, of course," I replied, trying to ignore my feeling of apprehension about the construction. "First I need to check at my office, in case Mrs. Schreier left any messages." The school closed early in the summer. The front door would be locked, but I always carried a set of keys in case of an emergency.

"Let's walk in the center median. Under the trees," he said.

He didn't walk beside me, but instead strolled about ten feet in front. I felt as if we shared a private bower. My heels sank into the moist grass.

We saw it together, Franklin and I. We both stopped suddenly, as if our minds couldn't comprehend what it was exactly that we were seeing. A splash of red—that's all it seemed at first. And then we were both running, Franklin struggling not to trip on his bike as he pushed it along. The splash of red turned into a pattern of red. The pattern turned into letters. When we were just opposite the door, still sheltered by the trees, we slowed. We stood side by side, staring.

"You should telephone the police." Franklin was absolutely calm. "There's a telephone in the school office, isn't there? I'll do it, if you prefer."

I was trembling. "I don't want to telephone the police."

"There's a threat implied here. You must."

"The police have never been called to the Macaulay School."

"Don't be ridiculous."

"My job is to protect the school."

"At least notify someone on the board, let him decide. Telephone Rumsey. This is serious. It was probably done by someone on your own construction crew."

"You don't know that. It could have been anyone."

"Not anyone. Only someone with knowledge—someone who knows what's going on here. First this, then they'll burn the building down."

"No. Then they'd be out of jobs."

"They'd have more jobs rebuilding it."

"Now you're being ridiculous."

"For such an intelligent woman, sometimes your naiveté astounds me."

I said nothing. Two words (what a sacrilege it was, to call them words) were painted in red across the broad wooden door. Forming a crudity for a Negro man brought in to replace union workers.

Yes, I knew these words were a threat. But I wasn't quite as naive as Franklin thought. I also knew that if I telephoned the police, the incident would be reported in the newspapers. It would be blown out of proportion. Because of the NACW convention, some people might make a link. Much would be made of the fact that Millicent Talbert attended the school—not as a charity student, but as an equal. The wisdom of that would be called into question. I needed to protect Millicent, the school—and myself.

So we found Mr. Houlihan, the maintenance man, who lived in the basement apartment that opened onto the back courtyard. He was a longtime widower, getting on in years, and he had trouble with his hearing. His loyalty to the school—and to me—was absolute. He was terribly upset when he saw the painted letters. No, he hadn't heard anything amiss. He too urged me to telephone the police. But I cut him off. This was my decision; I had made it.

He and Franklin went off together to get a bucket, turpentine, rags, and a ladder. Together they washed the paint away. The job was easier than I expected: although thick, the paint was still wet. The door had a heavy coat of varnish; except for a few spots, the red didn't stain; Mr. Houlihan said he would scrape those spots away and revarnish the door in the morning. While they worked, I thought about the dismal passions which had led to this incident. I felt thankful that this had happened during the summer, when Millicent wasn't here to see it.

Chapter Twenty-Two

I couldn't get the incident of the painted letters out of my mind, as each weekday morning I rose to the sounds of construction, hammering, sawing, and shouted orders cutting the birdsong. Whenever I left school or home and saw the workmen, I wondered . . . was *this* the man who'd painted the words: thin and bearded, lounging on the curb eating his lunch? Or was it this man, heftier and red-faced from labor, leaning against the school to rest? Or was it none of them: Was someone sent directly from the union, his sole duty to take care of such jobs; someone who could disappear in an instant, leaving the regular workers totally innocent if ever they were questioned? Meanwhile the two Negro bricklayers were no longer with us; their bit of work was complete.

The following Sunday, my presence was required at the Bastille Day costume ball given by the Milburns in honor of the French ambassador. I felt too vexed to look forward to it, but then again, I've always hated costume balls. Especially those for which I'm supposed to feel abjectly grateful for the privilege of being invited. Naturally the chandeliers twinkled. The banks of roses made newcomers gasp. The orchestra played waltzes with verve. The ladies shimmered with jewels even as their skin glowed in the July heat. Their elaborate gowns, ordered from New York, cost more than a laborer's yearly wage.

What more can I say? Only that by happy coincidence the Astors were visiting the Pan-Am that same weekend, so they too were in attendance. Judging from the deference offered them, they were more truly guests of honor than the ambassador himself.

The Milburn house looked very fine. In preparation for the exposition's stream of dignitaries, John Milburn had ordered a remodeling, converting terraces and verandas into receiving rooms and suites fit even for the President of the United States. On the exterior, the additions were already laden with ivy, the type which takes years to grow, and the whisper was that the ivy had been stolen from other houses in the dead of night and pasted on. There were other whispers too: that Milburn was having difficulties organizing the timely payment of the Pan-Am's debts. Nothing but cash flow problems, he'd explained to more than one impatient contractor and supplier, but there was a fluttering of nervousness in the air as the investors pondered their own hopes of repayment.

At any rate, we had a tradition of costume balls in Buffalo; masquerades relating to the novels of Sir Walter Scott were special favorites, because of the extravagant medieval and Tudor costumes required. For the Milburn ball, French history was the theme. Research had gone on for months. As I arrived at the Delaware Avenue mansion stylishly late at 11:15 p.m. (the ball began at ten), I wondered if Miss Love would attempt the challenging role of Marie Antoinette without her head; probably it was too much to hope for.

Nonetheless, when I came upon her in the oak-carved entry gallery, she surprised me. Her wrinkled bosom was pushed up and out by what must have been an exceedingly tight corset. Complicated panels of white silk fell from her shoulders, draping her ever so much like—well, window drapery. Although her feet were hidden, she must have been wearing very high heels, for she seemed even taller than usual. Adding to the sense of height was her grey hair, piled high atop her head, one thick lock twisting down to her waist.

"Miss Love, how . . . magnificent you look. I can't quite place—"

"The Spirit of France, my dear, the Spirit of France." She was tremendously pleased. "Mrs. Astor herself complimented me. She said I looked quite realistic!"

"How wonderful!" I said—and I complimented myself for the sincerity of my tone.

At the top of the grand, curving stairway, the French ambassador appeared to be relishing every moment of his receiving-line glory. He claimed to be Voltaire, and remarkably there was some resemblance—most notably in the self-satisfied smirk I recalled from busts of the great philosopher. Patty Milburn, the former schoolteacher, received her guests attired as the Empress Josephine, and somehow she managed to look demure despite a dress more revealing than a summer nightgown. Her husband, however, did not play the part of Napoleon. "I'm glad to say, I'm too tall to be believable as Napoleon!" he assured me. Instead he was the Sun King, inpointed shoes, silk stockings, brocades, and an exotic feathered hat. Recently Milburn had developed a swollen heaviness beneath his eyes, and his skin was pasty. He looked haggard. Judging from his appearance, the financial pressure of the exposition was taking a toll on him.

Despite a bit of velvet at my neckline (which was cut low enough to show off my mother's pearls), I was costumed as myself. Of course I spent my life in costume. Standing straighter, squaring my shoulders, I buttressed myself against Patty Milburn's condescension with the sharp certainty that she knew nothing about me whatsoever.

Nor did anyone else here tonight. I knew I wouldn't see Tom: he and Margaret never went to costume balls. With his absence, I could still be ever so much myself—a confirmed spinster, alone at the ball. The debutantes greeted me warmly, welcoming me like a prize their graduation had earned them. Behind their painted fans, they confided to me the identities of the young men with whom they hoped to dance. The newly married women claimed me to ask what books they should include on the autumn reading lists of their literary clubs. The matrons (those whose children were nearly grown) drew me into a discussion about proposed speakers for the Twentieth Century Club's fall and winter lecture series. There was also the pressing issue of whether to introduce fencing at the club; the older women were opposed to this innovation, while the younger women championed it. As the debate between youth and age grew more spirited, I drifted on.

I tried to avoid the clergy, the group with whom I was most often linked during the dinner segment of such gatherings. The clergy and the school principals—birds of a feather, hostesses generally assumed. In honor of the French ambassador, the Roman Catholic bishop was here, attired in the full regalia of his office and obviously enjoying himself. By contrast, the Protestant clergymen wore their usual black and glared with disapproval at the women's low-cut gowns even as they stared fixedly at them.

Suddenly Mr. Albright was next to me; not *with* me, but purely next to me, as if we'd been walking separately down the street and he had overtaken me.

"Have you passed on the Cloudless Sulphur to your student as you thought you would?" Instead of a costume, he wore elegant evening clothes.

"You mean Abigail Rushman?"

"Whomever," he said indifferently. "Did you tell me her name? I don't recall. Well?"

"Not yet. Miss Rushman received an art fellowship, as you may have heard. She's spending the summer with the Roycrofters. She left directly after graduation."

He mulled this over, never looking at me. "No, I never heard of such a thing—the Roycrofters giving fellowships? Well, I suppose they must, if you tell me this girl received one. Oh well, time enough to pass on the gift when she's in a position to appreciate it. You might mention that I mounted it—although she certainly wouldn't think you had mounted it!" He chuckled, looking at me at last. "More importantly, I don't suppose you ever gave my message to Sinclair."

"Yes, in fact, I did."

"Really? He never mentioned it," Albright said suspiciously, as if doubting me. "What was his reaction?"

"He laughed."

"Oh," Albright said in disappointment.

"Mr. Albright, exactly what—"

"Well, well, such is life." He pushed his glasses farther up his nose. "Do please excuse me." He moved towards the ministers who hovered at the drinks table with suitable expressions of censure even as they perused the selections.

Sighing in exasperation, I continued my walk around the room. There was Franklin, without costume and looking all the better for it as he stood in the middle of a crowd of my young ladies. As Susan Rumsey's cousin, of course he would be considered a catch, but I sensed that young society ladies would hold little appeal to him, despite their Macaulay educations. I felt profoundly grateful for his help at school the week before, even more so because as far as I could tell, he'd said nothing to anyone about it; he had respected my decision to pretend publicly that it had never happened. Onward I went: there were the Rushmans, speaking to Mr. and Mrs. Astor. Near the windows, Miss Love appeared to have cornered Frederick Krakauer, who was attired in the garb of an early medieval monarch—Charlemagne, perhaps. His eyes were level with her artificially swelled bosom. Eventually I came upon Mr. Dexter Rumsey, dressed in a plain suit that made him look exactly like himself.

"Where are you going, Louisa? I've been trying to say hello to you for ten minutes, but I've had to follow you round and round the room."

"I've been trying to escape the clergymen." Because Mr. Rumsey reminded me of my father, I could let my guard down a bit to joke with him. "I wanted to avoid the confidential lectures on how they really don't approve of costume balls but suppose they must graciously accept them because the French ambassador is here and Buffalo has become the capital of the world."

He laughed warmly, putting his hand on my shoulder. "Very wise of you, Louisa. My wife is off somewhere displaying her Empress Eugénie outfit—come, let us dance."

Thus he placed his blessing upon me. Desiring always to avoid attention, Mr. Rumsey seldom danced, and then only with family members. People noticed that we danced. Doubly noticed, when he asked me to dance again. He was showing them all that I was under his protection. Warning them. As I gazed at him anew—the close-cropped gray beard, the veiled astuteness—I wondered what he thought he needed to protect me from.

As we circled the ballroom, observing our friends and neighbors in their disguises, Mr. Rumsey sighed. "I can admit to you, Louisa, that these past months have been a burden to me. All this hoopla about the exposition, the vice president coming to town, royalty from every rightfully obscure nation of the world. I much preferred our city when it was staid and boring and we could focus on really important things, like business! And then on top of everything the deaths of Speyer and Fitzhugh to deal with."

"To 'deal' with?" I asked, trying to sound nonchalant.

He shrugged. "Anything dramatic comes under my purview, I'm afraid."

"Don't you believe both deaths were accidental?" I asked impulsively.

Startled, he paused for an instant in the dance, then abruptly resumed on the beat as if nothing had disturbed him. He glanced around. "Oh, how wonderful," he whispered with relish, changing the subject, "our friend Urban does look absurd." And so he did: Macaulay board member, flour king and cultivator of green roses, pudgy George Urban, Jr., was attired as feline-lover Cardinal Richelieu (who was thin and elegant in life), holding a none-too-pleased tabby cat on a red leather leash.

I, too, pretended to be at ease. "And what is your costume, Mr. Rumsey?"

Jauntily he said, "I'm a Huguenot. Willing to die for my cause. And I would guess that you are either a Protestant missionary—which seems unlikely from what I know of you—or yourself."

"Definitely the latter." I made myself laugh even as my forever-attuned vigilance pondered his words. What did he know, or think he knew?

I was still considering this when, on our next pass near the door, we observed the entry of Francesca Coatsworth. She was dressed in tie and tails like a man. Beside her, also in tie and tails, Susannah Riley. Their hair was swept up under top hats. They looked very handsome, especially Susannah, whose entire demeanor displayed a worldliness and confidence I wouldn't have credited to her. Inwardly I flinched, as much from the spectacle as from the fact that few would believe my putative liaison with Francesca now. Mr. Rumsey studied them probingly and then gracefully danced me into the crowd.

"You know, Louisa, when I was a young man, right here in Buffalo, women who dressed up as men were arrested! Of course they were a different kind of women. Ladies of the night—they were the ones who dressed up as men. Odd, isn't it? Though I suppose some men find such things alluring." He flushed. "Forgive me, my dear, for mentioning such a topic. I lost track of myself."

"Not at all, Mr. Rumsey. I believe I am mature enough to hear even a reference to ladies of the night."

"Sometimes I forget your maturity when I see your beautiful face." He chucked me under the chin, and now I flushed.

And so the ball continued. At about 1:00 a.m., I found myself with a group that included Mr. Rumsey, his daughter Mrs. Wilcox, and several recent Macaulay graduates. The ladies had just induced me to admit that I was in favor of introducing fencing at the club, when the Milburn butler materialized at Mr. Rumsey's side and whispered in his ear. Mr. Rumsey paled, but quickly recovered.

"Excuse me," he said. At a measured pace he walked toward the staircase, the butler following, while the rest of us watched and wondered.

After a few moments, however, the butler returned to whisper in my ear: Mr. Rumsey requested my presence downstairs in the entry gallery. The butler searched out another guest while I made my way to the staircase, feeling the eyes of the others on my back. This was so irregular, this summoning of guests from a ball. Something had happened. Fear catapulted through me. My foot slid on the thick stair carpet; I gripped the railing as I walked down.

At the bottom of the stairs, by the carved doorway, stood Mary Talbert and the man I assumed to be her husband, William. He was thin, straight, and debonair. Intently Mr. Rumsey questioned him, and William Talbert replied in a precise tone that was almost British. I was aware that the two men were business associates through their mutual real estate holdings. Police Superintendent Bull, dressed as a Musketeer, joined me on the stairs, summoned by the butler, who now glided past us to stand sentinel in the hall, undoubtedly guarding the house from "coloreds."

With the arrival of Superintendent Bull, I knew. Millicent.

In the end, we had to travel by water taxi. Mere streets couldn't take us there. And why should they? The place we were visiting was designed for railroads and lake steamers, not horses and carriages.

We journeyed less than three miles from the Milburn house. Mr. Rumsey, Mr. Talbert, and Superintendent Bull drove in the Rumsey carriage while Mary Talbert and I followed in the Talberts'. With the sweet night air flowing around us, Mrs. Talbert told me what had happened. Millicent didn't come home from the Fitch Crèche, where she was volunteering for the summer. Two hours after she was expected (time enough for her to run an errand or have tea with a friend), Mrs. Talbert went to the Crèche. She spoke to the matron, who had said good-bye to Millicent on schedule and watched her leave; nothing had seemed amiss. Mrs. Talbert telephoned several friends and they searched Millicent's route, through a mostly Polish neighborhood mixed with Slavs, Czechs, and Rumanians. Of the few who could speak enough English to answer questions, none had seen anything, none knew anything. A colored girl? They'd never in their lives seen a colored girl—even though Millicent walked the same route twice each day.

Mrs. Talbert returned home to await her husband, even as her friends and neighbors continued to search the vacant lots, the abandoned buildings, the factory yards. No, they did not telephone the police, would never telephone the police; for them, only Mr. Rumsey could telephone the police and expect a response.

Then, a short time ago, like a clumsy melodrama at a second-rate theater, a rock had been thrown through their kitchen window. The sleepless cook heard the sound. Wrapped around the rock was a note. The cook brought the note to the Talberts, who were in the drawing room waiting for whatever might happen. Mrs. Talbert couldn't show me the note, because her husband had it, but she described it to me. It was written in pencil, in barely legible script, replete with misspellings and with the diction of someone for whom English was most likely a second language. The note was an angry, racial diatribe. Mrs. Talbert could barely bring herself to say the exact words; I would never repeat them. The words were about Negroes getting uppity, taking jobs that belonged to white men, making trouble when they should mind their own business—if they knew what was good for them. If they didn't want to end up the way Negroes did in the South, strung from the nearest tree.

Such were the words, uneducated and fraught with hatred. But the paper was a lovely ivory vellum. This contrast between the writing and the paper was disturbing. For the poor, clean paper was a rare commodity; they often wrote their letters in the margins of newspapers, or above the lines of other letters, or on scraps ripped from advertising circulars. Where would a person with such writing and such beliefs find such paper? Had he stolen it, or had it been given to him? Or was the uneducated writing merely a ruse?

The Talberts didn't pause to decide. For the note told them where to find Millicent: at one of the grain elevators along the harbor. There was a certain logic to this, because Negro laborers were often hired to shovel grain during the frequent strikes and slowdowns that plagued the waterfront. With the knowledge provided by the note, the Talberts immediately went to Mr. Rumsey's Delaware Avenue home, only to be told that he could be found up the street, at the Milburn ball.

Slowly we made our way through the squalid, fetid slums along the waterfront. The immigrants who lived here were utterly powerless: Several years earlier when the DL & W railroad desired access to its coal trestles down a tenement-lined street, its laborers simply built the tracks during the night; in the morning the elected city fathers announced that they couldn't correct a *fait accompli* and the tenement children would need to be careful, what with a railroad outside their doors.

As we drove through the slums, the cityscape around us gradually became a maze of ship canals, commercial slips, stagnant estuaries, and railroad bridges; a dismal, reeking Venice. Coal trestles rose along the harbor like colossal insects, interspersed with giant hooks used to unload cargo. Upward of one hundred fifty vessels at a time could be docked at the Buffalo Harbor, and there were always more anchored just offshore, waiting for space. When there was no regular docking available for grain ships, "floaters"—grain elevators that operated on the lake itself—were brought into service.

Finally we reached the outer harbor, where huge breakwaters protected incoming vessels from lake storms. Opposite the "Chinaman's" lighthouse (so called because some thought its conical top resembled a coolie's hat), we left the carriages. Two police officers materialized from nowhere, to stand guard. I glanced at Mr. Rumsey; his merest nod provoked nervous barking orders from Superintendent Bull. The feathers on Bull's Musketeer hat tossed wildly in the wind. I shivered in that wind, even though it was warm and moist, like a wind from the tropics; it was everywhere—a force, a companion, a roar as well as a pressure. When I was a girl with my father in the mountains, I would lean into such a wind and let it buoy me up.

A red glow out on the lake, a pillar of flame, showed that one of the floating grain elevators was on fire, no doubt from spontaneous combustion. Tugs surrounded it, hosing it to little effect. The red glow lit and shadowed our way.

A police officer corralled two water taxis, one for Mrs. Talbert and me, the other for the men. The taxis were weatherworn, flat-bottomed scows propelled by a single oar, the boatman standing in the rear, shrouded in black against the black night. As we boarded, struggling against the boats' wobble, Mr. Rumsey's calm grew preternatural. Several police boats (not much bigger than ours but with two oars instead of one) joined us, and we formed a makeshift convoy as we moved toward the channel of the Buffalo River. This winding stream, which had once been a virtual swamp, had been reengineered over the years to become an extension of the harbor. Its only purpose was to provide more space for the docking of ships, more riverbank for grain elevators, and more land for the rail lines serving them both. Ship canals intersected the river at odd angles, creating still more docking space. Even with all this, however, there still wasn't enough room: the ships were docked chockablock, the elevators crowded against one another, and always there were ships waiting out in Lake Erie for space to open—such was our city's good fortune.

Now, in the night, the only light was torchlight, fire on sticks held by the police or propped in sockets along the shore, the flames pressed by the wind. A greasy slick covered the water, which smelled of garbage. Mrs. Talbert and I gasped as something large and white like a body rose suddenly before us, rolled, and disappeared. The boatman laughed, a rumbling sound shielded by his low hat and high scarf.

When we entered the channel of the river itself, the wind abruptly died. The masted sailing ships and funneled steamers, docked sideways along the shore, loomed beside us. Tugboats angled for space. In the interstices between the ships, we glimpsed the devil's promenade along the shore: prostitutes in flowing kimonos flaunting themselves to sailors bedecked in the colors of their shipping lines; vagrants bedded down in doorways; immigrant families trying to escape the stifling tenement heat, their children passively awake, staring wide-eyed at the ships and at us. There were no such amenities as safety railings along this shore; children fell in or they didn't. Many people lacked a hand, an arm, a leg, fingers, a foot—as if there'd been a war here, and the victims sat on stoops now nursing their wounds. Of course there *was* a war, and it was on-going: the inescapable war of employment in industry. I remembered Rolf, losing his arm; Maddie's father, his life. I thought about the Negro workman beaten outside the Albright Gallery, and the defacement of the school . . . even Speyer and Fitzhugh, although their deaths had been officially deemed accidents, seemed to belong on the list of casualties of war.

Even now men worked, transferring cargo in the torchlight. When there was no torchlight, they worked by touch and instinct in the darkness. On the horizon, there was a peculiar blackness against the sky, in the shape of boxes and pinnacles: the downtown skyscrapers silhouetted by glimmering stars.

Where Main Street met the water, passenger steamers were docked three-abreast against the piers. Some of these were excursion vessels that would set out in the morning for lakeshore beaches. Others would go farther, carrying the never-ceasing stream of immigrants that passed through Buffalo (like so much freight) on their journey west, to the cities of the Great Lakes—Cleveland, Toledo, Detroit, Chicago, Duluth. And always more canals and waterways were being built, to accommodate more ships: the Evans Ship Canal, Coit Slip, the City Ship Canal, Match Slip, Peck Slip—a warren of water paths lined with grain elevators, coal trestles, warehouses, and mills. Ornate jackknife bridges with fanciful towers traversed the waterways. And permeating everything was the sound of pianos. Waltzes and rags, blended into a single tinkling song. Saloons lined the waterfront, their doors open to dissipate the heat; every saloon had a piano, every piano gave its tune into the night. There were more pianos on Canal Street than on Delaware Avenue, a newspaper once reported, and their songs drifted achingly around us.

Slowly we approached the primary grain elevators. Two hundred and fifty feet tall, over forty of them were arrayed along both sides of the river like monsters spawned by the water itself. Somewhere among them there was even a Coatsworth Elevator, on its own Coatsworth Slip. Francesca never visited the elevator and rarely mentioned it; family agents managed the business and every quarter sent her a share of the profits, providing the income she needed to wear top hat and tails to costume balls.

The channel narrowed, elevators looming on both sides. All at once images of Millicent's death ran through my mind. How did people die at a grain elevator? They slipped (or were pushed) into the immense storage bins, where they suffocated in the grain as it pulled them down like quicksand. They were trapped (or tied) on a work platform when spontaneous combustion (or a match) caused a bin to explode. They were overcome by smoke poisoning from the slow, slow burn of a fire deep within the grain. They choked to death in the constant pall of grain dust. They fell off the open man-lift, onto the floor below.

Millicent. I remembered the first day she came to Macaulay, ever modest, oblivious to the stares of her classmates. I remembered when we reviewed together her first-term report, with its row of *A*'s, and the shy smile that ever-so-slowly lit her face. I remembered the evening she came to me in the snow with the story about Grace, her hands frozen, snowflakes touching her hair.

At a signal from Mr. Rumsey, who struck a match to double-check the note that William Talbert carried, we landed, pulling in between two freighters. Oddly, the elevator before us was deserted. With a start, I saw the large lettering painted on the exterior to guide the ships—this was the Coatsworth Elevator. Unused, tonight.

Mr. Rumsey came to my side while the police fanned out across the site, waving torches. We entered the building through the side door, away from the river entrance. Inside, the shadows curved, mimicking the giant wooden bins rising around us. The bins were constructed in intersecting rows and connected to one another like a patchwork quilt. Above them—far above our heads—was a labyrinth of delicate wrought-iron walkways. They were beautiful, like works of art, covered with designs of wheat and corn. Apart from our hollow footsteps, the only sound was the groaning pressure of the grain inside the wooden bins.

"Millie! Millie!" Mrs. Talbert suddenly wailed. The torches sent pillars of orange up the bins. "Millie! Millie!" She turned around—left, right, back—desperately wondering where her niece could be hidden in this maze. Her husband gripped her shoulders from behind, pulling her close against his chest to restrain her.

Dexter Rumsey took my hand, his palm warm and dry like well-used leather. Was he looking for comfort, or offering it? His face revealed nothing. The police went farther down the line of bins, leaving us in shadowed darkness. All at once I was lost. Disoriented. We all were; four of us bunched together, unable to tell even what direction we were facing.

Then from far away came a cry. Muted. It came again. Long enough for us to find a direction among the groaning bins. The cry became louder, a breathless call of anguish. Louder still.

"Millie? Millie?"

"Here. Here—Aunt Mary!" Suddenly the shout was clear, reverberating around the walls. But where was "here" in this echoing cave?

Almost by chance, we turned at a break in the bins—the police converging from the opposite side with their torches—and there she was, standing on a high, narrow platform. "Aunt Mary?" she shouted again, this time in surprise, as if she doubted herself. She appeared unharmed, although she was so high above me that I couldn't see her clearly.

She'd been taken up on the man-lift, a revolving metal belt with footholds that went from the ground floor to the roof, and left on an unprotected work platform above the open. bins. Any misstep would have toppled her into a quicksand of grain. Perhaps that was what those who'd done this had counted on: She would have fallen of her own accord and disappeared, and they could still take communion at their churches because they hadn't committed murder; her death would have been accidental, and months would have passed before her body was sucked down and blocked the lower chute from which the bins were emptied. How many other bodies were concealed within these bins? I shuddered at the question. And yet . . . Millicent didn't fall; she'd found just enough space up there to survive. The police started the man-lift and went up to get her. All at once, like an unexpected gift, she was with us.

On the way back, Millicent sat between her aunt and me, holding our hands. Her breathing seemed normal, but her palm was moist and clammy against mine. Her hair was properly pinned up, her clothes only a bit disarrayed. We made our way peacefully down the river as if we'd all been on an outing: a midnight picnic in the woods. The Talberts had decided not to let the police question her, at least not now. They wanted to take her home. So a contingent of police stayed behind to gather evidence at the elevator while we returned to the scows.

As we journeyed, Millicent was silent, her expression blank, her eyes terribly wide and somehow vacant. Yet she must have registered what she saw, for she turned her head when we passed a child with a dirty face (whether male or female, I couldn't tell) who stood alone at the water's edge. Millicent watched the child until we were too far away to see it anymore.

"Perhaps you'd best help at the Talbert house, Louisa," Mr. Rumsey said to me when we landed opposite the Chinaman's lighthouse.

At this instruction—Mr. Rumsey's "perhaps" was always an order—the Talberts nodded in silent acquiescence. When I entered the Talbert carriage I felt anxious. It was unheard of for a lady of my race to visit a home in the Talberts' community. The Talberts themselves glanced at me guardedly, while Millicent stared straight ahead, oblivious.

Standing at the window of the carriage and watching her, Mr. Rumsey sighed. "Well, William, you may want an officer to accompany you home. In case there's any . . ." He didn't say "trouble," but we knew what he meant. "And Millicent may wish to offer a statement. Later." He studied her vacant face. "After she's rested. There's no telling—" He paused, seeming at a loss. "Well, the perpetrators may have . . ."

The Talberts glanced at one another with understanding, and Mr. Talbert said, "Thank you, Mr. Rumsey, but no." Because of race, Mr. Talbert would always address Mr. Rumsey formally, whereas Mr.

Rumsey would say "William," not simply "Talbert" as he would for Milburn or Albright. "I think it best that the formal investigation end here. Millicent is obviously shaken but otherwise unharmed—more than we hoped for or expected. We will speak with her later, when the moment seems propitious. I will let you know what she says. There's no point bringing the police to our home. I assure you, our friends are . . . around us," he said meaningfully. "And undoubtedly the journalists would follow the police, creating a *cause célèbre* which would bring little justice and most likely produce similar incidents as people come to recognize the . . . possibilities of such endeavors."

Mr. Rumsey considered. At last he said, "As you wish." He bid us good-bye.

As we drove away, I imagined him returning to the Milburns' ball to find his wife. Would he say anything about the events that had transpired this night? Most likely not. "What took you away from the party?" Susan Fiske Rumsey might ask. "Only a bit of business," he would reply offhandedly as he offered her the final dance.

Chapter Twenty-Three

T he Talbert house, at 521 Michigan Street, was large and rambling, covered with ivy and surrounded by gardens, as lovely as any house on Lincoln Parkway. Although the time was now nearing 4:00 a.m., a small crowd was gathered outside.

I glanced at Mrs. Talbert. "Who—"

"Our neighbors," she said quietly. So the community was united, keeping vigil. But the crowd silently dispersed when we stepped from the carriage. Mrs. Talbert looked at no one, simply led Millicent to the door, and as I followed I realized that it was because of me that everyone left. Friends would say nothing until the Talberts gave some word or signal that I was to be trusted.

As if we were dressing a doll, we prepared Millicent for bed. We turned down the covers for her, lifted her legs, eased her down. Millicent said nothing through all of this, which worried me; but of course she was traumatized, and it was the middle of the night, so most likely Mrs. Talbert was right simply to encourage her to rest for now. Humming a lullaby, Mrs. Talbert caressed her forehead and hair for several minutes until she relaxed into sleep, looking all at once peaceful and calm.

Then, Mr. Talbert and the servants also went to bed and Mrs. Talbert and I were alone. We went downstairs and stood in the front hall that flickered with gaslight. We regarded one another warily. What were we to do now? Knowing that Millicent was safe, I wanted to go home, but I couldn't ask to be taken at this hour. Mrs. Talbert did not invite me to rest in a guest room upstairs, did not offer a dressing gown, did not make any of the overtures of hospitality that she might have made had she viewed me as an ally.

Instead she made tea. We sat at the formal dining table in the mahogany-paneled dining room, amid the shifting shadows thrown by the hall light, and we drank tea. The tea was brewed in a heavy silver pot, the surface shaped into vines and berries that I outlined with one finger. The thick Persian carpet was soft and inviting; I slipped off my shoes—my ballroom slippers—and rubbed my stockinged toes into it. The windows opposite me were thrown open, but no breeze touched the curtains. Why had Mr. Rumsey sent me here? To forge a friendship, or to be a spy? Or were the two the same for him?

Opposite me Mrs. Talbert was absorbed in her own thoughts. After some time passed, I grasped at a way to reach her; to make conversation, any kind of conversation at all. "This is a lovely teapot," I offered.

"Thank you. A wedding gift." She sounded indifferent.

Another step toward her: "I was proud of Millicent tonight."

She did not respond.

"Her resilience. Of course she was in a state of shock and there will be repercussions ahead, but she didn't break down in front of the police."

Still Mrs. Talbert was silent. I continued, "Her reaction revealed an in-born sense of dignity."

"Yes," she said thoughtfully, so I knew I'd finally said something that pleased her. "Millicent has always been modest and self-possessed." She turned toward the still-dark windows. "Like her mother. My eldest sister."

Abruptly her composure broke, and she hunched over, crying, her hands fisted against her mouth. I yearned to rush around the table to her; to hold her and comfort her. But I sensed that she wouldn't want that kind of comfort—at least not from me. Minutes passed while she wept. Finally she regained control and sat up. The horizon was beginning to lighten, the trees outlined like dark skeletons. The pendulum clock in the hall made its muffled gong for 5:00 a.m. Without looking at me, Mrs. Talbert began, "Sometimes I wonder if I've failed Millicent and my sister by taking on my burden of work. Maybe it is better to keep in the background, out of everyone's way, and protect your own. This never would have happened if I hadn't put myself forward and made myself so visible to everyone on the outside. I've had to make myself so harsh, for the work. Sometimes I sound sanctimonious even to myself. I feel like I've had to make my body into a shield to protect myself. Otherwise it's too hard to get up on crates and shout at people. And what's the purpose of it, anyway? Nothing ever changes. I should have been loyal to my sister and her daughter and kept quiet."

I waited for her to continue, and when she didn't I said, "You know you couldn't hide away. Hiding isn't your nature." I believed in her work, I admired her courage. Her choice had been the opposite of mine, and it was the right choice. "Things do change, bit by bit, not so as you can watch them changing every day, but so that you can turn around suddenly and see them changed, and you're astonished—the way you're astonished to realize suddenly how big a child's grown, and you hadn't noticed because you saw her every day. The risks you've taken, you've had to take. What you must do now is find a way to protect Millicent without surrendering your fight."

A freshening breeze picked up, the breeze of dawn that I welcomed each summer morning, pulling my blanket around me. Birds began singing in the garden—so many, so loud. I caught the sound of the mockingbird, sharp and close.

"Yes . . . protect Millicent," she said doubtfully. She seemed to sink into meditation.

"Why did you and your husband decide against a formal investigation?"

Here, at least, she was secure; she seemed to wake from reverie: "If anything had actually happened to Millie—if she'd been killed, is what I mean." I flinched when she said it, a real word abruptly taking the place of implication. "Of course William and I would have cooperated with the police. And the newspapers. We would have made it the greatest of causes: the lynching of a child." Again: a real word, forcing us to face reality.

"The lynching of a girl child." Closing her eyes, she expelled a long breath. "But as it is . . . well, we won't talk to the police now. We'll tell Mr. Rumsey anything we discover, of course: We can count on him to keep such matters private and do his own investigations. But we don't want any of this to become public. Why should Millicent go through life known as the girl who was kidnapped? Why should she become a symbol? Why should someone in my own family be made into ammunition for the fight? I don't have that courage." She studied me frankly. "Now there will always be something that holds me back—slightly back—from the barricades," she said with a trace of irony. "A secret. Now I understand you a bit better, Miss Barrett. You and the secret that holds you back. You'll always know my secret, so in fairness I ask you: What is yours? What is it that holds you back?"

I stared at her but said nothing. With dawn fully upon us, the room turned bright and clear, and the time for unfettered confession was gone.

"Shall I guess?"

"Guess all you like," I said more dismissively than I intended.

"I've pondered it more than once. And I believe I've discerned it. Not that I have any evidence," she noted quickly. "But in evaluating the alternatives I've allowed myself a speculation."

"Indeed."

"Yes. Indeed," she said pointedly. "Here is what I have decided: A long time ago, you fell in love with a man. You were reckless. He couldn't marry you for whatever reason. You paid the price. You bore a child. Even I, for all my sanctimony"—she cocked her head in good-hearted self-deprecation—"understand what love can make a woman do."

I burst out laughing, and my laughter was bitter. "I never 'fell in love' with a man." Immediately I realized that by protesting one supposition I'd virtually admitted the other.

She looked confused.

"Love would have been easy," I added, as if that were an explanation. And from her changing expression, I saw that it was, the truth slowly coming upon her.

"Oh. I see. I'm sorry."

Some words, like the words needed here, were too horrible to say, and we would never say them; words like rape, for example—that was a word neither of us would ever say.

"Who was he? Was he a stranger?"

"No, not a stranger. Although I suppose he was a stranger, when all was said and done. Some might consider him a gentleman."

"I understand."

Did she? "I was . . . young then, for my years."

"Yes. Couldn't you try, I'm mean, I don't wish to pry, but—wouldn't it be possible to pretend that the child is an orphan left to you by a deceased sister or a cousin, or something like that? Not that I've done that with Millicent, mind you. She's my sister's child fair and square, but I have heard of such solutions."

"When it happened, I made arrangements for—" Suddenly I didn't want the full truth known, even by her. Firmly I said, "I made arrangements."

"To your satisfaction?"

"I trust so." I felt my composure on the verge of breaking, but I couldn't allow it to break. Not now, not ever. "I hope so."

"Aunt Mary!" Millicent called from upstairs in a voice of terror. "Aunt Mary!"

Automatically we both stood, our moment of confidence over.

At first she screamed and cried so uncontrollably that I despaired of finding a way to calm her. Yet gradually she did calm, the Talberts and I sitting beside her, talking to her, reassuring her, holding her. At eight a.m. Mr. Talbert felt he had no choice but to leave for his office in order to keep up an appearance of normality. By then Millicent sat propped up in her canopy bed, her embroidered nightgown buttoned to her neck. As the day slowly wore on, Millicent, in shifting, jostling sentences, began to tell her aunt and me what had happened.

"I was walking home from the Crèche," she explained, "and I was walking on exactly the streets I'm supposed to." Defensively, apologetically, she glanced at her aunt, who nodded in reassurance. "Then all of a sudden there was something over me. Maybe it was a blanket? I think it was a blanket. It could have been a shawl. It didn't smell good, no matter what it was. I thought there were two men next to me, and they pushed me into a carriage and they tied my hands behind my back; the string hurt me." She massaged her wrists, although there was no sign of rope burns on her skin.

"And then?" I asked gently.

"When we got to that—place, that grain elevator, they took me up on that—belt, and it was scary because I couldn't see anything and I felt like I was swaying and I was going to fall off, even though the men kept pushing me against the belt so I couldn't fall. Finally when we got to the top, they pushed me out on the walkway and told me not turn or move or else I would fall in. And I really did think I would fall in—it was so small of a place to stand, and—" Reaching for her aunt, she again burst into tears, and while Mrs. Talbert hugged her close, my own eyes filled. After a few moments Millicent collected herself and continued: "Then they untied my hands and took away the blanket." She twisted and twisted the sheet in her hands.

"It's all right, dear," Mrs. Talbert said, stroking her head. "You don't have to tell us anything more now."

"No, I want to tell you." She pushed herself away from her aunt ever so slightly and looked at me. "That's when I opened my eyes. But I couldn't see anything. I felt like the blanket was still over me, because everything was so dark. Like I was blind! And by then the men were going back down the belt—they didn't even need any light, they could just do it by touch." Mrs. Talbert and I exchanged a quick glance: Was this a clue? Only men well-accustomed to the grain elevators would be able to use the belt in the dark. "When they got to the bottom, they lit some matches to find their way out. Then I was alone. All alone in the dark!" Her eyes became huge as she remembered her fear. Mrs. Talbert squeezed her shoulders, steadying her.

I asked, "Did they say anything else?"

She shifted her head. For a moment she considered. "Well . . . when we were going up the belt they told me not to be scared. But they laughed when they said it. That made me more scared."

"What language did they speak?"

"Sometimes they spoke English and sometimes they spoke a different language. I don't know which one. It wasn't French. And it wasn't German." Those were the two modern languages Millicent was studying in school. "And it wasn't Latin," she suddenly added with an impish grin that startled both Mrs. Talbert and me; it was a welcome glimmer of her former self, and Mrs. Talbert exhaled in relief. Of course she studied Latin at school too. But as suddenly as she had smiled, Millicent looked crestfallen. "Should I have asked them what language it was?"

"No, little darling," Mrs. Talbert said, hugging her close once more. "You did fine, just fine. You were wonderful."

"Why did they choose me to take?" She hit her fist against the quilt. "What did I ever do to them?"

"They weren't taking you, my darling. They were taking what you represent."

She looked confused. "I don't understand."

"You're a smart and lovely Negro girl from a good family. That makes them mad. And—well, I'm sorry to have to tell you that they were also taking me. And your uncle. Taking all of us who try to fight for what's right." An idea seemed to come to Mrs. Talbert, a way to help her niece. "So you see, you were part of our battle too. What you faced and overcame—well, you made your contribution. With dignity and bravery."

This Millicent understood. Of course she had met her aunt's friends and attended her aunt's church; she knew the language of the fight for justice. She brightened even as she became more serious. "Did I do exactly what I should have done?"

"You were wonderful. You were a heroine! A heroine for all of us! I'm so proud of you. All our friends are so proud of you!"

Looking aside in her modest way, Millicent seemed pleased.

"I'll always remember the day you were a heroine!" Mrs. Talbert exclaimed. Silently I blessed her, for she had found precisely the way to redeem all that had happened.

That day, Millicent slept on and off, and when she was awake Mrs. Talbert or I read to her from Sir Walter Scott's *Ivanhoe*. In the late afternoon we helped her to dress, and slowly, with our help, she made her way downstairs. At first she looked around in bewilderment, as if she didn't recognize her own home: the vase of peonies on the drawing room table, the tree branches tapping the long windows. She ran her fingers along the carved backs of the wooden chairs. At five o'clock we sat in the drawing room for afternoon tea, including cucumber sandwiches and little round cakes. Millicent ate in small, furtive bites. She seemed exhausted, which was natural of course and relieved my mind precisely because it was natural.

At about six-thirty, as we sat by the windows enjoying one last cup of tea, an impressive brougham drove up. Miss Love emerged. She regarded the house with narrowed eyes, then strode up the walkway. She banged on the front door and pushed past the astounded servant to find us.

Without greeting Mrs. Talbert or Millicent, she announced, "Louisa, you must come with me."

Mercifully she was no longer attired as the Spirit of France.

Chapter Twenty-Four

Even as the brougham drove away and I turned back to look, the neighbors came silently to the Talbert house. They must have been waiting all day for me to disappear. Miss Love and I drove through the neighborhood in the early evening glow of this long summer day. We passed the plain, brick Michigan Street Baptist Church, where Mary Talbert did much of her work. Once the church had been a stop on the Underground Railroad, and men and women slept on its padded pews and ate in its cellar. I felt a rush of optimism— for my friendship with Mary Talbert, for my own future.

"Don't upset yourself, Louisa. We'll find out who did this."

Startled, I turned from the window to face Miss Love. "I wasn't upset."

"You can't fool me, the way you were looking out the window. I can read your mind like an open book."

"Oh." Worried that I wouldn't be able to keep the irony out of my voice, I said nothing more.

"Mr. Rumsey has sources." She seemed to swish the word around in her mouth like fine wine. "Don't tell the Talberts," she cautioned, placing a restraining hand on my arm. "It's not that I don't trust them, but their acquaintances may not be—well, I'm sure you know what I mean."

Feigning innocence: "No, what?"

"My dear Louisa. The fact is, Mr. Rumsey is giving this matter his full attention. He told me so this afternoon."

"He visited you?"

"I visited him. To learn what took him from the party. Dexter keeps no secrets from me!" She laughed complacently. Dexter Rumsey and Maria Love had been children together, romping Delaware Avenue when much of it was still forest and farmland. "I imagine we'll be hearing shortly about an unfortunate accident befalling an unfortunate man or men. A slip along the slippery shore of the Niagara River, for example," she said with a disturbing hint of glee.

"What are you saying? You believe Mr. Rumsey would order people murdered—I don't believe it!" Even as I protested, an image of Speyer and Fitzhugh came into my mind.

"My dear girl." Again she placed a restraining hand on my arm. "I was only joking. Your night's adventures have made you sensitive. But don't you wish to see justice done for young Miss Talbert? You know very well there would be no justice for her in a public court. And I'm sure you don't want her name in the newspapers. I certainly don't want the Crèche publicly involved with this—and it is involved, don't forget, since she was walking home from the Crèche when she was . . . taken." Miss Love wrapped her large, gnarled hand around my upper arm. "I will not have my life's work besmirched. I'm grateful the Talberts saw fit to keep this matter private," she hissed. "Dexter's initial thought was to order a full police investigation—so he told me today. In this case the Talberts had more sense."

She let go of my arm. We rode in silence while the brougham turned onto Ferry Street, crossed Main and Linwood, and finally came to Delaware. As we drove up the avenue, the gardens and mansions resplendent around us, she said with reluctance, "Louisa, the time has come that I must warn you of something. Dexter doesn't know that I'm warning you, and I'm putting myself at risk by doing so. Nevertheless, it must be done. And I must rely on you to keep the matter *entre nous*."

I looked at her quizzically.

"You are poised on the brink of disaster."

I laughed at her melodrama. "I am?"

We turned onto Chapin Parkway. "Beck," she called to her driver, "continue to Lincoln, circumnavigate the park and the exposition." In a lower voice, she repeated, relishing the word, "Disaster."

"Miss Love, with all due respect, you must be exaggerating." I spoke lightly, indeed without due respect. But after missing a night's sleep, I had lost the ability to make myself tiptoe around her.

She glared. "You think it's a joke," she said quietly. "But it isn't."

With grand irony I replied, "Of course not." I felt giddy. Warnings in a carriage—whatever was she thinking of?

She didn't like my tone. "I know you young women make fun of me. Don't think I don't know it," she said bitterly. "But you don't realize how hard I had to fight to get what I wanted. It took years of fighting to be allowed to set up the Crèche. Years of fighting to get a woman like you named headmistress of Macaulay, to secure architectural commissions for Louise Bethune and Francesca Coatsworth. All in secret, this fighting, all in the background. Small steps, one at a time, that you and your friends take for granted, acting as if women were always allowed to enter the public domain. But we weren't—when I was young, we weren't. I couldn't fulfill a quarter of my dreams, not a tenth. Instead I had to spend my time charming and cajoling pompous fools like Ansley Wilcox to grant me 'favors'. I had to manipulate even Dexter, to make him think everything was his idea and pray he wouldn't realize. So don't laugh at me, Louisa Barrett."

Feeling like a schoolgirl, I inched away from her. "I'm sorry, Miss Love."

"Of course you are," she said sardonically. She gazed dully out the carriage window as we circled the exposition. "I wasn't always the wrinkled old lady you see now. I was young once too. Once I was the belle of the ball, not just pretending to be. Not just trying to steal the attention from the girls."

Were there tears in her eyes?

"Once I led the dances; once I gave the winner's cup for the sleigh races in the park. Once I even thought I would marry; I dreamed of being carried off by a shining knight—what girl doesn't?" she added derisively. She turned to me. "I will confess to you, Louisa, because you'll understand: I've known temptation. I've felt passion. I've punished myself for years, for minutes of indiscretion."

I studied her wrinkled skin, her ever-bright, flashing eyes. I'd never heard even a rumored hint of what she was telling me.

"I'm your friend, Louisa," she said with sudden, gentle reassurance. "For all these years I've protected you. Dexter and I, we've protected you. We've watched you develop and mature. And you've fulfilled our expectations. More than fulfilled our expectations. We've congratulated ourselves for choosing you. This community takes care of its own—have no fears on that score. You serve us well, you become one of us. Only this afternoon, Dexter said to me, you are one of us. You undertook a great sacrifice for us."

Cautiously I said, "I don't know what you mean."

"Of course not." She patted my leg as if I were a child. "That's as it should be. That's why I'm giving you this warning, heedless as you are." She paused, staring vacantly out the window. "They are planning a comeuppance for Thomas Sinclair. One that he deserves." She didn't look at me.

"I beg your pardon?"

She gave me a shrewd, evaluating glance. "Let us say they are displeased with his ambitions for the power station."

"His ambitions? Whatever do you mean?" Surely, I thought, the directors must be pleased by his plans to "waste" no water.

She smiled thinly. "I don't want you caught in the whirlpool, shall we say, when it comes. Who knows how things will turn out in the end? I fear they've met their match in Thomas Sinclair."

"Who are 'they'?"

"Men," she said, spitting out the words. "Who else? Thinking they control the world."

"What men?"

"Dear, dear Louisa. Disingenuousness does not become you."

So John Albright had once told me. Why did everyone assume I knew their secrets?

"You should extricate yourself from any . . . entanglements, as quickly as possible." She studied me for a moment. When she continued, she was completely matter-of-fact, without a hint of emotion, but she didn't meet my eyes. Like Patty Milburn, she gazed slightly over my shoulder. "And if you don't, or can't, rest assured that I shall look after Grace for you."

I couldn't breathe; there was a terrible pressure against my chest. All I could say was, "Pardon?"

"You need have no fear on that score. I will treat her as my own."

She couldn't know the truth.

"Grace will live at 184 and enjoy every advantage—as she should, given her true parentage. Her elevated heritage." Her face took on a look of smug complacency that terrified me. It was *impossible*, that she should know the truth. And yet seemingly she did.

I called to Beck, "Please stop. I wish to get out." I couldn't listen to any more of this. "Please. Stop." He began to slow the horses.

Miss Love looked startled and displeased, caught off-guard. "Where are you going?"

"It's hot. I'll walk home."

"You can't do that. Beck, continue," she called.

"Beck, *please*. I am unwell."

At this—the threat of a passenger being sick in his brougham—Beck did stop, promptly pulling over at the curb. With Maria Love's useless protests surrounding me, I got out and hurried away. Away from her warnings, and her knowledge.

In the warm, humid evening air, strands of damp hair clung to my cheeks. I was trembling. Struggling to steady my hands, to control my breathing, I looked around. Slowly the scene came into focus: I was near the exposition's Lincoln Parkway gate. People were bustling around me, alive with expectation. I followed them, separate from them and yet united with them, passing into the scene as if entering a painting. Accompanied by the brash American optimism of a John Philip Sousa march from the bandstand, I walked down to the park lake.

Now, nearing seven-thirty, the sun was low in the sky, lending everything in its path a luminous precision. The water bore the reflections of trees and rowboats, of playful birds and Spanish turrets. Well-dressed children with their stockings off threw cake crumbs to eager ducks along the shore. The boaters cavorted, splashing on the lake where Karl Speyer had drowned . . . how many months ago now? I had to pause, and carefully count to make up for the lack of sleep that set my mind adrift. I was floating; all my days, floating like a mist on the water. Five months, it was. Karl Speyer, the engineer-hero; no evidence, no hint of him remained here.

As I stood unmoored with my thoughts, the sky gradually turned ominous; dark clouds scudded across the horizon, sheeting the sky with an eerily greenish gray. The air itself pressed against me, as if I were breathing clouds. All at once the wind whipped up, lightning cut the sky, and with the thunder came the rain, torrential as a waterfall rippling in waves across the surface of the lake. The rain drenched me and I shivered. Then just as fast as it had arrived the wind died away and the rain became a gentle, soothing wash. In the boats on the water, men and women, young and old, lifted their faces and let the rain run down their cheeks, cooling them after the day's heat. I too turned my face to the rain, the precious rain that washed away at last the remembered stench of the harbor and the haunted faces along the waterfront.

The boaters, in a precarious position during a lightning storm, seemed not to understand what was happening—as if they, like me, had entered a dreamscape. After several minutes of suspended animation, they began to realize their predicament and to row fiercely toward the shore, some laughing, others anxiously counting the strokes that would lead them to the safety of the boathouse. I too awoke to the fact that I was beside a tree in a lightning storm, and I took shelter beneath the boathouse's second floor balcony. On the broad, formal staircase leading to the lake, the water level slowly rose, first one step, then two, then three.

And so the lazy storm rested upon us for about an hour. I stayed where I was, watching the night fall. Gradually I perceived that something was different. What was it? I looked around in confusion, and then I knew: The darkness was absolute. The electricity was off. The goddess atop the Electric Tower had no power, the Pan-Am's gaudy rooftops were invisible. We were taken back to the days before our hope.

The rain stopped. A warm mist, the consistency of floating dewdrops, hung in the air. People began to emerge from their makeshift shelters to feel their way home in the darkness. Several exposition workers appeared with emergency lanterns to light their way.

"A lightning bolt at the power station," someone asserted with great authority.

"Happens all the time," someone else affirmed with equal confidence.

I waited for the crowd to depart, wanting time alone. I was still in my "costume," I realized with a start: my schoolmarm's silk dress soaked, the skirts clinging, outlining my legs and articulating my body, a camouflage no longer.

The water smelled fragrant as I walked to the lake. What Maria Love had said in the carriage . . . could she know the truth? But no one knew apart from Tom, who'd only guessed because he saw Grace every day. Certainly some people knew smidgeons of the truth: Gilder, with his slick arrogance, who'd taken me to Cleveland; my acquaintance at the settlement house in New York, who'd found a doctor for me; Dr. Perlmutter, who'd brought the infant Grace to Buffalo at my instigation. Each of them knew a thread of truth (even Tom only guessed at one thread), but no one could weave the threads together into a complete picture; no one except me. I had to believe this—I couldn't survive otherwise. I searched my mind: There had to be a rational explanation for every one of Miss Love's pronouncements. *Rest assured that I shall look after Grace for you*: I was Grace's godmother, therefore I had a sacred duty toward her, especially after Margaret's death; Miss Love was referring to my position as godmother. Grace's *elevated heritage*: Through Margaret, Grace was a Winspear, undoubtedly quite elevated enough for Miss Love, especially when compared to Tom's background. And what of Miss Love's words about a comeuppance for Tom? Well, Miss Love had always spoken disparagingly of Tom and would be quick to exaggerate anything that might threaten his position. Most likely Tom was already aware of the dangers she alluded to, which were probably embedded in Albright's message, as well—the message Tom had laughed off. With every inhalation of the sweet, vaporous air, I felt my confidence growing, my equanimity returning, until finally I had convinced myself: Maria Love knew nothing about Tom or Grace. I could return home; I could resume my life.

Carriage lanterns guided my way up Lincoln Parkway. On my left was the Sinclair estate, stone wall and tall hedges concealing tennis court, formal garden, bathing pool; I saw them all in my mind. When I came to the house itself, the windows revealed the soft glow of candlelight instead of the usual starkness of electricity. I paused, staring. On the second floor there were candles in the library, and I imagined Tom at his desk in the corner, reviewing files about water. But more important to me was the bright candlelight that came from the third floor, Grace's floor. Perhaps she was finishing an evening snack of applesauce, graham crackers, and cocoa. Or maybe she was bathing, and the housekeeper held up the warm, thick towels that awaited her. Her lacy nightgown was smoothly—lovingly—laid out upon the bed. She was safe.

Secure in this certainty, I crossed Forest Avenue and continued on my way, walking more by instinct than sight, using candlelit homes as my landmarks, enjoying the sprinkle of raindrops that fell from the wet leaves onto my face. Gradually I became aware of the leisurely clip-clop of a hansom on the asphalt roadway beside me; the hansom was beside me but slightly behind, its lantern propped high to give off a wide circle of light. No surprise in that. What surprised me was the hansom's slow pace. I slowed my own walk, to let the carriage overtake me. But the driver matched my pace. I glanced over, but there was nothing to see: an open carriage, no passengers, a driver with his cap pulled down to shield his face from the weather. No doubt he saw me as a likely fare and was waiting for me to signal him. There was nothing threatening about him, and yet I was abruptly, irrationally overcome by fear. The slow clip-clop, clip-clop echoed through the mist-laden silence of the deserted streets.

At Soldier's Place I crossed onto Bidwell Parkway, and the carriage turned too. When I walked faster, the driver quickened his pace. I held down the urge to run, but I walked so fast that I virtually was running.

Finally I arrived at my door, breathless. I fumbled for the key, felt for the keyhole, turned the lock. Once the door was open and I'd put one foot across the threshold, I stopped, escape at hand, to see what the driver would do. He drove on, unhurriedly, into the darkened night.

At first my heart raced wildly in freedom and relief, but slowly I realized that I was completely alone. At this hour, even Katarzyna had gone home to her family. Through my own wish, my own desperation to keep a secret, I had cut myself off from companionship and affection. There was no one in the house to welcome my return, to wonder where I'd been, to listen eagerly to the tale. Through my own devices, no one was here to notice whether I returned home or not.

Everything had turned out exactly as I had planned. Exactly as I had hoped and arranged. Yet now I wondered if I had planned correctly, ten years ago, in the crisis of the moment, still a girl—or so I seemed to myself now. But then I had thought myself a woman. I was still hopeful, still optimistic—then. Four or five years, at most, would I spend at the Macaulay School. Then I would go to Europe to study geology. I would go on expeditions in the West as I had done with my father. Perhaps I would even fall in love, have a family . . . Certainly the Macaulay School would never turn into my life. Never would I be so alone that I'd be afraid of a hansom cab beside me in the dark.

Leaving the door ajar, I took several steps toward the street and looked down Lincoln Parkway to the Sinclair house. Glimpsed through the trees, the upper windows radiated a nimbus of candlelight. And I thought, this is the sum total of what I have willed: to be able to study that house from a distance, and know all was well.

Chapter Twenty-Five

A *boy*, read the note that Elbert Hubbard sent me at the end of July, *unusually large and healthy, considering the "sin that went into its making."* I could hear Elbert's parodying voice. *The wet nurse and her husband, a farmer, would be pleased to have him, if there are no other plans. They can be trusted to maintain privacy, and I know they would offer him affection, having recently lost their own, and only, infant.*

But there were other plans. All was arranged according to Abigail's instructions. Dr. Perlmutter had found a childless family in town. Even now a young woman, possibly a Macaulay graduate, was wearing padding and was well into her "confinement," having declared to family and friends that she'd kept the pregnancy secret for so long because of her years of bad luck and miscarriages. Nonetheless Dr. Perlmutter had strongly cautioned this unnamed young woman and her husband against relying on the adoption: The infant might prove to be ill, or dark-skinned; the mother might change her mind or make unreasonable demands. From his professional position, Dr. Perlmutter had frankly reviewed the possibilities.

With this in mind, I resolved to present Elbert's idea to Abigail. The more I thought about it, the more appealing his idea became. If the nurse and her husband took the baby, Abigail would always know where the child was and how he fared. Perhaps she could even visit him now and again (the child remaining ignorant of her true identity, of course). On the other hand, if the baby were adopted by an unknown family in town, Abigail would be left always wondering, always speculating—ever searching for the child who was her child.

Abigail herself would have to decide. Some might balk at entrusting such a decision to a girl not yet eighteen, but I could only do what I would want done myself, were I in her position. The idea that Abigail would keep the child was out of the question; her life would be ruined. She was no Alice Moore (Elbert's paramour), able to make her own way in the world, with family to assist her by caring for the child. Abigail was virtually a child herself. If she kept the infant, she would become an outcast.

The day after I received Elbert's note, having few duties at school on a beautiful summer's morning, I took the train to the village of East Aurora. The narrow gauge railway of the Western New York and Pennsylvania line carried me into the lush, rolling countryside to the southeast of Buffalo. This was horse country for Buffalo's Hamlin, Jewett, and Knox families. The Jewett farm was renowned for its covered, heated racetrack. A love of horse training and racing had originally led Elbert to East Aurora. The village was less than twenty miles from the city, yet it seemed strangely obscure and hidden, reachable only by a convoluted journey through vaporous meadows.

From the tiny station, I walked the short distance to Elbert's home. The quiet was immense; the only sound was birdsong. Over the years, Elbert had purchased house after house, taking over the village block by block to establish his Roycroft community of artisans. He wanted to create the atmosphere of an era before factories, before machines, and he had. Sheep grazed around the chapel, rhododendron bloomed deep purple, and the scents of burning wood and fresh-baked gingerbread filled the air. The Roycroft community glorified individual craftsmanship as opposed to modern mass production, and designers came from around the country to work in the print shop, the bindery, the metal and furniture shops. Many of the craftsmen executing the designs were local people, men and women escaping farm labor for a life of artistry. Elbert brought an intellectual life to East Aurora as well, with lectures and activities on every subject within the reach of his imagination. All this was financed by Elbert's commercial genius: by his ability to use advertising and direct marketing to convince the general public that handmade books and furniture were essential accoutrements of upwardly mobile life.

Elbert's home was a reflection of his beliefs, and I felt every tension melt away from me as I went through the door, entering a realm in which each object, no matter how minor or utilitarian, had been transformed into a thing of beauty. He greeted me with a brotherly hug. "We've told everyone that our young apprentice is laid up with 'fever,'" he explained, leading me to the stairs. "A very serious fever indeed, requiring a doctor and a constant attendant—although we advertise a full recovery. Meanwhile, the grandmother has been very helpful in the kitchen. She's there now in fact, whipping up a strudel concoction with early peaches. The young lady herself has shown an aptitude for watercoloring, under Bertha's direction. We've managed to keep her from prying eyes, I'm glad to report, and the infant has cooperated by not crying too much. So far."

Elbert's employees were fiercely protective of him; if a baby cried and Elbert didn't hear it, they didn't either.

We reached the third-floor landing, and I was grateful to see that Elbert had given Abigail and her grandmother the entire top floor. To the left, there was a comfortable parlor where a plump young woman sat knitting in a rocking chair. A calico kerchief covered her head, and a few strands of pale hair curled around her face. This must be the wet nurse.

"Mrs. Houghton, good morning," Elbert said in his most charming manner. He did not introduce me, however: If anything went wrong, my name wouldn't be brought into the situation. "I can't help but notice that the infant thrives."

Standing, pressing her knitting against her waist, she curtseyed and blushed. "Thank you, Mr. Hubbard." There was a hint of a Scottish accent in her voice.

"A fine job you're doing. We're most appreciative."

"Thank you, sir." She curtseyed again.

"Good day to you, then."

"And good day to you, sir."

Elbert turned and walked to the door on the far side of the landing. I had resolved to keep my attitude completely businesslike, and now I steeled myself to the task at hand. Before opening the door, Elbert whispered, "You should know that *Mère* Rushman has graced us with her presence. That fine woman told me in confidence that the infant should be dropped off at a church door somewhere far away, so that five or ten years hence his features will not be recognized in town and cause Maria Love to ponder a resemblance—a resemblance to whom, Mrs. Rushman did not reveal."

When Elbert opened the door, the first thing I noticed were the leaf shadows that danced upon the walls. The stained glass in the transoms showed a scene of white lilies against green fields. The chairs, the table, the bookcase, the bed and cradle beside it—all were handmade of solid, plain-finished oak. A peacock with a sweeping tail, in tooled leather, decorated the back of a hand mirror. I might have stepped into medieval England.

"I'm so pleased you're feeling better," Elbert said sympathetically, patting Abigail's arm as she lay in bed propped up by pillows. Embroidered blue herons walked up the hem of the pillowcases. Abigail held a Roycroft book, her thumb marking her place. The binding was a brown leather tooled into the image of an angel. *The Last Ride*, by Robert Browning. "As soon as you're out of this nagging 'fever' we're going to put you to work illustrating a manuscript—your apprenticeship is over!"

She smiled at him dreamily, under his spell like everyone else. Her long hair was spread around her, reddish-blond. "Miss Barrett, there are some of my watercolors on the table, just practices, but . . ."

I went to look. The paintings were lovely: flowering vines, gentle reeds, frolicking birds meant to decorate the margins of a typeset page. She'd also done dozens of initials, capital letters turned into miniature works of art.

"They're lovely, Abigail. Truly. I'm proud of you." She gave me the same dreamy smile she'd given Elbert.

I turned to the cradle. The sleeping baby looked strong and plump for a newborn. He had some fuzzy blond hair—nearly white—as though he were Scandinavian.

"Abigail," I said gently, pulling a chair beside the bed, "Mr. Hubbard tells me the nurse would be happy to take your baby. She seems like a lovely woman. Perhaps we should consider—"

"Isn't there a family in town?" She sat up, all at once beset by anger and worry. "I thought there was a family in town."

"Yes, there is. But perhaps—"

"I want the family in town. I told that to Mother—I told that to *you*, Miss Barrett," she added, her voice sounding strangled, as if I had betrayed her.

"You told me you wanted him to go to any family that could love him." I maintained my gentle tone. "If he's with the nurse and her husband—"

"I thought you knew what I meant! I don't want him to grow up to be a farmworker! I want him to grow up in the city and have a chance to become a lawyer or a doctor or the President of the United States."

The innocence of her hopes made me shiver.

"I want his new mother to be a graduate of the Macaulay School! I want him to go to the Nichols School and to college—an Ivy League college—I want him to become a millionaire!"

"Mmm," Elbert sighed. His impatience with just such sentiments had caused him to give up his position in business and come here to establish a community of artisans. Of course he'd already made his fortune by then, so the degrees of hypocrisy in his reasoning were difficult to sort out. "We must look to the person, my dear, not to the financial backing, nor to the academic degrees, which in the end don't mean much—begging the forgiveness of our highly educated Miss Barrett." He nodded at me graciously.

Abigail was not deterred. "I don't care what you think. That's what I want for him, and I won't let anybody tell me no!" She hit her fist against the quilt, her face scrunching up like a three-year-old on the verge of a tantrum.

Well, Dr. Perlmutter had found a fine family in town. The baby was healthy, his skin pale, so the fine family would presumably have no objections. "And if he's in town," Abigail continued, turning wistful, "there's a chance that I would see him now and then, isn't there?" She gazed at me with wide-eyed wonderment. "I mean, I wouldn't know him at first, but how many babies could there be, that were his exact age? After a while, I would figure out who he was, don't you think? And even if I didn't, after a while I could persuade Dr. Perlmutter to tell me, if I promised never, ever to tell him—" She glanced at the cradle. "Then I could always make sure he was all right, without ever letting him know who I was. But if anything happened, I would be there to look after him. To back him up, if he ever needed anything. I'll get a job, if I have to. I'll think of something I can do. Then I'll have enough money to help him, if he ever needs anything. I'll always be there for him." With a contented smile, she leaned back against the pillows, which puffed up around her.

She was utterly confident, as only the young can be. The absolute assurance in her face made me look away, tears smarting my eyes.

That evening, using the ruse of illness, I called on Dr. Perlmutter in his spacious examining rooms and told him about my visit to Abigail.

"You see the good we're doing here, Louisa?" he said with satisfaction, sticking his thumbs in the armholes of his vest. Although we were no more than acquaintances, he always called me "Louisa," no doubt assuming that the right to do so came with the Hippocratic oath. He was a large man, with florid cheeks and a big belly imprisoned by a tight vest. His office and examining rooms, on the ground floor of his comfortable home on Franklin Street, reflected a complacent ease. Someone who didn't know any better might look at him and his rooms and conclude from their serene, self-assured equanimity that he'd never lost a woman in childbirth, when in fact he had: Margaret, and so many of my graduates, dead from giving birth, regardless of which doctor attended them. Not the doctors' fault, of course, but my anger at the losses had nowhere else to go.

"Arranging adoptions always pleases me. Everyone benefits," he continued. "Now then, the family is eager to proceed. We should make the transfer soon. The grandmothers-to-be are already wondering why their grandchild is running late and what I intend to do about it!"

Having no emotional involvement, he could afford to be flippant.

"How often do you do this, Doctor?"

"Not frequently, Louisa, but not infrequently. How's that for an answer that tells you nothing!" He laughed pleasurably.

The good doctor and I made a plan: In one week, on August 6, I would go out to East Aurora again in a hired brougham driven by a hired man whom the doctor had reason to trust. I would bring the baby (soothed by a dash of brandy) to Dr. Perlmutter's home, where he would examine the infant. "Merely cursory," he confided. "With such good parentage—a Macaulay girl, after all, and a gentleman of society, as you say—I don't foresee any problems." Apparently the doctor, like so many do-gooders, viewed poverty as a genetic vice.

At any rate, after nightfall, with the baby asleep and ingeniously hidden under the voluminous coat Dr. Perlmutter was renowned for wearing in both summer and winter, the doctor would enter his ostentatious carriage—christened the "delivery coach" and designed especially to garner attention—and take the baby to the waiting parents. He would spend a good amount of time in the bedroom so the servants wouldn't talk, give the infant a hearty slap on the bottom at the appropriate moment to induce crying, and call in the nervous, waiting husband to witness the miracle: a son. Perlmutter would complete his night's endeavors with a hearty meal in the kitchen, and just after dawn, looking weary but pleased, he would depart the family home. If any neighbors happened to wander by, they would have it straight from the doctor that both mother and child were doing well, the mother a bit tired but blissfully happy, thank you very much.

There were no documents to be prepared, no papers to be signed. The arrangement was neither legal nor illegal. In a sense, it didn't even exist: Everyone participating would pretend it had never happened. The adoptive family had to trust Dr. Perlmutter's word that the baby was healthy and of good background. The only protection the family would have from Abigail attempting to reclaim her child was the absolute social rejection she would face if she did so.

We wrote the necessary notes, Dr. Perlmutter to the adoptive family, myself to Elbert and the Rushmans. The doctor wanted to wait a week because he believed the baby would do better during the long carriage journey if he were given a bit more time with his original nurse.

We felt no reason to hurry. The plan seemed clear and acceptable on all sides. All the parties agreed to it, or so we believed—although of course it was Abigail who had agreed, and the adoptive parents who had agreed, and the doctor and I who had agreed.

Mrs. Rushman had not agreed and felt no compunction to share her view with any of us.

One week. Not a long time, though time turns long or short

depending on what fills it. I worried about the baby—irrationally, I tried to tell myself. Elbert sent me a note saying he was going to Cleveland and Detroit to deliver lectures, but to rest assured—all was well.

Anyway, what could happen in a week? One day Grace and I cruised on Mr. Rumsey's yacht with his family and friends; we went to Falconwood, a private club on Grand Island in the Niagara River, where we picnicked along the water, liveried servants spreading blankets and unpacking baskets. Another day I took Millicent Talbert to lunch at the Twentieth Century Club. That very week a Negro was lynched in Elkins, West Virginia, and another in Port Royal, South Carolina. Mary Talbert was spearheading a protest campaign, and I could only imagine the anger and despair she must be suffering. I felt terribly protective of Millicent. We sat on the screened piazza overlooking the fountain gardens—seemingly far from the battles of the nation outside. Although she was quieter and more reflective than before, she seemed very much like herself.

Day upon day I woke to a cool breeze prompting me to pull the sheet over my shoulders. And then the week was over, and the time had come to set our plan in motion.

"Good morning, Mrs. Rushman," I said, meeting her on the path leading to the Hubbard home. She was coming out as I was going in. "A lovely day for a journey." The sky was deep blue, the air crisp, more like spring than summer. There'd been rain in the early morning, and now the sun sparkled over the wet lawns.

"Your intervention is no longer needed, Miss Barrett."

"I beg your pardon?"

"Two days ago I took the creature to the Infants' Asylum in town. Or rather, I dropped it off in the dark at the door." She gave a self-satisfied smirk. "Took it when Abigail was asleep. She didn't even know! Luckily your friend Mr. Hubbard was away giving lectures, so he couldn't interfere. Abigail was beside herself when she found out. She keeps ordering me to go to the asylum to find the creature! Hysterical, that's what she is. But she'll come around, sooner or later. What choice does she have, eh?" Mrs. Rushman made a little laugh. "We fed the creature a good dose of brandy to keep it quiet on the trip. I pinned a note to its blanket, saying it was Polish. I even wrote the note on the bottom margin of some Polish newspaper Fritz found. That should throw them off the trail!"

"But the Infants' Asylum—how could you!"

"That's what it's there for."

"Why wasn't I informed of your plan in advance?"

"Why should you be? You're not a party to this."

"But you asked for my help!"

"You protected Abigail very nicely, I'll grant you that. But I don't believe in this business of adoption. You probably think I'm cruel, Miss Barrett, but when you're not the one involved, it's easy to think you're better than everyone else. I'm telling you, we can't have some little urchin wandering around the drawing rooms who looks like Abigail—she'll be disgraced. And what if the creature turns up in twenty years and wants money from us? Or tries to blackmail us? I won't allow it."

"But the child will *die* at the Infants' Asylum."

"That is in the Lord's hands," she responded with determined sincerity.

"But I found a good family!" I called uselessly as she mounted her carriage. Her driver wore formal regalia.

"Good day to you, *Miss* Barrett," she said as she closed the carriage door. She stressed the "Miss" as if it were a badge of my inferiority; a scarlet letter that I wore.

"A baby boy," Francesca was explaining to Chief Nurse Clarkson. The infant's ward felt dank. Because I'd had no choice, I'd confided Abigail's misery to Francesca, who'd immediately become practical and forthright, bringing us here. "We've come to find a baby boy. Dropped off the day before yesterday. By mistake. His mother wants him back. Her family was misinformed, to bring him here. My friend has seen the baby and will make the identification."

Chief Nurse Clarkson, in her well-starched, well-pressed uniform, wanted to help. She was a gray-haired, thick-waisted woman, but quick-footed. She wore an unpretentious gold cross around her neck. Fetching her record book from her alcove office at the end of the ward, she found the proper page. Six infant boys had been dropped off the day before yesterday, she reported.

"This one was left on the doorstep, at night," Francesca said.

Four of the six had been left on the doorstep at night.

"Where are the four?"

"Well, well, two have died already, Miss Coatsworth. You see this mark in my book? The check mark?" She showed us her carefully prepared records, her printing small and precise. "That means the little varmint died. It's the will of the Lord." Her accent was Scottish, like that of Mrs. Houghton, the wet nurse at Elbert's, although Mrs. Houghton's accent was mellifluous and this woman's was as starched as her uniform.

"Where are the other two?"

"Well, well, let me see, I need to check the numbers on the cribs, it's a complicated system."

She walked down the ward, comparing her records with the numbers on the cribs. But the babies were taken in and out of the cribs to be fed and changed. Who could tell if they were always put back in the proper place? I glanced at Francesca.

"Nurse Clarkson," Francesca said, catching up with her, "shouldn't these babies have identification tags on their wrists or ankles?"

"Forgive me for saying so, miss, but that would never work. For sure it would kill them. Rubbing the tags into their mouths and choking, rubbing them against their legs, getting cuts and infections."

"Ah. I see."

Nurse Clarkson nodded in affirmation. She continued to walk down the ward conducting her mathematical reckoning. I wandered away from her, studying the babies, searching for the one I had seen just a week before swaddled in hand-loomed blankets, rocked in an oaken crib. The stench; the pitiful, mewling whimpers; the sheen of incipient death—all these I tried to ignore in my search.

Swiftly Nurse Clarkson was before me. "You are certainly free to look for this baby, too, ma'am," she said tightly, her voice indicating the opposite. "Look all you like." She gestured widely. "We are always open to inspection, whether Miss Coatsworth is here or not. Nothing is hidden. We are not ashamed of the work we do."

Francesca joined us. "We don't ask for your shame, Nurse Clarkson," she said pointedly. "We ask only for the baby."

Nurse Clarkson glanced at her guardedly before turning away to continue her tour of the cribs, leaving Francesca and me to search together.

Each baby was more pitiful than the last. By the window there was a wet nurse, holding an infant at each breast. The woman appeared as scrawny as the babies. I hesitated to examine too closely, but Francesca had no such compunction and walked right over to the woman, speaking to her in Italian, only to learn that both infants were girls.

"Oh, Miss Coatsworth, here's a boy who came in the day before yesterday," Nurse Clarkson called, excitement transforming her face. "I knew we'd find one." We hurried to her side.

The boy was strong and crying robustly. But he had dark hair.

"The child we want is Scandinavian-looking," Francesca said.

"Everyone says they're here for a Scandinavian-type baby," Nurse Clarkson observed with brisk condescension.

Unruffled, Francesca said, "There may have been an indication on his blankets that his family was Polish."

"Polish," Nurse Clarkson repeated flatly.

After a moment's pause, Francesca and I left her and resumed our own search. Suddenly Francesca gripped my arm.

"Here's one," she whispered.

I looked closely. It could be. The child was listless but blond. Very blond. It lay on its back beside three other infants.

"Nurse Clarkson?" Francesca called. When she joined us, Francesca pointed to the blond baby.

"Oh, that one. That one came in, let me see," she flipped through her record book, "He's been here awhile. Number 3/247—that one came in two weeks ago. Poor dear, he's not looking as good as he did when he first arrived. That happens. They just waste away. He's not the one you want, I'm afraid." She moved on.

Could Abigail's baby actually be dead after only two days? Surely God could not allow such a thing to happen; not after what Abigail had suffered already. I had to find a way to help her. Maybe we should just choose a baby . . .

"Louisa," Francesca whispered, holding my shoulder, stepping close to me. Her closeness, our closeness, the way our thoughts converged: these were my only comfort. "Why don't we just choose one. Save one. That blond one—it's scrawny, but let's take it."

I nodded.

Francesca went to the nurse. "Excuse me, Nurse Clarkson, there must be some mistake. Two babies have been confused. They don't have tags—confusions can happen. The baby that you say was brought in last week, we're certain that's the baby we're looking for."

"It cannot possibly be. The numbers don't lie, Miss Coatsworth. We do not get confused, no matter what you think." She swelled with indignation. "Number 3/247—I distinctly remember him. He's an Alsatian baby, not a Polish baby." She spoke with the venom of those for whom such ethnic distinctions mattered. "You have told me the baby came in the day before yesterday. Although it's against the rules, I would give that baby back to you, upon your detailed description, knowing how such things sometimes happen. But to give you a totally different baby, a baby you have no relation to at all, to let you simply walk out with it—absolutely not." She talked on and on, filled with righteousness. Possibly she had been lax about such matters in the past and had been reprimanded. Or perhaps she wanted money.

Once more Francesca's thoughts followed mine. She glanced around surreptitiously, making sure we were apart from the other nurses. Only the infants heard her words. "It's difficult work you do here, Nurse Clarkson. You must need many things. Things which are not covered by the regular budget. As head nurse, you know better than anyone, what is needed."

Nurse Clarkson flushed, but said nothing.

Francesca continued, "I for one would be pleased to entrust you with certain . . . discretionary funds, to use as you see fit. For the betterment of your patients, of course."

Nurse Clarkson regarded her with narrowed eyes. "Certainly we need many things here, Miss Coatsworth. I would accept with gratitude any donation you'd like to make on behalf of the Infants' Ward. But even so you cannot simply take a baby."

And that was the end of our search. As we went outside, I felt as if

I were falling into the sunshine, falling into the sky, with only Francesca's hand on my shoulder to hold me steady.

"What are we to do, Francesca?" I asked, filled with the image, not of Abigail's child, but of Grace—of what would have happened to her, if I'd been forced to bring her to a place like this.

"You must tell the girl—"

I tried to focus on her words but they disintegrated around me.

"Louisa, listen." She shook my shoulders. "Stop it."

I felt like a rag doll in her hands.

"Louisa, look at me." She held my chin so that I had to look. "You've got to think about this rationally." Of course Francesca didn't know why I had to struggle to be rational. "You must tell the girl that you found the child and turned him over to the doctor as you had planned. You must tell her that he's gone to a good home, otherwise she'll never be able to forgive her mother. She'll never be able to live with herself."

That evening, I sat at my desk to write to Abigail. I was calm, finally. Drained. Able to calculate. To weigh the cause and effect that I controlled. Regret filled me that I'd ever taken on this burden. Abigail was my student, nothing more. Was it within my rights to shape her future?

You must tell her that he's gone to a good home, Francesca had said. So she can live with herself. So she will stay in Buffalo forever, hoping to see the child, hoping to be there if he needs her. Most likely never marrying, because a husband and legitimate children would interfere with her devotion, her godlike watch over a child she can identify only through suspicion. Could I condemn her to that?

What would be gained if I told her that her baby was most probably dead? And if not dead, certainly lost forever. She would know that her child had died because of her own mother, her child's grandmother. Could there be forgiveness? I would never forgive such a thing—yet that was blithely felt on my part, for I had little recollection of my own mother. But knowing the child to be dead, at least Abigail would be able to get on with her life, continue her education, start a profession, I hoped, without worrying about finding her mirror image at a garden party. Without searching, always, every drawing room, every picnic, every sleigh race, for her child.

And yet . . . what if the truth unhinged her? What if it unleashed passions that led her into public revelations? Such revelations could destroy not only herself, but others as well. And why not, she might think. With her child dead, she would have nothing left to protect.

I tried to put myself in her shoes. How easy it was, to see my own life spread before me. All that I had done, and not done, as the result of decisions I had made long ago. How would I feel now, if I had chosen differently? Which of Abigail's two choices would I rather have had?

I would have wanted to know that the baby was alive. To know that he was more than alive—that he was flourishing and well cared for. Not taken to an infants' asylum to be misplaced or confused with other babies, or to die of starvation or dehydration or sickness with no one to comfort him or even notice. Only knowing that he was alive, could I live with myself.

With that conviction, I picked up my pen. I knew what I had to tell Abigail: I had found the child, and everything had gone according to plan. I also wrote to Dr. Perlmutter that day. With him I had no need to conceal; to him, I could tell the truth.

A few days later, I heard at the club that Lucinda Dann, one of my graduates, had given birth to a full-term but still-born baby. She was a lovely young woman who had hoped for a child through five years of marriage. She'd hidden her pregnancy from her family up until the seventh month, so as not to disappoint them with another miscarriage. She'd been filled with hope and excitement, until the end. Dr. Perlmutter, I heard, had attended her.

Chapter Twenty-Six

There's a conspiracy afoot to impoverish me," Francesca confided with the irony that for her always concealed the most serious truths. "Do you think it's revenge because I wore a top hat to the Milburn ball? Or perhaps I didn't meet the gentlemen's sartorial standards: Should I have ordered my suit from London tailors, do you think? Possibly my cravat wasn't properly tied. I should have asked Cousin Freddy to redo it. Wouldn't that have made him blush!" She tossed back her head in joyful mirth.

One week after our visit to the orphanage, we were reclining on the beach at the Coatsworth family compound on the shores of Lake Erie, on Abino Bay in Ontario, Canada, about ten miles west of Buffalo. We had come out by boat that morning, taking the ferry from the foot of Main Street across Lake Erie to Crystal Beach, and then a launch up the bay to the Coatsworth dock. Francesca and I were indulging in a four-day holiday together. I was trying to come to terms with my sadness and guilt about Abigail and her baby. I knew I had done all I could, and yet . . . the baby's apparent death, the actions of Mrs. Rushman, these haunted at me. Abigail was thriving, however: Elbert, home from his lecture tour, had written that she was out of bed and eager to begin work on the manuscript pages he had promised her. At least I'd done right by sending her to East Aurora and placing her under Elbert's care.

While I thought about Abigail, Francesca mourned the temporary loss of Susannah, who was visiting her mother in Fredonia for several weeks. Or so she had claimed. Without evidence, Francesca had been speculating jealously about more nefarious activities relating to the preservationists.

Although it was mid-August, amazingly we were alone here at

the family compound, except for the servants we had brought with us and the local caretakers. Such was the power of the exposition to readjust people's habits. So much the better. Our relaxation would not be marred by the shrieks of frolicking children or the sidelong glances of their curious parents, and I wouldn't have to maintain my dignity for the benefit of any Macaulay students, present, past, or future.

The Coatsworth compound consisted of five large, gray-shingled houses widely spaced along the shore. The houses were shaded and sheltered by tulip trees that rose high and straight, branches spreading at the top. Back from the shore, the lawns were manicured but always cool and moist, the grass thin; because of the age and spread of the trees, tulip giving way to maple, little sunlight sneaked through.

Even the beach was partly shaded. The sand was fine-grained and pearl-colored. Francesca and I reclined in the sun near the gently lapping water on large, oriental-patterned cushions. Wide-brimmed hats enveloped our heads to prevent the sun from reaching our precious skin, and fine netting covered both hats and faces to keep away the sand flies. For the same reason, we wore long white gloves that rose to our elbows. We wore ivory-colored tunics over our dresses in case the wind became strong, and certainly we would never dream of swimming.

The lake was aquamarine, the color of the sky. I felt content as the sunshine warmed me. To my right, Point Abino curved in a long green crescent out into the lake. The air was lightly fragrant, the scents seeming to rise from the water itself. The only sounds were rustling leaves and Francesca's lilting voice.

"What I don't understand is, if it's a conspiracy to make me poor, it will also make Freddy poor, and I'm sure he would never have agreed to that. But on the other hand, he has so many more . . . sources, he may not even notice."

"Oh, Frannie, what are you talking about?" I asked with tolerant good humor. She rarely discussed personal money matters; in her set, to do so was considered rude, although that never stopped her from gossiping about other people's finances.

"A certain person," she replied meaningfully, "has asked if we would be willing to make our grain elevator available now and again at night for certain . . . situations."

"*What?*" Startled, I sat up.

"That's precisely what I said when Freddy called on me to ask my permission. I said, 'Whatever do you mean? What does this person want with a grain elevator—at night, no less?' Apparently Freddy hadn't thought to ask. Or he'd been too intimidated to ask, more likely. I'm afraid I rather teased him." She gave me a coy look. "'Freddy, you don't mean this certain person is planning to change the locale of his costume ball, do you? Has he a hankering to dress up as a stevedore?'" She imbued the word with licentiousness. "Freddy has no sense of humor, I'm sorry to say, and he just squirmed. Another black mark for me, I'm sure."

I believe Francesca intended for me to laugh. To join her in the satisfying deprecation of Freddy, who as the current male head of the Coatsworth family behaved (in her opinion) as if his sole purpose in life was to thwart her. I'm sure she also intended for me to join her in the luscious gossip about this "certain person." But I didn't; I couldn't.

"When was this, that your cousin first came to you?"

"No need to get so grim about it," she said, put out because I wouldn't join in the joke.

"It was when?"

She shook her head in exasperation. "All right, if that's how you're going to be. It must have been in June sometime. A few weeks after the vice president's visit. When everyone was talking about the invitations to you-know-who's Bastille Day ball."

"Oh," was all I said.

Unable to gauge my reaction, Francesca looked almost comically confused. I was confused too, but I knew better than to reveal my thoughts even to those I counted my closest friends.

I'd shared the search for Abigail's baby with Francesca because I'd really had no choice, and also because I knew I could rely on her in an emergency. In her heart Francesca was trustworthy and loyal. But in something so layered, so fraught with ambiguities as this situation with Milburn, I had to keep my own counsel.

"Well," Francesca continued, "I certainly didn't object to closing the elevator for one night. But last week Freddy came back to say that Mr. Milburn would like a kind of *carte blanche*, and wonders if we could make the space available on an 'as-needed' basis. Of course Milburn didn't mention compensation, and stupid Freddy was too scared to ask; claimed it would've been an 'ungentlemanly' question! Particularly because Milburn says he doesn't expect to need it, but wants to know it's available, just in case. Apparently things worked out so well the first time, he wants his options open. He even claimed that it would be a 'comfort' to him, to know he had the option; it would let him sleep better at night!"

Impassively I studied her. Was this little explication beginning to sound contrived? Like a well-rehearsed performance? Or did I simply imagine that it was, because suddenly everything seemed so obvious— every detail clicking into place, forming a line like a child's puzzle spread out along the floor, at the end of which was the picture of a terrified girl standing on a narrow walkway above an open grain bin.

"Freddy's a great believer in the idea of *quid pro quo*," Francesca was saying. "We do a favor for Mr. Milburn, who knows what favor he may do for us? His debt is especially great because he keeps asking that we keep the arrangement 'private'. We all know what that means, don't we?" In a dramatic stage whisper, she confessed, "He's not going to tell Mr. Rumsey about it. Freddy said over and over that I mustn't tell anyone, not anyone. Poor Freddy seemed to think he couldn't trust me! His own cousin!" After a good bit of laughter, she became thoughtful. "It's dangerous, though, this business of keeping a secret from Mr. Rumsey. Our little . . . community has always presented a united front. *Tous pour un, un pour tous*. I would say that Milburn has opened himself to blackmail. It's useful to know the stakes are so high. Whatever his intentions, he considers them worth the risk. Which makes me wonder, what could Milburn be doing there? It must have something to do with the Pan-Am's profits. I was among the few wise enough not to invest, I'll have you know," she said pertly. "I think Milburn's walking a financial tightrope: investors wanting returns on one side, while suppliers and contractors demand payment on the other. Even so . . . a grain elevator," she mused. All at once her face lit up. "I could be wrong about the profit motive, however. Although it's not the sort of place to rendezvous with one's mistress, it would be the perfect place to meet one's *mister*, should one be so inclined. The atmosphere there is so very . . . masculine. And I wouldn't put it past our friend Milburn. All that charm for which he's so notorious, always makes me suspicious."

"Don't be ridiculous," I snapped.

"Why do you think it's ridiculous? It seems perfectly plausible to me," Francesca pouted while nonetheless eyeing me with shrewd expectation. "Do you know anything I don't know?"

There it was: what all of this had been leading to. She hadn't been able to bring herself to ask outright if I was privy to any currently circulating rumors.

"I know nothing about it whatsoever," I replied. "But if you're worried about your income, maybe you should speak to Freddy on that score."

"I did. He wasn't the least bit concerned. Retorted that he's the one with children to think of, and if he saw no cause to worry . . . Oh yes, it's easy enough for him to give up profits, when he has so many other sources—" I had no idea what she was trying to imply about Freddy by her repeated stress on that word, and I didn't want to know; the city was overlayered with secrets. "And I have only my limited share from the elevator revenues each quarter." She shook her head in mock despair. Both of us knew full well that her "limited share" was anyone else's tidy fortune.

For a long time we sat in silence. I heard the tinkling of glasses and silverware behind us, and I knew without turning to look that the maid was preparing a table on the screened-in porch for our tea. Francesca abhorred sand in her food and never ate on the beach or even on the veranda. I closed my eyes and tried to come to terms with what she had told me, so that I could get beyond shock and examine her news rationally. Yet shock alone continued to fill me, along with a worry: A few days ago at home, I had received an invitation to a reception for the President and Mrs. McKinley at Rumsey Park, the home of Bronson Rumsey, on the first day of their visit in early September. The invitation had been addressed to "Miss Louisa Barrett and guest." This was unheard of, that I should be invited to attend a party with a nameless 'guest.' I could only assume that the invitations had been made out by someone unfamiliar with our local customs; someone in the First Lady's entourage, or perhaps Mayor Conrad Diehl's secretary, who might be familiar with political mores but not the social ones, which also told me that the reception would be a large one.

At any rate, I had decided to take advantage of the error and invite Mrs. Talbert. No, I hadn't stood up for her at the Buffalo Club, nor at the exposition, but after what happened to Millicent . . . I knew I had to do something more. I would bring her to this party, where her accomplishments rightly placed her, and thus publicly display my support. She had accepted my invitation by return post and offered to call for me in her carriage. But now, with this news of Milburn . . . should I rescind the invitation? And if I did, what reason could I give? I didn't feel that I could share with Mrs. Talbert what Francesca had told me—the story was too entangled to go outside our circle. But anything less would seem so ill-mannered as to be a betrayal. No, I was trapped now within this invitation . . .

"Is something bothering you?" Francesca finally asked.

I knew I had to make some concession to her. I decided to tell her one small thing, to shift the discussion away from Milburn.

"Frannie," I said, opening my eyes and turning to her, "I never told you, but about a month ago someone—I assume a workman—painted something on the school door. Mr. Houlihan washed it away. It was something—indecent. About Negro workers. I remember you hired—forgive me, your contractor hired—"

Abruptly she sat up beside me. "Why didn't you tell me before?" she demanded, flushed with worry. "You should have told me. One incident like that can lead to more, and worse."

"I didn't think—"

"I could have done something about it then, when it happened."

"What could you have done?"

Her flush deepened. "Well, I could have"—she shook her head in small jerks—"I could have told the foreman to speak to the men about—about tolerance!" At this absurdity, she sighed. "Well, you're right: I couldn't have done anything—except to stop hiring Negro replacements, which we did anyway, because we didn't need any. All of this is a mess," she said, exasperated. "Last week I corresponded with a friend in Chicago, and he's having similar problems, and . . ."

On and on she talked, about unions and their violence; about their disputes ruining or delaying so many projects; about dynamite being stolen and stockpiled, one stick at a time; and what was wrong with these unionists anyway, didn't they want to work? Weren't they grateful to have work? Weren't they happy they weren't starving? Happy their children weren't starving? I might have been listening to the esteemed gentlemen of the Buffalo Club.

No matter. Whatever she said, I ignored her. I closed my eyes again and nestled against the pillows, her voice rendered a distant background as I pieced together, step by step, what had happened to Millicent Talbert and why. Perhaps Franklin was right and money was at the basis of all things: Mrs. Talbert's protests were perceived to be cutting into exposition ticket sales, therefore Mrs. Talbert's protests must be stopped. But why use a child to accomplish this? Why not go after Mrs. Talbert herself, or threaten her husband's business interests? Yet the more I thought about Milburn's plan, the more logical and clever it became. With lynching so common in the South, this type of attack, if it became public knowledge, would simply be viewed as part of a pattern. Furthermore, a child is more pliant than an adult, more easily controlled, which would make the actual kidnapping simpler. And if Milburn wanted to keep his action secret, targeting a child was the obvious choice. Most likely never intending for Millicent to die, he must have sensed that the Talberts would keep the incident private; they would never turn her into a living martyr. And Milburn had achieved his goal. Mrs. Talbert had in fact stopped her protests at the Pan-American after what had happened, and the entire matter had remained private.

Now my thoughts went farther. If Milburn was capable of conceiving such a plan against Millicent (and of course I had no proof, I reminded myself), was he also capable of formulating the "accidental" death of Karl Speyer or of James Fitzhugh? He had no obvious motive to do so, and yet . . . he was the attorney for every important business, every important person, in the city. He was the attorney for every member of my board—and for Tom and the Niagara Frontier Power Company. He straddled every center of power. Who better placed than an attorney to execute Fiske's Henry II/Beckett scenario? *Who will rid me of this troublesome priest?*

"Have you fallen asleep?" Francesca asked.

"No, I'm not asleep." I felt lost in a maze. Every time I thought I'd discovered something and defined it for myself, it seemed to slip away.

PART FOUR

Passion

And so to me it seems altogether well that all the froth and hurry of Niagara at last, all of it, dying into hungry canals of intake, should rise again in light and power . . . in cities and palaces and the emancipated souls and hearts of men.

"The Future in America: The End of Niagara,"
H. G. Wells, *Harper's Weekly*, July 21, 1906

Then there is electricity, the demon, the angel . . .

The House of the Seven Gables,
Nathaniel Hawthorne

Chapter Twenty-Seven

G ood afternoon, Miss Barrett. Might I speak with you for a moment?"

Susannah Riley, safely returned from Fredonia, was flushed and breathless from climbing the stairs to my office. She gave me a flirtatious smile. She wore a light-blue corduroy suit, too heavy for the warm day, and a navy-blue bow tie, but despite this confining outfit, she managed to look charmingly pretty. She carried a well-worn leather portfolio.

"Yes, of course," I replied. The date was Friday, August 30; close to five o'clock. I pushed aside the scheduling sheets I'd been working on, trying to balance advanced Latin with beginning botany so a certain student could take both. Every year during these weeks before the start of school, I despaired about the limitations of the curriculum and about teachers who were working by rote instead of bringing their subjects to life. I wanted my teachers to be both inspired and inspiring, to believe themselves revolutionaries forging an army of educated women. But I couldn't always make them realize that with the little things we taught each day—and not simply what we taught but the way we taught it—we could change the girls' lives. This year, distracting me when I could least afford it, the city itself was in an uproar: next week, President and Mrs. McKinley would arrive. Preparations surged on every street.

From her beguiling manner, I assumed that Susannah had come to ask to be assigned an additional section of painting; to present plans for a new course, perhaps in botanical drawing (which I might propose if she didn't); or even to request a raise in salary, which I would be willing to consider, recognizing that her salary was low.

"I hope I didn't cause you any embarrassment last month, attending the Milburn ball as I did." She looked down at her hands folded in her lap, glancing at me fleetingly through her eyelashes.

I studied her. "Did you cause yourself any embarrassment?"

The question flustered her.

"Well, I—I've been worried that you might think I've cast aspersions on the school. Through my too public—maybe in some people's eyes—association with Miss Coatsworth."

"Susannah, as I said to you some months ago regarding your politics, you must set your own priorities. The school survives us all," I added dryly. I hoped she hadn't disturbed me simply to discuss her reputation.

Susannah heard only that I had exonerated her. She exhaled in a happy sigh. "Thank you, Miss Barrett. Thank you very much. You see, I'm not really the kind of person people make me out to be."

"And what kind of person is that?"

"Some people think I'm—well, a fanatic in my politics, and with an irregular way of life to boot!" She glowed with merriment. "I've never thought of myself that way. I can't help what people say about me."

"Of course not."

"But I wanted to ask your forgiveness anyway, just in case you feel I've done anything at all that might have reflected badly on the school. I promise to be more careful in the future."

"No forgiveness necessary," I replied, impatience creeping into my voice.

As if making small talk at a garden party, she said, "I heard from a friend of mine who's a book designer with the Roycrofters that our apprentice is doing very well."

In an instant, she disarmed me. But she continued on, seemingly oblivious. "She was ill for several weeks with a terrible fever."

Was there a touch of irony in Susannah's voice? Did she know—had she guessed—the truth?

"They had to call in a doctor and hire a nurse. My friend said it was touch-and-go." Susannah paused to give me a brilliant smile, and all at once I was wary of her. "She recovered, thank goodness. My friend said she's still weak but her spirits are good. And she's making wonderful strides in her work. Really focusing and applying herself. I never found much artistic inclination in her during our classes and frankly I was surprised when you gave her the apprenticeship—oh, forgive me for saying so, Miss Barrett." Leaning forward, she touched the edge of the desk with her fingertips. "I guess that's why you're headmistress and I'm not: You recognize the hidden talents."

Again, the brilliant, beaming smile.

"Why have you come to see me, Susannah?"

Although I spoke gently, the question surprised her. Her cheeks reddened.

"You haven't come here on a summer afternoon simply to engage in flattery, I hope."

"No, no, of course not," she said nervously. She reached for her portfolio, seeming very young, and I remembered that she was indeed young, only in her early twenties, and probably still ill at ease when challenged, her every reaction out of proportion to the situation. She propped her portfolio on her lap.

"I wanted to see you because . . . well, I'm worried about one of the girls in the lower school." She stopped, looking a bit lost, as if expecting me to guide her. I said nothing.

"Well," she mumbled, "you know I tutor a few of the girls privately. Their mothers too, sometimes."

"Yes."

She opened the portfolio and took out a stack of papers which she shuffled through distractedly, more to avoid looking at me than to find anything, I sensed.

"Last week I went to one particular girl's home for my regular visit. I had set her some work to do during the week. Figure drawing. And since she's young I told her to draw her cat, or the carriage horses. But when I asked to see what she'd done . . . well, it wasn't what I expected."

Biting her lower lip, Susannah glanced at the window. Then she offered me a sheaf of pictures drawn on standard student art paper; it looked like an assignment ready to be turned in.

"I didn't feel I could mention it to her family," Susannah said too quickly, "and I didn't know who to turn to. You seemed like the proper person, because the girl *is* a Macaulay girl, and—"

Abruptly she stopped. She must have realized that I was looking at the pictures.

I readily admit that in certain ways I am a person of limited experience. My knowledge of the human body for example, especially the male body, is based more on Greek statuary than on living human beings. At that particular moment in my life, I had seen only one man naked—partially naked, that is—and he possibly not the best specimen.

But even I could tell that these drawings were perfectly rendered, with remarkable technical facility. They showed an adult man, muscular but lithe. The face was shaded; no identification could be made. Only the body was articulated. In different positions. Not poses precisely, not in the sense of Greek art—there was no sense of a person arranging himself for the artist. The sense was more of a figure in relaxation, a man drawn as he rested or slept, unaware or unconcerned that his body was exposed to the artist. On some of the sheets there was a second figure, intertwined with the first: this a female, though not a woman's body; in its simple lines, the figure could only be a young girl, the face also shaded, and much made of the contrast between the smoothness of her limbs and the muscularity of his. The drawings weren't lewd; they had a certain classical purity about them—except for the reality of what they showed.

I looked up at Susannah. She reddened once more. "What did you say when the girl showed these to you?"

"Well, I—I tried to be sweet and not at all surprised and told her they were beautifully done and I asked her if she'd done them from life."

"And?"

"She said she didn't do them from life, not from people posing, but from memory. She's a fine draftsman and I know she could do this from memory, especially since the faces are shaded. And so I asked her who the people were. She giggled and said she couldn't tell me, it was an 'artistic secret.'"

"Did you ask her what she thought the people were doing?"

"Yes. She said they were tired and they were resting. 'Just resting.'" Susannah imitated the disparaging tone of youth. "With that look they get when they think adults are too stupid for words. I kept thinking she had made it up—at that age they still don't always know the difference between what's really happened and what they're dreaming about or hoping about. But then she said something that was so upsetting, Miss Barrett. She said, 'It was a rainy day.' It was a rainy day! That made it all seem real; it made me know that she was the one in the pictures. Then she brought out some drawings of her cat, as if there was no difference between them. 'This is my cat, cleaning her face,' she said. 'I drew her from life—does it make a difference? Can you tell? Is it better from life?' She said things like that. She kept asking me questions and I didn't know what to say to her. But she didn't even notice that I wasn't answering. She just went through the pictures one by one explaining what they were and asking if I liked them—when all I could think was, 'It was a rainy day.'"

"How did the girl seem, in general?"

"Fine. Happy. Flighty, but they all are, at that age. Normal. For her age."

"How do you come to have these pictures?"

"Well, I am sorry, Miss Barrett. I took them. She went down to the kitchen to get some cookies the housekeeper had promised, and while she was gone I put the drawings in my portfolio without telling her."

"Don't you think she'll wonder, if she looks for them?"

"I know it was wrong, but I didn't know what else to do. She had such a pile of pictures, I didn't think she'd notice a few missing." She became terribly nervous. "I'll—I'll return them when I go back next week, if you think I should. But why should she even—" She broke off and began to smooth her skirt, over and over.

"It's all right, Susannah. You did the best you could. You were very brave."

Calming, she gazed at me in gratitude. "Thank you, Miss Barrett. Thank you. What should we do now?"

"I don't know, Susannah. Truly, I don't. I have to think about it. You can leave the drawings with me, while I decide; I'll take responsibility for them. This is very serious, but we must proceed cautiously. After all, the girl is not the one at fault. You were wise, the way you took it all in stride while you were with her."

She grinned, then quickly repressed her smile, no doubt thinking it unseemly.

"And tell me, who is the girl who drew these pictures?"

At my question, a sudden, radiant beauty transformed her face. "You know her, of course. Your goddaughter, Grace. Grace Sinclair."

Chapter Twenty-Eight

I managed to maintain my composure until Susannah left. Then names and faces rushed through my mind in a torrent as I asked myself who the man in the picture could possibly be. The groom, the butler, one of Tom's business associates—someone who knew his schedule? Or maybe what was shown in the drawings didn't happen at home; maybe it happened when she was visiting a friend: a brother home from university, a cousin visiting from out of town. Grace would appear vulnerable to a man with such an intent, Grace with her moodiness and her harkening to Margaret. In some perverse way the man might even think he was consoling her. Giving her a reason to live. Certainly Abigail Rushman had felt loved and comforted. All I could think was, thank goodness Grace had her talent for drawing, otherwise Tom and I might never have discovered what was going on.

There was no time for rationality or reflection. I had to act, now, to protect my child. I had to do something, anything, to safeguard her. Tom would help me—and of course he needed to know what was going on. I telephoned his office at the Ellicott Square Building downtown. Upon learning that he was at the power station, I began to telephone him there, before realizing that speaking on the telephone would do no good; I had to show him the evidence Susannah had brought me. I stuffed the drawings into my own portfolio, and leaving my schoolwork spread across my desk, hurried out. I hailed a hansom on Elmwood Avenue to take me to the station, where I boarded the electric train to Niagara. In less than forty-five minutes I was at the gate of the power station. Seeing me frantic (and undoubtedly evaluating me as a harmless old maid rather than a bomb-throwing anarchist), the guard directed me along the path to Powerhouse 3, the equivalent of several city blocks away.

During my walk I had time to consider the proper course of action, and my steps slowed. I would need to approach Grace gently, not like a whirlwind, which would only make her frightened and defensive. I couldn't scare her with the enormity of what had happened. In order to discover who the man was, I would have to be calm with her even as every urge within me screamed for revenge. Tom and I would have to act together. As I truly accepted what the pictures showed, I felt overcome by grief—for the pictures might have been of me; in a way they *were* of me, for I too was only an innocent girl when a powerful man exploited me. And isn't any man powerful in the eyes of a girl, able to hurt or help her as he sees fit?

When I reached the arched marble portal of Powerhouse 3, however, I realized this wasn't the best place to talk to Tom, or the best time. Dirt-smeared workmen pushed up their brimmed caps to stare at me. I took a deep breath, steeling myself against their stares as I walked through the portal. Inside, the powerhouse was crowded. There was a din of conversation. Elevators clanged as workers were brought up from the tunnels and other men took their places. Workmen pressed close to me. I didn't know where to turn. I was lost. How would I even find Tom amid this teeming confusion?

Then all at once I saw him in the distance: striding toward me, taller than the others. Like polished leviathans, the generators rose beside him. Everything about him was strong and bright and set off by contrast with the workmen, but as he came closer I saw the fear on his face. "Louisa! The guard telephoned—is Grace all right? Is she hurt?"

Of course he would assume that only an emergency would bring me here unannounced. But this was an emergency, an emergency as serious as if Grace had fallen from a horse or been hit by a trolley.

"Tell me! Is she all right?" Tom stood before me now. Time seemed to slow, offering every detail: his smooth skin, his brushed-back hair. He reached for my hands.

"She's all right," I reassured him.

"But?" he questioned. "What's happened?"

"She's—she's fine." I averted my gaze, deeply embarrassed about what I had to show him. "Everything is fine." I forced my voice to sound confident. "Forgive me, but I need—I need to speak to you.

Now." I studied the floor, no longer the dirt and planking I remembered from my visit with the girls, but meticulously designed decorative tiling.

I felt him watching me. "Yes, of course . . ." He looked around. "This has been a difficult day for me, I don't mind telling you, Louisa." Sighing wearily, he squeezed my hands before letting them go. I glanced up to find him staring at the balcony that went around the second level of the powerhouse. "There's a place upstairs . . ."

He led me to the circular staircase in the corner. The handrail was twisted into elongated vines resembling the eels that played upon the rocks in the Cave of the Winds. I touched the wall for support rather than hold that image. On the balcony, there was a small alcove with a carved oak table and several hard-backed chairs: Roycroft furniture, handmade craftsmanship set amid this mecca of industry. When we sat down, Tom leaned forward and waited for me to begin.

I felt reluctant to speak. The day was warm; my undergarments clung to me. I was still breathless from the stairs. My heart beat fast. "Well," I offered, looking around, reaching for anything to avoid the subject that had brought me, "everything has changed since my last visit." Indeed, although crowded with workmen, the powerhouse was pristine, every detail not only in place but shining; there was no memory of Rolf, nothing to mar the building's perfection. "Will you be finished in time for the President next week?"

Puzzled, Tom stared at me. "Mostly there's finishing work needed underground, in the tunnel."

"You'll make the deadline?"

"I don't intend to miss it." His bewilderment increased. "I suppose if I had time to see you more often, you wouldn't need to come out here to talk to me—as delightful as it is to have you. Now then, what is it that's brought you?"

I felt ill-bred, bringing out the drawings. I didn't even want to touch them.

"I need to show you some pictures." I tried to be as businesslike as he. "Drawings Grace showed to her teacher. As part of an assignment. The teacher took them—without Grace's knowledge—and brought them to me."

I smoothed the pile on the table between us, cringing at the knowledge of what they showed. He reached for them, then leafed through the pile, one at a time. "Who did you say gave you these?" he asked, without looking up.

"Grace's art tutor. Susannah Riley."

"Ah." He continued to study them. "They're very well done," he said finally. His nonchalance shocked me. "You realize Susannah Riley will stop at nothing to discredit me?" He pushed the drawings back haphazardly across the table. "Now she's circulating salacious nonsense and claiming my daughter is the author of it. Today, of all days. Well, yes, obviously. Today. She's planned it very well."

"What do you mean? Grace showed the drawings to Susannah without any prompting."

"We have only Miss Riley's word on that." His implication rested between us, confusing me. After a moment he asked, "You haven't shown them to Grace, have you?"

"I haven't taken them back to her, if that's what you mean."

"Grace had nothing to do with these pictures."

"You think Susannah made them up? I doubt it," I said firmly. "Susannah's description of Grace sounded very real—sounded like Grace." I stopped myself, realizing that Tom's first reaction would be an unwillingness to face the truth. Whereas I was responsible for Grace at school, he was responsible for her from day to day; denying the evidence was the only natural reaction. Steadily, trying to console him, I continued, "Tom, as difficult as this is, we must accept the fact that Grace did the drawings and that she is the girl pictured. Now we must try to discover who the man is. A servant, perhaps. Or a visitor brought in by the servants. Possibly your housekeeper and her husband aren't to be trusted. Or perhaps it's the older brother of one of Grace's—"

"Don't be naive. The man is supposed to be me."

"No!"

But even as he said it, of course it was obvious. Who else could it be, but him? I'd been blinded by my affection for him; by my memory of Margaret. Certainty filled me like a blood surge: it was *him*—his body spread around me in pencil, each intimate delineation set down before me. All at once I remembered: Grace had shown me similar drawings, before we went to the fireworks at the exposition. Well, not precisely similar, but intimate drawings nonetheless: Tom with his vest unbuttoned; Tom in his paisley dressing gown. How easily I could imagine the move from one scene to the next.

"I think it fair to conclude that Susannah Riley did these drawings herself and brought them to you today so that you would bring them to me today," Tom was saying. "To distract me."

I forced my eyes away from the pictures. Rage filled me. I held myself in check by focusing on the wood grain of the table, forcing myself to remain calm. "And why would she do that?"

"You don't know everything, Louisa, as much as you like to think you do." The rebuke made me more convinced that he was the one at fault. "Susannah Riley may be a skilled artist, but she is also a fanatic. I know this, Louisa. She is not to be trusted."

What else would he say, what else *could* he say, to defend himself?

He reached across the table and touched my shoulder lightly. I flinched away from him. "You don't really believe this, do you?" He motioned toward the drawings. "Of *me?* You think *I* would do such a thing?"

I heard the shock in his voice. The anger and hurt. But I wouldn't let them deflect me. "I'll talk to Grace about it," I said. "I'll be careful how I approach her, of course, so she doesn't feel threatened, but—"

"Oh, Louisa," he said sadly. "Please don't."

"There's no alternative. I'll show her one or two of the . . . less explicit drawings and see if she denies them."

"I would prefer that my daughter not see such drawings," he said, his voice hard. He was closing himself off from me, and still, in spite of everything, I didn't want to lose him. And yet . . . perhaps he was manipulating me as easily as Susannah Riley might have done. I didn't know where to turn for the truth.

"I'll believe Grace, if she denies them." Tenuously my allegiance began to shift from Susannah to Tom: If he were guilty, would he have admitted so readily that the pictures were supposed to be of him? On the other hand, most likely his sense of honor would not permit him to allow his staff or associates to be falsely accused of hurting Grace.

Nonetheless he would have no qualms about accusing Susannah Riley, falsely or otherwise. I felt unhinged; everything turned topsy-turvy: Was he worthy of trust, or not? How could I determine it? I who knew only too well what men were capable of? I had only one certainty: My sole loyalty was to Grace.

"Louisa." There was still a gruff affection in his voice. "Something will happen here tonight which will prove Susannah Riley's fanaticism. I would ask you to stay and see for yourself, before you rush to judgment."

Only Grace could tell me the truth. Standing and gathering the drawings before my resolve could weaken, I said, "Certainly not. I'm returning to town, and I'll go directly to Grace. I'll be gentle with her, but I will learn the truth."

"I can't let you go alone—and that's what Susannah Riley's counting on. Don't you see? She's expecting I'll return to town with you to set all this straight, and then she and her friends will have a free rein here tonight. Can't you just trust me for a few hours?"

Anger and sincerity mixed equally on his face. Who was this man? Our backgrounds were completely different; our frames of reference, completely different. He had progressed so far, so quickly: I had no idea how he'd achieved all he'd done, or what he was capable of. Even now I could not shake the memory of his final meeting with Karl Speyer. Apart from the public litany of his achievements, what did I truly know about Thomas Sinclair? Only that Margaret, my closest friend, had loved him.

"What is it that's supposed to happen?" I asked.

"Well, it's difficult to explain."

"Perhaps you should try." That sounded crueler than I intended.

He took a deep breath. "If you must know, the self-proclaimed preservationists have managed to get themselves some dynamite and they intend to use it to blow up the powerhouse—or, rather, part of the powerhouse. The part I've chosen for them to blow up."

"What?" I asked, shocked.

"I know it's a bit unorthodox—"

"But dynamite? And how—"

"They're walking into a trap. The damage will be only moderate.

One generator temporarily out of commission, tiles torn up, a lot of dust. I've worked out the risks, and the rewards."

"Is it safe to stay?" I asked doubtfully.

"There's a small risk," he admitted, "but I think the results will be worth it."

"All right, I will stay," I said slowly, keeping my focus on my own priorities. "But if I'm not satisfied, I'll go to Grace afterward."

"That's fine," he said. "Thank you."

About two hours later we knelt beside the balustrade on the balcony of Powerhouse 3. The building was apparently deserted, and the lights were off. Bands of moonlight lit the room. The generators gleamed in a black line below us, the Westinghouse-Speyer slightly larger than the others. The silence was absolute.

"Don't you have guards on duty?" I whispered.

"I sent them out." How calm he was. "They'll come running soon enough when they hear the explosion. I had to work out a balance between making the place accessible but still normal. I don't want to put anyone in danger. I have to make certain everything goes according to plan, and I can't leave that responsibility to anyone else. There's always the chance—"

Suddenly there was a sound. A muffled creaking. Then a brief flickering of light from a lantern, which left the cavernous building seeming darker than before. Whoever had come in should have trusted the moonlight. Tom covered my knee with his hand and began to whisper, his mouth to my ear, his breath warm against my cheek. "When I tell you, we must go down the stairs. We'll have more than enough time. Just go at a steady pace and don't stop. The stairs lead all the way into the tunnel—you remember, where Peter Fronczyk took you and your girls that day. You'll be perfectly safe. I'll go first and hold your hand. But even if we get separated you'll be able to find your way out. The tunnel slopes; just follow the slope." Beneath his reassuring tone, there was a sharp urgency.

Below us, on the main floor, there were furtive, fervent murmurings. We peered through the posts of the balustrade. Several shadowy figures were feeling their way toward the generators. Once more came the light, and I was able to make out a man: Was it . . . yes, it was Daniel Henry Bates. Although he carried a cane and moved slowly, he held his back and shoulders straight and strong; he wasn't the bent, aging prophet he publicly pretended to be. In his hand was a slender package. Dynamite, my mind said. I sensed rather than saw the others pushing close around him. Three at least, maybe four. A voice gave instructions. The lantern shone again—and there was Susannah Riley, her pale face flashing brilliant. As if sensing my gaze, she looked toward the balcony, blind triumph deep as a trance in her eyes. I stood, as if also in a trance, staring at her as she stared at me, although I couldn't tell for certain whether she actually saw me. Maybe she only felt me, like a vision in a dream, before Tom gently pulled me back to kneeling.

"You see?" Tom asked, grasping at my hand, clutching it tightly. "You understand?"

My quick inhalation alone told him yes. So . . . I had been duped by Susannah. Even the way she'd withheld Grace's name from me in my office until the very end, knowing Grace was my goddaughter, had been part of her snare. Tom put his arm around me in protection and possession.

There was work to be done below us. The small group positioned itself beside the Westinghouse-Speyer; they looked infinitesimal beside the mass of the generator.

"Why did they choose that generator, the one Speyer designed?" I whispered.

He shrugged. "I chose it. It's the strongest. The newest design. It'll get the most attention in the press."

"But Karl Speyer is dead." Suddenly I felt that Tom was committing a sacrilege. "And not only that, when they were putting the casing on, Rolf—"

Tom put his fingertips on my lips. "It's a piece of machinery, Louisa. That's all. It's not a person. It's a machine. It can be rebuilt."

No—to me it was more than a machine. It represented human hopes, efforts, and dreams, all sacred. "Why are you letting this go on?" I pleaded. "Why don't you stop them? Surely there's enough evidence already to prove—"

"I want to discredit them for good. Be rid of them once and for all.

They'll become nothing but dangerous radicals to the public. People are beginning to appreciate the importance of electricity, and they won't have any sympathy for so-called nature preservationists bombing the power station."

"But you could lose all you worked for here, all you've created."

"That won't happen." He shifted to see better.

Someone was lifted up on crossed hands; I heard the sharp exhalations of strain. The lifted man ran his hands over the metal casing of the generator, feeling his way, searching for the proper place. He whispered to Bates, who gave him the slender package. The man unwrapped it and began taping it to the generator; I heard the rips from the spool of tape. He asked for light—and I gasped to see the handsome face of Peter Fronczyk. He wore workman's overalls. Loyalty and betrayal crisscrossed through the moonlit darkness while Peter checked the dynamite, positioned the wires that led from the bomb, funneled the wires through his hands. How could Peter betray Tom? Was it because of the death of his father here at the power station? Or some unintended insult the evening we sat on Tom's veranda together? Or did Peter know something about the power station, and about Tom, that I didn't know and couldn't begin to guess?

I glanced at Tom. He simply stared at the scene below us with intermittent nods that told me everything was going according to plan.

At a mumbled signal, Peter was eased down again to the floor of the generator room. Someone began unraveling the line across the floor toward the door. The others followed, Peter instructing, correcting, cautioning in whispers. They reached the exit. I heard a match being struck and the hiss of burning as the fuse line was lit. Peter placed it on the tiled floor, and the group slipped out.

Ever so gently, Tom took my hand. We rose and went to the circular staircase and began walking down, Tom in the lead. Down and down, around and around, the curves tight, Tom walking first slowly and then faster as if sensing the danger growing—down and down, making me dizzy. What had O'Flarity said all those months ago—ten floors down, was that it? With every step I feared I would tread on the hem of my skirt and fall—fall onto Tom, both of us swept round and round into the center of the earth. The stones of the wall where I pressed my fist for balance changed from dry and warm to wet and cold as we progressed deeper underground.

Then we were in the tunnel. The water at my feet felt like melted snow as it seeped into my boots. The air was cold but fetid, the stink of it catching in my throat. Feeling his way confidently, holding my hand, Tom guided us. When we reached the interlink, he stopped. He pressed me against the wall with the side of his body while he fumbled for something. A match.

"Look, Louisa," he said, holding up the match. The cavernous interlink curved above our heads. He led me forward to the horseshoe-shaped main tunnel. "If anything happens, keep your hand on the wall and run in the direction of the fresh air. Downward, like I said before. At the end you'll be safe. You won't get lost."

Just as the flame touched his fingers, he blew out the match. He took my right hand while I kept the fingertips of my left on the wall as we ran. Suddenly there was a deep rumbling behind us and above. The explosion. We paused, listening. Then Tom tugged on my hand to urge me along.

All at once, a bit of the air turned sweet. Gradually we slowed to a walk. More and more, the air greeted us with waves of fragrance—not perfume; simply the pure smell of a summer's night. We reached the end of the tunnel and walked out onto the ledge which the workers used as a staging area during the day. It was piled with detritus: cast-off planks, broken tiles, shards of stone, wires and pieces of twisted metal. The Niagara Gorge rose before us. The roar of the Falls was all around us. I turned to gaze upriver. The Horseshoe Falls gleamed white in the moodlight and seemed terribly close—huge and exultant, soaring over me.

I turned to Tom. He placed his hands upon my shoulders. At that moment Grace seemed far away, the drawings nonexistent. The power station and its battles too: far away and meaningless. We had passed through danger together and now we might have been the last two people alive on earth.

Tom put his hands on either side of my face and drew me close to kiss me. He smelled like wildflowers, was all I could think of, but that might have been simply the air around us. His body was strong enough to hold me even as I yielded my weight against him. That feeling, as he kissed me—that touch, the warmth, simple and consoling . . . I'd never thought I'd know it; I'd never expected or imagined it, and I leaned into him to meet it.

Chapter Twenty-Nine

om and I climbed the construction ladder rivetted to the side of the gorge and picked our way among carts and cast-off timber until we reached the road and saw the Sinclair carriage, driver and horses waiting patiently. We got in and the carriage drove away at a steady pace as if nothing were amiss; the master was simply returning home from a late night at the office. By carriage the journey to Buffalo took some time. Tom said he would take me "home"—to his home, he meant, and I didn't object. I would be safer from prying eyes if I emerged from the carriage in the confines of his estate rather than on Bidwell Parkway in front of the school.

Trusting him to be a gentleman, I leaned against his chest. He held me close, his arms wrapped around my shoulders in the coolness of the evening.

"I'm sorry about Peter Fronczyk," I said.

"What do you mean?"

"That he was there, with them. That he—"

Tom laughed gently. "He was there, but he was with *me*."

Had I heard him properly? I pushed up against his chest, to look at his face.

"When I discovered their plan, I decided to guide them. Or rather, I let Peter do the guiding. I took a tip from union-busting tactics and infiltrated their meetings." His voice was cold now, and professional.

So this was why Tom had shown no reaction when Peter was revealed to us by the lantern light. Should I have condemned him for using Peter, or complimented him? At that moment the complexities of his decisions were beyond my comprehension, and I dealt on a simpler level: "Did Peter escape? Did any of them escape?"

"Peter at least. I hope. There's a path along the river. Once they're off the property, they're separating, so they can't be linked to one another. I've got a boat waiting upriver for Peter, if he can manage to get to it. He's a good lad." Tom shifted to nestle me closer.

"What makes you think this will discredit them and not simply bring them more attention?" I spoke against the soft underside of his jaw.

"People are sick of violence. And a power station's got more intrinsic glory in people's eyes than, say, an aluminum factory." His strong fingers massaged the back of my head. "No one will support them now. I wish all my critics were so easily thwarted."

"Which critics?" I asked, beginning to sit up until his arms tightened around me.

"None you need to bother yourself about."

"But—"

He caressed my cheek with the back of his hand. "Now, now, enough of this talk," he said, pressing me against him once more.

As the carriage swayed, we drifted into languor. We took the River Road, along the Erie Canal and the Niagara River. The pear orchards of the Tonawandas surrounded us, the fruit ripening, its weight pulling down the branches. A hundred thousand pears: the air was heavy with their scent. I opened my eyes and gazed out the window: moonlight on water; pear trees as far as I could see; and nothing else, no one else.

Closing my eyes again, slipping from Tom's shoulder to his chest as I rested, I dreamed a memory, of being on a moonlit summer journey with my father in the West. We traveled on horseback, at night because it was cool. I wore a jacket and trousers. We followed an ancient Indian route. The moonlight and the starlight were bright enough to read a map. The sky was huge around us. An exultant sense of my own singularity filled me. Safe within my father's love, I felt myself joined to a universe of infinite possibility.

From far away I heard Tom's voice. "Tell me you're Grace's mother."

Abruptly I was alert, my memory-dream cut short: "Her godmother," I insisted, afraid even now to have this truth set out between us, afraid that the truth would push him away.

"Her mother. Aren't you? You gave her to us, after all; told us about her, arranged for everything. She looks just like you . . . Tell me. I have a right to know." Then, as if he already knew the answer and would never judge me harshly, "Won't you kiss me, Louisa?"

"Yes." I lifted my face to his. "Yes," I said again, and I didn't know which question I was answering, but all at once there was only one answer, to every question, because I was finally tired of fighting, tired of keeping secrets, tired of being always careful, always wary. I wanted someone else to fight for me. I might never fully understand him, but at least on this I could trust him. I could sigh against his chest and offer him every worry I'd suffered, knowing he would keep me safe; knowing he would never use my secrets against me.

"I sensed it," he whispered. "These last months. So in a way we're married already, aren't we? Having a child together."

How easy my life suddenly seemed; easier than I ever would have credited.

"Who is Grace's father?"

"You are." This I could never tell him, my humiliation too deep.

"Don't tease."

"I'm not teasing."

"Tell me."

"I can't tell you."

"You must. I have a right to know that too."

I pushed against him with my elbows in order to see his face, but a shadow thrown by the moon concealed him.

"The man is no one from here, no one you know. A gentleman, I suppose we can call him. But no one you need to concern yourself about." He squeezed my shoulders and I sensed his discontent. "You'll just have to trust me on that," I added.

"All right," he agreed with a grudging laugh, embracing me once more.

Perhaps we slept in the carriage; we reached town sooner than I expected, and once inside the house, my fatigue lifted. Tom paced the second-floor library while I stood at the window waiting for the dawn. Grace was with Ruth Rumsey for the night, so I couldn't go upstairs to watch her sleep.

"Why don't you lie down?" Tom finally said. Preoccupied, he checked his watch. Without explanation he went to the desk, unlocked the bottom drawer, and took out a small red portfolio. He counted the money inside. I sensed he had counted the money many times. While he glanced at his watch once more, we heard a faint knocking upon the door downstairs.

"Excuse me, won't you? I don't mean to be rude, but I would prefer you to stay upstairs."

"Of course."

Nonetheless I went to the staircase. To the place where I had waited with Grace during Karl Speyer's visit five months before. I peered over the banister to see Tom leading Peter Fronczyk into the downstairs parlor. Peter wore a neat tweed suit and carried a new carpetbag. Except for his still-wayward hair, he looked all at once grown-up. He spoke excitedly to Tom, clearly relating the night's events, and he appeared utterly happy, his expression open, eager, and newly confident. Tom regarded him indulgently, with a slight smile, as he closed the parlor door behind them.

I felt my moral compass suspended, overwhelmed by all the explanations the night had brought me, waiting for the peace of reflection.

Tom and Peter spoke for many minutes in the study. I grew restless. When finally they came out, Peter was putting the red portfolio into the inner pocket of his jacket. At the door, Tom gripped Peter's shoulders. "Good luck," Tom said. Neither of them seemed saddened by the parting; their plan was still playing itself out and they were still united.

"Thanks," Peter replied buoyantly, and then he was gone.

Tom walked into the drawing room, and after a moment I went downstairs to join him. He was standing at the floor-to-ceiling French windows, staring into the garden, where amorphous shapes were being transformed by the dawn into irises and lilies.

"I'll miss him," Tom said. "He reminds me of myself—needless to say. Stronger than me, though, I think. I'm not sure I could have done what he did tonight."

"Where will he go?"

"He'll disappear into the West, I suppose; at least that's what I advised him. He doesn't have much choice right now. The police will be searching out tonight's perpetrators, and I don't want Peter even temporarily caught in the net."

"Is that fair? To make Peter a criminal in order to discredit Daniel Henry Bates?" I surprised myself with my quick, flaring anger. "He had a future here. A family."

Tom gazed at me calmly. No doubt this was the way Margaret had spoken to him during the disagreements that had loomed so large in Grace's mind: a man and woman in actual conversation, without simpering or manipulation.

"I made Peter Fronczyk a hero. In my mind as well as his own," Tom said matter-of-factly. "And I paid him well. He'll be able to get an education now. Become an engineer, which is what he wanted. With enough left over to help his family. And he'll stay in touch; I won't forget him."

"Exactly how have you made him a hero? A hero to your profits?"

He gave me a long, forbearing smile. "I'll forgive you that, Louisa, because you were speaking out of forgetfulness."

"I beg your pardon?"

"Come now. You know my dream. My goal." He spoke lightly, as if joking. "I told you that evening you came to see to me about Grace, back in March. Don't you remember?"

"I remember visiting," I said. I didn't say, what I remember best is that it was the evening Karl Speyer died.

"I bared my soul to you and you don't even remember?" he teased. But then he turned away from me, touching the curtain with his fingertips as he stared out the window. "How many of us have the opportunity to step beyond ourselves? To do something for the common good? Not many, I think. I would like to make an attempt, at least. Don't you remember"—he looked at me again—"my telling you that I wanted to be able to generate so much electricity that I could start giving it away? To make it a force for good in the world? To change the world? Don't you remember that?"

"Yes," I said hesitantly, trying to think back. Was this the explanation, then? The explanation that had eluded me all these months? The reason for the veiled warnings from Maria Love and John Albright, for Mr. Rumsey's inscrutable tactics? "But I thought you were talking about something in the distant future. A utopia. A dream. Not something you could achieve in the here and now."

"Well, cliché that it is, the future does have a way of catching up with us. The technology pushes us along. Makes the impossible possible. That's how I'll present it to the President next week."

"The President?" I asked with surprise.

"Certainly. Why not go right to the top?" Tom joked. "He'd make a noble convert to the cause. Especially because he's reputed to be at the mercy of the ever-so-magnanimous businessmen who put him where he is. That kind of dependency can't do much for a President's self-esteem. I'll give him a chance to shock us all with his courage and fortitude. I know, I know: It's doubtful he'll play along. But it's possible." Tom gave me a shrugging but still hopeful look. More soberly he continued, "After Margaret died I realized I had to make this happen sooner rather than later. She had some sympathy for Niagara. Not for the preservationists and their inanities, but for the Falls. We had so many arguments about how far development should go. Grace overheard those arguments, I'm sorry to say, and I know they upset her."

All they ever fought about was electricity. Grace's sorrowful words were imbedded in my mind.

"At any rate, Margaret thought my hope was absurd. Nothing but a pipe dream. But if she'd known it was real, she would have approved. She would have seen how worthwhile it is. Margaret of all people would have known that water falling over a cliff can't be compared to giving people electricity to operate their wells. Or giving children light to read by, to educate themselves. She would have understood that all that water shouldn't go to waste. But you see, Louisa," he explained in frustration, "to make this work, there has to be enough output for both profits *and* charity. I have to placate the powerful; let them see where their own benefit lies—give them a taste of what it means to be paternalistic. And to do that, I have to clear the air a bit: put a stop to these 'preservationists,' so that the investors can evaluate the issues clearly.

"I'll admit to you that I've had doubts about this bombing. I hope I've done the right thing. Of course I could have stopped their little plot at any point after they hatched it, particularly once Peter was involved. It was their idea, but I was the one who had to decide whether to let it happen. I believe it was for the best, but I can only wait now to see how it plays out."

A voice from behind us said, "I must say in my opinion it was very clever. Very clever indeed."

Chapter Thirty

W|e spun around. Frederick Krakauer stood at the door of the drawing room looking pleased with himself, his fingers propped in the armholes of his pinstriped vest.

I blushed that he should find me here.

Angrily Tom asked, "How did you get in?"

Krakauer waved his hand at the ease of his entry. Amiably he walked into the room as if he'd been invited. "It's a little trick I often use with big houses like this."

He looked at us hopefully, as if we could guess what it was.

"Don't you know?" He waited. "No? It's the kitchen door. Yes, the kitchen door!" he exclaimed, slapping his thigh. "This happens all the time: the servants go to bed and forget to lock the kitchen door. Or even if they do lock it, someone wakes up early, passes through the kitchen to get some breakfast, then goes outside leaving the door closed but unlocked behind him. The groom was the culprit in this case, and I'm grateful to him."

We stared at Krakauer, shocked. Complacently he glanced from me to Tom and back again. Finally recovering from my surprise, I said, "But Mr. Krakauer, this is completely unacceptable! How—"

Tom placed a restraining hand on my shoulder. "I don't mean to misunderstand you, Krakauer, but you feel free to trespass whenever you choose?"

"Not whenever I choose, but in cases of necessity."

"And what is your necessity here?" I could hear the wariness slipping through the surface confidence of Tom's voice.

"The explosion at the power station, naturally. I needed to locate you, Mr. Sinclair. To assure myself that you were all right. To protect the interests of the investors—I do nothing without the investors in the forefront of my mind. When I heard the news of the explosion, well, I hurried to your home. Strictly to make sure you were all right. We can't be too careful in this day and age, what with unionists painting graffiti in the best parts of town and little colored girls nearly getting themselves pushed into grain bins." He gazed at me knowingly. "You see, Miss Barrett—and what a pleasure it is to see you this morning—I may not manage to be everywhere at once, but eventually everything worth knowing comes my way, as if I'd actually been there to see it." He nodded slowly, taking a moment to appreciate his own ubiquity.

"Now then, what should I observe on my way to you early this morning but a young man approaching the house ahead of me. I recognized this young man! Yes, he was a former union agitator rumored to have thrown his loyalties to the preservationists. No doubt he carried a gun! A knife! Maybe he'd come to perform a cowardly deed against you, Mr. Sinclair, like that madman who attacked poor Mr. Frick in Pittsburgh."

In 1892, steel magnate Henry Clay Frick had been shot and wounded in his office by an anarchist. Krakauer's contrived arguments were taking on a watertight logic.

"Needless to say, and for your own protection, I had to investigate. Particularly after I saw this same young man about ten minutes later sneaking away from the house, patting his breast pocket. Well, I'm glad to find you hale and hearty, Mr. Sinclair. And you too, Miss Barrett." He beamed.

Businesslike and precise, Tom stepped forward. "Yes, as you see, Miss Barrett and I are quite fine, so you'd best be moving along. I'm sure there are other places where your services are required this morning."

"Most likely, Mr. Sinclair, most likely. However, we do have a bit of business to discuss, and this is as good a time as any." He slumped into a wide upholstered chair. "I would enjoy some breakfast, Miss Barrett. Or at least a cup of coffee." He rubbed his eyes. "I am not accustomed to these extra-early hours, I can tell you that."

"Miss Barrett has nothing to do with the running of this house, Krakauer. I would be happy to oblige your need for coffee, but unfortunately the cook has yet to begin her day."

Tom and Krakauer gave each other a long look. What balance of power was being worked out through this discussion of a cup of coffee? Krakauer finally looked away. He took out a pipe, filled and lit it, and began smoking. The tobacco smelled sickeningly sweet. With my stomach empty, I felt queasy.

"You've handled things very well, sir, if I may say so. Bombing your own power station—discrediting the opposition in one fell swoop. I salute you!" Amazingly he did. "I don't think even Mr. Morgan has ever thought of such a thing—although I'm sure he's done things that I have no knowledge of. He's deep, he is. Deep. If I worked for him for a hundred years, I wouldn't know everything that's on his mind. And the use of young Peter Fronczyk—again, brilliant. But getting back to the business at hand. Forgive me for saying so but Mr. Morgan has long harbored a suspicion in this regard. A suspicion about loyalties. Well, loyalties is the wrong word." He waved it away. "*Goals*. That's the word. The nation needs electricity to power the march of industry. But certain people, it seems, have their hearts set on giving the electricity away, so that—what did you say?—kids can read at night?" He studied Tom with condescending disbelief. "Throughout the ages kids have found candlelight highly sufficient for reading. Or oil lamps. Or kerosene lamps. Even gas—well, no need to go into all that now, I'm sure you see my point."

Tom said nothing.

"You're a sentimentalist, Mr. Sinclair, if I've ever met one. An idealist. Like that bright-eyed young man I just saw fleeing into the dawn, idealism written all over him. But the way to improve the lives of the poor is not to give them free electricity but to give them jobs, Mr. Sinclair. Jobs. Isn't that self-evident? Thousands are employed at the power station, thousands at the industries of Niagara, thousands at the steelworks at Stony Point. Those with ability will rise in the ranks—much as you have done, Mr. Sinclair. And the others—those who can't rise—well, they too are essential in their places. As they always have been!" He flourished his pipe through the air.

"Frankly, Mr. Sinclair, I would have thought the trip from where you were born to where you are now would have hardened you to this reality." He drew on his pipe, musing on his own words. "Well, well, we

can only take what we find." He sighed. "Pardon any unintended rude-
ness on my part, but it seems obvious, at least to me, that the investors
did not provide millions of dollars to construct the greatest hydroelectric power complex in the history of the world, to have even a portion of the electricity given away in some kind of socialist plot." He
tilted his head, as if to beg forgiveness for his blunt speech. "Now,
surely that is understandable. Logical, even," he said with a great show
of sympathy toward Tom.

Krakauer paused, waiting for Tom to meet him even partway. To
make some concession, however slight. But Tom said nothing.

"You've done a fine job managing the power project, I must say.
You've carried on with a minimum of strikes, you've gotten things
functioning beyond anyone's dreams. I've already heard a rumor
that Powerhouse Three will be ready for the President to put on-
line next week in spite of what happened just several hours ago.
Remarkable! Only we know that the explosion was a great 'sound
and fury, signifying nothing,' eh?" He inhaled sharply, like a snort.
"You see, Miss Barrett, little girls aren't the only ones who read
Macbeth." He gave me a long, satisfied look. "Now then, sometimes
I do ask myself, have we reached the point where Thomas Sinclair is
expendable?"

Tom laughed. "And what answer does your 'self' give you,
Krakauer?"

"Not quite yet, is the answer I get. Not quite yet. But soon. Sooner
than most people would think." His eyes narrowed.

"Then I'd best get back to work," Tom said good-naturedly.
"Before my time runs out." He made a move toward the door. "Very
kind of you, Krakauer, to come here at this odd hour to share your
views."

Slouching deeper into the chair, Krakauer crossed his legs. "I don't
think you understand, Sinclair," he said, pointedly leaving out the
"Mr." that was Tom's due from him. "This is a very serious situation. I
would be careful if I were you. Maybe you don't realize how high the
stakes have become. It is my duty to warn you. You have a beautiful
and talented daughter. I'm sure you hope she'll grow up to make a fine
match in this community—exactly as I hope for my own daughters.

You have a beautiful and intelligent"—he seemed to search for the next word—"friend here in Miss Barrett. She has a reputation in the community which I'm sure she'd be loathe to lose. I'm sure you'd be sorry to be the one to cause her to lose it. You'd best be careful, Sinclair. I'll tell you this only once."

At his threats my palms turned damp and I clutched at the folds of my skirt.

"You'll feel better after you've had some coffee, Krakauer," Tom said lightly. "Your hotel is sure to have a pot ready by the time you get back. A shower, a change of clothes—you'll be on your feet in no time."

"Always the joker, eh? Soon there'll come a time when the jokes will have to stop."

Tom gazed at him impassively.

"Even now, I'm prepared to reach a compromise. Yes, I must say, I'm authorized to offer you good terms, to keep everything going along just as it's been. We can maintain the status quo, no questions asked. Or failing that, there are quite a few important projects in the West that would benefit from your expertise. Dams, bridges, aqueducts—half the nation waiting to be born."

"If the investors are unhappy with the operation of the power station they may certainly contact me directly."

"They would prefer not to have matters become so confrontational."

He was right: Mr. Rumsey, Mr. Morgan, they would never want a direct confrontation.

"They'd prefer us to work this out quietly between ourselves. And I must say, it would be a marked failure on my part if I allowed matters to come to such a place that direct intervention was called for. Wouldn't be good for either of us. Or for anyone involved here." He glanced at me pointedly. "For example, how odd it would appear to most people if they learned that Miss Barrett was here this morning. Of course I understand her presence, but most people aren't like me. They aren't as tolerant as me. And how odd most people would think it was, if they learned how very close Miss Barrett is to her goddaughter."

I felt faint. Dizzy, I gripped a chair-back for support. Did he know the truth, or was he guessing? If I lost my reputation, I would lose everything I had worked for, everything I had built.

He appraised me astutely. "You see, Miss Barrett, I'm a lucky man. I make friends easily. I've got a gift for putting people at ease. Before you know it, they're confessing to me not just their own secrets but everyone else's too. I've been particularly blessed in this city by my friendship with Miss Love." Of course: How many times I'd seen, or heard tell of, her flattery towards Mr. Krakauer. And yet, could he really know? Nothing quite fit. My thoughts spun in circles.

"How many things get twisted," Krakauer continued, "once the public gets hold of them. And accidents do happen, let's not forget. The world is a dangerous place. Why"—he chuckled—"mature men have been known to drown in frozen lakes not a quarter mile from here. Strong young men, at the height of their professions, have been known to stumble on slippery rocks and be carried over the cataract of Niagara! Who knows what kind of accident could befall a young girl when she was riding her horse, or wading in the calm waters off Falconwood? Or even visiting a friend from a fine family?"

He would stop at nothing. I perceived his resolve from the narrow focus of his eyes and the studied nonchalance of his pose. He had a job to do and he would do it—by whatever means necessary. "Please, Tom," I implored. "Listen to him."

"This doesn't concern you, Louisa," Tom said quietly.

"But Grace—"

"This isn't about Grace."

Millicent flashed into my mind: Young girls could be made as much a means to an end as any of us. "Please—you can reach a compromise with him. Something, anything."

After pausing to let Tom respond, Krakauer said gently, "Wisely spoken, Miss Barrett. I'll take into account your point of view as the situation develops."

The telephone rang in the parlor.

"Ah, our friends from the press, I presume, eager to be the first to report the explosive events of the night. Did you yourself telephone in the tip? Yesterday afternoon, no doubt, before it happened?"

Tom maintained his silence.

"Well, I'll flatter you by presuming you did. Very clever, you've been—I give credit where credit's due, and you've been very clever, every which way."

Ignoring the telephone, Tom said, "Let me say again, Krakauer, how kind it was of you to come here this morning to share your views. Perhaps you'd care to leave by the front door, instead of the back." The clang of the telephone ceased.

"Certainly. And an honor it is." He rose. "Miss Barrett," he said, nodding his farewell to me. Tom followed him into the hall. "And where is your lovely daughter this morning, Sinclair?" he asked loudly, obviously for me to hear. "Graceful Grace. A wonderful future ahead of her. I had hoped to see her this morning. Well, another day." The front door closed behind him. I had thought I understood power: power to me had been expressed in the subtle maneuverings of Dexter Rumsey and even Thomas Sinclair. What Milburn had ordered done to Millicent seemed like stupid, cruel fumbling compared to Tom's and Mr. Rumsey's concise exercise of control. But Frederick Krakauer's threats operated on a different level—more public, more violent. In addition, Tom balanced many conflicting interests simultaneously, and Mr. Rumsey too worked on a broad canvas, indeed that of the entire city. Krakauer, however, had one goal only, and using logic and intelligence, he *would* achieve it.

When Tom returned he bantered, "Well, I'd better speak to the groom about locking the kitchen door when he goes in and out!"

"That's all you can say? Didn't you understand him?" I demanded. "He'll destroy you. All of us."

"I don't think so, my dear. Don't let him fool you." Tom put his hands on my face, then slid them to my shoulders; enclosing me, protecting me. He kissed my forehead.

"But he knows about Grace. He—"

"He knows nothing. He's guessing. Bluffing. He didn't even hear my plan to approach McKinley."

"How do you know?"

"Because if he had, he would have been more angry—more specifically angry, instead of generically angry, if you see what I mean. Don't let him worry you, darling." He caressed my hair. "His threats are empty. If it comes to it, I've got a few things I could threaten to reveal."

"Such as?" I asked, although instantly I understood.

"All the bribes we've passed to the state to let us get as far as we've come. Now, there's an unflattering tale guaranteed to please the newspapers. Are you shocked?"

I didn't reply. I didn't dare tell him that I'd read his papers. Once more my moral compass was unmoored.

The telephone rang again.

"I'd better answer this time. Get the story moving along. I'll have to go back to the station later, to supervise repairs," he added with bleak sarcasm. "You'll be all right here on your own, won't you? Of course you will." He squeezed my shoulders before going into the parlor to answer the telephone.

I stood at the long windows, breathing in the sweet morning air. It was calm summer day. Birds flitting; butterflies roving. The trellised roses hung in fat blossoms. I wanted to believe Tom's reassurances, I wanted to allow him to protect me. I wanted to stop fighting every second for my own survival and my daughter's. I could still smell him on me—on my clothes, my hair, my arms. I could still feel the pressure of his hands upon me. Of course there was a chance that the threats were empty: Grace was not Millicent Talbert, whose race alone made her vulnerable—there was an appalling history of precedents for what had happened to Millicent. Furthermore, Miss Love had told me that I was under Mr. Rumsey's protection and that she herself would look after Grace. Perhaps Tom was the only one of us truly at risk, and he had his counterthreats ready.

How peaceful the house was in the radiance of the morning. I could almost convince myself that everything Tom said was right.

Chapter Thirty-One

L ess than twenty-four hours had passed since Susannah Riley had come to my office with the drawings, but when I returned to my desk at school I felt as if I'd been on a journey of such length that home had become a foreign country. How strange everything was: Latin vs. botany, a class schedule to prepare— what was a class schedule? The papers before me turned into lines of indecipherable scrawl as my mind replayed all that had happened. I felt numb. I yearned for sleep to provide the quiet I needed to sort my thoughts. But I had no time for sleep, only for work.

Saturday, August 31, became Sunday, September 1. One day closer to the arrival of the President and to the deadline for putting Powerhouse 3 on-line. No arrests had been made for the explosion. Due to the lack of concrete evidence, the newspapers were predictably blaming everyone from the directors of competing hydroelectric power projects around the country (while affirming that no project could compete with Niagara) to the dark forces of the supernatural.

I went to church that Sunday morning. The 11:00 a.m. service at Trinity. Grace was there with Mrs. Sheehan. A Catholic housekeeper bringing Grace to an Episcopal church—it was so, well, inappropriate. If Tom were occupied, *I* should have been asked to take Grace to church. And furthermore, would Mrs. Sheehan be able to protect Grace from Krakauer if necessary? But then, I had to admit how cleverly the presence of the housekeeper deflected public attention from me.

After the service, the parishioners milled outside, all conversations turning to McKinley's imminent visit. He would arrive on Wednesday the 4th: the weather must be perfect, the streets must be immaculate, there must be no union protests, and nothing must disturb the First Lady, who was rumored to suffer from a nerve disorder. A challenging list of necessities. Everyone behaved as if the future of the city itself were at stake, and like a self-fulfilling prophecy, it became so.

Oblivious, Grace and her friends played hopscotch on the church-yard's shaded sandstone path. She pressed her straw hat down on her head to stop it from flying off, and her white-and-pink-striped dress bounced with every hop. Mrs. Sheehan sat on a nearby bench while I lingered at the edge of the churchyard, standing guard over my daughter against the threats of Frederick Krakauer, whether actual or feigned. I was relieved I would be seeing her later. She and I were hav-ing dinner together tonight at my home while Tom was working. When the adults began to collect their children, Mrs. Sheehan calling to Grace, I too headed home.

At four o'clock that Sunday afternoon—at the hour he could expect me to offer him tea—Franklin Fiske presented himself at my door. He looked tousled and tired, but when I asked him how he'd been, he shrugged off the question.

I hadn't been alone with him since our walk together the day the school was defaced. However, I'd seen him frequently in the past weeks at parties and receptions, and he'd always sought me out to exchange pleasantries, confide a bit of gossip, and in short be ever so much himself. But now he seemed angry with me, for reasons I couldn't comprehend. We sat in the shaded inner courtyard that my home shared with the school. Because it was the afternoon, because we were outside, Katarzyna used the "Russian" tea service: glasses and teapot held in silver filigree. Apart from our voices, the only sound was the gurgle of water playing through the Italian Renaissance fountain, a gift to the school from the Coatsworth family years ago.

Franklin came directly to the point, without pleasantries. "Last evening a messenger delivered an invitation to me." The statement was like an accusation. Waiting for my response, he stared at me stiffly.

"Yes? Something I should be jealous of?"

"Possibly. An invitation to brunch with Mr. Thomas Sinclair at his home this morning."

"Really?" I asked in surprise.

"You had no idea?"

"None at all."

"Good. Well, that relieves my mind." He relaxed a bit, his anger ebbing.

"Why?"

"Because he knows everything about me—my secret, in other words, and since you're the only one here who knows that, I began to worry about whether I could trust you."

"I would never tell anyone," I said sincerely. "I value my own secrets too much to reveal anyone else's." He stared at me, obviously waiting for me to say more about myself, but I avoided his gaze. "Did Mr. Sinclair tell you how he found out?"

Franklin stirred and shifted. "No, he didn't, and somehow I got the feeling that I shouldn't ask."

So. Franklin, as cynical and worldly as he was, had also been touched by a sense of Tom's power. All at once I felt an edge of intimidation: Tom was gentle toward me now, but what if I ever truly crossed him, stumbling into areas he needed to protect? Would he use his knowledge of me against me?

"Why did he want to see you?" I asked, trying to calm myself.

"He wanted to tell me something. And he certainly tried to impress me. Our meal was quite the elaborate event for just the two of us. Crystal and silver laid out on the second-floor veranda, cut flowers everywhere, a succession of courses and wines, servants disappearing at the proper moment."

"Don't let all that go to your head: It sounds like standard procedure in this neighborhood."

"Granted, but put on for me alone? The child was nowhere in sight."

"She was at church."

"Well, that was convenient. At any rate, the whole thing felt very much like a nonsexual seduction—forgive me, an entrapment." He nodded in recognition that his initial choice of words had been inappropriate for a lady, and I felt a wave of regret that he'd come to view me as prudish and proper. "Well, no matter. He shared with me some interesting information. Perhaps you already know it, from your lofty position as godmother."

"It was?"

"His plans for the power station. To begin giving electricity away. To make an ally of McKinley—although that seems unlikely. Have you heard about any of this?"

"He's told me in general terms."

"Do you believe him? I don't necessarily believe him."

"Do you ever believe anyone?" I asked brusquely, taking my fears and confusions out on him.

"Sometimes," he replied with a flash of a smile. "Anyway, he told me a complex tale about the bribery of water inspectors. He corroborated information I've gathered elsewhere, although he offered no concrete proof—while assuring me that such proof exists and can be produced whenever necessary. Although again, I don't necessarily believe him."

I said nothing. From his inquiring gaze, I knew Franklin suspected me of withholding something from him, but just as I wouldn't betray Franklin's secret, I wouldn't betray Tom's.

Finally Franklin continued. "Sinclair's a sly one. He was entirely too cavalier for my liking. As if he were engaged in a high-stakes game that only he fully understands."

I let Franklin's truth echo away. "Are you going to publish what he told you?"

"Not yet. Maybe never. First I really do need some concrete proof."

"I've never noticed mere questions of proof standing in the way of newspapermen."

"How right you are! But believe it or not, my fearless editor prefers that investigative stories be based on at least some kind of verifiable reality—assuming there is such a thing as verifiable reality."

I was beginning to doubt it myself.

"And he also prefers his heroes and villains crystal clear. Alas, Sinclair doesn't impress me as a Robin Hood-type. But I can't make him into the devil either: the deaths of Speyer and Fitzhugh—what an opportunity to prove something there, all gone to waste because nothing sticks to Thomas Sinclair. He's going to be in trouble now, though. He's making his life altogether too complicated, in my humble opinion. Trying to play both sides at once. Help the benighted while appeasing the investors. An untenable situation. I believe he wants to use me as a kind of insurance. When the pressure becomes too pressing, he can always say that he's told the whole sorry story to yours truly and if the pressure doesn't cease and desist, yours truly can be counted upon to write it up—especially if the universally beloved Mr. Sinclair is no longer available to defend himself personally."

Frederick Krakauer's dawn visit preyed upon my mind. I wondered why Tom had chosen Franklin to be his insurance. Perhaps because Franklin was outside the mainstream of journalists while still working for a crusading newspaper—the *World* could be expected to be in sympathy with Tom's goals. In addition there was Franklin's unusual position in society, welcomed as he was at every garden party. He could be a valuable, knowledgeable ally. If I told Franklin what I knew—told him about the papers I'd seen on Tom's desk—would that help Tom and Grace, or hurt them? I didn't know. How could I know? The prism of facts seemed to shift so quickly. Perhaps Tom was using Franklin not as insurance but for some other reason altogether, a reason hidden from me. I wasn't capable of discerning every nuance in this situation. The proof of bribery remained Tom's to give, not mine, I decided. And what about Krakauer: Should I tell Franklin about his threats against Grace and me? But to do so I would have to reveal the depth of my concern for Grace and the cause of my concern for her . . .

Franklin interrupted my thoughts. "Anything you'd like to add or comment on?"

"No," I said. Too quickly.

For a moment Franklin regarded me with probing skepticism. Then, as if changing the subject: "I must say my colleagues have come to feel obscurely set up in this business of the power station bombing. The whole thing seems overly orchestrated. But they can't pinpoint anything, so they're left reporting whatever sensational possibilities they can dream up. But I'll confide in you, at least, that if Sinclair even begins to do what he apparently intends to do, I don't think he'll live out the year."

"Why don't you help him, then?" I demanded.

"First of all, I wouldn't say—professionally speaking—that it's precisely my job to help him. And let's not forget that no matter what he intends to do with the electricity, he's going to need to take all the water from Niagara to do it. I must say I rather like the mighty cataract. I enjoyed our day there. Didn't you?"

I remembered my feelings that day: the comfortableness of him, the easy camaraderie. "I did enjoy it," I said sadly. Most likely our closeness wasn't appropriate now, as I contemplated the possibility of life with Tom and Grace, certain choices inevitably eliminating others.

"Thank you for saying that, at least." He gazed at me, and I looked away. "I don't suppose you'd consider marrying me?" he asked. Caught off-guard, I glanced sharply at him.

And I realized that I did like him. Very much. I was attracted to him . . . most likely I could even give myself permission to feel passion for him. Certainly a life with him would be constantly interesting and enjoyable. And yet . . . I couldn't even entertain his question. For me there was only one path, the path leading toward Grace.

His eyes were cheerless; he had sensed my answer.

"I'm sorry, Franklin."

"I didn't think so. But why don't you at least consider it. I wouldn't make any demands on you—apart from the usual ones entailed by matrimony," he said bleakly, unable to summon up the licentious irony that he might otherwise have given this reference. "I mean, I would never ask you to give up the school. And of course I do love you," he added, looking away. This was the first time a man had ever told me that he loved me. How odd. When I was younger, I had often imagined this happening to me, but now I felt too exhausted to appreciate it. "Well, think it over," he repeated, meeting my gaze once more. "We'll call it an open invitation." He managed to make his voice sound almost normal.

I wanted to reassure him of my feelings for him, but I didn't know how. Nor could I confess the reason that prevented me from accepting his proposal. I could only take refuge in politeness. What was it that ladies were supposed to say in such situations? "Franklin, I'm so very flattered—"

"Oh, don't mention it." Rising, he waved the conversation away. "Well, I'm off, then. Thank you for tea."

"Franklin—"

Hurriedly he saw himself out, leaving me to stare after him.

Returning to my desk at home, Franklin's words in my mind, I felt utterly drained. As I tried to work, the walls of my study seemed to imprison me. I couldn't escape the lingering sense of regret brought by Franklin's question. It would be lovely to marry him; what a wonderful companion he would be. But I couldn't desert my daughter or turn away from my commitment to Tom, tenuous as it was.

And I couldn't focus on my work now either; too much had happened in the past few days, bringing on more emotions than I could process. I needed to be outside, walking, running. Impulsively I got my bag and hurried out.

What to do? Where to go? The beauty of the late afternoon contrasted with the anguish inside me. I walked into the sunlight, toward Elmwood Avenue and its charming stores. Unexpectedly I felt a desire to visit the confectioner's. Momentarily all thoughts of Franklin, Tom, and even Krakauer were banished from my mind. I knew exactly what I wanted: a bittersweet-chocolate-covered marshmallow bar.

This summer the local branch of Huyler's was open on Sunday afternoons and early evenings, "exposition hours," they were called, and they were a godsend. Huyler's wasn't too far from the exposition's Elmwood Avenue entrance and so garnered a good deal of business; elsewhere, shops remained firmly closed on Sundays.

As I walked down Elmwood to Huyler's, I mused upon my forthcoming purchases. I would get myself the dark chocolate bar because I loved the luscious contrast between the sweet, fresh marshmallow and the bitter chocolate. For Grace I would buy the milk chocolate marshmallow bar because, well, because she was a child and children were supposed to prefer milk chocolate.

Huyler's was like an Oriental emporium. Molasses slip, butter crunch, almond turtles and almond bark, marzipan, fudge, mint patties, nonpareils, jellies of every size and color. All were displayed on shelves behind glass as if they were precious objects deserving the highest respect. The candy was made in the back, so the store always smelled like molten chocolate. The white-tiled floor and walls, the tin ceiling, the wooden counter, the gaslight fixtures—they looked slightly old-fashioned, reminding me of candy stores I visited in my girlhood, comforting me with the memory. But like all childhood memories, it was double-edged, and so I came to Huyler's only when I wanted to feel like a hopeful child rather than like a chastened adult gazing back at that time of hope.

There were two women ahead of me, which gave me a welcome respite to study everything before I was called upon to make a decision. I indulged myself in all the options I might enjoy, even though I knew very well what I was going to buy in the end: I did love marzipan, provided it wasn't too sweet, and also the crunchy squares of almonds . . .

The bell jangled, someone new coming in, and at first I didn't even look up. Then gradually I realized, by the shape and aura of the body, by the smell of pipe tobacco, that the person who came to stand beside me was Frederick Krakauer. I didn't dare step away.

"May I help you, ma'am?" asked the freckle-faced salesgirl. She spoke with a slight German inflection. She looked about twelve. Maybe she was the owner's daughter. Or perhaps she was living on her own already. Or the sole support of her family—alternatives swept through my mind as I tried not to focus on Frederick Krakauer at my side. "Ma'am?"

"Yes, of course." With relief I stepped forward and placed my order for the two marshmallow bars.

When I was putting my change away, Krakauer, ignoring the freckle-faced girl and moving just behind me, said quietly, "Look here—bars with almonds, bars with raisins, bars with peanuts. Bittersweet, milk." I felt his breath on the nape of my neck. "How is a man to decide?"

I must not let him see that he frightened me. Still like a child I was, hearing my father's voice as he taught me how to walk in the woods and the mountains: *Don't ever turn your back and run away from a wild animal*. I must make a stand.

"I recommend the bar with raisins," I said resolutely, turning to him and putting on my schoolmarm demeanor. "There's something satisfying about the contrast between the hardness of the chocolate and the softness of the raisins, even though the raisins are more of a texture than a taste."

"Is that so?" Krakauer gazed at me in surprised admiration. "How . . . astute of you."

So I had won whatever test he'd set for me, and my victory pleased him.

"But you bought marshmallow bars." Without a trace of irony, he bore a pouting expression that for him seemed exceedingly odd and made me even more wary.

"Marshmallow bars also have their place."

Abruptly he said to the salesgirl, "I'll have four milk chocolate marshmallow bars with caramel."

"Four?" I asked, incredulous.

"Well, I am quite a bit bigger than you," he explained.

When we were outside, Krakauer took one of his marshmallow bars out of the bag. I had been raised never to eat while walking on the street, and I taught my girls the same. But here was a man who either showed no compunction toward proper behavior, or came from a place where improper behavior was the norm. Or else I had become a prude as I'd grown older, failing to keep step with the times. Perhaps in the twentieth century it was perfectly acceptable for proper people to eat on the street.

Holding the moist, melting bar poised in his hand, Krakauer announced, "I'll walk with you." Inwardly I flinched; if he wished to walk with me, then of course I must allow him to walk with me. I must force myself to appear completely content, indeed pleased, with his company, when every part of me wanted to flee.

When we reached the corner and waited for a carriage to pass, he looked at the brilliant sky and loudly sighed. "Oh yes indeed, another gorgeous evening. How lucky we are. I just hope this weather lasts through the week. Don't want any umbrellas for President McKinley and the Mrs."

I nodded; what could I say?

As we crossed Elmwood Avenue, he took his first bite. "Mmm." He chewed on the caramel. The marshmallow would melt on its own—just thinking about it made my mouth water. "Nice and soft." Once more he sighed. He held the bar upright, so the caramel wouldn't pour out. In two more bites he'd finished. He licked the melted chocolate from his fingertips with a gurgling laugh of pleasure. He swept his tongue across his teeth, relishing the taste. Unembarrassed, he paused to wipe his mouth with his handkerchief.

"My daughters have always loved these bars with caramel and marshmallow. Now I understand why. And I thought they were for children! How wrong I was! So many years wasted." He shook his head in mock despair.

Apparently, in his eyes, we had become friends. We engaged in a seemingly companionable game of one-upmanship, comparing memorable chocolate bars we had enjoyed over the years and discussing the multifaceted glories of ice cream.

When we reached Bidwell Parkway, taking refuge in a bantering tone I asked, "Mr. Krakauer, you don't really believe you can walk into anyone's house any time you desire?"

He looked uncomfortable and straightened his jacket, pulling at the hem. "I have done," he said apologetically. "But only when it's absolutely necessary. I hope that doesn't lessen your respect for me. I have enormous respect for you, I'd never like to think . . ." He regarded me plaintively. "And besides, Mr. Sinclair might have been in danger—hasn't he been in danger before? Haven't people tried things before? Of course they have! Who knows what tactics these nature lovers might use. And these unionists too. Dynamite is so easy to come by these days."

He was sincere. Self-effacing, even. He portrayed himself as a man who performed a difficult job in the service of a greater good—as he himself defined that greater good.

We walked down Bidwell on the grassy, tree-lined center median toward school.

"This entire situation has become very frustrating for me, Miss Barrett. There's a chance I could lose my position. And if I lose my position, what will happen to my girls? I've been able to accustom them to a very comfortable way of life, I don't mind telling you. We live on Staten Island, you know. In New Brighton. A very comfortable neighborhood. I can't let my girls' comfort be compromised."

Obviously upset, he stopped walking and turned to me. "Sinclair won't listen to reason. He just goes along on his merry way without giving a thought to anyone. He's selfish, that's his problem. You know . . ." He gripped my arm but released it in an instant when he realized the inappropriateness of touching me. "I'm beginning to worry that he might feel the need to make some kind of announcement in front of the President this week. A public announcement. Putting everything out in the open so we can't negotiate anymore. Once the public starts agreeing with him, it's hard to negotiate. Has he said anything to you about an announcement?"

So . . . Krakauer *had* been too late to hear Tom's intentions. Don't blush, I ordered myself, *please*—don't give anything away. "No," I said, shaking my head. "He hasn't said anything." I forced myself to look bewildered. "Nothing at all."

"Or maybe a private announcement," Krakauer mused. "A whisper in the presidential ear about the good of the nation—although I don't think Mr. McKinley is the type to see any good in Sinclair's plan. But you never know if there might be some political advantage to it. That ring any bells for you?"

"No," I assured him. He studied me carefully. I forced myself to meet his gaze.

"Oh, all right, I believe you," he said finally. "I must say, you've always been generous with me, and I appreciate that in you. Not many people meet me so frankly. I always get the feeling that they think they're talking to my employer when they're talking to me. But you seem to be really looking at me. I like the way you tease me, like you're part of the family. To tell you the truth, I was waiting for you. Outside your house."

All at once I was terrified of him—watching, waiting.

"I followed you to Huyler's, hoping for a moment when we could talk. I didn't like to go knocking at your door, a woman in your position. A woman I have so much respect for." His eyes narrowed. "Even though other men don't seem to know the meaning of respect," he said derisively. I knew he was referring to Franklin. "Well, they have their standards and I have mine."

I said nothing, too frightened and horrified to speak.

"The problem is," he continued, "I'm worried my interview with Sinclair yesterday morning might have made him feel like I'm forcing his hand. Maybe I've mistakenly pressured him into taking action—into making some kind of announcement—before he himself intended. I'm worried I've made a mistake. I'm so worried about this that I've consulted my superiors." He took my elbow as though he needed my support, and I pulled away.

"Oh, it's not what you think, Miss Barrett," he said quickly and reassuringly. "I haven't corresponded with Mr. Morgan." He whispered the name. "I've been in touch with his representatives. His attorneys. His chief attorney, to be exact."

Francis Lynde Stetson was Morgan's chief attorney, as well as a close personal friend of former president Cleveland. I felt a pressure in my throat from the convoluted closeness of all these people to one another and to me.

"My superiors are growing impatient. With me and with Sinclair. I wish there was some way . . . something I could do or say, to make him realize the importance of all of this. No one wishes anything, well, unfortunate to happen to him, or to his child, or to you—especially not to him, if you'll forgive me. Seeing as he knows so much more about the power station than anybody else. And he has that talent of his for making union men work. That's the reason all of this has had to be so roundabout."

"Mr. Krakauer." Suddenly I was desperate; despite my best efforts, my voice was about to break. "Why do you make threats against my goddaughter? She's only a child. She's not involved with any of this. You have children yourself: How can you do this? Why can't you keep her out of it? Please, I beg you."

"Oh, I wish I could, Miss Barrett, I wish I could. But you see, life is so mysterious. We just never know what might happen. To any of us." He stared down the street to Soldier's Place. "Now, if I was a father—which I am, of course; that's not what I mean." He licked his lips. "What I mean is, I would never do anything to risk my daughters' well-being. I would want them to be always—basking in marshmallow bars! With caramel on the bottom! I would want them to be licking melted chocolate off their fingertips forever!" As he said these jesting words, his tone was deadly serious. I knew then that if he chose to harm Grace, nothing could stop him. "But that isn't always possible, is it? All too often something comes along to interfere with the way things ought to be. With the way we want them to be. Our supposed friends begin blurting out gossip to aid their own advancement. Problems begin to pressure us in ways we never could have foreseen. Things get to a point where it's too late even to correct our mistakes—once we've finally realized our mistakes. The time to take action is before it's too late, not afterward."

"That means you'll promise me to keep my goddaughter out of this, or you won't promise?"

"I wish I could promise, Miss Barrett," he said sadly, shaking his head as if to prove how much he wanted to relieve my anxiety. "For you especially. But she's already involved, whether we like it or not. You see, I'm helpless. Please believe me. Helpless. I'm only a messenger."

Chapter Thirty-Two

I*'m only a messenger.* I was trembling by the time I closed my door on Frederick Krakauer. What could I do to protect my daughter? What could I *do?*

Grace would arrive in about a half hour. Suddenly I didn't want her to be seen on the street, even with Mrs. Sheehan. She had to remain at home, where at least the walls of the estate might offer her some protection. I telephoned and told Mrs. Sheehan to expect me there; she mustn't bring Grace here.

That wasn't enough, however. I couldn't simply walk down Lincoln Parkway with my bag of marshmallow bars and dine with Grace as though nothing were amiss—as though Krakauer's threat were not out in the open, obvious and blunt. I telephoned Tom's office at the power station. One of his assistants answered, and after a long wait Tom himself came to the telephone. Struggling to keep a growing hysteria out of my voice, I explained to him what Krakauer had told me.

But Tom was reassuring and calm, as he had been the previous morning. "He's using you to get to me. He's got no other leverage. He's not as all-knowing and all-powerful as he'd like us to believe."

"I think you're wrong, Tom. I think we need to go to others for help." My mind raced through the alternatives. "I could visit Mr. Rumsey—maybe I could convince him . . ." But even as I said it, I knew this was no choice; or rather, it was a choice that might forever ally me with Rumsey and cut me off from Tom. "Maybe Franklin Fiske . . ." I didn't think Tom knew about my friendship with Franklin: "He's journalist who—"

"Louisa," Tom interrupted, though his voice was patient still. "I wish you would let me handle this in my own way. I know more about it than—" He paused; there were voices speaking behind him. "I really must go," he said distractedly. "Please, don't worry; everything will be fine." He hung up.

As I paced my study, I felt certain that everything would *not* be fine. Tom wasn't taking me seriously, however, and clearly I could no longer appeal to him. Who could I go to for help? Who would have power over Krakauer? *I'm only a messenger.* A messenger for whom?

For Francis Lynde Stetson, chief attorney for J. Pierpont Morgan and close personal friend, as well as former law partner, of President Cleveland.

Then I realized what I must do. The decision seemed remarkably easy. Obvious, even. I telephoned Mrs. Sheehan and told her that I wouldn't be able to have dinner with Grace after all. She should tell Grace that I was feeling a bit unwell (nothing for her to worry about), and that I loved her. I wrote a note to Mrs. Schreier, the school secretary, explaining that I'd been called out of town for a few days unexpectedly. I knew she could handle any inquires. Classes wouldn't begin for another two weeks, and Miss Atkins could deal with any emergencies. After I packed an overnight bag and was prepared to leave, I gave the chocolate bars to Katarzyna for her son.

When you're famous, people know where to find you. The newspapers report your whereabouts, hotels announce your visits, rail lines proclaim your arrivals and departures, advertising your name to enhance their profits. You may try to foil these forces and travel somewhere out of the way, vacationing in the privacy of a wilderness. But even a wilderness cannot guarantee escape from those determined to seek you out.

During the summer of 1901, former president and Mrs. Grover Cleveland and their children vacationed at Tyringham, in the Berkshires. The house they rented was close to the farm owned by their dear friends Mr. and Mrs. Richard Watson Gilder. The former president loved to fish, and there was wonderful fishing in this part of the Berkshires, particularly at the Otis Reservoir. The locals were highly protective of their esteemed visitors.

All this I'd read in the newspapers during the summer. From the descriptions, I could almost pinpoint the Clevelands' house. I'd grown up in the Berkshires and knew the countryside near Tyringham. I'd hiked the steep, laurel and pine-covered hills, bird-watched among the dense maples and ancient orchards of the valley, even collected butterflies in the lush meadows during a brief youthful fancy.

And so that Sunday evening I began the journey to the father of my child, to ask him to use his long-standing alliance with Francis Lynde Stetson to protect her. I was confident that—should he care to—Cleveland could eliminate the threats of Frederick Krakauer with the ease of a knowing smile and a collegial pat on the back.

I caught the night train to Albany. From Albany I would travel to Pittsfield, from Pittsfield—well, I would rely on my memory to guide me to one of the many inns that catered to summer visitors. The journey would be long and complicated, but what did that matter?

The night train was crowded and hot. I lay in my berth, unable to sleep, my thoughts in a riot. I hadn't seen Grover Cleveland in ten years, and I'd known him for only—what? Hours? Minutes? I tried to focus on the halo of Grace's hair, on the perfect sweetness of her face. But instead my mind kept clinging to the reek of Grover's Cleveland's cigars. His satisfaction, so smug. The slime upon my legs when I eased myself away from him. I had no illusions that he would remember me. He'd probably left dozens of women like me strewn across the great nation which for eight years he had ruled.

The house was called Riverside. Or so I had read in the newspaper. At midmorning on Tuesday, I stood at the end of the pine-shadowed path, staring. I'd ordered my carriage to wait. Because I'd spent Monday night at a nearby inn, my appearance, at least, was unruffled.

Riverside. Built on a gentle hill, the large house was white clapboard, with a covered porch all around. There was a flagpole, Stars and Stripes at rest on this peaceful morning. The air smelled of pine sap and summer warmth.

The Clevelands eschewed formal protection. Or so I'd read. As I walked up the path, the single guard patrolling the property glanced my way but did not approach me. To his eyes I probably had "schoolmarm" and "old maid" stamped clearly upon me. Such was my freedom. I traveled alone, I did as I wished—as no marriageable young lady or married woman could—and those who might enforce the laws of propriety dismissed me as irrelevant.

I knocked at the door. To the shy, uniformed girl who answered I presented my engraved card, "Miss Louisa Barrett, Headmistress, The Macaulay School, Buffalo." I asked if Mrs. Cleveland was at home. The round-faced maid, whom I pegged as the daughter of a local farmer, said she would check and invited me to wait in the hallway while she went upstairs.

Threadbare carpets; ancient umbrellas stuffed into a metal stand; watercolors of local attractions, the frames forever dusty. This was the hallway of any summer cottage, rented furnished.

I heard footsteps above me and then on the upper stairs. Suddenly Mrs. Cleveland turned on the landing, hurrying toward me, shocked to see me—her dress and hair perfect but her face in disarray. Frances Folsom Cleveland. I stared impassively at her worried expression. We'd been introduced a few times when she'd come to Buffalo to visit family and friends. Once at 184 I'd spoken to her briefly about women's education while Miss Love's canaries frolicked around us. She was only a year or so older than me. She was a college girl, a graduate of Wells. She'd given birth to her first child a few months before I'd given birth to mine.

She looked a bit stouter than she had been as a young woman, but even after bearing four children, she was strikingly beautiful, dressed in yellow lace, her hair heavy and dark, her round eyes framed by eyebrows thick and untouched by gray. She was the girl-First Lady still, she of the porcelain skin and the alluringly innocent tilt to her head; she who'd inspired songs, fashions, and fan clubs. In her way she was an inspiration, a stylish college graduate who'd married and raised a family in defiance of the cultural arbiters who proclaimed that education made women masculine. Despite the near-equality of our ages, I felt years older than she, like an aged crone filled with illicit knowledge— the knowledge of her husband's body.

She took control of herself when she reached the bottom of the stairs. Gripping the newel post, she paused a moment to steady her breathing. With dignity, she greeted me and invited me into the morning room. She was renowned for her dignity. Her dignity was the first thing people had remarked upon when, at the age of twenty-two, she had married the forty-nine-year-old president.

When we were seated in hard-backed chairs around the morning room's unlit fireplace, I offered the reassurance she needed. No disaster had befallen her family or friends in Buffalo to bring me here. She flashed a smile. She sighed in relief. She ordered refreshments. She would be too polite to ask me outright why I had come on this long journey.

After tea had been served, I began. "Fran—" I caught myself using her first name, as if she were a student. She seemed like a student to me. In private her husband called her "Frank," or so I had read. "Mrs. Cleveland, I'm so sorry to intrude upon you in this way. I wonder if . . ." What did one call him? I opted for aggrandizement. "I wonder if the President might be able to receive me privately to discuss a political matter of some pressing concern."

"The President has left all that behind him." Her voice was strained. I sensed that she was ever-so-slightly afraid of me, which brought me some small satisfaction: Perhaps being headmistress of a school like Macaulay did elicit respect.

"But this . . . this is a political matter with private implications. Affecting his former friends and associates. And I would appreciate his advice and guidance. Because of his history in Buffalo. He knows the entire cast of characters. It's quite important to me, and I—"

"He has always made clear that he no longer has any interest in Buffalo whatsoever. Perhaps you could tell me, and I'll ask him at some quiet moment when he's more likely to be sympathetic. I'll write you his response."

Did she ever wonder why "the President" no longer had an interest in Buffalo? Did she ever allow herself to believe the rumors which his enemies put out about his indiscretions? Probably she rationalized that enemies will always find some weapon, and this was the one they had found for him.

But Mrs. Halpin—she couldn't be rationalized away. Did this beautiful girl-First Lady ever wonder about what had happened to Mrs. Halpin, she who had been forced into an asylum and then bundled into oblivion? Possibly Frances feared that her husband would do the same to her if she challenged him. During the reelection campaign of 1888, Frances had felt compelled to make a public declaration that her husband didn't beat her. She was twenty-seven years younger than he. He had pushed her baby carriage—the carriage he himself had presented as a gift upon her birth. After her father's death when she was still a child, Grover Cleveland had become her guardian. This incestuous tangle of personal history made me recoil, yet also made me bolder.

"That's very kind of you, Mrs. Cleveland. But the matter is urgent."

She glared at me. "He's not at home now. He's taking his morning walk."

In the garden, children called to one another as they played. With her hands delicately crossed on her lap, she turned her head and stared out the window as if posing for a painting. A uniformed baby nurse comforted a little boy, four-year-old Richard, the youngest. Three girls spread across the lawn, tossing a ball. They wore ribbons in their hair, shirts with leg-o'-mutton sleeves, short skirts, thick stockings, high-button boots. They looked like—Grace. They were Grace's half-sisters. The oldest was just about her age. I hadn't thought, I hadn't realized, that I would see Grace's sisters, the family she might have had, the trusted companions of girlhood.

Taking a deep breath, I made what I knew would be my final attempt. I had no courage left. Quietly I said, "Perhaps I could wait for him at a certain point and talk with him on the path, and then be on my way. I won't trouble you for lunch."

She seemed relieved that she need not invite me to dine with them. She glanced at the clock on the mantelpiece. "Well, if you insist." She shook her head, as if trying to rid herself of some unwelcome thought. "If you walk down the drive . . ." Without looking at me, she described a nearby place. "I often meet him there myself."

I stood on the woodland path beside the ruins of an old stone wall, waiting for the father of my child. The ground was soft underfoot, cushioned by centuries of pine needles. After about ten minutes, he turned onto the path. He was about fifty feet away, walking toward me. He was much changed, which I knew to expect from the pictures

I'd seen, but nonetheless the transformation was shocking. Although still a big man, properly attired in a suit and straw hat, he looked deflated, like an overpressured balloon that has gradually lost its air and become wrinkled and pockmocked. His mustache, while still walrusy, had turned completely white. Liver spots dotted his cheeks. Instead of the curves of fat I remembered, he had a real chin now, his skin snapping oddly back toward his throat before sagging down to his neck. Rumor was that he'd been ill, that during his second term he'd had surgery for mouth cancer, although all had been hushed over at the time. His steps were cumbersome—he clutched a thick walking stick made from a rough-hewn tree limb. In his other hand he held his ubiquitous cigar.

I felt sympathy for him, made easier because, surprisingly, I saw nothing of Grace in him. He simply looked weak. Vulnerable. His wife's wariness seemed now a tender attempt to shelter him. This figure who had loomed so forcefully in my imagination had become nothing but a tired old man. Time had rendered him frail. For so many years I had feared him and anguished over what he had done to me, yet somehow in the process I had become the stronger of us. Heartened by that realization, I stepped forward, unashamed.

"Mr. President, I'm Louisa Barrett, headmistress of the Macaulay School in Buffalo." Despite my resolve, an image of Mrs. Halpin imprisoned in an insane asylum flashed through my mind.

"Louisa Barrett?" He said the name slowly, puzzled but not alarmed by my presence. "Do I know you?"

"We met in Buffalo, some ten years ago now, when you visited in May of 1891. I was a teacher then."

"Ah, yes. We met at one of the receptions?"

"Indeed. At the Cary house."

"Ah."

He seemed to relax. Of course the reception at the Cary house was the most prestigious of those he attended. My presence there would make him lower his guard.

"I remember one of those little birds made a mess in what I had intended to be my dessert," he said. I was taken aback by the kindliness in his eyes. The newspapers reported that he was wonderful with children. He would painstakingly teach them to tie fishing flies, and amuse them with stories for hours. I could imagine him entertaining his children with the story of Miss Love's canaries. Grace would have enjoyed that story too. "Not the sort of thing one forgets."

"No."

"And how is my friend Miss Love? Still doing good deeds?" he asked, chuckling.

"She's quite well." I forced a smile. "Doing more good deeds than ever." I braced myself. "Sir, in addition to meeting at 184, we also met afterward, at your—at the Iroquois Hotel."

Something seemed to dawn in his memory. "Did we?" he said cautiously.

"Yes, sir. Mr. Gilder brought me."

"Ah." He thought this through. "Have you come for a repeat performance?" he asked, not unkindly. "Have you been dreaming of me all these years?" Gentle indulgence filled his voice. There was even a twinkle in his eye. "You've come out here like some forest sprite to trap me on a lonely path and seduce me away from home?"

I hadn't expected the easy charm, the natural flirtatiousness. "I'm hardly laying a trap, sir. Mrs. Cleveland told me that I might find you here at this hour."

His anger was swift and startling. "You went to my home? You spoke to my *wife*?"

Surprised, I said, "Why, yes. Of course."

"A woman such as yourself? How dare you set foot in my home and show yourself to a virtuous woman? Have you no shame?"

Now I understood him. I saw the double standard he practiced, which allowed him to retain his much-proclaimed moral probity while still doing exactly as he pleased.

"Well, sir, please remember that I am the headmistress of a school and not—well, not something else. If you have the virtue to present yourself to your wife, then surely I do as well. For everything I did was done with your contrivance. Does not shame reflect upon us both, if it should reflect on one?"

"I hardly think—" he began.

"Furthermore the truth is that I went to your hotel all-unknowing.

Completely naive—as I was raised to be. What I remember best is you, sir, threatening the innocent girl who was my former self."

That silenced him. He resumed his walk, and I took the place beside him. With each step he pressed the stick hard into the ground. His legs seemed stiff, wooden. He puffed on his cigar, and smoke surrounded us, blocking out the forest scents. The path led along the edges of the house's clearing. Frances sat in a rocking chair on the porch, knitting. With a look of longing, and a trace of satisfaction, Cleveland tipped his hat to her. She stood to wave, holding her needlework against her abdomen.

On the far side of the clearing, we entered the forest once more. When we were safely hidden by the foliage, he grudgingly asked, "And what brings you here, lurking at my doorstep?" Disdain filled his voice, along with a touch of peevishness.

"I have an appeal to make. For the daughter I bore. Your daughter. She is the only reason I feel entitled to come here."

"A woman like yourself cannot give assurance that such a child is my daughter. A woman like yourself cannot know such a thing—innocent though you claim to have been at our first acquaintance."

On this he seemed confident, not at all taken aback by the notion that he had a daughter he had known nothing about until now. Most likely he had wide experience with this situation; perhaps many women had accused him of paternity, and he had his answers ready. *Ma, Ma, where's my Pa? Goin' to the White House, ha, ha, ha*—obviously the election ditty applied to more than one unfortunate child.

"A woman like myself can know such a thing, although I understand your reasons for hoping not."

"If you want money, I don't have any. Even if I did, I wouldn't give it to you. I'm far beyond blackmail now. Mrs. Cleveland is the only one who concerns me, and she will believe my word over yours. And I hardly think the newspapers will care anymore."

I could remember him naked. The mush of his stomach. His thighs white and dimpled. His face twisted with arrogant passion. "I don't need money. I would never come to you for money. My daughter—our daughter—was adopted into a fine family, where mercifully she has no need of money."

Angrily he turned to face me, blocking the path. "Why then, Miss, have you come here?"

"Because some . . . knowledge has come to me. Knowledge that threatens our—our daughter." I tried to be forthright, but I could barely go on, overwhelmed by a sudden yearning for Grace and by the necessity to keep her safe.

"What knowledge is this?"

"About the power station. At Niagara."

He turned thoughtful. "Yes, I've followed the work being done there," he said slowly. "I've been reading about the bombing in the newspapers. Now the police are leaning toward the nature lovers as the most likely culprits. I had assumed the unionists were responsible." He became suspicious, his eyes narrowing. "And what relationship do you have, my dear, to a power station? Have you thrown your loyalties to the fanatics? Have you come here to plead their cause?"

"Hardly. The family which adopted your daughter is a family with . . . an interest in the power station," I fumbled. The image of Grace filled me; an image of her half-sisters, playing here in safety, tossing a ball to one another.

"And?"

"There has developed a . . . tension among the investors and the . . . implementors of the project, about how the electricity should be used. Threats have been made to try to . . . force policy in a certain direction. Threats even against your daughter."

"I find that hard to believe." He paused. "Not the threats—standard procedure there. But threats against a child? That I don't believe."

"But it's true." Suddenly I felt like a child myself, stamping my foot petulantly.

"And who is making these threats against this putative daughter of mine? What big man, going after a little girl?"

As I studied him—smug and self-righteous, smiling condescendingly at my concern—something held me back from telling him the full truth. Something told me the truth would be dangerous in his hands, because it wouldn't be sacred to him. He would toss the truth in the air as a conversational gambit among his cronies.

Carefully I said, "Your associate—your friend—Mr. Stetson, has been involved with this . . . policy-making. He acts on Mr. Morgan's behalf. I'm sure what I'm saying is familiar to you. Perhaps a discreet word . . .'

He snorted. "Believe me, miss, my voice will do nothing against the forces involved in the construction of that power station. You truly are naive to think that it could." Choking on cigar smoke, he enjoyed a moment of sardonic mirth. As president he'd always claimed the same thing. He'd credited himself with no power except the power to acquiesce passively to the wishes of the wealthy. "No, I'm out of it for good. The country's heading down the road of that vaudeville act who managed to get himself elected vice president. Roosevelt!" He spat the name. "Well, any country gets the leaders it deserves."

Taking off his hat, he wiped his brow with his handkerchief. His hair was thin, wispy, and white. His skull was a mottled, sickly pink. We exchanged a glance, and he pressed his hat firmly into place. All at once his mood shifted. "Of course I have always found naiveté charming." He cocked his head at me, smirking. "My advice to you, my dear, is that you stop troubling yourself with matters like power stations. Leave such issues to the men who understand them. And believe me, such men have better things to do than make threats against a child—whatever her parentage."

The pine forest protected us from the gaze of the virtuous Frances. Still holding his cigar, he reached out and put his hand on my shoulder, squeezing the bones. Smoke wisped across my face. I stepped away from him.

"I must say, Mr. President, you have been a terrible disappointment to me. I never would have even spoken to you that night at 184 if I'd known that this is what you would become. That this is what you were. I had high hopes for you. That was before the Pullman strike, of course. Before you decided that government had no power except to help the powerful. You could have been a hero. Instead you were nothing."

He stared at me calmly. Finally he said, "How does that saying go, about a woman scorned?"

With that he turned his cumbersome body in the direction of the house. "Well, well, another battle I must refuse to fight. Good day to you, Miss—" Glancing back at me, he made a play of forgetting my name. "I'm sure you can find your own way to the road." Walking down the path he chuckled quietly, the blue haze of cigar smoke a ribbon in his wake.

Chapter Thirty-Three

I began my journey home, carriage to train. Although I was weary, I wouldn't permit myself to accept defeat, not when Grace was at risk. I puzzled through alternate plans, some of them extravagant, even crazed: to steal Grace away from Buffalo and escape with her to Europe, the school be damned; to offer myself to Franklin Fiske if he would publish the threats against Grace in his newspaper; to make my own appeal to McKinley, in the probably false hope that the President of the United States would have more power than Mr. Morgan; or even to approach Mr. Morgan directly, importuning him at his office—he had children himself, surely he would have sympathy. But even as I reviewed these options I realized they were absurd. For the moment, I would have to assume that Grace could be protected at home, on the grounds of the estate. Tom would have to hire guards, to make certain. I would prevail upon him to do so, and somehow I would explain to Grace the necessity of staying home—she had the equivalent of a city park at her command, with tennis court and bathing pool, even a butterfly garden. She could have friends to visit: Staying home would not be onerous. And then I would see what Krakauer would do.

As to Grover Cleveland, I shocked myself to find that I felt . . . nothing. His power over me was gone. Disintegrated. I saw that the looming figure he had been in my mind for so many years bore no relation to the reality of him. Seeing how time had rendered him narrow-minded and frail showed me how far I had come, how much I had grown. I remembered a difficult expedition my father and I had made when I was a child, and how much I'd looked forward to returning home at the end of the summer; when I got home, however, my bedroom seemed oddly small, the kitchen almost miniature compared to where I'd been. That was similar to the way I felt now about Grover Cleveland. He'd become insignificant—meaningless and irrelevant—compared to where I'd been. The place he'd occupied in my soul now felt free and soaring. I hadn't forgotten, or forgiven, the anguish he'd made me suffer, but I could see that anguish objectively now, as if it had been suffered by a different person—and I had been a different person then, inexperienced, with the skewed, innocent confidence of youth.

When I arrived at the train station in Albany, I was not entirely surprised to see headlines that assailed me from the newstands:

ARRESTED! FOR SHAME! A DISGRACE TO WOMANHOOD!

The stories reported the capture of the persons responsible for the bombing of the power station at Niagara. Each newspaper displayed a front-page litho of a defiant Susannah Riley being led to jail by a police officer who filled most of the picture with his jowly, mustachioed bulk. Quickly I bought a paper and searched for the names of those arrested: among them was an unrepentant Daniel Henry Bates, but nowhere was there even a mention of Peter Fronczyk. Despite the moral conundrum of his deed, gratitude filled me at his escape.

Please join me at the state hospital immediately, no matter what the time.

Such was the note, signed by Francesca, that greeted me when I arrived home early Wednesday morning, September 4, the day of President and Mrs. McKinley's arrival. At this hour, there was nothing I could do for my daughter, so hastily I changed and went out again, walking through the sparkling morning to the hospital.

As I walked up the sandstone path to the insane asylum's administrative building, pink roses were everywhere—hanging from trellises, crowding the patio, clustering in beds across the lawns, their sweetness making me gasp. Dr. Hoyt widely proclaimed pink roses to be therapeutic. Once I read about a Roman emperor who smothered a courtier to death with rose petals. Now I understood how such a thing was possible.

In the reception hall, the dark woodwork made the space feel small and cramped. The gaslight added to the lurking sense of darkness. It was only 8:00 a.m. and shadows still concealed the intricately carved central staircase.

The guard at the desk was a young man with a bad complexion. When I told him that I'd come to see Miss Coatsworth, he said I would need to get permission from Dr. Hoyt first. I had assumed that Francesca was here doing some urgent charity work, probably involving an ill orphan, but now a stark fear came to me, that she herself had been brought in as a patient because she'd gone against the wishes of her cousin Freddy or of Mr. Milburn.

After absenting himself for a moment, the guard ushered me through to the inner office.

"Ah, Miss Barrett," said Dr. Hoyt. This Santa Claus-like robber baron of the insane rose from his paperless desk. "A pleasure to see you." He leaned across the desk to shake my hand; his own was pudgy and as dry as parchment.

Patience and flattery—these were the ways to reach him. "You're here very early, Doctor. Your dedication is admirable."

He blushed. "Yes, yes. Well, well. The times require sacrifice. What a marvelous moment in the history of the city!"

"Yes. Absolutely. Forgive me, I've been out of town: Has the hospital garnered any special attention? Is a tour planned for the President, by chance?"

Sadly he shrugged, turning his palms up. "I would be thankful for the opportunity to conduct the President on a tour of the innovative work we do here, but alas, the committee has not deemed my suggestions appropriate. Most likely they are right, however, as the President shall be devoting his journey to the glories of electricity. And of course there are the unfortunate physiological and psychological problems suffered by Mrs. McKinley. A visit here might be too close to home, as it were." He shook his head in sympathy with her infirmities. "But you know, electricity may someday help the mentally ill. That is my hope. Research is being conducted—not here, alas, but—"

"Doctor, when I returned home this morning from a short journey I found a letter waiting from my friend Miss Coatsworth requesting my immediate presence here at the hospital. I trust her situation is stable?"

"Miss Coatsworth?" He looked confused. "Oh, no, no, you misunderstand. Miss Coatsworth is not a patient here."

I exhaled in relief.

"No, it is her friend Miss Susannah Riley who has been admitted as a patient—and being kept under police guard, I might add," he said with braggadocio, as though having a patient under police guard was a sign of his hospital's importance and fame. He leaned forward, taking me into his confidence. "She was arrested, you know. She's one of the band of fanatics who bombed the power station. At first she was in the common jail downtown," he whispered sanctimoniously. "Well, that would never do! An educated woman, a tutor in drawing and painting to the finest ladies of our city, a teacher at your own school! And there was more than a little indication of psycholo—well, suffice it to say, she was transferred during the night. I was honored by a telephone conversation with Mr. Dexter Rumsey that made the situation very clear. Very clear indeed."

"I'm sure it did," I said ironically. "Mr. Rumsey is known for his clarity."

Hoyt ignored my tone. "Yes, Miss Barrett, I agree. I have always found him extremely clear."

I glanced at Hoyt sharply, to find him looking at me with the same intensity. Now I saw his game: If Mr. Rumsey determined someone to be insane, Dr. Hoyt was glad to concur. Mr. Rumsey had a power equal to Grover Cleveland's over Mrs. Halpin, when it came to determining insanity.

"Mr. Rumsey asked me to oversee Miss Riley's situation personally."

"An honor."

He flushed. "Thank you. Thank you very much."

"May I see Miss Coatsworth?" I asked cautiously.

"Yes. Certainly! I will take you myself." Unlocking a desk drawer, he took out a set of keys. Motioning me out, he locked his office door behind him and led me down a curving, wood-paneled passageway lit by a single gaslight, and then on through a series of heavy doors.

"You see our fireproofing here," he explained proudly as he unlocked then relocked each door as we passed through. "Each ward is completely separate from the others, so any disturbance is quickly contained." I was struck by his view of fire as a species of disturbance. What other types of "disturbance" had he experienced here?

Unexpectedly he asked, "How is that girl we spoke about some months ago? Hasn't harmed herself, I trust?"

Was there sarcasm in his voice, or had I simply imagined it? "She's quite well. Thriving, in fact. How kind of you to remember."

"Not at all."

We entered one of the women's wards. The corridor was unusually wide, but the doorways into the individual rooms were oddly narrow; a person of average size might feel the need to turn sideways to slip into a room. At this hour, the attendants were organizing the patients to wash and prepare for breakfast. Each ward had its own dining room; scents of bacon and cinnamon filled the air. The patients appeared dazed and emotionless, but (on this ward, at least) they were compliant. Each of their small rooms had a long window overlooking the grounds: rolling meadows, huge trees, acres of flowers, farms, and baseball diamonds—an abundance of natural beauty which Frederick Law Olmsted himself had designed to sooth the patients' tumultuous minds.

Susannah Riley was being held at the end of the corridor, in a kind of suite: two narrow rooms with high ceilings, facing west. A severe but bored-looking police matron stood in a corner of the first room, while Francesca sat at a desk reading what appeared to be a formal report. Dr. Hoyt and I approached the open door in silence and waited a moment before Francesca looked up, startled, when she sensed our presence.

"At last!" she said, coming to embrace me.

"Well, well, I'll leave you to it, then," Dr. Hoyt said, taken aback by my friend's open affection for me.

Francesca pulled away from me and reached to grip his hand. "You are so kind, Dr. Hoyt," she said in her best *noblesse oblige* tone, which she used only for times of extreme condescension. "What would we have done without you? I'm terribly grateful."

Gazing at her worshipfully, he patted his stomach. Had Francesca given the hospital a substantial donation to make him so deferential? As Hoyt quietly shut the door behind him, Francesca squeezed my arm.

"Well, I've certainly won him over, haven't I?" she said with bleak humor. "That's why Susannah was given these *elegant* rooms. I'm hoping that with enough money he'll conclude that she's too ill to stand trial, and he'll release her into my recognizance and we'll leave the city for a while. But all that takes time, and plotting." She glanced at the police matron, who stared impassively at the wall, making a show of not listening. For the matron's benefit, Francesca continued, "Of course all my donations are to the hospital. Dr. Hoyt has never asked for anything for himself. He's totally dedicated to his work. Then quietly she explained, "It was Susannah who asked me to write you. She said she needed to see you. That it was urgent. Do you know why? Can you tell me?"

What could I say? That Susannah wanted to tell me that she had forged a series of drawings? Or—this flashed through my mind—did Susannah wish to tell me that the drawings had not been forged after all? I felt the cold sweat of dread. "I don't know, Francesca."

She regarded me skeptically, but how could I even begin to explain? Sighing, she said, "I'll tell her that you're here." But there was no need to "tell," for the two rooms were no more than adjoining cubicles.

Quickly squeezing Francesca's hand, I went into Susannah's room and closed the door behind me. She sat on the bed, her hair flowing loose to her waist.

"Thank you for coming, she said calmly."

"Why did you want to see me?"

Susannah stared out the window at the elm trees. The morning breeze would have been refreshing, but the window was locked shut, the air around us dank and stale. "We were set up—did you know?" Suddenly she turned to look at me, furious. "That man, Peter Fronczyk—Maddie Fronczyk's brother. We should have realized. So typical! *He* was the one who pushed us whenever we had doubts, *he* was the one who said it was a "perfect' plan. And now *he's* the only one who hasn't been arrested."

Her passion, reverberating against the walls, made me afraid of her, and afraid *for* her.

"Well, it doesn't matter now," she said, her anger receding. "At least I'll always know I've done something important—no one can ever take that away from me. Even if I go to prison for the rest of my life, I'll know to the end that I've done something important." She sighed, seeming drained and exhausted.

"Why did you want to see me?" I repeated gently.

Staring at her lap, she said, "I had to tell you that I lied. About those drawings. The ones I said belonged to Grace Sinclair. I did them, not Grace. Even I don't like a lie to go on forever. I'm not that far gone."

For a flash I felt a deep and terrible hatred toward her for what she'd done, but swiftly the hatred was replaced by relief as my hidden, lingering doubts were swept away. "Thank you, Susannah. I appreciate you telling me the truth."

"It was a lie for a good cause, though!" she blurted out defensively. "And I knew you'd believe me, because men do that kind of thing to women all the time, one way or another. But I realized afterward that it could hurt Grace. I'd never want to hurt Grace, even though her father is—well, I won't offend your sensibilities, Miss Barrett, by telling you what I think of her father."

There was nothing I could—or woud—say in response to her insult. I had heard her out, and now I felt free to leave. But as I moved to go she caught at me, hard, pulling me down beside her on the bed. Suddenly, unpredictably, she was close to tears. "I wanted to say also, I mean, I wanted to ask you, since I'm here and you're . . . I mean, I'm worried about Grace Sinclair. She's—I don't know exactly how to describe it; I feel as if she's like—like a thin pane of glass that's being pressed so hard it's about to shatter." I winced at her insight. "And I hope, now that I can't look after her, that you'll—I mean, you *are* her godmother . . ."

I grasped her hands to comfort and reassure her. "Yes, Susannah. I'll look after Grace. I always have."

"Oh, thank you. Thank you." The smile she offered me was pure and bright. "I knew I was right to talk to you. I knew you'd forgive me for lying before." Abruptly matter-of-fact she asked, "Do you think they'll kill me?"

"No, Susannah," I said, startled. "Of course not. You haven't murdered anyone; they won't give you capital punishment." I smoothed her hair, as if she were a child.

She nodded in agreement and then, as she stared at me, something seemed to shift inside her. Her eyes widened but at the same time became glassy. "No one ever thought it could be me," she said. "Not even you. It was as if I didn't even exist. No one ever suspected me."

"Pardon?"

"Do you ever feel as if you're invisible, Miss Barrett?"

I strained to understand what she was trying to tell me.

"It was Mr. Bates who sent me to meet him. In the lobby of the Iroquois Hotel. I went right up to him—a complete stranger! Mr. Bates always gives me courage."

"Who did you go up to?"

"The engineer, of course. Karl Speyer." She beamed with pride.

"Karl Speyer?"

Her expression turned to self-righteous anger. *"Engineer*—people say that word as if it's another word for God Himself. I hope I never live to see a world made by engineers." All at once, with her hair flowing around her, I saw her as a Cassandra staring into the future. "It would be a world of monsters. The machines and the people—all turned into monsters."

"Susannah." I gripped her shoulders, shaking her, trying to bring her back to sanity. "What did you say to Karl Speyer when you went up to him in the Iroquois Hotel?"

"Oh, I just went up and introduced myself," she said, as if to reassure me. "I said I'd done watercolors of the power station, and I wanted to meet the man who'd helped to create such beauty. Mr. Bates called it an 'encounter.' An approach. A way to find out the opposition's plans," she explained earnestly. "I can make myself very attractive to men when I want to. Right then and there, the engineer took my elbow and led me into the restaurant for lunch, which was delicious, by the way. Afterward he asked me to go upstairs with him, which of course I had to refuse, pleading my youth and virtue." She giggled. "He was married, with two young children—but there he was, trying to seduce me into visiting his room." She shook her head in incredulity, as if we were two young ladies sharing gossip over tea at the Twentieth Century Club. "I told him, however, that I would be honored to see him again, that perhaps if we got to know each other better . . . Well, he knew what I meant. And off he walked, whistling! From then on he wrote to me a week before each of his visits, arranging an innocent assignation. Luckily he never spent enough time in the city to learn my reputation for interests quite in the opposite direction!" How pleased she was with herself.

"Months passed like this. And the power development went ahead, more and more. We saw that Thomas Sinclair and his friends wouldn't be satisfied until they had taken all the water—all of it. To make aluminum and abrasives and God knows what else. People even began saying those words—aluminum, abrasives—as if they were quoting holy scripture. Something had to be done to stop them."

She gazed at me playfully. "I had the idea to kill him myself. I couldn't tell the others—then they would be implicated if I were caught. So I planned it on my own. I bought a special pair of leather slippers that didn't make an imprint in the snow at all. I even set up my easel on the banks of the park lake the day before so I could survey the scene at my leisure. I nearly froze! My fingers could barely hold the brush!" From her tone she might have been recounting the planning of a particularly successful surprise birthday party.

"As usual I'd received a letter from him a week before he came to the city. I left a note at the hotel, telling him to meet me at the park lake at eleven p.m. for a walk in the moonlight. I tried to hint that a romantic stroll was all that stood in the way of his attainment of his goal. I wrote that it would be 'the night of nights'! Isn't that silly?" She cocked her head at her own disingenuousness. "But he believed it. He met me at the lake, even though the moon was covered by clouds, just as I knew he would. He was a little late, because of a meeting at the Buffalo Club, and he apologized twice. I was glad he felt guilty, because it made him more pliable. I said I wanted to walk across the ice-skating area, which was marked off with ropes. It was snowing lightly, off and on. It was a beautiful night, as romantic as anything I could ever imagine. 'Oh, what's that?' I asked him, pretending to see something in the distance. I climbed over the rope, onto the snow mound that's always made when the skating ice is shoveled, and he followed me. And then—always pretending to look at this mysterious thing in the distance—I ran out across the uncleared ice, stepping lightly in my slipper boots. I was afraid of falling, but I never did. My feet were so cold, but I left almost no trail, I checked that, for certain!

"He called to me that it wasn't safe, that I should come back. Finally, when I was halfway across the lake, I pretended to realize where I was, and I pretended to be frightened, although I wasn't frightened at all. I knew what I was doing was right. Nature herself protected me. I felt her power all around me. I felt nature's power around him too—but against him. I called that I was too scared to move, that I didn't know what to do." She smirked. "He fancied himself a gentleman, so he came to rescue me. But the ice that held me couldn't hold him, the way he was trudging toward me in his heavy boots, with that great coat and that bourgeois bulk of his. He broke through the ice long before he reached me. Closer to shore than I expected. He cried out and tried to save himself, tried to pull himself out, but he was weighted down, soaked through. His coat pulled him down. He tried to take the coat off, but he couldn't. He became frantic, calling to me to get a stick, anything, to help him. He actually called to me, to help him." She regarded me with puzzlement. "How could he have thought that I would help him?"

She paused, actually waiting for me to answer her question. As I perceived the depth of her insanity, dread crept over me like a twitching in my arms and fingers.

"When he stopped calling, my ears began to fill with a screeching like a million birds singing. Singing, singing, singing—in victory! Nature herself filling me with her triumph! And I began to run as if I were skimming across the ice, not even touching it, not leaving any trail at all, nature protecting me, the snow falling to protect me, falling onto my face and blessing me and baptizing me and I ran and ran, until I came to a road.

"And then I stopped. The singing of the birds stopped. The snow stopped. I saw I was at Delaware Avenue. The cemetery was in front of me. I could just make out the monuments on the hill. The angels. They were illuminated by the snow. I didn't know what else to do, so I walked up Delaware Avenue to the circle, turned onto Chapin Parkway, and then I was home. And no one ever suspected."

She regarded me with a self-effacing smile, as if expecting congratulations.

"Susannah, you let him die a horrible death. You disagreed with what he did, granted, but he was still a human being, with feelings. He didn't deserve to die that way. He had a wife, and two children—"

Her hand cut the air in dismissal. "What are a wife and two children compared to the preservation of Niagara? Besides, he was happy enough to betray his family when given the chance. Oh no, he had no qualms about betraying them. He was like all those men who believe they're so high and mighty. They get away with being one way in public, where everyone thinks they're pure and good and noble, when all along, in private, they're lewd and selfish."

Insane as she was, of course she spoke the truth.

"His family's better off without him. My only regret is that even his death didn't accomplish what we set out to do. He was replaced by another."

"James Fitzhugh," I said, sick at heart.

She grinned sheepishly. "He was easier. There was no other choice, Miss Barrett. Some of my friends tried to get at Sinclair by throwing a torch through his window at home—that was useless and stupid; it didn't accomplish anything. But Fitzhugh—the simplicity of it was beautiful. He took walks, you see. Almost every day. I tried to be there, where he would see me. After a while he began to talk to me. To seek me out. To walk with me. He asked to see my paintings. He wasn't married, you know. He was timid, in his way. Anyway, he confided to me his doubts. He understood the evil he was doing. He wanted to die. He welcomed it."

"He told you that?"

"No. But I saw it in his face, at the end."

"The end?"

"After I led him to the waters. That place on Celinda Eliza where the current sweeps the shore. I took you there—remember?" She brightened at the memory. "I almost got you to walk into the water, didn't I?" she reflected gleefully. "I would have too," she assured me, "if that man Fiske hadn't come along."

All at once I saw that she would have killed me simply for fun.

How could I have been so blind? I steeled myself to self-control: "You were saying about Mr. Fitzhugh?"

"Oh, yes. It was such a hot day. I told him I often waded there, at that spot. He took off his shoes and socks—I had to throw them in after him!" she exclaimed. "It was over so much more quickly than I thought possible. The other one took so long, struggling under the ice. This one barely had time to realize what was happening, before he was swept away."

She paused, thoughtful. "Little Grace was with me that day. That was the same day you found us. Grace didn't see anything—I made sure of that. She was working. Hard at work. The man and I walked around the bend, just to that spot where I took you, later. Grace saw nothing. Afterward I told her that he had gone back to the power station."

I was enraged. I felt like screaming, like slapping her across the face, but I struggled to hold myself back. I needed to learn what she might say next. After a long moment I said cautiously, "You did well, to make sure Grace remained innocent."

She smiled like a young girl praised for getting an *A* in spelling. "So then you'll promise to take care of Grace for me?"

"Of course," I assured her again.

"And you won't tell on me? I mean, you won't tell anyone what I told you, about those men?"

I hadn't thought about this yet. If I told her story to the police matron standing outside, what would happen? The process of justice would be set in motion, and Susannah would face trial and the electric chair. She wouldn't show regret or repentance, she would consider herself a martyr. But no. More likely, she would never face trial: when Mr. Rumsey learned of her confession, he would never permit the scandal of a trial, not for this woman who had been admitted to all our homes as a trusted tutor. She would be done away with quietly—as if smothered by rose petals—and her death would be deemed a suicide. Or else she would simply be left to wither away here, branded a raving lunatic.

On the other hand, what would happen if I kept her secret? She would spend some time here, safe from the world, until Francesca maneuvered her release and took her far away. Maybe in that far away place she could heal, and find her own punishment and redemption. Did I have a duty to tell Francesca the truth? Would Francesca be prompted to protect her more or less because of the knowledge? Shouldn't Susannah herself be the one to tell Francesca? Dare I place myself between them? I didn't know, I couldn't decide. I needed time to think. All I understood was that Tom was innocent of the murders of Speyer and Fitzhugh.

Justice. I couldn't take Susannah Riley's fate upon me. Although she had determined the deaths of others, I couldn't take responsibility for whether she lived or died, was imprisoned or freed. The police would have to gather their evidence on their own—if they could. If she wasn't completely invisible to them, as she suspected.

All at once I discerned a kind of justice that was mine to dispense. "Susannah, I feel you should know that Karl Speyer actually opposed the exploitation of Niagara. At his death he was fighting the directors, to slow production. To *save* the cataract. He'd developed a new generator to produce more electricity with less water—that was the generator you and your friends bombed. Even James Fitzhugh, by your own admission, felt disturbed about the route development was taking. You should have let them live, Susannah. They would have been your best allies."

She studied me suspiciously, her brow knit. Had I reached her? Reached some area of sanity that must still lurk within her?

I continued, "So not only have you murdered your allies, but with this bombing your cause has been hopelessly discredited. You've achieved exactly the opposite of what you wanted. You haven't been a heroine at all."

The hatred grew slowly in her eyes. "You would say that. You've never stopped being jealous of Francesca and me."

"Whether I'm jealous or not makes no difference," I replied. "You've betrayed your own ideals. Your own goals. You've achieved nothing."

"At this moment our cause may seem 'discredited,' but in the end people will understand what we did and why. Our little group may be imprisoned, but others will take our place. In the end our cause will triumph."

"Perhaps. But *you've* committed murder. For nothing." I could tell by the fixed expression on her face that I still hadn't reached her. "Do I have to tell the authorities in order to make you understand the evil you've done?"

Abruptly she stood, fierce as a warrior. In a chilling whisper she said, "I had an assistant in what I did. A full assistant." I had to lean toward her, to hear her. "You would be surprised, should you ever discover who my assistant was. I knew every secret about the power station there was to know, because of my assistant." Her words were a sinister, threatening legacy. "I'll only say this to you once, Miss Barrett: If you report me to the authorities, I'll tell them who my assistant was and quick as can be"—she snapped her fingers in my face—"you'll have destroyed someone you love."

She was truly insane. Abruptly I turned and left her, calling my good-bye to the startled Francesca. As I strode down the women's ward, breakfast over, the patients sitting in loosely grouped chairs and staring straight ahead, I believed Susannah's threat was nothing but her madness speaking, and I dismissed it from my mind.

Chapter Thirty-Four

I passed through the asylum's gates and into the bustle of Elmwood Avenue. The city was coming alive, rejoicing in the arrival of President and Mrs. McKinley. The curbs looked as if they'd been scrubbed. Red, white, and blue streamers decorated every streetlamp. But the hoopla felt far removed from me. I blamed myself for the evil Susannah had done. I was the one who'd hired her when she'd first come to Buffalo, granting her the imprimatur of the school, which in turn opened the doors of society.

And yet, how could I have suspected? Her insanity was so intertwined with logic and reality; her outward demeanor was not simply normal but inviting—when she chose to make it so. Of course I knew she'd become passionate about Niagara, but even that day in my office when she presented the drawings to me, I'd picked up no hint of her inward disturbance. The terrible tragedy of the engineers, the disquiet I'd felt for months around Tom, the false leads which Franklin had pursued . . . she had touched each of us in a singular way. And she'd touched the girls she'd taught and tutored, to what ill effect I'd only discover over time. As much as my heart ached for the engineers and their families, I felt especially anguished over the ways Susannah had affected Grace: infiltrating her life because of her father, murdering Fitzhugh while Grace was only steps away. How easily Grace might have seen this murder. I could imagine her impetuously following Susannah down the path and stumbling upon the sight of her gently, like a touch of love, urging Fitzhugh toward the rapids. How easily Susannah could have done exactly the same to Grace, or even to me, seducing us into forgetfulness and death. I grieved at the thought of how little safety any of us can ever have. What can we rely on—truly rely on—that won't turn into water flowing through our hands?

Nothing. Not even God will bestir Himself to protect us from the threats all around to which we are blind.

I turned onto Forest Avenue, within sight of the Sinclair estate. Although tired from my overnight journey and from my time with Susannah, I needed to see Grace. I hadn't seen her since Sunday morning at church. I needed the simple reassurance of her presence, offering me a place and a purpose in life. And I wanted to tell her about Susannah's arrest. Tom wouldn't necessarily be attuned to his daughter's attachment to a teacher, even Susannah. Someone would have to tell Grace and much better it be me than a gossiping schoolmate.

Mrs. Sheehan's niece Blanchette, the shy, dark-haired maid who answered the door, told me that Tom had already left for work but she believed Grace was still on the terrace breakfasting with the housekeeper. That's where I found them, on the shaded second-floor terrace, where once we'd sat with Maddie and Peter listening to the sounds of the night.

"Aunt Louisa!" Grace exclaimed. "I'm so glad you came! You're here in time for the *spécialité du jour*: French toast! I had the idea to make it with cinnamon and nutmeg. Cook and I did it together and now it's the best I've ever had!"

"Good morning, Miss Barrett." Mrs. Sheehan sighed with the frazzled fatigue of a person who, however good-natured, has no tolerance for youthful exuberance in the morning. "Shall I bring you a pot of coffee?"

"Yes, please," I said as Grace prepared a plate of French toast and bacon for me from the buffet set up beside the dining table. Vases of roses, apricot-colored and white, decorated both tables. With apparent relief, Mrs. Sheehan went inside. "So, Grace, what have you been doing?" I asked.

Then came a litany of riding and Rowan, swimming and tennis, Ruth Rumsey did this and Winifred Coatsworth did that, and though these activities were trivial I savored every nuance. All at once my fears for Grace seemed exaggerated. What could happen to her in this protected haven? No wonder Tom didn't take Krakauer's threats seriously. How could he, coming out in the morning to have his coffee, surrounded by cut flowers, Grace bounding down from the third floor when she woke? Here on the estate all was well. Gratitude swept through me; despite the pain I'd endured from the decrepit old man in Tyringham, I was grateful that Grace had been born and that I was her mother. Parenthood transforms one's view of life, I thought, rearranging priorities and enforcing a vested interest in the future.

Mrs. Sheehan arrived with the pot of coffee, interrupting Grace's chatter. After I'd poured a cup, Grace asked, "What have you been doing, Aunt Louisa?"

I inhaled deeply. "Well, Grace, I have some rather unsettling news. Something rather . . . unfortunate has happened."

"To you?" she asked, startled.

"No, my darling," I reassured her. "To Miss Riley."

Grace looked confused. "Miss Riley? How could anything happen to Miss Riley?"

"Did your father tell you about the incident last week at the power station?" I didn't know how much Tom had shared with her, so I chose my words carefully.

She nodded. "He said some people tried to break one of the generators, but everything was okay and no one got hurt."

"That's right. Last evening those people, the ones who tried to break the generator, they were arrested. Miss Riley was among them."

"That doesn't sound like Miss Riley," she said, perplexed.

"No, it doesn't. But apparently—"

"Where is Miss Riley now?" she interrupted, her voice rising.

"Well, my dear, the men in charge of these things didn't want to keep her at the jail downtown, because conditions there are so . . . unpleasant. So they've given her a set of rooms at the state hospital."

Grace studied me, trying to figure this out. "If she's in the hospital instead of the jail, then I guess she didn't really do anything wrong?" Grace asked hopefully.

"Well . . ." I began, trying to formulate a response she could understand, one which would reveal some of the truth but not too much.

"How long will she have to stay there?" she demanded.

"I don't know."

"But she's supposed to give me a drawing lesson this afternoon.

Will she be here in time for my lesson? I did all the assignments—how is she going to see them?" Petulance filled her voice, and I sighed at her childishness—before realizing how important her childishness was. Indeed it was vital. She reacted as a child would react, with selfishness and self-involvement, seeing only her own side of the situation. Perhaps Susannah hadn't affected her as deeply as I'd feared.

"Don't worry, Grace, everything will work out. One of my best friends is taking special care of Miss Riley, so I know she'll be fine. Then we'll see what happens about your lessons."

Grace was still young enough to have a limited sense of time, and I hoped she could be put off by this idea of wait-and-see. Susannah couldn't hurt her now, so why give her more details than she could handle? Wait, I always advised parents and teachers, until the child herself has thought to ask a question about sensitive issues, and then answer only that specific question. Don't feel called upon to explain the meaning of the universe. Grace was worried about her lessons. She was missing her tutor. I was thankful that these were the only concerns I would have to deal with on this clear, sharp morning, because frankly I didn't have the strength to deal with anything more.

Unexpectedly Grace brightened. "While she's in the hospital, I can keep practicing. She wants me to work on drawings of people doing things. You could pose for me, Aunt Louisa. Pretending to play the piano. Let's do it now!"

So after I finished breakfast, we went downstairs to the music room. I was willing actually to play the piano, but Grace said no, the movement of my hands would muddle her. I must simply rest my fingers upon the keys as if I were playing and let her create the image. In this way we passed a peaceful half hour, the only sound the scratchy noise of Grace's pencil on the drawing paper. When Grace was ready to fill in the background, she gave me permission to rise from the piano bench. She herself sat on a low stool in front of the credenza; behind her, on top of the credenza, I noticed a bag from Huyler's.

"Did you and Mrs. Sheehan go to the chocolate store?" I asked, suddenly desiring the marshmallow bar I never did get to eat. "I was there the other day."

"No, we didn't go," Grace said, preoccupied with erasing an unwanted smudge. "Yesterday afternoon a man came to visit, and he brought the chocolates. He walked into the garden when I was reading a book."

Krakauer.

"He said he was a friend of Papa's," she continued. "But Papa wasn't home. The man just walked into the garden instead of knocking on the front door. At first I didn't know what to do." She looked up from her work, and I sensed the matter had been troubling her. "I know I'm not supposed to talk to strangers, but I'm not supposed to be rude, either. So I was just polite. I said, 'Good afternoon, sir. May I help you?'" She imitated herself with a tad of pride for thinking of this grown-up greeting. "Anyway, I could hear Mr. Duffy's shears on the roses, so I knew I wasn't alone outside." Mr. Duffy was the assistant gardener. "Then I remembered seeing this man at a party at Ruth Rumsey's cousin's house, so even though we hadn't really met, that made talking to him all right. He said I could call him Uncle Frederick."

"What happened then?" I forced myself to sound calm.

"He wondered what I was reading; it was just my *McGuffey*, but I showed him and he said his daughters had the same one. Then he gave me the bag from Huyler's. It had three caramel-marshmallow bars—I love those! He said his daughters love them too, which was why he thought of bringing them to me."

That odious man. He'd purchased four when I was with him and eaten one in my presence. Had he planned even then to bring the others to Grace? He was only a messenger, he'd said, and this was his message: He could reach Grace at any time, even within the confines of her house and garden, even in the middle of the day, the staff working all around her. He was the messenger, and his message was that no one was safe.

"Then Mr. Sheehan came out and told him to go, because Papa wasn't home, and so he went."

"Does your father know he came to visit?" I heard the tension slipping into my voice.

"I don't know. Papa came home after I went to bed last night and left before I got up this morning. I don't know if Mr. Sheehan told him.

I have to let Papa know, though, because the man wanted me to tell him something."

"What was that?" I dreaded her response.

"He said to give Papa his very best regards. He was particular about it. He said, 'Give your father my *very* best regards.'" I could almost hear Krakauer's unctuous condescension, almost see his ruthless smirk.

"You must never speak to him again."

"He seemed nice," Grace insisted.

"Believe me, Grace, he's not nice at all."

While she ran off to the kitchen for a postbreakfast snack, I went to the parlor to try to telephone Tom at the power station. The assistant who answered said Tom was inspecting the new tailrace and was unreachable until early evening, so I left my name and hung up. I would have to decide what to do on my own. Debating with myself and finding no solution, I glanced around. Margaret had designed the parlor as Tom's room, for business meetings and telephoning; it had leather chairs, an unadorned fireplace, prints of various castles in Ireland, a lingering scent of cigarettes despite the open windows. I sat at the telephone table, an intricate piece of furniture with cubbyholes and shelves for pencils, pens, and ink, notepaper as well as engraved stationery for home and office. Into this room Tom had brought poor Karl Speyer seven months ago to fight over water. Into this room Tom had also brought Peter Fronczyk, only several days ago although it seemed like months, and given him the funds to begin a new life, to buy himself safety.

Safety. Grace. I rose, set on doing what little I could to protect her. I found Mrs. Sheehan in the kitchen discussing the day's menu with the cook while Grace ate oatmeal cookies. I gave instructions that Grace must stay on the estate and the staff must guard against trespassers. If Grace went into the garden, someone must be with her at all times. Particularly she must not be permitted to speak to Mr. Krakauer, should he turn up again. Mrs. Sheehan nodded in agreement, perhaps not understanding my concern but too well-trained to challenge it. In addition, Mrs. Sheehan must tell Mr. Sinclair about Krakauer's visit as soon as he returned home tonight or if by chance he telephoned.

Grace was upset. My edict prevented her from going to the country club for her usual Wednesday riding lesson. I found myself impatient with her, an unfamiliar emotion between us. I instructed her to practice the piano for a full hour this morning, and then she could have a marshmallow bar. She nodded her head in compliance.

And that's how I left her at midmorning, practicing the piano, the sound of Czerny *Études* reaching me as I hurried down the drive. Of course the most reliable protection would have been for me to stay with her all day; no one else would have my vigilance. But I'd been away from school for several days, and I needed to check in with Miss Atkins and Mrs. Schreier. In addition, the formal welcoming reception for the McKinleys was scheduled for late this afternoon at Rumsey Park. I would have to attend; not attending would be a public admission that something was terribly wrong. Besides, I had invited Mary Talbert as my guest and she would be calling for me in her carriage at four o'clock. If I wasn't so beset by worry for Grace, I would have been looking forward to seeing her.

The reception at Rumsey Park spilled out across the manicured lawns, all of us floating in the afternoon radiance. Liveried footmen served champagne in fluted glasses; white roses were thick upon the trellises. The house was a Beaux-Arts palace, the long French windows reflecting the city around it. My board of trustees was present, of course, along with Miss Love and what seemed like the entire memberships of the Twentieth Century Club and the Buffalo Club (most of them married to one another). But this reception was unusual because there was also a cross section of the city in attendance: the operatives of the major political parties and ethnic groups, including the Irish, Italian, and Polish; our figurehead mayor, Conrad Diehl, scion of the German community, and his cronies; churchmen of virtually every faith in full regalia, including even the rabbi of Temple Beth Zion.

Although Tom himself had sent regrets to the Rumseys, the air was filled with talk of the miracle he was performing at Niagara. Word was out that on Friday the President would be able to put Powerhouse 3 on-line as originally planned, despite the bombing. Tom was hailed as a hero. Almost as if he were one of them, my board members were forced to acknowledge this admiration from the widely drawn crowd (not to acknowledge it would have been blatantly rude), and then they deflected it. According to them we were all heroes. Nothing could stop us. We were triumphant. As a city, as a nation.

One group notably lacking official representation at this reception was the Negro community. I had hoped that here, at least, they would have been included. Mary Talbert stood out, the only member of her race in attendance. Nonetheless we took our place on the receiving line, and for a few moments I was able to put aside my anxieties about Grace and appreciate the scene. From a thronelike velvet chair beside her husband, who stood, Mrs. McKinley greeted her visitors. Her face was tightly wrinkled and immobile. Most likely she was in her fifties (her husband was fifty-eight), but she could easily have been mistaken for eighty. Independently wealthy, she was stiffly shrouded in jewels like the Empress Theodora in a Byzantine mosaic. After the deaths of her two daughters from childhood illnesses, Mrs. McKinley had become an epileptic (or so it was said); she was subject to seizures and debilitating headaches. Nevertheless the President adored her and solicitously devoted himself to her comfort and happiness. He would place a handkerchief over her face if she suffered a seizure at a public event. She spent her time crocheting bedroom slippers by the thousands, distributing them to family and friends. Some friends boasted over a dozen pairs.

Mrs. McKinley could not bear to shake hands at receptions, so she held a bouquet of pansies on her lap to remind everyone not to reach for her hand. When I was introduced, she nodded without seeming to see me—or anyone, not even the exquisitely dressed but inescapably dark-skinned Mary Talbert who was next in line.

The President was his wife's opposite. Jovial, expansive, gracious, tolerant. A Civil War hero, at ease with himself and others, he caught every name, questioned every visitor, relished every tiny coincidence. How lovable he was, his large midsection girdled by a vest, his suit jacket carefully buttoned, his expression unfailingly kind and welcoming. He was everyone's favorite uncle. He swelled with the joy of shaking hands, but his handshake was sweaty. I wiped his sweat onto my skirt when he was safely occupied in a brief but pointed discussion

with Mrs. Talbert on the merits of Booker T. Washington's Tuskegee
Institute.

"Needless to say," Mrs. Talbert confided after we escaped to the
terrace, "I pretended to full approval of Tuskegee." We strolled down
the terrace steps. "That's all these white men want to hear: Tuskegee,
Tuskegee, training excellent cooks and shoemakers by the hundred."
We crossed the lawn and made our way to the formal garden. "Well,
the day will come when more is required from these white men than the
vocational training at Tuskegee."

"I trust when that time comes, you'll make yourself available to
explain exactly what is required?" I teased.

Her smile was slow but generous when it came. She took my arm.
"I hope so."

Huge stone pots overflowed with flowers—red, blue, purple, bold
and full-blooming. The laburnum walk turned luminous in the mist of
afternoon. Sculptured nudes gleamed on their pedestals. Suddenly I
spotted Frederick Krakauer beside a statue of Diana the Huntress. He
was exchanging what appeared to be pleasantries with John Milburn.
What sort of pleasantries would those two have to share? Undoubtedly
something to do with the persistent rumors that McKinley would soon
nominate Milburn to be Attorney General. At least then he'd be far
away from us. I thought. The McKinleys were staying with the
Milburns during their visit, and Milburn appeared more smug than
ever. I was relieved to see Krakauer, however: if he was here, he wasn't
attempting to reach Grace—although of course he could easily hire
someone to do such work, as Milburn himself had once done. I
resolved to keep Krakauer in my sight line as Mrs. Talbert and I wandered through the crowd.

I saw Franklin Fiske on the far side of the lawn, exchanging jokes
with a group that included the mayor. Seeing him, knowing his regard
for me, made me wish I could confide my fears about Grace to him. But
I felt helpless. He was not disinterested enough to respond objectively.
The only one who might be was the woman at my side. I studied her
honey-toned face. Her expression was complacent; she'd noticed
nothing amiss in my mood. Yet even now something held me back from
unbridled confidences.

Around us the fountains flashed, throwing water into the air to sparkle like fireworks. Franklin had once described Rumsey Park as a Versailles, and he was right, although it was an incongruous Versailles—for when I turned to look behind me, skyscrapers loomed above the trees. They were only a few blocks away and creeping closer. This estate was one of the last enclaves of the old city. The business district was fast expanding, and I expected the Rumseys, ever practical, would soon subdivide this land to immense profit.

In the center of the formal garden was a wide, round fountain that had in fact come from a French chateau. Its tiers gleamed, its waters fell in transparent sheets. Mary Talbert and I paused to admire it.

"I wouldn't object to a fountain like this in my garden," Mrs. Talbert observed.

"It would certainly cool the surrounding area when the wind blew across it," I said.

"Indeed. From that point of view, a fountain like this can be considered a practical necessity."

"Yes, you're right," I agreed.

We watched two blue jays frolicking in the upper tier, flicking droplets from their wings. I always felt surprised when I saw blue jays, never quite believing how truly blue they really were.

And then, through the sheets of falling water, Mrs. Talbert and I saw that a conference was taking place in the distance among three men and a woman. The leaders of the exposition and of the city. John Scatcherd, John Milburn, Miss Maria Love, Ansley Wilcox. Where was Krakauer? I glanced around and found him beside Mayor Diehl. More confident knowing where he was, I looked again at the impromptu conference: there were disapproving glances in our direction, nods of acquiescence, a plan being laid out and approved. Milburn appeared flushed with upset.

"Do you think they find my presence disturbing?" Mrs. Talbert asked matter-of-factly.

"I hope not," I said. "I would be appalled if—" But even as I spoke, Miss Love turned from the group and began to walk purposefully in our direction.

"I believe I'd best be going," Mrs. Talbert said lightly.

Suddenly I felt both offended and frightened. What had they planned, what was Miss Love going to do or threaten? "You mustn't go!" I said angrily—my anger directed at the group in the distance. "We can face down Miss Love. I won't allow them to force you to leave. We'll fight them together."

"Not today."

"You've always gloried in a fight."

"But my dear Miss Barrett, there won't be a fight. What will happen is that Miss Love will ask to walk with us, and we will not be able to refuse her. She will guide us—because we are too polite to resist, and because she cannot walk in the sun, or so she will claim—she will guide us to the shelter of some concealed bower where she will stay with us, because we are too polite to resist, until the party is over. Exactly as she would stay with a drunken relative who must be kept firmly out of the way. No thank you. I'd much rather leave at a moment of my own choosing. Which is now."

"You are my guest. If you are leaving, then I will leave with you," I declared resolutely.

"I disagree. My departure is wisdom but yours would be melodrama."

I realized how foolish I'd been to invite her. "I'm so sorry to have put you in this position. I never properly considered the . . . ramifications of—"

"Don't be sorry. I enjoyed every minute. Literally. I especially enjoyed the invitation. And now I can say I've discussed political issues with the President, which makes me more credible in the arena of national debate. Good day to you, Miss Barrett," she said abruptly, and with that, she strode around the fountain and toward the house, nodding her head in pleasant greeting to the startled Miss Love. Rather than wait for my own fast-approaching Lovian encounter, I turned and walked across the lawns in the general direction of the Rumsey woods, which were the equivalent of a full city block away. Guests clustered all around, and soon I considered myself safely lost in the crowd. I was pondering my next move when I heard a woman call, "Miss Barrett! Oh, Miss Barrett!"

Having no choice, I turned to see Mrs. Rushman disengaging

herself from the Freddy Coatsworths and approaching me with suspicious eagerness.

"Miss Barrett!" she repeated. "Have you heard?" She spoke loudly, for the benefit of those near us. "Abigail has been asked to stay on at the Roycrofters after the end of her fellowship. She certainly will become an artist now, in the great tradition of Mrs. Cary and Mrs. Glenny." She glanced around to see if those esteemed women were anywhere nearby but mercifully they were not. "She says she'll never marry, but we shall see, we shall see!" Mrs. Rushman leaned close to me. A bit of canapé had fallen on the bosom of her dress. "Every door will open to her now," she whispered. "She'll be able to marry anyone now. Oh, look who's there! I must tell him the news." Flashing her feather boa around her neck, she hurried off to greet Mr. Albright, who perambulated through the crowd with his long-limbed, sloe-eyed wife Susan on his arm. He appeared absolutely placid as he faced her.

I thought about what Mrs. Rushman had told me. So I had indeed bestowed upon Abigail my own life, except without a real child to watch over. Now she would resist marriage and spend her days searching for the boy she believed to be hers. However, if she also became a professional artist, well, at least I would feel a touch of redemption for the decisions I had made on her behalf.

My encounter with Mrs. Rushman had made the party feel oppressive. With the conviction that Krakauer would remain here until the end (there were too many important people in attendance for him to depart early), I decided to seek refuge for a while in the quiet of the woods.

In their own way, the woods of Rumsey Park were as manicured as the lawns and gardens—every woodland tree planted, every bubbling cascade shaped with the overall effect in mind. I had walked here many times over the years, and I welcomed every opportunity. From the moment I followed the path into the woods, trees sheltered me and silence enveloped me. These woods were famous in the city and laden with romantic mystery. In their midst was a serpentine lake where generations of children had learned to ice-skate and row boats. A spired, Gothic gazebo graced the lakeshore. Near the center of the lake was a small island with a Grecian peristyle just large enough to shelter a boating party from the rain. Today, because of a passing noontime shower, the woods were moist and shimmery, fragrant with the scents of late summer. Simply breathing those scents gradually eased my mind and restored the focus I needed to deal with the difficulties that besieged me.

After the path curved around a stand of birch trees, unexpectedly I came upon Dexter Rumsey relaxing on a bench in a clearing. His eyes were closed and he basked in the sun. This was like him, to wander off from big groups; to leave public panoply to his elder brother, Bronson. Hearing my step, he sat up and opened his eyes, then greeted me with a guilty grin.

"Miss Barrett!" he said with mock surprise. "Haven't you met the President? Haven't you attempted to overhear each and every word the President is saying to each and every person who comes to shake his hand?"

"Oh, yes, indeed I have. And a delightful experience it was," I replied, my voice sounding less jaunty than I would have wished.

Nonetheless he laughed appreciatively as he rose from the bench. "Walk with me, will you?" he asked, taking my arm. "My brother is much more suited to these events than I am. I think he actually enjoys them! But what's an older brother for, if not to give me the chance to roam in the woods? I need a calming interlude after the excitement of the past few days. I haven't been able to take my yacht out all week. There's a kind of fever at work in the city, have you noticed? Did you hear that some silly boys from the Nichols School risked their lives to hang a banner welcoming the President around the third floor of their school building? When they found out that McKinley's travel route would take him down a different block, they lobbied Milburn to change the route so McKinley would see the banner! What foolishness. Macaulay girls would never do something like that, I'm sure. Well, I'm grateful presidents don't condescend to bless us with their presence very often."

Late afternoon was turning to early evening and birds were coming out to feed: goldfinches making their way south; red-winged blackbirds, their wing bars flashing crimson and yellow against black.

Mrs. Talbert's escape was fresh in my mind, and I'd been wondering what to do with the information Francesca had given me at Abino Bay about Milburn. I decided to appeal to Mr. Rumsey in the only way I was allowed: quietly, and with subterfuge.

"Mr. Rumsey, do you remember the incident in the summer involving my young student, Millicent Talbert?" How blasé I made my voice sound.

"Oh yes," he replied, matching my tone as he gazed amiably at a redheaded woodpecker tapping its way up a tree trunk. "Unfortunate, indeed. I never could discover who was responsible, in spite of my best efforts."

"Well, I have no proof, but I believe I've learned something rather . . . surprising about it."

"Have you, now?"

"Yes," I replied. Then I told him the story Francesca had told me on the beach.

"Well," he said when I finished. "How very interesting." He spoke as if the matter neither startled nor concerned him. But of course Dexter Rumsey fought his battles beneath the surface, so his seeming indifference disturbed me not at all. Quite the opposite, in fact. It assured me of his full attention.

We walked in silence for several turns of the path, following the course of a meandering stream and its picturesque waterfalls. The wind rippled the surface of the water.

"Did you know that we've been having some financial problems with the Pan-American?" he confided. "No, of course you didn't," he said before I could answer, thus telling me that he preferred not to learn whatever gossip I might have heard. "I like to keep my ladies away from these tawdry details of business," he added. "But I'll trust you with the truth, Louisa. The fact is, debts have been incurred, plumbers aren't being paid, suppliers of every stripe are lurking in wait for whatever pennies turn up. The bonds issued to the investors will never be repaid. And who's to take the blame for this financial debacle—that's what I've been asking myself. It wasn't my idea to have an exposition here; certainly not—too much trouble altogether, for no particular reward." He contemplated a troop of nearly grown ducklings trailing their mother. "Well, well." All at once he smiled broadly. "What a perfect afternoon for a walk."

Thus were our battles fought and won.

"Thank goodness for the arrests in the power station bombing," Mr. Rumsey said, clearly intending to change the subject. "That's a blessing at least."

"I saw Susannah Riley today." I told him this because I wanted to hear what he would say—to learn the official explanation, as it were, for her deeds. "She told me some rather unsettling things."

"The woman is obviously insane. Poor creature. If I were you I wouldn't listen to a word she says. Imagine, a woman being involved with dynamite!"

In spite of the seriousness of the matter, I smiled at him. "You don't believe women capable of—"

"Now, now, don't start in on *me*, my dear." With mock terror he pulled away. "No lady of *my* acquaintance has ever used dynamite. As a matter of fact, I view it as a compliment, to consider a dynamite-toting woman insane rather than criminal. Don't you?"

I regarded him skeptically. We were such skilled actors. Where had we trained, to develop such skills? A silly question: Every instant of our lives constituted our training.

"You and I are mutually incorrigible, aren't we?" he asked. "But granted, it's my age talking too. Seventy-four. Very respectable, I must say, and deserving of respect—although I don't always get it, regardless of my well-earned reputation." With a self-deprecating shrug he shook his head. "I can't help but sense a new world growing up around me, filled with forces beyond my control. Nature lovers. Unionists. Socialists—even here, in Buffalo! Yes, there are socialists here," he assured me. "I used to feel that my friends and I could guide our city's future in exactly the way we wanted, and for the betterment of all, but now everything's slipping through our fingers. Even at the power station, we have to make *requests*, instead of knowing that our views will be accepted by right. It's not a situation I'm accustomed to. Although I suppose I'll have to become accustomed to it." He sighed.

As he spoke, fears filled my mind once more. Perhaps Grace wasn't safe even with the strictures I had placed upon her. Maybe Krakauer had left the party early after all. Maybe even now, while I walked in the woods . . . I breathed deeply as I struggled to steady myself, and had no retort ready for Mr. Rumsey when he finished speaking. He glanced at me with concern.

"What is it, my dear? You aren't your usual self today." He rubbed my shoulder sympathetically, like a father to a child. "Too much excitement?"

"No, I—" Suddenly there was no question of battles to be fought and won, secrets to be kept, strategies to be plotted and fulfilled—there was only *feeling*, despair, spilling over, out of my control, tears filling my eyes and rendering me helpless. "I need your help, Mr. Rumsey," I said as I wept. "Miss Love once told me—"

With soft humor he interrupted, "If Miss Love said it, then I'm sure it must be true."

"She told me you would help me, if I ever—"

"Yes," he interrupted again. He held my shoulders. He let me rest my forehead against his chest.

"I'm frightened."

"About what?" So patient he was. So gentle.

"About Grace Sinclair."

"Ah yes. I see her fairly frequently, you know. She's a close friend of my daughter Ruth. Well, I'm sure you know that. Grace has seemed more cheerful, the last few times I've seen her. Her mother's death was an awful blow. As it would be to any child."

"Mr. Rumsey, she's of special concern to me because—"

I was about to tell him about Krakauer's threats, but he touched my lips to silence me. "There is no need to look back, my dear. To reopen wounds best left forgotten."

"Pardon?"

"That may seem harsh now, but when you've had time to think about it, you'll understand."

What could he possibly mean? "But I haven't told you everything, Mr. Rumsey. Grace—there've been threats. Against her. Mr. Krakauer said he would hurt her, and me, if Mr. Sinclair didn't do—I mean, if Mr. Sinclair did do, certain things at the power station. Mr. Krakauer said . . ." But I couldn't go on. I raised my head to look at Mr. Rumsey.

He was staring at the trees with a quizzical expression on his face.

Finally he said, "I know of no threats to Grace, or to you. And I know everything, or so I am told."

"But you don't know about this," I insisted. "Mr. Krakauer actually went to Grace's home, trespassed onto the property and spoke to her. And he seems to know things about Grace that . . ." I choked on my tears. Mr. Rumsey rubbed my shoulders reassuringly.

When I'd regained control, I continued, "I've been so upset, Mr. Rumsey. I haven't known what to do or where to turn. I even went to see President Cleveland to ask him—" I gasped that I had said Cleveland's name aloud.

Offhandedly Mr. Rumsey asked, "Did he remember you?"

And at that moment, like a mist slowly lifting to reveal the world in exquisite clarity and precision, all became self-evident. I saw everything afresh, with true meanings revealed. Maria Love's talk of protection . . . the suspicious lack of suspicion, all these years . . . the Macaulay board's acquiescence to my every desire . . . they had known . . . they had even arranged . . .

We stared at one another, Dexter Rumsey and I. I felt tears pooling in my eyes; one rolled down my cheek and Mr. Rumsey brushed it away. He smiled sadly.

"Don't judge us harshly, my dear. We needed to do what was best. For the city. Not for ourselves."

"For the city?" I repeated numbly.

"Yes. To show him we were trying to make amends. We trusted he'd be reelected in '92. We wanted to have him on our side. On the *city's* side. Issues arise . . . a sympathetic ear in the White House can sometimes be helpful. Do you understand?"

I shook my head no, though comprehension unfurled before me.

"You see, we knew he'd be looking for someone. That was his nature, always, to want someone. I myself find it hard to understand a man so ruled by pleasure that he would risk everything for fleeting satisfaction. However," he sighed, "we must deal with the world as we find it, not as we wish it would be."

"Yes," I said, stunned.

"Why not guide him, we thought. In the right direction, that is. To someone we could trust. For his own protection. So he wouldn't embarrass himself—and us—as he did with Mrs. Halpin. What a sorry mess that was, with journalists swarming everywhere when the story broke. And the lewdness of it all, with that woman drinking and being bundled off to an asylum. Really, I didn't see how any of us would get through the newspaper frenzy with our self-respect intact. But somehow he managed to get himself elected in spite of it all, and then he had the gall to blame the city for his problems." Mr. Rumsey shook his head in distaste. "But he was still president, you see. We needed him. We wrote off his first term, when he was so angry with us, but we hoped to do better in the second term. When we finally convinced him to visit Buffalo in May of '91, we made our plan. You seemed perfect in every way. The logical choice. I asked Miss Love to invite you to her reception. I pointed you out to him. I said he might enjoy your conversation. That was all. But he understood me. He knew what I meant. And he was pleased. Oh yes. More than pleased." Rumsey chuckled bleakly at the recollection. "But I knew he would be. How could he not be pleased with you? So tall and beautiful and well-educated. So amusing, with that dry, ironic wit I've always found so appealing. Not unlike his wife, in certain ways." Mr. Rumsey caressed my cheek with the back of his fingers, the way he might comfort a child who'd fallen on the terrace steps. "We knew you were trustworthy. Not another Mrs. Halpin. No, no. You were suitable in every way. And you seemed to understand the necessity too."

"I understood nothing," I said, somehow summoning up the strength to speak. "I was innocent."

For a moment he pondered this. "Ah," he finally said. "So you went to the sacrifice unknowing. There's something reminiscent of Greek tragedy about that, isn't there? Every time I reread those plays I find more truth in them," he mused wistfully. "At any rate, none of us has ever forgotten what you did. We've always shown our gratitude. Haven't we?"

What could I say? For years I'd blamed myself. I'd struggled to reconcile myself to what had happened, to find a way to maintain control over my life, and now he'd told me that I hadn't been in control at all.

With sincere concern he pressed, "Haven't you been happy with how we've treated you all these years? Is there anything we could have done that we didn't do? Anything we could have given you?"

"Who is 'we'?" I managed to ask.

"A few of us—what does it matter? Milburn, Wilcox—they were the ones most closely involved in controlling the mess when the Halpin story broke in '84. There were a few others too. Never mind who. Not Larkin, of course—he's much too upright!" Mr. Rumsey smiled fraternally at his friend's exotic trait. "Maria naturally, but she only guessed, she wasn't part of our decision-making. She saw you drive off with Gilder that night and came to me irate, insisting you must be removed from your post forthwith for your indiscretion with Gilder, she thought!" Jovially he laughed at the memory before turning serious once more. "And you've never suffered from it, Louisa, have you? We've tried to see to it that you've never suffered. Please reassure me on that. Assuage my heart. Even I—the all-knowing one—doubt myself when I turn off the light at night."

I could see from his face that he did doubt. That he did care. How strange, that he could simultaneously use me as a pawn and fret over my well-being.

"But I bore a child."

"Yes. Although I am the only one who knows that absolutely for certain. Again Maria has guessed, putting two and two together with the dates and so on. And Grace looks so much like you—not at all like poor Margaret Winspear. How terribly sad, her dying so young. I know you two were close friends." He patted me sympathetically. "Anyway, I must admit that several of the original group have guessed. But I am the only one who knows for certain, and I shall never betray you."

Did I hear an unspoken "if"? Did I hear his own threat, as strong as Krakauer's, to destroy me if I didn't do as he wished? "Exactly how do you know?" I asked.

"In New York, when you went there," he hesitated, "I couldn't let my prize teacher go off alone, now, could I? I had to assure myself that all went well for her. Especially because I had the headmistress position awaiting her."

For the first time in my life I wanted to hurt someone—to hurt him, to watch him suffer the anguish I had suffered. I stared at his kindly face, his silvery beard, his welcoming eyes. In that same moment I realized I wouldn't lift a hand against him. I still had to protect Grace. Undoubtedly Mr. Rumsey knew that Grace would be my paramount consideration and gauged his arguments accordingly.

"Come now, my dear. Dry your eyes. Your daughter is well cared for. All has worked out for the best, has it not? We've grown, we've prospered—the city, I mean. Beyond our wildest dreams. The school too. You've made it exactly what I wanted it to be. You've fulfilled my trust over and over. We've all been very lucky. Come, let us walk."

Putting his arm around me, he led me along the path. Once *A Midsummer Night's Dream* had been performed beneath these trees by our amateur theater group, organized by Dr. Cornell. We in the audience had followed along from scene to scene. Evelyn Rumsey Cary had been Tatiana; Dr. Cary had been the donkey-headed Bottom. Grace had adored Bottom, and Margaret had held her daughter's hand as we strolled amid the forest sprites.

Finally Rumsey said, "Since we have been speaking about personal matters, there is something I feel honor-bound to bring up with you. Forgive me, but I must say it. Thomas Sinclair is perhaps not the best friend for a woman such as yourself. Not at the moment, at least. He's not one of us, really, if you see what I mean. We must let him find his own way, as he seems determined to do. His situation will play out according to its own rules—and the conclusion has by no means been fully determined. Much is still up to him. I would warn you—no, ask you, my dear, please," he again rubbed my shoulder tenderly, "to keep your distance from him while others evaluate the best course. All of this is so terribly difficult. For me too. I feel like you're a daughter to me. I would welcome you as a daughter, I admire you so. Your pluck and determination and independence. You've remained an ideal to me, all these years, alone in your tower, devoting yourself to your students and your books. Don't let your good heart lead you to be drawn in by the struggles of Thomas Sinclair. I myself have always found a hint of demagoguery in the Robin Hood story."

He meditated for a moment. "In fact I'm afraid I must ask you to stay as far as possible from Thomas Sinclair. Things may happen to him. It's unfortunate but unavoidable—and quite outside my control. For your own safety, and for the reputation of the school, I would urge you to keep your distance."

We came to the grape arbor, the fruit hanging in heavy clusters of translucent green. Each year Bronson Rumsey let the grapes freeze upon the vines, picking them in January to make ice wine.

"And my daughter?"

For a full minute at least, he said nothing. Then: "I know I'm requesting a great deal of you, my dear. Therefore I will tell you that as far as I'm concerned, it's out of bounds to involve a child in matters of politics or business. Unworthy of gentlemen."

This, I sensed, was meant to be his promise that Grace would not be harmed and that Millicent would be avenged.

"Thank you." I forced all emotion away. I needed rationality to deal with him, not pain, not anguish.

"I wish I knew a young man who would be your equal. I'd like to see you married—and still the headmistress of Macaulay, of course. It would please me, to see you married."

He paused. Then, as if surprising himself with the idea, he said, "Young Franklin Fiske has much to commend him. A thoughtful young man, artistic, apparently, but hardworking. And thoroughly respectable, from a fine old family, and Susan's cousin to boot—what more could you ask for?" His eyes twinkled. "He's got a wicked sense of humor, but he's well-intentioned nonetheless. A thoroughly honorable man. Furthermore he's probably got no notion of asking a wife to supervise dinner parties and flower arrangements—at least not to the extent that she must give up her good and decent labor. Being artistic he isn't likely to object to . . . previous entanglements. He's more likely to find them interesting. He has altogether much more to recommend him than the complexities of a Thomas Sinclair. Yes, yes, Franklin Fiske." As he considered this, he looked more and more delighted.

"Thank you for your concern, but I shall never marry Franklin Fiske." Regardless of my feelings for Franklin, I wouldn't allow Rumsey to manipulate me on this, too. I made myself impassive. Unreadable. Up ahead, a single elm tree was taking on its autumn colors, becoming a patchwork of yellow and green.

"Yes, yes, I'm meddling, I know. You have every reason to be annoyed. I know you young people like to work these things out yourselves. It's just a thought, anyway. Thank you for indulging an old man by listening. And no matter what you decide, rest assured that you are under my protection. You and Grace, both."

The path turned, the trees thinned, and we were within sight of the house. In the sunset the windowpanes glowed like fire.

"My deepest protection. As you always have been."

Chapter Thirty-Five

On Friday afternoon, September 6, at 4:07 p.m., President McKinley was shot at point-blank range at a public reception at the exposition's Temple of Music. His assailant, Leon Czolgosz, was a twenty-eight-year-old former factory worker born in Detroit of Polish immigrant parents. Czolgosz called himself an anarchist, although the anarchist parties quickly disavowed him. Yet his faith in himself and his deed remained strong. At his arraignment, Czolgosz said, "I have done my duty."

In the days that followed the assassination attempt, the city seemed to retreat into a state of suspended animation, with nothing but the newspapers to define the days. The details of the events at the Temple of Music came out bit by bit: The President, the newspapers explained, had a passion for shaking hands with the public. He had insisted on the open reception at the Temple of Music as a way to exercise this passion. He prided himself on being able to shake upward of forty-five hands per minute. There was an art to it: face a line of citizens arrayed perpendicularly to yourself. With your right arm, reach to the left, grab a hand, squeeze hard, pull the hand to the right, let go with a little push and swing your arm back to the left for the next citizen.

McKinley had enjoyed a magnificent day on Friday, the culmination of three magnificent days during which he'd toured the exposition; given a speech on trade policy before an audience of over fifty thousand; toured Niagara and put Powerhouse 3 on-line. By the time of his reception at the Temple of Music, he was in an ebullient mood and eager to greet the common folk of the Republic. He was shaking hands at full speed—potted palm trees framing the line, star-spangled bunting all around, an organist playing Bach—when suddenly the next man to approach him held a pistol concealed within his handkerchief-wrapped hand.

The weapon was a .32 caliber, short-barreled, six-shot automatic Iver-Johnson revolver which Czolgosz had purchased easily for four dollars at a local firearms store. After the attack, as he gripped his abdomen in pain, McKinley's first thoughts were apparently for the man who'd tried to kill him: "Go easy on him, boys," he cautioned the police and security agents who were grappling Czolgosz to the ground—or so reported the *Evening News*. "Let no one harm him," was the stentorian quote offered by the more respectable *Express*. Other newspapers offered their own variants on this statement, and I considered them one by one until realizing that I would never know what McKinley had really said. I was left understanding only that on some basic level history itself was forever unknowable.

After the shooting, the President was taken by automobile ambulance to the hospital on the grounds of the exposition. There he underwent emergency surgery to repair internal damage and remove the single bullet which had entered his body. Much was made of the fortitude of the surgeons: Because there was no electricity in the operating room, Dr. Rixey, the President's personal physician, had held up a mirror to the lowering sun to reflect light into the abdominal incision.

The surgery was deemed successful—even though the bullet was never found—and afterward McKinley was taken to John Milburn's home to begin the process of recovery. The weather was hot, and huge blocks of ice were brought in; electric fans, powered by a portable generating system, were set up beside the ice to cool the kindly President, who never complained.

In the hours that followed, chaos seemed to rage across the nation, whether real or invented by the newspapers was difficult to determine. In Pittsburgh, fifty thousand men continued their strike against the United States Steel works; their women burned the cots intended for nonunion laborers. In McKeesport, Pennsylvania, rioting Hungarian strikers set upon a group of replacement workers and beat them. Editorialists assured us that a massive anarchist, socialist, or "Red" revolt was at hand. If I should see any anarchists, socialists, or "Reds" lurking behind the trees, the *Evening Times* assured me, it was quite all right to shoot them—particularly if they were Polish.

Alas, such ridiculous notions did inflame the common people on the street. At Katarzyna's local shops, the butcher and the grocer refused to wait on her. Since the shopkeepers were German and hated the Poles anyway, Czolgosz's supposed nationality was only one more excuse for confrontation. I told her to use the shops in my neighborhood, where the shopkeepers would assume her purchases were for me. Katarzyna's American-born seven-year-old son was harassed by older boys while playing baseball with his friends in the street—he was punched within clear sight of a police officer, who did nothing. She would keep her son home now, she said, lock him in, were she not afraid that their tenement would be set ablaze. I told her that she and her son could move in with me. This did not console her, because with me, she would be far from her sisters, and she refused.

That Friday night, after I learned the news from the evening paper, my first thought was for Grace. I needed to be with her, to explain what had happened and console her if she was afraid. After closing the school, I went to the Sinclair house, where a guard at the gate stopped and questioned me, a welcome surprise. I found Grace peacefully swimming laps in the pool. Mrs. Sheehan, who was hemming one of Grace's dresses, made a grateful escape upon my arrival. I sat in her place and watched the sky turn from pink to magenta with the sunset. I resolved not to break the serenity of the evening by telling Grace about the shooting yet.

I heard steps and turned to see Tom coming toward me, a glass in his hand. He had planned on speaking to McKinley privately in the late afternoon, but then came the assassination attempt, and so his hope to enlist the President's help in providing electricity to the poor had come to nothing. Grace called her greeting, then continued swimming; she was trying to break her own record for uninterrupted laps.

"I went to the club," Tom said wearily, sitting beside me. He seemed drained. "I thought I could get some new information on his condition, but there wasn't much to come by."

I studied him. The light had almost faded; we were surrounded by shades of bluish gray. It was dusk, that time between light and darkness when the air itself seems impenetrable and details turn indistinct. "I'm sorry," I said.

"Thank you."

"You may still have a chance . . ."

"Yes," Tom sighed, "but timing is vital. Politicians have to see what's in it for them. Agreeing to it now, after putting Powerhouse 3 on line, McKinley would have been riding a path to glory, as it were. After what's happened, I doubt he'll be in that frame of mind again. I could simply go ahead with the plan on my own, of course. But it's so complicated, setting up the lines, increasing our output. It would be a massive project, and I'm not sure I can manage it without federal support."

I said the unsayable: "If he dies, perhaps Mr. Roosevelt would . . ."

"Perhaps," he agreed.

"Tom, on Wednesday, when I was at the reception for the McKinleys, Mr. Rumsey indicated that, well, that if you didn't give up on this idea . . ."

"Curious, isn't it," Tom observed after a moment, "that men like Rumsey and even Albright think of you as the best conduit to me?" Quickly, in case I'd mistaken this for an insult, he touched my arm. "I'm well aware of these indications, so please don't worry yourself."

He said no more. Mr. Sheehan brought out a kerosene lamp to light the garden, and uncharacteristically Tom didn't acknowledge him. Although he watched Grace swim, he seemed closed off within himself, and I simply let him be.

On Sunday after church, I went to 184 Delaware Avenue for what had been planned as a postpresidential-visit celebration luncheon for the select. The group was fairly large, perhaps a hundred people. Nonetheless Tom wasn't there (whether he'd been invited I didn't know) and neither was Francesca. Her absence made me ache for her. This was just the sort of event she would have relished in the days before Susannah, and I would have appreciated seeing it through her eyes. I feared I'd lost her forever, her life subsumed into another's. Franklin Fiske was there, however, acknowledging me with a simple nod. It was only a week ago today that he'd proposed marriage, and I felt awkward about facing him so soon. And of course Frederick Krakauer was there, standing in a corner of the drawing room observing everyone. I couldn't stop myself from keeping an eye on him from wherever I went in the room.

The canaries were under lock and key, and the mischievous grand-nieces and nephews were out of sight and hearing. Without the tumult of canaries and children, 184 was a somber place, all dark-wood panel-ing and dark-green wallpaper. The buffet luncheon too was a somber affair. Everyone was nervous, analyzing with an unnatural urgency each bit of news about McKinley's condition. There was no talk of heroes now. Today the conversation had a flickering edge of self-pity that our glorious exposition had been blighted by national tragedy. Hovering in all our minds was the unspeakable question: What if McKinley died?

The only person who seemed to be thriving was Mr. Milburn. He was even more pompous than usual, and his tired, hooded eyes were like a badge of pride—for he was the keeper of that most valuable pos-session, information. With McKinley recovering at his home, Milburn knew as much as the doctors. He apportioned tidbits of news around the room with the same beneficence and discrimination he had dis-played earlier in the summer when dispensing local accommodation for visiting royalty.

After dessert, Dexter Rumsey came to stand beside me in front of the drawing room's unlit fireplace. He didn't say hello, and taking his cue I said nothing to him. For the first time in all the years I'd known him, he looked shaken. I realized that the assassination attempt against the President was what Mr. Rumsey and his cadre must fear above all else: the freak event, unforeseen and unforeseeable, the lone individual, acting out of nothing but his convictions, willing to sacrifice his own life for a cause. Czolgosz was a man who, with nothing to protect, could not be controlled.

Unlike myself. I remained inextricably bound to the very man who had conspired in my ruin, maneuvering to introduce me to President Cleveland right here at 184, ten years ago. I still had to appease him; indeed, behave as though I were grateful to him. After the party at Rumsey Park last week, I'd berated myself for my delusions. For a decade I'd thought myself strong. I'd once made a foolish mistake, but I'd survived it and taken pride in my survival. Then at Rumsey Park I'd learned that my mistake and even my survival had all been plotted for me, as if I were nothing but a character in someone else's story. I felt deeply humiliated that Mr. Rumsey and the men of the board, even Maria Love, had known or at least surmised the most intimate details of my life.

And yet . . . as I'd prepared for the start of school, I'd gradually been able to look back on all I had done not with despair but with some sense of accomplishment. Mr. Rumsey had not given the infant Grace to Margaret and Tom, I had done that, and she had thrived. Mr. Rumsey had made me headmistress at Macaulay, but I was the one who had transformed the school and made it great. Even though I was bound by the chains of my secret, nonetheless I enjoyed a peculiar freedom, of a kind few women ever achieved. Today, standing beside Mr. Rumsey at the fireplace, I felt a hint of independence, as if in spite of all that had happened I too had become a force to be reckoned with.

After a few moments, we were joined by Macaulay board members John Scatcherd, the lumber magnate, and George Urban, Jr., the flour baron. They stood close to us and began to speak—strictly to each other, in one of the oddest interchanges I have ever heard, for they were obviously exchanging information they both already knew.

"I've been told the most incredible story," Urban began. "Incredible, although I do credit its truth."

"What have you been told?" Scatcherd asked rhetorically.

Surreptitiously they both glanced at Milburn, then brought their faces close again. Mr. Rumsey stared across the room, pretending they were nowhere near him.

"Last night, several days' proceeds from the exposition were concealed in the automobile ambulance and taken to Milburn's home."

"Not in the automobile ambulance?" Scatcherd asked indignantly.

"Yes, the same vehicle the President rode in after he was wounded."

They shook their heads at this disrespect.

"The money might have been taken to Williams's home, not Milburn's—my source was unclear on that point, but it's irrelevant." George L. Williams was the exposition's treasurer.

Mr. Rumsey did not countenance financial irregularities. For example, he insisted—as he should—on absolute, thorough precision in the Macaulay accounts I prepared for him each quarter. Although he showed no emotion, in fact no reaction whatsoever to this story, the hiding of money in an ambulance would not please him.

"What did Milburn do with the money?" Scatcherd asked.

"Right then and there, in the middle of the night, he reimbursed some mortgage holders—none of *our* group, of course. It seems he was trying to avoid a sheriff's lien in favor of small vendors."

Their conversation continued. Obviously the exposition suffered from more than cash-flow problems, as Milburn would have us believe. Indeed it was a huge financial failure—that was clear even now, before the exposition closed, and if McKinley . . . died—they didn't say the word, although it was understood—who would pay to visit the exposition then? Promises had been broken, fortunes would be ruined. Carpenters, plumbers, plasterers, the grounds crew—they would never be paid.

"How did this happen?" Mr. Scatcherd demanded. Again the two men glanced surreptitiously toward Mr. Milburn, who held court across the room before a group of ladies eager to learn any minor detail about the President's condition.

Evidently Milburn's place among the chosen was wearing thin.

After telling this story, Urban and Scatcherd each took a half step back from Rumsey and me. As if on cue, other board members joined us. Mr. Larkin forthrightly briefed the still-impassive Mr. Rumsey on a new, "robust" soap scent his company had formulated for the Christmas market, aimed at women buying gifts for their husbands. I took this as a proper moment to escape outside, into the garden.

Miss Love's home was even closer to downtown than Rumsey Park. The formerly extensive grounds had already been profitably sold off, the land subdivided for small businesses in low-rise buildings. The huge, three-story Gothic house seemed to overwhelm its meager plot of land. The garden now consisted of a strip of grape arbor, a path though roses, a birdbath instead of a fountain, and one marble bench half-hidden by shrubbery. Yet the garden remained fragrant, indeed lush, the grape arbor thick enough to conceal me, the roses heavy and profuse.

"Miss Barrett? Miss Barrett, a moment, please."

I turned to find Frederick Krakauer.

"So. Miss Barrett, at last. An honor."

"What do you want?" Suddenly, there amid the roses, I could no longer keep up the pretense of civility that ruled my life. My anger burst from me—not simply anger toward him, but toward Mr. Rumsey too, and toward all the men who tried to control me. "Leave me alone! Why can't you leave me alone?" I shocked myself with these words, but I couldn't stop them. "Why can't you leave the people I love alone? Why can't you just *go away*?"

Krakauer remained silent, his eyes shrewdly evaluating me. Then he spoke. "I regret if I surprised you, coming up behind you like this," he said quietly. "The fact is, you'll be happy to know, your wish is granted: I've come to say good-bye."

"To say good-bye?" I repeated suspiciously.

"Sadly, yes." He sighed in mock regret. "That's the unfortunate part of my job, isn't it? To become involved, to make a difference, and then to say good-bye. It seems I'm needed elsewhere."

"Where?" How far away?

"Ah, my dear lady, that I'm not at liberty to reveal. Well, well, I am sorry to have to say good-bye. To you especially." He lingered over this phrase. Could he possibly have formed a romantic attachment to me, or did he simply regret losing the opportunity to torture me? Or were the two the same to him? "I've enjoyed getting to know you."

Abruptly he turned and went down the path toward the house. I stared at his tweed-covered back. With Krakauer gone, I could let myself believe Grace was finally safe. A sudden, profound sense of relief overwhelmed me. After he entered the garden door, I looked up and saw Mr. Rumsey at the window, studying me. By his very presence he said, this, then, is what I have done for you.

Day by day the medical bulletins about the President became increasingly optimistic. Mrs. McKinley was unexpectedly strong and spent her time as usual, crocheting bedroom slippers for friends and family. The mood in the country stabilized, and a sense of routine developed. Members of the Cabinet were in and out of the Milburn home, maintaining the steady business of government amid the opulent surroundings of the nearby Buffalo Club. The Milburn stables were transformed into a telegraph office. Troops from the Fourteenth U.S. Infantry Corps, recently returned from suppressing the democratic insurrection in the Philippines, roamed the streets, bayonets at hand, but there were no signs of disturbance. Journalists created tent cities on closed-off side streets and purloined lawns. When Secretary of State John Hay arrived for a visit, he rode from the railroad station to the Milburn home in an automobile, to general amazement at this modern choice of conveyance. There was talk of moving the President to the White House on a special Pullman car of the Pennsylvania Line. Mrs. McKinley went for a drive in the park, which was interpreted as an extremely positive reflection of her husband's condition. The President enjoyed some broth. A package of pork and beans was sent anonymously to Czolgosz in jail and it was promptly confiscated in the belief that it was poisoned. Food was an appropriate gift, however, because Czolgosz, according to the police, had an extraordinarily hearty appetite.

Vice President Roosevelt came to Buffalo for a few days to see the President. He behaved with studied informality. After receiving the usual optimistic reports on the chief executive, Roosevelt toured the park zoo, admiring especially the polar bear and the baby elephant. Soon he departed the city, confident that the President was on the mend.

Monday, Tuesday, Wednesday, Thursday . . . bit by bit our civic pride returned. Mercifully we had escaped the stigma of being a city where a president had been murdered. Americans for generations to come would not say "Buffalo" with a mixture of derision and embarrassment. The sense of suspended animation ceased. And although I wasn't yet aware of it, the accepted fact that McKinley would recover brought a recognition of certain realities back to certain people. Plans were formulated. My life was used once more as a weapon in other people's arsenals. On Thursday at 5:00 p.m. a messenger arrived at school from Dexter Rumsey, bringing me a note inviting me to come to his home later that evening to discuss a matter of some importance to Macaulay.

The fine weather had ended that afternoon, and dark storm clouds had come in from Lake Erie. When I arrived at Mr. Rumsey's estate at nine, as he had instructed, the sharp scent of autumn was in the air.

Nine was late for such a meeting, but I wouldn't question Mr. Rumsey's sense of timing. Uundoubtedly he had many obligations pressing upon him.

I ordered the hansom to drop me off at the corner of Delaware and Summer. I felt like walking a bit. I had no reason to suspect anything was amiss. The school year was about to begin, and naturally many matters related to Macaulay would come up. Furthermore, Mr. Rumsey had eliminated the burden of Krakauer, so I had let down my guard. Delicate wrought-iron pineapples decorated the fence around his estate. Pineapples, the symbol of welcome, of a place to call home when one is lost in the wilderness. A light rain began to fall, and I opened my umbrella.

My first intimation that this might not be a routine summons was the sight of a familiar carriage driving out through the front gate as I approached. I thought I recognized Tom's black-haired groom turning onto Delaware Avenue, though with the rain I couldn't be certain. I stared after the carriage for a moment, straining to be sure of its markings, then gave up and turned onto the cobblestoned Rumsey drive. The downstairs maid answered the door and guided me through the wide, shadowed halls to the library. There was no sign of Susan Fiske Rumsey or their children. The house seemed silent, but in the Gothic library there was a big, warm fire that made the room cozy. Mr. Rumsey rose from his chair to greet me, putting down on his desk the leather-bound book he'd been reading.

He was gracious. So very gracious. As if graciousness existed in inverse proportion to the difficulty of the tasks he faced.

"My dear Louisa. Thank you for coming at such short notice." He sat down at the library table and motioned me to the chair opposite. At first he simply smiled at me. Disquieted by his unrelenting gaze, I glanced away, at the books of philosophy that filled the shelves, the books on scientific matters—he was so well read, erudite even, like my father.

"What a week," he sighed. "Well, at least the President is clearly on the mend. But there's been so much to think about. Ever since our walk in the woods at my brother's, well, my dear, I've had so much to think about." He shook his head. Then he stopped. As the silence lengthened, I became aware of the clock ticking on the mantel. Of a dog barking somewhere in the house and being shushed.

So he would force me to speak, force me to inquire. His silence was part of his play of power. "Is everything all right, Mr. Rumsey?"

"Well, thank you for asking. Actually I think things are better now . . . yes, I've come to believe they are. The President is better, and other things are better too. Everything is falling into place."

He paused once more, but this time I kept silent, hoping to put him on edge, to make him take the initiative—this was a small point of course, but my success felt like a triumph: "Yes," he continued at last, "I feel more comfortable now. Perhaps I'll even get a bit of sleep tonight, who knows?" he jested. Hurriedly, but as if offhandedly, he confided, "Mr. Sinclair was here this evening."

"I thought I saw his carriage driving away."

"Did you, then?" Mr. Rumsey seemed surprised, as if this coincidence were somehow improper. "Well, he stayed longer than I expected, that's why your paths crossed inadvertently. He had to stay, because we were having such a very interesting discussion. Did you know he's planning to move to the West?"

"No, he isn't!" I exclaimed, utterly abashed.

Mr. Rumsey appeared confused. "But he told me so himself, this very evening."

"I haven't heard anything about such an idea!" Then I paused to reflect, to caution myself. If Mr. Rumsey was telling me this, it was most certainly true.

"I'm not surprised you haven't heard," Mr. Rumsey continued. "I believe it was decided just today. This evening, in fact. Right here. That's why he stayed so long, sharing the details with me. Which was kind of him. I've never been to the West and it was interesting to see the opportunities through his eyes. Don't be put out that he hasn't told you, my dear. I'm sure he'll let you know in due course."

"I still don't believe it," I insisted—because that was the reaction that would be expected of me, and the only one that would buy me time to absorb the news and figure out its ramifications. I couldn't believe Tom would have made such a decision without consulting me, and yet apparently he had.

"I can understand why he wishes to move on. He's accomplished everything he can here. He's needed much more on new projects out there. Well, that's what happens to ambitious young men, always moving on to the next challenge. We're lucky he's stayed here as long as he has."

Things may happen to him, Mr. Rumsey had warned as we walked in the woods, and this was the result—but better this than the physical danger Krakauer had threatened.

"He plans to take his daughter with him. I offered to let her live here with Ruth, so she could benefit from your continued nurturance and from all Macaulay has to offer, but—"

Like a blow, I comprehended the full import of what Mr. Rumsey was telling me. Without pausing to think I interrupted, "If Grace stays in Buffalo she should stay with me, board with me. I'm her godmother, after all . . ."

"Oh, my dear, that would be quite inappropriate." Condescension edged his voice. "If Grace stays in Buffalo, she will stay with me. With my family, I mean."

I gripped the edge of my chair and forced myself to remain calm and focused. If Grace stayed with Mr. Rumsey, he would hold her as a kind of hostage to Tom's continued compliance. Much better that she go to the West. Tom understood Mr. Rumsey better than I.

"However, the question is irrelevant because he quite insists on taking Grace with him. I feel we should allow him that." So Mr. Rumsey inadvertently let slip the truth of his own involvement. "What an adventure it will be for her," he observed. "For them both. You spent time in the West when you were young, didn't you? I recall you did. How happy you must feel to see her following in your footsteps."

He gave me his benign, frightening smile. What threat had Rumsey used that was strong enough to make Tom capitulate? Tom had withstood even the threats of Krakauer, but now he'd given in. Why?

"Well, well, there's been so much news lately I can barely keep up," Mr. Rumsey was saying. "I'm so pleased that Mr. Krakauer's employer has seen fit to call him away to more pressing duties. I never liked Krakauer, I can tell you now," Mr. Rumsey admitted with a wry look.

"Always tagging along, everyone feeling obligated to invite him every-where—good riddance." Mr. Rumsey waved his hand through the air as though brushing away a fly. As he spoke of Krakauer, I made a decision. If Tom and Grace were leaving, I would leave with them—with *her*, come what may. I would be Mr. Rumsey's pawn no longer. "Mr. Rumsey, I believe after our long acquaintance I may be frank with you."

"I certainly hope so. If ever I can be of assistance . . ."

"If Grace is leaving the city, then I'm sorry to say I must leave with her. I must resign my position at Macaulay. Mr. Sinclair and I have dis-cussed marriage, and I realize you would disapprove, but it remains, well, not a certainty but a possibility between us. But no matter, I must be with Grace, whether married to her father or not."

"Oh, my dear girl," he sighed deeply. "I feared you would say as much." He shook his head sadly. "Now I must say more, and with regret." He took a long breath, summoning the strength to continue. "Here is how it is. Through a great deal of effort, I have saved your daughter's life. I have saved Mr. Sinclair's life. I have maneuvered a compromise. And I have convinced Sinclair to give up his plans to become a Robin Hood."

Rigidly . . . hesitantly, because he waited for the question, I asked, "How have you done that?"

"Through you of course," he replied smoothly.

"Pardon?"

"I simply told him that if he didn't give up his position and his plans, things simply wouldn't go well for you, my dear. Certain facts that we would all prefer to keep private would become common knowledge. I must say Sinclair immediately understood the logic of avoiding this situation—absolutely understood," Mr. Rumsey assured me firmly. "For you see he is a gentleman after all. I hadn't entirely thought so, given his background and whatnot, but now I must accept that he is, for who but a gentleman would sacrifice his own good to uphold the reputation of a lady? Well, well, well." Mr. Rumsey leaned back in his chair. "Everything is resolved, and so neatly too. There'll be a bit of time before Mr. Sinclair can organize himself and the power sta-tion for his departure. At least two weeks. Plenty of time to get everyone acclimated to the idea. We may even arrange a hero's farewell for him." He gazed at me contentedly.

Through this long peroration my shock had turned to rage. Maybe Tom wouldn't fight him, but I would—for if I lost Grace, if she went to the West, I had nothing left to lose. "Mr. Rumsey, perhaps Mr. Sinclair didn't feel comfortable discussing this with you, but I myself have seen proof of bribes being given to state inspectors to make them ignore the extent of water use at the power station. If the public were to learn of this—"

"Oh, please—do not speak to me of bribes," he said with deep frustration. With one hand he rubbed his forehead and eyes, his public mask slipping away. I saw that he was exhausted; he was seventy-four years old, and weakness gnawed at him. "The notion of these bribes has been advertised far and wide. No one has ever proven that there've been bribes—*I've* never seen any proof of bribes. And besides, I haven't heard any groundswell of opposition to the idea of bribes, except from a few discredited nature fanatics—and I praise God that Sinclair managed to get them to discredit themselves, saving me a lot of work in the process."

I had never heard him speak so unguardedly.

"Nobody cares about those bribes—if there were any—and no one ever will."

Abruptly his tone shifted to the gentle and cosseting: "But what are bribes compared to your reputation, Louisa? I have devoted myself to your reputation all these many years."

How he twisted the meaning of words, pretending to one thing while we both knew he meant another—for of course he was the very man who'd created the situation by which my reputation was put at risk. His counterfeit kindness left me chilled.

"I sincerely believe that this is by far the best course. I believe I am protecting you from yourself and from any impetuosity that might carry you away. I only wish the best for you."

Suddenly the room was lit by lightning, and then we heard the crash of thunder. Mr. Rumsey paused, as if to count the seconds, to know how far away the lightning was and whether it was coming closer. I counted too—ever since I was a child I'd counted the beats between the lightning and the thunder. My father and I used to count together during huge electric storms in the mountains of Colorado, when the sky was almost green with rain and I felt I could reach across the valleys to touch the peaks beyond.

Another flash of lightning . . . three seconds to the thunder. Another . . . five seconds. A third . . . four seconds. The storm was hovering over us. Mr. Rumsey said, "Now then," Mr. Rumsey said, "do please accept a ride home in my carriage, won't you? I don't like to think of you out in the rain alone."

The storm continued through the night with increasing ferocity. I didn't attempt to sleep, I didn't even change. Instead I sat in my study turning my choices over and over in my mind. By midnight I decided to walk to Tom's. What did I care anymore that someone might see me entering the Sinclair home at midnight? With Grace leaving me, my reputation seemed worthless—even more so when compared to the goals Tom had given up for me.

During the rain-swept hours, I had made a resolution. I would break loose from the control of men like Dexter Rumsey and take Grace away. With Tom's financial support, escape would finally be possible. We would change our names if necessary. And we would be together. Nothing was more important than that. Once Grace and I had found our freedom, Tom would regain his freedom to do what was right.

While walking through the storm, I reviewed what I would tell him. He would see the reason of it—I knew he would—and he would acquiesce. For how could he raise Grace without me? It wasn't possible. A child must be with her mother, or at least with a woman who cared for her. Even my father relied on my grandmother to maintain our household and tend to my daily needs. Tom would understand this—or so I told myself.

When I arrived at the Sinclair gate, Grace's third-floor lights were off, but the library light was on, so Tom was still awake. The house was no longer guarded. I walked up the path and knocked on the front door. After several minutes Tom himself answered. This was like him, not wanting to wake a member of his staff simply to answer the door when he was up and dressed. He still wore his business suit.

"Ah, Louisa. Come in." He took my folded umbrella and put it in the stand by the door. He helped me to take off my cloak, then hung it, dripping, on the peg in the vestibule. With both hands, he rubbed my shoulders to warm me. "Come into the parlor. I'll light the fire. It's the warmest in the house; I've never been able to figure out why." He sounded very calm. Taking my cold hand, he led me to the parlor and pulled a chair close to the fireplace. In a few moments, the logs were blazing. He closed the parlor door to keep the heat in, so the only light in the room was from the fire, touching us with its glow. He pulled a chair for himself next to mine.

"I assume you know, or you wouldn't have come here."

"Yes. Mr. Rumsey asked to see me at nine. I saw your carriage leaving."

"Did you? I wish I'd realized. I wanted to tell you myself, but I didn't feel comfortable visiting you so late. I see you have no such compunctions about visiting *me*." For an instant he smiled.

I was too upset to respond to his small joke. "Tom, all these hours since I left Mr. Rumsey, I've been thinking . . ." I began the speech I'd formulated in my mind and practiced on the walk over, although it now sounded stiff and trite: "I appreciate what you've done for me, but you shouldn't give in to this. You should fight on. What you're doing is too important. You can't let them win. And besides, if Grace leaves, there's no future left here for me. You must understand that. You go ahead with what you've been planning, and I'll take Grace somewhere. We'll change our names, with your help we won't have any difficulties. If Peter Fronczyk could do it, I . . ." That's where my planned speech ended, and I found I had nothing more to say. I was drained of words and had only the strength to wait for him to agree.

He took my hands within both of his, pressing them together, and blew his warm breath onto my fingers. "I've used these hours to think too, and I'm grateful for what you say. But you see, if you lose your reputation, Grace loses hers as well. No one will chase after Peter Fronczyk, he's not important—not like you and Grace. If you tried to hide, the moment I went to visit the two of you, you'd be discovered and exploited again and again. That's not the kind of future I want for Grace. And you'll need to teach too, or be involved in some kind of work. You wouldn't be happy hidden away in the woods somewhere with a child."

"But—"

"Someday we may decide to marry—who knows? I don't want to worry about this whole sorry story being brought up over and over." His words were firm, but his tone was sad and resigned. "Our only choice is to give in. Accept defeat now, and hope to fight another day."

"How, 'fight another day'?" I felt numb.

He brightened a bit. "This new project I'll be going to, did Rumsey tell you about it?"

I shook my head no.

"It's still in the planning stages, but it's a huge dam project. In a canyon of the Salt River, in Arizona. About seventy miles east of Phoenix. For electricity and irrigation. It's a tremendous opportunity, a tremendous challenge. I'm surprised they offered it to me, all things considered. Shows how desperate they must be for people who can do this kind of work—self-interest never being far from their minds, of course. Grace can visit you here at Christmas, and you can visit us in the summer."

He looked to me for agreement, but he must have seen the unhappiness on my face: He would be leaving for something that was wonderful to him, whereas I would be left here alone. He shook my shoulders gently. "Don't you understand? We can't be victimized by them if we hold on to our own goals as firmly as they hold on to theirs. Keep looking ahead, and we'll see what the future allows us. How old is Rumsey, anyway? In his midseventies, isn't he? Who's going to replace him when he goes? If we hold steady and plot as they plot, we've a chance to win in the end."

He was right. There was no choice but to accept this new burden and try to focus on the times I would see Grace, instead of the times I would not. After a long moment I asked, "Have you told her yet?"

"No. She was asleep when I got home. I'll tell her tomorrow. I hope you'll talk to her soon too."

"Yes."

"Rumsey wants us to go in a few weeks, so we will. What's the point of waiting?"

"Yes." What could I do but agree?

"My deputies will take over the running of the station, each in his own area, and the head of operations will supervise them all. I don't want anyone brought in from the outside who might have different ways of doing things." By this I knew he meant a more stringent approach to the unions.

The telephone rang, jolting us. Tom and I both glanced at the clock on the mantel: 1:30 a.m. The ringing continued. Grace was sleeping safely upstairs, so for once I didn't have to fear for her. Tom and I stared at one another quizzically. Neither of us had grown up with a telephone, so to hear it clanging in the middle of the night—what could this mean?

Tom leaned toward the telephone table and picked up the receiver. His words were clipped: "Hello . . . yes . . . I see . . . of course . . . thank you for calling." He hung up and turned to me.

"That was Albright," he said. "McKinley collapsed this evening. He's in a coma. The doctors say he's dying."

Chapter Thirty-Six

On Saturday, September 14, in the early hours of the morning, President William McKinley died of assassin's wounds. I awoke to the sound of church bells ringing before dawn and immediately I understood. The jovial, kindhearted man I'd shaken hands with, gone now. The city's frank optimism and illusions—delusions—of glory, gone too. The autopsy would show that unbeknownst to anyone, least of all his doctors, gangrene had spread along the path of the bullet through his abdomen. The widowed First Lady was reported to be sitting crouched in a chair, praying for her own death. The nation went into mourning, the newspapers were banded in black. I felt as if I were banded in black too, my private sadness playing out against the public drama on the streets as the President's casket was taken by military escort to lie in state in the City Hall rotunda. My grief would only grow stronger as the days passed.

On Friday I'd been too busy with meetings at school to visit Grace, so it was on Saturday that I finally went to her, feeling my loss already, missing her even though she was still here, preparing myself to be cheerful in her presence. I'd checked out an atlas from the school library and held it cumbersomely in my arms during my walk up Lincoln Parkway. I tried to picture the Salt River, the Arizona Territory, the city of Phoenix—what were these places? To me they were nothing but names on a map, footholds in a wilderness. When I thought of the Salt River, all I could imagine was the Dead Sea, so salty it would hold Grace up if she tried to swim. Sitting with Tom and Grace in children's chairs in the third-floor playroom I feigned a different view, however. "It's like a dream come true, to live in the West!" I enthused. "The mountains are so high that some of them are covered with snow all year round. And the canyons are so deep, sometimes you can't even see the bottom. You're especially lucky, Grace, because you're the perfect age to appreciate everything . . ."

She believed me. Her eyes came alight. "Show me where we'll live," she said excitedly, reaching for the atlas. "How will we get there?" She propped the wide book open upon her knees, and Tom pulled his chair close to hers to trace, page by page, the long train route that would bring them to their new home. The atlas, seldom used, smelled musty and damp, and some of its pages were stuck together, as though the book had survived a flood.

While Tom, Grace, and I studied maps, Vice President Theodore Roosevelt, age forty-two, was sworn in as twenty-sixth President of the United States. The makeshift ceremony took place in the library of the home of Roosevelt's friend Ansley Wilcox. Roosevelt had been fetched to Buffalo from a hiking vacation with his family on Mt. Marcy in the Adirondacks, and he wore borrowed clothes—the trousers of one man, the jacket of another. A silent crowd of several thousand stood outside the house as the oath was administered. In a short speech, Roosevelt promised to uphold the policies of his predecessor "for the peace, the prosperity, and the honor of our beloved country."

School did not begin on Monday as scheduled, because of several days of national mourning. Finally on Wednesday I welcomed back my girls. Instead of the somberness I expected, they showed relief to be gathered once more among themselves, away from eulogies and black bunting and the obsessive reading of newspapers. As the week continued, I sought out Grace each day and observed her in class and with her friends. I saw that her initial excitement was being tempered by sadness as she told her classmates about her move and grasped the reality of leaving. Meanwhile I struggled to convince myself of how valuable the experience would be for her. Over and over like an exercise I forced myself to put aside my own feelings and focus solely on what she would gain.

On the following Saturday morning, I worked at my desk at school as usual. In the afternoon there would be a farewell party for Tom and Grace on Goat Island at the Falls. The party was being given by the workmen from the power station and their families, so I had resigned myself to not seeing Grace today.

"Hello." But there she stood at the door to my office.

"Good morning," I said, surprised and happy that she'd thought to visit me before the party.

"I saw you with my spyglass." She held it up from behind her back.

"I thought you'd be spending this morning getting ready for your party."

Slipping the spyglass into her pocket, she came into the office. "I am ready." She showed off her outfit: blue sailor dress, white stockings, black patent-leather shoes, and a wide-brimmed straw hat, her hair falling in perfect, Mrs. Sheehan-induced ringlets down her back. "We're leaving at one o'clock. Papa had to do some work at his office downtown. Because we're leaving next week. The day keeps getting sooner and sooner."

Yes, the day did keep getting sooner and sooner. Be cheerful, I ordered myself, even though I ached. "Just think of all you'll see on the train trip. You'll cross the Mississippi River! It's wider and browner than you can imagine."

"I know." She walked to the window and stood there, looking out. "At first it seemed exciting, but now I don't want to go. I don't want to be missing my friends. I want to be with them, not missing them. They're more important than the Mississippi River. I want to be with you, not missing you."

At first I couldn't answer her. "I'd rather be with you instead of missing you too, Grace," I finally managed. "But when you come to visit at Christmas, you can tell me all your adventures. I'll give a special party for your class." I bit my lip with the effort of not letting her see my tears. "And even though we'll be far away for a while, I'll still love you, and if we think about each other, we'll still be together."

"When Mama got sick, right before she . . . went away, she told me you'd always be with me and look after me. Because you're my mother in God. And there isn't much difference, is there, between a real mother and a mother in God? At least that's what Mama said."

"No, there isn't much difference." For the first time I wondered, had Margaret guessed the truth, seeing through my subterfuge, noticing the resemblance between Grace and me, as Tom did? Had she been afraid to speak about it to me? Had we therefore kept our mutual knowledge secure from one another, letting the truth separate us when it could have united us? If she did know, however, during her final hours this knowledge must have offered her the most profound consolation possible—she herself would be gone, but Grace would be with her mother still. I prayed now that Margaret had felt such a comfort in those hours when she was still alert, lying in bed in the candlelight, Tom and me struggling to stay awake in chairs beside her, even the nurse dozing. Throughout that final night, she—the soonest to depart—was the only one of us awake to regard the darkness.

Grace began to study the books on my shelves. "There's another reason I'm not very happy today. I mean, not just going away."

"Really? What?" Expecting some childish response, I rearranged the papers on my desk to give myself a moment to regain my emotional equilibrium.

"Papa is angry with me."

"And why is that?"

She turned to look at me, her face oddly blank. "Have I always been such a bad girl as I am now?"

At once I was alert. "Bad girl." This was the phrase she had used with Millicent Talbert on that evening in March when she had talked about killing herself. Automatically I replied, "You're not a bad girl." Then I was brought up short by my recognition that such a pat answer would close her off from me. "What makes you say so?"

"Papa says I'm a bad girl." She breathed deeply, holding back tears.

"What does he say you did, that was bad?"

"I'm not sure I can tell you."

"You should tell me. Who else can you tell?" I said gently.

She gazed at her shoes, moving one foot slightly back and forth, studying the shifting reflections in the patent leather. "Well . . . He came to see me this morning before I got up and before he had to go to his office. He was dressed in his suit and he smelled all clean." She gazed at me hopefully, as if asking me to confirm these facts for her. I nodded in encouragement. "He almost always stops to see me before he goes to work because he usually doesn't get home until after I'm asleep. Anyway, this morning when he came in I was already awake and I was playing with Fluffer. He doesn't like Fluffer sleeping on my bed because she sheds fur all over, but sometimes I let her anyway because she really wants to." She gave me a shrugging smile. "Well, I always let her sleep on my bed. But that's not why Papa said I was bad. He was looking at some drawings I'm doing. Lately he's always asking to look at my drawings. I was showing him everything, especially the people doing things that Miss Riley wanted me to work on before—"

Grace paused, a look of bewilderment on her face as she realized again that Susannah was gone from us. Reassuringly I said, "Yes, I know."

She nodded. "He really liked the picture of you playing the piano," she told me. "And then he found, he found—" Suddenly she began to cry, slowly at first, then the tears burst from her uncontrollably.

I hurried to her and held her close. I pushed back her hat and caressed her hair. "What did he find?" I asked, filled with a sudden fear. "What was it?"

When she calmed enough to speak, she said, "Some papers."

"Papers?" I asked, taken aback. "What kind of papers?"

"Papers from his desk."

"Papers from his *desk*?"

She pulled away and turned to stare out the window again. To study her own house in the distance. "This is the part I'm not sure I should tell you."

"But you must," I insisted.

She knit her brow doubtfully.

"How can I help you, if you don't tell me?"

This she accepted. "Sometimes, because Miss Riley asks me to, I borrow things from his desk. Papers. About water. About the power station. I only borrow them for one day," she said, glancing at me for confirmation that this made it better. "On the mornings Miss Riley is coming to see me for my lesson. I take the papers and hide them with my drawings and then she reads them during my lesson and sometimes copies them."

A picture came into my mind of Daniel Henry Bates standing at the podium at Lyric Hall in May, waving his folded piece of paper and threatening to reveal the names of state inspectors who had been bribed.

"I return the papers before Papa gets home from work. Except the week before last, Miss Riley was supposed to come for a lesson and she never did, because she was . . . and then President McKinley . . . and then we were going away, and everything got into a muddle and I forgot to return the papers." She pressed her face against the windowpane, her breath misting the glass.

With dread, already knowing the answer; indeed the answer was obvious, making me heartsick at my own blindness, I asked, "Did Miss Riley tell you why she wanted to see the papers?"

"To help Niagara Falls."

So it was Grace whom Susannah had meant when she told me she'd had an assistant. A child. The woman's derangement reached even to subjugate a child.

"Miss Riley said she was trying to help Niagara Falls," Grace continued, "so the bad men wouldn't take all the water. Mama wanted to help Niagara Falls too. That's what Mama and Papa were fighting about on the day I interrupted them and surprised Mama and she fell because I surprised her and . . . " She stopped, unable to go on.

I didn't know which strand to follow: Margaret's death after her miscarriage, which we had discussed before, or the "borrowed" papers. I decided, for better or worse, that I should address the papers. I have berated myself over and over, in the years since, that I followed the one strand and not the other. I have berated myself even more for the anger that crept into my voice. "Grace," I said firmly, "didn't you realize your father would be unhappy if he knew you were showing his papers to someone outside the family? Didn't you know that some things have to be kept private?"

"I knew that! But Miss Riley said Niagara Falls was more important. She said I was a 'heroine.' She said almost nobody in the world gets a chance to be a heroine, and now I was one."

I shivered at how close her words were to Tom's when we stood together in the drawing room the morning after the bombing at the power station.

"She said she wouldn't keep tutoring me if I didn't do what she wanted me to do, and I wanted her to keep tutoring me. She said Papa was bad. She said he was more than bad, she said he was evil." She sighed in befuddlement and despair. "But now I'm not so sure, because they put her in the state hospital. Winifred Coatsworth told me that only crazy people get put in the state hospital. Is Miss Riley crazy? Is Papa evil?"

"No, Grace, no. Of course not." Which question was I answering? I couldn't tell. My mind was overwhelmed and reassurance was all I could offer.

"But he was trying to take all the water from Niagara Falls. *That* was evil. Even though Papa doesn't seem evil to me. I mean, he never acts evil—not to me, I mean." She stared at me in confusion.

"I understand how hard it is to figure all this out." And now I did understand: the frailty that Susannah Riley had recognized in Grace— like a thin pane of glass being pressured to the breaking point, she had described it—this frailty Susannah herself had created by forcing Grace into this terrible predicament. "Miss Riley never should have asked you to betray your family."

"Then if Miss Riley's wrong, and she must be wrong because they put her in the state hospital, she's the bad one. So she's bad and Papa's good, and I did the worst thing anyone could ever do. I'm the worst girl . . ."

"But you're a child. You didn't know. You didn't understand. Miss Riley made you do it."

"But at Sunday school they say even children can choose between right and wrong and good and bad. I chose bad."

I felt so tired. "Grace—you can't look at things only as good or bad. Things aren't that simple. You thought you were doing the right thing when you did it. You have to try to see the shades of gray, the way you do when you're drawing, and forgive yourself and promise yourself to do better. That's how God forgives. By seeing the shades of gray. By seeing into your heart, and what you truly feel and what you truly are, deep down. And how you learn from the things you do wrong and try to do right the next time."

Grace seemed to consider this. After a moment I asked, "What did your father say, when he saw the papers?"

She shook her head sharply. "He got so upset that he took hold of my shoulders and started shaking me and shouting. He was scary but at the same time it was like he was crying too—like he couldn't understand how I got to be such a bad girl who would let someone see his papers, especially Miss Riley. Then he stopped shouting and he just said, 'I trusted you, I trusted you,' like he would never trust me again. And he said didn't I know that he was trying to help poor people get electricity to make their lives better, just like Mama would have wanted him to, and I made it harder for him to do that by showing the papers to Miss Riley. Now we were leaving and he wouldn't be able to do it at all except maybe somewhere else. And then he got angry all over again and—and—the look on his face, Aunt Louisa, like he was going to kill me. And then he slapped my face—he never did that to me before—and then he looked as if he was going to do it again, but then he just turned away and said I had to stay in my room until it was time for us to go to the party." She stopped.

"And then?"

"He left. He shut the door behind him. He didn't lock it, though, so I guess he trusted me to do what he said and stay in my room. But I'm such a bad girl I didn't even do that. After a while, I heard the downstairs door and I looked out the window and saw him drive away in the carriage. I knew he was going downtown to work, so I knew there'd be a few hours before he got home. I waited awhile more and then went down the back stairs and snuck out without anyone seeing me and I came here." Again she sighed. "Do you think he'll forgive me?"

"Yes, Grace." I was quick to promise forgiveness, but what else could I say? "He loves you. I know he'll forgive you. Shall I talk to him?"

She brightened. "Will you?"

"Yes."

"I knew I was right to come to see you."

"You must always come to me if you're worried about something—or write to me," I quickly corrected myself. "We'll create the most wonderful collection of letters while you're away."

That look of expectation and eagerness which I cherished so much came into her face. "I promise to write every detail of what I'm seeing, so it'll be like we're seeing everything together. Even the Mississippi River!" she added, trying to please me.

"Yes." I rubbed my forehead in exhaustion. "I hope so."

She glanced out the window again. "Look how the leaves are turning yellow." It was true. Autumn was sneaking up on us. Grace took her spyglass from her pocket and pressed it against the glass. "I've never spied on my house from here—have you ever done it?"

I managed a laugh. "I have looked over at your house and wondered how you are, Grace. But I've never taken a telescope and tried to look in the window."

"But you can! You can borrow my spyglass! I'll leave it here for you. You can keep it as long as you want. Until we leave, I mean. You can look into our house anytime. I'll tape messages on the windows for you—secret messages, no one will be able to read them but us!" Unexpectedly she became solemn. "I wish Mama was with us. Don't you?"

I placed my hand upon her shoulder. "Yes, Grace, I do. I think of her often."

"I do too. Do you remember how when fall came Mama used to take me out to rake leaves because there were always so many everywhere, more than Mr. Duffy could manage—like an ocean of leaves, Mama used to say, and we'd rake them up until we had huge piles and then we'd fall back into them and lie there and watch the sky?"

"Yes, Grace, I remember." And when Margaret stood up from a leaf pile, there were leaves stuck in her hair and clinging to the back of her cloak. Grace too had leaves in her hair, shocks of red and brown against the yellow of her hair, and they used to brush them off one another, first Margaret brushing Grace, then Grace brushing Margaret.

"Sometimes I hear Mama's voice telling me what to do. She always gives the best advice." Grace smiled even as tears filled her eyes once more. "I don't mean I really hear her voice; I imagine her."

"I understand."

"Sometimes I think if I imagine her enough, then she'll really be there. Not like a ghost, I mean like an angel." Her expression turned ineffably sad. "Sometimes I wonder if she'll be able to find me after we move. I'll be going to new places where I won't ever have been with her, and she won't ever have been there, either. She might not be able to find me."

"She'll always find you, and you'll always find her, because she's in your heart."

She regarded me quizzically.

"You have her inside you, in your soul."

"Then she's not an angel?"

"An angel is . . ." But I couldn't fight my way out of this quagmire, so I surrendered to her simple Sunday school faith. "Angels never get lost, Grace. They follow you wherever you go."

"Oh, good," she said, apparently happy again. I exhaled in relief. So much of my energy was devoted to the process of ensuring that she was happy, as if the mere fact of her happiness could redeem the sorrow of her conception.

"Sometimes I think I'm so bad that I wish I wasn't even alive anymore. I wish I could just be dead. Then I'd be with Mama forever and I wouldn't have to worry about what was right and what was wrong."

Suddenly I felt light-headed, as if I would faint, every fear I'd ever had for her fused into this moment. I groped for what to say—what *could* I say, to stop her from having such thoughts? To make her want to live instead of die? "Oh, Grace, please don't talk that way, about not wanting to be alive anymore," I implored. "I couldn't live if you weren't alive." This was my one chance—perhaps my only chance—to help her, but in my shock and anxiety, I didn't know what to say . . . I didn't know where to begin. "Grace, it's a terrible sin, a terrible, terrible sin, for someone to take their own life. God never forgives it. Never. People go to hell for it. You can't be buried in hallowed ground." What was I doing, invoking hellfire, citing the teachings of the Church, doctrines I didn't even believe in? Whatever was I thinking of? But I was desperate to reach her, and I didn't know what else to say. "Your father and I, we couldn't . . ."

"It's all right, Aunt Louisa," she said, patting my arm solicitously. I could see by her concerned expression that she was more affected by the drama of my emotions than by her own worries. She giggled nervously. "I meant only that sometimes I *wish* I was dead, not that I . . ."

My clock chimed twelve noon.

"Oh, Aunt Louisa!" In an instant her face was flushed with excitement. I was stunned by the shift in her mood. "I have to go. We're leaving at one, and I don't want Papa to figure out that I didn't do exactly what he told me and stay in my room the whole entire time! You won't tell him I came to see you, will you, Aunt Louisa?" she asked. I felt as if my mind couldn't keep up with her, as if she'd leapt far ahead of me.

"No, Grace, of course not," I promised helplessly. "I won't tell him."

"And you're sure he'll forgive me? About the papers, I mean?"

"Yes, Grace. I'm sure."

"Thank you!" She gave me a quick hug, then bounded out, eager and happy.

I let her go.

Chapter Thirty-Seven

I never knew precisely what happened that afternoon at Goat Island. How could I? I wasn't there. God at least granted me that mercy. I heard only interpretations. Hearsay, which I painstakingly wove together like skeins of yarn for a tapestry. Even if I had been there to see it, would I have had a clearer comprehension of it than anyone else? Of course not. I would have seen only my own sliver of truth, as everyone else saw theirs.

Many people realized that something was wrong and ran to help. There were many witnesses, as the newspapers put it, but the waters are treacherous, and there was nothing anyone could do. Every witness said—every single one—that she slipped. She was playing a game. All the children were playing. On the rocks. By the cascades.

The center of the party was on Goat Island itself. That's where the food was laid out, sliced turkey and ham, bread and cheese, cold chicken, and cake for dessert. The type of food that's easy to eat at a picnic. The drinks were laid out on Goat Island too. There was nothing stronger than beer, which was for the men. The women and children had unfermented apple cider. The children bobbed for apples, and someone had brought a cider press for them to use. Grace used it, or so I read in the newspaper. She pressed three apples and then enjoyed the fresh juice.

As at most picnics, groups wandered off, congregating here and there, forming and re-forming from one place to the next. With a group of mothers and children of about her age, with some younger ones in tow too, Grace sat on the banks of Goat Island near the bridge to Asenath, the first of the Three Sisters. The waters are quiet there, at the Hermit's Cascade. I remembered that I'd pulled Franklin back from wading there—out of irrational fear, not reason. The afternoon turned hot. Of course it was all right for Grace to take off her shoes and socks, to sit on a rock and wet her feet. The mothers allowed it. All the children did it.

Tom wasn't watching Grace, but he didn't need to. She was old enough to place limits on herself and even self-control didn't necessarily matter because so many mothers were there. Tom made certain, before he went off with the men—congratulating them for the years of work they had shared in creating the greatest hydropower project in the country, if not the world—he made certain the mothers knew they were to watch Grace. Besides, it wasn't a man's job to watch a child. No one blamed him for what happened, though he blamed himself—through all these years he's blamed himself. The children were watched, Grace was watched. Even at the moment when she took the greatest risk, she was being watched.

She'd been explaining to the younger children how the Three Sisters Islands got their name. She decided to show them how—to do what the daughters of General Parkhurst Whitney had done in 1816. Excitedly, she stepped into the water before anyone realized what she was doing. The water there is calm, the cascade is lovely, but the current is treacherous. Nonetheless she walked across to Asenath, thus proving that what the three sisters had done could still be done today.

The mothers didn't like her walking across to Asenath. They consulted together in Polish or Russian or Italian or whatever language they had spoken in the countries of their birth, each group unto itself. But the mothers were reluctant to say anything to her in English because she was Mr. Sinclair's daughter. They couldn't bring themselves to criticize or correct Mr. Sinclair's daughter. They didn't want to overstep their position or give Mr. Sinclair cause to be angry with their husbands, even if he was leaving soon. And Grace was so self-possessed and confident, they convinced themselves that she was safe. Yes, the mothers convinced themselves that she knew what she was doing. Born and bred as she was in this part of the country, she must have more knowledge than they did. Or so they told themselves.

Nonetheless, as a subtle way to curb her, one mother asked Grace if she'd ever been to the Hermit's Cascade before. Grace said yes, her mother used to bring her here. Then the women, one after another, asked about her mother. They had heard tell of Margaret: the good she'd done, the compassion she'd shown. Grace said her mother was an angel now, and sometimes, if she spun around quickly and then stopped suddenly, she could see her mother like a glow at the edge of her vision. Then Grace did spin around—around and around as she had that day at the cemetery after the spring blizzard. Standing on the riverbank, she spun and spun, determined to make herself dizzy. When she tried to stop herself—to stop suddenly, to see Margaret at the periphery of her vision—she slipped on the slick black rocks of the shoreline. She was barefoot . . . she was spinning . . . she tried to stop . . . she slipped—it all happened in one graceful movement, like a ballet. Graceful Grace. She fell backward into the water.

Later the coroner surmised that her head hit the rocks on the bottom. When she surfaced, witnesses said she was initially dazed, and the current pulled at her. Only seconds later—when they realized she wasn't faking—the mothers began screaming. Inexorably, the current began to draw her under the water again and downstream. She struggled to right herself, but she was in the middle of the stream now, and the more she struggled the more the current imprisoned her, pulling her into deeper waters, pulling her under. Even men were screaming now at the bank. One of them found a broken tree branch and lay it upon the water for her to grasp, but she was panicked by then and couldn't reach it. She came to rest some twenty-five yards away, on the Goat Island side, in a serene, gentle cove, face down amid the reeds. Her hair floated in a perfect circle around her head.

This was the story Tom told me when he came to me late that night. I was in my study reading the first essays the seniors had written for our philosophy class, and I was marking up the papers in frustration at their simplicity and brevity. Then I heard the knock. Perplexed at a visitor arriving so late, I hurried to the door. As soon as I saw him—his ashen, contorted face—I knew something horrifying had happened. He told me the story there at the doorway, struggling to stop himself from weeping. At first what he said made no sense. Then, once I understood the meaning of the words, I didn't believe him. And then finally when I comprehended the actuality, the truth of what he was saying, I felt a kind of paralysis come upon me, imprisoning me from the outside, as if the air were too heavy for me to push my body through. I could only watch, not move. I have little memory of what I did during the rest of that evening. Little memory at all.

Chapter Thirty-Eight

I passed the weeks after Grace's death in a daze. I recollect people coming up to me at school, on the street even, offering condolences, their faces familiar although often I could not recall who they were. There was a funeral of course, at Trinity Church. A burial on a hillside at Forest Lawn, beside Margaret. At both services I was only a godmother, allowed to stand near the front of the crowd next to her godfather, Mr. Albright, but not at the very front where Tom and the Winspears stood. I tried not to let anyone see how much I cried.

After the burial Mr. Rumsey—kind, generous, as supportive as a father—took my elbow, led me to his carriage, and drove with me to the Albright estate because Mr. Albright as her godfather was giving a luncheon in her honor. No children attended this luncheon. Amid the board members and their wives, Miss Love, the Winspears and their friends, and various businessmen who'd worked with Tom, I heard no commemoration of Grace. For these people she had become merely an excuse for a party, an opportunity to lunch with Mr. Rumsey. My friends weren't here, not Francesca, not Elbert, for what right did I have, as godmother, to invite my friends to this luncheon? Even though none of Grace's schoolmates was there to remember her, the Albright house seemed to burst with children, "three under four," Susan Albright described them at the club. Their nannies shooed them away from the guests, and their tears or laughter were heard from corridors, or from outside as they played chasing games across the lawns—reminding Tom and me, as we stood silently side by side at the windows to stare at them, of what we'd lost.

Turning to Tom, I studied him, the strong features, the pale brown hair, and a memory pushed through of the night he'd come with the news about Grace. We'd gone into my study, and he had begun to cry. As a sense of disassociation seeped through me, bewilderment was all I'd felt. Who was this large person, weeping in my arms, telling me that he'd done this dreadful deed, telling me that through neglect he'd murdered our daughter? As that night wore on, I'd felt myself separating from him, not because I blamed him, but because there was no room inside me for any feeling but the loss of Grace.

That day I realized Tom and I would never marry. Not because of the machinations of others, but because Grace would be always between us. Indeed she *had* always been between us. Tom and I had always known one another through Margaret and later through Grace; to one another we had been simply necessary adjuncts to the people we truly loved. Nonetheless I felt connected to him, because of all we had shared and the memories we had in common; I trusted we would remain friends.

Within a week, Tom closed the house, paid the staff for a month, arranged for a caretaker, and left the city. He wasn't ready yet actually to sell the house. He spoke briefly of giving it to Macaulay, so the tennis court could become the school's and the formal garden turned into a place for girls to play field hockey. He smiled a bit at the thought of a troop of girls playing field hockey across his lawns, but held off making a final decision. In the meantime, he took very little with him. He was accustomed to moving from one place to the next, he explained. He gave me the keys so I could sort through Grace's things, which we would donate to the Fitch Crèche, and then he went to hide himself in the West. He had his cause, and gradually it seemed to sweep him up in its embrace, allowing him some respite, at least, from the anguish he suffered each day. Yes, he continued to blame himself. Years have gone by and have not relieved Tom of the burden of blaming himself.

I was luckier. I hadn't been on Goat Island that day. I couldn't hold myself immediately responsible for her well-being at the picnic. Nevertheless, night after night I imagined her death, the image of it twisting through my mind, my imagination supplying every detail. I never realized how fervent my imagination could be, until it filled in the feel of the wind and the warmth of the sun and the whiteness of her skin, as a doctor (who happened to be on a visit to the Falls) tried to resuscitate her on the shore. Soon I found as much blame to put upon myself as Tom did: I should have gone with her to the Falls that day, even though I hadn't been invited and my presence would have been inappropriate. I should have disciplined her more strongly from the time she was little. I should have, I should have . . . Every day of her life played over in my mind as I searched for ways I might have saved her. But then again, she'd always been heedless, boundless, rushing from one place and one thought to the next. Tom and Margaret were reluctant to curb her, offering only love to restrain her. And my love for her, well, it was different from the love I gave my students. For them I held the firm stance, the rational evaluation, the commitment to make them sit still and listen. With Grace I could never muster such resolve.

Over the years I have come to believe that there was a certain inevitability about what happened to her. Her *being* created her death. Because of the way she was, she died the way she did. Accident followed character—the character which put her on the rocks to begin with. Accident followed society—the watching mothers who were afraid to offend the daughter of their husbands' employer. And it also followed medical knowledge, which was so limited that a woman who suffered a miscarriage had a good chance of dying from it, and eventually her death destroyed the child she left behind. If Margaret had been at that party, Grace may have splashed in the water, but she never would have been allowed to spin on the rocks. But of course she would have had no need to spin on the rocks, for she only did that to create a fleeting vision of the woman she missed so much . . .

Such were the thoughts which coiled ceaselessly through my mind, leading always back to myself. What if I hadn't given her to Margaret and Tom? What if I'd stayed with her in New York City among the faceless masses? Would we have done better, perhaps, living in a room attached to a schoolhouse on a prairie in Kansas, where I would call myself a widow? Or somewhere in the South, where I could have taught the children of freed slaves? Would we have done better alone together in Chicago or San Francisco or in any city wild enough and new enough that the only thing that mattered was what you could do in the here and now, not what you'd been or done in the past?

But of course I hadn't made that decision. I'd done what had seemed best at the time—best for Grace, for the tiny infant that she was, helpless and vulnerable. Eventually I accepted that I was right to give her to Margaret and Tom; or at least I became reconciled to the fact that she'd had a good life in their care. Perhaps the problem was that the circumstances of her life were too easy. The horse, the art studio, her every desire met. If she'd had to work in a factory, as many girls did at her age—a textile factory, say, in the Carolinas—would she have had time to spin in circles to recreate her lost mother?

What is the measure of a child? Why does one survive and another not? What is the measure of a mother? How have I endured these years? I don't know. But my nature has always been to keep going, to work on from day to day. Grace's nature was riskier than mine. And so each morning the sunrise surprises me—that I am still here to see it, when Grace is not. On my bedroom windowsill I keep the spyglass she left behind. Every now and again I pick it up, as if by holding it I could hold her, as if by looking through it I could find, there in the distance, a note she'd placed for me upon her window.

In the immediate aftermath of Grace's death, I, like Tom, had my cause to keep me moving forward. Apart from the funeral, I couldn't take time off from school. Godmothers didn't need to take time off, to go into retreat, to let mourning consume them. It was just as well that I was busy all day. Grace could fill my mind only at night, when I tried to fall asleep, or in the middle of the night, when suddenly I woke and remembered she was gone, or in the early morning, when the time came to rise. Each day I made myself get out of bed, get dressed, brew tea, and drink it because teachers, staff, and students were waiting for me, depending on me, asking me questions from 8:00 a.m. until 6:00 p.m., awaiting the decisions I made for them—one decision after another, all through the day, pushing Grace's face, her words, her being, out of my mind.

Even my friends couldn't help me. Francesca visited, but I couldn't confide to her the level of my grief. I never wanted to hear her say, "She was only your goddaughter, you've got to get over it." Concealing the truth from Francesca became irrelevant, however, because within a few weeks she was gone: She'd managed to get Susannah released from the hospital and together they were on their way to Angkor Wat, the two of them transformed into female explorers attired in khaki skirts and followed by a line of bearers.

Franklin came to see me, and he too was unaware of my shattering grief. As usual he arrived in time for tea, which we had in my study because of the early autumn chill.

"I'm sorry about your goddaughter."

"Thank you." I kept my hands folded in my lap. I had begun doing that lately, so I could squeeze my hands together tightly, painfully, if ever I needed to stop myself from crying.

"She was always wild, though," he observed. He shook his head in sadness.

"Yes."

"I mean, at least she seemed to me—" He stared at me with perplexity, obviously trying to gauge my reaction, but I steeled myself to remain impassive—impassivity was now the mask I wore each day. "I meant no offense to her memory."

"Of course not, Franklin," I said generously. "You're right, she was wild. Sometimes. Now then," I said, clapping my hands together and briskly changing the subject, "what have you been doing?"

He sighed in apparent relief that our required commemoration of Grace was complete. "Well, frankly, I've been annoyed. I'd thought this would be the ideal time to publish all my revelations about Niagara, especially what with Sinclair forced out, but lo and behold the death of McKinley has rendered irrelevant all other news from the Niagara Frontier. There isn't any more space in people's minds right now, my editors inform me, for stories that include the dateline 'Buffalo.'"

I paused to take this in. I was finding it slow-going lately, to comprehend even the simplest explanations. "So what will you do?"

"Bide my time, I suppose. See if anything else strikes my fancy. Ingratiate myself with the new operators out at the power station, in case they have anything useful"—he raised his eyebrows meaningfully—"to offer me later on. Some of what I do depends on you."

"It does?" I asked, feigning surprise, though I wasn't at all surprised that he'd brought the conversation around to this.

"One of my cousins once told me that many girls make it a point of honor never to accept a man unless he's proposed three times."

"I'm not a girl." I smiled ruefully to hear the outrage in my voice, and I realized that most likely I would never marry. Not Franklin, not anyone. I didn't think I'd ever have the strength to open my soul to anyone to the extent that marriage, to me at least, required.

Smoothly Franklin shifted the conversation to some gossip he'd heard at a party, to the new topics he was considering for his next story (while not leaving Niagara behind for good, of course), and my interest waned. Soon I found I could barely register the words he said. Eventually he rose to leave, and I was grateful to be alone once more.

The first Monday of October, just two weeks after her death, my salon resumed, as it always did. I couldn't postpone, to do so would reveal a period of mourning unseemly for a mere godmother. But I was glad of the salon, in the end. So many came to show me support. How many of the board came pretending not to know the truth about Grace I couldn't tell, but what did it matter? They were there for me. Mr. Rumsey arrived early and stayed to the end, as did Franklin, who engaged Mr. Rumsey in passionate conversation about, of all things, the Rumsey herd. In November, the exposition land would be bulldozed and sold to developers to create upper middle class housing. Would those famed cattle never return to western New York for him to admire? Franklin wondered. Mr. Rumsey regarded Franklin with bemusement and confessed that the herd would remain at the Rumsey ranch in Wyoming, where it had found refuge during the exposition. From the way Franklin kept glancing to find me—to know where I was in the room at each moment—I couldn't help but think this conversation was staged for my benefit. Was he trying to prove to me how well he fit in? I already knew. Were Franklin and Mr. Rumsey in some sort of collusion about me? After the levels of collusion I'd previously experienced, I wouldn't let myself be bothered by that. Nonetheless I appreciated Franklin's concern. He looked terribly handsome, almost exotic, beside Mr. Rumsey, that paragon of ministerly rectitude. I could recognize Franklin's attractiveness while still knowing I wouldn't act on it.

Elbert arrived, and after giving me a quick hug devoted himself to business matters with the other guests, making notes on his little pocket pad. Watching him, I smiled inwardly. Wherever he went, he was always, and unapologetically, himself. I'd invited the Talberts and they came, which flattered me considerably. The only notable absence was Mr. Milburn. The week before, his portrait at the Buffalo Club had been defaced (every past president of the club had his portrait displayed in those hallowed halls). This act of revenge for the exposition's losses was not Mr. Rumsey's style, but was most likely committed by younger men whose fortunes were less secure to begin with and were gone now. In early 1902, Milburn, rendered an outcast, would move to New York City.

The autumn passed. School brought its usual rewards and frustrations. The holidays were soon upon me. Mr. Rumsey invited me to Christmas dinner with his extended family at Rumsey Park, which was kind of him, and I did appreciate the company on that always difficult day for spinsters. In the past I would have spent the day with Margaret, Grace, and Tom, or with Francesca.

I used the school break between Christmas and New Year's to sort through Grace's things. The house was lonely with dust covers on the furniture. While I went through the closets and shelves brimming with her possessions, I felt a pang of guilt that I hadn't done this before Christmas so the children at the Crèche could have these things as presents. But I consoled myself that they would enjoy them just as much at New Year's. Some things I left at the house: her drawings of course; the infant clothes which Margaret had put aside in a special box to save; and her hats, which reminded me of the tilt and turn of her head. I took nothing home with me, for I couldn't bear to be reminded of her any more than I already was.

In January, Miss Love requested my presence for lunch at 184, just the two of us, as her way of thanking me for the donation to the Crèche. We talked about the after-school vocational program she was instituting for older children at the Crèche—"Get them started on the proper path while they're still controllable!" she explained. We talked about the memorial to President McKinley that was being proposed for Niagara Square. We talked about a replacement for Francesca at the Infants' Asylum (mercifully Miss Love did not ask me to fill the position, showing more sensitivity than I'd given her credit for). We talked about anything but Grace. To distract myself from my memories, I offered my slice of lemon cake to a yellow canary who was as fat as a powder puff. As I watched him eat, I thought how much Grace would have enjoyed the sight. I could almost feel her squeezing my hand in the pleasure of it, knowing we must not reveal any giggles or even smiles to Miss Love, who regarded the feeding of her canaries as nothing but their due.

I kept myself close to home during the early winter, but ironically, as the February cold gripped the city and snow encased the ground, I felt ready to get out a bit. In that spirit, I accepted an invitation from Mary Talbert to visit the conservatory in Olmsted's South Park, not far from the steel mill at Stony Point. At first I queried her about the desti- nation of our excursion: a botanical garden in February? Yes, she insisted. We would go only on a sunny day, and I would be surprised. So on a sunny Saturday we took the train, hiring a carriage when we arrived at the Lackawanna station.

Surrounded by snow, the conservatory seemed like an overgrown dollhouse, its arches and cupolas lending it an Anglo-Indian look, like a play-palace built for the daughter of a rajah. Inside, the conservatory was warm and humid. Walking through the central, domed pavilion with its palm trees, and on into the orchid collection, Mrs. Talbert asked me a simple question, as simple as something like "How are you?" or "You haven't seemed yourself lately." Without taking time to think or reason, I began to unburden myself to her. I told her every- thing: the night at the Iroquois Hotel, the birth of Grace in New York, my decision to give Grace to Tom and Margaret, the blame I placed upon myself for Grace's death. I was prepared for her judgment, for her condemnation that I'd been so naive as to go with Gilder that night. But she offered only sympathy, revealed by a kind of density in her eyes which welcomed me toward her soul. "How strong you've always had to be," she said. "Much stronger than me." And I felt for her a kind of surge that I can only describe as love.

Near the end of our visit, as we left the fern and hydrophyte house with its two-story waterfall, she turned to hold the door for me. A gaudily dressed young couple nearby nodded sagely to one another. I realized that Mary's holding the door had answered a question for them. They had been taken aback to see a well-dressed Negro woman walking with a well-dressed Caucasian. Now they understood that Mary was my maid, and all was well with the world.

Mary raised her eyebrows in good humor. "There you are, ma'am," she said in an ersatz southern accent before letting the heavy door close directly in the couple's faces. How we laughed afterward. Sitting side by side on the train ride home, I studied her profile, the golden skin, the rounded cheeks, the straight nose, the warm half-smile, and I felt—here is my friend, the friend I have yearned for since Margaret died—but even closer, because I have trusted her with everything important to me. I have confided all and found acceptance. A friend now, finally, to call my own.

Epilogue

Early September, 1909

T his year, Grace would be graduating from Macaulay. She would be seventeen, applying to college; Margaret would be making arrangements for her coming-out party. If only Margaret had lived, if only Grace had lived. I stand now by the lake in Delaware Park where Karl Speyer drowned. Looking across the water, I see the cemetery hillside where Margaret and Grace are buried. Although I cannot actually see their graves, I do see them in my mind: the angel that marks Margaret, the child holding a water pitcher that marks Grace. So many hopes, brought to naught, commemorated only by stone.

And yet, I reassure myself that I've been blessed in these past years by those who have lived, one after another fulfilling dreams I'd nurtured for them. Maddie Fronczyk is a physician who works with Dr. Alice Hamilton in Chicago in the new area of industrial medicine. I used Tom's endowment to fund her medical education. Millicent Talbert is in training to be a pediatrician. During this past summer, she worked at a Negro settlement house in Richmond, Virginia. I feared for her safety in the South, but Mary tells me that Millicent doesn't recognize personal risk; she seems to have overcome the fear of risk on that summer's night eight years ago. Abigail Rushman has stayed on at East Aurora with the Roycrofters and is one of their most skilled book designers. I see her at the club now and again when she visits the city, though she never refers to the necessity that took her to East Aurora and greets me with no special acknowledgment of gratitude or memory. Which is how it should be. She is a professional now, confident in her path. She has not married.

After several years in the Orient, Francesca returned to the city alone. Susannah, she told me, had confessed to her the murders of Speyer and Fitzhugh and then disappeared in Singapore. Francesca explained to those who asked that Susannah had died of an Asian fever—"so dreadful, those Asian fevers," she said forthrightly at my salon. Despite Francesca's homecoming, Mary Talbert has remained my closest friend, even as she travels widely for her work against discrimination and lynching.

Tom did donate his home to Macaulay, and now girls play field hockey across his lawns. He asked that a small plaque be put on the gate: "The Margaret and Grace Sinclair Campus of the Macaulay School." I would have preferred not to have the plaque, with its daily reminder of their loss, but of course I acquiesced. Recently the board has been encouraging me to move into the house, so that my home, beside the school, can be converted into classrooms for our growing student body. Over three hundred fifty girls will attend Macaulay this year, as we welcome more daughters of the professional class and the burgeoning middle class, who can now afford—and desire—the level of education Macaulay provides. But I'm not tempted by Sinclair House. I fear I would wake in the night and imagine Grace or Margaret on the stairs.

There have been deaths too, of course. President Cleveland died last year, but his passing left me strangely unmoved; I felt as if I had long since left him behind. Touching me more personally, Mr. Rumsey died in 1906, at the age of seventy-nine. I found that I missed him, his steadiness, his quiet yet reassuring presence. Oddly, I no longer felt anger toward him. I had reached a plateau in my own life that allowed me to offer him forgiveness. After his death, no one was capable of stepping into his place as leader of the city, and a fluidity and diversity entered our midst, much as Mr. Rumsey himself had foreseen. The directorship of my board now rotates from member to member each year, and the power vacuum regarding Macaulay, at least, has been filled by me. The board looks to me for my opinion, and defers to it— for wasn't I close to Mr. Rumsey, didn't he trust me always? Thus part of his power has become mine.

Franklin Fiske has continued reporting for the *World*, roving from one story to the next. He passes through Buffalo frequently, and when he's here he always comes to see me. He has never married, but of course he is never long enough in one place to marry. I sense him hovering still, waiting for any move, any approach I might make toward him, unwilling perhaps to risk that crucial third proposal until he is certain of success. Sometimes, every now and again, I find myself imagining a life with him, but I've never told him this.

Tom continues work on the Salt River Project in Arizona. Construction began on the massive Roosevelt Dam in 1903, under the Federal Reclamation Act, and continues. With its federal support, the project is intended to aid the common people of the area rather than industrialists. Tom and I exchanged letters frequently at first, and then less often but still regularly. He hasn't remarried. The last time I heard from him, he reported that he's made Peter Fronczyk (now an experienced engineer) his second in command. Somewhat wistfully, it seemed to me, Tom wrote that Peter still believes that through his work he creates on earth the light of God.

The light of God. Often I catch myself wondering, what would Grace be like now, if she'd grown up? Would she be tall for a woman, as I am? Slender, lithe, her still-blond hair pulled back and up? Of course by now her hair may have darkened to pale brown, but I think not. Mine hasn't darkened, after all. Or instead of being lithe, she might be strong and firm, a horsewoman, for she always loved horses. She might be a fine artist too, planning to continue her training at an art school in Europe—in Paris, perhaps, and next summer I would visit her there. Would she have beaux already? Of course she would (no one serious yet, I hoped), boys from the finest families, a Rumsey, or a Cary.

In recent years I've enjoyed such fantasies about her. Such fantasies bring me pleasure, not pain. They lighten my being. More than once Miss Atkins has caught me smiling for no apparent reason in the front hall at school, where we are surrounded by girls hurrying to class, and teasingly brought it to my attention. Except for the anniversary of her death, I almost never imagine Grace slipping on the rocks at Niagara. I don't believe the Church's teachings about heaven, and I don't believe in angels—not as physical entities, the way Grace did—so I don't know where she is now, and I don't sense her presence with me. Nonetheless each year she has grown up for me along with her classmates, along with Winifred Coatsworth and Ruth Rumsey. When I see them, their hair pinned up, their long skirts rustling, I see her. I see what she would be. She is a young lady now.

September. Once again the faculty is gathering for the autumn term, and the students will arrive next week—those girls whose minds must be opened for the good of the city and the nation. Thus has God given me a second chance at motherhood, granting me the ability to forgive myself and offering me redemption.

In the calm waters of the park lake, there is a mirror of the sky, dense blue and touched by a dazzle of radiant, gray-bottomed clouds. My city's sky, a gift from the shifting currents and ever-changing winds of the Great Lakes, those vast inland seas, the source of our prosperity here at the place where shipping lanes converge with rail lines and electricity flows unending. I am poised between water and sky, in the park that Olmsted made, in the city that grain made—grain and lumber, steel and iron, their inexhaustible abundance granting us a riot of skyscrapers and mansions.

One last time I breathe deep the sweet scents of fresh-cut grass and thickly laden trees. Then I turn toward home and school—an unassuming, unremarkable woman in high-collared navy-blue dress, a blank slate upon which anyone might write anything whatsoever.

Historical Note

T he struggle to preserve Niagara Falls was the first major environmental battle in the United States. In 1906, the preservationists appeared to achieve victory when Congress passed the Burton Act, which strictly regulated the amount of water which could be diverted from the Niagara River for use in the generation of electricity.

But it was a pyrrhic victory. The Burton Act was superseded in the years that followed, particularly during wartime. Today, 50 percent of the water of the Niagara River is routinely diverted from the Falls to generate electricity during daylight hours in the summer, 75 percent at night and throughout the winter, with what is claimed to be no appreciable change in the scenic effect.

Although electricity is now taken for granted, electrical use among common citizens in the United States came relatively late, compared to some nations in Europe. In Europe, electricity was considered a public service and distribution was controlled by governments. But in America, electricity was a commodity. There was no profit in individual electrical use, so there was no incentive for privately held utilities to provide it. As Thomas P. Hughes observed in *Networks of Power*, "Power systems embody the physical, intellectual, and symbolic resources of the society that constructs them."

Buffalo never regained the sense of glory it had experienced before the assassination of President McKinley. The city's economic prosperity continued for many decades, however, until the completion of the St. Lawrence Seaway system in 1959 made its harbor obsolete, and the steel plant at Stony Point—by then called Bethlehem Steel—stopped production in 1983. The Pan-American Exposition was a financial disaster for its investors, and John Milburn's portrait at the Buffalo Club was indeed defaced. Mary Talbert protested the exclusion of African Americans from the exposition planning committee, but Milburn never took action against her for this. In 1902, Milburn moved with his family to New York City, where he once again rose to prominence as an attorney.

City of Light is a blend of fact and fiction, of characters and events real and imagined. Louisa Barrett, Tom and Grace Sinclair, Franklin Fiske, Abigail Rushman and her parents, Francesca Coatsworth, Susannah Riley, Frederick Krakauer, Karl Speyer, and Millicent Talbert—all are fictional creations. The Macaulay School is based on the Buffalo Seminary, a girls' school which still exists. The power station at Niagara is modeled on the Niagara Falls Power Company's landmark Edward Dean Adams Station, which pioneered the use of alternating current in the United States. The Adams Station ceased operations in 1961, and its beautiful powerhouses were bulldozed into their wheel pits. The site is now the Niagara Falls Wastewater Treatment plant. The character of Daniel Henry Bates is loosely based on J. Horace McFarland, president of the American Civic Association, who fought relentlessly, albeit nonviolently, for the preservation of Niagara.

Of those characters who actually existed, Dexter Rumsey's daughter Ruth grew up to marry (over her family's objections) Irish-Catholic Buffalonian William "Wild Bill" Donovan, who later became the director of the OSS, precursor of the CIA. Elbert Hubbard, who by then had married his paramour Alice Moore, died in the sinking of the *Lusitania*, in 1915. After John J. Albright died in 1931, his goods were sold at auction, his home torn down, and his estate subdivided; he had suffered business setbacks, but more important, he had given virtually all his money away to worthy causes and castigated his colleagues for not doing the same. Although he did indeed marry his daughter's governess, there is no evidence that he fathered an illegitimate child. Mary Talbert became a vice president of the NAACP and worked as a Red Cross nurse in France during World War I. In 1922, she received the Spingarn Medal, the highest honor bestowed by the NAACP, for her human rights work. She died in 1923. Maria Love lived on at 184 Delaware Avenue until 1931, when she died at the age of 91. The Fitch

Crèche, the first day-care center in the United States, closed two years later, a victim of the Depression. And Frances Folsom Cleveland lived until 1947. Before her death she made the acquaintance of future president General Dwight D. Eisenhower. To him, she must have seemed an emissary from a different world.

Acknowledgments

I am beholden to David E. Nye for his two remarkable books on technological development in the United States, *Electrifying America* and *American Technological Sublime.* Daniel M. Dumych's *Niagara Falls*, Patrick McGreevy's *Imagining Niagara*, and Paul Gromosiak's *Soaring Gulls and Bowing Trees* expanded my understanding of the Falls. I am also particularly grateful to Karen Berner Little for her book on Maria M. Love, Lillian S. Williams for her work on Mary Talbert, Ann K. Finkbeiner for *After the Death of a Child*, Margaret Leech for *In the Days of McKinley*, Walter Lord for *The Good Years*, and Michael N. Vogel, Edward J. Patton, and Paul F. Redding for *America's Crossroads*. My research has been made possible by the dedicated librarians of the Buffalo and Erie County Historical Society; the Buffalo and Erie County Public Library; the Niagara Falls (New York) Public Library; the New-York Historical Society; the New York Public Library; and the New York Society Library. Doris Hampton and the staff of the New York State Office of Parks, Recreation, and Historic Preservation, Niagara Frontier Region, generously provided information. Many Buffalo residents graciously assisted me, among them Cornelia Lewis Dopkins; Mary Rech Rockwell; Nancy A. Fredrickson at Lucas Varity; and Gary Sutton and Kristen Pfaff at the Buffalo Seminary. I enjoyed many walking tours with the Preservation Coalition. In addition to their books on the Pan-American Exposition and the waterfront, Elizabeth Sholes and Thomas Leary offered their insights and hours of companionship in our mutual excitement for Buffalo's history. And I am proud to be indebted to the late Austin M. Fox, educator, scholar, gentleman, who shared not only his encyclopedic knowledge but also his literary acumen.

I am deeply grateful to Carole Welch, my British editor, for her wisdom, commitment, and support. In addition, I offer my appreciation to Susan Kamil, my American editor, for the sensitivity and precision which have enriched this book beyond measure. I must also express my lasting gratitude to my agent, Lisa Bankoff, for her faith in *City of Light*, for her humor, and for her unending encouragement. At Sceptre, Sarah Ballard, Katie Collins, Alexandra Heminsley, Alasdair Oliver, Sandie Steward and Diana Riley generously contributed their multifaceted talents and advice. Many friends sustained me during the six years I worked on *City of Light*, especially Alexandra Isles, Carol L. Shapiro, Elisa Shokoff, Ruth Shokoff, and of course Richard M. Osterweil; their careful readings helped me at every stage. Finally I thank my husband, whose profound generosity of spirit gave me the time, nurturance, and stability in which to write, and I thank my son, for being himself.